THEY LOVED HER;
THEY FOUGHT HER.

CALEB BATES
A bounder who married Pastora, took her to California, and left her with two children to raise.

ELIZABETH BATES
Pastora's daughter. A willfull girl whose impetuous marriage to a Georgia gentleman might have ruined her, but for her mother's wisdom.

ABEL BATES
The boy Pastora took as her own. Educated at Harvard, he married an aristocratic bride who turned up her nose at his family and his hopes for the future.

FRENCHMAN JACK
Pastora's business partner, until shady dealings made him walk out on her.

HENRY FEARING
The wealthy banker who wanted to marry her, but ran off when his fortune changed.

SETH SLADE
The railroad man, miner and vineyard owner who offered his life for Pastora's happiness.

"A STORY OF PRIDE, COURAGE AND DETERMINATION"
Chatanooga Times

PASTORA

JOANNA BARNES

AVON
PUBLISHERS OF BARD, CAMELOT AND DISCUS BOOKS

AVON BOOKS
A division of
The Hearst Corporation
959 Eighth Avenue
New York, New York 10019

First Avon Printing, November, 1981

AVON TRADEMARK REG. U.S. PAT. OFF. AND IN
OTHER COUNTRIES, MARCA REGISTRADA, HECHO EN
U.S.A.

Printed in the U.S.A.

WFH 10 9 8 7 6 5 4 3 2 1

for A.W.B.

Acknowledgments

I am indebted to Dr. Gloria Ricci Lothrop whose lectures on western history, given at U.C.L.A. in 1976, first sparked my interest in attempting to faithfully portray the early days of northern California, the manifold character of its people and the kinds of events that shaped their lives.

To John Caughey, Professor Emeritus of History, U.C.L.A., I am profoundly grateful for the generosity with which he gave this project his consideration, his wisdom and his encouragement.

I thank Kathleen Roy Lindsay whose research on the genesis of Saint Joseph, Missouri, proved invaluable and Clement L. Grant of the History Department of the University of Georgia, through whom a trio of Georgians, namely J. Britt McCarley, assisted by Charles Gilbreath and Dan Brown, Historian at Kennesaw Mountain National Battlefield Park, provided material essential to this story.

Among the many friends and acquaintances who contributed unsparingly of their time, expertise and interest are Roger H. Licht, Beverly McEwan, Jacob I. Zeitlin, Doctor Joe Golenternek, Larry E. Mead of *Sheep Breeder* and *Sheepman* publications, Johnny W. Thompson of the American Sheep Producers Council and Jack Davies of the Schramsberg Vineyard in Calistoga, California.

I am deeply obliged to the following institutions and to their very helpful staffs: The Bancroft Library, The Wells Fargo History Room, the U.C.L.A. Research Library, the Public Libraries of Saint Joseph, Missouri, and San Francisco, Los Angeles and Beverly Hills, California. In particular, my thanks to Mary Ann Grasso of the Warner Research Collection, H.M. Lai of the Chinese Historical Society, M.D. Swingle of the California Historical Society and Clayla Davis of the Napa Valley Wine Library Association.

I

THEY WERE forty-three in number. Five of the voyagers were women, including the child, Tessa. They traveled toward the setting sun. The days disappeared behind a horizon retreating as they advanced and offering no sign of welcome or haven. In the darkness they pulled together like a small flotilla riding at anchor in some unknown, unnamed gulf. Like most travelers, they gave the places names of their own. Here was Vermilion for the color of the sunset. This place was Whitewater and this one Windover.

Lucy herself had never seen the sea but she knew it must be like this, behind them, before them, boundless, spreading out beyond sight. To every side, the land rolled away in great, lazy, green swells. From overhead, the scudding shadows of the clouds dappled it with swift-moving patterns of light and dark, causing the surface to ripple and shimmer to the eye like water skimmed by a squall. Ahead of her, swaying like a windjammer, its canvas bleached pale in the sun, rolled the Whitons' ungainly craft. Lucy fancied it might be mistaken for the Ark, being so overloaded with what seemed like two of everything and trailed by the Whitons' pair of dogs. Each evening Mr. Whiton disappeared inside and emerged from its abundance with his wife's rocker. He carried it to the fireside where Mrs. Whiton settled into it and rocked, if a trifle unsteadily, on the strange ground, doing her mending by the wavering light. Celia Whiton was a small, sallow woman with an unpleasantly pitched voice. It was generally conceded that her husband had made an error in bringing her along. "A useless piece of baggage," Mr. Bates called her, and Lucy had to agree.

1

Their own conveyance, hers and Mr. Bates's was nothing so grand as the Whitons'. Theirs was a narrower and lighter wagon and required a span less oxen. If there were any luxuries to be found inside, they were her mother's looking glass and her father's books. Mr. Bates had allowed her to bring them along since they were all that was left to her, although he had chided her at first. "It's well known that blood is not supposed to rush to a lady's head. It deprives her of the circulation needed for chores and childbearing." Lucy had blushed crimson, and Mr. Bates, breaking into laughter at the sight of her color, had relented. The incident put her in mind of something her mother used to say. "Don't fill the child's head full of dreams. We women haven't time for dreams." This last statement was supposed to remind Lucy's father that he had no time for such things either, and that reading aloud from Shakespeare over the noon meal was not to divert his attentions from the rest of the day's tasks. Her mother had also held that if one could afford the time to read at all, one should choose a passage from the Bible. Her father insisted Shakespeare was written better. "A sacrilege," she charged, but Shakespeare prevailed. Lucy herself had been named Lucy Cordelia Curtis, in a tribute to *King Lear*, and her brother had, in turn, been called William.

Her parents had made an unlikely pair. It was difficult to understand what had drawn them together, and they rarely spoke of the past. They had come from back East, and there had been another farm before the one Lucy knew, but that had failed when she was still an infant, and they had moved farther west to Missouri. If there was family in the East, they had never mentioned it. Her mother's parents had been English, she knew. Of her father's side, she knew nothing, save that her mother called them "fine folks."

Her father was indeed a finely sketched figure, small-boned but very tall, with a thin, aquiline nose and high forehead. He was a lank scarecrow of a man and yet, for all his appearance, unsuited to farming. He tried. He loved the land even more than his books, perhaps even more than his wife and children. He hungered to be a physical partner with nature. He was more at home out in the solitude of those fields than he was in the cabin he had built for them. But try as he might, the land rebuffed his attentions. And he, like an obstinate suitor, persisted, growing more taciturn and melancholy with each blighted hope. Yet his inner passion was only fired by his frustrations. He plodded on, determined to carve his mark on that farm. In the end, it carved its mark on him instead, fashioning deep furrows in his forehead, hollows in his cheeks and jagged ruts at either side of his dry and cracked lips.

Her mother, on the other hand, was a broad-boned, solid woman with a round, bland face. She looked as wholesome as milk and hardy as the earth itself. But she wanted nothing more than to quit the farm. "We must be getting away from this sad place," she would say. But her husband refused, and her words only angered him. He would open a jug of whiskey and stalk outside into the night with it. They could hear him bellowing in the darkness, hurling passionate passages of poetry out over those fertile bottomlands which bore exuberantly for everyone but him.

One day that last spring, over a year ago now, Lucy and her mother were making soap, and Willie was helpin Pa sow corn. They could hear Pa reciting to Willie as he planted each handful of five kernels in its hill. "One for the blackbird, one for the crow, one for the cutworm and two to grow." Her mother, leaning over the tallow barrel, straightened up suddenly.

"This land doesn't want us, Lucy. Push on when you're grown. Find a place that wants to hold you to itself. You'll know when you feel it."

"Did you ever know a place like that, Ma?"

"I've forgotten. Stop asking questions, there's work to be done. Just mind what I said."

Spring planting had been late that year of eighteen forty-four because the floods had come. At first the river rose slowly, obscuring the snags and sawyers along its banks. Gradually it swallowed the lower clearing below the barn and still kept coming. Its color changed, muddied by the earth it swept along with it, and its current became more rapid, until the roar kept them from sleeping. They could do nothing but watch as it swept along trees and brush and portions of what might have been boats or buildings from places far upstream. When it finally receded, it left behind a dead doe in the lower clearing, its body rotted and swollen and reeking.

3

When summer came, it appeared that for once the crops would flourish. There would be plenty to lay up against the winter, perhaps even enough to repay some of their debts. But on one of the warmest days, so sultry that the dog lay listlessly in the shade of the woodpile, unwilling to stir even for a raucous flock of geese in the clearing, Willie's teeth began to chatter.

Oddly, her mother was the first to go. She had insisted she felt fine, that Willie needed tending. By the time the malaria forced her to bed, it was too late for even that sturdy body to fight it off. Willie went in his sleep. Pa lingered longer than either of them. His already haggard form was simply worn away by the caprices of disease, first chills, now fever, until it was too wasted to endure. He had raved in his delirium, sometimes in Latin which Lucy did not understand and felt powerless to respond to. He recited fragments of the fanciful yarns he had concocted for her and Willie, tales of seafarers and shipwrecks and such. Once, after Ma and Willie were gone and shortly before he fell senseless for the last time, he took her hand in his and held it. She looked down at that great trembling paw and heard him say quite clearly, " 'Upon such sacrifices, my Cordelia, the gods themselves throw incense.' " Perhaps he had been lucid. Perhaps not.

There was no preacher living in Saint Luke's Plains, so the doctor spoke at the funeral. His manservant, a listless ebony slave, sat slumped in his master's wagon, the reins drooped over one arm, his eyelids sinking lower and lower as the doctor droned on.

One tall wooden marker served the three of them: "Hamilton Pindar Curtis, Annie His Wife, William Son Of The Above." And below that was written in smaller letters, "They are in glory, the world in tears." This addition struck Lucy as curious, since they knew so few people thereabouts.

Almost everything went to pay off the debts. Lucy herself had presided over the process. She was not only a good reader but quick with figures. When it was done, there was a little over thirty dollars left. This, her mother's looking glass, a worn Bible, *The Collected Works of William Shakespeare*, a copy of *The Iliad* and the *Sketch Book* of Washington Irving were what remained to her.

According to Mrs. Vose, Lucy had been "saved by the good right hand of God," and it had been His will that

4

she be spared. To what purpose it was difficult to discern, but Mrs. Vose was willing to take it on faith that Lucy was among the chosen and therefore an amulet of good fortune. She welcomed her to the Empire House and showed her to the loft where she would sleep. The Empire House was the only two-story building in Saint Luke's Plains. It rose imperiously above the dozen or so other structures on the town's street, with a steeply peaked roof which added to the effect. Over the door and nailed to the clapboard was a printed sign, its letters slightly askew, which read, "Empire House—Fine Food and Lodgings." The food was prepared and served on the ground floor, which also had a parlor and, across the vestibule, Mr. and Mrs. Vose's quarters. Up a narrow staircase were the lodgings, six identical cubicles, each with its bed, chamber pot, mirror and washstand. On the walls, freshly white-washed each spring by Mr. Vose, were clothes pegs for the guests' convenience. At the far end of the dim hallway was a ladder to the loft. Mr. Vose had cleared away one end of the attic and strung an Osnaburg partition across it to conceal the heap of trunks, storage chests and furniture piled on the other side in the windowless gloom. Lucy's mattress and quilt lay tucked near the eaves, along with a white china chamber pot, a pitcher and basin, both cracked but watertight, and a slop bucket.

Within a few months, besides the household chores, Lucy had taken over the books of the Empire House. Neither Mr. nor Mrs. Vose had a mind for sums. They were barely schooled at all, which embarrassed Mr. Vose and led him to pretend to more facility than he possessed. But Mrs. Vose never ceased to marvel. "Only fifteen years old, with the mind of a professor!" She was an ample, motherly woman who, lacking children, babied her guests as best she could. She cajoled them into eating if she felt they weren't taking enough, and held over them threats of scurvy and dysentery as a result of improper diet.

Lucy liked the Voses but felt no closeness to either of them. Mr. Vose was a short, spindly, narrow-boned man, gone completely bald. With his own complexion and abrupt, jerky movements, he reminded her of a plucked fowl. When spoken to by Mrs. Vose, he would thrust his head forward attentively, bobbing it up and down in agreement. It was this habit of pecking at Mrs. Vose's

5

words which forced Lucy to bite hard at the insides of her cheeks to keep from laughing aloud.

The transients were, for the most part, a jolly bunch. Some were men traveling to Independence or Robidoux's Saint Joseph in hopes of establishing themselves in trade there. Some were trappers heading east to Springfield to see their wives and families after months, sometimes years, on the trail. Mr. Vose and the men ate together. Mrs. Vose stayed in the kitchen while Lucy waited table. The men traded stories of wide rivers teeming with beaver and otter, prairie fires which blazed for weeks, mountains topped with snow in summer. They laughed at the peculiar ways of the Indian savages who sold their daughters for a pony and a bolt of calico. They debated the relative beauty of the handsome Chippewa and Gros Ventre women. Some even dared to boast about their China articles, the Indian wives who taught them to live off the land and dressed their kill. Lucy took it all in, relishing every morsel. There was a red-haired giant, they said, a Colonel Chiles, who had traveled twice with wagon trains of whole families, all the way to Alta California. The West—that was where America's destiny lay.

Sometimes Lucy lay awake at night, trying to reckon where her own destiny might lie. If Ma and Pa had lived, they'd have seen to it that she made someone a proper wife. Pa would have preferred a man who worked the land. "Honest work," he called it. Pa had an abiding suspicion of commerce. Her mother would have wanted her to marry a tradesman and live in a town. To Ma, that was a secure position for a woman.

Now, of course, there would be no family quarrels over the choice of a husband for Lucy. And if she missed Ma and Pa, knowing that they had cared enough to fight over her, she supposed there was some consolation to be found in being allowed to choose for herself what kind of life she might have. The only thing she knew for certain was that she did not want either of the alternatives they had anticipated. Farm life meant constant toil and disappointments. And the life of the merchant's wife would be stifling. She could not imagine herself in dimity and lace, dispensing just the proper greeting to each customer, never too shy, never too fetching, the model of etiquette. So it must be a different choice, though she didn't know what. The only young men of her age in Saint Luke's Plains were the Foster boys, a thick-set, doltish pair who lazed around their father's livery stable, doing their best to shirk their chores. They called her the Voses' "hired girl" and commented rudely on the development of her bosom. They were slow-moving oafs, and she and Willie could have beaten the tar out of them with ease. She missed Willie. He'd been small for his age, but wiry and tough, and though she'd always bested him at arm-wrestling, he was a real battler. On those nights when loneliness overcame her and she missed the folks so keenly that she couldn't keep from tears, it was for Willie she wept most. He'd had so much life to live, and it seemed a vicious, mindless sin to take a boy of twelve, even if he was in glory while she was in tears.

"The Lord will lead us," Mrs. Vose was fond of saying. "The path may look dark to us, but His hand will guide us to the light." To Lucy, Mrs. Vose's God sounded rather like an Indian guide, one of the trappers' China article wives. But if what the woman said was true, then the Lord would somehow show her a way out of working for her keep at the Empire House. Maybe He would even show her a road away from this sad place. To where, or to what life, she couldn't fathom, but there was no future for her here.

Winter was a slow season at the Voses', a time of solitude and snows and silences interrupted only by the sudden snap of a log on the fire. But by the middle of April, business was back to usual. Even the rain-swollen rivers couldn't deter those hardy men eager to get an early start in a new settlement. The promise of spring was infectious, and the elements were a minor inconvenience. So they came, their animals caked with mud, their provisions saturated, their clothing still damp from the last storm.

At dusk one April afternoon, Lucy went to fetch a loaf of sugar for Mrs. Vose. Three doors away was an establishment which bore the sign "Apostle Provisions—Fair Traders" and smelled pungently of coffee beans and spices and the musky piles of hides and pelts taken in trade.

When she left, her parcel under her arm, it was raining again. Lucy darted for the front door of the Empire House, praying Mrs. Vose's loaf of sugar might stay dry. She fixed her eyes downward as she ran, trying to sidestep

7

the troughs of water which had formed in the ankle-deep mud of the street.

Perhaps it was the sound of the downpour that rendered her oblivious. She neither heard nor saw the approaching horse until it was upon her. She glanced up only as it rounded the corner of the Empire House, its heaving, wet, amber chest inches from her face. Startled, she cried out. The horse reared back as she slipped in the thick mire and fell headlong under its belly. Horse and rider swerved and foundered, the frightened beast flailing its legs and whinnying in alarm as it rolled sidelong into the street.

"You there!"

She raised herself on her elbows in the slime and looked up.

He had the face of an Indian, swarthy and sun-blackened, with a prominent nose and dark, deep-set eyes. His hair, slicked by the rain, streamed like India ink down over his forehead and into his heavy brows.

"You, girl! Can you move?"

"Yes, sir." She scrambled to her feet and retrieved the filthy parcel of sugar. "I'm sorry, sir."

He raised his horse slowly, soothing it with soft words and stroking. His pack mules stood numbly by, the water trickling down their hides.

"Is there anything I can do?"

"You've done enough, I'd say. I've a lame horse here."

She stood wet and shivering, clutching her package to her chest. "I didn't see you coming, and the rain—"

"Here now. No cause for tears. I was traveling too fast for the weather. Should've known better."

"Yes, sir."

He approached her, leading his mount. He was holding his side as though it pained him. Lucy stared at him. She had never seen so dark a white man. But he wore good clothing, soaked and muddied now, and had spoken in a most civilized manner, considering the circumstances. Suddenly he halted and threw back his head in laughter and then with a sharp "Ah!" pressed his side and winced. "Ah!" he said again, but he smiled, his teeth strikingly white against his skin. "What a mud pie you make!" He cupped a hand under her chin. "Don't be afraid. We must both be a sight. Can you point me the way to the livery stable?"

8

"It's there, sir, Foster's, the building just beyond the trader's."

"Good enough. Watch where you're going now, girl." He turned and led his animals away.

When she had scrubbed herself clean and dressed again, she went down to the kitchen. Mrs. Vose was standing over a steaming kettle of rabbit stew, salting it as she stirred. "We didn't lose the sugar. Most of it stayed dry. Certainly dryer than you, at any rate. The man's trousers want mending, but his rib wants mending more. Mr. Vose says it's cracked or broke. We can thank the good Lord it was nothing worse."

"Yes, ma'am."

"You'll take supper to Mr. Bates in his room. And don't you forget to tell him how sorry you are."

Lucy set the tray on the floor of the upstairs hall and rapped at Mr. Bates's door.

He lay propped up on two pillows which she recognized as Mrs. Vose's own. He was wearing a clean white linen shirt and reading a book by the candlelight. Lucy set the dishes on the washstand.

"If it isn't the mud pie! You look a bit different with a washing. The lady of the house told me it was you out there."

"I'm sorry about what happened." She backed toward the doorway.

"Nothing to it. I'm only resting in bed to appease that large mother hen downstairs. I'll be up and about in the morning."

"And your horse? Is it all right?"

"Nothing serious, but your livery stable couldn't spare me another mount. We'll lay over for a while, rest him and feed him up. There's a long way ahead, and I've been pushing hard. A rest won't hurt either of us. So long as we make Saint Joseph by the beginning of the month."

"Mrs. Vose wants to know if you need anything."

"Could you spare me another light?"

Lucy fetched a candlestick and brought it to him.

"That's an improvement. The better to see Mr. Cooper by."

She glanced at the book on the bed. *The Prairie.*

"You read? Well?"

"Quite well, sir."

9

"You must be a handy lass to have around. Well now, don't let me keep you from your chores."

She left quickly, thinking she had overstayed her welcome. Mr. Bates had made an elegant picture, with his dark skin and jet-black hair, dressed in fine linen, resting against his pillows with his book. He had the look of a grand gentleman taking his ease.

"He's a charmer, all right," Mrs. Vose commented, after he had lavished praise on every meal she had served in the space of two days. "A bit too much the charmer, judging by the look on your face, young lady. It's the Irish in him, I expect."

Lucy continued sweeping the kitchen floor, making a small detour around Mrs. Vose. "Do they have darkies in Ireland?"

"Heavens, child, the questions you ask. But I'll admit I suspected a touch of the tarbrush myself. 'Stuff and nonsense,' says Mr. Vose, 'there's dark Irish as well as light.' Lucy, fetch me a basket of potatoes from the root cellar."

"He's going west to be a sheep farmer."

Mrs. Vose dropped a chunk of salt pork into a big iron skillet and set it on the back of the stove. She watched the fat glide slowly across the black surface. "With those hands? Not likely. Get a move on before my pan's ready."

Mr. Bates was sitting on the cutting stump outside the kitchen door, dubbing a pair of tall brown boots. "Hello, mud pie. Getting a bit of the noonday sun, are you?"

"No, sir. Potatoes for dinner." She hurried by him.

As she emerged from the root cellar, she could see him watching her, wiping his hands clean of the boot grease with a dry cloth. He moved his hands in slow, meticulous, circular motions, as though the rite gave him pleasure. Lucy dragged the heavy wooden door into place over the cellar and picked up the basket brimming with potatoes, its load still smelling faintly of earth.

"You're a strong lass. That's good in a woman."

Nobody had ever called her a woman. She didn't know what, exactly, she should say.

He held out his arm, blocking the door to the kitchen. "Did someone make off with your tongue?" He smiled and folded his arms on his knees, crouching toward her. His hair shone in the sun like a blackbird's wing. His face went solemn. He lowered his voice in mock gravity.

10

"Come now. You may tell me. Why is it you're frightened of me?"

Lucy felt the color rise in her cheeks. "I am not frightened of anyone!" She brushed past him, hearing his deep, rich laughter behind her.

Mrs. Vose had made it clear that Lucy was never to enter a lodger's room without leaving the door open wide to the hallway. "Men have been known to take liberties," she said. Lucy was not altogether sure what liberties those were, though one fellow, a brash, fiery-haired tinker scarcely older than herself, had stolen up behind her in the parlor one morning as she swept, slipped his arm around her waist and raised her off the floor, kicking and squealing like a piglet. That incident had provoked Mrs. Vose's lecture on liberties.

Lucy carefully placed her bucket against the open door to Mr. Bates's cubicle, so it would not swing shut as she scrubbed the floor. The room's occupant sat on the bed, absorbed in his reading.

The weekly floor scrubbing was a ritual demanded by Mrs. Vose. "Men are untidy creatures by nature. I'll not have them wallowing in filth and giving our place a foul name." Actually, it was one of the chores Lucy minded least. She liked the fresh, aromatic scent of the wet wood. She had never lived in a house with wood floors before, and the odor smacked to her of a luxury worth tending.

"Are you about making an island of me?" Mr. Bates folded his book and glanced at her as she drew abreast of his bedside.

"I won't be long, sir."

He swung his legs onto the floor directly in front of her. She looked up.

"Why do you take me for such a monster, girl? A bit of pleasant banter never hurt. You're far too young and pretty to be such a somber sort."

She scrubbed as rapidly as she could. "I have my work to do."

"You're a vigorous worker, and that's the truth. And a good girl, too, I'll wager. How old are you?"

"Sixteen."

"Have you no family?"

She shook her head.

"No suitors?"

11

"No."

"There's a pity. A fine-looking girl like yourself ought to have choice pickings."

She stopped. Raising herself on her haunches, she asked him, "Am I? Fine-looking?"

He caught himself before he laughed. The innocence of the question sobered him. "Do you never take a look in the glass, girl? There's a fair young lady there with hair like ripe wheat and eyes as blue as a morning glory."

"Irish talk."

"What?"

"Mrs. Vose says when you speak like that it's the Irish in you."

He chuckled. "She's right, you know."

"I know."

"You're a spirited lass, aren't you? A good trait in women and horses. I don't suppose you'd care to come with me to California."

"You're teasing, Mr. Bates."

"Ah, but I made you smile."

"What is it like there, in California? Do you know?"

"Blooming with opportunities, girl. They hang like honeysuckle on the vine, ready for the picking. The climate is kindly and temperate, they say. December is as green as April. And there's land enough for any man to make his own kingdom. The Mexicans are a shiftless lot, too busy fighting amongst themselves to heed a few newcomers. There's room to grow, girl."

"You'll send for your family then."

Abruptly, he stood. "I have none." He sounded vexed. "I'm alone. But I shall remedy that in good time." He lifted the small leather trunk that was part of his baggage, moving it out of her path.

"I hear there are no women out there. Only Indians and Mexicans."

"There are women everywhere, girl. Take yourself."

She was not sure she liked being teased this way. It was not fair of him, though he had no way of knowing just how sorely she yearned to be a part of one of those exotic excursions to the West. She looked quickly around the room to see if she had missed scrubbing anywhere.

"Here, give me your hand, I'll help you up." He pulled her to her feet and, as she rose, stepped toward her. She

12

moved backward and felt the wall behind her. He stood close, raising an arm on either side of her so that she could not slip away. She felt the heat of his body through his clothing.

"I'll not touch you," he said softly. "Not unless you want me to."

She shook her head.

"As I thought. You are a good girl." He dropped his arms and retreated a step. "Look at me."

Lucy raised her eyes to his face.

"You're a pretty thing, you are. Strong and lithe as a sapling."

Lucy saw his dark eyes flicker as though his mind had wandered briefly to something that troubled him. Then he smiled faintly.

"Be about your chores now. We'll talk again."

She lifted the bucket away from the door. As she turned to go, she caught his gaze. "I don't really mind the Irish in you, Mr. Bates."

He threw back his head and laughed. "You don't!"

"No, sir."

"Well, girl, I'd say that was a lucky thing for us both."

"I have eyes," Mrs. Vose said sternly, "and what I see looks mighty like a moth drawn to a flame."

Lucy didn't reply.

"They come and they go, these chaps. It's no good to become partial to any one of them. One thing I've learned —though they may have different names and faces, in the end they're all more alike than not."

"Mr. Bates is a gentleman."

"By whose yardstick? You know nothing about him. Where does he come from?"

"He told me, 'the East wind blew me here from a place full of troubles and grief.'" Lucy paused to savor his words. "Where do you think that was?"

"No matter. There isn't a mortal among us can outrun his own cares. I'm not your ma, Lucy, but I'm warning you all the same, don't let your heart rule your head."

Lucy raised a hand. "Listen. It's him."

"He has a sweet voice, I'll give him that." Mrs. Vose nodded her head in time to the strains of Mr. Bates's singing in the parlor.

13

> "It's meeting's a pleasure
> And parting is grief . . ."

The parlor was warm and still suffused with the aromas of supper when Lucy and Mrs. Vose finished their kitchen chores and joined the others. The lamplight, reflected on the circle of faces, burnished them to a sheen. Mrs. Vose, perspiring slightly from her recent exertions in the kitchen, shone like a ten-dollar gold piece. There were seven, the five men seated about, Mrs. Vose close to the lamp with her quilting and Lucy on a footstool at her feet. Mrs. Vose's toes beat lightly on the floor in time to the music. Mr. Vose's head bobbed jauntily up and down as he sang.

After a rousing chorus of "Good Old Colony Times," Mr. Bates launched into a solo rendition of "The Golden Vanity." Lucy listened to his strong, mellow voice pour out the sad song, holding her breath in anticipation each time he reached the end of a verse and paused, then echoed the refrain of the lonesome lowland sea in a soft, mournful croon that faded away like a faraway call in the night.

When he had finished, the room was silent. Mrs. Vose, who had put down her quilting, sat with her eyes closed and her hands clasped in her lap. She looked like someone asleep. Slowly she parted her lips, and in a full, sweet soprano that swelled to the corners of the room she sang "I'll Give My Love an Apple," caressing each stanza with such an outpouring of tenderness as Lucy had never heard before. Stealthily, Lucy glanced at Mr. Vose. Puffed with pride, looking like a banty rooster, he perched on the edge of his chair, beaming blissfully, caught up in some private reverie. Lucy realized suddenly that she knew nothing at all about either of them.

The circuit preacher, a squat, rotund man who came around every several weeks, led the group in "All Hail the Power of Jesus' Name." He stood to conduct them, as though it would have made a difference; he was little taller on foot than seated in his chair. As he waved his arms in cadence over his bulging vest, Lucy thought he looked like nothing so much as a suet pudding in motion. She tried to suppress her smile, and failing, found Mr. Bates grinning broadly back at her as though they shared some special secret.

"Ah," Mrs. Vose sighed happily, "that was a good sing."

"It's the voices of the ladies that sound the sweetest."

"And singing the songs of home. It puts me in mind of my own dear girls."

"There's no doubt," said the preacher, "that music cures the heartsick. Day after tomorrow ought to bring the judge by. Now there's a fine tenor for us."

"The judge?" Mr. Bates flicked at a speck of dust on the toe of one boot.

"Circuit judge. Comes round these parts regular as rain."

Mr. Bates stood up. "Good. I hope I shall still be here to harmonize with His Honor."

When the gentleman travelers had repaired to their rooms and the fire was banked, Lucy took her candle upstairs. Her skirt gathered in one hand, she trudged up the narrow stairway and tiptoed along the hall toward the loft ladder.

"Here."

She drew in her breath sharply, but a hand covered her mouth so that she could not cry out.

"I want to speak with you. I'm sorry I alarmed you. It seems we're great ones for startling each other." Mr. Bates dropped his hand and drew her gently by the arm into his cubicle.

"Sir?"

Mr. Bates seated her on the bed. He reached down and held her face in his hand, drawing it upward until she met his eyes. "You are going with me, girl, aren't you?"

She was silent, not knowing what he meant.

"You're a strong, healthy young woman. You've an agreeable way about you. I'm in need of such a one as you."

"What for?"

He smiled broadly, his teeth gleaming against his skin, darker still in the shadowy room. "Why, girl, for a wife, of course! A man can use a helpmeet to make the crossing. You have the spirit in you to do it, I can tell."

"Mr. Bates? You want me?"

"You'll make some man a fine wife. Why shouldn't I be the fortunate fellow? And what's to keep you here in this dull place? You're little more than a scullery girl. Haven't you an appetite for enterprise? California, the land of enterprise, that's what I'm offering you."

She sat motionless, her eyes fixed on his, as though to

15

move at all, to so much as take a breath, might jar and shatter the moment. When she spoke, she replied as softly as she might have spoken to one asleep. "Thank you, Mr. Bates. I shall accept your offer."

To her consternation, he burst into laughter. "Ah," he said, catching himself short of breath, "the maidenly dignity of that response." He took her by the shoulders and drew her to her feet. "Get your belongings together. I'll make the arrangements. After the preacher says his words, we'll be off for Saint Joseph. And then . . ." He paused and looked upward, as though reading an announcement inscribed in the air. "Mr. and Mrs. Caleb Bates, late of Saint Luke's Plains, will set out westward to find a new life in that grand land beyond the Line. How does that sound to you, girl?"

"Fine, sir." Her face was flushed, her cheeks burning with the sudden fever of excitement.

"Then run along now and rise early. There's a lot to be done, and we mustn't be dawdling."

Once in the hall, she glanced back only in time to see his door shut, leaving her alone in the dim passageway.

When times were hard, her Ma used to say, you had to keep a keener lookout than ever for opportunities. To Lucy, lying wrapped in her quilt near the eaves, unable to doze, it seemed that keen lookout or no, Ma and Pa had encountered precious few opportunities. And now, thanks to Mr. Bates, one had been handed to her like some miraculous gift. She thought Pa would have liked Mr. Bates. He admired adventuresome spirit in a man. "The soft life softens everything in a man down to his moral fiber. One has only to look at the fat banker and his greed." Her mother would have found in Mr. Bates a dashing figure of a man, clearly a gentleman of substance and fine manners. He was, Lucy thought, the best of both worlds. And if there had been no time for courting, well, that was the way of men in a hurry to settle out West. Certainly she was vastly preferable to some China article who could not even speak his language. She would be a good helpmeet, she vowed, and together they would make a home in that far place with the alluring name that glided on her tongue like honey. California.

"Set down that milk pail," Mrs. Vose told her as she came in from the shed. "Mr. Bates has just informed me

16

of his intentions." She pulled the iron biscuit pan from the oven and upturned it over the breadbasket, shaking the fragrant rolls out of their steaming molds. She wiped her hands on her apron and faced Lucy, her arms akimbo. "Why would you want to do such a thing, child?"

"You said that the good Lord always shows us the pathway. He's shown me the path to California. That's where I want to go."

"Whatever for? On account of all those tall tales the lodgers tell over dinner? Child, that's nothing but table talk. It's hard country out there, swarming with half-naked savages."

"It's hard everyplace, one way or another. So my Pa said. And Mr. Bates will take care of me."

"What do you know of him? Who is he?"

"He told me about sheep farming. He says some people in Alta California are already raising sheep. When we've settled there, he'll come back East and drive a great flock of Merinos across the country to our farm."

"The man is no farmer. He has the hands of a riverboat sharper."

"He saved a great deal of money for the venture. And he came into a sizeable inheritance of late."

"I'll grant you, he does appear to be comfortably off. You didn't tell him, did you, that you've thirty dollars of your own?"

"No."

"It's a fortunate woman with a dot of her own money."

"Corrie!" Mr. Vose stood in the doorway. "It's all right, Corrie, I spoke to him. The man's a Protestant."

"Thank heaven," said his wife. "That's one thing to the good. Child, are you still sure you want to do this?"

"Yes, ma'am."

"Jacob," she said to Mr. Vose, "would you be good enough to leave the ladies alone?" She waited until he had gone. "Lucy," she began, "there are some things about marrying that a woman should know." She bent over the big skillet, her back toward Lucy, turning spattering slices of bacon rapidly with a fork.

"Ma'am?"

"Men, all men, must have their wives' obedience and loyalty. It's a wife's duty to do as her husband wishes."

"Yes, ma'am, I will."

"There are times," she said slowly, "when it can be

17

difficult or even unpleasant to obey the wishes of your husband. But that's no matter. Whatever he wants, you must submit yourself to his will. That's the woman's lot. It's been that way since the beginning of time. So you do as he says, always, even when it ain't easy. A good man appreciates obedience in a woman and finds a hundred ways to repay her for it. That's what makes the partnership work, and don't you forget it."

"Yes, ma'am."

"Understand this, too. I don't know that I approve of what you're doing. But Jacob and I have always known that sooner or later such a thing might happen. A young woman like yourself is a prize in these parts. It was only a matter of time, and I cannot force you to stay here if you don't wish to. We've done our Christian best by you."

"It's not that I don't appreciate all you've done. I'm very grateful. Truly I am."

"I know you are, child. You're a sweet girl, to be sure. If you were my own, I'd forbid you to go like this. I'd invoke the devil himself, if necessary, to make you stay. You're neither old enough nor yet wise enough to know how great a mistake you may be making. Sometimes there's no way of telling until it's too late."

"It's what I want to do, ma'am."

"And what we want isn't always what's best for us. I'm telling you what I would tell my own daughter, if I had one. It's all I can do for you, if I can't make you give up this idea and stay. If you feel you must leave us for this stranger, I warn you now, Lucy, the decision rests upon your own head."

She stood her ground. "I shall marry Mr. Bates."

"So be it. I tried, and that's all a body can do. Mr. Bates maintains that he has treated you in a gentlemanly fashion. I trust he's telling the truth?"

"He didn't take liberties, if that's what you mean."

"Oh, child," she said, shaking her head from side to side in futility, "you know so little of the world."

"But now I shall see a great deal of it."

II

BLUE FUSED with blue. The breadth of the sky lay mirrored in her eyes, and like a mote of dust on their watery surface floated the reflection of a distant hawk making wide, graceful circles above the earth. The silence of the land around them was violated only by their intrusion. To the hawk flying overhead they might have appeared a band of bungling musicians invading the still, green prairie with the creak of rolling wheels, the snorting and braying of the teams, the hoarse shouts of the drivers and the constant din of goods jostling against each other as they traveled.

Lucy had grown used to the mingled sounds of the journey and the motion of the wagon. She had learned to disregard the dust that settled on her skin and ran in rivulets down her neck in the warm midday sun. And though she hadn't yet learned to disregard the mosquitos which attacked them in ravenous hordes, she at least abided them in silence.

Despite the bonnet Mr. Bates had purchased for her in Saint Joseph, her fair skin had burnt and darkened. It made a peculiar contrast to her pale blonde halo of hair. Mr. Bates had said that she looked like a tarnished angel—a remark that had prompted Celia Whiton to warn that jokes about falling from grace courted the devil. "What a surprise!" Mr. Bates had whispered to Lucy. "I'd have doubted she'd recognize a joke if it scampered up her skirts!"

Celia Whiton, a tiny woman, though nonetheless a

19

grave presence, was given to dwelling upon her ailments and discomforts, a preoccupation which left little time for humor or for interest in anyone other than herself. She had lately suffered a fit of the gravel, subjecting them all to her complaints accompanied, as was all her conversation, by a series of small, sibilant sighs like the sound of ice slipping off of a roof.

Her husband, a prosperous, hearty, red-faced farmer from Illinois, saw to her every comfort without protest, seemingly unmindful of her dour character. He was as genial as she was somber and faced each new day of their journey with the unfettered exhilaration of a beaver sprung from a trap. He had been a widower, raising four daughters until, as he said, "My hens outgrew the coop and roosted elsewhere," leaving him to marry a widow lady with a grown brood of her own. Lucy could not conceive why such a jolly fellow would choose a woman like Celia. "We've a hankering for a new adventure, the two of us," he had said that first night on the trail. Celia had stared into the firelight, coughed faintly and drawn her shawl closer around her. She liked to point out that she had "highly susceptible lungs" which suffered from the unremitting dust. Toward the end of their second week's travel, the school-teacher, Reed Pierce, had offered Mr. Bates a wager. "I've a gold eagle that says Celia's hardy as a she-wolf. She'll outlive us all."

Lucy liked the Pierce family, Reed, Kate and the little girl, Tessa, who was five. Tessa was a sprite, lively and full of childish curiosity. Sometimes she would run and skip beside the wagons, gathering bouquets of wildflowers for her mother. Other times, she rode perched upon her own little pony, riding bareback, her small hands firmly grasping its black mane.

"Schoolteacher or not," Mr. Bates had told Lucy, "Reed Pierce is a man of property. I can make out a man of property at a hundred yards. He's a real Virginia gentleman, that one." It was true that he had about him a certain native elegance. And his wife, timid though she might be, was obviously a gentlewoman. She was possessed of delicate chiseled features, a slim upturned nose, prominent cheekbones and a high forehead. Her bearing was that of a refined and cultured lady, and Lucy might have been awed by her demeanor were it not for the fact that Kate was very shy and had about her eyes a look of sadness so poignant as to be almost palpable.

"A handsome family," Mr. Bates had judged the Pierces when they'd met in Saint Joseph. "We'll be traveling in fine company."

"Did you look in her eyes?" Lucy had asked him.

"Girl! We've only been married a matter of days! My gaze isn't wandering so soon!"

"She's troubled."

"Perhaps she has misgivings about the journey. Now, shall we pay a visit to the wagonwright to see if he has finished or shall we go down the street to the cooper's?"

They went to the cooper's, a large barnlike building smelling pleasantly of wood shavings and sawdust. Barrels of every size lined the walls and hung suspended from the rafters. Mr. Bates jingled his gold coins impatiently in one hand as the cooper totted his figures. They bought barrels for water, flour, molasses, salt, bran and cornmeal, and a tar bucket to hang on the real axle of the wagon to grease the wheels and the kingbolt. The cooper advised Lucy to store her eggs in the cornmeal barrel against breakage and hams in the bran where they would be safer from the heat.

"Mr. Bates, we have spent a great deal of money," she said as they left. "I didn't dream it would be such a costly venture."

"Ah, girl, not to worry. Caleb Bates is a man of means. Nothing but the best will do. Hey there, look at the pile of buffalo robes in that fellow's wagon. Shall we see what he wants for them? Mind you don't touch them until I've had a look. They may be crawling with vermin."

She hung back until he had examined them and beckoned her forward.

"November robes, girl. The finest. Have your pick, one for each of us."

Saint Joseph was the first real town Lucy had ever seen. Unlike Saint Luke's Plains where buildings rose at random like plants sprouting from seeds dropped by passing birds, Saint Joseph appeared to have been carefully plotted in precise, rectangular sections of land, some already lined with newly built homes and places of business. To the north and east, beyond the surrounding hemp fields and pasturelands, rose the Blacksnake Hills.

21

On the western side, a cluster of warehouses marked the busy river landing at the town's edge. Below, to the south, black oaks and hazel bush dotted the landscape, and here and there a limestone block indicated the future course of Saint Joseph's expansion. Even to Lucy's unseasoned view, this was a burgeoning town, a place full of prospects and promise, of commerce and conviviality. Wide-eyed and giddy with pleasure at such a glorious excursion, she tagged after Mr. Bates like an eager puppy, breathlessly trying to keep pace with his long strides. He took great amusement from her delight. "It's a holiday every day for you, girl, isn't it. Whoever thought that buying an ox team would provide amusement for a lady!"

"But sir, you paid two hundred dollars! I never saw the like of such a sum."

"Money, my dear girl, is for spending. We need those eight beasts, six under yoke and two spares. Mules cost nearly twice the price. Besides, the Indians are partial to mules. They won't steal oxen."

"Why not?"

"Who can fathom the primitive mind? Perhaps because their women are their beasts of burden."

"But if that were so, they'd have no need of mules either."

"Now, girl, don't be contentious. It's not a pleasing trait in the female of the species."

Thus rebuked, she trailed obediently after him down the street. Mrs. Vose had been right. There were peculiar lessons to be learned as someone's wife. Lucy tried her best to do his bidding amiably, though it was not so simple an endeavor as she had thought.

He had frightened her that first night in Saint Joseph. They had repaired to their room, far more spacious than any at the Empire House, with clean white leno curtains at each of the two windows and a wide wooden floor which someone other than herself would kneel to scrub. She had just unfolded the Star of Bethlehem quilt which Mrs. Vose had given her in parting and was laying it across the bed when she felt his hands on her shoulders, drawing her upward. He slipped his arms around her waist and brought her back against his bare chest. She could feel his heart beating between her shoulders.

"Look, girl, what do you see?"

22

She gazed into her mother's looking glass across the room and watched his hands caress her.

"Those are fair and tempting regions, they are, begging to be discovered. A man knows how to make use of such territory." He held her there, his mouth close to her ear, making her watch as he disrobed her, all the while whispering his pleasure at the smoothness of her skin and the still childish roundness of her body. Finally she thought she could stand it no longer, that he had become deranged, that she would snatch up the quilt to cover herself and run from him. But abruptly, he doused the light and forced her downward onto the bed, covering her small form with his own. She cried out in terror, but he muffled her sounds with a pillow. She sobbed at the pain and fought him blindly, gasping for breath. Aghast, she realized that he was doing to her what barnyard animals did to each other, panting and heaving in brutish convulsions. She lay still, hurting, mortified. He had abused her in such a grotesque fashion that she did not think she could ever again look into his face. Mrs. Vose had been right. He was a stranger. She had known nothing about him. And now she was alone with him in this unfamiliar place. She could not return alone to Saint Luke's Plains, humiliated and used by a madman.

He pushed the pillow to the far side of the bed and brushed her hair from her face. "You're a spirited one for sure. Are you all right, girl?"

"I want to die."

"Ah, now, it's not as bad as all that. You'll become used to it, they all do. And tomorrow I'll buy you a fine bonnet to wear on the journey. Would you like that?"

Their wagon was almost ready, save for the covering on top. It was indeed a substantial sight, solidly built, with five graceful hickory bows arching over it to support the gray oiled canvas sheath. She wondered if it would, at the last, prove commodious enough for all their stock of provisions. It seemed to her that they had purchased enough to outfit several wagons. Only that morning, Mr. Bates had bought her a spinning wheel, though she hardly knew how it might be wedged in among their sides of bacon, sacks of dried peas and beans, smoked beef, sugar, coffee and dried fruit, not to mention the three hundred pounds of flour they had set aside for the journey. She

23

had few belongings of her own, but Mr. Bates's baggage included his small, heavy leather chest, two rifles and a shotgun, a canvas tent, flannel shirts, heavy trousers and a sparse but bulky library of volumes on animal husbandry. It seemed there was no end to the furnishings they must carry.

"Be a good girl and run back to our room. I left some coins on the washstand. Bring them to the dry goods merchant's. I must buy some ribbons and cloth for Indian trade. Hustle now, will you?" He turned and strode away toward the dry goods shop, a cluttered, dingy maze of supplies which advertised itself as "The Great American and Territorial Mercantile Emporium, H. Haskins, Prop."

"Young lady." A strapping, broad-chested man reined up his horse beside her. "Might that have been Blackie Collier with whom you were passing the time of day back here?"

"Who, sir?" She looked up into his face, a grizzled uneven beard, weathered skin and eyes barely visible under his worn, wide-brimmed hat. "The gentleman is my husband."

"His name isn't Benjamin Collier? Blackie?"

"We are Mr. and Mrs. Caleb Bates. We've come here from Saint Luke's Plains."

"Mrs. Bates?" It was Reed Pierce walking toward her. "This fellow isn't giving you any difficulty, is he?"

"None at all, friend," the rider told him. "I had thought to pay my respects to an old acquaintance, but I was mistaken. No offense intended, ma'am." He touched his hat brim and gave his mount a light kick.

"None taken, sir," she called after him.

Across the way, Reed Pierce's wife Kate waited, hanging back from the bustle of the street as though to make herself invisible under the overhanging eaves of the storefront that sheltered her. Lucy waved. The glimmer of a smile passed over Kate's face, then disappeared as quickly as a frightened sparrow.

"Where are you bound, Mrs. Bates?"

"To our lodgings, Mr. Pierce. I've an errand to run for my husband."

"We'll accompany you. A lady can't be too careful here. There are probably any number of rogues in Saint Joseph, bent on getting beyond the Line and away from United States' laws." He took her arm and led her across

24

the street to Kate. "And at any rate, half the fellows passing through here haven't seen a white woman for far too long. The mere sight of one as pretty as yourself is bound to bring out the worst in them."

"I thank you for the compliment, but it was my husband who caught the man's interest, not myself."

"A likely tale!" He smiled warmly and held out his other arm for Kate. "At this moment, I am the envy of every fellow in Saint Joseph, with two lovely ladies at my side."

She saw Kate raise a hand in front of her face, fluttering her fingers nervously as though to ward off an insect. But it was her husband's flattery which had caused her distraction. Lucy felt suddenly overwhelmed with pity for the woman, and wished there were something she could say or do to put her at ease. These two handsome people with their fine bearing and elegant accoutrements puzzled her. She had watched, spellbound, as they packed their wagon with sets of pewter plates and goblets, brightly flowered bandboxes, even a delicate set of scales of bronze and brass. And when Reed Pierce struck his lucifers to light his pipe it was on a shining, slim silver box which bore his initials elaborately engraved on its side. When Kate jotted down lists of provisions they must buy, she wrote in an ornately filigreed silver case with him ivory leaves that fanned out like a hand of cards. Both of them seemed to take such possessions for granted. They carried their splendid appurtenances wholly without affectation. Lucy wondered what else it was they carried with them. Whatever it might be, it was neither shiny nor pleasing and it weighed heavily upon them both.

Lucy could not help but be curious about the travelers assembling in Saint Joseph for the westward journey. Strange faces became familiar ones as the day of departure drew nearer. What had been a motley confusion of souls straggling into town from points unknown began to take shape into an orderly band of emigrants sharing their burdens, their knowledge and their hopes. They voted as one to elect White Russell as captain of the train. White was the elder of two brothers, both Kentucky backwoodsmen and experienced in the ways of the frontier. He was a smithy by trade and though not a tall man, he had about him an air of dignity and purpose which inspired confidence. His face was nut-brown and leathery as cured hide, and his dark hair was streaked by a milk-white shock which grew from the center of his forehead as though cleaving his head in half. The younger Russell brother was taller by a head and had a mop of kinked, flame-colored curls which had earned him the name Red. He was the more outspoken of the two, a headstrong, energetic fellow who fairly pawed the earth in his eagerness to get on with the journey. Red Russell was a gunsmith and carried not one but two Colt Patersons on his person at all times.

There were a number of farmers, plain folk and hard workers, and some who claimed to be professional men, including one who said he was a saddler but seemed woefully inept at handling horses. There was a short, somber French-Canadian who spoke little English and kept to himself. Reed Pierce, who knew some French, said that he was a carpenter named Jean-Jacques Louet. Everyone called him French Jack. The only other foreigners were a German father and son, both cutlers, who made themselves understood in broken but adequate English. Old Burger was an arrogant, quick-tempered martinet, given a wide berth by most of the others. Young Burger was a pale, taciturn shadow of his father, who smiled only rarely and always in the direction of his wife, Ellie, a sweet, quiet, round-faced girl from Ohio. She was not much older than Lucy. Sometimes she gazed in Lucy's direction and nodded, as though she wished to become friends. But she was afraid of Old Burger's capricious outbursts of anger and refrained from conversation.

There were several children, though none as young as Tessa Pierce. Save her, they were all boys. The youngest was Joe Mason. He was eleven and frisky and spindly as a colt. He had fair hair which fell like a shiny mane over his freckled forehead. He would brush it back impatiently, only to have his father give it an affectionate tousle and throw it once again into disarray. It amused Lucy to watch John Mason tease the boy. There was between father and son such a fond devotion that one might almost warm one's hands by its glow. Mr. Whiton said that Joe was the only surviving child of half a dozen boys to the Masons. Even now, Mrs. Mason was at home in Springfield, awaiting another birth. Next year, God willing, she would join them in the Oregon country.

The Masons were not the only ones bound for Oregon.

26

Over half the party would strike off onto the northern route when the time came. But now that time seemed very far away. White Russell had a detailed waybill which would take them as far as Fort John. The travelers would supplement their information with whatever news they might learn along the way to guide them from Fort John to Fort Bridger, Fort Hall and beyond.

They were a confident crowd, to a man. On that balmy, clear day in the middle of May when they crowded about, waiting for White Russell's starting shout, were it not for the teams and the wagons they might have been celebrants at a spring fair, so giddy were they with the mixture of adventure and high hopes.

As the moment of departure drew nearer, the excitement of the undertaking mounted, racing through the throng, possessing them all. Celia Whiton sat fanning herself rapidly in the still cool air of morning. The oxen shifted restlessly under their yokes. The horses pranced fitfully in place, eager to be off and going. The spare mules clustered around their bell mare, biting and kicking each other, jostling for closer position. Two of the Pierces' mule team set to braying lustily, jealous of those near the mare. Kate glanced quickly at Reed who gave her a reassuring smile. All around them, the gentlemen were calling to each other, their voices raised and filled with bravado like men intoxicated. Mr. Bates coiled his whip in his hands, loosed it, then coiled it again. "Hey, girl!" he shouted up to Lucy in the wagon. "Are you set?"

She nodded and then suddenly began to laugh, a gay, delirious, exuberant giggle which would not be contained.

White Russell raised his whip and snaked it out with a resounding crack. "Wagons, ho-o!" he bellowed. A tumult of cheering burst forth. Tessa Pierce, clinging to her pony's mane, squealed with glee, kicked her tiny feet against its sides and pursued by the Whitons' two dogs, Rudi and Rusty, made west for California.

It was a glorious excursion, Lucy thought, even if it took some getting used to. Most of them were unaccustomed to camping, the women in particular. At first Celia Whiton was shocked to learn that she would have to wait until they laid by for a day or two to wash her clothes. But there were breakdowns early on, with wagons and equipment to be repaired, and she soon got her chance, though her freshly laundered wash was darkened again with dust in no time.

Sometimes Lucy would wake from her sleep and lie listening to the night noises. Next to her lay Mr. Bates, snoring softly, his fingers lightly touching the stock of the rifle beside him. From somewhere not too distant came the mournful howling of the wolves that dogged their trail. But more than anything, it was the sound of the constant wind to which she listened. It washed over them, moaning as it streamed and swirled, buffeting the canvas over her as if attempting to wipe the landscape clean of such intruders. And each day, as they moved on, the wind was at its business again, sweeping away all traces of their camp. She did not tell Mr. Bates that the wind frightened her.

After all, it was spring, and the lush green prairie was resplendent with wildflowers and the promise of good grazing for their animals. The streams were high and had to be taken with caution, but water was plentiful and as sweet-tasting as any she had ever sampled. At daybreak, the aroma of fresh coffee wafted over the landscape as the women tended the breakfast fires and padded about in the dew-damp grass, serving up crisp bacon and bread and molasses. They bustled about, helped by the younger boys, cleaning up and breaking camp. White Russell gave the call, "Catch up!" and the teams were yoked and harnessed for the first pull of the day.

Often as not, Mr. Bates and another of the men rode scout, departing ahead of the others to find a place for nooning. Lucy had learned to handle the oxen, walking beside them, urging them on. Mr. Bates had taught her to crack the whip over them so as not to let it fall on their hides. She enjoyed watching it snap and curl in the air, a thin black ribbon against the blue sky. Celia Whiton pronounced her proficiency "unseemly," but Celia Whiton's opinions had long since ceased to matter to anybody.

In the late afternoon each day, they made a new camp. While the women and boys gathered brush for the cookfires, the hunting parties rode out in search of game. Sometimes there was fresh meat, sometimes wild turkey from which Kate Pierce made a savory stew, shaving into it small flecks of nutmeg from a solid silver grater shaped and carved like the nut itself. There were beans and biscuits and dried fruit and songs by the firelight. John Mason played the fiddle, and as the dusk around them deepened, the rousing strains of "Yankee Doodle" rose into the moist night air. French Jack tapped his boots on the ground and sang out at full voice, trying to mimic the words of the others, invariably coming in a bit late. Ellie Burger always led the hymns in a surprisingly full, rich contralto. "Fellows," announced Mr. Whiton, "we've no need of firearms with Mrs. Burger along. She sings sweetly enough to convert any heathen savage's soul." Old Burger scowled and muttered in German to his son.

In the first week of June, they reached what French Jack called *la côte de la Nebraska.* It was a strange place, this coast of Nebraska, as barren-looking as the full moon that shone coolly down on the vast, treeless landscape. It extended to the rim of the horizon, offering not a single thicket or shady grove to mark a milepost on its great grassy shoals. Here and there along the wide river itself an occasional willow or cottonwood rose from the banks and arched gracefully over the water, but the few sparse stands only brought more sharply to mind the peculiar desolation of these outlands.

The green of the grass had begun to fade with oncoming summer. In places it was grazed short where buffalo herds had passed, leaving poor browsing for their cattle but plenty of chips for the cookfires. Celia Whiton expressed a vigorous aversion to collecting the buffalo chips. "Madam," said Mr. Bates, "I suggest you overcome your delicate sensibilities or in the absence of firewood you will have to consume your antelope raw. Is that your preference?"

"Why do you bait her so?" Lucy asked when the woman had marched sullenly out of earshot.

"She's got no place here, a weak feminy thing like her. If she were my wife, I'd see to it she did her full day's work or she'd be left by the wayside."

"Surely you don't mean that, Mr. Bates."

"Fetch me my chisel, girl. If I don't clean out these animals' hooves they'll be infected. And mind you take my other pair of trousers to the river with you."

They had laid by for repairs that day. Reed Pierce and some others had formed a hunting party so they might make meat, and the women had taken advantage of the stop to wash the piles of dusty clothing that had accumulated since they last laid by. Lucy knelt on a soft, sandy promontory of the riverbank, wringing out the wash. Upstream, the mules were noisily sucking the water in through their teeth. It was a particularly ugly sound, and each time the beasts would sidle closer to where she was, Lucy would flap a piece of wet clothing at them, backing them away with the noise. She could tell without looking up that they were coming closer again. She seized Mr. Bates's shirt and shook it out. But just then she heard another sound, a mewing which rose to a high whine and then higher still, a shrill, piercing wail that cut through the quiet air like the agonies of a dying animal. She turned and shaded her eyes from the sun.

Above her on the bare, grassy bluff stood the figure of a woman, Kate Pierce, outlined against the cloudless sky. She stood alone, unmoving, a dark shadow screaming wordlessly into the stillness around her. Once Lucy had seen a tree struck by lightning. It had stood traced against the sky like Kate Pierce did now, black and burnt-out.

She made a move to scramble up the banking, but she saw Mr. Bates and Red Russell appear at a run. Red gripped the woman by the shoulders and jolted her roughly back and forth. The sound continued, quavering as her body shook under his grasp, subsiding finally exactly as it had begun. Then Kate did something which was almost more peculiar. She stood stiffly erect and as complaisantly as a lady taking a sociable stroll, she laid her arm on that of Mr. Bates and walked serenely away with him in the direction of the wagons.

No one spoke of the incident, not even when Reed Pierce and the others returned. They brought with them the carcass of a buffalo cow, its udder still full of rich milk. That evening there were tasty hump steaks for dinner. When the rest of the meat had been cut and hung and the night watch posted, they repaired to their tents.

"What do you think happened, Mr. Bates?"

"Not a thing. Nothing at all happened."

"But we both saw it."

"Nothing happened to her. Did it?"

"But the way she shrieked . . ."

"Girl, Pierce's wife is quite mad. That's all there is to it."

She was silent for a moment. "Are you sure?"

30

"I know that kind too well. Go to sleep."

Celia Whiton and some of the others shied clear of Kate Pierce after that. Not that they could very well avoid her altogether. They simply ceased to make conversation unless the occasion demanded it, and Kate, sensing this, withdrew into her shyness as though it were a refuge, busying herself silently with her chores, speaking infrequently and then only to her husband or Tessa.

Lucy made attempts to draw her out, timidly at first since she had never before known a madwoman and had no idea what to expect of such a creature. But Kate seemed mild enough, wrapped in her singular isolation, and Lucy thought that, mad or not, the woman must be wretchedly lonely despite the presence of the others. Her overtures met with little success, perhaps the tremor of a smile, perhaps only a gaze of mute distress so acute that Lucy sensed it as sharply as a scream. Finally Lucy decided it could do no harm to broach the subject delicately with Reed Pierce, out of the others' hearing.

"Mr. Pierce, Kate's not herself of late. Is she feeling poorly?"

"Don't trouble yourself over it, Mrs. Bates. She means no discourtesy. My wife is inclined to spells of melancholy. And please, do call me Reed."

"What makes her so very sad?"

"Now surely," he said, giving her a slight smile, "even one as sunny as yourself sometimes carries a heavy heart. It happens to some extent to everyone, from time to time."

She thought a moment. "Not to Mr. Bates. He never has any pangs at all."

"Then he is either not human or a great dissembler. Lucy, you've been most kind to my wife, and I'd count it a personal favor if you would be patient with her. She needs more tender sympathy than I am able to afford her. Don't be put off. Do what you can. Please."

Later that day she told Mr. Bates, "He is a sad one too, Reed Pierce. He tries to justify it by saying that everyone has qualms now and then. I said that my husband never did."

"And what did he say to that?"

"A sorry thing, really. It was as though he needed to defend himself. He said that you were either inhuman or a great deceiver."

31

"Were I you, girl, I would steer clear of that strange pair."

"I thought you liked them. You said they were people of quality."

"And so they seem. But some of the most tempting streams hide dangerous depths. Keep a distance from those two."

She had given her word to Reed that she would try to be Kate's friend. Yet it was a wife's duty to obey her husband. She would follow Mr. Bates's bidding, but surely it wouldn't hurt, if he was gone scouting or hunting, to show a little kindness toward Kate Pierce.

Tessa's disposition was as different from her mother's as day from night. Her laughter pealed like the clear, pure chiming of a small bell. Lucy, hearing it, found the sound a rare and special grace in this remote, barren place.

Back in Saint Luke's Plains, June had always been a month lush with promise. The crops would be growing tall, the landscape dotted with flowers, and fat, furry bumblebees would be droning lazily over the verdant fields.

This was no such country. The land was seared brown by the blazing sun. The nights were not like summer nights full of sweet scents and the soft conversations of owls going about their bosky business. Here the evenings grew chill, even though it was almost July, and in the pale light of the moon, the land looked gray and lifeless.

"I shall be glad to see Fort John," Ellie Burger said as she peered into the large, iron pot of beans and gave them a stir.

"Soon," Lucy replied. "Mr. Bates tells me we are only a few days away. Ah! I've gone and spilt the saleratus." She laid her mixing spoon on the ground and carefully, with one finger, brushed the saleratus into it. "We've been eating dust for weeks. I don't suppose a bit more in the biscuits will kill us." She rose and emptied the spoon into her mixing bowl. "Look, Ellie. There are the scouts riding in."

They reined up their horses and dismounted. Young Burger quickly unsaddled his mare, calling to his wife. "Pierce says the Frenchman thinks a storm is coming."

"But Mr. Burger," Ellie protested, "there's only one small cloud yonder."

It moved toward them at amazing speed, growing larger and darker as it came.

"Secure your belongings!" White Russell ordered. "And round up any strays!"

"How cold it's growing!" Lucy shivered suddenly and went to fetch a shawl from the wagon. A flash of lightning blanched the blackening sky. The canvas wagon top shuddered noisily as the wind sliced across it, making a curious, sharp sound somewhere between a whine and a whistle. The wind rose, strident and irritating, and above it swelled the roar of the storm. The lightning flashes came in quick succession now, followed by deafening thunderclaps. Mr. Bates jumped into the wagon, saying something which Lucy could not hear. When the crash of thunder had subsided, he spoke again. "It's damned near to freezing out there."

"In here too." Her teeth were chattering.

Suddenly it began to pour. The water came down so hard that it penetrated the canvas in seconds, running in rivers down the interior sides of the wagon and splashing from the roof, soaking them both. Mr. Bates threw her a dry blanket and wrapped himself in another.

Lucy peered out into the teeming rain. She could see the mules huddled nearby, their hindquarters to the wind, being pelted by hail. Around their hooves lay a thickening layer of white stones. Some of the animals were gashed and bleeding. They stood, heads drooping, unable to lie down on the icy, jagged surface of the ground.

She clasped her hands together, flexing her fingers, trying to keep them from the numbness of the cold.

After a time, the hail stopped falling, but the rain continued until dawn. When they emerged from the wagons, the earth had become a slough of mud. They moved slowly, encumbered by wet clothing, still chilled, exhausted. There were no cookfires. The buffalo chips had dissolved in the downpour. For breakfast they ate some jerked buffalo meat and raw bacon with a ration of brandy for all but the youngest children. The water in the stream next to the encampment was thick and brown, roiled from the storm. Lucy carried two buckets to the wagon and sprinkled them with cornstarch to settle the silt. "Get out your palm and pricker and set to mending that canvas, girl," Mr. Bates told her. "Two of the wagons are badly mired. I'll be with the rest of the men, hauling them out."

She did not see him again until noon, when he came running toward her through the mire, almost tripping in his haste. "Gather the women and children together," he ordered her. "Sing as loud as you can. Don't stop until one of us tells you."

She looked at him blankly. He was soiled with mud from head to boots and his hair fell in a tangle over his face. He had the look of a wild man.

"Damn you, girl!" he bellowed. "Do as I say! Get everyone together and sing! Red Russell slipped from the wagon tongue, and it rolled over him. His leg's crushed. It has to be taken off. We must distract the young ones' attention."

Lucy summoned the women and children. She stood in the center of the small flock, waving her arms fervidly in rhythm to their songs. She marched around the inside of the circle, beckoning the voices out of the half dozen children, pulling them forth, it seemed, by sheer force. From behind the gathering of singers came the excruciating screams of Red Russell's suffering, penetrating the sound of their songs, filling the air with his agony.

"Who did it?" she asked Mr. Bates that night.

"White Russell started, but he vomited. Your friend Pierce took over. Did a decent job of it, I'll say. It took most of the rest of us to hold Red down. He's a strong one. Damned if we didn't retch our bellies dry, one by one."

It passed through each of their minds that it could have happened to anyone. They perceived the presence of danger more closely now. It lay in ambush among them, assailing the senses like some dank, sour-smelling effluvium that gradually faded and was gone, only to recur when least expected.

They laid by at Fort John, a small post of the American Fur Company, rising incongruously from the vast naked plains along the Laramie. It was a rough-hewn, poorly equipped station, and Lucy, remembering the tales she had heard of places like Bent's Fort with its tasty food and billiard room, could ill conceal her disappointment. But they made repairs, conducted a bit of trading and procured a waybill from there ahead to Fort Bridger. By the time they moved on, Red Russell was making his way about on a wood crutch he'd carved for himself. Robust fellow that he was, he bore his anguish stoically. Only the deep hollows beneath his eyes and the stiff set of his jaw betrayed his distress.

Now the journey became a rough, toilsome route up and down dismal, somber-colored ridges dark with pine and cedar. It seemed that having wished so long for the sight of trees, they were now to be rewarded by the oppressive gloom of these interminable hills.

When they reached the North Fork, the water was far too high for fording. It was clear they would have to ferry the wagons across. They set to caulking the seams, stuffing them with strips of cloth and melting pitch over them to render them watertight. Red Russell sat with young Joe Mason on the riverbank, teaching him how to fashion steering oars from the soft limbs of the cottonwood trees which arched over them as they worked. Twice Reed Pierce had been forced to lance Red's stump of a leg, draining it and dousing it with spirits. "My husband says it is a stubborn infection," Kate confided to Lucy. "Mr. Russell is weakening."

"If only there were a doctor among us."

"My husband knows his business, Mrs. Bates." With that, Kate lapsed into one of her silent moods and retired from conversation. Lucy had learned to ignore these spells of Kate's. They no longer surprised or alarmed her. She simply took them as a part of the woman's character. Lucy's tacit acceptance elicited an unspoken fondness in return. When Mr. Bates grew short-tempered, she could rely on seeing the trace of a sympathetic smile on Kate's lips and a slight inclination of her head as though to say, "Well, that's the way it is. We must all live with such things." When Lucy's chores overtaxed her, Kate always offered the extra pair of hands to help. Mr. Bates expressed no objection to the friendship, as long as the two women refrained from conversation. "There's a lot to be said for a man having a dumb wife," he commented as they prepared for the river crossing.

"Do I distract you with my small talk, Mr. Bates?"

"It's Pierce's wife. Better silent than screaming."

The ferrying of the wagons was an arduous task made more difficult by the strong, swift currents of the river. They drove the oxen across first, to have them ready for hauling up the wagons on the opposite bank. Then came the bell mare and the mules. Almost to the shore, the mare was seized by the current. Sensing the peril, she swerved and tried to swim back, but in that moment of turning she left herself prey to the force of the stream and was carried downriver. The mules panicked and followed, some by instinct, some victims of the river current. The hapless animals crushed against each other, wild-eyed, braying in terror, a maelstrom of tumbling bodies and legs sinking and reappearing, desperate to reach the side of the bell mare.

The men scrambled down the banks on either side, running abreast of the drowning beasts. Some bounded into the water with ropes in an attempt to bring the nearest to shore. John Mason, overseeing the oxen on the far side, kicked his horse and rode hard to a point just beyond the frantically swimming bell mare. He urged his mount into the river and made for the mare.

"Pa!" Joe Mason cried out. Lucy ran to the boy and clasped her arms around his shoulders, holding him close. Together they watched as Mason's horse struggled against the current. For a moment it appeared that Mason had miscalculated the speed of the flow. The mare was drifting by him. But he took a coil of rope from his shoulder and with a profound effort, sent it flying, holding both ends in his hands, catching its curve under the neck of the bell mare. Feeling the sudden pressure of the rope against her, she started and attempted to turn against the current. Mason's horse rammed into her and overturned, rolling over its rider.

Joe hid his face against Lucy's chest, and she held him tightly to her. "He's strong, Joe. He'll come out all right," she murmured, but she scanned the roiling water in vain for some sight of the boy's father.

They found John Mason's exhausted horse almost a mile below the ferrying point, where it had stumbled onto a shoal at the curve of the river. Too weak to climb the bank, it stood there, its head bent low, unable to move further. Hanging from one stirrup, grotesquely twisted, was John Mason's leg. His body lay face down in the shallows. What had once been his head, battered to an indistinguishable red mass against the rocks and snags of the riverbottom, sent out a widening rust-colored flush in the water around it.

The bell mare survived, though several of the mules perished. The Whitons' wagon, that ponderous overburdened ark, struck a submerged rock during the crossing. Its axle broke, and its contents were sent tumbling into the current, gone beyond recovery. Celia's rocking chair bobbed like a cork on the surface of the water until it disappeared around the curve where John Mason's body had come to rest.

Between the North Fork and Independence Rock, Red Russell's strength failed him at last. They buried him in parched brown earth by a brackish stream so full of some copper-colored mineral that it looked like blood flowing from a wound in the ground. They drove the oxen over his grave, as they had John Mason's, so that no animals, four-footed or two-footed, might discover the place and disturb his remains.

The dust billowed around them as they traveled across the scorched land and rose into the air like gusts of smoke caught up in the hot, dry wind. The earth had long since sucked up what little water there might have been. Here and there they came upon reeking mineral pools, their edges thick with a white, briny crust. Even the animals refused to drink. They lay in the water and cooled, and when the moisture on their hides dried in the sun, it left them frosted with fine, shimmering crystals. As they moved on, some of the cattle, compelled by thirst, overcame their distaste and drank. In a matter of days, most of the poor beasts sickened and died.

When at last they reached a freshwater stream, they fell upon it, men and beasts alike. But now it was fuel for the fires which ran in short supply. There were few buffalo chips to be found, and though they hacked out strands of artemisia, it burned too quickly, like a torch, backing them off with its great heat and dying as fast as it had flared.

They traveled now along wide, gentle slopes, moving gradually higher with each passing day. The nights grew cooler. Darkness brought with it a deep chill, leaving a frost that glistened on the earth at sunrise, and a thin film of ice on the water buckets.

One morning, White Russell called them together around the smoldering remains of the breakfast fire, his manner solemn and worried. "We'll have to lay by for a bit. We've half a dozen men unfit to travel. Reed Pierce here has something to tell you all."

"Keep clear of those who are ill," he began.

"Whoa, there," one of the men interrupted. "What kind of talk is that? They need tending. We're not a bunch of Indians, you know, leaving the old and infirm to die alone by the wayside."

"Listen to me. It's cholera. There was an outbreak among the Osage in 'thirty-four. They only survived by scattering."

"Like the man said, we ain't Indians!" another voice called out.

"Sir, I assure you I know of what I speak. There are other cases in which quarantine has appeared to save lives. We must try everything possible, or all of us, one by one, might perish here. If you've any better suggestion, I'd like to know what it is."

"You'll not keep me from caring for my husband!" shouted Celia Whiton. "My place is by his side, and I'll not pay the slightest attention to your heartless, hare-brained ideas!"

"Very well, Mrs. Whiton. I cannot rightly stand between a husband and wife. Do as you must. As for the others, French Jack has volunteered to assist me in looking after them. The rest of you will please go about your business."

"Do as the man says," White urged them. "It can't hurt."

"Don't see how it can help us much, either," Old Burger muttered.

"The disease must be attacked at its very onset," Pierce told him. "We are doing our best. We'll keep you informed. If anyone of you falls ill, make sure I hear about it right away."

"That Pierce makes a mighty curious doctor, if you ask me," Mr. Bates told Lucy as they prepared to bed down for the night. "It's a pity we've no one more qualified."

"Perhaps he's read books about doctoring."

"Celia came back for her bedding this afternoon. She told White Russell she thinks the man's a charlatan. Just as daft as the wife and maybe dangerous. Seems she begged him to bleed Whiton, and he refused."

"Celia makes a fuss at the best of times. I daresay she's quite hysterical with Mr. Whiton so ill."

"My, my, how quickly you spring to champion Reed Pierce. To what does he owe such a stalwart defense? Girl?"

"To nothing!" Lucy's cheeks were fiery. "He's a decent man, that's all! He's trying to keep us alive, and though he may be no trained doctor, I'll wager he's more capable than that old biddy hen."

"You're young, girl, and foolish. Reed Pierce is playing on your sympathies like a man plucking on a fiddle. I have eyes to see with."

"Mr. Bates, begging your pardon, but I do believe you may have misjudged him."

"The devil you say. Do you think he's content in the company of that madwoman? Use your head, girl. Why do you think he made such a fuss over you back in Saint Joseph? Because some stranger chanced to hail you on the street? Not likely. And why would he then proceed to assail your husband's honesty? Answer me that!"

"He did no such thing! He merely meant to say that he thought you concealed your tribulations better than he."

"So now you are also Reed Pierce's interpreter. The man had no business talking to a woman about her husband behind his back."

"It was I brought up the subject. It was my fault. I'm sorry. I'd no idea it would rankle in you so."

He looked at her in silence for what seemed a very long time. Then he raised his hand to his eyes and rubbed them hard with his finger and thumb, as though to clear away some irritating substance. "Ah, girl," he said finally, "spirit's an asset in women and horseflesh, but it has to be checked now and then or it'll run wild."

As they were assembling for supper in the gathering gloom of dusk the next evening, they heard the unmistakable sound of hammering from across the slope where Reed Pierce had set up his small infirmary. "French Jack," Young Burger said quietly in answer to Lucy's questioning look. The carpenter was building a coffin.

By noon the next day, they had buried two of the stricken men. They consumed their dinner in silence. Tessa Pierce looked on as her mother ladled stew from the large iron cooking pot into a smaller one to carry to the makeshift infirmary.

39

"Take some biscuits with you," Ellie Burger said, wrapping them in a cloth. "We've enough to spare."

"Only three." Kate returned the rest to her.

"The others aren't taking any nourishment?"

She shook her head and walked away from them toward the hill.

"Mama!" Tessa was up, running after her. She caught her mother's skirts and held them tightly in both fists. "Mama, don't go there again! I don't want you and Papa to die!"

White Russell bounded after her. He pried the child's hands loose and scooped her up. "Here, now. Your Ma and Pa are fit as can be. Nothing's going to happen to them." He raised her to his shoulders and placed her there. "Be a good girl, and I'll let you ride my dapple-gray mare until your Ma comes back. Hush now."

"What wonders children are," Ellie said to Lucy, watching Tessa bounce happily atop White's horse. Her small legs stuck straight out on either side, unable to straddle the animal's broad back. She held tight to its mane as White, holding a lead rope, trotted the mare around him in circles. "They change like milkweed in the wind, blowing one away one minute and another the next."

"And a blessing it is, too. Poor Joe Mason's just old enough to know what a fix he's in."

"Will they leave him at Fort Bridger like they say?"

"It's the best thing. Vasquez there has a China article wife. The boy will be looked after. An eastbound trading party can take him and his Pa's wagon back to the States."

"To come all this way and have to go back . . ." Ellie shook her head.

"He's all his mother has for a man in the family."

"I wonder if the poor woman's had her baby, and all the time not knowing John's lying dead in some lonely place."

Of the four men remaining alive in the infirmary camp, Whiton and two others survived through the following Sunday, but Celia had begun to suffer stomach cramps.

"*Ach*," said Young Burger, "the woman imagines herself sickly always."

Kate glanced at him and shook her head.

40

"Speak up, Mrs. Pierce," White told her. "This is no time to fall tongue-tied."

She stared at the ground by his feet. "My husband requests one of the ladies' assistance to care for Mrs. Whiton."

"Then you must go, of course."

"No!" She reared up her head and stared at White. "No! I cannot help!" Her eyes were those of a trapped, terrified animal. There was panic in the pitch of her voice.

Tessa began to weep.

"Control yourself, Mrs. Pierce. You're upsetting your daughter."

Kate was screaming now. "I cannot help!" she cried. "The woman will die! I am an angel of death. I am an angel of death. I am an angel of death." She continued to repeat the words. They came tumbling out of her mouth, over and over, rapid, slurred, in a frenzy.

White raised his voice over Kate's. "It appears to fall to either Mrs. Burger or Mrs. Bates."

"No!" said Bates.

"One of the women must tend to Mrs. Whiton," White said firmly.

Young Burger stepped forward. He looked back at Ellie, who lowered her eyes. Old Burger moved to stand behind hs son.

"I am an angel of death. I am an angel of death . . ."

"Mr. Russell," Young Burger said quietly, "my wife expects a child. I cannot allow her among the dead and dying."

"Then you three will please escort Mrs. Pierce to her wagon and stay with her until she comes to her senses."

"Russell," Mr. Bates said, "I'll not permit my wife to serve as Reed Pierce's sick nurse. It's an occupation unfit for a lady."

"I'm ordering it, Caleb. Celia Whiton needs her. We can't abandon the woman to the ministrations of a man who ain't her husband. Go, Lucy, and gather up your things."

For a moment, she thought Mr. Bates was going to strike White. He stood rigid, his fists clenched at his sides. Then, "I'm coming with you," he told her. "Let's go."

The stench of the camp was almost unbearable. Lucy gagged as she rinsed out the fouled, reeking clothing of the sick. They lay listlessly, too wasted to stir, sometimes

41

calling weakly for water, more water. Lucy herself could consume nothing, save a sip or two of Mr. Bates's brandy.

Celia's body seemed to shrink inward, drawing upon itself until her skin clung to her bones. Her eyes were sunk deep in her face, and her pallor had a ghastly grayish-blue hue to it. Her voice was feeble. Lucy bent close to hear her. She tried not to recoil from the woman's sour, fetid breath.

"My husband—"

"Mr. Pierce thinks the danger's passed, but he's still very weak."

"Lucy?" Reed entered the tent. "How is she?"

"She still wants you to try bleeding her."

"There's too much risk. That's a fact. We've nothing that works much better, but I'll not weaken them further by loss of blood. Has she been taking her liquids?"

"She said you were trying to drown her."

"Keep her drinking that stuff."

"What's in it, Reed?"

"Salt."

"What?"

"You heard me. It's nothing but salt water."

Lucy wondered if it were possible that Celia had been correct, that there was not one but two lunatics among them. Mrs. Vose used to say the world took after Noah's ark. Like paired with like. "Mr. Pierce? Reed? Why would you feed them salt water? Won't they die? The cattle that drank at the salty pools died. Perhaps one of the other gentlemen might have a better suggestion."

"Trust me. I know it's not medicine. It's folklore. But if I'd tried it sooner on the three other men, I think I might have pulled them through. I didn't remember having read it until it was too late for them. It's rumored to work."

Gently, she suggested, "Maybe we are in need of stronger stuff than rumors."

He did not answer. He was taking Celia's pulse, concentrating on the faint palpitations of her wrist.

Something in the sure way he touched the woman's flesh with his fingers caught Lucy's attention. She watched his face, seeing there a look of preoccupation so absolute as to prohibit intrusion.

She followed him outside the tent and caught his arm. "You are a doctor, aren't you, Reed? Not a school-teacher."

He halted. "I do not practice medicine, if that's what you mean."

"But you're not a teacher."

Reed hesitated.

"Pierce?" interrupted Mr. Bates. "Whiton's calling for you. Says he feels hungry.

She looked after the men as they walked away, wondering what kind of people the Pierces really were.

The three men and Celia survived, whether because of or in spite of Reed Pierce's treatment no one could say. Too frail yet to walk, they lay inside two of the wagons, emerging only when the company came to a halt.

The way to Fort Bridger was a hard stretch. White Russell had ordered every available vessel filled with water and each wagon loaded with cut grass to sustain the animals. They had redistributed their personal goods among all the wagons, so that none might be unduly weighed down by the added burden of the sick. Still, the wheels sunk deep in the sandy soil. The sagebrush tore the animals' bellies and blocked the wagons. The men hacked away at it with axes, gasping in the shimmering blaze of a relentless sun. There was no shade, only the inescapable scrub. Hardly a blade of grass sprouted along the way. Occasionally the withered land was scarred by the trace of a streambed seared dry by the unmerciful heat. Water was rationed now. There were no longer any spare oxen. Some had strayed off at night, searching for better grazing. The weaker ones simply gave out. They lay helplessly in the bushes by the trail, too far gone to stir, waiting for the wolves.

It was not only the wolves that tracked them. At night, high on the hulking sandstone buttes in the distance, a scattering of signal-fires burned.

"Why do they follow us, Mr. Bates?"

"For the leavings. They're waiting for us to have to lighten our loads or abandon a wagon, maybe with a few odds and ends inside."

"Scavengers. Would they attack, do you think?"

"Only if we appeared to be in dire straits."

"All the same, would you teach me how to use your pistol?"

"When there's time to spare. When we reach Bridger's."

By the time they drew near the station, four more of the party had become ill. Old Burger and two others had been sunstruck, faltering and dropping in mid-stride, grown men collapsed into motionless bundles of clothing, like fallen scarecrows. In the Pierces' wagon, French Jack lay gamely fighting the cholera. At White Russell's insistence, the others had given up most of their water rations on his behalf. They slaked their thirst by sucking on rags soaked in vinegar.

"So help me," Lucy said, half to herself, "before I let this infernal country get the better of me, I'll live on vinegar and dust just as if they were nectar and ambrosia."

"Stubborn," Mr. Bates muttered, but there was a note of approval in his voice.

They laid by at last at Fort Bridger. The place was nothing more than a few cabins and animal pens, but there was good water to be had and meat, something they'd not tasted since the last of the buffalo, long back. During the four days they remained at Bridger's station, French Jack began to improve, and the others regained their strength. Mr. Bates, in his free time, instructed Lucy in the firing and cleaning of his pistol. "You've a keen eye, girl, but you hesitate too long. Delay spoils the aim."

"I shouldn't like to fire without thinking."

"You'll do it if you have to, mark me."

When the time came to leave, Lucy took Joe Mason's hand in hers. "I shall think of you often. You're very brave, Joe. I know you'll make us all proud of you."

As the wagons neared the crest of the cedar-covered hill beyond the fort, she caught a glimpse of him through a break in the trees. He stood outside one of the huts, his red shirt bright against the weathered logs, his fair hair shining in the sunlight, a small, distant figure no longer waving.

The two weeks' journey northward to Fort Hall was less difficult than they had feared. There were deer and antelope to be had, and sufficient water, though some of the springs tasted strongly of sulphur. "It's the devil's own territory," Celia pronounced darkly. "Once again, he makes himself known."

"Rot," Lucy countered, provoked at the woman's incessant pessimism. "Don't listen to her, Ellie. Have we

44

any dried fruit left, Kate? It would taste grand with the roast venison."

Kate shook her head.

"Perhaps we shall find some at Fort Hall."

But there were fewer supplies to be found at Fort Hall than at the other trading stations. They made repairs and rested. No one spoke of the fact that soon the party would break up. Those bound for Oregon would press on to the northwest, and those for California would split off to the south. One of the trappers at the fort played the fiddle. They hadn't heard the sound of a fiddle since John Mason died. They sat together and sang in the summer dusk, their animals browsing peacefully in the plentiful, cool grass, the firelight sputtering low, their voices mingling with the soft sounds of the night birds and the crickets.

III

THERE WERE only fifteen remaining in White Russell's party. Twenty-two had made for Oregon. They'd elected their own captain and determined a new order of procession. Solemnly, they'd bade Lucy and the others farewell. How different the leave-taking was, she thought, from that spring day in Saint Joseph. Gone was the blithe, jaunty air of folks setting out on a lark and the foolish audacity with which they had so roundly dazzled themselves. They clasped each other's hands, said little, and parted.

Where were they now, she wondered. Somewhere far north of this place, following the signs and the stars like themselves, bound for a distant place full of promise, beckoning them like a light on another shore. Sometimes she thought they must all be a bit mad. Not herself necessarily, for she had no home or anyplace where the especially belonged. She was traveling from nowhere to another nowhere which, from all accounts, at least sounded more rosy than the one she had left behind. But the rest of them had quit their homesteads, the fields they'd tilled, barns they'd raised, trades they'd plied. And why? They were not like the Pilgrim fathers, sailing forth under a billowing standard of noble and holy resolve. They were, she concluded, dreamers, adventurers. She found the notion titillating. Imagine what Ma would say, seeing her in such a company. Her father, though, would have understood that even stolid Old Burger and the prosaic Mr. Whiton were pursuing some private dream. It was Pa who said all sailors were daft to begin with. Lucy had caught the grudging admiration in his voice, the way he shook his head and smiled in awe of such a madness.

And when her Ma was vexed with him, she sometimes said to Lucy, "I swear, I think that man is moonstruck."

She supposed it was that trace of madness that had enabled Pa to believe the farm might actually reward him one fine day, that fed his dogged perseverence and sustained him as it did the Burgers and the Whitons and the rest of them. It was, Lucy decided, a worthy madness, dangerous perhaps, but one she must acquire if she wished to do more than simply survive.

She did not think of Mr. Bates in the same way she did the others. Mr. Bates, unlike the others, never lookd back. He acted as though he had come from noplace at all and left nothing behind him. He talked about sheep farming and boasted of the bags of fine wool he would sell and the profits he'd gain, just as the others talked about the land and the trades they would ply when they reached California, but Lucy gradually realized there was something missing in his speech. He lacked the madness she heard in the others. It was as though the journey in itself was his purpose. It frightened her to think he might be like the Wandering Jew, rootless always, condemned to blow before the wind like thistle-down. It scared her all the more that she was his wife and she was going to have his baby.

The heat bothered her the most. September was almost upon them, and the late summer sun beat down with a force so palpable as to stifle all but necessary conversation. They plodded on silently, weary of sage and snakes and the monotonous, faded terrain. The dry air shrank the wooden wheels of the wagons. Time and again they halted to drive wedges under the iron tires to tighten them. The perspiration on their skin dried as quickly as it appeared.

This was Digger country. White had seen them through his spyglass, squalid creatures wandering about on foot, all but naked.

"How could they exist in such a place?" Lucy wanted to know.

"In holes, ma'am, dug in the ground. They grub for roots and vermin."

She gave a small shudder in spite of the warmth of the evening fire.

"Mangy animals. Thieving as pack rats. That's why we

camped here in the clear, ma'am, and cut down the bushes nearby."

"I shall sleep better thanks to you, Mr. Russell."

But she did not. She lay awake listening to the calls of life · in the night, wondering which were genuine and which might be made by Indians, until weariness finally overcame her.

The crack of rifle fire splintered the silence. Lucy sat upright, then, seized with vertigo, lay down again, trying to keep still, listening to the bawling of men and animals, counting the shots. She reached out to where Mr. Bates lay, but he was not there. That meant he had gone to stand watch. She raised her head slowly. It was still dark, but she knew it must be near daybreak if he had relieved the earlier guard. She wanted to cry out for him, to run into the midst of the melee to find him, but she checked herself. Motionless, she lay there, her hands clenched tightly into fists, feeling her heart pound against her chest as though it were trying to break free and escape.

In the first light of dawn, they assessed their losses. The arrows of the Diggers had overflown the clearing. They had aimed for the animals, to cripple as many as possible so they might be killed and left behind for them to feast upon. They had got two of the mules. The bellmare, wheezing blood through a wound in her neck, had to be destroyed. One of the Whitons' milk cows was missing, and the larger of the two dogs was nowhere to be seen. The smaller, the black and white spotted pup named Rudi, ran aimlessly about the carnage, sniffing at the fallen animals, searching in the confusion for its companion.

"Get the dog away," Mr. Bates told Lucy. "I have to kill the ox."

She lifted Rudi into her arms and turned away from the sight of the dying animal, its belly pierced deep by an arrow.

They put the Whitons' remaining cow under yoke in its stead. Tessa Pierce walked beside Lucy, Rudi trailing at her heels.

"Why did the Indians take Rusty?"

The child had made pets of the dogs. There was no sense telling her. "Because they wanted to play with him."

"Do Indians have little girls?"

"Yes."

"Will they comb out the brush from his coat like I did?"

"Of course."

"Ssh." Mr. Bates came abreast of them. "Keep walking." He lifted Tessa under one arm and raised himself and the child into the wagon. He reached for the rifle in its sling. "Damn." He recoiled as his fingers touched the sun-scorched barrel. Gingerly he lifted the weapon onto his knees.

Lucy scanned their surroundings. She saw no movement.

"That's it," he said, "keep going."

She fixed her eyes on the ox team, watching the movement of their flanks, bone and sinew clearly visible in the gaunt, swaying bodies.

He fired. There was a sound in the bush, a harsh cry like the screech of a startled crow. Mr. Bates bounded down, pulling his pistol from his belt as he ran. Mr. Whiton followed, his Yager in hand. Bates fired into the scrub. The two men kicked at something on the earth. Rudi, the dog, trotted over to investigate.

"Rudi! Here, Rudi!" Tessa jumped down after him.

"No!" Lucy ran toward them. "Tessa!" She reached the child and held her back. "Go to your mother and father at once."

"Got him." Mr. Bates pushed aside the brush. "Give a look."

It was a small, dusky form, its back running crimson, its black hair filthy and matted, its legs drawn up under its chin as though sleeping. Mr. Whiton prodded one shoulder with the toe of his boot. The body rolled over. Lucy quickly glanced upward from the barely covered loins. It was an ugly face, darkly mud-colored, with a low forehead almost meeting the brow. Yet it was the still, staring face of a very young boy, its mouth agape as though astonished.

It occurred to her that it must have a mother and a father, if savages kept track of such things. But some wretched female somewhere had carried and delivered the child, just as she would the one within her. She vomited on the blood-soaked ground.

They nooned the next day by the banks of a stream, a puzzling body of water, lukewarm to the touch and appearing to flow directly eastward.

"It can't be Mary's River, can it, Mr. Bates?"

49

"If it is, we've come upon it well below the head-waters."

"But running east?"

"White Russell and I are going to scout ahead. Perhaps it takes a turn."

"May I fetch you more coffee?"

He spat on the ground. "Vile stuff. Can't get the taste of it out of my mouth."

"It's the water."

"You're sure there's no more sugar to be had?"

"None." They had used it all. For dinner there had been only beans and a watery stew of sage hen flavored with bacon, rancid now with the fat all but melted out of it by the heat. If this was not Mary's River, they were off their course, farther still from good game and good water. "Who would have thought we could run short? I remember thinking we'd supplies enough for an army." She remembered too those early days when the journey had seemed a continuous picnic and each wagon a cornucopia of victuals, the ladies trying to outdo each other in their preparations, John Mason fiddling by the firelight as they supped. How almighty confident they had been, carefree and innocent and blind as kittens.

Mr. Bates rose. "We'll be back by sundown. See that you do the washing, girl. At least the water'll do for that."

Lucy had been waiting for Mr. Bates to absent himself, and now, though she had thought about it for days, she felt suddenly apprehensive and ashamed to be seeking out Reed Pierce behind her husband's back.

"It is . . ." she paused. "It is a matter of some delicacy, Reed. I should appreciate your confidence."

"You have it." Reed looked up from the rope he was splicing. "Lucy? You have my word. Sit down."

She rested on her haunches next to him. Timidly, she told him. There were answers she must have, things she must know.

"But it's not an illness, Lucy. You'd do better talking to a midwife, if we had one, or another of the ladies."

"Kate?"

"No." He glanced up sharply. "You'll not mention the subject to my wife, whatever you do."

"I've spoken to Ellie, but this is her first. And I'll be hanged if I'll hand Celia Whiton a key to meddle in my life. Please, Reed, I'm only asking you to tell me what to expect. I was too young when Ma birthed Willie. I don't remember. Is it like the animals did on the farm?"

"Ah, Lucy." He sighed and laid the rope beside him. "Go ahead. What is it you think you need to know?"

He chose his words judiciously. Kindly, discreetly, he tried to set her mind at ease.

"I know I have put you in an awkward position, Reed. I thank you for indulging me."

"Caleb Bates must be a happy man. And his child will be a native-born Californian to boot."

"I haven't told him." And Mr. Bates, wearied to the point of inertia, had not bothered to uncover her secret.

"Good grief, why not?"

"I don't know. Something—" She frowned. "I'm not sure why, but I don't think it will altogether please him He's a man who fancies being footloose."

"He must have had his reasons for bringing you along."

"He wanted a helpmeet for the crossing, he said."

"But so few of the men brought their wives. He might just as easily have come by himself. And he has plans to settle down to a rancher's life. That's life on a tight rein, Lucy, hardly the design of an impetuous spirit."

"Yes." She looked at him, aware of the misgivings in her eyes.

"What is it?"

"I know that's what he says he wants. But sometimes I wonder. When I listen to him talk, it seems as though it was the leaving that mattered most to him, not the arriving in California. Do I make any sense?"

"No." He smiled. "I expect you're feeling a little fearful, that's all. What's unknown always scares us a bit. Put your mind to rest. You'll do fine. You're a strong and determined young woman."

"Determined? What an odd thing to say. I don't think I am."

He laughed aloud. "Lucy, Lucy. What a strange picture you must have of yourself. Didn't you tell me you wanted to escape from that hamlet back east? You dreamt of coming west, didn't you? And lo and behold, the handsome Mr. Bates presented himself at your door."

"But it was his doing, not mine."

51

"You underestimate yourself. Women have ways of getting what they want."

She was taken aback at the suggestion. "Reed? You make me sound like a seasoned coquette. I assure you, I'm no such thing."

"Don't misunderstand. I meant no offense. In fact, most people manage to get what they want, barring certain strokes of fate. I simply meant to say that you've a large measure of grit in you. I'll wager you'll prevail against all odds."

"Right now I should be content just to prevail until we reach Sutter's Fort."

"There. You see what I mean? There's the spirit in you."

That evening as she lay next to Mr. Bates, listening to the deep breathing of his slumber, she felt somehow reassured that everything would be all right. They had found Mary's River in this vast, trackless waste. They had simply to follow where it led, almost within sight of the Sierra Nevadas. Four hundred miles would bring them to the mountains and, beyond them, to California. She had grit, Reed said. She could weather the trials ahead. If it was true that people had ways of getting what they wanted, well then, all that she wanted in the world was to reach California. She could not imagine wanting anything more than that.

They crossed and re-crossed the sluggish, clouded stream and crossed it again, plodding laboriously along its path. In places, the dust lay fully six inches deep and fine as powder. The mere effort of walking through the soft stuff exhausted men and animals alike. Each footfall, each turn of a wagon wheel sent up blinding gusts of dirt which settled on their perspiring faces, graying them to a deathly pallor. A ghoulish breed, they appeared, ashen-skinned, red-eyed, rasping, hacking, spitting creatures, stumbling foggily up against bushes and wagons, spectral shapes enveloped in a great gray-brown cloud which remaind suspended in the air long after they had passed. Lucy heard White Russell swear bitterly as another of the animals fell wheezing and snorting to its knees.

Under White's orders, they lightened their loads. The teams were flagging, and only by consolidating the efforts of the strongest could they hope to push on. Out from under the canvas canopies came their treasures, souvenirs of home, remembrances of a genteel life, sacrificed now to heat and dust and distance. The Burgers' grandfather clock lay face up between two artemisia bushes. One of the horses relieved himself upon it. From the Pierces' wagon came a set of fine treenware, bottles and phials of every shape and size, and a large trunk which gave way as it fell to the ground and broke open. Lucy stared with undisguised wonder at the spectacle of such finery. Velvet the rich, deep color of violets. Maroon silk trimmed with lace. Pink satin slippers with dainty, pointed toes. It looked for all the world as though a garden had blossomed in the sand.

"Girl, give me a hand here." Mr. Bates eased her mother's looking glass over the side of the wagon. Lucy grasped the bottom and laid it against the spokes of a wheel. She brushed at the coating of dirt with her forearm and peered into the clear, round pool of light.

It was not she, this apparition. Lucy rubbed feverishly at her face with her palms and ran her splayed fingers through her hair, shaking loose a floury sifting of dust. She looked again. The blonde hair had coarsened and bleached in the sun until it was almost colorless. The plump, childish countenance had been whittled away, and in its place had emerged the sharply hewn features of a woman. She had a heart-shaped face with a wide, high forehead above a slim, newly prominent nose. The bones of her cheeks were pronounced above the hollows beneath, and her chin firmed almost to a point. Her brows were pale, her eyes bloodshot. Her skin was burnt brown and weatherbeaten, and the flesh of her lips had shriveled and cracked. She stared at the haggard, dirt-streaked reflection and suddenly felt moved to speak, to introduce herself to this stranger, this dazed young woman who looked not unlike a survivor of Pompeii. As she parted her lips, the figure in the glass did the same, and Lucy knew once and for all that this woman's face was her own.

She bounded into the wagon, almost colliding with Mr. Bates who knelt over his small leather trunk. "Mr. Bates! Such an astounding sight! I looked into—" She stopped. "What is that you have?"

He glanced down as though he had not noticed what he was holding. "This? It's a daguerreotype."

"May I see it?" She held the marvelous thing in her hands, tilting it to the light. On the bronzy, burnished metal surface lay a picture of four people so lifelike, so detailed, that she might as well be gazing into the room where they sat. In the center was a slim, shy-looking woman sitting primly upright against the back of a chair, her right arm resting on a cloth-covered table. Her light hair was parted in the middle and drawn back. Her lips were slightly pursed. Her wide eyes had the look of a small, soft creature unsure whether to hold quite still or to scurry away to safety. She wore a ribbon pinned at her neck, and over her dark dress she carried a light shawl. Around the ruffled flounce of her skirt were seated three children, soberly posed, hands folded in their laps. Three little girls in luminous, creamy dresses, two dark-haired, one fair.

"What a miracle," she said softly. "How is it done?"

"I don't know. By chemistry."

"How wonderfully real they look. As though they might speak at any moment. Where did it come from? Who are they?"

"My brother's wife and children. From Philadelphia."

"But I thought you had no family."

"My brother is dead."

"Perhaps that explains why she looks so very anxious."

"She does?" He took it from her and held it at arm's length. "She always looked like that, for as long as I can remember."

"You're not going to leave it behind, surely?"

"I've no need of it."

"But it weighs so little. Your leather chest is so very heavy. There must be something in there that you could dispose of. It seems a pity to leave such a keepsake. Let's look in the trunk for something else."

"No." He moved in front of the chest. "I need it all. There's nothing in here I can spare. It's type."

"Type?"

"Printing type. Metal blocks."

"What would you want with type?"

"I might set up a press if I could get the supplies. I've often thought about it."

"You have? But what about the sheep ranch?"

"There's nothing says a man has to tie himself to one way of making a living. Now think, girl, what else can we do without? Not the books. I'll need the books. Any of the cooking gear?"

Lucy stared in wonder at the vista ahead of her. Rivers did not evaporate and vanish before one's eyes, but the Mary's had. The river simply disappeared. It dwindled and sank into a stagnant, yellow-green swamp, its shores lined with salt-encrusted rushes. The water gave off a stench and tasted of alkali.

The men set to the task of cutting the meadow grass and bundling it in the wagons. The four women prepared food for keeping. There was naked desert ahead, void of grass for grazing or brush for fuel. There would be no camping until they had passed it, only short respites to rest the teams. It could be crossed in a day and a half, White said. Every serviceable container must be filled with the bitter water. They would start before daybreak.

But no amount of forewarning had prepared them for the crossing itself. In the worst of dreams, Lucy could not have conjured up such a sight. The earth leveled out on all sides, flat and unrelieved, white as chalk, baked hard by the searing sun. Not so much as a lizard trespassed in this lifeless landscape. Even the wind had perished. The heat of the still air punished her lungs. Her temples throbbed. Her eyes burned from the glare. Each step felt as though she were walking on banked coals. The far horizon deviled them as they went, advancing, receding, wavering and shimmering, veiling itself behind a writhing haze. It was as though the darkest of nightmares had reversed itself, appearing in the cloudless blaze of day, bleached white as bone.

Ellie Burger walked beside her. She stared ahead and spoke. "The valley of death," she said, and she began to whisper the Twenty-third Psalm to herself.

"Look!" Lucy pointed. The others saw it too. Hovering near the horizon lay a large, blue lake, its shores lush with woodlands.

Mr. Bates moved past them. "Mirage. The devil's own torment. Keep going."

The water supply had long since been exhausted. They paused again to rest. Two scrawny mules lapped at the hollow barrels on the back of a wagon and wandered away, heads drooping. They stood soundless and still until they dropped. There was no time to strip the carcasses for meat. Another of the wagons had to be abandoned for lack of a full team. The men contrived pack saddles and emptied the wagon of goods. "Faster, boys," White Russell urged. "There's no time for delay."

Young Burger, helping the others, handed down a large pile of bedding to his father. The old man caught it in his arms and fell.

"Mr. Burger!" Lucy ran to him. Suddenly she swayed like a sapling in the wind and toppled forward.

They roused her with vinegar compresses. Groggily, she tried to raise her head, but it was too heavy. She opened her eyes and blinked dazedly in the harsh light.

"Mr. Bates?"

"I'm here." He touched her arm.

When she had regained her senses, they put her on one of the horses. Mr. Bates walked beside her. "It's the child," he said.

"You knew?"

His parched lips made a grimace of his smile. "Foolish girl."

"Mr. Burger . . . is he all right?"

He shook his head and glanced away from her to the horizon. "We'll bury him when we reach the other side. He's in their wagon."

She gazed across the desolate land. Far in the distance a whirlwind danced, but not a breath of air stirred where she rode. She thought of Old Burger, come all this way, only to die in the desert. Too many had died. First Ma and Pa and Willie and now the others. She must not die. The baby inside her must live. She and the child were all that was left. Without them, there would be nothing to show for Ma and Pa having ever existed.

The loudness of her own voice surprised her. "I didn't come this far just to die in some godforsaken place!"

The two men in front of them turned around, perhaps thinking her delirious. They stared a moment and trudged on.

In the night, they came to water. Ellie stood next to her, gaping at the sight.

Illuminated in the pale, waxy light of the moon were springs the like of which Lucy had never seen. Gurgling, boiling water sending up a milky mist which hovered over them, swirling and churning like sinister clouds. She started and leapt back as one of them spurted skyward, gushing forth a column of steam.

"Out of limbo and into the regions of hell," Ellie said softly. "Nearly dead of thirst, and the devil mocks us."

"Don't stand there, men," White commanded. "Dam up the flow where you can and lower the buckets. The quicker you move, the sooner we'll have it cooled enough to drink."

At dawn they gathered to bury Mr. Burger. Young Burger, convulsed by grief, leaned against his weeping wife.

Little Tessa stared up at them for a moment and backed away through the crowd. You couldn't blame the girl, Lucy thought, so much sorrow and toil and pain to bear, and only a child of five.

They lowered him into the earth. The shovels rasped against the ground. In the stillness, Tessa's voice shrilled out, "Rudi! Rudi!"

Lucy turned and saw Tessa grasping frantically at the empty air, trying to keep her balance on the brink of the boiling spring. As the child tottered, Kate screamed and sprang toward her. Lucy threw herself upon the woman with all the force she had. White and French Jack ran to her side and held Kate down. From her slack, open mouth came a hideous bellowing, hollow and roupy, as though she had been struck violently in the stomach. She fought the two men, writhing and wild-eyed, crazed as a steer at gelding. The brute force of the woman was overwhelming.

"Rope, Mrs. Bates," White shouted. "Hurry."

Lucy ran to the wagon, her chest heaving with sobs. The horror of what she had seen surged over her like a palpable, clammy chill, and she retched and dirtied herself. Shaking, whimpering, she loosed a coil of rope from the side of the wagon and ran back to them. Mercifully, Kate had fainted. Hands and feet bound, she was carried into the Pierces' wagon and placed on a quilt.

They pulled the bodies of the child and the dog from the steaming spring and covered them quickly. The sound of the shovels hollowing out the earth grated on Lucy's ears until she thought she could not control the scream of anguish that welled up in her. She clenched her jaw tightly and felt the tears cascading down her cheeks and neck, their salt stinging her skin.

White tried to force Reed Pierce to ride, though he insisted he could walk. He repeated himself over and over, as though he had desperately seized upon the argument to stave off contemplating what had happened to his child and to his wife. At last, dazed and swaying drunkenly, he did as White ordered.

"We'd best be leaving this satanic place as quick as we can," White told them. "Get a move on."

They traveled in silence across a low, sanded ridge. The animals struggled knee-deep in the soft powder, bawling and braying their misery into the still air. One of the lead pair of oxen stumbled and was gone. Mr. Bates unyoked the others.

Now it was their own wagon, so handsome and solid, which must be unloaded and abandoned. But Lucy had no tears left to spare upon a wagon. Numbly, she handed down their belongings to the others.

Several times she looked back. The wagon lay partially sunken in the sand, bleached and picked clean like the hulk of a beached galleon in one of Pa's tales of shipwrecks and desert isles. Finally it disappeared from sight behind them.

For a while, Lucy kept silent, afraid that what she saw might be another mirage. But no, as they descended toward the faint green smear ahead, there emerged the distinct shapes of cottonwood trees rising above a grassy bottomland.

"Hey!" cried out Mr. Whiton. "The river! We've done it!"

But there was no echo from the others. They moved like sleepwalkers, too spent to cheer or to rejoice.

In the early morning, Lucy sat in the shady meadow, watching Tessa's pony graze, taking in the fragrant perfume of the lush grass around her. Nothing, she thought, would ever smell quite so sweet to her as long as she lived. She caught sight of Mr. Bates and White Russell riding back into camp. They had scouted ahead, hoping for a glimpse of the mountains, the last barrier to their Promised Land. Beyond them lay California.

She ran toward the men. "Did you see them?" she

gasped, out of breath. The weight of the child was beginning to tell on her.

Mr. Bates grunted and dismounted.

"What do they look like?"

"A jagged stone wall, my girl. Something the Lord might have erected to repel trespassers." He unsaddled his mount and sent it off with a slap to the rump.

"Will we be able to get across?"

"I plan to. Don't you? What happened to the lass who was so determined to reach California?"

"Nothing. Nothing, sir. Only—"

"Spit it out, girl."

"Ellie's due any day now, she says. And I don't know how I'll be at climbing in this condition. Then there's Kate. She can't be loosed. She goes berserk. This morning Celia Whiton untied her for a moment, and Kate tried to gouge out her own eyes."

"Women," he sighed. "Pierce's wife's gone altogether, has she?"

"They say so. She doesn't even make a sound anymore, just tries to strike out if she's not tied."

"We shall drag her up if we have to. See here, girl, those mountains are not called the snowy range without reason. We'll be into October by the time we reach the top. White says the snows can come at any time. They've been known to have early storms up there. There's no safety until we've reached the valleys on the other side. So I suggest that if you cannot climb, you'd do well to crawl. One way or another, we have to move on as quickly as we can."

By Lucy's count, they had crossed the river's meandering course more than twenty times before she stopped keeping track. The icy, clear water which days before had seemed like milk and honey quickly became nothing more than another trial, another hindrance to their pitifully slow upward progress. The animals' hooves, softened by constant immersion, pained them so greatly that they refused to move at all unless the men walked beside them, hip-deep in the frigid stream, urging them on. But were it not for the water, the wagon wheels would have splintered and broken on the rocky river bottom. As it was, overhanging limbs ripped at the wagon canvas, tearing to shreds those canopies which had for so long been their protection against the elements. No effort

59

was made to repair them. Time was short. Each passing night felt colder than the last.

Mr. Whiton and some of the others were suffering badly from dysentery. Too weak to stand the numbing cold of the water, they left it for the other men to drive the teams and were forced to walk behind with Lucy, Celia and Ellie.

Here and there the stony banks of the river gave way to green glades softly illuminated by the slanting rays of the sun angling through heavy stands of fir. The trees were so tall, the woods so dense, that only patches of light penetrated through them. In the desert it had seemed the sky was so close and overspreading that it all but threatened to swallow them up. Now Lucy found that she had to stand still and look directly upward in order to search out a small fragment of blue far above the web of branches that enclosed them.

They hacked and hauled away the wind-felled trunks that blocked their path. She had never seen trees of such girth; giants they were, dwarfing the men as they worked. And late one afternoon they came abruptly to a place where there had been a fire in the forest. All the way down to the river's edge the ground was blackened. Charred stumps pointed skyward like great skeletal fingers. Not a creature stirred there. No birds sang. Through the burnt-out columns they glimpsed clearly for the first time the mountains ahead. No one spoke.

A towering gray fortress of sheer granite reared up in front of them. Along the top, against a brow of clouds, lay jagged escarpments glinting in the waning light like shards of broken glass. Below them, shadowed and somber, stood lofty pillars of rock, some of them in formations of such precision as to have been sliced by some monstrous hand. In places, huge boulders hovered on the outcroppings like weapons from immense catapults. Tall pines stood ranked along the sides of the cliffs, armies in green, standing guard. At the foot of the precipice there lay cascades of granite, as though falls of rock had poured forth from its side and dwindled finally into rubble.

"How long, do you figure?" Young Burger asked White Russell.

"Two, three days."

"Are you sure?"

"No more'n you."

There were not even game trails to offer an indication of the way upward. Time and time again, they reached a higher ledge to find that it led only to a wall of granite. Once more they would stop. The men would haul rocks into position, loosen the hard earth and pack the rocks together to build a rough ramp to the next level. The women and ailing men were led up first. Then came the Pierces' wagon with Kate lying inside, and behind it came the others. The mule teams made their way, surefooted as goats. The oxen faltered on the craggy footing. The wagons swayed precariously as they clambered ahead.

Lucy, pausing to take a deep breath, heard Ellie give a cry and turned to see the Burgers' wagon lurch sideways, wide of the path. For a moment it moved so slowly that it appeared to hang there, about to roll back and right itself. But it had pitched too far. It fell, crashing against the outcroppings as it slid down the steep ravine, dragging the hapless, yoked animals behind it.

All but two of the oxen had to be destroyed. They saved what they could from the wreckage. White and Young Burger went down by rope and stripped the canvas from the bows. They gathered up most of the scattered contents and bundled them in the canvas. When the packs had been hoisted to the top, White and Young Burger made their way up.

"We're going to unload," White told them. "It's the only way. We'll camp here and make packs for the animals, all of them, the oxen and Tessa's pony too. No one will go a step without carrying something. The women and the sick will take rolls of clothing."

They toiled toward the summit for the rest of the day, bending under their burdens. "Mr. Bates," Lucy said, "you must reconsider. You can not tote that thing up by yourself." Since early morning, she had watched with alarm as, heaving and sweating in the cool mountain air, he had lugged his heavy leather trunk upward, reeling under its weight.

"Keep your peace, girl." He set it down on the ledge and caught his breath.

"Please. It's too much for you. Put it on one of the oxen."

"And have it knocked off? I don't suppose you saw

how they've been trying to throw off their loads. It's my own personal property, and I don't aim to lose it. See to our food, girl, and don't bother me."

"Oh, Lucy." Ellie Burger stood beside her, shielding her eyes against the strong afternoon sun.

"I know." Lucy looked ahead. There rose a sheer rock overhang, perhaps all of nine feet high, and not a break in it for them to pass.

Silently, Ellie began to weep. She made no effort to dry the tears that rolled down her cheeks.

"The men are looking for a way. Sit down. Rest."

Ellie made a small sound in her throat.

"Ellie? What is it? Are you all right?"

She nodded.

Lucy glanced at Mr. Whiton, who lay on the ground next to her. He blinked in the sunlight. At least he's still alive, she thought. Two of the men had recovered, but Mr. Whiton and two others were failing rapidly. They were so weak, so consumed by dysentery, that their skin hung on their bones, loose as an ill-wrapped shroud.

"Here, man." Reed Pierce bent over him. "Put your arm around my shoulder. They've found a cleft in the side. Let's go."

The rock had split clean, opening a crevice barely wide enough for one animal at a time to push through it. The mules and horses were led up first. The oxen balked. Only by pulling them onward by ropes and beating them from behind with sticks could they be forced through the fissure. They slipped on the smooth stone surface underfoot and fell. The men struck and prodded them until they got up again and made their way through, leaving a trail of blood in the narrow passage. Once up, they were yoked again and hitched to chains let down over the cliff and fixed to the tongues of the empty wagons below.

"Where is my husband?" Ellie Burger asked as she watched the men bring Kate through the passage, cradled in a blanket.

"Below," Celia told her, "pushing up the wagons with the others."

Shoving with all their might, the men on the lower ledge heaved their shoulders to the wagons, as the teams hauled from above. The wagons bounced and clattered as they were drawn slowly higher, one by one, dangling like spiders against the face of the rock.

"We are almost to the top, Ellie," Lucy said. "Follow Reed Pierce and the others. The rest of the men will come when the wagons are up."

"I don't know . . ."

"Is anything wrong?"

"I think it's my time. The baby is coming."

"I've had five of my own, Mrs. Burger," Celia said, seeing Lucy's frightened look. "It's nothing to fear. Tell me when the pains come, and I'll know when you're ready. For now, let's move as fast as we can. You'll be more comfortable if we can reach the top before the baby arrives."

"Mrs. Whiton!" Reed Pierce called down. "Hurry!"

Celia ran ahead of them. The old woman's energy amazed Lucy.

"Hurry!" he shouted again.

Celia stumbled and fell. Crawling hand over hand, she scrambled toward the sharp peaks of the escarpment where he stood.

Ellie looked after her. "Mr. Whiton's dead."

"We aren't. Keep walking."

"Are we almost there?"

"Yes. Give me your hand. Some of these rocks are loose."

Slowly, unsteadily, the two heavy women made their way up the boulder-strewn crest of the ridge, panting like dogs with every step.

"Look!" Lucy cried. "Look up now!"

The sky was full of fat, gray clouds, so thick and seemingly so close that she might reach out and scoop them up in her hands. From behind one cloud, the sun sent out a silver wreath shining on the piney plateau where they stood.

A short distance away, Reed Pierce and Celia Whiton bent over Mr. Whiton's body. The two other ailing men who had gone ahead with Reed lay nearby, themselves more dead than alive.

"You didn't have to come to tend me, Mrs. Whiton," Ellie told her.

"I said I would. And there's no more I can do now for my man."

Lucy held the girl's hand. "What a soft blanket the pine needles make, Ellie. Don't they smell sweet?"

"Is my husband here yet?"

"Soon."

Ellie gave a deep moan.

"Push now!" Celia cried. "That's it! Hold her down, Mrs. Bates. She mustn't thrash about so. Here it comes."

It was a tiny, glistening thing, smeared with blood, moving ever so slightly as Celia wiped it clean and swaddled it.

"How is she?" asked Reed Pierce, seeing Lucy approach the campfire.

She shivered in the chill of oncoming dusk. "Celia says she's bleeding a bit much. The boy's a listless little thing. Reed?" She looked around her at the men making camp. "Where's Ellie's husband? Hasn't he come yet?"

"He's not coming. There was an accident."

"What's going on here?" Mr. Bates strode up to them. Lucy moved a step away from Reed. "What happened? Ellie keeps calling for the baby's father."

"One of the wagons broke loose and fell back on him. He went down almost forty feet. He was dead by the time we reached him. His neck was broke."

Before nightfall, they had buried Mr. Whiton and Young Burger at the foot of a large, dome-shaped, granite outcropping. A breeze had come up, damp and cold. They stood, their hands clasped more for warmth than prayer, listening to White recite the passages he knew too well by now. When it was over, and they started to file away, Celia Whiton spoke. "Jeremiah," she addressed the place where her husband lay, "sleep well in California."

It was true, Lucy realized, they had arrived. She tried to feel something—elation, a trace of thankfulness or satisfaction, but nothing came. There was a stinging on the bridge of her nose and, touching it, she found it moist. Snow had begun to fall. Fine, icy flakes swirled in the darkness like specters dancing in the wind.

Later that night she pulled the heavy buffalo robe close around her and walked to the tent where Ellie and the baby lay. The snow groaned softly under each footfall. She crouched and slipped inside the canvas opening. "Celia? How is she?"

"In and out of dozing. She wakes now and then and calls for him. I tell her he's on his way. She has no idea of time. Did you feed the Pierce woman?"

"Just now. Here, I brought you some pieces of meat. It's mule, but it's food. We've nothing else, not even beans left. White says we have to be getting to the valley right away. We must find a safe place to lay by and hunt."

Celia inclined her head toward the sleeping woman. "She's not well enough. She's weak from bleeding. It won't stop."

"Have you spoken to Reed Pierce? Perhaps he could help."

"Are you mad? What decent woman would allow a strange man to gape at her body? Have you no sensitivity?"

"He seems to know something about doctoring."

"Jack at all trades, master of none. If only I'd been able to give her some rhubarb tea, her labor wouldn't have been so punishing. She's in the hands of the Lord now. His wisdom will prevail."

"And the baby?"

"Sickly. I never knew an infant that wouldn't nurse. It seems he hasn't even the gumption to suckle. French Jack brought the cow to see if he'd take that milk but he spat it up."

Lucy pushed the blanket aside and gazed at the slumbering baby. He had a faint halo of golden fuzz, a blond like his father and grandfather. She touched the soft down on his head. "Celia? He's cool." She moved her hand to his chest. Slowly, she pulled the wrap over him, covering his lifeless face.

Celia sighed. "It's God's will."

The meek submission in her tone irritated Lucy, but she thought better than to rebuke a woman who had lost her husband only a few hours earlier.

Ellie stirred fitfully. She whimpered and in a voice not much more than a whisper, she said, "Fritz?"

"Soon," Celia answered.

Lucy woke to the sound of the oxen bawling out their hunger. The ground was covered with a blanketing of white. The harsh contours of the landscape were softened now, and she thought for the first time in many weeks of the gently rolling fields of home. The sun shone on the dazzling surface, almost blinding in its brilliance, and the snow lay on the branches of the trees like gobs of thick, rich cream.

There was no coffee, only some weak tea for breakfast and what remained of the butchered mule, no more than a mouthful for each of them. They ate quickly and broke camp.

"But Mr. Russell—White, please." Lucy was trying to make him change his mind. "Ellie's too weak to travel, even in a wagon. And if she's to die, we must see to it that she is buried here with her husband and child where she belongs."

"I doubt it'll matter much then, ma'am. And if we don't reach the valley and decent pasture for the animals, we could all be buried here with them. We've no more provisions, nothing. Your lady friend is in good hands."

"Don't tell me she's in the Lord's care, Mr. Russell! I have my doubts about that!"

He gave her a small smile and touched the brim of his hat. "Most of us do, now and again, ma'am. Shall we go?"

On their western flank, the mountains showed a gentler side, sloping steadily away from the snowy summit toward the valley ahead. But the way was strewn with boulders and dense underbrush. Everywhere sprang up a maddening round bush, flat-leafed and speckled with withered reddish berries which they dared not eat. In places, the earth underneath showed through vivid and coppery, as though the fruit had drawn its coloring up through its tough, wiry branches from the ground below.

Where the slope dipped downward, unbroken by any level resting place, they snubbed ropes around the staunch pines to check the descent of the wagons. But the going was hard. French Jack's wagon suffered a broken axle on the rocky incline and was left to the wind and weather and the curiosity of the ubiquitous foxes.

Toward the end of the third day of their descent, the pines began to give way to leafy trees, and the path became less rugged. They glimpsed broad meadows, green from the recent rain, spreading out before them like wayposts to Eden. And beyond the woods and ridges came gentle foothills dotted with spreading oaks. The golden autumn sun filtered through the graceful branches of the willows that lined the sweet-tasting streams. Grazing and game abounded, and so benevolent and hospitable was

66

the countryside that they laid by at last to rest and to bury Ellie Burger.

Lucy sat on the ground by the cookfire, watching the grassy hills rippling under a balmy breeze. She turned and spoke to Celia. "It looks like home."

"Missouri?"

"No," she said. "Home."

IV

WHAT A spectacle they must have presented as they straggled across the flat bottomlands toward Sutter's walls. The Indian laborers in his fields looked up and watched the procession in silence. They must have thought them the dregs of the white man's race—haggard, tattered men, their eyes hollowed and red. The two women walking with them, their skin shriveled and burnt to the color of a dried leaf, their collarbones sharply protruding from their gaunt frames. And one of them obviously with child, shuffling along with her awkward, rolling gait, clasping her frayed shawl self-consciously about her as though she were wearing her pride on her shoulders. It would have been impossible to judge her age, the elements having taken their toll. And when she saw her image in a looking glass, she wondered herself if she had not traded her youth for a waybill west. She was a drawn, scrawny figure of a woman, her ungainly, swollen stomach a preposterous accessory to the rest of her body.

While Mr. Bates and Reed Pierce and White Russell journeyed to Yerba Buena for supplies, she stayed with the others camped near the reassuring walls of the fort. She and Celia cared as best they could for Kate. They changed her clothing, fed her, wiped her mouth. She was little more than a helpless infant. Lucy often wondered about her own baby, thinking of what had happened to Ellie, and trying to imagine how she would cope when the time came. Celia would be there, of course; that was some small comfort.

They had decided among themselves that the Pierces, White, Celia, French Jack and Lucy and Mr. Bates

68

would push on together to a place about forty miles east. There was an old man settled there, a mountain man named Luther Moore who'd acquired a flock of sheep and a squaw wife and built himself a cabin. It was a fine place for stock, they heard tell. And there was plenty of wood to be had and a small, clear river nearby. Between them, they would manage, and Moore was on friendly terms with the savages hereabouts.

The Indians here could hardly be thought of as red men. They were a dusky lot, and were it not for their straight hair, they might be taken for blacks. Some of those in Captain Sutter's employ spoke Spanish and were said to be Christians, though they looked to Lucy as heathen as could be. Shouting and whooping, they pursued the cattle across the broad, green plains outside the fort, waving noosed ropes called *reatas* in the air. They rode in large Spanish saddles with wooden stirrups and wore huge spurs, wide as the span of her hand. They would wave the rope in the air above them and, with almost flawless aim, send it whipping forward to slip over the head of the running steer. None of them had ever seen such a sight. They applauded these *vaqueros* and marveled at such dexterity. Captain Sutter shrugged and in his heavily accented English told them, "Children, they are all children."

And like a stern schoolmaster, he ruled over them. He was a canny, keen-eyed Swiss with a prominent nose and an oddly boyish roundness to his cheeks when he smiled, which was rarely. Lucy had never encountered a man of such ironclad determination and industry. He presided over his small empire, single-minded in his ambition, attentive to the smallest detail. And though he was unfailingly hospitable to the travelers who came to his bastion, there was no denying his beneficence was bestowed with a distinctly lordly flourish.

Still, she wondered when she would enjoy such luxury again. And in the weeks that followed, her glorified recollection of the place would have warmed the Captain's heart, so high and secure were its mud-brick walls in her memory, so hearty the simple fare and genteel the surroundings.

Not that Mr. Bates stinted in providing for them. He had returned from Yerba Buena laden with everything and anything that might be found in the holds of the

69

ships trading there. "Caleb Bates was born to live well, girl, and after such a journey, nothing is too good for us."

"But how did you do it? We'd nothing to trade."

"Leave that to me."

Indeed, it seemed ungrateful to question his bounty, especially since he had brought with him half a bolt of nankeen for her very own. Perhaps when spring came, after the child was born, she would have time to make herself a dress.

For now, they lived as they had on the trail, in tents, while the men cleared the ground and hewed the trees for their cabins. They'd had no trouble finding Moore's place, perched as it was on the crest of a rolling hill above the stream, visible for miles and affording Luther Moore a view from the heights of all who ventured near. Whether or not he welcomed the prospect of neighbors they never knew. "I reckon there's land aplenty." As he turned and walked away, they heard him say, "Couldn't stop you anyhow."

Lucy regarded him with open curiosity, this hoary old trapper with his leathery skin and peculiar ways. He dressed like a savage in fringed buckskin adorned with a hideous array of porcupine quills. And he had taken for a wife a squat, swarthy, moon-faced squaw, shapeless as a sack of meal, who shuffled silently about in buckskin skirt and mocassins and an evil-smelling deerskin cape, her face daubed with clay. Moreover, she had the unsettling habit of chanting each morning at the break of day. From inside Moore's cabin walls would issue a strident, unmelodious incantation loud enough to wake the living and dead alike.

The offspring of this odd pairing was a small, tanned boy, perhaps a year and a half old. He was a sweet-tempered little child of the woods, his face as smooth and round as an acorn and his dark hair shiny and sleek as a wet otter. Abel was his name, though the woman never called him that. She watched after him impassively and nursed him when he was hungry, but not once did Lucy see her fondle or play with him.

Savage ways or no, the Indians had to be dealt with. Each day as the men went out for wood Captain Wally would appear to extract from them whatever payment he could, a shirt perhaps, or some beads or dried peas.

70

"Why do they call him Captain, Mr. Bates?"

"Because he's the Miwok leader. Would you have him called Admiral?"

She couldn't imagine a body less captainlike than this short, sparsely clothed figure loosely wrapped in skins about the hips. It was rumored that Captain Wally could understand the white man's talk. Conversation came to a halt when he approached.

"He-kang-ma." Captain Wally extended his hand.

"I know," said Lucy, used to the ritual by now, "he's hungry. I'll fetch some dried peas. Why does he always say he's hungry?"

"Because we're using the oak trees for firewood," Mr. Bates replied. "They grind the acorns to make flour."

"Good morning, Mr. Moore," she waved as he approached. "Bit of a nip in the air today."

"Rain's coming," he said. "Came to tell you to hurry up your roofing." He nodded to Captain Wally.

"Hai-et-kem."

"Rain's a little way off yet, but nearing, he says."

So Captain Wally understood at least one word and probably a good many more than he let on. She drew her shawl about her and scanned the horizon. "Mr. Moore! Look there, below!"

He turned and watched as his wife immersed the baby in the chill waters of the river.

"He'll catch his death of cold!" she cried.

Moore called out something to the woman, who stared at him for a moment as though she might defy him, then laid the child in the basket beside her on the bank.

Captain Wally spoke, curt and contemptuous.

"Silence!" Moore thundered. "Stupid son of a carcajou!"

"Wuk-si-mus-si," the Indian said as he turned to leave.

"And to hell with you!" Moore shouted after him.

"What on earth did he say?" asked Lucy.

Mr. Bates cast her an admonishing look. "You must forgive my wife her childish curiosity, Moore."

"Dog's nest," he called it."

"The basket?"

"The Miwok make fancy baskets for their babies. He said the woman's was fit only for a dog."

"She is not one of them?"

He shook his head. "From the north, a Modoc."

"Oh." Lucy nodded as though she understood the difference.

"I'll be off now," Mr. Bates told her. "Roof ought to be done by this evening."

Theirs was the largest of the cabins. Lucy swept the dirt floor smooth and clean each day and cooked the kill from Mr. Bates's hunt in the fireplace made from stones she had gathered by the river's edge. For the first time since she had left the farm she began to feel that here was a place she belonged. Perhaps it was having a home of her own. Perhaps it was the kinship she felt toward the others, toward all of them who had come so far together to find this place. She found even Celia tolerable. The draught of adversity appeared to have purged her of her petty complaints. Reed and White and French Jack had raised her a small cabin, and in return, she cooked and did for them and Kate, having no means of her own.

Reed had discovered a spring in the dell behind his place and named the settlement Castalia after the spring where the Muses drank. "Hell," Luther Moore spat on the ground, "it's a place, that's all. Just another place."

Lucy liked the old man, though his China article wife made her feel uneasy. How was one to approach this stolid creature who gazed sullenly from eyes dark as charcoal, watching everything, revealing nothing? Lucy gave her a wide berth. But she liked Luther's tales of stalking and trapping, of blinding blizzards and rollicking rendezvous. "Ain't hardly any beaver left," he mourned. "Damned if I'll play guide for the greenhorns. No offense, little lady. But there comes a time when a body's got nothing left but to stay put."

"He's almost sixty years old. Imagine, Celia!"

"I don't suppose he's thought of what will become of the half-breed brat after he's dead and gone."

"Maybe her people will look after him."

"Never."

Lucy lay very still under the buffalo robe, feeling the child move inside of her. No longer did her protruding stomach seem such a grotesque attachment to her body. Rather, it had swelled so large and so fast that her own small figure now seemed instead to be its property. It led the way and she followed, accommodating herself to its size and its stirrings. Sometimes she resented the situation, shuffling along behind it like a reluctant servant. At

72

other times, she lay as she did now, touching it lightly, amazed that such a miracle had come to pass within her.

"Any time now," Celia promised. "Any day it will arrive."

It was one night late in February when her time came. Celia sat by her, fretting over the lack of rhubarb tea to ease her pains. Mr. Bates waited outside, under a full, milk-white moon, smoking a pipe with Luther Moore, who, nocturnal as a hedgehog, prowled the hilltops in the night. Lucy could hear the low murmur of their voices in the stillness. She tried not to cry out sharply, not wanting to embarrass Mr. Bates. But at the last she found that she could not control herself. The spasms were excruciating. She gasped and screamed, unable to contain her suffering as the throes continued.

There were two, twin girls, tiny, wrinkled, red-faced mites squirming in Lucy's arms. They appeared to be identical, to the sparse thatch of raven-colored hair like the down on a pair of small, black birds.

"I am surrounded by wenches," Mr. Bates, said, inspecting them, and he let her sleep.

Lucy lay nursing the babies early the next morning. "Mr. Bates, have you a middle name?"

"Have I what?"

"Any middle names."

"Why do you ask?"

"Perhaps one of them might be named after you."

"Oh." He rose and walked to the doorway, his back to her. "Suit yourself. I have but I rarely use it."

"May I know it?"

"Collier. It's no name for a girl-child."

They were called Susannah and Elizabeth.

After two day's rest, Lucy rose and resumed her chores. French Jack brought her a gift, a long, low cradle, lengthy enough to lay both babies end to end. "All one tree, *le berceau*," he told her.

Lucy lined it with deer and rabbit skins and tore the nankeen from Yerba Buena into swaddling clothes for the little things. On fair days, she dragged the cradle out into the sunshine. How extraordinary, she thought, to have such weather in the dead of winter. February here was like the first cool days of fall back home. The verdant hills were full of deer come down from the snows. Fish and wildfowl abounded. No one could go hungry in

73

such a place. And when spring came, and the rains abated, they would plant their first crops. Looking at the sleeping babies, she saw in their small, plump faces the promise of all living things that grew and flourished here.

Toward the end of March, the storms came with less frequency, and a faint tracery of wildflowers began to be visible on the hills. The river ran high and swift, fed by the rains and the mountain snows. As Lucy trudged up from the banking with her wash, she saw Captain Wally on the opposite side of the clearing. He didn't usually come to their settlement at this time of day. Did he know, she wondered, that the women were alone? She felt her heart begin to pound.

Abruptly, he raised his arm in a gesture of command, bidding her to halt, but Lucy was not about to take orders from a savage. She walked toward the cabin. He made a frenzied pushing motion with both hands, as though to ward her away. And then she saw the snake. It lay between the Indian and the shallow cradle, inching its way toward where the babies slept. Lucy glanced at Captain Wally and opened her mouth, whether to scream or speak she did not know, for he silenced her before she made a sound. As she stood there, he padded toward the snake from behind. Before it could turn and strike, he calmly raised his foot and crushed its head under his heel.

Lucy ran to the cradle. The babies were asleep. "Captain Wally! Thank you! Do you understand? Thank you."

He sliced the head off the snake with a sharp stone and, rising, gave her a perfunctory nod. He peered into the cradle. *"O-ti-ko?"* He held up two fingers.

"Yes," she said with a laugh.

"O-ti-ko."

"Two. *O-ti-ko,*" she repeated.

He laid a finger on Susannah's cheek, his calloused skin dark against hers so soft and creamy. Lucy started to reach out. Indians were filthy creatures, and Lord knew what he might do. But he withdrew his hand without a word, scooped up the dead snake from the ground and walked away.

When the men returned from the hunt, she told them what had happened. "I didn't know what to do. Should I have repaid him somehow?"

74

"No need," Luther Moore told her. "He killed himself a fine dinner."

"Girl, can't you keep the twins quiet?" Mr. Bates demanded. "They're wailing like a pair of bobcats."

The sound of the babies' crying plagued him. He was one of those men to whom infants were simply small, troublesome animals to be tolerated as best one could. Perhaps next year, when he would have gone away and come back again with his sheep from the East, perhaps then he would hug them and dandle them on his knee and find them as wondrous as she did.

"Celia, can babies have catarrh?"

"What a foolish question. Of course. Is it the twins?"

"They're so fretful and feverish. All I do is wipe their eyes and noses. I'm glad Mr. Bates has gone to Sutter's. He hates it when they fuss."

"I'll have to look at them. Give me a hand with Kate."

Reed Pierce's wife was scarcely recognizable as the quiet, elegant lady Lucy had admired in Saint Joseph. In her place was a wretched shadow of a woman, pitifully emaciated, her hair unkempt, her eyes wandering, wild and furtive as those of a trapped animal. She was less than human, this silent wraith kept tied like a dog in her cabin. Celia slipped a spoonful of food into her mouth. Automatically, it was swallowed. It was neither savored nor chewed, merely gulped like a scrap thrown to a hungry cur.

"Here, Lucy." Celia handed her a rag. "Wipe what falls out. Then I'll clean her up and see to the twins."

"Look." Lucy halted as they came out into the sunlight. "What is she doing?"

Moore's wife stood in the doorway of Lucy's cabin. She was staring inside.

"Out!" Celia bustled toward her. "Get away from there!"

Lucy brushed by the squaw. "My babies are ill," she said.

For a moment, the Indian woman remained in the doorway, her short, thickset body looking like little more than a haphazard pile of pelts outlined against the sun. Wordlessly, she turned and padded away.

"She heard them whimpering, I expect. Celia, how are they?"

"Too warm. Cold compresses might help."

"I wish Reed hadn't gone with Mr. Bates."

"Oh, Lucy, stop fancying Reed such a medicine man. It's a woman knows what's best for babies."

"I think he is a doctor."

Celia gave a contemptuous grunt. "Never yet heard of a doctor who refused to bleed his patients. I'll grant you Reed did his best on the trail, but we'd no one else, had we? Fetch some fresh, cold water and bathe their foreheads. I can't leave Kate alone long. She rolls onto the floor and dirties herself."

"Go along, then. I'll get the water."

When Lucy returned to her cabin from the spring, Moore's wife was there again, in the doorway, standing still as a stump and gazing at the two infants in their cradle. Lucy cleared her throat as she came up behind her, and the squaw stepped aside to let her pass. She set the bucket on the floor and dipped a cloth into it. "They're burning up," she said, as though the woman could understand. "They're so small," she went on, knowing she was speaking only to herself, "and I'm so afraid for them. They're all I have. I know," she said, prattling in her anxiety, "you would say I have Mr. Bates, but it's not so. He's restless. I can tell. He wants to be away from here, to go back East for the Merinos. He has no inclination for staying put. I must take care of my little girls myself. They are everything to me."

When she looked, the woman was gone.

Mr. Bates found Lucy sitting by a cold hearth in the dark cabin.

"Susannah is dead," she told him numbly, nodding toward the blanket-wrapped bundle lying on her buffalo robe. "Last evening."

"How did she die?"

"Of whatever babies die of. A fever. I don't know."

"And the other one?"

"She is not 'the other one'!" she flared. "Her name is Beth!"

"Lower your voice, girl. Let's have a look at her." He bent over the cradle and recoiled. "What the devil is that?"

"Moore's wife's work. She came last night and saw that Susannah was dead. She went away, and when she came back, she had that with her. It's the skin of a freshly slaughtered lamb. She rubbed the baby all over with grease and wrapped her inside it."

"Have you taken leave of your senses? It's some pagan rite she's performing."

"I think not."

"What in God's name do you know about it?"

She could see the anger in his face, but she stood her ground. "The child's fever has broken. The Indian woman did it."

"I've no stomach for superstitions."

"Nor I, Mr. Bates. I'm telling you the cure worked, that's all."

"I suppose next you'll be painting your face and chanting at the sunrise."

She looked at him defiantly. "If I thought it might improve your disposition, yes!"

He gave her a hard, sharp slap with the flat of his hand. "Don't ever raise your voice to me again, girl."

She touched her face where he had struck her. Nobody, not even Ma or Pa, had ever hit her before. Her jaw was throbbing. The pain brought tears to her eyes.

"You've turned, girl. Curdled like sweet milk. Gone from a pleasing, obedient young woman to a contentious, hare-brained baggage. You test my patience too severely." He lifted the dead child in his arms and went out.

Lucy stroked Beth's forehead and crooned softly to her, as if it were the baby and not she who wanted comforting.

"Done," Mr. Bates said when he returned. "I laid the body in the leather trunk. It was the right size."

"You could have made a coffin. She needed such a small one."

"It's dark out, and raining."

"Where did you bury her?"

"In the grove behind Castalia Spring. I walked the horse over it. The Indians won't disturb it."

"I suppose I shan't be able to find it either." She handed him his food. "What became of your cache of type?"

"Buried."

"Mr. Bates? Whatever for? Nobody would take it from our cabin. And my thirty dollars in gold pieces was in your chest. You put it with your type for safekeeping."

"So? It's safe there."

"Where?"

"By the big rock. Eat something, will you, girl? Let your supper stop your mouth."

But she had no appetite. She washed Beth and covered her with a clean cloth and blanket and laid the child next to her in bed, as though her nearness might safeguard the little one against the fears she felt for both of them.

"I'll be going, girl, in two weeks' time," Mr. Bates told her.

"Must you?" But she knew that nothing she could say or do would keep him here.

"There's a party leaving for the East. The trapper, Peter Stewart, is leading."

"And when will you return?"

"We'll reach the States before fall. I'll start back in the late spring, after lambing."

"How will you buy the sheep? We have no money."

"I've funds in the States."

She wondered if he would be able to give up his roaming once he had his fine Merinos. Or would he hire Indians, as Luther Moore did, and leave his flock to them to oversee. His restlessness pricked him like an itch he couldn't scratch, always spurring him to rove. Lucy knew better than to think she could follow him each time, uprooting her child and her household to trail along like the squaws did with their tribes. She would have to stay here, safe among White and Reed and the others and make a home for him to come back to. It was all that she could do.

April came like a gift. Not even Mr. Bates's leaving could prevent Lucy's spirits from soaring as high as the myriad birds that wheeled about the clear blue skies. Every part of the land, hills and ravines alike, blossomed exuberantly in a lavish blaze of color the likes of which she had never seen. There must have been a hundred varieties of blooms bending gracefully in the breezes that carried their fragrance through the air.

"Mr. Bates," she said, watching as he filled his saddlebags, "how can you leave such a paradise?"

"Paradise is seductive, girl. It can trap a fellow. The minute he grows complacent, that's when he's tangled and stuck there, caught like a fly in amber. It's a wise man carries his comforts with him."

"And when you return? Will you still have such a wanderlust?"

"Now see here," he quickly countered. "I only meant that I must be off and going if I'm ever to fetch those Merinos. The first man to arrive here with pure stock will put Moore's wretched breed to shame. And having you standing there singing me a siren song doesn't make the leaving any easier. At the moment my mind is attuned to the journey. Now where's my other flannel shirt? I can't find it."

"It wasn't with the rest of the clean wash?"

"No."

"Moore's wife or Captain Wally. I'll see if I can get it back."

She walked up the hill to Luther Moore's, waving to White and Reed and French Jack who were clearing the slope for planting. "Hello there, Luther."

He was sitting on a stump, honing a knife, the blade hissing against the whetstone as he stroked it. "What can I do for you?"

"My husband is packing to leave. He needs his flannel shirt. Perhaps your wife might have it?"

He got up and went inside the cabin.

She could not bring herself to call the woman "Mrs. Moore," for who knew if any rites, savage or otherwise, had formalized their union? She could see the squaw now, on the crest of a near hill, the child beside her, gathering roots in a basket. It did not matter that it was the hill behind Reed Pierce's place for which he had paid Captain Wally and his tribe a substantial amount in goods. In the Indian woman's mind, the plants, like Lucy's washing, were there for the taking. They thought all things belonged to everyone and nothing to one alone. Captain Wally would plunge his fingers into Lucy's bowl of stew and help himself, unbidden. She could not bring herself to reprimand him after he had killed the snake that had threatened her babies, and so she would simply push the bowl into his hands and serve herself another.

"I have it, Mr. Bates." She waved the shirt that Luther had retrieved from his cabin.

He pulled tight the rawhide thongs around his clothing

roll. "Well, girl," he said, turning to her, "what's to say? Look after yourself and the little one."

"Take care."

"Don't worry your head about it. In the meantime, you'll be in good hands. And by the time I return, I daresay Castalia Spring will be thriving, with vegetables put down for the winter—and for all I know, a whiskey still."

"Not if Celia hears about it."

"Give us a peck, girl. I must go."

Spare horse and pack mules trailing, he led his mount along the riverbank to the west, toward the rendezvous at Sutter's. She watched until he was gone from sight.

With the coming of summer, the garland of flowers faded from the hills and was gone. The grass grew brown in the weeks of unbroken sunshine. Here in California it seemed the earth reversed itself, lush and green in the winter rains, and in summer as withered and colorless as December back home. Only the oaks and pines and some few shrubs retained their greenery. But around the spring in back of Reed's cabin wild blackberries grew, and down by the river, grapes ripened on their vines among the rocks on the bank. Anything could grow here, White Russell said, if only it had water.

Lucy worked alongside the men in the fields, hoeing, sowing, weeding and watering under the warm sun. Beth lay on a blanket nearby. When the baby cried, Lucy would straighten up, brushing off the soil, and carry her to the shade of an oak tree to nurse.

It had fallen to Celia to do most of the cooking, since she was bound to the cabin with Kate. Lucy helped, but on those days when they were short a man gone hunting, she stayed late in the fields with the rest of the men, pulling her weight with the others.

One Sunday late in July, when they had rested from their labors, Lucy laid the child in her cradle and went outside, taking the Bible with her. She opened the pages of the book to Deuteronomy and read,

> "For the Lord thy God bringeth thee
> into a good land, a land of brooks
> of water, of fountains and depths
> that spring out of valleys and hills . . ."

"Lucy! Lucy!" French Jack preceded White on horseback, the two coming at a canter along the rim rising above the stream.

"Where are the others?" White shouted.

Reed and Celia emerged from their cabins. "What's going on?" Reed called, as they reined up short in the clearing.

"A war!"

"It was true, what we heard, *l'affaire du quatorze juin*," said French Jack, "*à Sonoma.*"

"The U.S. has captured Monterey and Yerba Buena," White told them.

"When?"

"Over two weeks ago."

"Is there fighting there?"

"Not now."

"What will become of us?" Celia asked quietly.

"Nobody's going to bother with a little settlement like Castalia," Reed assured her. "Our forces will push the Mexicans back southward before they know what's happened. Chances are, there'll be no fighting at all this far north."

The weeks wore by with little or no word about the War. The weather grew hot as September approached, and even the breezes became torpid, barely stirring the cornstalks in the field.

The child, Abel, toddled among them as they tended the crops, chattering unintelligibly, cheerful and tanned and full of curiosity. He was a winning little boy, half-breed or no. "Will you look, Reed," Lucy smiled as she stood up from the garden with her basket of turnips, "how he loves to play with Beth."

Abel squatted next to the baby on her blanket, tickling her with a handful of corn silk. He giggled with glee as her tiny hands reached out toward it. Both children were black-haired and sun-browned. In truth, they bore a striking likeness to each other. Beth was going to be dark, like Mr. Bates, a sloe-eyed beauty, Lucy fancied, the belle of California.

"One can't help but pity the boy," said Reed. "Did you know that Moore won the woman on the turn of a card?"

She glanced at him.

"It's true. From another trapper."

She looked at the children playing so happily together

81

under the cloudless sky and shook her head slowly from side to side.

"My land!" Lucy sat in the doorway, rocking Beth in the early dusk. "Who'd believe autumn could be such an inferno?"

"Nothing about this country could surprise me anymore," Celia said tartly.

Lucy laughed. "We have seen a lot of it, haven't we?"

"I suppose some poor devils like ourselves are out there now in some godforsaken spot, wondering if there is such a place as California and if they'll ever find it."

"Evening, ladies." Luther Moore reined up his horse and dismounted. "Captain Wally says he heard that the south of California has fallen to the Americans. The Mexicans have surrendered the pueblo of Los Angeles."

"And how would he know that?" Celia inquired.

"The tribes pass the word along."

"Do you think it's true?" Lucy asked him.

"There's a lot of them speak that damnable Spanish. And there's Mexicans around, lying low I should think, but they're around. The Captain's information is usually reliable."

"The word of an Indian?" Celia said.

He turned to face her with a thin, cheerless smile. "Yes, ma'am, the word of an Indian." He led his horse away up the hill.

"Celia! Why did you say that?"

"It slipped out. At any rate, I can't always be thinking to accommodate Luther just because he took himself a China article."

"We must tell the others. I'll bed down the baby and tell Reed, if you'll find White and French Jack."

Lucy laid the baby in her cradle and hurried to the Pierces'.

"Reed?" She rapped at the open door.

"I'm here."

She stepped into the cabin, her eyes searching him out in the darkness. He stood in back of the chair where Kate was bound. Gently, lovingly, he was kneading her neck and shoulders, as though through his touch he might awaken some response in the woman. She sat there, her head slumped forward, her body moving pliantly under

82

his ministrations. She might as well have been a sack of grain.

"Shall I light a candle, Reed?"

"No, it's a fine night. Let's sit outside."

She told him the news. "So the War will end soon, won't it?"

"Who knows? There's Texas, too. The Mexicans stand to take a great loss. They won't give up easily."

"And what will you do?" she asked suddenly. "Will you stay here always, in Castalia?"

"It's home now."

"Earlier, Celia and I were talking about more settlers coming. For all we know, there may be dozens of wagon trains heading this way, especially if they've heard Yerba Buena is in American hands. Why, Castalia could become a real town like Saint Joseph."

"You're going at rather a gallop, aren't you?"

She chose her words cautiously. "I meant to say that we'd have need of a man of your abilities. We do now."

"Anyone can plant a row of corn."

"That wasn't what I meant."

He gazed up at the star-filled sky, saying nothing.

"Why, Reed? Why would a man give up doctoring and leave all his medicines in their fine treenware to rot in the sand?"

"You knew what they were."

"It seemed such a short-sighted thing to do, when you knew how much your services might be needed."

"My services, as you call them, are a good deal more successful at tending to the life of the crops than they are at tending to humanity."

"If you ever truly believed that, surely what you did for us on the trail changed your thinking."

"We lost Red Russell and Whiton and the others who had cholera."

"But you saved the rest."

"I've lost too many, Lucy," he said wearily. "And I've lost my Kate, too."

"That's not your doing."

"But it is. I'd thought that leaving the States would mean a new life for us. I was a fool not to see the dangers." He shook his head. "I was so sure that Kate would recover if we could only begin all over in another place."

83

"Then you knew she wasn't feeling right when you left?"

"Not since the baby."

Lucy kept silent.

"It was born . . . wrong. Not so much a baby as a monstrosity. Kate never had a strong constitution. I knew she couldn't cope with it. There was an interval, I don't know how long, when it was having trouble breathing. I did nothing. She tried to take it away from me, but I prevailed upon her not to. We sat there and watched our son die." He took in a deep breath of the cool night air. "I think that Kate began to die then, too."

Lucy reached out and placed a hand on his arm.

Moore's wife squatted on the riverbank, the child Abel beside her. Lucy watched the woman's hands skillfully twining a basket from the rushes she had gathered. How quickly and surely her fingers moved. Now and then she glanced up and spoke to the boy, who seemed as intent as she upon the work. Beyond the two figures, Lucy saw White Russell approaching on horseback, coming slowly along the stream-bed, the pack mules behind him. She ran up to the clearing. "Celia! White's come back. It must have been the rain that delayed him. Maybe he has news of the Mexicans."

"It wasn't the rain," he told them when they ran to meet him. "Sutter's is under U.S. occupation. They're calling it Fort Sacramento."

"Then surely we've no more worries. Sutter's was the only Mexican flag within fifty miles of us. If the Americans have taken over, we're safe."

"But the *Californios* have retaken Los Angeles. The news arrived while I was at the fort."

Lucy frowned. "I hope that's not a sign the tide's turning in their favor."

"If I might have a word with you, ma'am." He walked away a few steps toward the cabins.

Lucy followed. "Ma'am? Why, White Russell, you haven't called me 'ma'am' since we set foot here. Whatever's got into you?"

He halted and turned. She could not make out his face clearly. She squinted against the strong, pale-colored sun and held up a hand to shade her eyes.

"There's other news. About the Peter Stewart party.

84

They fell afoul of the Paiutes near Mary's River. There were only two left alive when another party came upon them, and those died soon after."

"I don't believe it," she said slowly. "Stewart has a reputation as an experienced trapper. Everyone knows he's on friendly terms with the Indians."

"It happened. I don't know the details, but you'd best take it for the truth."

"But the Mary's! That's so close to California. It must have happened months ago. Today is the last day of October."

"In June."

"But we heard nothing, not a word of it," she argued, as if by sheer will she might compel him to contradict himself.

"Two of the men who found them rode back into Sutter's a short time ago."

"You spoke to them?"

"They'd gone. But everyone at the fort knew."

"Tales spread and become exaggerated."

"Ma'am? Lucy?"

She glanced at him.

White shook his head. He reached out to steady her.

She cleared her throat. "It's all right. I shan't faint. I need to sit down, that's all."

BACK ON the farm, when times were bad, which they were more often than not, Pa took stock. He said the important thing was to figure out what you had left after the rains and the rot and the ravages of birds and insects. That way, he said, you knew exactly what means you had at hand to make a fresh start. It could only have been that faint streak of madness in him, Lucy thought, that enabled him to take heart from the meager remains of his hopes and set about starting anew, believing, against all evidence, that this time he would make a go of it. She could do with a bit of Pa's madness now. But instead, it seemed she had inherited Ma's dour sense of the reality of the situation.

She tried not to be frightened of what the future might hold. She tried not to be sad or to indulge in self-pity. But sometimes, in spite of herself, she awoke drenched with perspiration from a nightmare in which she saw Mr. Bates at the brutal hands of the savages and heard his voice so clearly, crying out as they butchered the innocent travelers. She would try to shake her mind free of the grisly scene, gathering up the sleeping Beth in her arms and holding her close, as though whatever part of the child that was Mr. Bates was here, near to her, and safe.

Lucy could understand death. She had seen enough of it to view it as one of those things like sickness or drought which simply happened and must be accepted. Yet his death haunted her. He had died in some nameless waste, gone from his home and family, among people she did not know and never would, a stranger among strangers. She understood now what John Mason's wife must have felt when young Joe returned to tell her she had been made a widow in some faraway place she would never know on some ordinary day as she went about her chores, seeing the patterns of the sun on the floor and hearing the birds warbling outside, untroubled and calm. But at least Joe had been there when John died. He could answer her questions. Lucy had only the threads of an account, nothing more than a scant handful of loose ends, and try as she might, she could not stitch them together to make a shape which she could understand and accept.

Whatever was left, Pa said, were your assets. When Ma despaired, he would remind her to count her blessings, such as they were. Well, Lucy thought, we are safe, Beth and I. We shan't be allowed to starve, and I shall do my part to see that we don't. The men would take care of her as they had Celia, yet there was no way of telling if one day some of them might want to move on, and what would she do then? She wished there might be some way she could fend for herself, so as not to be dependent upon the whims of the others, but she had no skills to barter, save her willingness to work in the fields with them.

"Nonsense," Celia countered. "How old are you?"

"I was born in 'twenty-eight, so I shall be eighteen this year."

"Young lady, there'll be a fair swarm of men coming West like ourselves. You remember how the traveling fever swept Saint Joseph. I'm past marrying, but an able-bodied girl like yourself will have her pick. Why even now, I'll wager White Russell and French Jack are just waiting a decent length of time before they think to ask your hand."

"I doubt White's the marrying kind. It doesn't seem to fit him. And half the time I don't understand a word that French Jack is saying. Besides, I'm not contemplating marriage. Perhaps I've lost my taste for it."

"It's too soon, that's all. You wait. Why, after the shock and the mourning wore off when my own dear Samuel died, I looked up one day, and there was Jeremiah Whiton, alone like myself and looking for a companion."

And now, Lucy thought, you are alone once again. Even Celia, prudent and practical as she was, had had a trace of that lunatic optimism, thinking that she could make a fresh start with her Jeremiah and that the end would be different this time. But it had not worked out that way, and Celia lived here in her tiny cabin, doing for Kate and the men, as Lucy had worked for her keep at the Empire House.

No, Lucy had no mind to remarry. There had to be another way. Mrs. Vose had steadfastly insisted that the Lord would show the way, and to be sure, whether it was the Lord's doing or Mr. Bates's, Lucy had prayed to leave that place, and her prayers had been answered. What she needed now was to make her own way, but she hadn't a waybill to guide her, much less any notion of where she might be heading. She had developed rather a firm distrust of the Lord, having seen too much of what everyone insisted was "His will." Yet without Mr. Bates, with no one to guide her, she had no alternative. She decided that praying, while it might not help, probably could not hurt, either.

Lucy stepped out into the sunlight. "Mercy, what a pleasure this is, after nearly a week of nothing but rain. I began to think I was going to mildew at any moment."

White smiled. "Just to see you cheerful, Lucy, that's all the sunshine we need."

"If I didn't know better, White, I'd say you had a bit of Irish in you. Are you and French Jack off to hunt?"

He nodded. "Might as well use the break in the weather. No way of knowing how long it'll last." He squinted and scanned the hills to the north.

"I swear," she said, "I believe you can make out a deer at a mile's distance."

"No, I was thinking of Reed and the rain."

"Reed Pierce?"

He shook his head. "There was a Mr. Reed came to Sutter's. His party was still on the trail, in a bad way, to hear him tell it. The Captain gave him food and animals and two *vaqueros* to go back to them."

"He went back up into the mountains at this time of year?"

"Six days of rain in Castalia means six days of snow up there."

"Perhaps not. Maybe the storm didn't reach that far."
He grunted, unconvinced.

"Morning." Reed Pierce emerged from behind his cabin with a bucket of spring water. "Didn't mean to interrupt you."

"White thinks there may be some folks snowbound in the mountains."

"Poor devils, I should hope not. Good hunting, men!" Reed called as White set off with French Jack. "And you, how are you feeling, Lucy?"

"I suppose we must do the best we can with bad times."

"I said it before and I'll say it again. You're a determined young lady. I wagered on your spirit then, and my bet still stands. You've drive and ambition uncommon in a woman."

"Your eyes find things in me that escape my own entirely. Ambition, indeed. That's for men. Women haven't any such thing."

"Had you no ambition to come to California? Did you not succeed? I wonder what you'll accomplish next."

"I suppose I should be content to survive."

"A melancholy outlook. I hope you haven't been dwelling on our sorrows these past dismal days."

"It's difficult not to, cooped up in the cabin in the rain. For a while it got the best of me, but I finally resorted to Mr. Bates's books on sheep-raising. I now understand all about shearing and castration and diseases like the scab." She smiled. "Perhaps Luther Moore can find a place for me with those Indian herders of his. It's a shame my spinning wheel is lost in the desert somewhere."

"Don't lose your spirit, Lucy. You're doing fine." He lifted his water bucket. "I'll be getting along now."

From the quiet shade of the cabin, Lucy spied Moore's half-breed son toddling downhill on his chunky, brown legs. She could not help but smile. How droll he looked, his child's face grave and intent, making his way toward Beth's cradle which lay in the sunshine by the door.

"Here now, boy! No!" She pried his arms from around the baby. "Child, Abel, you must not try to pick her up."

He stared up at Lucy, crestfallen, his solemn brown eyes like those of a scolded puppy.

"Oh, for pity's sake. Give me your hands." She took his small hands in hers and wiped them with her skirt. "There, now you may play with her."

He stood still, his arms at his sides.

"I declare, the Indian race is second only to the mule in stubbornness." She grasped his hand and stroked Beth's downy black hair with it. "It's all right to touch her, but not lift her. See? Isn't her hair soft?"

He looked at Lucy quizzically.

"Dear heaven, doesn't Luther teach you anything? Hair." She pointed first to Beth's, then his, then her own. "Hair."

"Hai."

"Hai-r."

"Hai-rrr," he growled and giggled.

"Close enough. Lord, child, you're almost three years old. Don't you know any English?" She tried to recall, but other than the gibberish he spoke with Moore's wife, she had only heard him say "Papa," nothing more. She sighed. "A crime. Here." She touched her finger to their three noses in turn. "Nose."

"Nose."

"Hair?"

After a moment's hesitation, he pressed his palm to his head and grinned broadly.

She nodded. "Yes, hair. Well, boy, you're not slow-witted. Now, eyes."

She was patiently trying to teach him the difference between "mouth" and "lips," when a shadow fell between them. She glanced up. The old man stood there, his eyes fixed on his son. Lucy rose, smoothing her skirt. "I was only—"

He cut her off. "Wasting your time."

"How can you say that? He's a bright little boy!"

"So he is. And I won't have you baiting him."

"Baiting him! Luther, I was teaching him a few words of English, which is a sight more than you've done!"

"He ain't a toy for you to pick up to amuse yourself and then put aside."

"All due respect for your years, Luther, but I was not using your child for my own amusement. The poor little thing wants teaching."

"I ain't got no such patience. Anyhow, I couldn't teach him much of anything. I ain't a writing man."

"But he ought to learn English. California will belong to the States any day now. How is he to get along?"

Moore snorted derisively. "With white folks? Hell, he could spout like President Polk, but nobody'd have him or his mother inside the door."

90

"He's not much darker than Beth. Look at them together." She tactfully omitted mentioning Moore's wife.

Abel, oblivious of the discussion, played quietly with the baby.

"Listen, Lucy Bates, there's only one thing that boy has to learn about white men, and that's to protect himself. And from Indians, too. He's not one of them either."

"Then he must learn to speak our language."

"Yes, damn it!" he shouted. "Of course he must! But we ain't got any teachers! I'll teach him every trick I know to defend himself, and that's plenty. But the boy should be taught proper, not teased and tantalized with play words from some silly woman when it suits her fancy."

"Bite your tongue! You see, I can shout full as loud as you! How dare you assume I'm having sport with the child? You are a mean-minded, suspicious old man, Luther Moore."

"And I got a right to be."

"I suppose you also have a right to leave him in ignorance until some fine gentleman professor decides to build a college to your liking in Castalia?"

"Damn you, lady!" he thundered. "Can't you see how bad I want that boy taught? But I want him taught right! I don't want someone playing games!"

She spoke softly. "Little children learn by playing word games. I shall be happy to have Abel spend a few hours a day with me, so that I can teach him what he has to know."

He squinted as though assaying her sincerity. "What do you want for it?"

"When I want something from you, Luther, you'll be the first to know it."

The Indian woman led the boy to Lucy's cabin each day and deposited him there without any sign that she either knew or cared why he was brought there. Sometimes she would pause a moment, standing a few feet away from Lucy, and give the child a slight push toward her. Her dark eyes would meet Lucy's and hold the glance, betraying nothing, expressionless and cold as stone.

"See, Abel, what's Papa riding?"
"Horse."

"Good boy. Look there, on the hill, what do you see?"

He pointed at Moore's flock. "Sheep."

Luther brought his horse up beside them. "Time for me to take the boy home."

"He's quick as a fox, Luther. Abel, show Papa the sheep."

He pointed toward the hilltop and repeated the word.

A smile creased Moore's grizzled face, displaying the spaces of his several missing teeth.

"Luther, how many sheep have you?"

"Maybe fifty."

"Are they difficult to raise?"

He spat on the ground. "Stupid animals. Eating's all they do, but there's no lack of grazing. Most trouble's keeping the coyotes away. The lambs will stand there, dumb as dirt, just waiting to be carried off. Imbeciles, all of them."

"You don't like farming sheep?"

"A man like me? Hell, no, begging your pardon. You spend all your life trapping animals with a bit of craft and wile, and you end up playing nursemaid to a flock of foolish sheep that ain't got a whole brain to call their own. Any damned fool could do it. It's for lazy Indians and old men like me."

"Then I could do it."

"Beg pardon?"

"If I had some sheep, I could raise more. Do your Indians try to steal them?"

"I shoot too straight, young lady. They'll make no trouble with me, so long as I have a few trinkets to trade for the work."

"Mr. Bates bought a number of things in Yerba Buena to trade. I've some cloth and beads left."

"You ain't got no sheep."

"I would if you traded me some for teaching your son. And I've some dollars in gold hidden nearby, if I could find the place."

"Gold's no good hereabouts. Maybe someone like Sutter would take your money if he had sheep to sell. There's Indians with flocks between here and Mission San José. Sheep and sickness, that's what the Pope's men left them."

"But you agree I could do it. I've read my husband's books on raising sheep."

"Trouble is, the sheep ain't read those books. Look

92

here, Lucy, book-learning won't help you. It's a damned fool idea for a woman, anyhow."

"If I'm willing to teach your son to speak proper English, why aren't you willing to trade me some sheep and teach me how to care for them?"

He gazed long and hard at her. Finally, he said, "I'll think about it. That's all. I'm promising nothing." He dismounted and scooped up the child, setting him in front of himself in the saddle.

"I'm counting on you, Luther."

He grunted. "Ain't a white woman alive won't hound a man into the grave to get her way." With a snap of the reins, he turned his horse away and rode out of the clearing at a trot.

Lord, she thought, what have I done? The idea had surfaced in her mind for weeks, shining and elusive as a fish breaking water in the river below. And now she had seized onto it, hardly knowing how to handle such an enterprise.

The money. She must find her thirty dollars. If Sutter would take it, perhaps he would also accept Mr. Bates's printing type. White Russell said there was an American newspaper now in Monterey. Perhaps Sutter could trade the type to someone in Yerba Buena. Surely now that that there were American troops there, they would soon have a paper of their own. Lucy was giddy with the audacity of what she was considering. But it was, on the face of it, no more foolhardy than leaving Saint Luke's Plains and heading west to California, and a sight less dangerous, to her thinking.

She saw Reed walking past White's cabin with Captain Wally. "I must ask you both something." She hurried breathlessly to where they stood. "The big rock. Where is the big rock?"

Reed looked confused. "What big rock?"

"That's what I have to know. Mr. Bates said there was one nearby."

"There are a lot of them. The hills are strewn with outcroppings."

"But this was a special one. He mentioned it. Captain Wally," she said to the Miwok, picking up a pebble from the ground, "a rock." She held the stone under his eyes and made a wide arc with one arm. "Like this, but big. Big rock."

Captain Wally shrugged and looked at Reed, bewildered.

"Reed, does he understand me?"

"As well as I do. But I'm afraid neither one of us can help."

"But Captain, you must know of such a place."

He gazed at her impassively.

"You are an exasperating creature sometimes, Captain."

"The Captain," said Reed, "chests his cards. But I'm sure he'd assist you if he could. He promises me he can cure the headache I've been suffering for three days. He's taking me to his sweathouse."

"You're going to their village?" She looked from one to the other. "Are you sure it's wise?"

"I should think it unwise to refuse such an offer of help."

"Of pagan foolishness, is more like it."

"All in the interest of science, my girl." He saluted her. "I hope you find what you're looking for."

The setting sun cast long shadows across the ridge above the streambed. Lucy leaned against her shovel, disheartened. The two largest rocks within view of the cabin were both here, lying on the downward slope to the riverbank. She had trenched around them, to no avail. Moore's wife was still observing her, sitting on the ground by her doorway, twining a basket, watching the silly white woman dig circles around a pair of boulders.

"How right you are, madam," Lucy muttered. "And don't think I don't feel the clown, too."

After supper, when she had bedded down Beth, she stood in the door, her arms folded, staring out over the clearing. She could see little. The night was overcast. Only the flickering lights from the other cabins illuminated the darkness.

But it had been dark that night, too. Raining, it was. She tried to imagine where she might carry something so heavy in a steady downpour. Near the house, for certain. Perhaps the rock was not the largest in the settlement, but the largest nearby their home. Of course, she thought suddenly, it wouldn't be between here and the river because the rainwater would be running down that way and fill up the excavation. Until now, she had thought he might have buried the child near Castalia Spring because it was the place from which the settlement took its name, so logical a spot in which to return the dead to the earth whence they came. But Mr. Bates had no such sense of poetic justice as she. The grove behind the spring was on higher ground, that was all.

She tucked the blanket securely around the sleeping child and threw a shawl over herself.

The trees loomed dark around her, their topmost branches merging indistinguishably with the moonless sky. Her foot falls ruptured the quiet of the night. Unseen creatures fled from her approach, darting into the whispering grass or rising in a sudden, startling flap of wings. She stood amid the grove, the wind soughing in the leaves about her, her eyes straining to search out the shape of a boulder on the hill ahead. Over and over, her eyes swept the shadows, seeing nothing. She turned back toward the cluster of cabins below. In the dim glow emanating from the houses, she saw at once the faint outline of a large rock lying low, like a slinking animal overlooking the settlement. There was no other. Surely she had found the place.

In the first cold light before dawn, she climbed the ridge again and began to dig. She still felt a bit foolish, but if it was a wild goose chase, no one would be the wiser. Besides, the thirty dollars was her legacy—and a tidy sum, considering the circumstances. And Mr. Bates's type, providing she could trade it, was as good as currency.

"I knocked at the door," Celia said as she entered Lucy's cabin, "but you didn't . . . Land, child! Why are you sitting on the floor? You look as pale as a ghost." She scanned Lucy's face. "You're not sickly this morning, are you?"

Lucy's mouth was dry. Her words came out in a hoarse croak. "I didn't sleep well."

"I came by to ask if you'd watch Kate while I do my washing. Reed's not returned."

"In a moment. If you'll just give me time to finish up here, I'll be over directly."

When the woman had left, Lucy rose and looked again at what she had hastily concealed beneath her skirts. She dropped to her knees beside the piece of canvas spread on the dirt floor. A sudden attack of vertigo seized her,

95

and she leaned forward on her hands for support. Like an animal on all fours she crouched over her quarry. The baby stirred fitfully in her cradle, but she paid the child no mind. Once more, she counted, her palms growing moist as she whispered the numbers. It was the same as before, over four hundred dollars in coins, glowing like a pool of sunlight on the stained cloth.

Her fingers trembled as she unwrapped the small oil-cloth packet that lay beside them. She lifted a yellowed, spotted fragment of newspaper from the face of the daguerreotype inside and stared again at the timid woman posed uncertainly above the three small girls at her feet. Mutely, they returned her gaze. She laid the thing face down on the canvas, picked up the newspaper and un-unfolded it. "Bank Clerk and Cash Missing," she read. "Benjamin Collier, for many years a trusted member of the banking company of Walsh and Taylor, has been reported as missing by his family and employers. At the same time, a sum in excess of two thousand dollars is believed to have disappeared from the firm's vault. It is not now known if there is any connection between the rumored cash loss and the whereabouts of Mr. Collier, long a resident of Philadelphia and the father of three young children. His wife and friends suspect foul play. Banking officials say only that an investigation has been commenced . . ."

When Lucy had finished reading what was printed there, she raised herself unsteadily to her feet, took the paper to the hearth and laid it between two burning logs. She watched it flare, blacken and disintegrate.

If she had ever had any doubts as to why he had needed her as his wife to make the journey, she understood now. She'd been a part of his ruse, nothing more. Their marriage had been a sham, his past a lie—and worst of all, their children the bastard offspring of a thief, a bigamist. Lucy felt ashamed. She felt guilty, too, that the fact of his death relieved her. At least, she thought, Beth would never be disgraced by the truth about Benjamin Collier. It was nothing but ashes now. "Caleb Bates," Lucy whispered, as though the name were one she had never heard before.

The Indian woman saw her throw something in the river, but it did not matter. She quite probably thought

96

Lucy a queer sort anyhow. And had she so much as glimpsed the picture, so lifelike, of the woman and children, she might well have taken it for sorcery. Lucy walked back up to the clearing in time to see Reed approaching from the other side.

"Kate's not got much appetite," she told him. "I fed her for Celia this morning."

"I'll see what I can do. Aren't you going to ask me about the sweathouse?"

She shook her head as if to clear it. "I forgot."

"Is anything wrong?"

"No. What was it like?"

"Fragrant. They came each with piles of wood, most of it green, from the smudge it sent up. They stacked it around the door of a round, domed building covered with thatch. There was no escape, you see," he went on, "not until the fires burnt down. We lay close to the floor, men all, no squaws, hot as in hades, with dense smoke all around us. Lucy?" He stopped short.

"Yes?"

"I'm boring you with my account."

"No. No, Reed, go on."

He hesitated, frowning. "Nothing more. It cured my headache, but there were times it all but cured me of breathing. After a brisk dip in the creek and a drink of acorn tea, bitter as gall it was, Captain Wally pronounced me not only cured but blessed to be lucky at deer hunting. I say, Lucy, you're acting like a sleepwalker. What's the matter with you?"

"How interesting," she said.

"What's happened?"

"Your evening with the Miwoks."

"Yes." He paused in front of his cabin. "Well, I shall attend to Kate now." He stood watching as Lucy walked on.

What Luther had said was true. Gold wasn't of much use hereabouts. But in a place like Fort Sacramento or Yerba Buena it was good for something. If there were only a way for her to purchase the materials she needed, she could seek out the Indian flocks Luther said lay south of here and trade them for sheep. But it was no task for a woman, and her place was here with Beth. She lay in the darkness, the baby asleep by her bed, reflecting on the irony of her situation.

By any standards, she was a rich woman, but her fortune was no help to her here, and certainly she could not strike out on her own and establish herself elsewhere. In fact, there was no place to go. There was a war on, and for any of them to leave the safety of Castalia was unthinkable. But somehow, when the time came, she would use Mr. Bates's money as Mr. Bates had used her. There was fortune in the word misfortune, Pa used to say, and if it had been her misfortune to serve Mr. Bates's purposes, at least she was well compensated, no thanks to him. Nobody would trace the money to this place. It was hers now, to do with what she might. She wondered if the Lord punished those who profited from tainted money. Mr. Bates had died at the hands of savages. But then, the men with him had died too, and such was not their case. Obviously she could not return it to anyone. And if she could use it for some good, perhaps the Lord would kindly ignore its origin. She folded her hands and prayed.

It rained Christmas Eve and the next day, as it had through most of December. But they came together, all save for Luther's family, to celebrate the occasion. Lucy and Celia cooked, and Kate Pierce was made comfortable on Lucy's bed. Reed said grace over loud wails from Beth, who was teething and feverish, and set to carving the splendid venison roast. When the dinner was done, White Russell brought out his brandy for toasting. Hymns were sung, and French Jack, tone-deaf though he was, gave them a song in French which sounded passably pretty, if incomprehensible. White and Celia stayed to clean up, and when Celia at last ventured out into the mud and the damp, White insisted upon remaining to bank the fire and have a second tot of brandy while Lucy nursed the child.

"Did I do wrong, White, not to invite Luther and Abel and the woman? I fear it was not the Christian thing to do. But do they observe Christmas, people like that?"

He stared into the hearth. "I expect not."

A log popped and hissed on the fire, sending up an iridescent flurry of sparks and illuminating the craggy profile of White's face. His head, once marked by that odd, silver streak dividing left from right, was now wholly frosted over, like the planes of some rugged escarpment softened by a capping of new snow. "Do you miss your people, Lucy Bates?"

"I have none." She laid Beth to rest. "I am with my people. Here. And you?"

"The same. My brother, Red, took a wife, but she died in childbirth. Probably a blessing, considering."

"Come now, White. We shall be in a new year soon. No sense turning our thoughts back or we should all meet the fate of Lot's wife. Do you suppose 'forty-seven will bring more settlers to Castalia? Celia says so."

"Would you like that?"

"It's a fine place to live. It would suit me to see it become a real town like Saint Joseph."

"I expect a young lady like yourself misses the quilting bees and socials."

"I never had such things. But you know, when John Mason played the fiddle, I did long to know how to dance." She smiled, a trifle embarrassed.

He dropped his eyes to his hands in his lap and pressed his broad palms together, "Well, I can't show you how. Never learned myself. But Celia's right, you'll find plenty of fellows to teach you."

"Dancing is the least of my concerns. It's making a life for Beth and me that comes first."

"So it should. And I'll be glad of the chance to assist you."

"You have already. I'm very grateful to you and the others, White."

He glanced up. "It's not your thanks I'm after."

"I never suspected it was."

"It's marrying."

She saw revealed in his face all the apprehensions of a very shy and very brave young suitor, suddenly afraid of himself and of her. He seemed at once so exposed and so fragile, this rock-hard man, that she all but ran to him and clasped him to her for assurance. But she went toward him slowly and knelt on the floor in front of his chair, taking his huge, calloused hands in her own. "It's Christmas," she said. "I expect we all feel a bit lonely. Perhaps it's the brandy speaking."

His voice was low. "No, ma'am."

"You've paid me a great compliment, White, and given

me a wonderful Christmas gift, too. But I'm ashamed to say I cannot reciprocate. And that is my fault," she hurried to say, "not yours. I'm not yet ready to marry again. But may I ask a favor of you?"

After a moment, he nodded.

"If the time does come, will you promise not to think me forward if I tell you it has arrived?"

He smiled "Done."

"But in the meantime, I shan't hold you to anything. I've no right. And who's to say there won't be a bevy of young ladies coming to Castalia? Why, you and French Jack may have to fend for your lives. You're a good and honorable man, White, and only a fool or a woman in my predicament would be daft enough to say no to you."

"Whatever you want, ma'am, I'll do. Anything I can do for you and the little one."

"I believe you mean what you say." They sat in silence, both gazing into the firelight. After a long while, she spoke. "Tomorrow morning, will you come here? It's late now, and I need time to think out something that's been preying on my mind. Say you'll come, please."

The following morning, White returned, as he had promised. He listened in silence as Lucy spoke, his eyes on her face. The white winter sun streaked through the window, casting a bleached stripe across the table where they sat.

"Will you do it for me?" she asked. "It's a long journey for this weather, and you'll need another man, but I believe I can get Luther Moore to loan me one of his Indians. I expect he'll be relieved it's not his sheep I'm after. And I hope you'll agree to the money. Have I offered you enough?"

He shook his head dazedly. "More than enough. I can't accept it, Lucy."

"Nonsense. Mr. Bates left me well off, and it's a difficult undertaking. You'll have to go first to Sutter's and maybe Yerba Buena and then over half the countryside. At least the sheep are down from the mountains for the winter."

"It's a foolhardy scheme. You've no experience in such things."

"Luther Moore owes me a debt. I intend to collect it. It's time he started teaching me what I need to know. As

100

I see it, the only problem will be keeping my flock apart from his, but there's no shortage of land."

"I still say you shouldn't be in such a rush to rid yourself of the money."

"Money doesn't grow, White Russell, and sheep do. Besides, I shall have a lot more use for sheep to trade than coins."

"You're determined to do this?"

"If you won't do it for me, I shall ask the others. And if they won't, perhaps by next year someone will arrive and accept my offer. But I aim to do what Mr. Bates intended here. They may not be Merinos but wool is wool and mutton is mutton. Between Luther Moore and my husband's books, I shall do the best I can."

"Ain't nothing but madness, if you ask me."

She laughed aloud, seeing the startled expression on his face. "Yes! I hope it is, White. I shall need such a madness to see me through. Please, say you will do it for me. However many you can find, I shall pay you by the head. Agreed?"

"It may take as long as a month. And I got things to do before I can go."

"Very well, I shall use the time to have Luther show me everything he can."

"Begging your pardon, Lucy, but a genteel young lady like yourself taking up business, much less ranching, what are folks going to say?"

"Celia will be scandalized. Reed will be amused. Luther finds white women exasperating anyhow, and French Jack, praise God, will be hard put to make his opinions understood. As for strangers, I expect they'll respect me if I make a go of it." She took his hand. "White, so much depends on you. You know what I want, as many ewes as you can muster for the price, and the larger their size the better. I shall need at least one ram for each two dozen. I want no irregularities in the jaws. See there's no poke underneath. No spaces between the teeth and no foot rot. I want thick, greasy fleece, and be sure there are no hidden lumps about the heads or on the ewes' udders."

He shook his head, smiling incredulously. "Lady Lucy, you do beat all."

She went to him and kissed his cheek. "You've shown yourself a good friend, White, at a time when I sorely need one. I shall find Luther now. I'm sure he'll let one of his men go along to help you."

She trailed the old man like a yapping pup, accosting him with every argument she could summon to mind. At length, he stopped protesting and fell to muttering to himself under his breath.

"Hear Papa grumble, Abel. Like thunder far away. Give Papa a kiss."

The child smacked one chubby palm and blew it toward him.

"On the cheek," she prodded. "Kiss Papa on the cheek."

He crawled up on Luther's lap and bussed him noisily on his whiskered jowl.

"You make your point, woman," Luther growled. "The tall one, Chuto. Take him and leave me be. Thanks to you, I got to train me another Indian. You're a damned fool and a pest, Lucy Bates, but you're a good woman, I guess, and spirited as a wildcat. I wish you luck."

"You're a good man yourself, even if you are the most irascible creature I ever knew. I thank you. As for the luck, I doubt I shall need it with your assistance." She turned and dashed quickly down the hill, pursued by the old man's outburst of protest.

They came along the bluff above the stream, moving against the current below in a great, gray tide of their own, billowing and bobbing and bleating as they meandered along the embankment. There were thirty-two ewes, some showing lambs on the way, and a pair of fine, healthy rams.

"We lost two ewes," White said, dismounting. "They strayed, and Chuto made signs he thinks the Indians got them."

"But you did it!" She hugged him. The animals crowded around, curious, nuzzling against her skirts.

"Chuto knows sheep. He's a good man."

Lucy smiled and held out her hand to the Indian. He stared at it for a moment then extended his own. She shook it, and he nodded approvingly.

During supper that evening, White listened patiently to Lucy's plans for her new flock.

"Now tell me, White," she said when she had cleared the table, "what news is there?"

"Well, folks in Yerba Buena are trying to get used to saying San Francisco."

"But that's a Spanish name, too!"

"The town ain't. It's full of sailors and soldiers and a bunch of Mormons aiming to make a profit from them. There's a newspaper, even, the *California Star*. And everyone is saying the War's all but over down south. All the same," he went on, "there was a skirmish near Santa Clara just before I reached there. That fellow from Sutter's, Reed, was trying to find volunteers to go up into the mountains, but most folks didn't want to leave with things so unsettled."

"Who would go up into the mountains in winter?"

"Not many. But Reed's people are still up there."

"White? That was the man you met at Fort Sacramento last autumn."

He nodded, frowning.

"Luther says the snow up in the Sierra Nevadas doesn't melt away between storms, like back east. It just keeps piling higher and higher until spring. He was caught there once. The bears hibernate, and most other animals drift down hereabouts. He said if he hadn't caught himself a fox, he might have starved."

"That's what Reed's afraid of. There were women and children, too. Irish and Germans from the sound of the names. Murphy and Spitzer, Donner and Keseberg and the like. Whole families."

"They must all be dead by now. God rest them. How they must have suffered. The poor things are better off." Suddenly she recalled how it felt to go hungry. Raising a hand, she ran it over her hair, smoothing it, as though to brush away the memory. "White," she said, "how am I ever to thank you for what you've done for me?"

"You've paid me well and Chuto, too."

"You deserve it. And Luther is training two other Miwoks to tend the flocks. He'll give one to me. Of course, now he wants his boy taught figures as well. He's only just turned three, but I'm determined to teach him."

Lucy squatted on her haunches and hugged Abel close to her waist. "Watch," she told him. "Here come the forelegs."

103

Slowly the small creature emerged from the ewe, coated with orange-colored mucus. Lucy placed it close to the dam's head and waited. The exhausted ewe nudged the slippery little thing and began to lick away the sticky sac.

Lucy rose. "Chuto, that ewe looks to be a bit listless—" She stopped, noting the puzzled expression on the Indian's face. "Oh, hang it. Chuto—" She pointed at the lamb and made motions of cleaning its mouth and nostrils.

Chuto nodded and crouched over the two beasts. White had been right about him. He possessed a sixth sense when it came to sheep. Day before yesterday he had examined this ewe and raised his hand, pointing up at the sun. *"O-ti-ko,"* he had said, and sure enough, in two day's time she had given up her lamb.

"That's the last of them for this season. Abel, give me your hand. Let's go and count the others."

They stood on the wind-washed hill. Around their feet, the first flowers of spring quivered in the breeze. The sheep herded about them, the lambs wobbling close to their dams on small, spindly legs. There were fourteen, though Abel had got only as far as ten. Six male and eight ewe-lambs. Three others had come stillborn, and a fourth had weakened and died. Lucy bent to pet one of the soft, woolly babies. It nosed inquisitively about her hand and arm.

"Say, now, if you don't make a pretty sight." White sauntered up beside them and surveyed the flock.

"It's all thanks to you."

"It's not me who's been up in the wee hours all those nights. I've seen you and Chuto going out with the lanterns."

"I wonder why most of the ewes lamb at night."

He shrugged. "Celia asked me to come and tell you Beth wants feeding."

"I'm on my way. Will you take Abel with you to help in the field?"

He hoisted the boy onto his shoulders. "That squawman's a queer one. You'd think he'd pay more attention to the child."

"White, please don't use that word. Abel learns too quickly. As for Luther, he's old and he's testy. He hasn't much patience. You don't mind looking after Abel until I get there, do you?"

Celia was waiting for Lucy when she came to feed Beth, but her only greeting was a curt nod. As Lucy picked up the baby, Celia pressed her lips together and sighed in that annoying fashion which signaled her disapproval. For a moment, Lucy was tempted not to inquire what bothered her, but she knew she would hear about it anyhow. "Well?"

"What?"

"Don't be coy, Celia. Out with it."

"Coy, indeed. Look who's speaking."

"I hardly think the word applies to me."

"Young lady, you are mistaken. I'm not blind. I see what a shameless flirt you can be when it suits your purpose. It's White Russell I'm thinking of."

"White has proven a great friend to me. That's all there is to it."

"For you, perhaps. Lucy," she said, not unkindly, "White's a backwoodsman out of Kentucky, not some worldly rogue like your Mr. Bates."

She started. "A rogue, did you think him?"

"At a glance, my girl."

"Back home, in Saint Luke's Plains, someone tried to tell me that, but I turned a deaf ear. He was quite the handsomest man I'd ever seen. I could hardly believe he'd have eyes for someone like myself."

"May he rest in peace. It's the living I'm concerned for. White Russell follows after you like a devoted dog. He's a strong man, God knows, but the mighty topple hardest. Don't toy with his feelings, Lucy."

"Do you think I have been?"

"I always said you were headstrong and heedless. But up to now your ways never hurt anyone. We are all of us in White's debt for seeing us through to California. I shouldn't like to have anyone turn against you out of loyalty to White."

"How dare you threaten me, Celia! And you know very well you're speaking only for yourself."

She drew herself up, and as tiny a woman as she was, stood stern and imperious as a spire. "Listen to me, Lucy Bates. It's for your own good I'm speaking. You are willful and determined. No," she said, silencing her with an upraised hand. "It's true. And though I find those traits unseemly in a woman, I do not dislike you. But I am warning you not to loose your ambitions to ride roughshod over others. Or to use others to suit your own devices. I wish you success at this sheep-farming venture, and that's the truth. But not at the expense of honor."

"That was quite a sermon, Celia. Perhaps you missed your calling. I assure you, my conscience is clear. If I may suggest, perhaps you harbor some secret feelings of your own for the gentleman. Might that be the reason for this tirade?"

Celia slammed her hand down on the table, shaking it, waking Beth who began to wail. "Stupidity!" She spat out the word as though it were bitter alum. "I come to you with good advice, and you reward me with stupidity! You are not a stupid girl, Lucy, so it must be that I am right, and you refuse to face it. Be it on your own head." She turned and left.

Celia was a meddlesome old woman, Lucy thought crossly. It was her business and hers alone how she handled White's attentions. Still, something Celia had said struck a chord, not that Lucy would have given her the satisfaction of admitting it. Pa used to bridle when Ma, trying to coax him away from farming, spoke admiringly of this or that fellow's success in trade. "The first thing the merchant trades is his conscience," he'd retort, and the argument would be on.

Lucy was no merchant, to be sure, but she was a rancher now, an eighteen-year-old woman with a livelihood. And she did not mean to fail, no matter what. She needed White's help and encouragement for support, but not if he mistook her attentions for devotion. She had no wish to deceive him. She came to the sudden, jarring realization that she had bought more than a flock of sheep with Mr. Bates's coins. She had traded them also for a new position in life, an unfamiliar and confusing situation which she did not fully understand. Women were the gentler sex, dependent upon men. Yet if she must use her femininity to make a success of the venture, she would be abusing White's affections and trading her conscience in the bargain, like Pa said. What kind of a transaction had she made, she wondered. Lucy was not at all sure that she liked this new and strange place in which she found herself. She felt uncomfortable. Yet like it or not, she had unwittingly made the trade.

VI

"SLOW, ABEL. Walk slowly. She can't keep up." Lucy and the boy, holding Beth between them by the hands, walked beside the flourishing rows of corn toward the far field where the men were working. Occasionally the little girl stumbled and righted herself with an amazed look of pride. She kept up a steady chirrup of baby talk, sweet-sounding, cheerful and utterly unintelligible.

"Gentlemen," Lucy called, raising the bucket in her left hand, "I've brought some cool spring water for your parched throats."

She sat with the three men under the shade of an oak. Abel had disappeared among the corn rows, teasing Beth with a game of hide-and-seek. "I swear I can see those stalks growing before my eyes," she told them.

Reed Pierce spoke up. "We've got our work cut out for us, all right. Crops grow so fast here, it's all a body can do to keep abreast of them."

"Luther tells me you're going to be shearing next week," White said, sounding a bit disgruntled at having received the news secondhand.

"I'm just doing as he tells me," she replied. "He says August is the time to shear in these parts. I remember we always sheared in the spring, back home. You know, gentlemen, I've been thinking, and it seems to me that Luther makes a mistake taking all that wool down from here to trade. Granted, the wife doesn't know how to use it."

White snorted. "Hell, if she did, she'd probably still prefer to wear those stinking skins."

"And Luther, too," said Reed. "Don't stand downwind of him on a hot day."

107

"But my point is, we do want the wool. We have use for it here, for ourselves."

"I thought you had plans to make your fortune from those sheep," White said.

"Someday, perhaps," she answered, "but meanwhile, we need blankets and clothing, don't we? I've no illusions about the wool. It's no fine quality stuff. But it would do nicely for blankets and the sort of rough capes we saw on the *vaqueros* at Sutter's."

"Lucy, are you being fair to yourself?" Reed asked. "You've worked like your Indians over those beasts. It's right that you should profit from them. It's not your responsibility to clothe us."

"Nor yours to have sustained me all this time."

"You work in the fields whenever you can. You've earned your keep along with the rest of us. You and Celia do all the cooking."

"Celia does most of it. I've no wish to argue, but I think the wool belongs to all of us for this first year."

"Trouble is," White interrupted, "we got no means of carding and spinning and weaving. And no time to spare for it."

Lucy smiled. "I believe Captain Wally has offered me a solution to part of that problem."

Reed looked puzzled. "What do the Miwoks know about wool?"

"Absolutely nothing," she said gaily, "but bear with me. I confess I could have sent Abel up here with the water, but I was hoping to ingratiate myself with French Jack."

French Jack raised his head in surprise and pointed at his chest.

"Yes, you. Reed, what is the French for spindle?"

"I've no idea."

"Oh, dear. Well, look here, French Jack." She pointed at the sheep in the distance and pantomimed the act of shearing them. Then, as they looked on, she proceeded to card the imaginary wool and to spin it on a drop-spindle. Arms flying, she threaded weft through warp, working a nonexistent loom at a feverish pace.

French Jack nodded. "*Et voilà, la laine, c'est . . .* the cloths."

"Exactly. You're a carpenter, French Jack. I know you could make me a loom. And cards," she said, illustrating

108

her words with her hands, "and drop-spindles. Many of them." She counted in the air with her index finger. "Reed, do help me. Am I making myself clear?"

"Comprenez, Jack?"

"Oui, oui. Elle veut tisser la laine." He turned to Lucy. "We make cloths."

"You will help me?"

He shrugged and raised his palms as though he were not quite sure what he was getting into. *"D'accord.* Sure."

"Where the devil does Captain Wally figure in this scheme?" White asked.

"Evidently he has seen the handwriting on the wall and assumes the Mexicans are done for. He's watched me teaching English to Abel. Now he's asked me to teach some of the Miwok boys. I intend for them to work the wool in return."

"Spinning is woman's work."

"Well, White, I shall just have to trust you not to tell them that, won't I."

Lucy found the Miwok boys quick and willing to learn. Only Luther Moore appeared to have misgivings. He stood in the clearing, arms akimbo, the reins of his horse drooping from one hand. "I don't like it," he said, casting a glance over the assembled children.

"What sort of a greeting is that?" Lucy countered. "You traded all your wool, I presume. What news have you brought back?"

"I don't like it," he repeated.

"Luther—. Dear me, wait a moment. Child." She took the spindle from one boy's hands. "It's tangling because you aren't feeding the wool onto it fast enough. Here." She sorted out the twisted wool and showed him the proper rhythm. "They're good children, Luther, and hard workers."

"I thought we'd agreed you were to educate my boy."

"And I am."

"My boy's the son of a white man."

"And that entitles him to particular consideration, I suppose."

"Damn right."

"Luther . . ." Her tone softened. "I love that boy almost as if he were my own. Indeed, he's such a part of my day

109

that he might as well be. He watches after Beth from morning 'til night. She's his favorite toy. He's no trouble at all. And he almost never uses Indian talk around my house. Why, he'll be speechifying like Patrick Henry one of these days. I'm not giving him short shrift just because I'm teaching the others."

"It's trouble. It's wrong for them to know too much."

"Why? So they can understand the cruel things white men say?"

He spat on the ground. "Remember how your man died, lady."

"He was not murdered by these children. The Miwoks are a docile lot, and you know it." She went to him. "I never met a man who didn't want the best for his son. And I give you my solemn word that I am teaching him as I would my own child. I am doing my best for him, nothing less. Now please, Luther, tell me what news there is."

"Newcomers aplenty and trade thriving and too damn much civilizing for a man of my likes." He spat again, for emphasis. "Heard tell there was a steamer in the bay of San Francisco. And Sutter's taken on a partner from back in the States to build himself a sawmill."

"He must be thinking of expanding his little empire. The American occupation appears not to have set him back a whit."

There was peace in California, Luther told her; the War was being fought in Mexico by General Scott's troops. And the families in the Sierras, the Reeds, the Donners and the others had been brought out, the last of them in April.

"They survived? All of them?"

"Half only." He told her what had happened in the mountains.

"Stop!" Lucy pressed her hands to her ears. "I don't want to hear another word!"

"Keseberg won his case in court, but that hasn't stopped folks from talking. Those who know say he's guilty as sin. Thievery and murder and—"

"No!" she cried. "I won't hear of it. You're making me quite ill, Luther."

He gave her his toothless smile. "Got a bellyache myself. Can't seem to get rid of it."

110

"I should think not, after hearing a tale like that." She wondered if he had made up the sordid saga of cannibalism just to upset her. Luther was not above embellishing his yarns to suit the occasion, and he was, after all, piqued at her for sharing her attention with the Miwok lads. He was a cantankerous old codger at best, and she had long ago given up trying to understand his ways.

For several evenings, French Jack had sat at Lucy's table, poring over the plates in one of Mr. Bates's volumes and making brief notations in French inside the cover. When he was satisfied with his calculations, he'd set to work, laboring long into the nights.

"It's splendid," Lucy had declared at the sight of his finished work.

He stroked the loom lovingly with his hand, a look of satisfaction on his face. *"Pas splendide, mais utile,"* he pronounced.

"My first task is to make a fine cape for you. It's coming on winter soon."

But Lucy found the endeavor more difficult than Mr. Bates's books had led her to believe. "Clumsy baggage," she'd mutter, scolding herself as she slowly reworked the weft across the loom, squinting intently so as not to make another mistake. Her eyes smarted. Her neck ached from the unaccustomed motion. But in the weeks that followed, she began to enjoy her labors. The rhythm of working the loom took on the familiarity of a pleasing ritual, and her fingers flew unerringly as she manipulated the wool. Her hands, softened by the greasy fibers, became smooth as China silk. And when she had mastered the craft sufficiently, she began to teach the boys to weave as she gave them their daily lessons.

French Jack's cape was hardly a handsome garment, sand-colored and coarse and dotted with lumps here and there, but it was heavy and warm, and the autumn rains seemed to roll off the rich, oily wool like water off the feathers of a teal. The *serape*, as Reed called it, was a grand success. And Celia, though she said little, blushed crimson at receiving a new blanket. A tacit truce was declared between the two women, though neither would give the other the satisfaction of overt amity.

"That's a nice shawl you're knitting, Celia."

111

"It's your wool."
"It's a pretty pattern."
"It's for Kate Pierce."

It was a late November evening, and Lucy was alone with Kate, who sat huddled in Celia's shawl, staring dully into the flame of the candle on the table. Lucy wiped the spittle from her slack mouth. "I hear Reed coming back," she said to Kate. She found it hard not to chat with the woman, believing, against logic, that she might one day miraculously respond, if only with a look of comprehension. "I'll be leaving you now, Kate. Good night." She took her lantern and closed the door behind her.

The evening was illuminated by a full moon that sent sharp-edged shadows slicing across the clearing between the cabins. Reed came toward her, emerging from patterns of light and dark like a chameleon changing its colors. She set her lantern on the ground. "How is Luther?"

"There's nothing I can do for him."

"Reed, I'm sure that's not so. The poor man's had a stomach ache for weeks and weeks. Celia made him some herb teas, but they didn't help. Surely you know what to do."

"It's past helping," he said, "not that I could have done anything anyway. It's a tumor, a huge mass in his midsection. I could feel it with no trouble."

"You're positive?" The night was quiet. Not even an owl broke the silence.

"Yes."

"Will it go away?"

"I never heard of one that did."

"Perhaps it's an abcess."

"It is not."

"He's been in great pain lately. He hardly stirs from the cabin. The Indians have been managing the sheep by themselves, though I make an inspection now and then."

"He must have had it a long time. He's a Spartan, that old fellow, but it's going to get worse. It'll drain whatever strength he has left in him."

"He's going to die?"

"His time's near, Lucy. I doubt he'll live to see eighteen forty-eight."

"But what about the boy? That woman can't give him any kind of a life."

"I don't know." He sighed wearily. "Lucy?" He touched the tears that glistened on her face in the pale light. "Here now, don't weep. Nothing has happened yet." He put his arm around her, muffling her sobs against his chest. "I know you love the child."

She took comfort from his embrace. She was no longer weeping. She rested her body against his, restored by the warmth that swelled from them against the coolness of the night. She raised her face to his and found him looking down at her. She knew then that what she saw in Reed's eyes was mirrored in her own, and she grew alarmed, though she did not move from him. They stood like two mute animals, sensing without words the feelings that had come unbidden, instinctively as dumb beasts were drawn to each other. When they drew apart, she felt the sudden assault of the cold against her skin, as though without him she was helpless even to protect herself against the chill of evening.

"I must go now," she murmured. She turned and left him, knowing that he stood there looking after her.

Luther's health continued to fail. Mercifully, Abel was too young to understand. Carefree as ever, he ran his green ways, full of childish enthusiasms.

"Mrs. Bates?" Abel opened his palm and displayed his treasure.

"What a beautiful big shell. Where did you get it?"

"There."

"Perhaps a bird dropped it in the grass. How lucky it didn't break. It has only one small hole in it."

"It's pretty."

"It surely is. Now what shall we do with it?" She turned the shell this way and that, admiring his find. "I know. Christmas will soon be here. Perhaps we could make a gift for your mama. We could make a sash and hang the shell on it. Would she like that?" She held the shell to her bosom and showed him how it would look.

He nodded eagerly. Giving him a smile, Lucy turned and called out to Celia.

"The soap's coming to a boil," Celia called back. "Wait a moment." She brushed her hands on her skirt as she came. "What is it?"

"You had some of that nice heavy yarn left over from Kate's shawl, didn't you?"

"What of it?"

"I wondered if you'd be good enough to teach Abel how to knit. Just a small thing, about an inch wide and a yard long."

"I'm a busy woman."

"So you are, but the child wants to make a Christmas gift for his mother. He wants to make a sash to hold this shell."

Celia glanced at Abel. "I am not going to waste my precious time on gifts for that kind."

"How do you suppose we are going to teach the child the Christian way, Celia, if not by our example?"

"He can hang it on a strip of hide."

"He could also make a braid, but they're both too easy. Children like to labor over presents. Besides, it will keep him occupied and away from what's happening in that cabin. Do say yes."

Celia turned to her soap kettle, saying nothing, but Lucy knew she had won. The old trapper was dying hard. Each passing day gouged deeper hollows in his face, whittling away without mercy at that once formidable man. He was as weak as a baby, his muscles flaccid, his hands palsied. He lay in the cluttered cabin day after day, his sunken eyes staring up in silent fury that a man of his kind should be destroyed like this. He was a great, fallen grizzly being gnawed away, bit by bit, by an enemy he could not even strike at.

When Lucy's eyes adjusted to the gloom of the cabin, she saw him lying on his bed of skins, the woman squatting next to him, both of them silent.

"I brought some broth, Luther. Here, let me raise your head." Gently, she spooned the liquid into his mouth, until he could take in no more. "I'll leave the rest here. Perhaps you'll have it later."

He rolled his head over to look at the Indian woman. Weakly, he raised a hand to shoo her away. He waited until she had gone out. "The boy," he whispered hoarsely, "take the boy."

"Take him where, Luther?"

"With you."

"To live?"

He nodded.

"Are you sure that is what you want for him?"

"I'll not have him—" he paused, grimacing at the effort of his words, "eating roots with the rest of them."

"But what of his mother?"

"I'll send her north. Back to her people."

"She'll not leave you now, Luther."

"After. Lucy, the sheep. They are yours. To pay for taking my son."

"I want no pay."

His hand fluttered in protest. "Take them."

"Luther, you must give all this more thought. I shall send White Russell and Reed Pierce to talk to you. They will know what's best."

"A damn congress," he muttered.

Lucy smiled. "That sounds just like you. I pray the boy is made of such stern stuff as his father."

Evening came. Lucy sat holding Beth on her lap while Abel fed the baby small mouthfuls of mush. She looked up as Reed entered. He came no farther than the doorway. "It's his wish," he said, "exactly as he told you. Are you going to do it?"

"I can not refuse. What kind of a life could she give the child?" She stroked the boy's head protectively.

"It's the right thing." He turned and went.

They buried the old man behind his cabin in a curious, strained ceremony that was neither wholly Christian nor wholly heathen, though the woman placed in the grave with him all of his personal belongings. They tried to dissuade her from laying his bag of coins beside him, but she stared them down, fierce and suffering and mute. At the last, she set some root-flour next to him and stepped back. She stood unmoving, watching the shovels at work. Once, her eyes strayed to Abel, solemn and silent, clutching Lucy's hand, and then they moved away.

Christmas day was clear and cool. Smoke plumed high from the cabin chimneys, rich with the scents of the feast to come. French Jack had made the boy a little bed as a present, just right to fit in the corner by Lucy's hearth. Abel, of his own doing, presented her with a tiny, twined basket like those he had so raptly watched the woman make. She, in turn, gave him a small wool cape like French Jack's.

They said grace and dined, with toasts and hymns. Once again, French Jack gave them a song, this time in

English, though it was hardly any easier to understand him.

At the end of the day's celebration, White Russell rose from the table and raised his cup. "To our neighbor, Luther Moore. He's free from pain now, and may God rest his soul."

"And to Abel," said Lucy. "A new beginning."

Before she fell asleep, she listened for a time to the steady rhythmic breathing of the two sleeping children. The Lord giveth, she thought, and the Lord taketh away. He had taken her husband and child, but He had given her a son, an amiable, bright-as-brass little boy whom she had grown to love as though he were one of her own. And now he was. She smiled drowsily and slept.

Lucy yawned as she slipped from bed the next morning and donned her clothes. "I expect it will pour before the day is out. There's damp in the air. Abel, put your *serape* over that shirt. I won't have you catching a chill." She peered out the window at the dawn-streaked sky.

Very slowly, she turned back to the room, her hands gripping the sill behind her, the knuckles pale. The children were playing on the floor. She stood there, frozen, numbed by what she had seen from the window. She began to tremble violently. Abel made a move to stand. "No!" She steadied herself. "Child," she said calmly, "I want you to stay where you are. Play with Beth on the floor until I come back. Mind you don't go near the fire. I shan't be gone long. Will you do as I say?"

"Yes, ma'am."

"Good boy."

When she had shut the door behind her, she ran. Her heart was hammering, her cheeks streaming hot with tears. She averted her eyes from the eastern sky, overcast as it was, yet light enough for her to have clearly beheld the sight at the top of the hill.

"Reed!" She beat on his door with her fist. "Reed," she gasped, as he flung it open. But he was looking past her. He had seen it for himself. Like a trussed animal waiting for the skinning knife, Luther Moore's wife hung from the limb of an oak, turning ever so slightly in the wind.

"Oh God," he said hoarsely. "I'll cut her down. Quickly, help me bind Kate first so she can't hurt herself."

116

"I'll come with you. We must get the woman out of sight before Abel sees her."

She must have planned it thoroughly, knotting the woolen belt Abel had given her with care, gauging its length against the several branches of the tree until she found the one just high enough. She must have tested the limb to see that it would support her. She had secured the sash around its bark and around her own neck. Then she had kicked away the sturdy, twined basket on which she stood. Above her head, the opalescent shell dangled, luminous against the gray sky.

They carried her inside old Moore's cabin and laid her there. "You will bury her without Abel's knowing," Lucy told Reed. "I'll tell him her people sent for her."

"I'll fetch Jack or White. We can wrap the body in a blanket and put it over a mule. We'll find a place away from the settlement."

"Wait." She scanned the cabin. Picking up one of the large baskets, she put into it all that she could find that might have belonged to the woman, no more than some feathered ornaments, her deerskin cape and a pair of mocassins. On the top, she placed a small basket of root-flour. "See that you don't spill it."

He took the basket and held it, looking at Lucy with a faint smile.

"It's her way," she said. "Bury them with her. Here," she said, handing him the belt Abel had made. "Like it or not, she must have this too. It was hers."

Lambing season was coming on again. The ewes, heavy-bellied, browsed on the bright green hills like reflections of the fat, woolly clouds dotting the sky. Lucy came up from the river and found Reed sitting on a chair in the sun outside his cabin, repairing a bridle.

"Look." She dangled a pair of trout in front of him. "Abel caught them."

"Only four and a fisherman—that's quite a little fellow you have."

"He's a joy. Ah, Reed." She laughed and tossed her head, "What a glorious day. The breeze smells so fresh and the spring flowers are showing their first color. She stopped and closed her eyes. "Listen." From somewhere in a thicket, a lone bird poured out a sudden, splendid stream of song. The sound hung in the air like a yellow ribbon fluttering and shimmering in the sunlight. "How blessed we are," she said quietly.

He stood abruptly and shaded his eyes. "Here comes White, riding as though the fiends of hell were after him."

"He'll lame that horse, bringing him downhill through those rocks at a pace like that."

Reed called out to him, "White?"

"Gold!"

Lucy looked at Reed. "What did he say?"

White reined up his sweating mount. "Gold!" he shouted again. "There's gold in the water!"

She wondered if he had been riding too long in the sun. "And there's silver in the sand, I expect."

"In the American River, gold!"

"How nice," she said, casting a baffled glance toward Reed.

"Streams of it, there for the taking."

"The only thing I'll be taking from a stream is my washing."

"How do you know?" Reed asked him.

"Mormons. I ran across a bunch of them coming from Sutter's. They were off to join some others picking gold off an island."

"Oh, White," she said, "they were having a joke with you."

"No. I saw samples. There's gold at Sutter's sawmill, too. Chunks of it, lying in the riverbed. I say we go have a look."

"Whatever for?" she asked him. "We have everything we want here."

"You, maybe. But if there's a fortune to be made, I aim to get my share. Reed? What do you say?"

"You go if you like. Take French Jack, if he's of a mind to chance it. Between myself and Captain Wally, the ladies will come to no harm. But don't desert us, White. You're needed here."

"Ten days at the most," he promised. "I'll ride up there and see if I can verify the news. If there's truth to it, I'll stay long enough to bring back plenty of proof."

"Our fields want tending," Lucy reminded him. "We can't eat gold, and the weeds won't wait for your return."

"My dear girl," Reed said with a laugh, watching White as he headed toward French Jack's cabin at a lope. "You couldn't have kept him here on a tether."

118

"Do you think it's true?"

"I daresay we'll know soon enough."

"Won't the Mexicans be furious if they find they missed their Golconda." She held the two fish at arm's length. "Do you suppose these things have been swimming unconcerned through rivers of gold? Perhaps California is awash with the stuff."

It was. No sooner had White and French Jack returned with bottles of flakes and nuggets from the American, than they discovered a shoal downstream from Castalia where traces glinted in the rocks of the riverbed. They pried out the flecks with their knives and came shouting into the clearing, clutching the evidence in their fists.

"What did I tell you," White said, "we're sitting on top of a fortune!"

Lucy eyed the sprinkling of bright metal in his palm. "Were I you, I shouldn't bellow about it. You'd best keep it quiet."

Each morning at sunrise and each dusk after chores, Reed, White and French Jack made for the shoal. Squatting on their haunches in the shallows, they poked at the rocks, scraping bits of gold loose with their jackknives, scooping up water and sand and stones in various containers and swirling the lot about for a glimpse of color. Celia shook her head at the sight. "They look like a bunch of savages grubbing for roots. Mark you," she warned Lucy, "if word gets out, we shall be the Mormons' next target. Castalia will be swarming with those greedy, adulterous saints."

"At the moment, I am more concerned with the greedy coyotes. They've gotten both a ewe and a lamb in the space of one week. Are the beans done? I see the men coming up for supper."

White with his skillet, French Jack with his wooden bowl, Reed with his Indian basket, trudged up the banking for the evening meal. Reed raised his hand and rattled the tea caddy he held as he entered the cabin where Lucy and Celia were preparing supper. "Hear that sound, ladies? Four good chunks. There's a natural trap down there in the curve that makes a rich pocket."

Celia glanced up from feeding Kate. "And what do you plan to do with all your wealth?"

He set the tea caddy on the table. It was a moment before he replied. "Not one of the things I want most can I buy with gold."

Lucy turned from the fire. He raised his eyes from Kate and looked at her. If only she could reach out to him. Such a small gesture, merely to touch his arm, to comfort him in his distress. But fearing one of the others might glance up, she could only turn away. She ladled the beans from the pot and set the food on the table.

"Abel?"

"Mama Bates?"

"You may say grace."

He stumbled haltingly through the short prayer. She patted his hand approvingly.

"Are the rains over, do you think?" she asked White. "I shouldn't like to see the cabbage rot again like last year."

"Last year we planted them too soon. April's near gone now. I shouldn't think we're in for much in the way of storms from here on."

"How I love those long summer days with the hills baked brown like fresh loaves of bread."

"Moi, j'aime les nuits d'été. The night, she is warm, *douce comme une caresse.* She has the soft feel like a lady."

Lucy laughed. "Why, French Jack! Such a poet!"

He flushed and bent to his plate.

Kate's head lolled to one side. Celia wiped her mouth. "Reed?"

He rose from the table, untied his wife and lifted her frail body into his arms.

"Is she asleep?"

"She falls into these slumbers of late. They come on without warning. I'll make her secure in bed and be back presently."

When he had carried her out of the cabin, White spoke. "If you ask me, it would be a blessing if she never woke."

"Don't say such a thing!" Lucy flared.

"The sleeping spells come closer and closer together," Celia said. "I expect that poor body lives more on rest than food."

White shook his head sadly. "The man endures the trials of a saint."

"Beth!" Lucy cried. "Oh, baby, take your hands out of

your food. Look what you've done!" She wiped the child's dripping fingers. "Watch Abel. He uses his spoon like a gentleman."

"Here." French Jack held out his arms. "Give her to me. I feed her."

He held the little girl on his lap, humming tunelessly, making grimaces to amuse her between mouthfuls. Lucy smiled. There was not one of them, even Celia, whom she didn't cherish as her own family. Surely, to live among such people in such a place as this was as close to heaven as a mortal could reach. California was an earthly paradise, Mr. Bates had promised. At least he had been honest about that.

Captain Wally crossed the field to where Reed and the others were working. He pointed in the air with his fishing spear. "Strangers yonder."

"There?" Reed asked.

He nodded. "By the water."

"How many?"

The Captain held up one hand.

"Men!" Reed called, "Captain Wally says there's a gang of five fellows working the river between here and the Miwoks. Drop what you're doing. We'd best go post a clearer claim on the section we've been panning."

There were four more just beyond the Indian village, prowling along the shore, washing their test pans, inspecting them for color, tilting them this way and that to catch the summer sunlight. By nightfall, they had found what they came for. In one place where the river widened and slowed, they had raised between five and a dozen grains to the pan, none of them bigger than a pellet of shot, to be sure, but enough to set them whooping and shouting over the richness of their claim.

"The five are Mexicans from San Francisco. The other four are sailors, Americans."

"Sailors? Here?"

"The way they tell it, they came off a bark out of Boston. They landed, heard the news and spent their pay on spades and pickaxes and blankets and provisions. There were eight. Four heard Bidwell made a strike on the Feather and went there. The others came here. They'd heard Reed Pierce paid gold for supplies at Sutter's."

"Then they're deserters."

121

"The whole city's deserting. One of those fools is working with a warming pan. Said it was all he could find in San Francisco."

By shearing time there were still more of them. They came along the river with their tools and tents like wandering tribes, camping on their claims, filling the warm, still August air with the sharp sounds of their picks and their hoarse voices echoing from the sides of the gully where the streambed lay.

"These men are quite mad," Lucy told French Jack, coming upon him one day outside his cabin where he was working. "They come here with only the clothes on their backs and sleep in them, wet from the river, with their boots for a pillow. They exist on salt pork and slapjacks and they want to pay an ounce of their gold for my rusty shovel and three potatoes. I doubt most of them take out more than a half-ounce a day at best."

"Non," he corrected her, "that Jim Fowler fellow, he make one good strike. Maybe twenty ounce yesterday."

"That's over three hundred dollars! A pity it had to be Fowler. He's a surly one, mean as an old bull. He stamped into my weaving shed this noon and offered me three ounces to make him a blanket."

He stopped hammering and looked up. "You tell him *non?"*

"Quite the contrary. His gold shines very brightly, even if he doesn't."

He threw back his head and roared with laughter. *"Ah, Madame Lucy, toujours sagace."*

"I do hope that was complimentary. But I've a nose that tells me there's more to be gleaned in commerce hereabouts than by standing up to one's knees in water nine hours a day."

"Pas le nez." He put his finger to his temple. *"La tête."* He returned to his hammering.

"How many of those cradles have you made?"

"Six."

"And how much to you get for them?"

"Five ounce."

"You're a bandit, French Jack. No wonder you're not down there on the sand bar with Reed and White. You can sit here dry and comfortable and pan other men's gold. I'll grant you, those things aren't near as beautiful

122

as the cradle you made for my babies, but they're a sight more profitable."

"Amigo!" A pair of short, swarthy men in wide-brimmed hats approached them. *"Buenos días, Pastora,"* one of them said, bowing to Lucy. "Frenchman, ready?"

"Un moment." He pounded the last two nails into the rocking handle of the cradle. *"Et voilà."*

The Mexican opened the drawstring of his leather pouch. French Jack glanced inside and, taking it from him, disappeared inside Reed's cabin. The two men followed, anxious to observe the formality. Nightly, men trooped to Reed's door to use his small weighing scale. They stood in a ragged line in the clearing, disheveled, unshaven, exhausted and, often as not, laden more with hopes than gold.

Reed and White halled her as they returned from the river. Reed glanced down at French Jack's handiwork. "Don't tell me you've gone and got yourself a cradle."

"Hardly. The infernal things are playing havoc with my woolen factory. They wash the gold out so fast that the miners are trying to hire away my Indians to fetch and carry dirt for them. If it weren't for Captain Wally insisting the boys stay with their lessons, I should have a mutiny on my hands."

The three men emerged from Reed's cabin. The two Mexicans shook hands with French Jack and, touching their hat brims, nodded in unison to Lucy. *"Adios, Pastora."* They lifted the cradle between them and set off.

"Pastora." Reed smiled. "It amuses me that they call you by that name."

"Evidently it amuses them also, though I scarcely see myself a sheperdess."

White grunted. "It's for sure they never saw a white woman raising a herd of sheep. *Loco,* they call it, crazy."

"Indeed. It's they who are *loco.* Gold fever on the brain, every one of them."

It spread like an epidemic. As the summer merged into autumn, the water in the river fell, exposing even richer placers, and word spread that a team of four with a cradle could take out eighteen ounces daily, almost a hundred dollars a man. Tents sprouted on the slopes along the stream like toadstools rising in the night. The remains of campfires scarred the hills like a black blight. And the clear, placid water became a roiled and muddy flow, its music drowned under the rasping and pounding of the digs.

And still they came. Old men, boys, American, foreign, there must have been nearly a hundred of them poking at the rocks, shoveling into the shoals, squatting in the shallows and washing as many as fifty pans a day. The cradle gangs worked faster, urging each other on with raucous shouts, cursing and blaspheming the heat, the water, God and each other.

"Damn!" said Abel, as he stubbed his toe on the hearthstones.

Celia recoiled, clutching her bosom.

"Young man!" Lucy caught him by the britches and turned him over her knee. She brought her hand down hard. "Never! Never, never." When she had set him on his feet, she saw the two large tears rolling down each cheek and drew him into her arms. "Abel, my son, there are good words and bad ones, and I know sometimes it's hard to tell the difference. Don't listen to how the newcomers talk. You speak like me and Celia and Reed and White. If you do that, I shan't have to thrash you again."

"They're a plague on my ears," Celia muttered. "They've no consideration for womenfolk."

"They're a plague on all of us," Lucy retorted. "Chuto has had to drive the flocks still farther away from the settlement. Captain Wally's men can't fish in the river anymore. And each morning and night we have to search the seams of our clothing for the lice these gentlemen so kindly brought with them."

"They're a rough lot. Half of them can't even speak the language."

"And the ones who can are teaching my boy foul words." Hearing a knock, she turned. "Captain Wally, what brings you here?"

He paused in the open doorway and nodded to the two women. Then he stepped aside, revealing a small boy behind him.

"Why, it's one of my weavers. What happened to you, child?" She cupped her palm under his chin and raised his head. There was a bloody gash in his upper lip, and the flesh around it was bruised and inflamed.

"White man," he mumbled through his swollen lips.

"Who?"

"Big man, no hair, red shirt."

"Lucy," Celia said, "it's that Jim Fowler."

"How did it happen?" she asked the boy.

"We three watch. He puts gold on his blanket. Then he—" The boy crouched on all fours, his eyes close to the ground, bobbing his head up and down.

"He was counting his take."

The child rose. "Like big bear eats. We laugh. Make him angry."

"What happened to the other boys?"

"Run. I fall."

"And he struck you?"

He nodded.

"Let's let Reed Pierce have a look at you."

"No." Captain Wally put an arm around the boy's shoulder.

"It's a white man's fault, Captain, and a white man should help. Besides, I want Reed to speak to the fellow who did this. It won't happen again."

"The very idea, a grown man attacking a child, even if the boy is—"

"That will do, Celia," Lucy interrupted. "I shall be back in a moment." She took the Indian boy by the hand and walked across the clearing. Captain Wally followed at a distance.

Outside Reed's cabin, the line of men waited in the gathering dusk to weigh their findings. Lucy scanned the soiled, restive crowd. "You there, Mr. Fowler!"

"Hey, Pastora, you're a pretty sight for tired eyes!"

"Well, this," she said, pushing the child in front of her, "is not! How dare you hit this boy?"

"That little bastard, begging your pardon, him and his playmates was mocking their betters. He learned his lesson."

"They laughed because you were creeping about like an animal on all fours. I daresay I would have laughed too. Child, tell these gentlemen what Mr. Fowler looked like."

The boy glanced up at her, his dark eyes wide with fear.

"It's all right, nobody will hurt you." She squeezed his hand. "Tell them."

"Like big bear eats."

Howls of mirth filled the twilight air. "Bear Fowler,

browsing for his berries!" They hooted with laughter, pointing at his girth. "Hey, Bear," someone called and growled.

When the hilarity had subsided, Lucy spoke. "Now, Mr. Fowler, you have been mocked by your equals." Turning, she pushed her way through the men into Reed's cabin with the terrified child in tow.

"Don't cross Pastora, boys!" someone called out after her.

Reed examined the cut and cleansed it. "Have Captain Wally bring him back to me if it becomes infected," he told her.

"I trust Mr. Bear Fowler will reimburse you for your services," she said tartly.

Reed looked at her for a moment. "I believe he will."

"Pierce?" One of the men looked up from the scale. "Are you a doctor?"

He stiffened. His eyes caught Lucy's and held her gaze without expression. After a minute, he replied. "More or less."

"Are you or ain't you?"

"I am."

"Doc, I'm sore as all get-out, and my mouth hurts like the very devil."

"Open it." Reed flinched at the fellow's foul breath. "It's the gums that are sore?"

He nodded, his mouth still agape.

"What have you been eating?"

He shrugged. "Ship's biscuits, coffee, a bit of bacon now and then with my slapjacks."

"Scurvy. Lucy, have we any greens to spare?"

"I'll ask Celia. But there are wild onions growing in some of the oak groves. They're very tasty."

"Doc, there's some of the men got what they're calling the river fever. It's fever and chills like the ague, but quinine don't seem to help. You know what it is?"

"My dear sir, you stand in frigid water up to your waists while the sun beats down on your upper body at over a hundred degrees, and a dry wind parches every drop of moisture out of your exposed flesh. Certainly I know what causes the ailment. Avarice. And the cure is moderation. I speak from experience, having had the cursed thing myself."

They came to him with their wounds and ailments after that. The hot-tempered Bear Fowler got into an argument over a bottle of whiskey, and Reed reset his dislocated jaw. Fowler's first coherent words were an oath of abstinence forever more, which proved to be an eternity of exactly six and one-half days.

"You'd have done a bigger service had you not laid a hand on him," Celia testily told Reed. "Now that his mouth works again, we must all hear the profanity that pours out of it."

"Take heart, Celia. He'll be going to Sacramento at the end of the week. The rains are discouraging some of the men."

"It would suit me if the rains washed the lot of them out of our hills."

"But so many are staying," Lucy said. "There are at least two dozen cabins going up between here and the Miwoks' village. Captain Wally is afraid his people will be wanting for acorns, the way the miners are felling the oaks."

White spoke up. "Come spring, the others will be back, and more with them, I'll wager. There'll be no stopping them now that the word's out there's rich pickings in Castalia."

"And they'll live on flour and pork and jerked beef," Reed said resignedly, "and wonder why they all have scurvy. They trade their health for gold without a second thought."

French Jack looked up from his whittling. *"Tant mieux, pour vous.* They need the doctor, they pay the doctor."

"Jack," Lucy said to him when the others had left, "I've been thinking about what White said and what you said."

"Eh?" He held up the tiny wooden animal at arm's length and examined it.

"Mama!" Abel exclaimed from his bed. "Look at the ears! It's a mule! French Jack is making me a mule!"

"Not yet." French Jack smiled at him.

"It's not finished, child. Don't bother Jack. Go to sleep." She sat down across the table from the carpenter. "There are more people bound to come here, White said. And you're right, they'll pay for what they need. But Jack, they need everything! Why, I've sold over thirty *serapes* for four ounces each. These men haven't even

127

suitable clothing. They want for everything, from candles to nails."

He nodded, bent over his handiwork.

"We must lay in supplies."

He glanced up at her.

"Of everything. Picks, spades, sugar, pickles, tobacco, boots—"

"Hey, *un moment!*" Laughing, he held up a hand to stop her.

"And you," she went on, "can make a sight more profit by building a number of cradles and renting them. Had you thought of that?"

He had not. He laid his knife and his whittling on the table and looked at her attentively as she went on.

"You know how gold-crazy these fellows are. You've seen how on the hottest days last summer it was all they could do to break off work for a few hours at midday when it was at least a hundred and five in the shade."

"So?"

"They're loath to turn a hand at anything but panning or rocking. But they're willing to pay for what they need. What do you say, Jack, shall we give them what they want?"

"*Moi?*"

"Both of us. You made money in the river and making your cradles. How much?"

"In dollars, near nine hundred."

"Well, I made over two thousand from my weaving factory. I can keep books and write in English, and you cannot. You can travel to the *embarcadero* at Sacramento for supplies, and I cannot. But together, Jack, we might make a profitable partnership. I'd provide twice whatever amount you're willing to risk, but we would be equals. I cannot do this without you."

"Lucy? Why you ask me?"

"Who else? Reed spends his spare time doctoring. And when White's not in the fields, he's panning. Anyway, my presence seems to gall him, often as not. I expect we'd quarrel. Besides," she reminded him, "didn't I just give you a better idea of how to profit from those cradles of yours? You were the one who told me I have a head for business." She gave him a look of reproach. "I thought that you meant what you said."

He gave a long sigh and shook his head. "Ah, Pastora,

the miners, they are right. They never saw the like of you."

"At least promise me you'll think about it."

"D'accord. That much. I will think. The—" he paused, searching for the word, "flood, is it, of men?"

"Yes, what about it?"

"Not until spring. Three, maybe four months, from now."

"But we would have to stock up well before that. We'd need provisions and a roof over our heads, and you'd want time to put together a supply of cradles."

"Like I say, I think about it."

"Don't think too long, or some sharp fellow like that San Franciscan, Sam Brannan, will be a step ahead of us. I hear tell he's rich as Croesus, thanks to an eye for trade."

"But Lucy, is a risk, all our gold for these things. We do not know for sure what happens."

"How can you sit there, French Jack, and tell me you're afraid of risking your poke, when with my own eyes I've seen you playing euchre night after night with that pair of sailors? I assure you, I'm a good deal more trustworthy with a dollar than a couple of bounders who've jumped ship. I am not afraid," she challenged him. "Are you?"

"You ask me to think. I am thinking. In words."

"Jack," she told him soberly, "I am almost twenty years old. Already twice in my life I have lost everything. It does not scare me anymore. But when we live smack on top of a river of gold I hardly think it's such a great chance we're taking."

"What about your flocks, Pastora, and your weaving?"

She paused, gathering her thoughts. "I have four able-bodied and dependable Indians. I shall give Chuto more responsibility over the others and reimburse him well for it. As for my weavers, I shall pay them in goods. The ones who choose not to stay with me can find jobs in the digs. I have taught them enough of the language to get along."

"You plan this a long time, then."

"No!" She laughed and lowered her voice, not wanting to wake the children. "I am planning aloud as I go. The full force of the idea struck me only tonight."

129

"Comme un coup de foudre." He smiled. "Maybe you make too much haste. Better we go slow."

But "we" was all she needed to hear. By the time the candle had dwindled to a stump and the stars had begun to fade with the approach of dawn, they were partners. Partners with lists of goods to purchase from the riverboats, money allotted for pack trains to bring them up country and a small sketch of a shed, only slightly larger than the weaving factory, three sides of logs and a fourth open to display their wares. At the last, French Jack added a canvas flap to be pulled down nightly and in the event of rain.

It was rain, weeks of it, which threatened to sink their enterprise in a sea of mire before it was so much as launched. Above Castalia, in the mountains, great snows filled the glens and ravines, sending the waters in the rivers below rising high along their banks, obscuring claims, filling the digs, washing away the work of months. It poured unceasingly for days at a time, dampening virtually everything, Lucy thought, save their hopes. There was word that the Sacramento had overrun the lowlands. Boats could sail inland almost to Sutter's Fort. "Laden with everything we want, no doubt," she complained, "and no way to get from here to there."

"Patience, Pastora," French Jack told her.

"It's only that I am so sure of our success that I'm afraid someone will steal a march on us. There are hundreds of men, they say, camped on the high ground by Sacramento, just waiting for the deluge to stop so they can move into the hills. What if someone is struck by the same bolt of lightning we were?"

He shrugged. "Then we pray he goes to Hangtown. But you don't worry, Pastora. The first two, three dry days, I go. My horse, he swim the rivers like a fish."

"Let us only hope you manage to find mules and drivers willing to make their way up here through the mud and the wet."

"For gold? For gold, Pastora, the devil himself would learn to swim."

VII

"Whiskey!" Celia sounded like a spitting cat. "You didn't tell me you were going to traffic in spirits! Have you lost every trace of decency?"

"I'm not going to drink it, Celia, only sell it."

"And in the bargain send many a man reeling from the strait gate and the narrow path."

"That's their folly, not mine. If a man wants liquor, he's bound to get it somehow."

"Young woman, you've shed your principles like a moulting fowl. And your new plumage, may I add, is most unappealing."

"Do be still, Celia! Can't you see I'm totting up figures?" Lucy bent her head to her ledger as though to burrow in its pages. The truth was, Celia had a point. Like a troublesome, indigestible morsel of food, her conscience refused to be so easily consumed by her practicality. Moreover, she was aware that she was in the process of becoming the very thing which Pa had despised most. Still, she thought, this merchant had not yet traded her conscience. Instead, it lay heavy and discomforting inside her, continually calling attention to itself. But hadn't Pa regularly bought whiskey from the folks at Apostle Provisions, back home? Who was the worse, they for dispensing it or he for buying it?

The more Lucy ventured into business, the more she realized that it was not an outbreak of liver rot in the sheep or the exorbitant fees of the muleteers that crowded into her thoughts as she lay sleepless in the blackest hours of the night. She could deal with those things. They were real and tangible. Rather, it was the amorphous side of

131

her affairs, questions and doubts that stirred in the darkness like nocturnal spirits loosed from their sheets. She was no longer sure exactly what was proper and virtuous for a lady, though despite Celia's disapproval, she felt no less decent a woman than when she had left Saint Luke's Plains. And try as she might to be just in her dealings, she was never altogether sure, as in the case of the whiskey, what was quite right.

"Lord knows," she told Reed Pierce, "I mean to be a lady and a good mother and honorable in my transactions, but I am so confused sometimes. Am I wrong to let the men banter with me and call me their Pastora? I tell you the awful truth, I find it flattering. And as Celia would be the first to say, flattery is a device of the devil. And is it wrong for me to expose Abel and Beth to such a rough lot? I want my children by my side, but only yesterday Abel giggled with glee as one chap told how they'd beaten and chased the Mexicans off their claims up near Sutter's mill. The man sounded like a barbarian, and my boy laughed right along with him!" She shook her head in dismay. "I wonder if I was even fair to Captain Wally. I promised I'd teach his lads, and when it no longer suited my purpose, I stopped the lessons." She leaned forward across the table. "Reed, I trust you to tell me the truth."

He tilted his chair back against the open door of her cabin. For a moment he sat in silence.

"Please, don't just gaze at me like that. Whatever you say, you won't offend me."

"Dear girl," he said quietly. "I've less reason to offend you than anyone on earth. I was considering what you've said."

"Tell me. I am a farm girl, Reed, not a woman of the world."

"But you are fast becoming one."

"Am I allowing myself to be compromised entirely?"

"Lucy." He brought his chair back to the table and, reaching across it, took her hand in his. "The men chat and laugh with you because the sight of a pretty woman is rarer than gold in these parts."

She looked down at the table. Her eyes rested on their two hands clasped together.

He went on, as though he did not notice. "And I have heard you set Abel right often enough to know that he will not grow up a barbarian. As for the Captain, your

132

conduct must be on your own conscience, but you didn't promise to teach those children for the rest of your life, only until they could speak sufficiently to get along."

"But there are others now, younger ones. Who will teach them?"

"Most of the able-bodied boys are washing gold for the white men. They'll learn soon enough."

"But think what they'll learn!"

"You can't be the world's conscience. You've enough trouble with your own."

"Sometimes I wonder if there's much left of it."

He smiled. "Now you are really wrong. Do you think you'd be bothered so if you were an unscrupulous character? That's the test, mark you. As long as you suffer these pangs, you've nothing to fear."

"I detest worrying and fretting. Are you telling me there's no solution?"

"The more you learn of life, Lucy, the more you'll find to question. And if you are ever absolutely sure that you have discovered the one true answer to such a question, my dear, you may also discover that you've become a damned fool."

"I need answers, and you promise me only more questions," she said irritably. "I should think it much easier to be a sinner without remorse. I daresay they sleep like babies."

He took his hand from hers and rose. "Don't," he said. "Life is too full of temptations to joke about them."

"Oh, Reed, I didn't mean it."

"I know. But I did." He was gone.

Despite her disapproval, Celia could not conceal her curiosity at the cornucopia of goods displayed in the shed beneath the newly raised sign "Castalia General Store." There was a second sign, lettered on the canvas draped over the single plank-and-barrel counter. It read, "No Credit." Hidden beneath the canvas were sacks of beans, flour and meal, and still another smaller pile of sacks behind the counter afforded Lucy a place to sit. Picks, at fifteen dollars each, hung from pegs in the wall. Under them were stacks of shovels for the same price and pans for ten dollars. Every inch of space on the floor and walls was lined or piled with goods. Dried apples lay side-by-side with gunpowder, flannel shirts next to vinegar, jerked beef beside Celia's hated rum, beloved, though, by the customers, even at twenty dollars the bottle.

"It's the New England traders making the fast fortunes," Lucy complained to Celia. "We must compete with the other merchants to meet their outrageous prices —and on top of that, pay the lighters and the boats that bring the goods to Sacramento and then the packers. It's no pleasure for me to have to charge four dollars for a single pound of coffee or six dollars the bottle for pickles, not when I suspect I am keeping the ladies of Salem in silks."

"Buttons," Celia said. "Could we have buttons?"

"Buttons . . ." Lucy added it to her list. "French Jack, see if you can find more cheeses, but store them in the cornmeal next time. I don't like asking six dollars for a moldy cheese, though heaven knows they're willing to pay it."

By June, the waters had subsided sufficiently to make the digs accessible, but the deluge of men was just beginning. What had been a trickle in April became a river in July and a torrent in August. And as feverishly as Lucy and French Jack worked to bring in provisions, it seemed they disappeared before so much as a mote of dust had the chance to settle on them.

"Madness!" Lucy said to White as they stood watching French Jack unload more supplies. "How else can one explain it? These fellows' minds have been addled by gold. What sane man would pay two dollars for one cabbage? White, they hire French Jack's cradles for a hundred dollars a day! May God forgive me, I no longer wince at asking a dollar for an egg. Jack," she called out, "were you able to get any molasses?"

"Two jugs only," he answered, unloading a sack of beans.

Lucy sighed. "They'll be gone by evening."

"Pastora, here. For you." He reached inside his shirt and withdrew a folded newspaper.

"You brought me the *Alta California!*"

"*Non.* Look." He unfolded it and spread it on the counter.

"New York City! Land, I never saw a newspaper from New York City." She bent over the yellowed page and began to read, smoothing the creases where the printing had all but worn away.

"It's near a year old, dated July of forty-eight," said White, leaning over her shoulder. "The *New York Sun*."

"I bought it from a Scotsman who bought it from another fellow who got it off the Pacific Mail boat a few months back."

"Damned foolishness," White muttered, poking a finger at the page. "See here. Women's rights, indeed. Some silly biddy hens cackling like there's a fox in the chicken coop."

"Where?" Lucy peered at the faded print. "The Seneca Falls Declaration of Sentiments and Resolutions," she read. "My goodness, what cheek."

"Those biddies think they're a man's equal, then let them fell trees and build cabins."

"Find something interesting to read to me while I take stock." She opened her ledger and began to write. Flour, pocket knives, tobacco, combs and, praises be, wine.

The foreigners liked wine. Of the thousand or so men crowded into and around Castalia, at least a third were foreigners. They came from Marseille wearing loosely flowing blouses, from Dublin with their clay pipes, from Guayaquil in their wide, woven hats. In their strangers' faces, Lucy saw come to life all the exotic places of Pa's fanciful tales. Names of places that had once seemed as farfetched as the phantom face of the moon were bandied about across her counter as though they were common as rabbit tracks. From the Sandwich Islands, Buenos Aires, Valparaiso, from Aberdeen and Amsterdam, they came. In the warm summer nights, they told of Baltimore vessels tossing like corks in the Straits of Magellan, of filthy Peruvian tubs and stinking Nantucket whalers. She listened to them raptly, overlooking the broken English and the blasphemy that accompanied their accounts. It seemed to her that they came with the gift of a world which, though she would never see it, was as close and remarkable as each of their strange and singular souls. They came on foot, as she had, by mule and dugout across the Isthmus, by ships with names that sang and soared like great, glossy birds. *The Celeste, La Pluma Roja, Orient Cloud, Flying Lady, L'Espérance, Gypsy Belle, Aurora*. It did not seem to matter to them that they had existed on rice cooked in sea water, fought off the ships' rats, suffered from dysentery, cholera or Panama fever. When their bodies failed them, their dreams sustained them. What a breed they were, Lucy thought, so like Pa. There was no doubt in her mind that had Pa lived, he would have been one of them. She understood them and their dreams.

Sometimes, mistaking her insight for something more, they tried to court her. She refused them as gently as she could. Mostly, they were homesick. Even Celia had her share of courting. Her denials to the contrary, she flourished like the last, late bloom of autumn, rosy and full of life. For her favorites, she cooked. It occurred to Lucy, a trifle meanly perhaps, that Celia was worthwhile courting, if only for a decent meal.

White Russell was lately making a tidy sum, providing everything from bear to quail for those willing to pay. Last spring, he and Reed and Jack had sold off their claim for a large price to a company of Sonorans. The Sonorans had worked like beavers, clearing away the soft surface soil to reach the rock layer. They had picked and pounded and dug at it to no avail, and when the last rains of the season had raised the river and it washed over their holes, filling them with dirt and debris, the Sonorans simply waited for the river to fall again and sold the worthless digs to a pair of greenhorns from New Orleans.

Lucy wiped Beth's face clean of the remnants of breakfast. "Go find Abel, dear, and bring him to the store. We'll have a numbers lesson this morning."

The child climbed down from her chair and scampered out the door. She paused at the foot of the hill to watch two Mexican women cooking *tortillas* on a sheet of tin.

"Beth! Do as I said, at once!" The Mexican women seemed fond of the children, but smoked black *cigaritos* and gambled nearly as recklessly as their men. Lucy had never seen such a race for wagering. They raced their horses at breakneck speed, threw dice and thought nothing of betting ten or twenty pounds of gold on a single game of monte. Worse, their devil-may-care ways had caught on with the white men. When they broke off their work on Saturday afternoons, Castalia became a town of gamblers. Faro, *vingt-et-un*, dominos, any game would do. Only the Irish showed any indifference to the lure of luck; but then, they drank themselves nearly senseless and brayed out mournful ditties loud enough to rouse the dead with their sorrows.

On Sunday mornings, the limbs of every tree within sight blossomed forth with a profusion of freshly washed shirts and stockings and drawers. Tools were mended, rabbits, deer and birds hunted, and services, such as they were, were held. The Americans were given to brief Bible readings and hymns. The Papists carved a cross on one of the oaks and knelt before it, muttering in rapid Latin. But nothing, not chores, nor food nor worship was allowed to stand in the way of gaming. With the last "Amen," out came the flasks and bottles and jugs. Those who had, not five minutes earlier, begged the Lord's pardon for past misdeeds, bowed their heads once more and plucking judiciously at their cards, arranged them in their hands.

"Mama!"

That boy has the lungs of a coyote, she thought. She went to the doorway. "Don't shout so!" she called.

Abel stood on the bluff above the stream, waving both arms, beckoning her.

The men made a path for her to pass between them. She made her way to Reed's side.

"Abel said you knew him."

She looked down at the figure they had pulled from the tent. "He came into my store yesterday. He complained of a pain in his stomach. Said his horse had rolled over him."

Reed glanced over the crowd. "Anyone know who he was?"

"Newcomer. He was alone."

"Nobody heard his name?"

"They called him Chick," she said. "But it wasn't his name."

"All right, fellows." Reed dropped his hat on the ground. "Give me a hand. We'll truss him in his tent and bury him on the slope over there."

"First let me try on his boots." Bear Fowler dropped to his knees and tugged at them.

"Mr. Fowler!" Lucy cried. "Have you stooped to robbing the dead?"

"Lady, they're a sight more use to me than they are to him, and I'm willing to pay for 'em by digging his grave.

That's fair, ain't it?" He pulled them on. "Tight, but they'll do."

"I hope they pinch your feet at every step!" Seizing the children's hands, she marched away.

Lucy placed two bottles of Doctor Hooper's Pectoral Compound on the counter. "Now it's Beth's turn. How many, child?"

"One," she said, pointing with a chubby finger, "two."

"And if I put another pair next to them. How many new ones?"

"Two."

"And how many in all?"

Beth frowned intently as she silently mouthed the numbers. "Four!" she cried triumphantly.

Lucy laughed and hugged her, then started as she heard a noise behind her. "Why Captain Wally, I didn't see you." She gathered up the bottles. "That's all for now, children. You may play until we go home for dinner." She looked after them, smiling, as they went. "Well, Captain, you cut a splendid figure."

Captain Wally's straw hat was so large that it nearly covered his eyes. He wore a red neckerchief and a checked woolen vest over his bare chest. His legs were covered by a pair of buckskin breeches thickly encrusted with grime. "The shirt," he said, "there."

"The red one? I fear it's much too small, but you may try it." She glanced quickly out of the front of the shed, hoping no one might see an Indian slipping into the shirt. If the scene were observed, she'd be obliged to lower her price in order to sell it to anyone else. "It won't fit across your chest. I can't fasten the buttons."

"I take it."

"Captain, I don't want you to have a shirt that doesn't fit. Wait until French Jack comes in with the freight."

"How much, Pastora?"

"What a stubborn fellow you are. Fifty dollars. I declare, for a race that cared nothing for gold, you are fast acquiring the white man's taste. I never saw such gaudy getups as you folks wear."

"You got more blue calico, Pastora, and rum?"

"No rum," she lied. "A small scrap left of the calico."

"Whatever you got. Some chest medicine, too."

"You're determined to get around me, aren't you?"

138

She set the Doctor Hooper's on the counter. "Don't get caught, you hear?"

"Medicine, Pastora. Good for everybody. Good to help a man sleep when the loud ones shoot off their guns and sing and holler."

"You'd be safer to use the sweathouse."

"Good day." He made an elaborate gesture of raising his hat to her. It all but swallowed up his head as he replaced it.

It was time for the noon meal. Lucy tidied up and loosed the canvas flap over the storefront. She stopped. From behind her came Abel's voice, clear and piercing.

> "What was your name in the States?
> Was it Jackson or Johnson or Bates?
> Did you murder your wife
> And flee for your life?
> Say, what was your name in the States?"

Flushed and suddenly shaking, she glanced out over the clearing.

"What was your name in the States?" he chanted again.

The two of them, Beth and Abel, were perched on the back of the weary mule working the *arrastre*.

"Was it Jackson or Johnson or Bates?"

"Stop that!" she screamed. "Stop it!"

They stared at her, mouths open, as she ran toward them.

The mule plodded in circles, turning the huge grinding-stone over the piled rocks, crushing them as he went. Atop his back sat the children, Abel holding Beth in front of him.

The Mexicans backed away from the *arrastre* as she wrenched Beth from his arms. "Get down from there!" she cried to Abel. "Immediately!"

Silent and fearful, he slid off the mule.

She grasped his chin and raised his face to hers. "Don't let me ever again hear you chanting that abominable rhyme!"

He stared at her.

"You heard me! Never again!" She pushed the children ahead of her. "Go home. It's time for dinner." She brushed past the baffled Mexicans, her chin raised defiantly as she blinked back her tears.

With autumn came the storms. The sky was overspread with thick, leaden clouds that hovered oppressively above the dun-colored hills, bringing with them the scent of oncoming rain. The damp and the chill penetrated walls and clung to clothing like an ever-present shroud of hoarfrost. Not even the warmth of the hearthfires could diminish the dankness and the cold that burrowed into the bones. The days were short now and dimmed by the constant downpour. They slept to the sound of rain and woke to the sound of rain. The men dug channels around their tents and raised their bedding on logs, to little avail. The swollen river roared along its course, a turbulent tide that swept away everything in its path. It seemed to Lucy that the whole world had darkened and dulled to shades of brown and gray. The waterlogged earth became a morass. Horses and mules struggled overland in slime up to their bellies. Muddied and shivering men huddled together in soaked tents, too drunk to know or care if their brandy had allayed their misery.

With the first break in the weather, hundreds left. It did not matter to them that the way down from the hills was all but impassable or that Sacramento itself lay half-drowned under a murky yellow flood. Any place was better than this.

Those who stayed, built. They attacked the groves with their axes and saws, filling the damp air with a din of hammering and cutting and the great, wrenching groans of the trees as they toppled. All around, there sprang up log cabins, board and canvas shacks and dwellings of roughly hewn stone with shingled roofs.

They worked until they dropped with ague or catarrh or pleurisy or pneumonia. And then they rose, those who could, and resumed their labors.

The clearing had become the main street of Castalia, ascending from the bluff above the river, past the earlier cabins and on up into the hills where it dwindled away. It was lined cheek-by-jowl with buildings, and behind that first row of dwellings, tiers of other houses perched on the hummocks on either side.

140

"We're a city!" Lucy marveled.

"Not quite," Reed corrected her, "but it appears we shall soon have all the problems of one. Look there."

"I know, I saw it arrive. How on earth do you suppose they brought such a heavy wagon through in this weather?"

"But look what it's carrying."

She watched the two men unloading the wagon. "Dear heaven, it's enough spirits for a saloon."

"Precisely. Hey, fellows! What do you aim to call your place?"

One of them straightened up and doffed his hat. "Will Crane, at your service. We'll be known as The Miner's Friend, and you're welcome day or night. Care to give us a hand?"

"Sorry, but I've patients waiting. Doctor Reed Pierce, at your service day or night." He tipped his hat jauntily and strode away.

"Paco can help you," Lucy suggested. "Paco?" she called to the Mexican who was helping French Jack hang the door on the newly completed wood facade of their store. "Can you spare a moment to lend these men a hand with their goods?"

Will Crane came before her counter later in the day. "Pastora, is it? I'm in need of a pair of lanterns. By the way, that Paco is a good worker. Thank you."

"I was glad to help."

"From a fine old family of *Californios,* he was telling me. Noble stick, if you believe him. Seems they lost everything, though I didn't catch how. He works better than he makes himself understood."

"Here you are." She set the lanterns on the counter.

"You got a lot of those greasers here?"

"A good many."

"Our place won't serve them. No greasers and no Indians. Makes for too many fights."

Not to be outdone, the Mexicans built their own watering hole at the end of the street and named it, with waggish accuracy, *El Palacio de las Pulgas,* The Flea Palace. But of course they, too, refused entry to Indians.

Despite the ban against furnishing alcohol to the Miwoks, Captain Wally seemed never to find it scarce.

141

He wandered about the town in one or another of his absurd costumes, appearing perpetually dazed, whether by spirits or bewilderment it was hard to tell.

"I know very well you've been drinking, Captain," Lucy scolded him. "When you've been at the bottle, you forget yourself and speak perfectly good English. Here, take some coffee."

He made a grimache of distaste.

"Take it. There's plenty of men like Bear Fowler who like nothing more than to bait a drunken Indian."

The Captain closed his eyes and took a deep gulp. He coughed and wiped his mouth on his sleeve.

"You're setting a poor example for your people, you know."

He grunted contemptuously. "They need no Captain. Now they do what the white man tells them."

"Lucy!" White Russell burst through the door. "I heard the Captain was here. Damn," he said, assessing Captain Wally's condition, "better not let him leave just yet."

"What's wrong, White?"

"One of the Miwoks made off with a side of bacon. A bunch of the men gave chase."

"What happened?" She raised her voice over the tumult in the street outside.

"Don't go out there," White told her as she made for the door.

There must have been thirty of them. Wild men, they were, their patience and tempers worn thin by the weeks of rain and mildew and mire. Men boiling with frustration and acrimony and now, vengeance. They had tied the Indian by the ankles behind a chestnut stallion, the ropes made fast to the pommel of the saddle. From one end of the muddy street to the other raced horse and rider. Cursing and howling, the men lining the way took aim and fired their weapons. Back again the rider came, dragging the bleeding mutilated body through the slime underfoot. Again, they loosed a volley of shots, causing it to jerk and writhe as though still living.

"I told you not to go."

Lucy leaned against the door, staring at White.

"His squaw tried to protect him. They cut her up bad. Chuto brought her to Reed."

"Can he save her?"

142

White shrugged and poured a generous dollop of whiskey into the tin coffee cup in Captain Wally's hand.

"What in heaven's name are you doing?"

"Getting the Captain here dead drunk. When he's thoroughly stupefied, we can wrap him in a blanket, and I'll throw him over my horse and steal out of here with him. It's the safest way." He glanced at her. "What's the matter? Afraid I won't pay the lady merchant for her precious whiskey?"

"Damn you, White Russell!" She gasped at the sound of her own profanity. "Captain Wally, he means to have you drink yourself senseless. It will make you sick."

He held out his cup for more. "I am sick. My spirit is sick a long time."

"White, spare me a bit of that. I can't stop shaking. Thank God the children are safe with Colin."

Captain Wally looked up. "No one is safe!" he said loudly. "Not even on the land that is his since the coyote created man."

Lucy prayed he would fall unconscious quickly, before he made trouble.

"He was a thief," White said. "There's no getting 'round that."

"You know very well, White, the Indians don't understand. They think the world's goods belong to everyone."

"Then they'd better change their thinking."

"The white man," Captain Wally intoned morosely, "calls the Indian a thief."

"White didn't mean you, Captain."

He held up a hand to silence her. "But he cuts down our trees. We have no acorns for food. He spoils our waters. We have no fish. He drives off our game. He comes like a cloud of bugs covering the land and laying waste to it. So, Pastora, who is the thief?"

"Pour him another whiskey, White. I'm going to find the children. Don't let anyone in." She took the small shingle on which was lettered the word "Closed" and, shutting the door behind her, laid it on the outside sill of the store window.

"Mama," Abel asked, as they sat at supper, "is it true they killed an Indian?"

She cast an accusing glance at Celia.

"I told the boy there was an argument," Celia said.

143

"It's true," Lucy told the boy. "There was a fight. He died."

"Oh." He resumed eating his supper.

Lucy sat behind her counter, leaning forward, her arms folded on her knees. "Reed, I am afraid for my children."

He looked surprised. "They'll come to no harm. The men are fond of them."

"Too fond. Yesterday Will Crane held a cat and dog fight in back of The Miner's Friend. He pitted that fierce amber mongrel of his against a wildcat one of the others had trapped. They took Abel along with them. They gave the child a pinch of dust to wager for himself, can you believe it? He chose the cat and won. He was all too delighted to describe how that cat seized hold of the dog and tore it to pieces."

"Hardly an instructive experience for him, but I doubt he's any the worse for it."

"I don't want him wagering. A boy of six keeping company with ruffians? There's something else, too. They killed the Miwok and his squaw. Indians are dirt to them. Even the law won't protect them."

"We few are the only ones who know about Abel."

"The Miwoks know."

"They've no grudge against you or the child. Were I in your place, I wouldn't think or speak of it again. Abel is light-skinned enough to pass for one of our own, and that is what he must be, for his own safety. Does he ever mention the woman?"

"Never. But he hasn't forgotten. He amused himself sometimes by twining small baskets. And now and then, early in the morning, he croons to himself in bed, peculiar sounds like the woman's chanting. I haven't the heart to scold him."

"Time will change all that."

She supposed he was right. Time was fast changing the face of Castalia and their lives with it. By the time the hills had turned brown under the summer sun and the dust rose from the digs and hung in the warm air like a fine mist, the town had grown still larger, spreading out on either side of Main Street and eastward toward the Miwok village. It seemed the new tax on foreigners hardly mattered. There were companies of Keskydees,

144

the French, who inevitably argued and insulted each other and disbanded, every man for himself. The Dutch, Germans and Swedes worked their long toms diligently, gruff laconic men with dour countenances. The Kanakas, near-naked barbarians from the Sandwich Islands, dove like otters into the deepest waters of the river, surfacing with their catch of nuggets clasped in their brown paws.

They arrived on foot, on mules and horses and more by wagon. There were even whole families from the East. The Spences, the Websters, the Stokes, the Booths. And some had brought their children. There were George and Hannah Booth and the Stokes child, Ella.

There were others, too. A pair of Negroes, Moses Cooke and Gabriel Cousins, who claimed to be from Ohio. But they made no trouble and knew their place. The same could not be said for the remainder of the new arrivals. "That kind," as Celia called them, made camp in the cluster of wood-framed canvas shanties so eagerly erected for them by the miners, at the far end of town. Word had it, there were at least half a dozen of them.

"Surely you won't allow them in the store," Celia said.

"I suspect I already have," Lucy answered. "Only today I sold some nankeen to a woman I'd never seen before. And when she went to pay me, I saw she had only one arm. The other was withered away just below her elbow."

"Then it's true what they say."

"Nelly One-arm, who else? I didn't believe it until I saw for myself."

"What was she like? How did she behave?"

"She had a stubborn jaw, a nose too small for her face and rather hard, dark eyes. But she gave a modest appearance, I must admit, and she spoke in a pleasant voice."

"The song of the siren. Heaven help us."

"It's not us they're after, Celia. I suppose I shall have to accommodate them like any other customer."

"You wouldn't!"

"I would," she argued tiredly. "I can't be held accountable for the virtue of every woman who crosses my threshold. I daresay a lot of the chaps who come to buy are less than virtuous. I'll confess, though, that keeping abreast of the times taxes my forbearance to the limit."

"And fills your purse to the limit."

"Who are you to stand in judgment?" Lucy flared.

"You offered no objection when Bear Fowler and his boys proposed building an eating hall for you. Surely you expect to make a profit of the venture. Who will take care of Kate Pierce when it's finished? You'll be too busy cooking for the men."

"Reed's home most of the time now. I asked Julia Spence, but she's expecting. She's afraid to be around a madwoman for fear it will hex the child. Priscilla Webster said she'll see to Kate, providing I repay her with meals for herself and Luke."

"So, Celia, you're learning. Bargains must be made. You will keep yours with the Websters and I mine with the harlots, as long as they give me no mischief."

In mid-August, the sheep were driven down from the far hills beyond the Miwok village and penned once again for shearing. Abel and Beth played among the soft piles of wool, frisky as lambs themselves. The Indian youngsters, mostly girls now, though Lucy had managed to retain some few boys, set about carding, spinning and weaving the fleece with the placid complaisance so characteristic of their tribe. One had only to give them a bit of direction and they became the most amiable of workers. Even Celia had taken two of the young girls into her employ at the Castalia House after first furnishing them with suitable attire and subjecting them to a lecture on cleanliness which they may or may not have understood.

"Celia, you waste time. Why do you make them wash after every single task? They wash when they arrive. They wash before they serve the food. They wash before they clean up. They even wash before they wash the pots!"

"They're a squalid breed, and someone has to keep after them. Hand me those apples for the pie."

Celia's establishment boasted a hearty bean soup for a dollar and meals of baked fish, beef stew or venison at a dollar and a half each. Mashed or sweet potatoes might be had for another fifty cents and pies, stewed prunes or bread pudding for seventy-five.

"I've brought you the two dozen tacks you ordered," Lucy told her. "That will be three dollars."

Celia laid the crust over the pie and pressed down the edges. "I shall give you credit."

"No you won't. French Jack and I could never keep

our accounts straight if you kept giving one or the other of us credit."

"I won't handle money while I'm cooking. Mary," she addressed one of the Miwok girls, "my money box." She pointed. "There."

"Mary?" Lucy said.

"Their names are unpronounceable. I call them Mary and Sarah."

Lucy smiled. Reed had guessed right at first glance. Celia would outlive them all. Whatever strength had preserved her up to the present, she now aimed single-mindedly and with full force upon her new enterprise. Not even her natural aversion to Indians or the unpronounceability of their names would interfere with serving her diners.

"I declare," Lucy said, "it's a blessing for us that food prices are lower this year than last."

"Not that it makes such a difference. The teamsters take up the slack with their exorbitant charges. I paid one hundred dollars for that barrel of flour!" She pointed a doughy finger at the offending barrel. "I told them they'd as soon see an old woman starve as blink an eye."

"Celia, there's not a doubt in my mind that you'll never go hungry again. Especially not with folks pouring into Castalia from all corners of the world, and every one of them hankering for a decent meal."

On either side of Main Street, tacked to each building, hand-lettered posters stirred slightly in a breeze so faint and so hot as to be little more than a sigh. "GENTLEMEN," Lucy read, "THERE WILL BE A TOWN MEETING." In smaller print it went on, "for the Purpose of Enacting Resolutions for the Internal Government of the Encampment of Castalia. Six o'clock this evening at Abner Gibbs' Hall of Fortune."

No doubt it was the work of one of the Massachusetts companies. They considered themselves missionaries of morality and jurisprudence, ordained to convert wayward California. "The Massachusetts of the Pacific," they promised. Lucy found them sanctimonious and patronizing and took great satisfaction in noting that only Abner Gibbs' large gaming hall might possibly accommodate the throng.

"Will you go, Reed?" she asked him.

"Of course. If only to see those New England lawyers turn Abner's lewd paintings to face the walls. They mean to elect an *alcalde*, though I suppose they'll want him called the mayor, and a sheriff. With every inch of land claimed, there are bound to be squabbles unless every man knows his rights and limits."

"Castalia is no longer ours, is it."

"Not since the first of them raised color in his pan. They are two-thousand strong, Lucy."

"They've stolen our peace for gold."

"Whoa, there! Look who's talking. I never saw you turn away a pinch of yellow dust."

"Nor you," she retorted. "I've seen you bleeding three and four men at a time, and for what? All because they insist they feel better afterward. The truth is," she said quietly, "I take the yellow from their veins and you take the red, and we each make a profit. We are no better than Abner Gibbs or Nelly One-arm and her girls."

He smiled and shook his head. "Dear Lucy, you continue to see life as though it existed always in the blaze of noon, either pure light or black shadow. Why must you be so hard on yourself? There are subtle shadings which you stubbornly refuse to perceive."

"You're wrong, Reed. Each day I see more of what you call the shadings. The trouble is, I begin to wonder if the time will come when I can no longer see the light and the dark of the situation. I allow Velvet Annie to bounce my daughter on her knee. I sell Captain Wally patent medicine laced with alcohol. I refuse credit to a man who can't find a speck of pay dirt, and that night he draws a razor across his throat."

"But only after he went into debt at Abner Gibbs'."

"Hardly a consolation. I am bone-weary, wrestling with my conscience. Life seemed so simple once." She felt his hand on her shoulder and glanced up.

"It's not your dealings with the harlots or the Indians or the miners that trouble your conscience, is it?" His gaze was unwavering. "And it's not our profits that make us no better than the others, is it? No." He cupped her face in his hand. "Look at me."

"Please, Reed."

"Please what?"

"Don't. Someone will come in. French Jack is due any minute. He went to meet the teamsters."

He released her. "So long as we both know. There is still some virtue in honesty."

The bylaws of Castalia, enacted under the watchful eyes of the lawyers, professors and military men from Massachusetts, numbered eleven articles. Claims were restricted to a width of fourteen feet, running back from the middle of the river. No man might hold more than one claim. A claim left without tools for three days or unworked for one week might be considered abandoned. Provisions were made for the election of an *alcalde* to record claims and resolve disputes. In the case of murder, theft or assault, there would be a jury of twelve American citizens. The administration of laws, civil and criminal, would conform as nearly as possible to that of the United States, favoring no state's laws in particular From this time forward, no person coming directly from a foreign country might be permitted to stake a claim within the jurisdiction of Castalia. With the rest of the bylaws approved, White Russell was elected sheriff, and the new *alcalde*, Will Crane, and his partner, Charlie Woods, opened the saloon to all comers to celebrate the charter.

"If you ask me," Celia told Lucy the next day, "their fancy meeting brought more lawlessness than order. Bear Fowler was shooting off his pistol outside The Miner's Friend at three this morning, and those women were laughing and shrieking in the street so's no decent soul could sleep."

"I hear tell the men from Massachusetts were rather taken aback. I believe those were not the results they had in mind."

"I'd as soon we did without any more laws and decrees. I prefer my peace."

But before the month of October was out, the news came. A girl named Mary Helen Crosby had disembarked from a ship in San Francisco, carrying a sheaf of documents she had brought wrapped in her umbrella across the Isthmus. California was admitted to the Union, a free state. President Fillmore's signature was there for all to see. San Francisco was reeling with the celebration, officially to be observed on October the twenty-ninth of this providential year of our Lord, eighteen hundred and fifty. And what was good enough for San Francisco was surely good enough for Castalia, California, U.S.A.

149

VIII

ACROSS THE front of The Miner's Friend, hanging from the roof, was stretched the Bear Flag. Its canvas background was not quite white, to be sure, and was slightly spotted, having of late served as Will Crane's wagon tarp. The brown bear in the center resembled nothing so much as a large and rather shapeless mud pie, but that, too, was cheerfully overlooked.

Beneath the hastily contrived banner, French Jack had erected a small, square platform for the speakers. There was no bunting to be had, but a gay swag of red-and-white checked gingham from the store hung draped from the center of the box and down across either side of the portion facing the street. In the space between was tacked the only American flag to be found in Castalia, a tattered silk standard, faded, wrinkled, little larger than a handkerchief, proudly provided by Velvet Annie.

By the time the morning mist had burnt away, people were already filling the street in expectation of the day's events. A celebration was a celebration, and it did not matter to the foreigners that this one belonged to the Americans. To a man, they were turned out in their Sunday best. Often, it was only a clean red silk neckerchief or a feather slipped into the crown of a straw hat or a freshly dubbed pair of boots. The Mexicans wore their brightest *serapes,* despite the warmth of the day, and some of the Keskydees sported jaunty *bérets* at a rakish tilt.

Abner Gibbs had donned a dove-gray vest which, together with a matching high-crowned felt hat, must have been intended to furnish him the image of a respectable banking man. A banker he was, Lucy thought, though the vest and tall hat gave him neither the respectability nor the stature he lacked. Abner Gibbs was a small man, his head reaching only to Lucy's chin. He toddled about the town, his stiff little legs working like busy scissors, introducing himself, passing the time of day in a high, nasal voice, telling one and all of the easy riches awaiting them at his Hall of Fortune. Beneath his heavy brows, his bright blue eyes moved about restlessly, appraising this fellow or that, reckoning the man's worth and susceptibility to the gaming tables. Between Abner's brows and his beard was a face so densely pebbled with wens that it was difficult to discern his small, round nose among the mass of protuberances. Despite his unattractive appearance and unsavory occupation, Lucy thought him a congenial little creature, so courtly toward the female sex that were it not for the obvious flaws, he might have passed for quite a gallant.

He doffed his hat and waved it with a flourish. "Your servant, Pastora." He bowed. "A grand day for us all, isn't it?"

"Especially for you, I expect. The men are in high spirits.

"Equal only to the beauty of the ladies, ma'am. Here, son," he said to Abel, "you won't see a thing down there." He raised him to his shoulders.

"Morning, Lucy, Abner." Reed made his way through the increasing press of people. "You've a fine view, Abel. Beth," he said, lifting the four-year-old into his arms, "you must see too."

Lucy hushed him. "The speeches—"

Will Crane stood on the platform, his hands raised high over his head, calling for quiet. The throng grew still.

"We are here," he shouted, "to salute that great lady, California!"

He was interrupted by a roar of cheers. A volley of shots burst into the air, leaving wisps of blue-gray smoke and the pungent odor of gunpowder over the crowd.

"The Union's thirty-first state!"

Another fusillade rang out amid the ovation.

"But first and foremost, the belle of the western world! Wooed by Spain, England, Russia and Mexico, she spurned their attentions. Like a virtuous and regal maiden, she chose to bide her time, waiting for an alliance of honor, of nobility, of greatness, of strength—"

A murmur spread among the crowd, interrupting him. "Will you look at that," Reed said softly.

Advancing from the far end of Main Street, four abreast, arms linked, came two rows of harlots. In the first group walked Velvet Annie wearing a prim, brown bombazine dress brightened by a pink ribbon tied at her throat. As the noise of the mob swelled to whoops of laughter, a smile spread across her face. With the exception of Velvet Annie and Nelly One-arm, dressed in deep purple, the women were Chileans and Mexicans. The Chilean girls, their glossy black hair hanging in plaits down their backs, wore a motley assortment of threadbare clothing. One, very young and scarcely developed, struggled along in a red silk dress over which she tripped repeatedly. The three Mexicans, although there was not a pretty face among them, were gaily turned out in calico and bright sashes. Necklaces and eardrops shone against their olive skin, and on their heads were scarves which skimmed their shoulders and lay draped over their bosoms. Across the street, Lucy saw Priscilla Webster move slightly to face the speakers' box, leaving her back to the approaching women. The marchers halted at the edge of the crowd and stood respectfully waiting for Will Crane to continue.

"Well, I never!" Lucy laughed, as Reed and Abner set the children down after the final hurrahs. "My ears are ringing from the speeches and prayers and cheers and all that shooting."

"Will I see you at the races?" Reed asked.

"I wouldn't miss them. After I give the children their dinner and a nap, we'll be back."

Abner touched the brim of his hat. "Until this afternoon, Pastora. Doctor Pierce, would you care to be my guest at Mrs. Whiton's eating hall? I've an appetite like a handsaw."

As the children slept, Lucy sat with her mending, listening to the chorus of men from Celia's Castalia House. The diners were singing. She smiled and quietly hummed along with "Home, Sweet Home." There was a pause and a babble of conversation, and then they started again with renewed gusto.

152

"Oh, Susannah, don't you cry for me,
I'm off to California, with my washbowl on my
knee . . ."

She laid her mending on the table. Susannah was dead,
buried somewhere in the grove behind the spring. Lucy
turned in her chair and gazed at Beth's sleeping face, trying to imagine the other child, her face so like this one's.
The long, thick eyelashes against her skin, the sun-
burned cheeks, the silky soft black hair, the pink lips
pouting slightly in slumber. She had a sudden feeling of
emptiness. So many should have lived to celebrate this
day. Old Luther, Red Russell, John Mason, the Burgers,
even Caleb Bates. Tessa Pierce would have been ten
years old now, old enough to understand the importance
of what was happening. And Kate, she thought, Kate with
her quiet, elegant ways, what would she make of this
rowdy, jubilant Babel of Keskydees, Kanakas, Chilenos,
Welsh and all the others? But Kate would pass this day as
she did the rest, unseeing, unhearing, slipping in and out
of sleep. Lucy despised herself for wishing Kate Pierce
dead, but that was the truth of it. What disturbed her
even more was the thought that she might wish the
woman dead not so much to end Reed's heartache as her
own.

By early afternoon, the town, fueled and restored, took
up the festivities again. "Children!" Lucy cried, clutching
hold of their hands. "Don't run off. Stay close." She
threaded her way through the noisy mob lining the street.
"Oh!" She recoiled as a splash of whiskey stained her
skirt.

"Pastora." The black man made a fumbling attempt to
brush away the spot.

"Never mind, Moses. It's too late."

"Mrs. Bates!" It was Charlie Woods, standing on the
wide wooden step outside the entrance to The Miner's
Friend. "Bring the little ones here. There's room."

She glanced around, wondering what the other ladies
might think of her. But it was a fine vantage point, and
Abel and Beth might otherwise be jostled and lost among
the throng.

"From the state of the crowd, Charlie, I'd say you've
been doing a brisk business."

153

"We can't pour the stuff fast enough. You've missed the mule race already."

"Who won?"

He shrugged. "Some tawny. I can't tell them greasers apart. The three-legged race is next. Me, I got to go back inside and help Will. You'll be safe by the door here."

"Lucy?" White Russell joined her. "You going to wager on the race? French Jack's running with Reed Pierce."

"Oh, but look!" As the contestants hobbled to the starting line, she began to laugh. "Abner Gibbs drew Bear Fowler for a partner! Did you ever see a more comical pair?"

A shot rang out, and they were off. Poor Abner was dragged along like a pup who'd seized the big man's trouser leg in his jaws. Bear, his broad shoulders hunched forward, cursed the little fellow roundly as they struggled on. The pair in front of them stumbled and fell. Bear looked bewildered. Abner, panting, seemed momentarily relieved. Reed and French Jack, both doubled over with hilarity, hopped gracelessly around the two. Luke Webster had drawn as a partner some pathetically scurvied soul whose limbs were swollen and stiff. With each step he winced in pain, and perspiration cascaded down his florid cheeks. Of the dozen pair of racers, only eight were still wobbling toward the finish line in front of the saloon.

"French Jack, French Jack!" Abel leapt up and down excitedly.

"French Jack!" Beth echoed.

"Reed! Faster, you two!" Lucy called. She caught her breath and broke anew into peals of laughter as they collided with a puffing pair of Mexicans. "Come on! Tom Booth and Ira Spence are catching up!"

White was shouting at the top of his lungs, waving them onward.

Gasping, Reed and Jack hurled themselves across the finish line, falling into the dusty street as a roar went up from the crowd.

When they had loosed themselves and got up, Reed was still laughing. "No offense, *mon ami*," he said, brushing the dirt from his trousers, "but I'd sooner try to flog a toad through tar."

"Drinks are on the house, doctor!" Will Crane shouted from the doorway.

"Oh, Reed." Lucy giggled. "You two did make such a

154

funny sight." She stepped aside as two boisterous Irishmen staggered from the saloon, blinking like bats in the glare of the sunlight.

All afternoon long, there were relay races and jumping contests and roping exhibitions put on by the Mexicans. There was even a dog race, won handily by a spotted mongrel belonging to the negro Gabriel Cousins. And when the shadows grew long and the chill of dusk came on, a parade was formed. Giddy with exhaustion, the disorganized band sang out at full voice as they marched.

"Yankee Doodle came to town, a-riding on a pony . . ."

Up to the top of the highest knoll they went, gathering around the high-piled wood and brush which had been assembled for the bonfire. With a flourish, Will Crane laid the torch to it. There was a flicker, and then a great, hollow rumble as the oil-soaked fuel ignited. Whoops of joy soared into the night air. The crack of shots punctuated the roaring of the flames. Dogs yapped in confusion. To Lucy's left, three Germans, their eyes glazed with drink, their faces glistening with sweat from the heat of the fire, were harmonizing in song. Their voices were slurred, but despite the fact that she understood not a word, Lucy could not help but nod, smiling, in time to the lilt of their tune.

Beth was tired. She rubbed her eyes with her fists.

"Mama," Abel asked, "now that we are in the United States, will we get to meet the president?"

Lucy heard Reed's chuckle at her elbow. "Son," he told him, "now that we are in the United States, perhaps you will get to *be* the president!"

"Reed, don't," she said swiftly. He knew as well as she that half-breeds were not allowed the vote. "You musn't fill his head with such ideas."

The boy looked up at her. "I'd rather be sheriff like White Russell."

She had to smile at his earnestness. "I'm afraid the sheriff will have his hands full tonight."

"He does already," Reed said. "There was a nasty brawl at Abner Gibbs' place after the final race. I just patched up a Dutchman with a bad gash in his scalp. Poor Abner was knocked unconscious for a bit. Someone overturned one of his faro tables on him as he was crawling under it for protection."

"What was the fight about?"

"One of the women."

She shook her head incredulously. The crowd had begun a rhythmic chant, "Cal-i-for-nie, Cal-i-for-nie, Cal-i-for-nie, Cal-i-for-nie . . ."

Lucy gazed at Reed. Waves of light and shadow played across his face. The firelight flared and dimmed and blazed again, illuminating, now eclipsing his features. She felt his hand on her arm in the darkness. "Reed," she and, barely audible above the steady chanting, "I miss our old Castalia."

"It was never really ours, dear girl. It only seemed so for a while. Come now, this is a great day for us and a great day for the Union."

"Cal-i-for-nie," they cheered, "Cal-i-for-nie . . ."

"Shall I walk you and the children home?"

She gave one last look at the assembled throng. The light of the flames flickered over the motley gathering. Those who weren't drunk with whiskey were intoxicated with joy, their gazes fixed on the glowing bonfire. It seemed to her that they and the fire were one, their spirits fused with the shimmering heat, soaring upward with the rising smoke, spreading over the outlying, silent land like a boundless, overhanging canopy. It was their land now. They held sway over every gully and slope and crag of it, and they would do with it what they wished.

"Cal-i-for-nie . . ."

"I'm ready, Reed."

They walked in silence down the hill, each holding a child by the hand. The sound of the chanting continued behind them. In the main street, groups of rowdy celebrants brayed and bawled like packs of addled animals. From The Miner's Friend came the tinkle of Velvet Annie's hurdy-gurdy.

"Into the house, children. I'll be with you in a moment."

"Good night, my Lucy." He laid his palm against her cheek.

She reached up and touched his fingers with her own. He took her hand in his, grasping it so tightly with such a fierce, sudden surge of strength that she gasped and started. "The children," she said. "I must go."

Though their lives were little changed, the fact of statehood seemed in the minds of many to validate the existence of the town of Castalia. By the time the autumn rains came, and with them, breeding season for Lucy's ewes, still more permanent homes had been put up. They dotted the hillsides as far as the eye could see, like closely ranked troops, erect, stalwart, abiding watchfully over the business of the village. There was an assay office, a third saloon and several streets with names ranging from "Plymouth" to "Paris," depending on who had built there.

"Chuto tells me that Captain Wally's people may have to uproot again and move still farther from us." Lucy was giving the merchandise a cursory dusting while French Jack presided over the counter.

"It's not their country. We grow, they go."

"It will play havoc with my woolen industry. I can't carry on without my Indians."

"Pas de tout. Ici nous avons—"

"Jack, please."

"We got here all sorts of fellows who don't find pay dirt. Others, their claims run dry. The foreigners, unless they already strike it rich, they got to work for someone else."

"I've yet to see one I'd take for a sheepherder. One rumor of a run someplace else, and my flocks would be left to the coyotes. I'll keep my Miwoks, though heaven knows how, if they unsettle themselves again."

"Mama?"

"Close the door, Abel."

"Doctor Pierce wants Mr. Louet, in a hurry."

"Go ahead, Jack. I'll close up. Where's your sister, child?"

"Playing with Ella Stokes. Mama, may we go explore the new houses?"

"I'll walk around with you before supper. I don't want you climbing over unfinished buildings. It's far too dangerous."

"Mama." He stood his ground.

"You heard me. Go play with the others. I won't be long."

As she strolled the newly named streets, the passersby nodded or raised their hats to her. She smiled, addressing most of them by name. Although these constitutionals were the children's sport, Lucy enjoyed them almost more than they. Abel and Beth skipped along, peering through

157

open doorways at the men laying hearthstones, waving to those above who were hammering shingles. They took note of who had moved in and who had hung shutters. To their delight, the town sprang up around them like a constantly changing plaything. Lucy, too, couldn't help but be stimulated by the industrious bustle on every side. The sounds of sawing and pounding, the calls of the workmen, the fresh, sweet scent of stacks of lumber, all filled her with the heady excitement of promise and prosperity. She bore a certain proprietary interest in the burgeoning town. Castalia belonged to her as much as to anyone and more than most. And she had belonged to Castalia, long before there was such a place as this.

Beth tugged at her hand. "Mama, can we have a new house?"

"May we," she corrected. "Ours is fine the way it is."

"It's old logs," Abel complained.

"And very solid," Lucy countered.

"But it's old," Beth insisted, unwilling to give way so easily.

"Only as old as you, Beth. Are you so old? Come now, both of you. It's time we went back for supper." She turned the corner onto Main Street, the children trailing behind her. Outside The Miner's Friend, a knot of men stood by the door. Two of them were steadying a ladder for Will Crane. He stood perched on a high rung, hammer in hand, tacking a strip of black bunting over the entrance. Lucy stopped to watch. "Will?" she called up. "What is that for, may I ask?"

"Bear Fowler." He began to descend the ladder.

"Bear Fowler's dead, Pastora," one of the men told her. "Them savages up the way killed him and wounded two others, only a couple of hours ago."

"Our Indians? Not the Miwoks."

"The same."

"You must be mistaken. They're too peaceable for such a thing."

Will Crane's jaw was tensed. "Try telling that to Bear. Half a dozen of them attacked while our boys were hewing wood. Just minding their own business, felling an oak tree."

The acorns, she thought; we have taken away their food. She took the children's hands and held them tightly. "What will happen now?"

"One of them's dead, maybe two. Bunch of fellows have gone after the others. We ought to get rid of them Indians once and for all."

"Where is Sheriff Russell?"

"Gone to Hangtown, early this morning. Never you mind, Pastora, we'll take care of this."

One of the men gave a curt laugh. "They'll be peaceable, all right, when our boys are through with them and they're three feet under."

She nodded and walked on a few paces. "Children," she said quietly, "go directly home. Stay there in the house. I'll be with you very soon. Now, go."

Inside Reed's cabin, she found Priscilla Webster sitting on the edge of Kate's bed, combing the woman's sparse, gray-streaked hair. The form on the bed lay staring upward, motionless.

"Where are they," Lucy demanded, "Reed and French Jack?"

"They rode out after the others. Doctor Pierce bandaged up the two men who were struck, and then he left with French Jack."

"They'll get themselves killed! Those men have gone spoiling for a fight!"

"Mr. Fowler's dead. The Indians did it."

"I know that, but there's no use in any more bloodshed."

"So Doctor Pierce said. The two of them went to try to prevent it."

"Oh, God." Lucy sank into a chair and pressed a hand to her forehead. Her temples were throbbing.

"Mrs. Bates?" Priscilla asked. "Are you ill?"

Lucy glanced up and saw the solicitude on her face. "I'm frightened."

"Our men are well armed. The Indians are not."

"Yes." She rose. "Would you be good enough to tell the doctor I stopped by? I should like to see him."

"You employ some of those heathens, don't you?"

"I do."

"Then I see your concern," Priscilla said tersely. "I can't for the life of me think how you can stand to be around such creatures."

Lucy flushed with sudden anger. "And I cannot for the life of me think how you can stand to sit here combing that living skeleton as though it were some ghastly doll!"

"She is a Christian woman!"

"She was, once. What she is now I do not know. But it is not human."

"And your savages are?"

"Priscilla—" She stopped abruptly and felt the tears rush to her eyes. "I'm sorry." Hurriedly, she left.

"Almighty God, boy! Put that down!" Lucy stared in horror at the Bowie knife in Abel's hand.

He stood in the center of the room, facing the door, his father's knife in his fist. At her words, he lowered it and reached for the leather sheath on the table. "I was afraid they would come here."

"Who, child?" She knelt and took his hands in hers. Beth crouched in a corner of her cot, her hands clasped around her knees, her eyes wide. "Bethie, come here. It's all right. Abel, who are you afraid of?"

"The Indians. And the men who want to kill Indians."

"Will the Indians murder us, Mama?"

"No, Beth." She slipped an arm around her waist.

"Mama," Abel said, "those men want to kill the Indians. You heard what they said."

"There are no Indians in this house."

"Mama?"

"You heard me, Abel. In this house, there are only my two children, Beth and Abel Bates. They are the son and daughter of Caleb Bates who died four years ago."

"How did Papa die?" Beth asked her.

"By accident. On the trail. His horse threw him."

Abel was studying her face. He held out the knife in his hand. "Whose is this?"

"It's yours. It belonged to Luther Moore, our neighbor."

The boy gazed at her, his dark eyes solemn and unblinking.

"I know you are nearly seven years old, child, but you are still too young to be using it. Put it away now, or I shall have to take it from you and keep it myself."

He stood there a moment, looking at her. Then he did as he was told. Lucy's eyes followed him. I must leave this place, she thought, and then, just as quickly, she banished the notion from her mind.

She sat alone that night, staring into the flickering candlelight as the children slept in their beds. Outside, she heard the sounds of distant voices, men on their nightly rounds of the saloons, Abner Gibbs' and the harlots' dens. She waited. When the knock came, she sprang to the door. "Reed!"

"*Non, c'est moi.* Reed, he cannot come."

"Is he all right?" She drew Jack outdoors, into the darkness.

"Sure. There was no more fight. He told them they already clear the score. They get two and the Indian Captain. He is worth all the rest together."

"Captain Wally?"

"They hamstring him."

For a moment she thought she was going to vomit. She put a hand on French Jack's arm to steady herself. "Did they leave him there?"

He shook his head. "We wait 'til dark and bring him to Reed's. The Indians, they no take such good care of cripples, maybe leave him for the coyotes."

"Jack? Is it safe for Reed? What will they do when they find out?"

"Reed is their doctor. They respect him. They give him no trouble. You know them, Pastora, tonight they get drunk, tell how they cut up the Indian, and tomorrow is a new day. Besides, White Russell be back tomorrow. He keep everyone calm.

"Oh, Jack, what's happened to this place?"

He shrugged. "People. America. I am an American too, now. It's funny, no? We Americans got no use for damned Indians."

"Thank you for stopping by."

"You don't worry about Reed, Lucy."

She glanced at him.

"Reed can take care of himself."

"Thank you, Jack," she said quietly. She turned and entered the cabin.

Captain Wally remained in the Pierce cabin, dragging his useless limbs along as he pushed himself about, tending to the fire, watching over Kate, assisting Reed with his practice. The townsfolk paid him no mind. More often than not, they overlooked his presence entirely, as though his dusky form were nothing more substantial than a

161

shadow stirring with the changing light that filtered through the cabin windows.

That winter of fifty-one there was talk of rebellious Indians up and down the length of California. The Mariposa Battalion was organized to bring in some of the outlaws. Rumors swept through Castalia from one end to the other, occasionally making the circuit twice and colliding with startling discrepancies. The town fed on gossip. It was said that Downieville, to the north, had the choicest new diggings. No, Sonora was the place, down south . . . Abner Gibbs wanted to hire Nelly One-arm as hostess in his Hall of Fortune . . . In Sacramento, Lewis Keseberg's boarding house was filled with lodgers who either didn't know or care that he might serve them up for breakfast, as he had the unfortunates of the Donner Party. There were bandits in the hills, the rumors had it, though no one had actually seen them; greasers they were, robbing and killing their victims without mercy. The only safe place for a man's money was Henry Schliemann's bank at Front and J Streets in Sacramento, where it was guarded by a band of armed men . . . Abner Gibbs had escorted Nelly One-arm to Sunday services, the two of them brazen as bluejays . . . Down in San Francisco, spring brought out the Sydney Ducks again. Gangs of the Australian roughs were setting fires and looting. Three-quarters of the city was in ruins, with Sydney town suspiciously untouched. By the end of August, the Vigilance Committee had hung three of them, and the rest scattered from the city. There were two new faces in Castalia, purported to be Ducks and given a wide berth, just in case. Abner Gibbs was keeping steady company with Nelly One-arm, who had abandoned her calling to keep house for him.

"In sin!" Celia pronounced.

"Oh, Celia, how can you be so sure?" Lucy said. "Perhaps Abner simply had need of a housekeeper."

"He could have hired an Indian. An Indian with two arms, at that."

"You have a point," Lucy admitted with a smile.

"It's up to the ladies of the community to do something. We're the only ones who can exert a civilizing influence."

"That's what the gentlemen from Massachusetts thought."

"But they were only men."

"What did you have in mind?"

"I'm telling all my diners to stay clear of Abner Gibbs' Hall of Fortune. That will pinch Abner where it hurts the most. And you must pass the message to your customers."

"With about as much effect as a snowstorm in Hades. For pity's sake, Celia, let well enough alone. They live as quietly as a pair of fieldmice, while Castalia bursts at the seams with new saloons and fandango halls. There are monte games on nearly every corner and rowdy, drunken rascals reeling about in broad daylight. What's so dreadful about Abner and Nelly?"

"It's not what, it's where. They don't belong in the decent end of town where respectable folks live. That strumpet actually attempted to strike up a conversation with Rebecca Booth yesterday. Becky was aghast."

"I had no idea that Becky Booth's morals were so frail that a mere how-de-do from Nelly would pose such a threat."

"Don't you start baiting me, Lucy Bates. I'm onto your ways by now."

"Then you should have known better than to try to enlist me in your scheme. I'll not cast the first stone. Hello there, Bethie," she said as the child came into the store. "Where's your brother?"

"The assay office."

"You run and tell him," Celia said, "that if he wants the job of sweeping out the eating hall, this is the time he should be there. He can dillydally around the assay office later."

"Go on, Beth, do as your Aunt Celia says." Lucy watched her go. "Is he doing a passable job, Celia? He must learn respect for honest labor. It's a difficult lesson to teach, what with all the bad examples loitering about."

"He's a conscientious boy, but a mining town is no place to bring up children. I can't say I envy you the task."

They were well-behaved children, all the same, not mischievous or unruly like Hannah Booth and her brother, George. In Lucy's opinion, those two scamps would cause Becky Booth a good deal more trouble than Nelly One-arm.

Beth, at the age of five, already had the clear indications of a great beauty in the making. With her dark hair and eyes and full, bowed lips, she looked like a small, lush bloom, a violet, Lucy thought, dainty, soft and exquisite. The child was not unaware of her looks, since not a day went by without a shower of compliments and coddling. Children were still a rarity around the mines, and one as winning as Beth was bound to be a pet. But Beth set little store by the attention paid her. She received it with a trace of impatience, as though it were something which grown-ups felt compelled to foist upon her through no fault of her own. Since this was, in fact, the truth of the matter, Lucy could hardly begrudge her the slightly petulant pout and languorous look which these blandishments evoked.

Abel had a more serious disposition. He seemed to Lucy less childlike than most boys his age. He was as active as any of them, darting here and there, full of eager curiosity about the workings of the town. Plucky and industrious, he would volunteer to work on this project or that, anything at all which might afford him a new scrap of knowledge or expertise. Other boys might gather birds' eggs or rocks or insects, but Abel occupied himself with his hoard of information, examining every fragment with the absorption of a collector. He carried each new treasure home with him and displayed it as proudly as a kitten bringing home its first mouse. Full of earnest enthusiasm, he would tell how a series of sluice-boxes were joined to make a long tom or how Charlie Woods had explained glass-blowing to him as they unloaded a shipment of whiskey for The Miner's Friend. He could show why monte was a loser's game, thanks to Abner Gibbs, and how Reed Pierce had taught him to make a tourniquet. Above all, Abel liked the doings at the assay office. The weighing scale there was nearly as tall as he was and appeared to him a wondrous work of art, with its gleaming copper and brass pans, sleek steel arm and carved ivory handles. He pored over the box of weights, holding one after another of them in his hands, his eyes shut tight, until he could guess the value of each of them almost unerringly. His pursuits both pleased and amused Lucy. She could not imagine what sort of a livelihood the boy would choose when the time came, but whatever it might be, he'd surely know all there was to know about it.

Castalia continued to flourish like a fast-growing tree, sending offshoots of its streets up and down the hills, sprouting houses and business establishments, increasing in size and population until Lucy wondered whether there were any folks at all left back East. Once again, the store was enlarged to accommodate the trade. There were new playmates for the children and enough of what Celia pronounced "decent women" to have an occasional quilting bee.

"Do you think we should invite Dolly Todd?" Celia wanted to know.

"Good heavens, do as you please." Lucy moved out of the way so that Abel could sweep behind the counter.

"The rest of the ladies aren't sure. Someone said . . ."

"Said what?" Lucy looked up from her ledger.

Celia waited until Abel had taken his dustpan outside. "She wore bloomers."

Lucy laughed incredulously. "She did? Truly?"

"Coming overland."

"What a sight she must have made."

"She'll not wear them in Castalia if she wants to keep her customers."

Lucy tried to envision the plump, robust Dolly Todd attired in a pair of bloomers. "Land, she must have looked squat as a mushroom. But she seems a nice enough woman, and she works night and day taking in washing. He daughter is a friend of Beth's. They take lessons together from Julia Spence."

"And Julia says there's never any mention of the father."

"Perhaps Dolly's husband's dead."

"Of the shock of seeing her in bloomers, no doubt. If there ever *was* a husband. One can't tell about that kind."

"I swear, Celia, I can't tell about any of them anymore. Time was, I knew the name of every customer who came in, but I fear the town's quite gone beyond me. Everything's changed. Not even the river runs on course anymore, what with the flumes and the sluices shifting off the flow. And one can't even hear a bird sing for all the sawing and hammering that goes on around here." She stood and smoothed her skirts. "Afternoon, Reed," she said as he closed the door behind him.

"Ladies." He nodded. "French Jack says you've some fine cheeses, Lucy."

"Over there," she said, pointing. "Best take all you can use. They won't last long. Where is Jack, by the way?"

165

"He stopped by Wells Fargo to make a deposit. Said to tell you he'd be back directly."

"With all the news of the day." Lucy smiled. "There isn't anything happening that doesn't pass through that office. There's more gossip there than in The Miner's Friend."

"I doubt that," Celia put in. "The only difference is that when they leave Wells Fargo they're in a condition to remember what they've heard. Do you know anything about Dolly Todd, Reed?"

"Last seen, she had two of my shirts. Why?"

"Celia wants to know if she's a lady."

He laughed. "Ah, Celia, they're all ladies to one man or another. I hear tell Abner Gibbs is planning to make a lady out of Nelly one of these days."

"He is?" Lucy said. "My word, what next?"

Celia smiled, complacent as a cat with a bellyful of cream. "I believe it was pointed out to him that a man who doesn't live an upright life can hardly be expected to run an upright gaming operation."

"Lordy, lordy, Celia," Lucy said with a laugh. "I'll be hanged if you didn't do it after all. You've made Nelly One-arm an honest woman. I expect," she went on soberly, "that you'll ask her to join the ladies at quilting."

"She's only got one arm."

"Lucky for you, I'd say. Let me wrap that cheese, Reed. Hello, Jack," she said as he came in. "Take the doctor's money, will you, while I do this up?"

French Jack laid the Wells Fargo receipt on the counter. "You give them gold, you get paper. I don't know, Pastora, it don't seem so safe to me."

"It is," Reed assured him. "What with bandits like that Joaquin marauding about, it's a lot safer there than here. Good day to you all."

Lucy watched through the window as he strolled up the street. He doffed his hat to Rebecca Booth and stopped for a moment to speak to her. Lucy felt a slight pang of jealousy and turned away. "Did you pick up any news at Wells Fargo?"

He shrugged. "Some. You know, talk."

"What talk?" Celia pressed him.

"This, that."

"For pity's sake, Jack," Lucy told him, "don't be such a clam. Is it bad news?"

"No." He paused. "Up north, by Weaverville, they stop some Indian trouble."

"I'd call that good news," Celia said. "Why—"

He cut her off. "Over a hundred Indians dead. Only a few children they let live, maybe two, three."

"Obviously they were troublemakers. I'm sure they brought it upon themselves," Celia said staunchly.

"Celia, please." Lucy sat down, resting against the counter.

"Lucy," Celia said quietly, "I know what's going through your head—"

"Do you?"

"There's a vast difference between those heathens and him. Past is past."

"You don't seem so quick to overlook Nelly's past or the silly rumors about Dolly Todd. Who's to say somebody doesn't know? Everyone at Sutter's knew about Luther Moore."

"Hey, Pastora." French Jack fixed her with a steady look. "Nobody says nothing. Nobody knows."

"Sometimes I think we would be safer away from here. Somewhere where there aren't any Indians. He hears these things too, about tracking them down and killing them. I often wonder what passes through his mind."

"Children forget."

"I wonder."

"Excuse me," said Celia, her eyes on the doorway, "I must be going."

"Good afternoon, Pastora." Nelly One-arm hesitated on the threshold. She glanced at Celia. "Perhaps I should come back another time."

"Miss Nelly," Lucy rose, "you must know Mrs. Whiton."

"We ain't been introduced."

"Now you have."

"Ma'am." Nelly nodded guardedly in Celia's direction, receiving, in return, the faintest inclination of her head as she made her way out the door.

"What can I do for you?" Lucy asked.

"I'd like to order some goods, if you please, ma'am."

"Jack? Miss Nelly wants to place a special order. Will you take care of it?"

He threw Lucy a reproving look and reluctantly spread a sheet of paper on the counter, making no effort to take pen in hand.

Lucy felt a twinge of pity for the woman. Save for the men who made their furtive way to the harlots' quarters in the dark of night, there was scarcely a soul in Castalia who would grant any of them a civil word. And those whom Lucy suspected most of being on all too intimate terms with such as Nelly made an elaborate pretense of shunning any of them cheeky enough to show their faces on Main Street in daylight. Only under the pernicious influence of liquor or lust was their presence recognized. Lucy, who still bore the memory of Mr. Bates's carnal incursions, thought their lot a wretched one. They seemed resigned to suffer all that was ugly and vile in the nature of men, with hardly a token of human kindness in return. She, for one, didn't begrudge them whatever money they earned at their odious trade, though she would not have dared express her views aloud.

"Blue silk," Nelly was saying. "Enough for me and Annie to sew a dress. With thread to match and buttons."

Jack gave Lucy a glance dark with displeasure, but he continued writing. *"Oui, les boutons."* He tapped his pen impatiently against the side of the inkwell.

"Could you be getting some lace? We could make such a pretty chemisette."

"Why, Miss Nelly," Lucy said, "are we talking about your wedding dress?"

"Yes, ma'am. Abner says to get whatever I want and he'll pay you. The cost don't matter none."

"You must have a hat then, too."

She brightened. "A straw bonnet! With ribbons, any color so long as it's gay."

French Jack flushed and continued writing.

"Have you and Abner set a date?"

"As soon as I have the duds, ma'am. He says if we're going to have a respectable wedding it's going to be the best, most damnedest respectable wedding anyone ever had."

Lucy couldn't help but smile. "I'm sure it will be."

"Thank you, ma'am." She paused in the doorway. Timidly, she said, "Abner says the whole town's invited. Anyone who'll come is welcome."

"That's very generous of him."

"Yes. Well—" She gave a small smile and a shrug and left.

"Poor thing, I hope somebody shows up."

"Pastora, you wouldn't—"

"I don't know. Maybe I would. Abner has been a good customer, and more than that, he's very sweet to Beth and Abel."

"Mon Dieu, comme elle est folle!"

"It does seem to me that if Abner wants to make her a proper wife in a formal ceremony we should celebrate the woman's redemption. Didn't Jesus forgive Mary Magdalen?"

"You are not serious."

She laughed. "I was testing my argument. Just in case the occasion arises."

"But what would people think?"

"That I was a forgiving, Christian woman. I hope," she added.

"You're not going to do it."

"You heard Nelly. It will be a respectable wedding. What's wrong with that? It's not as if it were some sort of saturnalia."

He pressed a hand to his forehead in exasperation. "In the company of a gambler and a loose woman?"

"Oh, Jack, you're as bad as the rest of them. You'll do business with the likes of Abner and Nelly if it's to your advantage, yet you set yourself up as better than they. Who are you to be so sanctimonious?"

"Hey now," he said slowly, "not me. I got no objection to go to Abner's wedding. But it's no place for a lady like yourself."

"That's for me to decide. I'm sick of hearing what's proper for a lady and what isn't. White tried to tell me sheep-farming wasn't proper. Celia thought storekeeping wasn't proper—that is, until she acquired a taste for profit herself. I don't feel the least bit tainted by either venture, and doing business with Nelly and the rest of her kind hasn't corrupted me a whit either. I'm at peace with my conscience at last. And I think it's sheer hypocrisy to invite their patronage on the one hand and damn them on the other."

"So?" he challenged. "You going to invite Velvet Annie and them into your home where your children live?"

"I am not," she retorted, "but Abner is a friend, and I shouldn't like to hurt his feelings by slighting his wife, even if I don't approve of her past."

"Ah, now we come to the truth," he said thoughtfully.

"You are trying to make a trade, Lucy. You are afraid for the boy's past, like Celia said. You make a trade with God—maybe if you forget the past, nobody else will remember either."

She looked up sharply.

"It's true, no?"

"I hadn't thought of it," she answered slowly. "Perhaps you're right."

"Superstition, Lucy."

"Is it? But I meant what I said. I'm tired of this nonsense about what's proper. I'm a rancher and a merchant and I'm proud of it. I shan't be mealy-mouthed and two-faced. Nelly behaves respectfully toward me. Why shouldn't I treat her the same way?"

"The world is not so honest as you, Pastora. You got to take that into account or you make trouble for yourself."

"I don't care. What can they do?"

"Who knows? Call you names, maybe."

"A lot that matters. White said the Mexicans call me crazy. And Priscilla Webster thinks me an Indian-lover. You know, Jack, it occurs to me that I no longer give a fig what strangers think."

"You be careful. Me, I am an independent man, but it's not so easy to be free either. Sometimes it is more simple to obey the rules."

"Not if it means having to be a hypocrite. I'm quite willing to take responsibility for my conduct."

"I tell you again, you shouldn't go to that wedding. But if you're going to insist, then better I take you. It don't look so bad that way. Everyone knows Abner does business with us both."

IX

It was, as Abner had promised, a splendid occasion. Inside the Hall of Fortune, the tables had been cleared away against the walls to accommodate the guests. From one end of the room to the other, along both sides, the banked tables were laden with food and drink. Lucy, who had never so much as peered into the gaming establishment, scanned the barnlike surroundings for some evidence of the dissipation that dwelled within these rough board walls, bare, she noted, of their infamous pictures. But the only visible temptation was the lavish abundance of the wedding feast. The room was filled with the delicious scent of roast bear loin and venison, of brandied fruits and apple and mince pies baked by Celia Whiton who, though she disapproved of the festivities, saw no harm in profiting by them. Lucy was so busy craning her neck for a better look at the bountiful spread, the platters of sardines and oysters, the bowls of almonds and raisins and figs, that she failed to notice the curious stares which were cast in her direction. When she turned to speak to Jack, she saw at once that there was a conspicuous space around the two of them. Despite the growing throng, they stood alone, as though a small gulf existed between them and the others.

"Why?" Lucy whispered.

"A lady don't belong here. She's no part of this crowd. They make a special place for her."

"Out of courtesy? Or to make me feel like a leper?"

He smiled, without committing himself to an answer.

She spied White Russell across the room and nodded. He frowned and shook his head like a parent reprimanding a troublesome child. She looked around the assembled men for the familiar faces of her customers. Here and there she received a flicker of recognition, but it was clear that her presence was not appreciated.

"Jack," she said, "I do believe I'm not welome here."

He gave a short grunt of annoyance.

"But I thought I was doing Abner and Nelly a kindness."

"Maybe so. But I guess when the men come here, they don't want to be around no ladies."

A murmur swept the guests, and the crowd parted. Nelly One-arm, resplendent in her lace and sky-blue taffeta gown, her bonnet tied in a yellow bow under her chin, walked primly through the path made for her, on the arm of Charlie Woods. At the far end of the room waited Abner Gibbs with his witness, Will Crane, and the preacher, a gangling young man, blonde and studious-looking. He had been imported from Volcano, presumably innocent of the circumstances, after no one could be found in Castalia to bless the occasion.

The couple stood stiffly at attention as he spoke, Nelly towering over the dapper little Abner, and when the benediction had been pronounced, the groom grazed the cheek of his bride with a single chaste peck.

"Gents," he announced, "me and the wife want you all to have a fine time. Dig in."

There was a scramble toward the tables, and somewhere in the back of the room someone began to saw noisily on a fiddle.

"I'd best be paying my respects and leaving. Will you lead the way, Jack?"

She greeted them both warmly, ignoring the look of astonishment on Nelly's face.

"Pastora," Abner said, seeming relieved to be able to produce a lady to introduce to the preacher, "shake hands with Mr. Whiting here."

"So you're the famous Pastora," the young preacher said, a look of surprised pleasure on his face.

"I am?"

"The lady sheep-farmer. Word gets around. We've some fine, healthy flocks in Volcano, too. Just arrived from the East. Merino sheep."

"Merinos? You're sure?"

"Yes, ma'am."

172

She beckoned to Reed Pierce. "Did you hear that? Merinos. Over in Volcano."

"Someone finally did it."

She stepped aside as well-wishers jostled about the newlyweds. " '*Mene, Mene Tekel Upharsin.*' Weighed and found wanting. I believe the value of my flocks just diminished considerably."

"It was bound to happen sooner or later," Reed answered. "And you have the store, after all."

"I must find a buyer for them as soon as possible. Where did Jack go?" She searched the throng. "He was going to take me home."

"May I have the honor?"

"A dubious one, I'm afraid. I made a mistake in coming."

"Your intentions were charitable."

"Reed, why didn't you warn me that I'd be unwelcome?"

"Because you weren't to Abner and Nelly. And because you are an uncommonly mulish little lady once your mind is made up. If you're determined to be so obstinate, you're going to have to swallow an occasional mistake."

"I didn't ask for a sermon," she retorted.

"Aren't you the one who complains that I don't answer your questions? You might as well stay and have a bite to eat, as long as you're here."

"I shouldn't want to disturb the other guests," she said tartly.

"After the first round of drinks, nobody will give it a thought."

Lucy eyed the tempting array of food.

"I'll escort you away before the party gets out of hand. Which it will," he warned.

"For a little while, then. Do let's eat. Everything looks so tasty."

The guests set upon the food as if none of them had ever before been favored with such a feast. Lucy stood with Reed and Jack, popping the last of several luscious figs into her mouth.

"May I fetch you anything?" Reed asked her.

"I don't want you risking your life among that hungry horde. Who are all these men? I only recognize a few of them."

"Rolling stones, I expect. You wouldn't expect to find any of Castalia's august citizens here. Certainly no family men."

"You're here," she countered.

"Reed's the doctor," Jack said. "A doctor, he can go anyplace. People respect a doctor, no matter what."

"I guess that leaves you and me."

French Jack shrugged. "Me, I come so some stubborn woman don't make such a big damned fool of herself."

"I have already heard that speech from Doctor Pierce, Jack."

"Oh?" He exchanged glances with Reed.

"If I didn't know better, I'd say you had both conspired to try to teach me a lesson."

"Give a look," Reed said, "the dancing's begun."

As the fiddle squawked, Abner gave Nelly a courtly bow and took her in hand. His head came only to her shoulders, but he steered her adroitly across the floor, accompanied by cheers and whistles. Presently they were joined by a pair of Mexicans, hands held high above their heads, performing a sprightly fandango.

"Why are there no women?" Lucy wondered aloud. "I'd have thought Velvet Annie would be here."

"I expect," Reed told her, "she had the good sense to stay away. I doubt that Mrs. Gibbs would take kindly to such a reminder, especially on her wedding day."

"I guess I should be going along now."

"Yes," said Reed. "Some poor dunce has got himself drunk senseless already." He nodded toward the doorway, where two men were supporting a third between them.

"Make way!" one of them called, pushing through the crowd in the entrance.

Lucy glanced quickly away from the vulgar spectacle. Then she turned and looked again. Something in the small, spindly shape of the man they carried tugged at her attention. His head, bald as an egg, lolled forward on his chest.

"Great heavens." She bolted from Reed and Jack and elbowed her way through the press of revelers. "Sirs!" she called to the two men. "Wait up!"

One of them glanced back at her.

"The gentleman—" she said.

"You know him? He said he came over from Fiddletown, and some greaser robbed him."

"His name is Jacob Vose. Is he very drunk?"

"Don't ask me. He was in need of something to eat, so we brought him along."

"Reed!" She motioned to him and Jack. "I know this man. Could you take him back to my house and make him comfortable?"

Reed and Jack carried him back to the cabin and laid him down. Reed loosened Mr. Vose's shirt. He bent close to his prostrate form. "Lucy, is he much of a drinker, do you know?"

"I never saw him take a drop. Why?"

"I don't smell liquor on his breath. I think he's ill."

"With what?"

"I've no idea." He grasped Mr. Vose's hand as it moved ever so slightly. "Can you hear me? What seems to be ailing you?"

Mr. Vose's eyelids fluttered and opened. He stared up silently.

"I'm a doctor. Can you tell me what seems to be wrong?"

The door burst open. "Mama!" Abel cried.

"Not now," she hushed him. "Someone's ill."

"Hannah Booth pushed Beth in the mud!"

"Come." French Jack took his hand. "We go have a talk with Hannah Booth." He led the boy outside.

"You go too," Reed told Lucy. "I want to examine Mr. Vose."

"Well?" she asked anxiously when he came out of the cabin. "What is it?"

"He has a severe pain in his side, near the liver. Unless I miss my guess, it's that peculiar pleurisy I've been seeing lately."

"Are his lungs congested?"

"Somewhat. But that doesn't mean much with this kind of ailment. It's a puzzlement, Lucy. There's not much I can do. It doesn't look good for him. You'd best just try to make him as comfortable as you can."

As Reed left, she bent over the suffering man and raised his head slightly on the pillow. "Mr. Vose? It's me. Lucy. Remember? Lucy Curtis. Caleb Bates's wife."

He stared up at her and blinked once or twice, as though a harsh light had dazed him.

"Lucy Curtis," she repeated, "from Saint Luke's Plains."

"Mercy," he breathed.

She smiled. "I'm as surprised as you are. Have a spoonful of soup, won't you? It'll keep up your strength."

"Lucy."

She fed him as much as he could take in, but he had hardly sufficient strength to swallow.

"Where's your mister?" he whispered.

"Passed on, six years now. But I'm doing fine. What about you and Mrs. Vose?"

"Corrie."

"Yes."

"Going to bring her back a hill of gold. But the greaser got it. Two saddlebags." He closed his eyes tightly against the pain.

"Joaquin, I'll wager. He's everywhere these days."

"Lucy." He reached out and took her hand in his feeble clasp. "Do something."

"Doctor Pierce is a good man. He'll do his best for you."

"No," he said, "write a letter for me. To Corrie."

She sat beside him, holding the paper on a book in her lap. Sometimes his voice faded away, and she glanced up, alarmed, waiting for him to summon the strength to continue.

"My Dearest Wife," he had dictated, "I am feeling unwell right now but, God willing, I'll recover soon. I've had one good piece of luck, though. I'm being cared for by our little Lucy Curtis. She lives not far from Fiddletown, where I found some rich diggings."

He paused again, exhausted. When he went on, he said, "But I regret to tell you, I lost the harvest of weeks of work at the hands of one of the Mexican criminals loose out here. It is no easy place, Corrie."

Before morning, he was dead.

They buried him in the Castalia Town cemetery, a trim, sloped clearing on the side of a hill above the assay office. When it was done, Lucy returned to the store and, drawing his letter from her pocket, she spread it on the counter and took out a clean sheet of paper. She began to copy it. ". . . Rich diggings," she wrote and stopped there. She crumpled Mr. Vose's letter into a ball, dropped it on the floor and continued to write.

"I am sending you what I hope will be enough money to keep you for some time," she wrote in closing the letter. "I wish it could be more." Lucy signed it as he had told her. At the bottom, she added, "Mrs. Vose, he died peacefully. I was with him. He is resting now nearby my house in a pretty place overlooking our town. I send you my sympathy and affection. Your friend always, Lucy Curtis Bates."

When Jack returned to mind the store, she took the letter to Wells Fargo and made the arrangements.

"Abel, dear," Lucy cautioned, "do your sweeping a bit less aggressively, if you will. You're raising a bothersome dust in here." She turned to Priscilla Webster, who continued to cough daintily behind her handkerchief. "I'm sorry. Will that be all?"

"Quite." She counted out the correct amount and handed it to Lucy.

"I hear Luke's been feeling poorly. I do hope it's not serious." Lucy paused and nodded a greeting as Dolly Todd bustled into the store.

"Mr. Webster—" Priscilla paused to clear her throat. "Mr. Webster," she repeated, in case Lucy had missed the point, "is recovering nicely."

Lucy's face was innocent of any expression. "I'm glad. Do give Mr. Webster my best regards, Mrs. Webster."

Priscilla gave a curt nod.

" 'Day to you, Priscilla," Dolly called after her. "Land! Didn't anyone ever tell that woman not to slam doors? Acting a little peevish, ain't she?"

"Mother," Abel said, leaning his broom against the wall, "I don't think Mrs. Webster likes you."

"Nonsense. Her husband's been sick abed. She's probably worn out from tending to him."

"No ma'am," he persisted. "George Booth told me his ma and the other ladies said you should be ashamed of yourself."

Lucy felt the color rising in her cheeks. "Help yourself to what you need, Dolly. I'll be with you in a moment."

"Oh, don't pay attention to me," she said brightly. "I'll take care of myself."

Lucy sat down behind the counter. "Abel, come here. Do you know why the ladies said that?"

"Because you put a stain on womanhood."

Dolly looked around sharply and then, catching herself, returned to her perusal of the yard goods.

Lucy's face felt as though it were burning. She spoke as

calmly as she could. "And did George explain that statement?"

"No. But I know why, anyhow."

"You do?" she asked, taken aback.

"Because you went to—" He wasn't quite sure how to put it. ". . . You know."

"To Abner's wedding."

"Yes, ma'am. To that—" He stopped and glanced at Dolly Todd. "Mother," he whispered uneasily, "if I use that word, you'll punish me."

"You're right. I will. Now, Abel," she said, slipping an arm around his waist, "do you think I did wrong to go? Abner's been a good friend to us."

"The ladies think you did."

"But do you?"

"I don't know . . ." He frowned. "What was it like?"

"Any other wedding, except there were lots more people."

"George said it was near to a riot."

"George wasn't there. And it certainly was no such thing while I was present. Tell me, should I have slighted Abner because he took a wife most people disapprove of?"

"Mrs. Webster slighted you."

"That's between her and me. Do you think I did the wrong thing?"

"I like Mr. Gibbs. Sometimes he gives sugar candy to me and Beth."

"What would you have done in my place?"

"Go. I guess. But I would have been scared."

"I was," she admitted. "But I felt I acted in good conscience. If you have any trouble on my account, either you or Beth, you let me know. Any woman who takes revenge on children for the doings of their elders is no Christian. It's those women who should be ashamed, if you ask me."

"Bravo! Well said!" Dolly Todd beamed. "I couldn't have put it better myself."

Embarrassed, Lucy rose. "Let me measure that gingham for you. Run along, Abel, and remember what I said."

"He's a fine young man." Dolly looked after him. "And I expect that daughter of yours will break a few hearts in her time."

"They're good children," she acknowledged. "Things are well with you?"

"As long as these strong arms hold out. Who'd have thought there was a fortune to be made over a laundry tub?" she said with a smile. "Did you find a buyer for your sheep?"

"From Amador City, but they only fetched eleven dollars the head. The news of the Merinos has spread like a prairie fire. I'm afraid the price would have dropped even lower if I'd waited. Dolly—" She stared over the woman's shoulder and out of the window beyond. "Merciful heaven, will you look there!"

They hurried to the window and peered out. "Well, I never!" Dolly gasped. "Listen, they sound like a flock of gabbling geese."

It was a strange sound, a peculiar singsong chatter like no language Lucy had ever heard. She stared at the half-dozen faces, yellowed like old ivory, as they nodded and jabbered. Their dark, almond-shaped eyes appeared set in a perpetual squint, and their black hair hung in single long braids down their backs. Two of them wore wide, shallow, cone-shaped, straw hats. The others had small close-fitting black caps perched far back on their shiny, sallow pates. Each of them was clothed in the same curious, baggy costume, a loose smock hanging down over a pair of absurdly wide pantaloons.

"Whose are they?" Dolly whispered.

"I don't know. They're using them in Auburn. They're cheap enough, only two dollars a day."

"But this is Castalia! What do we want with a pack of heathen Celestials?"

"Mama! Mama!" Beth dashed in, leaving the door flung wide. "The Chinee!" she wailed, pointing across the street.

"I see them, Bethie."

"Ella Stokes says they eat children!"

"They do?" Lucy glanced at Dolly Todd, who looked as bewildered as she. "Well, I shan't let them near you. Stay here until dinner time and walk home with me."

Lucy sat outside with Reed in the warmth of the early autumn dusk. He leaned back in his chair and stared into the darkening distance. The air still held the heat of the day. A slight haze shimmered above the hills, making

179

watery ripples on the pale purple horizon. It was that lull between the day, now gone, and the night, not yet begun, when everything seemed to hang suspended in the balance. They might as well have been becalmed, Lucy thought, floating somewhere on a glassy sea with only the faint whisper of a breeze stirring. They sat without speaking, watching the sky grow dark and the stars appear. The sound of Velvet Annie's hurdy-gurdy roused them from their silence.

"I think Bethie was quite relieved, Reed, to have you assure her that the Chinee don't feast on little girls."

"But they do drown them."

"Don't tease."

"They do. Any woman who delivers a surfeit of daughters can expect to have them consigned to the deep."

"They'd murder their own flesh and blood? How could anyone do such a thing, heathen or no?"

"Girl-children are worthless articles to them. They've no value."

"Why, not even Indians stoop to such practices! The Chinee must be the lowest form on earth."

"You'd find any number of people hereabouts who'd agree with you."

"This afternoon, I took the children for a walk to have a look at them on the digs. I confess, I felt a bit sorry for them wearing those neck yokes hung with overloaded baskets of rock. But I shan't waste a moment's pity on them anymore."

He stretched his arms wide and took in a deep breath of the night air. "These poor yellow devils here are only the flotsam and jetsam of a fairly civilized people. Don't forget the China trade."

"Reed," she asked, "have you ever seen the sea?"

"Of course."

"My Pa used to tell us tales about ships and sailors. He came from back East. He said when he was a boy there were great, brooding Atlantic storms that hovered about for days, blowing a gale."

"Where was he born?"

"I don't know. He never spoke about his folks."

"What kind of a man was your father, Lucy?"

She thought for a moment. "A dreamer. He farmed

180

dreams because that was about all the land allowed him to do."

"Caleb Bates was a little like that too, wasn't he? Filled with dreams of ranching. Odd, isn't it, that you became the sheep-farmer."

"No," she said quietly, "he knew exactly what he was doing. He had a plan, and I was part of it. I don't know whether or not he was serious about the ranch."

He glanced at her quizzically. "What a peculiar thing to say. He was so determined to go east to fetch his Merinos."

"He had money in the States, I think."

"So he said."

"I suspect it was the money calling him. He was a strange man."

"You knew him better than I."

"I never knew him. Certainly not as well as I know you."

"I suppose that's true. You were married for only a short time. We have been through a lot together, haven't we, Lucy." His hand found hers and held it.

"Reed," she said in a low voice, "anyone could come strolling by."

He acted as though he had not heard. "Do you miss him?"

"No."

"I try to remember—" He stopped and cleared his throat. ". . . to remember the sound of a woman's voice in the house. The way a woman sometimes hums to herself as she does her mending or folds the laundry—"

"Reed, don't." She rose and stood over him. His head slumped forward in his hands. "Why must our evenings always end in sadness?"

He looked up at her. Placing his palms on his knees, he rose tiredly. "You know why as well as I. Good night, dear girl. Thank you for the fine supper."

In time, the gentlewomen of Castalia thawed toward Lucy. It was not that they suffered any regrets, but rather that they suffered a need for the Castalia General Store, despite their views of its proprietress. "There's no small advantage," Lucy told Jack, "in being indispensable."

"Hey, look here." He raised his eyes from the newspaper on the counter. "Ain't this the fellow from the

Donner Party who was supposed to have turned cannibal?"

She peered over his shoulder. "Well, well." She gave a grim smile. "It looks as though that dreadful man has had a foretaste of the fires of hell. 'The Lady Adams Hotel,'" she read, "'owned and managed by Lewis and Philippine Keseberg, was also lost to the flames. The blaze spread rapidly from J to K Streets, spurred by a strong northwest wind. By morning the magnitude of its destruction was apparent . . .'"

"Be glad we ain't in Sacramento, Pastora. Me, I'm used to a roof over my head in the winter rains."

"Mother!" Abel stood in the doorway, grinning broadly.

"Shut the door, child. You're letting in the damp."

"But look, mother, outside!"

"Heavenly days—" She hurried to the door and poked her head out into the chilly street. "I scarcely believe my eyes! It's snow, Jack! Here in Castalia!"

"It don't last, Pastora. We're not high up enough."

But it snowed again and again that winter, despite all probability, despite the curses of the miners and the prayers of the preachers who were no less anxious to get back to the business of extracting gold from the scarred hills. Sometimes it sprinkled lightly down, leaving only a scattering of white to melt quickly in the noonday sun. Other times it spread over the town, heavy and silent, muffling all but the shrill squeals of the delighted children at play. In the night it swirled and eddied, its currents pale against the darkness. It buffeted about the buildings, pushed by a raw wind that banked drifts against the doors and skated across the roofs of the houses like a blade whispering on a whetstone. It lay thick on the drooping branches of the bushes and enveloped the rocks and stumps and mining furrows under an icy shroud. There was no passage into or out of the town, save by a few hardy Norwegians who braved the way from Fiddletown as a lark on long snowshoes made from green oak.

"Morning, Pastora." Will Crane was shoveling a path in front of The Miner's Friend. "Looks like God's featherbed's got a hole in it."

"Looks that way," she called back gaily. "If He

doesn't mend it soon we'll have to send those snowshoers down country for food."

But in spite of the fact that they kept a wary eye on their supplies there was not much chance of privation. The town, resigned to an enforced holiday, became as giddy and frivolous as its children. A man walked at his own peril down the streets, prey for a sudden, glancing snowball from an unseen marksman. Lucy watched from her window with considerable pleasure as one missile landed squarely on Julia Spence's ample bosom, causing her a most unladylike loss of composure. "I couldn't have aimed better myself," she murmured contentedly.

"How's that?" White Russell raised his head from the nail keg. "Drat, now I've lost track." He spread open his palm and counted his handful of nails.

"Is there any news of Joaquin?" she asked him.

"Not lately. Not even that thieving coyote can get about in these snows. You going to the snowshoe race tomorrow?"

"If the weather holds. You?"

"I'm firing off the starting shot. Sure is going to be a sight. Those Norwegians sat down and made another two pair of the clumsy things. Twelve foot long, they are, and not one of those fools in the race has ever so much as tried them on."

"It hardly sounds worth the risk. Someone's likely to break his leg."

"Oh, it'll be worth it, all right. The winner takes home six ounces. You plan to make a wager?"

"First I'll have a look at the contestants."

"I thought so. You're a tomboy, Lucy Bates, and that's a fact."

The spectators stood under the stone-colored sky, swathed against the cold, shifting impatiently from foot to foot. At the top of the hill, the half dozen contestants waited while the Norwegians attached the snowshoes to their feet. Those with the wooden slats already in place stood awkwardly immobile, bound to their boards. They were a motley group, to say the least. One of the Keskydees, his *béret* tilted jauntily down over one ear, shouted spiritedly in French to his companions below. Next to him stood two Kanakas, appearing utterly bewildered. There was a stoic Chileno, a frightened-looking Chinee

183

who worked for old Ebenezer Beal, and an Irishman, his long clay pipe clamped firmly in his teeth, who swayed slightly in the wind, having fortified himself for the ordeal at The Miner's Friend.

"Pastora?" Abner Gibbs stopped in front of her as he made his way through the crowd. "Would you care to wager a pinch?"

"On that shabby batch? You might as well throw the dust to the wind."

"Oh, Mother," Abel exclaimed, jumping up and down excitedly, "do!"

"Do," echoed Beth, "just this once, Mama."

"Which one of the daredevils will it be, Pastora?"

"Only a pinch, mind you." She scanned the six on the crest of the hill. The Irishman, being half-seas-over, might be the likeliest to survive to the bottom. But the Chinese, abject creature that he was, had the least of all to lose. So be it. "On the Chinaman."

Abner's eyebrows raised perceptibly.

"No, Mother," Abel put in, "the Frenchman!"

"You're going against the odds, Pastora," Abner whispered.

"Mama, don't do it."

"Hush, Beth. I've made up my mind."

Abner shrugged. "No use arguing with a lady, children."

The racers stood poised in a line. White raised his pistol and the crowd hushed. At the crack of the shot, the six contestants lunged forward.

The taller of the two Kanakas fell flat on his face, over his boards and lay wallowing in the snow at the top of the hill, trying to right himself. The Frenchman sailed past him, wagging his arms for balance, shouting continuously as he came, his voice rising in alarm. He narrowly missed striking the other Kanaka, who sped downhill in silent terror, his face frozen with dismay. The Chileno veered wildly from side to side, propelled by the boards under him, trying valiantly to stay upright. Suddenly he gave a great lurch and plunged sidelong into a drift, sending up a small explosion of white. Through the flurry emerged the Chinee, hunched forward as though about to pounce upon the slope, his black tail bouncing behind him as he hurtled downward. Ahead of him, the Irishman, his pipe lost to the snow, sped on, wearing the stunned expression of someone just rudely awakened. As the Chinaman came abreast of him, he let out a startled whoop, tottered for a second and tumbled backward, grasping at the air as he fell. The crowd roared with laughter.

The Keskydees at the finish line were sending up a great outcry, waving their comrade onward. Down he came, passing the stricken Kanaka who swayed dazedly and slid slowly lower and lower until, with an audible thud, he sat lodged like a stump in the snow. The Chinese pressed on without a sound. The crowd was in a frenzy of cheering. Lucy craned her neck, trying to follow his progress. The children were squealing with glee. "Come on!" she cried. "Hurry, Chinaman!" Looking neither to left nor right, he darted on. The Frenchman, casting a quick glance to his side, saw that he was about to be overtaken. He thrust his body forward, his arms wide, and like a gawky fledgling trying to take wing, he flapped once and plopped gracelessly down, his snowshoes crossed one over the other.

The Chinee crossed the finish line alone, smiling at the hurrahs of the onlookers. Ebenezer Beal gave him a hearty whack on the shoulders, which almost sent him flying farther into the crowd. He stood nodding and grinning as his snowshoes were unfastened. Then seizing his bag of gold from Abner Gibbs, he scurried off through the throng like a pleased pack rat.

Lucy brushed a dusting of cornmeal from the counter and handed Will Crane his change. "Sorry about the pickles, Will. I'll have French Jack try to locate some in Sacramento."

"Never mind, Pastora. Now that the weather's cleared, Charlie'll be leaving for there tomorrow. He can pick them up."

"I guess we're all a bit relieved to have the snows finally disappear. Afternoon, Eben," she said, smiling at Ebenezer Beal as he entered the store. "What brings you in? I haven't seen you since your Chinaman won the big race."

He gave an angry grunt. "And I haven't laid eyes on the yellow scum since. Last seen, he was gambling his way from one end of town to the other. Got his hands on a bag of dust and never did another day's work."

"Abner Gibbs told me," Will said, "that the fool keeps

trying to get into the Hall of Fortune to play. Abner chucks him out near every night."

"The devil take him. Pastora, you're looking uncommonly well. The cold put roses in your cheeks, did it?"

Will laughed and cuffed him amiably on the shoulder. "Don't waste your breath, Eben. The lady's deaf to flattery. Nigh onto every bachelor in town has tried to charm the Pastora."

"And they have all succeeded," Lucy put in, smiling. "I find each and every one of them delightful."

"Then how come you ain't married?" Eben challenged. "It ain't natural for a pretty young woman like you not to have a husband."

"I'm afraid the poor fellow would have a bad time of it. I've two children to raise, a house to keep and the store to manage. A man would be hard put to compete with all that. And besides," she added, flashing a grin at Eben, "how on earth could I choose among all you fine handsome fellows?"

Eben reddened perceptibly. Will, laughing, collected his purchases. He gave a nod to White Russell as he passed him in the doorway. White closed the door behind him and removed his hat. "Been looking for you, Eben."

"What for, Sheriff?"

"Your Chinee, the snowshoer. He's dead. Found him this morning between two shacks on La Colina Street. His head's bashed in."

Eben scowled. "What's that to do with me?"

"Thought you'd want to know. And I need a hand to bury him. That's hard ground after a cold spell like we've had."

"Ain't no way I'd raise a finger for that ungrateful heathen, not even as a favor to you, Sheriff. Maybe one of them other Chinamen will help."

"Have you any idea who did it?" Lucy asked.

White shrugged. "La Colina's mostly Chilenos. Likely he got into a fight over a dishonest game. He was plucked clean when he was found."

"Wait a bit, would you, White?" she said. "Just let me tend to Eben here. I'd like a word with you."

When Eben Beal had gone on his way, she asked White, "Do you think you'll be able to find the person who killed that Chinee?"

"Not a chance. Not even if there were witnesses. Ain't nobody's going to snitch on anyone just for doing in some crazy Chinaman."

Lucy reached under the counter and withdrew a small, round, wooden box. On the top was printed "Bateman's Vegetable Pills." She handed it to White.

"What's this for?"

"It's my winnings from the snowshoe race. I put them in there. I wasn't quite sure what to do with them, seeing as they weren't rightly earned. They'll pay for someone to help you dig the grave."

"The Chinaman's no concern of yours, Lucy." He laid the box on the counter.

"I doubt you'll find anyone around here who'll offer so much a dime on his behalf. Take it."

White gazed at her in silence and pocketed the box. He turned to go, then hesitated and turned back. "I heard something this morning that you should know about. Could be just a rumor, nothing more. You know how many cock-and-bull stories fly around this town."

"What is it?"

"Like I said, it's probably nonsense, but if there's any truth to it, you ought to be told."

"Out with it, White."

He rubbed his fingers uneasily over the furrows of his forehead. "It's about Abel."

187

X

LUCY SLAMMED the cabin door with such force that Beth dropped her rag doll and stood still as a startled fawn, staring at her.

"Where is your brother?" Lucy demanded.

"Sweeping out Aunt Celia's place."

"And do you know where he was last evening, while I was dining at your Aunt Celia's with Doctor Pierce?"

"He said him and George Booth were going to catch themselves a Chinaman and cut off his tail."

"Indeed. Well, we'll see what he has to say for himself when he comes home." She knelt beside Abel's bed and peered under it.

"What are you doing, Mama?"

"Never mind." She rooted in the darkness underneath, where he so methodically stored his belongings. Out came his shirts and trousers, a carefully looped fishing line, his primer, Luther Moore's knife, a small basket holding several acorns, each painted with a droll little face, and several painstakingly drawn sketches of a long tom. "Hand me the lamp, Beth." She reached up and took it from the child, setting it beside her on the floor. Far under Abel's cot, lying flat against the wall, she could see a narrow roll of canvas. Lucy rose and lifted the bottom of the bed from the wall. She picked up the rolled cloth, astounded to find it so heavy. Behind her, the cabin door opened. She turned and faced Abel. "How much does this weigh?"

He looked at her in silence.

"Close that door and sit down."

He did as he was told. Lucy laid the bundle on the table in front of him. "Answer my question."

188

" 'Bout seven pound."

She glanced at him, stunned, as she unrolled the canvas. At seven pounds, there was nearly two thousand dollars in gold inside. "And where," she said evenly, "did you come by this fortune?"

He shifted uncomfortably in his chair. Beth looked from one to the other of them, unsure of what was happening. Abel gazed down at the tabletop. "Sweeping," he mumbled.

"What?" Her voice rose with anger.

"Sweeping. You know, the store and Aunt Celia's. There's dust in the leavings, and if you just wash it out—"

"In the floor sweepings?"

He nodded. "When the people pay, sometimes some falls on the floor."

"Look at me," she demanded. "What kind of takings? In a week, how much?"

"Maybe twenty dollars." He glanced away again.

"And you never told me." Rapidly, she multiplied the sum in her head. "All right. That would account for some three hundred dollars, more or less. Go on."

He shrugged sheepishly.

"Boy, if you don't come out with the truth, I swear I'll take a strap to you!"

"Mama!" cried Beth.

"You hold your tongue! Abel?" She seized him under the chin and forcibly turned him to her. "Now!"

He was shaking. "Abner Gibbs said I could," he told her tremulously.

"You could *what?*"

"Play. I know how. George Booth and I practice with his cards."

"Then it's true. You, a nine-year-old boy, gaming with the men in that sinkhole of vice."

"Mama," he whined, "you went there! And I saw you make a wager on the snowshoe race!"

Her words came sharp and rapid as blows across his face. "I am an adult! You are not. I went to no gaming hall but to a wedding. And as for the wager on the race, I see clearly now that it was a grave error!" She caught her breath. "Good Lord in heaven," she exclaimed, "what's to become of you?"

He looked down at the table.

189

"Let's go," she said wearily. She stood and took him by the shoulder. "Beth, you wait here for us."

Nelly Gibbs opened the door, her jaw dropping visibly at the sight of Lucy's face.

"I was told I could find Abner at home. Let me in, please."

Nelly stood aside, too surprised to speak. Lucy pushed Abel ahead of her and entered. Finally, Nell found her voice. "He's at supper. In here." She led the way.

Startled, Abner rose from his plate of stew and wiped his mouth on his shirtsleeve. He frowned and cleared his throat.

"Before you say one word, Abner Gibbs, I want to know why you lured this child into a gaming hall."

"Ah, now, Pastora—"

"You've attempted to corrupt my child. You have betrayed my friendship. Why?"

"Now, now," he said easily, "where's the harm . . ."

Lucy stiffened with rage. "You despicable little man, how dare you—"

"Pastora," he continued, unruffled, as though he had not heard, "sooner or later young men gamble. And those who know the game are better prepared than those who don't. Besides, didn't he come away a winner?"

"That is not the point!" she shouted. Out of the corner of her eye, she saw Abel cringe at the sound of her voice. "You have repaid my kindness with treachery. And you have led astray a child of nine. What kind of a creature are you?"

"Pastora," Nelly interrupted, taking a stand next to Abner, "if you please, ma'am—"

"I do not please," Lucy retorted harshly. "My business is with your husband, madam."

Nelly's eyes were blazing. "You got no right," she snapped, "coming into my home screeching like a crow."

"The devil I don't. And when I'm in need of a lesson in etiquette, thank you, I'll find me a tutor a lot better qualified than yourself!"

Abner took a step forward. "Lady, you thank your lucky stars you're not a man, because if you was—"

"If I was," she shot back, "you'd be needing a doctor by now."

Abner attempted a conciliatory smile. "Ah, now, let's suppose I thought the boy had your permission to play."

190

"Abel? Did you tell him that?"

The boy shook his head.

"You have no excuse, Abner. None. And after I went out of my way to make a display of Christian charity toward you and this woman——"

"You sermonizing, self-righteous slut," Nelly spat. "You ate your belly full with the rest of them, and now you talk like you made some big sacrifice enjoying our hospitality! You ain't no better than any of us, storekeeper. And anyone who ain't blind can see the shameless way you feast your eyes on that Doctor Pierce, and him with a wife lying helpless at home."

Lucy recoiled as though she had been struck. She glanced swiftly at Abel. He looked bewildered and frightened, and suddenly very small. "Come." She held out her hand to him, "We're through with these people." She made her way to the door with Abel. She paused only once. "Under no circumstances are either of you to approach me or my children as long as you live."

Abel was silent as they walked back to the house. At last, he asked, "Mother, is it still my gold?"

She stopped and shook him by the shoulders, hard. "Is that all you can think about," she cried, "greed?"

He began to sob.

"There now. Calm down. You'll make yourself sick, weeping like that." She knelt down beside him. "I will take the gold to the Wells Fargo office. It will be safe there. You must grow a little older before you can handle such a large sum. Every bit of dust you raise from your sweepings is to be washed out and returned to the store or Aunt Celia. It wasn't altogether right for you to keep it in the first place. And, Abel, for the next two weeks, you are to come to me after your lessons. You are forbidden to play with the others."

"Yes, ma'am."

"That's better. I'll be having a talk with Rebecca Booth about George's playing cards. I don't want ever again to hear that my son has been gambling. Is that clear?"

He nodded, wiping his tear-stained face.

"I begin to think," she said, more to herself than the boy, "that we'd be well-advised to leave this place."

But as it had before, the idea receded in her thoughts, borne further and further away by the coming of spring and the warm summer months. Sometimes, watching

191

Reed Pierce's face, Lucy would see clearly the etching of despair there, and abruptly the idea of leaving would bob to the surface of her mind. But she found it almost impossible to reconcile such a notion with the surge of tenderness and longing that accompanied such moments. Once again, she would allow it to drift off.

In the street outside the store, Lucy and French Jack stood in the scorching noonday sun, overseeing the perspiring teamsters as they unloaded a shipment of merchandise. Jack shook his head and said something which she didn't catch. "What?" she shouted. "I can't hear you. The confounded hydraulickers are making too much noise."

He made a grimace and nodded in agreement.

"Finally," she breathed when the commotion subsided, "blessed quiet. They've knocked off work for dinner. Well, that's the last of the goods. We can unpack them this afternoon." She placed the "Closed" sign in the window.

Lucy and Jack walked back toward the cabins. Only the buzzing black flies seemed indifferent to the oppressive heat. "Look there," Jack said sadly, pointing toward the bluff.

On the far side of the bank, the hydraulickers had done their work. Their canvas hose snaked out along the bluff, its length stretched across a series of wooden braces, then descended toward the streambed where its long iron nozzle lay braced against a foundation of piled rocks, like a mighty cannon aimed at the hillside. The force of the water was appalling in its destruction. It had eaten deep into the high ground, undercutting the grassy crest and sending it sliding down in a cataract of tons of earth and stone and toppled trees. Where once willows and wild grapes had scaled a green and flourishing bank, only a gaping crater remained, its bedrock walls yawning dark above the rubble below.

French Jack shook his head in awe. "They destroy our world. The fields, the hills, the river . . . Hell, they destroy the town if they think they find pay dirt under it."

"Before another summer comes there'll be nothing left of the land the way it was. Do you remember how I used to think these hills looked like loaves of fresh brown bread? They devour the earth with those machines.

When they've gorged themselves and plundered us clean, they'll move on to attack some other lovely place."

"It ain't never going to be the same, Pastora. I been thinking." He paused and walked a few steps in silence. "Maybe I move on sometime. You could buy my share of the store if you like, no?"

She halted. "Jack? Where would you go?"

"He shrugged. "Who knows, maybe San Francisco for a while. They make a big city down there, maybe they need good carpenters to show them Chinese workers how to do."

"You're not serious, are you?" she challenged him. "Come now, Jack, confess. I'll wager you only want a peep at Lola Montez."

"Not me," he said, grinning. "I don't pay a hundred dollars to see any woman dance with a spider. No," he said soberly, "I been meaning to talk to you. Ain't no more Castalia. They tear it down all around. I like better to be someplace where men build things."

"I see," she said, and they walked on. "When would you go? Autumn will be here soon. I hear it's difficult to find lodgings then, with the number of men who leave the digs in the rainy season."

"You don't worry, Pastora. I take my time, make it easy for you. Come spring, perhaps I go."

"Jack," she said quietly, "I've been thinking about it, too. Not a word of this to anyone, mind you." Lucy glanced quickly toward him, and he gave her a nod. "What if we were to open a store in San Francisco? We know how to manage it by now, and a thriving city always has room for another merchant."

"Now I think it's you who's not serious."

"I'd have a proper school for the children. This town's no place for them, especially not for Abel. But I don't want the whole world to know what you and I are thinking, not until we're both sure."

Like the pendulum of a clock, Lucy's intentions continued to sway between leaving and staying. Castalia was still her only real home, though it seemed the very ground under her feet might be blasted away at any moment by the explosive force of the hydraulic machines. Gabriel Cousins's spotted dog had carelessly dashed into the path of one of the monitors and been killed instantly by the mightly arc of water, though nearly two hundred feet from its source. The heartbroken Negro had packed his belongings and left town that same evening. Lucy saw him depart, a small, bent, black figure trudging disconsolately away down the street, his old mule at his side.

But it seemed that for every one who left, another came to take his place. At the end of Spring Street, there was a hotel going up. It was a towering three-story structure, its wide doors opening onto a stone-paved colonnade where guests might sit and while away their leisure. Overhead were two tiers of rooms, with bay windows opening onto a veranda supported by slim white wooden columns and fronted with a lacy balustrade. It was a grand edifice, little less than palatial in Lucy's eyes, and she wondered just what sort of gentry might occupy the Saint George Hotel.

"Never you fear," White Russell told her. "If James Birch brings his stage line in here like they say he will, there'll be no lack of folks passing in and out."

"Mama?" Abel rested on his broom-handle. "Does that mean we could take a trip on the stagecoach? Could we go to San Francisco?"

"Whatever put that thought into your mind?"

"Because I could see Joaquin's head. Look." He withdrew a frayed scrap of newspaper from his pocket and unfolded it for them to see.

"Joaquin's head," it read, "is to be seen at King's corner of Halleck and Sansome Streets. Admission one dollar."

White laughed. "One dollar. The bandit's dead and he's still stealing money."

"I assure you," Lucy told the boy, "that if we ever go to San Francisco, it won't be to gape at a dead man's head." She handed the paper back to him.

"I heard you and French Jack talking about San Francisco," he persisted. "Couldn't we go, just to see what it's like? I've never seen the ocean."

"Neither have I, and I'm none the worse for the omission. Get on with your work."

That night, as they were closing the store, she told Jack about Abel's eagerness to see the city. ". . . So it seems at least one of us is ready to go."

"Two. Me, I made up my mind. After the rains, I go."

"Oh, Jack." She sighed. "I don't know which way to turn. I'd stay here forever if I thought there'd be anything left of the place. It was the prettiest spread of land I ever saw."

"Ain't nothing left, if you ask me. Only one thing keeps you here, Pastora."

She wiped off the counter in silence.

"You stay because someday that woman has to give up the ghost, and that's the truth."

The color drained from her face. Quickly, she sat down and rested her head in her hands. When she finally spoke, her voice was low. "You make me sound like some sort of leech wanting to suck the life out of her."

He put an arm around her shoulders to comfort her. "No. But all the same, it ain't no way to live. It's no good you should ache for a life you can't have. Maybe better to go someplace and forget. Why do you think I go to Saint Joseph and join the wagon train?"

"I didn't know." She looked up at him, surprised. "And have you forgotten the lady?"

He gave her a rueful smile. "No. But it don't hurt so bad no more. You find a new place, new people, and one day you wake up and you discover you still got the memories, but you ain't got the pain."

"All the more reason to leave," she said without conviction.

"I don't try to make you go, Lucy. But I don't want to see you so sad, neither."

"I know, Jack." She clasped his hand. "You're a good friend."

The first fall rains began on a Thursday and continued for five straight days. There followed a brief respite, a weak, waxy sun shining coolly down on the glistening black mounds of mud. It proved only a false promise. Within another day came an even heavier storm, reducing the already wasted land to a continuous avalanche of ooze. Work in the digs came to a halt. There was little else for a man to do but pass his time at gaming or drinking. Lucy wondered which depressed her more, the constant cold and wet or the inescapable presence of a town full of restive idlers groggy with spirits. There was bound to be trouble if the rains continued, and the gray clouds hovered low overhead, unbroken by so much as a glimpse of blue.

Lucy drew another chair up to the hearth. "Sit here,

Celia," she said quietly so as not to wake the children. "What on earth inspires you to brave the downpour at this hour?"

Celia settled herself close by the fire and clasped her hands in her lap. She made a slight movement in her chair, which might have been a suppressed shiver but appeared to Lucy more like the jouncing of an impatient child. She gave a smile and whispered, "News."

"Good news, I hope."

She nodded, her smile still in place.

"Well?"

"There's going to be a wedding."

"Oh," said Lucy. "I think I've had my fill of that sort of thing."

"It's not that sort of thing! It's mine!"

She stared at her. "Celia?"

"Yes." Her head bobbed up and down eagerly. "I came straight away to tell you. Ebenezer Beal has asked for my hand."

"Eben? My land. I'm at a loss for words." She grinned dazedly. "I had no idea this was going on."

Celia pursed her lips. "He is a wee bit younger than I am. But," she hastened to say, "ever so staunch in character and very prosperous. He said to me, 'A good woman is rarer than a buffalo in these parts, and I don't aim to let one get away.'"

Lucy leaned over and kissed her cheek. "I'm delighted for you. I wish you both great happiness."

Celia drew herself upright in her chair, stretching like a proud, sleek tabby. "We'll be married on New Year's Day. I need time first to do some sewing. My, it's been so long since I had me a fancy dress."

"I promise you the best stuff Jack and I can ferret out. We'll send to San Francisco if we have to. You're a lucky woman, Celia. There's plenty of men who'd come courting just for the gold you've panned in your eating hall. Eben's not that sort, thank heavens." She started at a rap on the door. "I declare," she said, rising, "tonight seems full of surprises."

White Russell stood in the doorway, rivulets of rain cascading from the brim of his hat. She hastily beckoned him inside. Beth stirred in her bed. Abel raised himself on his elbows and glanced sleepily around the room. "Lie down, dear. It's just Sheriff Russell stopping by."

196

The boy rolled over on his side and burrowed into his pillow. White motioned the two women to the far end of the room.

"It's the Indian girl, Mary," he said.

"My Mary?" Celia asked. "My hired girl from the Castalia House?"

"I've locked her up in the jail."

Celia's hand went to her heart. "Whatever for? She's perfectly well behaved and meek as a mouse."

"Celia," White said grimly, "your mouse just stabbed a man to death."

Celia faltered. Lucy reached out a hand to steady her. "What happened?" she asked him.

"One of the boys was having some fun with her. There was two of them, actually. The other one was busy trying to get rid of the girl's mother, and the old squaw was putting up a fuss, so he didn't see it happen. Just saw his friend grab his belly and fall. The girl had a knife."

"What kind of fun, exactly, were they having?" Lucy demanded.

"The fellow, Josh Peck his name is, he says she and the woman were walking down beyond the hotel with a basket of roots and such. These boys came by and walked alongside them, and the girl started like to flirting with them—"

"Never," Celia countered. "Not Mary."

White picked up Celia's shawl from the table. "I come to take you to her. She won't say nothing to me."

"White," Lucy said as she opened the door for them, "you can't keep a girl in that jail."

He gave her a dour look. "You want me to let her loose in a town full of restless drunkards? Hell, I'm doing her a favor."

The trial of Indian Mary assumed all the aspects of a welcome diversion from the gloom of those raw, damp days. It was conducted in the only building large enough to hold the crowds, the Hall of Fortune. The ladies of Castalia, Lucy included, kept their distance from the proceedings. Celia was the sole exception.

"Lucy," Celia told her after she had given her testimony, "I don't think I've felt quite so helpless since my Jeremiah died in my arms."

197

"You did your best. Reed says you painted a strong picture of the girl's good character."

"For nothing. I can't help her."

"But you already have."

"No," she said, "no one can. I know, sure as I'm standing here, that Mary told me the truth. She was only defending herself. Poor child, she sits there unable to say a single word."

"That's the law, Celia," Lucy said bitterly. "Indians and half-breeds can't testify in trials involving whites."

"But it's she who's involved," Celia protested. "Even if it was a white man who died."

"Don't you understand?" she flared. "When it comes to Indians, they interpret the law as they please."

Celia glanced at her and started to say something, but she just shook her head, silently.

The only other witness was the dead man's companion, Joshua Peck. The hearing concluded at noon, in time for the spectators to place their wagers as to how long the jury would take to deliver its decision before they hurried home for dinner.

Celia had closed the eating hall for the day. "It wouldn't seem right to carry on like nothing was wrong." Now, as she waited for the verdict, she sat with Lucy and the children at their table, stirring her tea over and over with one hand while the other fidgeted with her shawl.

Beth frowned gravely. "How do you know Mary isn't telling a fib?"

"Beth," Lucy answered, "Aunt Celia knows the girl well. I'm sure her judgment is sound."

Abel folded his arms across his chest. "Mrs. Spence says they haven't God, so they have no conscience, either."

The two women glanced at each other.

"Abel," Lucy said evenly, "Julia Spence's opinion is of little importance right now."

"But she's our teacher!" Beth objected.

"And," the boy continued, "she told us they have to be taught the difference between right and wrong, even if it's a harsh lesson."

"Child!" Celia cried, her fingers trembling on her shawl. "Oh, child," she said again, "Mary's only fourteen. Not even a woman yet, just a young girl."

Abel shook his head. "I heard what Mr. Webster said

198

to French Jack down at the store. He said she ain't nothing but an animal, and an animal's got no morals."

Lucy felt a sudden wave of nausea. She gripped the table's edge to keep her hands from shaking. "We are not the jury," she said, her throat dry. "It is not for us to make judgments."

It took less than an hour to reach a verdict. White Russell, his face grim, came by the store in the afternoon to tell Celia and Lucy.

"Celia, don't weep." Lucy gave her a new handkerchief from the shelf. "White won't let them do it."

He shook his head, his lips pressed tightly together.

"But surely there must be some way to prevent it! She's only a girl!"

"No."

"In the name of God, White, how will you live with your conscience?"

"I don't make the laws, Lucy. I got to abide by them like everyone else. Nobody ever said it was easy. I'll be getting along now."

She put an arm around Celia's shoulders. "Why don't you bring Eben by for supper tonight? There's comfort in company at times like this."

"Afternoon, Pastora." Sam Stokes held the door open wide as White passed him. "Looks like the sun's going to break through."

"So it does, Sam. Celia, do go find Eben and tell him he's invited, won't you?"

Sam watched the tearful woman leave without comment. He closed the door berind her and walked to the counter. "Sundown," he said.

"I know."

The pale winter sun cast long shadows across the muddied street as she closed the store and made her way home. The unaccustomed brilliance seemed harsh against her eyes. She was relieved to reach the dimly lighted cabin. Beth sat on her bed, her primer on her lap, painstakingly copying a page of printing.

"You'll lose your sight, working in such darkness. Where's Abel?"

"With George Booth."

"Well, he's got no business letting the fire go down like this." Lucy stirred the embers and laid on more logs. "He

199

should be here. It'll be suppertime soon, and we've company coming."

Beth slid off the bed. "I'll help," she said. "How many plates?"

"Two extra, for Aunt Celia and Mr. Beal. Where did those boys go?"

Beth stood on tiptoe, taking the plates from the shelf. "To the hanging. They said I wasn't—"

"Stay!" Lucy cried. "Stay here! Mind the fire!"

She ran as fast as her legs would take her, her skirts caught up on her hands. She darted through the wet streets, dashing around the glassy puddles of water, splattering mud to every side. Gasping for breath, she climbed the slippery slope below the cemetery and saw illuminated beyond the fenced knoll the glistening, moist trunk of a tree, its branches still dripping, its largest limb furnished with a noosed rope. She strained for a glimpse of the boy in the throng around the wagon where the blindfolded girl stood. She pushed through the edge of the crowd, averting her eyes from the overhanging branch.

"Come." Lucy seized his arm with such a wrench that he started and slipped on the wet ground. She yanked him up so violently that he cried out. Without a word, she shoved her way past the waiting mob, the boy struggling to keep pace with her. She held his wrist tightly, dragging him past the pale gravestones glowing in the last rays of the dazzling, disdainful sun. She heard the crack of the whip and the creak of the wheels as the wagon lurched forward. The crowd roared. She released the child. "Run," she screamed, her voice thick with tears, "run away from here!" She followed after the scampering boy, crying aloud as she went, "We must leave this place!"

"They hang criminals in San Francisco, too, Pastora," French Jack warned her.

"You know that isn't it."

"Charlie Woods, he come up with a good offer for the store. Will Crane's going to buy him out of The Miner's Friend. Charlie says he don't want to keep those hours no more. Says he's getting too old to deal with rowdies."

"So all that remains is to make the arrangements and wait until after the rains. And one other thing," she said quietly. "For me to tell Reed . . ."

The wedding of Celia Whiton to Eben Beal took place

in the parlor of the newly opened Saint George Hotel. The long, spacious room still held the scent of new wood and fresh paint. As the preacher read the service, Lucy could not keep her eyes from straying from the bride and groom to the sumptuous surroundings. In all her life, she had never seen so grand a room. Her whole house could have fitted inside it. Every one of the four walls was hung with paper, a leafy scrollwork of wine-colored vines against a gray field. At the far end, a single tall Argand lamp on a brass column stood on a polished drop-leaf table with carved, clawed legs. The light gleamed through bunches of grapes cut in its glass shade, so strong that the candles on either side of the fireplace across the way seemed wan by comparison. She glanced into the gilded pier-glass above the ornate, high-backed sofa. In it, she saw the preacher's face as he spoke to Eben and Celia. In back of him the pale candles flickered under the watchful eye of the mahogany eagle perched atop the mantel clock. The preacher raised his eyes from his book. The Beals turned from the fireplace, both beaming.

Lucy arranged herself on the damask seat of one of the pair of side chairs that flanked the doorway. She searched out the children among the thirty or so guests buzzing about the room. Abel was seated with George Booth at Sam Stokes's feet, listening quietly as Sam played "Amazing Grace" for them on his mouth-organ. Beth sat on the sofa next to him, less engrossed in the music than in running her small hands over and over the rich maroon plush of the cushion underneath her.

"You're smiling." Reed stood above her chair.

She laughed, a trifle embarrassed. "I was thinking. I was seeing Bethie stroke that fine upholstery stuff and hoping someday she'd have a house of her own filled with such grand trappings. Am I a fool?"

He smiled but didn't answer. "May I fetch you anything from the table?"

She shook her head. "How do you suppose Eben ever persuaded Celia to allow spirits at the party?"

"*Omnia vincit amor*, and praises be." He lifted his cup and saluted her. "You're looking very lovely this evening, Lucy."

She lowered her eyes from his face. "Reed—"

"Don't tell me you're blushing!"

201

"No," she said hastily, "it's something else." She stared down at her hands in her lap. "It's time I told you. I'm going away from here."

"When?" he asked, his voice suddenly flat.

"As soon as the rains stop."

"May I ask where?"

"To San Francisco." She looked at him. "I want the children away from this place, Abel especially."

French Jack joined them and Reed moved aside. "I believe my throat's dry. I'll be back as soon as I refill my cup." He turned and made his way through the press of people surrounding the bride and groom.

"Come," Lucy said to Jack, "I must offer my congratulations."

She pressed her cheek to Celia's. "I don't know which shines brighter, that rosy silk dress or the smile on your face."

"When she smiles," Eben boasted, "she's all of eighteen years old."

"Oh, now," Celia chided him, obviously relishing his every word, "what girl of eighteen would have the good sense to find a man like yourself?"

"I declare, Jack," Lucy said as they moved away, "I believe that woman's discovered the fountain of youth." She looked around for Reed, but he was nowhere to be seen. She paused to greet Dolly Todd, casting an occasional glance past her toward the doorway, but he did not reappear. After a while, she began to think he might have left, though it would be quite unlike Reed to go without saying anything.

Lucy saw his reflection in the glass above the sofa. He stood uncertainly scanning the room, looking slightly bemused. She wondered how long he had lingered at the punch bowl.

"There you are," he hailed Lucy and Jack. "Getting a bit close in here, isn't it?" He lifted his cup and took a long swallow. "Well, Jack, I expect you'll be finding yourself another partner."

French Jack raised his eyebrows quizzically.

"The lady tells me she's leaving us. Seen the elephant, so to speak, and now she's moving on."

She found his banter unconvincing. "No, Reed," she replied quietly, "you didn't let me finish. Jack and I are going to try our luck at a store in San Francisco."

He glanced at Jack. "Both of you together."

Jack shrugged. "We do good in Castalia, so why not there?"

"Why not indeed," he answered smoothly. "I had no idea you'd been laying such plans."

"It's for the children," she repeated.

"It is? And you, Jack? I suppose you're going for the children's sake."

"There's no call for sarcasm, Reed," Lucy told him.

"Time to move on," said Jack, "that's all."

"Is it?" He turned away from Jack. "You know, Lucy, Red Russell passed on an interesting piece of intelli-gent—" He corrected himself, "—intelligence to me. Seems there was a Canadian named Louet, just like our friend, here, a trapper, though—"

She interrupted him, "You're being quite rude to Jack, Reed."

"Hear me out. This fellow quarreled with his partner all the time. And wouldn't you know, one year Louet ap-peared at the *rendezvous* without him. A bad business, having a partner disappear like that. This Louet couldn't find anyone who'd join up with him afterwards. Had to quit trapping. Probably found himself another trade."

"Reed!" she cried sharply and glanced around them, embarrassed.

He gave an oddly sheepish grin and patted Jack on the shoulder. "No offense, *mon ami*."

Jack nodded. "Maybe better you lay down your cup, Reed."

"I think I'll take the children home now," Lucy said.

"No." Reed caught her arm. "They know the way. I'll take you. I believe I could use a breath of fresh air."

They walked the length of Spring Street in silence. The night was damp and cloudy. Lucy pulled her shawl close around her. "You behaved wretchedly toward Jack. What possessed you to tell that unpleasant story?"

He walked on without answering.

"Are you drunk?"

"A little."

"I suppose that's some sort of excuse."

"You're right," he said brusquely. "I'll offer my apolo-gies tomorrow."

She steadied him as he stumbled into a muddy rut and righted himself. "Reed, let's not walk here where people might see their doctor in his cups." She led him through a narrow alleyway between two buildings. "We can go around the back way, along the foot of the hill."

It was quiet behind the town. Their way was lit only by the occasional fleeting appearance of the moon from behind the swiftly scudding clouds and here and there a ray of lamplight from a rear window.

"Stop," he said.

She turned in alarm. "Are you all right?"

He placed his hands on her shoulders. "Don't go," he said. His eyes sought out her face in the darkness.

"I must."

"No." He clasped his hands behind her neck. "Look at me," he told her, tilting her face to his.

"Please—"

His fingers slid into her hair, and his mouth covered hers. He was holding her so tightly to him that she could not move. She twisted away, but he brought himself up against her and, sliding one arm to the small of her back, held her pressed close. The scent of him filled her nostrils. She felt flushed and light-headed, as though his body were some kind of overpowering influence. She felt herself yielding to his embrace. He murmured against her lips, words she couldn't hear. She answered him with her mouth, warm and pliant. He moaned and shuddered against her and pulled his face aside, burying it in her hair. "Oh, God," he whispered, "if only I were free to go with you."

She was afraid that if he took his arms from her she would collapse. "Hold me," she begged.

"May God forgive me for my thoughts."

"Reed." She rested her head against his chest and felt his heart pounding under her. "Now you see why I must leave." She felt his breath rise and fall rapidly until it slowed finally and he composed himself. "Never," she said softly, "did I know what it was to want a man. Not until I knew I loved you."

"Don't leave, Lucy. I promise you this won't ever happen again."

"But don't you see? It would happen. Because now I would want it to."

"I was an idiot. I was jealous of Jack."

"I know. There are many reasons why I'm going, but he's not one of them. Walk me home, Reed."

When they reached the door of the cabin, Reed said, "Promise you'll reconsider."

"I would be lying to you."

"It's my fault. I've driven you away."

"I am removing us both from temptation. I suppose I should be thankful that Jack has given me the opportunity." She tried to smile.

Reed took both her hands in his. "How sad you look. Is that what I've done to you?"

"You know better than to think that." She shivered suddenly in the chilly air.

He embraced her and just as quickly released her. "God in heaven." He shook his head. "I can't imagine being here without you."

"I'm not leaving yet. And who knows, perhaps sometime you'll come to San Francisco."

He drew her hand to his lips and kissed it. They looked at each other in silence. At last she turned and slipped into the house.

He did not ask her again to stay. As if by mutual arrangement, they kept their distance from each other. In truth, it was a kindness, given freely but not without sacrifice. Sometimes, seeing him across a street, she yearned to run to his arms, to pour out her doubts and fears about the journey. Strange, how she had felt no such qualms about setting off beyond the Line with Caleb Bates. But Castalia was her home. And Reed's. When by chance they met, she would see in his face the same sorrow she felt inside herself, a pain that lay beneath the surface like the ache of a deep, irreparable wound.

The store itself, Lucy reckoned, was Jack's to sell, since he had built it. That meant that by the time Charlie Woods had paid them for the building and its inventory, they each had somewhat over eighteen thousand dollars, thanks partly to her sheep and Jack's cradles. It sounded like a great deal of money, but they had been warned that San Francisco was an expensive city and to rent a place of business might easily cost them two thousand dollars a month. Despite the price, there seemed little risk, since it was a beehive of commerce and neither she nor Jack harbored a taste for extravagance. The final arrangements were made for Wells Fargo to transfer their funds to the new office at California and Montgomery

Streets. "Imagine," she said to Jack, "that bank is four stories high and the land alone is worth a hundred thousand. I'm almost afraid to do business with such a grand place."

He smiled at her. "You're no more a country girl, Pastora. You get used to the city quick, you'll see."

"I wish I could be so sure."

"You wait. We give ourselves six months, no? By then I bet we make one fine profit."

Six months, that would be October. She brushed away the last crumbs from the supper table and glanced around the cabin. It seemed suddenly too small for herself and the two children. And truth to tell, it wasn't much of a house, compared to the newer buildings. She'd been lucky to find a buyer who'd pay a decent price, an unmarried fellow from Kentucky who said it reminded him of home. She turned the log in the fireplace and banked the embers back from the hearth, remembering how she had laboriously carried each of these hearth stones up from the river so long ago.

"Mama?" Abel asked. "Why do we have to leave?"

"Must we go through this again? I told you. They've proper schools in San Francisco, and Jack and I are tired of paying so much to transport our merchandise overland. We can buy goods more cheaply there, and because it's a bigger place we'll have greater opportunities. There now. Are you satisfied?"

"But Mama," Beth said, "we won't know anyone. We won't have any friends."

"It's an adventure, Bethie. A chance to go to a fine new place and make a lot of new friends." She wondered if she sounded as unsure as she felt.

"But I like it here," Beth pouted. "Why do we have to go?"

"Because I said so!" she retorted. But it was not the children who upset her, she knew. "Make yourselves ready for bed," she said gently. "I'm going for a little walk. I'll be back in time to hear your prayers."

The moon was nearly full. Lucy walked down Main Street, her eyes scanning the land beyond the ranks of buildings there. Above the high wooden facades, above the lines of fire-buckets on the roofs, the silent hills lay dark against the horizon. At night like this, it was almost possible to see them as they once had been, before hordes

206

of men had swarmed over them, gouging out their secrets. Another April, unlike this one, they would have been covered with wildflowers scenting the evening air. But nothing grew there now. Thousands of pairs of feet had trodden down those slopes, and every kind of device known to man had been used to tear away the earth. She paused at the corner of Plymouth Street and looked up to where Luther Moore's cabin had stood. No trace of it remained. The place had long since been dismantled and its lumber sawed into planks for sluice boxes.

She walked up the steep street with its jagged outline of houses rising like a staircase on either side. She stopped to catch her breath outside the Wells Fargo office. The heavy iron shutters were closed tight. She wondered if her money was still in the big steel safe inside. Probably not. That part of her was gone from here already, along with the rest of her past, into Caleb Byles and the baby, Susannah, the lambs that had gamboled on rickety legs in the green fields and now, the store. All that was left to hold her here was Reed Pierce. But it was he, more than this place, that she must leave. She turned and quickly made her way along Spring Street. The light from the windows of the Saint George Hotel cast bright patches across the ground before it. A trio of guests sat under the colonnade, taking the night air. She nodded as they raised their hats to her. Strangers all, not a familiar face among the shadows. From somewhere, most likely The Miner's Friend, came the sound of men singing. It was a song she didn't know, and she couldn't make out the words. From the darkness of a small alley echoed a woman's laugh. As she passed, a couple ducked furtively deeper into the narrow recess. She walked faster. There were the children to be put to bed and some few last items to be packed for the journey. Perhaps there had been some truth in what Reed said. She had seen the elephant, and it was time to move on.

"It was good of you to come, Celia." Lucy clasped the woman's hands in hers.

"Oh, dear." Celia shook her head in chagrin. "I promised myself I wouldn't cry. White Russell said to tell you he would have been here to see you off if it weren't that he had to go to Volcano for the day."

"I understand." Her eyes swept the busy street, but

207

Reed was nowhere to be seen. "Children, stop fidgeting so. The stage will come when it comes. Your jumping about won't bring it any faster."

"I hope it's one of the new Concords," Abel said, barely containing his sudden eagerness for the adventure.

Jack stood in the shade of the hotel entrance where the stage would draw up, keeping a wary eye on their belongings.

"Look, Mama," Beth cried. "Here come the fresh horses for the coach!"

The six handsome, prancing beasts, their heads held high, paraded to the hitching rail alongside the hotel, where they were tethered in readiness.

"There's Emma Stokes waving, Bethie. Do say good-bye to her. Celia," she said, "you haven't by any chance seen Reed today, have you?"

"Perhaps he's with a patient and can't get away."

"Of course. How foolish of me. Children, we must find Doctor Pierce."

"But I want to see the stage come," Abel protested.

"You've seen them come before. Do as I say." She took them each by the hand.

"If you don't mind," Celia said, "I believe I'll run along. I'm not much for good-byes. Oh, Lucy!" She kissed her cheek and stepped quickly away, scurrying down the street, her skirts raising a small flurry of dust behind her.

Lucy and the children hurried to Reed's cabin. She knocked at the door and waited. Slowly, it opened. Captain Wally looked up, blinking like a brown owl against the strong spring sunlight.

"Pastora?"

"Captain." She nodded to him. How old he looks, she thought, and feeble, as though he were wasting away pent up like this. "We have come to make our farewells. Is the doctor at home?"

He dragged himself aside and motioned them in.

"Reed."

He looked up from his desk. "Ah." He cleared his throat and pushed back his chair, rising. "I must have lost track of the time. I was just . . ." He waved his hand absently at the open book on his desk, his voice trailing off.

"We knew you must be busy," she said gently.

"Abel, Beth, come to me." He bent down and opened

208

his arms wide to them. "You will be good children, won't you? And helpful to Mama?" He looked from one face to the other, then abruptly pulled them to him, stroking their hair and murmuring low. He kissed them each on the forehead and laid his cheek against Beth's as he cupped the boy's chin in his hand, gazing silently into his face.

In the shadows beyond, almost obscured in a dim corner of the room, lay Kate's bed. Only the slightest swelling of the covers betrayed the fact that it was occupied. Lucy wanted to look away, yet she couldn't help but wonder that this thing still lived. Her arms lay across the coverlet, thin, brittle twigs like the limbs of a stick-doll carelessly abandoned on a child's cot. Her motionless fingers were little more than bone. Lucy was reminded of the talons of a dead bird and glanced quickly away, her stomach churning with revulsion. She looked around the cabin, at once despising herself for leaving him like this, alone save for the presence of a half-dead lunatic and a maimed Indian.

"We must go," she said, startled by the urgency of her own voice.

Reed stood, still holding the children in his embrace. He looked at her across the room, saying nothing. He dropped his hands from their shoulders and turned them each to face their mother, giving them a gentle push. "Go now," he told them, making no move to follow.

She took their small hands in hers. "I shan't say goodbye, Reed—"

"Don't," he replied swiftly.

She turned from him, blinking back the tears. The Captain sat in the doorway. As they passed, he reached up and grazed the boy's arm. Lucy paused. "Captain," she said, "you were always a good friend to us—"

"*Ku-ni*, Pastora. Thank you."

She brushed past him into the bright sunlight, hurrying blindly down the street, the children struggling to keep up with her.

"Mama, Mama!" At the sight of the brand-new Abbot-Downing coach, its red paint still shiny under a film of dust, Abel broke from her and ran. He dashed to the front, then to the rear, then back to the front, jumping up and down for a glimpse of the driver's box on top.

"Do move out of the way, dear. They have to change the teams."

209

"Look, Mama. The rear wheels are as high as your head."

"So they are. Now give Jack a hand with the luggage."

"Your boy's first ride?" The whip was a broad-shouldered fellow with slate-blue eyes and smooth, nut-brown skin. He shot an expertly aimed quid of tobacco under the rear baggage platform.

"The first for all three of us."

"We're going to San Francisco," Beth piped.

"Are you now?" He smiled. "Whoa, Tim!" he shouted, as one of the lead horses shied and whinnied. "Ma'am, may I have a word with you?" He drew Lucy aside.

When the baggage had been loaded and the green, iron-bound boxes of gold stored in the front boot, the passengers stepped aboard. French Jack held open the door for Lucy and the children.

"Abel, Bethie, I have a surprise for you." She glanced up at the coveted seat atop the coach, beside the driver. "You two have been invited to share the seat of honor."

Abel turned to the driver, speechless with pleasure, an awed grin spreading over his face.

"Is it safe, Mama?" Beth asked, eyeing the lofty perch.

The driver threw back his head and laughed. "Never you fear, little lady, with old Charlie Parkhurst in charge."

"New Englander, aren't you?" Lucy inquired. "I caught the accent."

"Right you are, ma'am. Upsy-daisy now, children." He lifted them onto the coach.

"You behave yourselves," she called up. "Mr. Parkhurst, if they're any trouble, they're to come inside at the next stop." She waved at the two delighted children and, gathering up her skirts, entered the coach.

Once, on the outskirts of town, she looked back out the window, then drew her head inside.

"No, Pastora." French Jack wagged a warning finger.

"No tears," she assured him, a little surprised at her composure. "Not for this Castalia. The one we knew is long gone."

Two of their fellow passengers, a newspaperman from Baltimore and a sandy-haired preacher with a German name, disembarked at Fiddletown. They were replaced by a pair of grizzled miners and a young midwestern couple bound for Drytown to visit relatives. Drytown, for all its name implied, hardly seemed in danger of withering away. It was crammed cheek-by-jowl with sturdy brick buildings, every other one of which appeared to be a saloon. "Land," Lucy giggled when the midwestern couple had left the coach, "it's a wonder anyone here ever draws a sober breath. Ooh!" She seized the windowsill as the stage lurched forward. Overhead, she could hear Mr. Parkhurst calling to his six-in-hand.

"Git along, boys! You, Mackie, git!"

The coach sped along the tortuous, rutted roads, its wheels rattling, its passengers jouncing with the motion. Great gusts of dust billowed out behind them as they wound through the green hills and shady, gray gorges. Gradually, the rock-strewn ridges gave way to a smoother landscape, fields dotted here and there with cabins and animal pens.

"Just to think, Jack. There wasn't a soul to be seen, last time I passed this way from Sutter's to Luther Moore's. Why, it's farmland now."

"You must be an old-timer," one of the passengers remarked.

"I suppose I am, at that," she answered, amused at the thought.

Lucy marveled at the number of towns where the stage stopped, always at a busy hotel or a local Wells Fargo office. And as the land grew flat and they approached the broad plains surrounding Sacramento, she couldn't help but recall the haggard, dirt-streaked girl, lumbering under the weight of her belly, who had walked this way ten years before. "Mr. Bates was right, you know," she told Jack matter-of-factly. "He said California was blooming with opportunities ripe for the picking. Of course," she said, giving a curt laugh, "he neglected to mention there might be thorns."

"The thorns don't stop us, Pastora. Not then, not now. We ain't hardly begun."

In the late afternoon, the coach drew up at the Orleans Hotel. "Heavens, but it's warm here," Lucy exclaimed. "A day's travel, and we're in another climate altogether."

"Mother!" Beth cried excitedly as she clambered down from the top of the coach. "Mr. Parkhurst let Abel and me share the reins with him most all the way in from the edge of town!"

Lucy shook the driver's calloused hand. "You've been very kind. I hope they weren't a bother."

211

"Young 'uns? Never." A grin creased his sunburnt face. "Good luck to you, ma'am." He tipped his hat.

Jack hired a porter and quickly assembled their belongings.

"Abel," Lucy called, "don't stray! We must go to the boat right away."

Behind Jack and the porter, each laden with luggage, walked Lucy, hanging on tightly to the children. What a bustling place this was. Buildings of every shape and design spread out on all sides. Two-story brick buildings with tall iron shutters, gaudily painted wooden structures with showy verandas and ornate carvings, now and then a church steeple rising behind the continuous parade of markets, milliners, gaming halls, restaurants, boarding houses, saloons and dry-goods shops. "Stay close," she whispered to the children as they made their way through the thickening crowds around the *embarcadero*.

"You folks come down with Old Charlie," the porter said. "The best, he is. I'd a lot sooner trust myself to him than these river steamers. Don't suppose you heard about *The Secretary*. Blew up a few days back. Over twenty people dead on them boats just since the first of this year. Comes from the damned fools racin'."

"Hey," Jack said, "no more, you hear?"

Beth tugged at Lucy's hand. "Mama? Will the boat explode with us on it?"

Lucy silently cursed the stupid fellow. "I'm sure not. *The Golden Phoenix* is a safe, staunch vessel." She devoutly prayed she was telling the truth. "You wait and see."

Above the hubbub of the wharf, above the broad-beamed sailing ships, the lighters and the dinghies plying their way along the teeming river, rose *The Golden Phoenix*. She was a long, sleek, majestic sidewheeler, two decks high and topped by a lofty black stack. Her immaculate white paint glowed in the sunset like burnished copper. Her paddleboxes were adorned with trim red and green stripes, and fore and aft her flags fluttered lazily overhead, stirred by a mild breeze. Lucy stopped at the foot of the landing plank. "Mercy, what a splendid sight."

"Une grande dame, n'est-ce pas?"

Grand she was, from her brass chandeliers and stained glass windows to her marble tables and red plush upholstery. The children, flushed with excitement, scampered about the ship, investigating every nook and cranny. Lucy stood by the gangway, watching the last of the passengers troop aboard while the final trunks and boxes were stowed away and the bulging sacks of gold were carried to the ship's bullion room. Below, on the landing, the well-wishers clustered, waving to their friends on board as the plank was drawn away. "Children," she called, "come here and wave to the people. Don't be getting in the way. Where's Jack?" She glanced about the passengers and saw him descending the stairway from the upper deck. "Is everything safely stowed?"

"Oui." His answer was all but drowned out by a loud blast from the ship's whistle, as she slowly pulled away from the wharf. The mighty engines throbbed, and the water churned and splashed under the rolling of the paddle-wheels. Beth moved closer to her mother, clutching Lucy's skirt tightly in her fist.

"Is it going to blow up, Mama?"

"Mais non," Jack reassured her. "This captain, he don't race. We take our time, have a fine supper, and tomorrow you have breakfast in San Francisco Bay."

It was a trifle easier said than done, what with both children beside themselves with curiosity. At last Lucy bedded them down with a promise that if they could not sleep, they would at least try to rest quietly, snug in their bunks.

French Jack was deep in a hand of cards with three other gentlemen in the social hall. Lucy stepped out onto the deck, closing the door behind her. Two couples were taking a postprandial stroll, talking softly among themselves. A few lone souls lounged at the railings, gazing into the river as it passed below. Overhead, the moon sent ribbons of light playing across the placid water. She stood at the stern of the ship, watching its wake widen behind them until it disappeared toward shore. Like a great, luminous queen, poised and impassive, *The Golden Phoenix* swept through her domain, the stately rhythm of her engines pulsing like the beat of a powerful heart.

On either side of the river, the grassy lowlands leveled out into obscurity. Here and there a few bushes hovered darkly over the banks. Occasionally the ship passed a campfire burning brightly through the night to ward off the ever-present mosquitos. Voices would call from shore, and shadow would wave to shadow as they slipped away.

Lucy felt herself drifting, carried like a leaf along the glassy surface of the water, borne through the warm night far away from the roots that had sustained her for so long.

"Hey." French Jack touched her arm. "Pastora, you dreaming?"

"No." She gazed out into the darkness. "I was thinking of Castalia."

"Better you get some sleep. There's fog ahead. You don't want to catch a chill from the damp. We got a lot to do tomorrow."

Lucy woke early and found the children still sleeping soundly. The ship's engines were still. Quickly, she dressed and stepped out into the passageway.

The Golden Phoenix lay at her mooring with her bow headed into a choppy tide. Lucy stood on the sun-drenched upper deck, her hair blowing loose in a cool, brisk wind that smacked of sea spray. She took in a deep breath, savoring the freshness of the scent. Suddenly she realized that save for the gentle lapping of the water against the sides of the ship, the ocean made no sound. She stood still, listening. The flags of *The Golden Phoenix* billowed and snapped in the wind. But the sea was quiet. She had expected, from all Pa's tales, to hear it roar and thunder, but it merely swished and splashed in a most peaceful and soothing rhythm. Lucy decided that this ocean must be quite unlike the one Pa had known, and that was clearly why it had been called the Pacific.

She gazed across the shining water. Ships of every description and registry swung at their cables. She wondered that such an abundance of large vessels could maneuver their way through the bay without colliding. Pacific Mail steamers, lumber barges, whalers and China clippers lay floating side by side, all but touching. Amid the forest of masts thrusting skyward their fluttered ensigns of all colors, whose origins she could not possibly identify. She watched spellbound as the huge square sails of a glossy black bark were unfurled. What a spectacle it was. Lucy wondered if people hereabouts took such awesome sights for granted.

Along the line of the shore, rows of long, narrow wharves extended into the bay on pilings. Still more ships were berthed alongside, and early as it was, scores of men busied themselves about the docks and the warehouses beyond.

From the sandy strand at the water's edge rose great, rolling headlands, their heights disappearing into a silvery halo of mist. The land was covered with a bright yellow-green carpet of spring growth. In places, the hills were cleft by ancient streambeds, their paths marked by a march of low-lying shrubs down to the bay-side. As she scanned the clusters of peak-roofed houses rising along the precipitous slopes, it struck Lucy that, verdant as these hills were, she saw not a single tree.

She turned and looked about her. Across the way lay a small island, its shoreline rocks turned white with the droppings of the myriad flocks of sea birds that wheeled and swooped above. Its high grass rippled in the breeze, and a scattering of wild mustard gilded its crest, but there were no trees there, either.

She glanced back at the city. Some of the larger buildings, warehouses and places of business most likely were made of brick or stone, but most, by far, were wooden. How peculiar, she thought, that a city would flourish here where every scrap of building material had to be fetched from somewhere else or contrived by hand. This San Francisco was an improbable place.

XI

Lucy stood with French Jack beside the redwood-planked street, seemingly oblivious of the clatter of carriages and the press of passersby. Her body, poised against the persistent buffeting of the bay breeze, was thrust forward slightly like the shapely figurehead of a ship making its way into the wind. Several men turned to stare at her as they walked by, taking note of the fair tendrils of hair blowing loose about her smiling face and the clear contours of her figure revealed through her skirts as the gusts pressed them to her. She appeared not to notice.

"My eyes," she was saying. "My eyes don't lie to me, Jack."

He frowned. "Pastora, already you make me a rich man, but I'm not sure you're so wise this time." He raised his arm in a wide arc, taking in both sides of the street. "What about them, eh?"

Above the succession of shops to left and right fluttered an unlikely array of banners. Assorted garments of every shape and color swung from high poles. Red flannel shirts and homespun trousers, capes and coats and gilded uniforms stirred in the wind. Like the vestiges of some motley mutinous crew swinging from the yardarm, they danced against the bright blue sky. French Jack pointed to a name on one of the storefronts. "How you going to compete with Mr. Levy there and the rest of his kind? Look at those flags of Jerusalem, hanging clear down to the docks! Why you're so keen on selling dry goods?"

"I've no intention of vying with Mr. Levy and his tribe. Anyone can cater to waterfront riff raff. Why must you set your sights so low, Jack?" she said a trifle impatiently. "I declare, you'd still be making rockers for greenhorns if you'd been left to your own devices. Times have changed. This is eighteen fifty-four. Don't you see what I see? Everywhere you look there are grand gentlemen in frock coats with fine silk lapels, wearing embroidered waistcoats and ruffled linen shirts. That's money, Jack. In this place, folks wear their money for the world to see. Why, the richest fellow in Castalia would look a pauper here in San Francisco. See there, in that doorway," she said, lowering her voice, "the swell with the gloves and gold-headed cane and velvet waistcoat."

Jack gave her an exasperated look. "Pastora! That ain't no gentleman! Gentlemen don't wear velvet on the streets in the middle of the day. And they don't wear gloves, neither. That fellow's a sharper, a gambler most likely."

"Nevertheless," she maintained, marching airily around the corner with Jack following, "these birds sport fine feathers. I saw two women this morning in the Wells Fargo office. What a striking picture they made. One was dressed in pale green silk embroidered with roses, and on her bonnet were sewn more clusters of roses to match. Imagine, an entire costume strewn with roses!"

"Pastora—"

"The other one," she continued, keeping up her brisk pace, "wore a gray riding skirt with a violet velvet jacket and cascades of lace on her bodice. They were chatting with one of the clerks at the weighing scales, and when they had moved along, I inquired who they might be. He looked at me, shabby as I was in my plain clothes and knitted shawl and said, 'I've no idea, ma'am,' and he came around the counter and stood between me and the two women, blocking my view." Lucy stopped, bringing Jack up short beside her.

"I don't see—"

"I know you don't. Hear me out. I walked right past him to the door and watched them step into a splendid barouche with bright scarlet upholstery."

French Jack groaned.

"Next to them, Nelly One-arm and Velvet Annie dress like beggar-women. These ladies hereabouts are their own best advertisement. Plumage, Jack. This is a place where plumage counts for everything. By the way, the two I saw were French."

He stood here a moment without speaking, scanning her face as though he was not altogether sure he recognized this prattling woman with the steady, challenging blue eyes. Finally he gave a low chuckle. "Lucy, Lucy. You still call yourself a country girl?"

"Indeed I do," she replied jauntily. "Only a country girl like myself would notice such things. You," she teased, "are too jaded."

"Comment?"

She took his arm. "Come, let's walk the long way back to the hotel. We must give this city a hard look. You have to see for yourself how these birds preen. I shan't try to convince you anymore, I promise. It's for you to decide."

Lucy felt a constant sense of excitement here. The wind tugged at her clothing and grazed her cheeks to a rosy glow. The heady tang of the sea filled her nostrils, hinting of deep and distant mysteries. The majestic parade of ships gliding in and out of the bay piqued a sense of wonder and romance which she had never known she possessed. Even the sunlight that shone on the steep hills and sparkled on the water's surface seemed brighter than the soft, golden light that had slanted through the groves and glens of Castalia. Here it beamed down, brilliant and clear, on the brush-covered heights and clusters of narrow wooden houses that clung to their slopes. It reflected against the glossy black iron balustrades of the tall stone and brick buildings that rose on the lowland near the bay. It cast abrupt, sharp shadows across narrow alleys and broad thoroughfares alike and turned the dazzling surface of the sea to silver.

But it was gold that was the lifeblood of this place. Gold alone had brought forth a city on these sand spits and brushy hills. San Francisco existed solely for commerce. Except for gold, it would still be only a remote military outpost with a small village that catered to the needs of transient ships. The irony of this fact was not lost on Lucy. Gold *in situ* could destroy a Castalia, but gold once removed could build a San Francisco. Here on this rough, inhospitable terrain flourished great banking houses and newspaper offices. The streets were lined with shops to serve every whim. Shoe shops, saddlers, gunsmiths, watchmakers, apothecaries, cigarmakers, bakers and daguerreotype galleries thrived on the gold that poured into the city from the faraway fields. Along the bay's edge, whole pine trees brought from Oregon were being sunk to build new wharves. The rhythmic pounding

218

of the pile drivers filled the air with the sound of progress. Already some of the planked streets were being replaced by pavement, and everywhere one looked, more buildings sprang up. There were bowling alleys and saloons and tall brick gambling houses that looked like ornate palaces. Carriages of every sort passed by, and for a small fare, one could board a public coach line to one's destination.

And still the city grew. Miners who had made their pile came here to spend it. Keen-eyed tradesmen came here to help them spend it, and the croupiers, dealers and trollops came with the same intention. From every corner of the globe, from every walk of life, they flocked here. The streets of Little China teemed with almond-eyed men in their loose-fitting blue cotton jackets and wide straw hats, bent on getting their share of the wealth of California. And now, thought Lucy, we are here too.

The dry-goods firm of Pastora and French, a name they both reckoned would be known by anyone who'd passed through the gold country, was located in a narrow three-story brick building on Clay Street. The location could not have been more suitable.

To the far west, up the length of Clay Street, was Fern Hill, its contours obscured by the heavy underbrush which had so far discouraged settlement there. At its foot, however, along Powell and Stockton, lay the well-kept homes of some of the more distinguished residents of San Francisco. In order to reach the places of business on Montgomery Street or the wharves beyond, these upright citizens would likely choose to pass through Clay Street, rather than Sacramento, the Chinese street to the south, which was thronged with yammering Orientals hawking odd-smelling foodstuffs, or Washington Street to the north, which filled with promenading perfumed ladies hawking even more questionable goods. It was rumored that over a hundred houses catering to gentlemen were crowded around Washington and Kearny. And if the chaps who passed by in that direction weren't bound for the offices of doctors or lawyers or the gaming halls that bordered Portsmouth Plaza on the next block, well that was their affair, thought Lucy. There was trade surrounding Pastora and French in all four directions, and what that trade was mattered little, as long as it brought people past the two tall, iron-shuttered windows where their merchandise beckoned invitingly.

More often than not, it was the women who paused in passing to study the display of silks and wools and linens, the gimps and galloons, the rolls of ribbons and the bright array of shining silk threads that spread a rainbow of colors across the front counter just inside the glass. They would peer and point and chatter among themselves, touching their sleeves or throats or bosoms, adorning themselves with possibilities.

Lucy made no distinction between the well-bred ladies of Stockton Street or South Park and the well-used ladies of Dupont or Pike Streets. Indeed, there was no need to, for the wives and daughters of the city seemed curiously intent upon blurring the distinction themselves. As soon as Mademoiselle Blonde or Red Kitty stepped out for a stroll, attired in the latest Paris fashions and handing out visiting cards, the gentlewomen of the neighborhood, determined not to be eclipsed in the shade of such tainted glory, would flock to rival them. The city was filled with men who had struck it rich and decided to settle down, and while demure maidens were in short supply, a wealthy man never lacked charming company. The same girl who last week needed a new frock for her ritual Saturday walk through the streets, this week needed a gown to accompany her husband to the charity ball for the good nuns of the Sisters of Mercy.

This was a place of beginnings. Each evening the fog washed in from the bay and swept the hills, brushing softly against the buildings, swirling in milky pools in the light of the gas lamps on the street corners, obliterating all that remained of that day and that place under its pure, clean-scented billows. And when the mist flowed back out to sea and the city glistened moistly under another sunrise, sparkling as though it had been freshly washed for the occasion, it seemed to Lucy like a boundless, immaculate slate upon which she could inscribe anything she pleased. There was no past here, only the urgency of the present and the promise of the future.

The children took to their new life like ducklings launched in a congenial pond. They chattered incessantly over each discovery, clapping their hands to their ears at the racket of the carriages over the newly paved streets, squealing with pleasure at the sonorous clamor of the bell of Engine Company Number Six around the corner, running outside to watch the volunteers of Big Six race by with their pumper and hook and ladder wagon. They tagged after Wong, the Chinese laundry man, imitating his singsong speech, darting into doorways when he turned, baskets swaying on his shoulder pole, to fix them with an angry stare. They reported daily on the upward progress of Saint Mary's clock tower and each new fireproof brick building that sprouted in the neighborhood. But most of all it was the sounds they loved, the cries of the peddlers and tinkers, the newsboys and the Chinese ragpickers. At the ringing of the charcoal vendor's bell, Abel would crane from the window to watch the dour Mexican unload the panniers on his cantankerous mule.

"He bit him again!" Abel called gleefully. "On the arm."

"Shut that window and wash up for supper."

"Oh, Mama—"

"One more word and I shall take away *Uncle Tom's Cabin.*" She had only to hint at curtailing Abel's reading privileges to bring the boy to heel. As if the books they used at the public school weren't enough, he had wheedled his way into the good graces of the custodian at the Y.M.C.A. reading room. Each afternoon, he trotted quickly from school to the second floor of the Post Office building down the street, emerging from the reading room only when hunger pangs reminded him it was nearly suppertime.

"Beth," Lucy said to the girl, "I want you to work on your sampler tonight. When Jack brings me home from the theatre, I expect to see you've made some progress. Leave it on my bed for me to look at."

"What are you going to see?"

"Something of Laura Keene's at the Union. Jack will be here shortly. You can ask him."

"Mama, why doesn't Jack live with us?"

The question took her aback. She glanced at the child, then smiled. "Jack wants his own kind of life, Bethie, and I want mine. Besides, he liked his lodgings because there are some French-speaking people there."

"But he could be our father," she persisted. "I'm the only girl in my class without a father."

Lucy went to her and held her close. "I'll wager you're the only lucky little girl in your class who has a grown-up

221

gentleman for a dear friend. Didn't he take you children to the pantomime show and to an outing on Telegraph Hill?"

"The goats on the hill scared me."

"They only wanted your food. But Jack wouldn't let them get a bite, would he? You see what a good friend he is?"

Lucy repeated the story to Jack, her eyes merry, as they were seated at the restaurant that evening. "That child has marriage on her mind already! Yours and mine! What a dog-and-cat match that would be."

"You're a stubborn, pushy woman, *ma chère.* I'd sooner keep house with one of them steam pile drivers they use on the wharves."

"And I with one of those great, gray wharf rats. At least the creature wouldn't gamble his nights away like certain people I know."

"*Touché.* You must have an appetite after the play. Shall we order?"

Lucy scanned the menu card. "You'd best do it for me. I can't read this outlandish language of yours."

He ordered the *consommé, l'homard, le porc braisé aux légumes* and something called a *gateau à la neige* which was cake and ice cream. It was, as dining went, a tasty late evening snack. Lucy had fast become used to the fancy eating habits of the city. It seemed, after Castalia, a place where everything, both good and bad, was done to a surfeit. And though she might find fault with some of San Francisco's more lurid excesses, the food would never be one of them. One had only to go hungry once to appreciate the wonder of a table lavishly spread with steaming dishes and wine glasses shining ruby-red in the candlelight.

She laid a hand on Jack's arm. "This tastes a sight more appetizing than a chew of mule meat and a swallow of melted snow. Remember?"

He nodded and looked around the crowded restaurant at the well-dressed patrons enjoying their meals. "Makes you wonder, don't it," he mused. "Who are all these folks and how did they come to be here like us?"

"Not me." Lucy wiped the cake crumbs from her lips. "I don't ask questions. Who they are, who they were, how they got here, that's their affair. But I know one thing for sure," she continued quietly. "I know what makes them tick."

"Eh?"

"Dreams, Jack. Just like the hordes that rushed to Castalia with visions of gold. This is a city that has risen from dreams."

He shrugged. "That's America, *non?* Your Boston, Providence, Philadelphia, ain't those places built from men's dreams?"

"But these are not the same ones. The men you speak of were full of noble intentions. I'm not talking about idealists, Jack, I'm talking about daydreamers. Not principles, Jack, but fantasies. The folks who made this place flourish were chasing after rainbows. What is it the Chinese call it?"

"New Golden Hill."

"So they are no different from the others. They all come with their dreams of riches. There's a lunacy in California that wasn't here when we arrived. People believe in *El Dorado* all over again, and they flock here daft as geese crowding to the feed-bucket."

"You and me ain't no different, Pastora. We didn't come to San Francisco to get poor."

"Perhaps it's contagious," Lucy said lightly. "I've a certain affection for such madness. If it weren't for a touch of it in myself, I'd probably be down on my hands and knees, pulling up turnips on a farm somewhere back East." She glanced up and caught the look of disbelief on the face of the waiter pouring their coffee. She smiled to herself. The woman who sat here in her fancy gilt chair, dressed in silk that matched the wine in their goblets, must look a far cry from a farmer's wife. Lucy was not vain but neither was she blind to her own beauty. Even if she had been, the men of San Francisco would soon have enlightened her. The simplest purchase of a few yards of broadcloth became a protracted affair as this or that chap turned the occasion into a social introduction. Had she wished, she could have had her pick of suitors any night of the week and spent her evenings dining in exotic Chinese, Spanish or German eating places, dancing at balls, listening to Christy's Minstrels or watching the latest performance of Shakespeare with a different escort for each. But flattered as she might be by the barrage of attention she received, she held herself aloof. Jack was right. There was no way of knowing anything about a man's past. And she had no intention of becoming involved with another Caleb Bates now that she was wise enough to know better.

There were the children, too, to look after. She wanted to see to it that they partook of all the abundance the city had to offer. She had joined the Unitarian Church on Stockton Street so that they might attend Sunday school. She took them on outings in the park near the Mission and to hear the German bands play in Mr. Russ's gardens. She read to them at night as they lay in their beds insisting on "just one more page," though their eyelids were all but closed. They were bright children and some-day, all too soon, they would vanish, leaving grown-up strangers who bore their names. But for now, they and the store were all that mattered. The store, as Lucy saw it, was her means of getting the life she wanted for them. As soon as she could accumulate enough money, she in-tended to make some investments and accumulate even more. There were fortunes to be made, and she saw no reason why she should not fare as well as any other dreamer aiming to strike it rich.

All this was true, to be sure. But she also knew, though she tried not to think about it, that there was still another reason she spurned the offers of courtship that came her way. Despite time and distance, despite the urgent busi-ness of the store and the demands of the children, despite the pleasures of the city, she loved Reed Pierce still. Try as she might to crowd him out of her thoughts, he re-mained with her. Sometimes, in dreams, she saw him so clearly that she could reach out and touch him, and wak-ing, she despised the daylight for fading his presence away in its impertinent glare.

She did not speak of Reed, nor did Jack, and the chil-dren seemed to have forgotten Castalia entirely. What-ever passions Lucy felt were betrayed only by the ardor with which she attacked each day's work. Save for the children, her only purpose in life appeared to be the suc-cess of Pastora and French. And if such dedication to commerce was either peculiar or unseemly in such a pretty woman, then the world would just have to think her queer as a three-legged mule. Lucy needed the store, not simply for its profits but as a means of filling the emp-tiness deep inside her that struck sometimes like a sud-den, acute spasm of hunger, unexpected and unnerving in its intensity. She contemplated the displays of merchandise, switching the bolts of linen and dimity, flannel and serge to suit her eye. She pondered the customers' requests, jotting small notes to herself on the newest length and width of skirts and sleeves and sashes. She brooded over orders of notions waylaid by storms at sea, and spent her evenings, after the children were asleep, poring over her ledgers until the pages were frayed and gray.

Early each morning, Jack would go down to the wharves for news of incoming cargoes or to the auction marts where newly arrived goods were put up for bidding. Sometimes, when the wooden telegraph on the hill signaled the arrival of a ship whose captain he knew, Jack would rush to board any craft he could hire to reach its side and inspect its manifest before the other merchants were alerted. He studied the waterfront, the ships and their masters as assiduously as did the conniving crimps who lurked about the docks and saloons in search of human cargo. Though it made Lucy uneasy, he cultivated their acquaintance, too, along with that of the respectable shipowners and importers. The trade of San Francisco was dependent upon merchant vessels, and every rumor, every scrap of intelligence that could be gleaned from any source, high or low, Jack put to use. He was not above running a secondary trade in information, and with his methodical carpenter's mind, he would fit together the reports and bits of hearsay until they formed a discernible and usually valuable piece of knowledge.

"Pastora, don't count on getting on time those English worsteds we ordered," Jack said, closing the door of the store behind him.

"Why not?"

"That captain, his wife run off with his brother last trip he was gone. He took to drinking, and they say he ain't reliable no more."

"Drat, times like this I could use my sheep."

"We'll make it up at the auctions, don't you worry."

"And pay a sight more than we would have. No mind, we need the wool goods. This is the woolenest place I ever did see. I suppose it's the constant fogs and the sea breeze that make this city more suited to Merinos than men. If it weren't for wool clothing, the place would be uninhabitable on the best of days." She rose as the door of the shop opened. "Mrs. Pitt, how nice to see you."

The woman in the doorway all but filled its space. She was easily as tall as Jack and seemed as broad abeam as a wide-bottomed ferry. She advanced majestically into the room, her great weight listing from side to side as she moved. She waved a hand at Jack, her swollen fingers chubby as a baby's. A tiny crocheted hand-bag dangled incongruously from her fleshy wrist.

He nodded. "Queen Rosie, good day to you."

"Carlotta?" The woman turned to look over her shoulder. Her massive head and neck seemed one, and the features of her face, small and childlike, were barely distinguishable, all but lost in her corpulence. It was as though her eyes, nose and mouth might sink out of sight at any moment, engulfed in that sea of suet. "Carlotta!" She stamped her foot, causing the floor to reverberate under her. For several seconds a tidal wave of flesh undulated across her bosom, and her gold lapel watch bounced against the breadth of black bombazine that swaddled her.

From behind Queen Rosie emerged a slight girl with brown hair and a sharp, vulpine face. She stood at the woman's side, blinking uncertainly.

"Give the gentleman a smile," Mrs. Pitt ordered.

Obediently, she grinned, displaying two gleaming gold incisors.

"Ain't that a treat?" Mrs. Pitt asked.

French Jack cleared his throat. "I'll be leaving you ladies. Pastora, I'm going upstairs to the storeroom."

"She ain't Mexican!" Mrs. Pitt called after him. "I know her name's Carlotta, but she ain't Mexican! I don't have Mexicans!"

"What may I do for you?" Lucy asked.

"We got to dress up this little girl, don't we, dearie?" She gave Carlotta a shove in Lucy's direction. "Something bright, orange maybe." She rested her huge bulk against one of the display cases, obscuring its contents. "Jenny," she said suddenly. "That's a better name. I won't have folks thinking Queen Rosie Pitt has Mexicans under her roof."

When Lucy had wrapped the girl's purchases, she took them to the front counter, where the newly christened Jenny was gingerly fingering a piece of Brussels lace. "I'm

226

sure the dressmaker will do something lovely with this,"
Lucy said as she handed over the parcel.

"And the lace?" Jenny said in her tiny, breathy voice.
"How much is it?"

"No lace!" Queen Rosie boomed. "Lace hides the
bosom. Ribbon. That green stuff there," she said, pointing
a round, gold-ringed finger.

Lucy laid it on the counter for Jenny's inspection. The
girl unrolled a length of it and held it up to the light from
the window behind her.

"She don't say much," Mrs. Pitt confided to Lucy, "but
she plays the pianoforte like an angel at the harp. You
should see how the gentlemen smile."

Lucy cut the ribbon and tucked it under the string of
Jenny's parcel.

"I'm home, Mama." Beth stuck her head in the door.
"I'm going upstairs."

"Don't be rude, dear. Say hello to Mrs. Pitt here and
Jenny."

Beth opened the door wider and gave a brief curtsy, a
new refinement instilled by her schoolteacher. Lucy
couldn't help smiling at the child's natural grace.

"Come here, little one, and let me have a look at you,"
said Mrs. Pitt. "Land," she said as she stroked Beth's
cheek with her thumb, "what a beauty. How old is this
child?"

Lucy slipped an arm around Beth's shoulders and held
her close. "She's not quite nine."

"So young," she said, "and pretty as a black-eyed
daisy. So young," she repeated in a whisper. She withdrew a lace handkerchief from her mountainous bosom
and dabbed at her eyes. "Children . . ." She shook her
head apologetically. "Ain't never had none of my own, so
I guess I was just born to love everyone else's. Ain't a one
of them I don't want to hug to smithereens."

Lucy felt Beth stiffen slightly at the prospect of being
enveloped by this elephantine presence.

"Here, my little daisy." Queen Rosie reached into her
crocheted bag and pressed a gold coin into Beth's hand.

"My name is Beth, ma'am," she said politely, "and
thank you."

"Mrs. Pitt, really, you mustn't," Lucy told her.

"Pshaw. Won't do me a bit of good when I'm laid out

and candle-lit. Good day to you, Pastora," she said as she opened the door to leave, prodding Jenny ahead of her.

Beth opened her palm and looked at the coin. "Mama, ten dollars! The lady gave me ten dollars! Why?"

"I expect she's lonely for a family and she wants children to like her."

"Ain't no way she can have me for ten dollars."

"She meant well, dear. That's all that's important. And don't say 'ain't.'" She glanced out the window. "Look, here comes Abel. Go upstairs to the second floor and tell Jack it's almost closing time."

Lucy stirred the coals in the stove and settled herself in a rocking chair. Abel looked up from his book. "You came from Missouri, didn't you, Mama?"

"I did."

"Did you have slaves there?"

"Heavens no, we were much too poor."

"My teacher says slavery's sinful."

"Your teacher is from Quincy, Massachusetts. Most New Englanders feel that way. But there's plenty of them that made their fortunes shipping black ivory, believe me."

"Would you have slaves now, if you still lived there?"

"Son, if I still lived there, I'd be close to a slave myself. Farming does that, unless you're lucky."

Beth laid her embroidery hoop on the table beside her. "We're not poor now, are we?"

"I should say not."

"You're not poor," Abel told Beth. "You've got ten dollars from that fat lady. Do you suppose she likes boys, too?"

"She'll want to hug you." Beth shuddered. "She'd squish you like a bug."

"I'd rather be poor."

"Children, what's all this nonsense about poverty? Go back to your work and let me read the *Alta*." She spread the newspaper in her lap.

"I can make two bits for every rat I catch," Abel said. "A lot of boys do it. You get a sack of them and sell them to the grog shops by the docks for the rat and terrier fights."

"Young man, don't you dare!" Lucy shook the paper at him. "If you didn't get bitten, you'd be knocked over the head by one of those crimps down there and wake up as a cabin boy on some wretched ship bound for China. Now do your lessons! I want you to be through with them before supper." She turned the pages of the *Alta* to the commercial and financial news. The railroad across the Isthmus would be finished within a few months. That meant still another, faster way for folks to come to San Francisco. She scanned the columns rapidly with a practiced eye. Each evening she sought out the news of the city's business, preparing herself for the time when the weekly sums she deposited at Wells Fargo would finally amount to enough to invest. She was still at sea as to what kind of investment she should make, though it seemed that in a place where men were willing to pay over a thousand dollars for a single concert seat and a Chinaman could get rich telling fortunes on the street, nearly anything she turned her hand to was bound to prosper. The enterprise, she'd decided, must be one which demanded very little of her time, since the store and the children came first. She was ignorant of the workings of the securities market, which seemed to her as capricious as the whims of the weather. Jack had purchased a small interest in a shipping concern, but then, Jack knew something of ships and trade. She had no intention of placing her hard-earned gold in a venture over which she had scarcely any control. No, she wanted an investment she could see with her own two eyes and watch over, a lodging house perhaps, or a small building she might rent to a shopkeeper. Already she and Jack had tried to buy the store property, but the owner seemed determined to hold fast. She understood that. Land, Pa used to say, was the only wealth he wanted. Land was real and tangible. But the land had never produced for Pa, and if she were to put her scant fortune into the ground, it must be ground upon which something flourished. Lucy set the newspaper aside and rose to prepare their evening meal.

"Wash up, children. It's nearly supper time." Lucy poured a pitcher of water into the kettle and set it on the stove to heat. "Abel, light another lamp. The days are shorter now, and I expect you to come home earlier and have the lamps lit by the time I close downstairs." She peered outside into the October dusk and reached up to shut the window against the evening fog. Suddenly the sash flew from her fingers and fell with a crash. The floor lurched under her. The house shuddered and swayed, throwing her against the fall. Again and again it happened. She heard Beth cry out in the bedroom as another convulsion shook the building. The kettle clattered and splashed on the iron stove. The door of the china cabinet swung open, sending a cascade of cups and plates crashing to the floor as the house rocked and groaned. In the street outside, there was the sound of precious glass panes splintering. A horse whinnied in panic. A brick plummeted past the window and fell to the ground.

Just as suddenly, the motion stopped. "Bethie!" she cried. "Abel, are you all right?"

Abel stood dazedly in the doorway, still clutching his unlit lamp. Beth ran into the room and flung herself into Lucy's arms, weeping. "I broke the wash basin, Mama!"

"No, dear." Lucy patted her. "It was an earthquake. It made a grand mess of the china, too. We'll be lucky to find a plate to eat supper off."

"I'm not hungry," Beth sobbed. "I'm afraid. Is it going to happen again?"

"Of course not," she told her.

"Five," said Abel. "I counted five jolts, one right after another."

Lucy laughed in spite of herself. "Gracious sakes, only you would think to count. Where you came by such a studious little head I'll never know. Come, we'll go down and have a look at the store. We can clean up here later."

When Jack found them, Abel was sweeping up the shards from the large mirror that had toppled from the wall, while Beth and Lucy crawled about on all fours, trying to gather the notions which had scattered in every direction. "Mind, Jack! Watch out for spools of thread. Abel took a bad spill on one. Mercy!" Lucy caught sight of the bloodied handkerchief he held to his temple. "What happened?"

"Piece of stone cornice come raining down on me. The fellow next to me was hurt bad. Me, I only got a cut."

"Let me have a look at it."

Jack winced as he took away the cloth.

"It's an ugly thing. Come upstairs and let me wash it. I've a drop of brandy to steady you, if the bottle didn't break."

Beth barely touched her supper that night. "I don't like

230

it here," she said abruptly. "I want to go back to Castalia."

"Here now," Jack replied, reaching across the table to squeeze her hand. "These things happen everyplace, just like thunder and wind. You be brave like your brother and your mama. You ain't going to let yourself get shaken out of your own home, are you? Didn't you sit up there with old Charlie Parkhurst on top of that high coach, bouncing and rattling all the way to Sacramento? You ain't afraid of a little shaking, eh, Bethie?"

But it was almost a full week before the girl slept through a night without waking and crying for Lucy. Unlike Abel, who seemed a born stoic, Beth was as sensitive as a weather vane. The slightest breath of a disturbance spun her into confusion and fretfulness. Only time and patient soothing restored her.

"Sit next to me, Bethie, and I'll read to you," offered Abel.

"Don't you read her any of those Poe tales," Lucy cautioned. "I won't have her frightened out of her wits."

"I wouldn't do that, Mama," he said soberly. "Don't you know how much I love Bethie?"

"Of course I do. And you're a good boy to read to your sister." She gazed at them, their heads bent over Abel's book, their black hair glossy in the lamplight, like the shining coats of the sea lions that romped on the rocks by the bay. Abel was so affectionate toward Bethie, so earnestly protective of her, that he mothered her almost as much as Lucy herself did.

"Watch me." Abel stood on one of the gravel walks that crossed Portsmouth Plaza, Beth's hoop in his hand. "It wants speed. The faster it goes, the less chance it will fall." He gave the hoop a push and chased after it, waving his stick.

"Let me! Let me!" Beth followed him and struck the hoop with her own stick. It rolled ahead, bouncing on the gravel. The blonde young man who had been watching them jumped backward onto the grass to let it pass.

"Children, don't make a nuisance of yourselves," called Lucy. "It's time to go home. Jack's coming for Sunday dinner."

Down the sloping street they went, the two children running after the hoop as it careered along ahead of them.

231

When Lucy stopped at the door, waiting for them to retrieve it and bring it back, she saw the blonde young man from the plaza again. He had stopped too, three doors away, and as he caught her eye he tipped his hat politely. He seemed less interested in the contents of the shop window in front of him than in her and the children. As Abel and Beth trudged up the stairs, Lucy gave a last glance behind her. He stood across the street, looking at the sign over the window, which read "Pastora and French—Dry Goods."

In the morning, as she did each Monday, Lucy rearranged and refreshed her displays. She ran her feather duster lightly over the rainbow of spools on the front counter and turned to brush it across the window sills. As she looked through the glass she spied the fellow she'd seen in the plaza the day before. He couldn't have been much more than twenty, a tall, pleasant-looking chap with his fair hair and mustache. He was well dressed, too, in clothes that looked to be nearly new. He paused for a moment, as though undecided, then crossed the street toward her door.

"Ma'am." He doffed his hat.

"Good day to you. You're the young man my children all but tripped yesterday. I trust that's not what brought you here."

"Not at all. Would you be either the Pastora or French on your sign?"

"The Pastora. It's a nickname, actually."

He spread his arms wide and laughed aloud. "I knew it! I was sure I was right! You look different, but not that different."

She shook her head, puzzled. "Have we met?"

"Yes indeed." He laid his hat on the counter and approached her, his hand outstretched. "You're Mrs. Bates, aren't you?"

She nodded.

He took her hand in his and shook it warmly. "I'm Joe Mason, ma'am. Remember me?"

She stared. "Young Joe Mason? John Mason's boy? Oh, land—" Her voice broke as her eyes filled with tears. She hugged him to her, then pushed him away and held him at arms' length. "Look at you! Joe, you're a grown man! And a handsome one, too, if I may say. How old are you? What are you doing in San Francisco?"

"Twenty-one, and I'm visiting my mother. She married again, a gentleman from Saint Louis. They moved here last year."

"And you, are you married?"

"Not yet. I went to college after we sold the farm. I've just secured a position with Page and Bacon here. I start work next week."

"The banking house? I'm impressed, Joe. A banker, for pity's sake, who'd have thought it?"

"And you, ma'am? You're prospering, from the look of things. It agrees with you, I'd say."

"We're fine, thank you. Mr. Bates passed away some time back, and I've moved here with my two children. Joe, you know my partner, French Jack, Monsieur Louet! Do you recall him?"

"The carpenter from Canada?"

"The same. We started a small store in Castalia. That's in the gold country, and then—" She broke off, laughing. "There's so much to tell. Where shall we begin?"

"That's why I came by. I was sure yesterday it was you. I told my Ma, and she sent me to invite you to dinner next Sunday. You will come? Please bring your family and Mr. Louet."

"All of us? Are you sure she'd appreciate such a crowd?"

"Yes'm, I'm sure. She knows what a comfort you were to me when Pa died on the trail."

Her eyes looked past him, and she frowned slightly, as though trying to glimpse something in the far distance. "How long ago that seems."

XII

THEY DINED on those past years. Polly and John's daughter, Martha, who was nine, sat glancing from one speaker to another, rapt. By the time the Negro servant, Octavia, set two steaming apple pies on the long mahogany dining table, the tales had been told, passing from teller to teller, from one side of the table to the other, unfurling like a ribbon that intertwined among them, joining them together.

Joe's mother, Polly Fearing, was a solid, round-faced little woman, an unimposing figure by any standards, yet she presided over her table with queenly dignity. One would never suspect, thought Lucy, the rigors and suffering she must have endured, alone on a remote farm with two children. There was something determinedly cheerful about the woman that Lucy admired. She appeared to have somehow discovered that she would never run dry of the means to cope with anything life dealt her, and having limitless resources, she was free to share them without stinting.

Albert, her husband, was a beanpole of a man, tall and sharp-featured, but his genial character belied the severity of his looks. He laughed readily, and his bright blue eyes were alive with secret merriment.

Seated between Abel and the shy, spellbound Martha was Albert's brother, Henry Fearing, a more serious and reserved version of his elder. Quiet though he was, Lucy found herself glancing every now and then at Henry. His long, elegant hands manipulated his knife and fork so deftly that they might be the instruments of an artist. He had a way of pausing to listen with his head held high and motionless, like a proud stag harkening to distant sounds on the wind. His slightest gesture possessed a quality of artless grace that she found fascinating. He seemed incapable of making a clumsy or unbecoming move. True, he was not as striking as Albert, but in his subtle way she found him the more attractive of the two. He was not handsome, she decided, yet he was, in his own way, wholly pleasing.

Both Fearings were men of independent means, educated at Yale University, well-traveled and cultured men who had evidently resolved to invest a good part of their fortune in the future of San Francisco. They conversed easily with young Joe on the subjects of stocks, municipal warrants and their investments in mills and foundries. They were a new breed to Lucy, men who saw the whole city simply as an enterprise, not unlike her store, a place containing certain materials which, if properly exploited, resulted in gain. Lucy had never conceived of the city in such a light. To her it was a home, one with vast possibilities to be sure, but until now she had never viewed it as objectively as they. The Fearing brothers were not dreamers pursuing fantasies of a fortune. They already possessed money beyond their needs. They were, instead, cool-headed, practical men who, looking for a new medium of profit, had cannily selected San Francisco, all of it, as their concern. There was, she decided, a good deal to be learned at this table.

"Mrs. Bates," Joe said as he laid down his fork, "what sort of inducement can I offer you and Jack to bring your banking across the street from Wells Fargo to Page and Bacon?"

"Heavens, Joe, I doubt it would mean a drop in the bucket for Page and Bacon, though I'm flattered you think me worth the invitation."

"They're a fine firm, Mrs. Bates," Henry Fearing assured her.

"What Henry means," Albert put in, "is that their roots are in Saint Louis like our own. We've family connections with the firm. You couldn't ask for a better banking house, solid as a sound old oak."

"Naturally, Mrs. Bates, we're a bit prejudiced," Henry said.

"Please, do call me Lucy."

"Well, then, Lucy," Albert continued with a twinkle,

"seeing two such upstanding products of Saint Louis as my brother and myself, you'll give some thought to Joe's idea."

"Never you mind them," Polly Fearing said gaily, "they eat, breathe and dream business. Albert, Henry," she chided them, "we've a lovely guest here, not one of your cigar-smoking cronies. You mustn't bore Lucy with business chatter."

"Ho!" French Jack raised a cautioning hand. *"Madame,* let me assure you that the lady is probably enchanted. You got sitting here one smart woman. She can even drive an old donkey like me to make money."

Lucy felt the color rising in her cheeks. "Well," she said hesitantly, "I do find all the possibilities hereabouts rather exciting."

"Then perhaps you'll allow me to contribute a suggestion now and then," Henry said. "May I call on you at home?"

"Why—" Lucy glanced around the table, realizing suddenly that everyone was silently poised for her answer. Flustered, she answered him. "I suppose—that is, I should be delighted."

"Didn't I tell you," Joe said proudly, "how much you'd like her?"

Albert pushed his chair back from the table. "You didn't oversell the lady by a whit, Joe."

"Tavie!" Polly called toward the kitchen. "You may clear now! Come," she said, taking Lucy by the arm, "let's go into the sitting room, my dear. We've still so much to talk about."

Lucy emerged from her bedroom, smoothing the silk folds of her skirt. "Bethie, why on earth are you crouched on the floor?"

The child turned from her place at the window. "Ooh, Mama, you look so pretty in blue. Another new dress for Mr. Fearing?"

"You didn't answer my question."

"I was watching for his carriage with the silver horses."

Lucy smiled. Henry's pair were actually dapple-gray, but Beth's imagination, as always, revealed her penchant for splendor. She embellished the night sky with diamonds and saw satin ribbons in the colors of the sunset behind Fern Hill. She decked her dolls with scraps of bright cloth

236

from the store and sewed on bits of lace and beading until they resembled a pair of Queen Rosie Pitt's girls out for the Saturday promenade. "You mustn't spy on callers," Lucy told her. "If you want to watch for Mr. Fearing's carriage, stand up like a lady. Abel," she said to the boy sitting in her rocking chair, "have you no schoolwork to do? Why are you reading the *Alta?* When did you take to reading newspapers? I declare, you'd read the label on a bottle of liver compound for lack of anything else."

"My schoolwork's done. What does 'franchise' mean?"

"I don't rightly know. Something to do with privileges, I think. Why?"

"It says here the Franchise League of San Francisco wants Negroes to have the vote. If they're not slaves, Mama, why can't they vote?"

"Because it's the law. Men of color don't vote."

"Why?"

"People who aren't educated in politics shouldn't be allowed to vote. Ignorant folks will do whatever they're told to or paid to."

"Do the China boys vote?"

"No."

"Some of them must be educated. They read their queer newspaper."

"Who knows what it says? It's probably a lot of heathen gossip."

"Do Indians vote?"

"There are no Indians in San Francisco. Give me the *Alta,* please. I want to read it while I wait for Mr. Fearing."

Henry raised his glass to her. "To your health, my dear lady, and that of your captivating children. Silver horses, indeed!"

"Sometimes the things they say amaze even me. Especially Abel. Trying to keep up with that boy's mind is like chasing a running deer."

"Obviously he takes after his clever mother."

She studied the menu card. She was fast becoming familiar enough with foreign fare to identify the dishes offered her. Henry preferred German food, rich and heavy and accompanied by foaming amber beer. "Abel is his own little man," she replied, "far brighter than I."

"Nonsense. Did you read those figures I gave you on

the railroad that Wilson wants to build out of Sacramento?"

'I did, but I don't know what it has to do with us here."

"Expansion, my dear. Wilson, if he succeeds, will be shipping tons of freight daily from Sacramento up the American River to Negro Bar. It will be the signal for an outburst of rail lines here in California. Possibly a very shrewd investment."

"It all sounds a bit far-fetched to me. I prefer to have my funds where I can see them."

"That's all well and good, but meanwhile your gold is gathering dust at Wells Fargo. Money that isn't working for you isn't serving its full purpose. Money has to circulate and flow, like water. Stagnant water's no good. But you dam up a little pool of money, save it until it reaches a serviceable level, then you let it flow out in the right direction at the right rate and you create power, just as you turn a waterwheel to power a gristmill."

"It's not power I'm after, Henry, only a bit of security."

"Money and power go hand-in-hand. You have one, you have the other."

She laughed at the notion. "I wouldn't know what to do with power."

"You wouldn't have to do a thing. It's not like money. You don't have to use it unless it's called for."

"My Pa was always suspicious of that sort of power, peerhaps because he had mortgages foreclosed on him more than once."

"But if it's you with the power, you're the one who does the foreclosing. You'd be quite safe, don't you see?"

"You make it all sound very appealing to a widow like me with children to provide for."

"There are other alternatives, of course . . . But your reputation is that of a woman who cares only for commerce." He set his beer down carefully and patted his lips with his napkin. "Surely you've considered marriage, Lucy."

"No," she confessed, "not really."

"But think of the alliance a smart woman like yourself might make with the right man. What an association! The combination of two minds with the same drive and resolve—there'd be nothing could stop us." He looked up quickly, realizing what he had said. "Pardon me, my dear. A too-eager slip of the tongue, I'm afraid."

"You flatter me, Henry," she said gently.

"Lucy, this city is the future. California's the future. My brother and I are convinced of it."

"You remind me of an elated child who's just been presented with a new set of blocks," she teased. "What will you build with all this power of yours, Henry?"

He glanced down at the table, then looked up at her with a hint of amusement in his eyes. "For you, my dear, nothing less than an empire would do." He reached across the table and laid his hand on hers.

"I'm afraid it's all I can do to manage what I already have. An empire is quite beyond me." Despite her protest, she made no move to draw her hand away from his.

Henry Fearing, charming though he might be, was not a man to air his thoughts without deliberation. Obviously, he saw in her an ambition as strong as his own. She turned this notion over and over in her head. She looked at it this way and that, like a miner holding a nugget to the sunlight, scrutinizing it, assessing the value of his find. It had once seemed quite sufficient for her just to survive, but she realized that was no longer the case. Something had changed. When, she wasn't sure. Perhaps the ready riches of the gold fever had affected her more than she'd thought. She was sure of one thing. She relished every scrap of talk among the Fearing brothers. She listened with rapt attention to their discussions, speaking only to interject a question when she failed to grasp a point. Neither Henry nor Albert concealed the fact that they considered her absorption a compliment. Not only was it flattering to have a lovely woman fascinated by their expertise, but Lucy was a willing acolyte. Their convictions became hers, and the prospect of boundless prosperity, something which had always seemed to her as unthinkable as flying, appeared not only to be possible but also exceedingly inviting. As her horizon enlarged, so did her ambition. Though she kept it to herself, she saw no reason why, woman or not, she couldn't play this game. That's what it was to men like Henry and Albert, a game. You placed your money here and there, withdrew it if it failed to pay and redoubled it where it reaped the greatest profit. The simplicity of this strategy struck her with the force of a Delphic revelation. She was not yet sure how she would apply this new lore. She was keenly aware of her own areas of ignorance and the need to invest prudently in a venture with little or no risk. But she was determined to play the game, and money, every dime of it she could save, was her ticket of admission.

Neither the bleak days of winter nor its raw winds and rains dampened her exhilaration. "What I think," Jack said, smiling, as he unloaded his bolts of cloth on the counter, "is that Page and Bacon made themselves a mistake. They should have hired you instead of Joe Mason. You may look like a woman, *ma chère,* but you got inside you a mind like a man. And since Henry's been paying court, you sound more like one of them Fearings every day. He's angling to make a partnership, you mark my words."

"Jack, please!" She inclined her head in the direction of Queen Rosie Pitt and a second customer, a small, primly dressed lady who was keeping the greatest possible distance between herself and Mrs. Pitt. "The partner I have is nuisance enough, thank you. Shall we tend to business?" She carried a bolt of Swiss muslin to Mrs. Pitt. "This is the finest we have. Feel how soft it is."

Queen Rosie bent close to her. "Confidentially, partners ain't worth the trouble. Had one myself, and all he ever did was drink up the profits. Go it alone, dearie. That's the best way. You take me, for instance. I got a solid business that don't depend on seasons or tides or weather. Not even this stuff," she gestured toward the downpour pelting against the window panes, "keeps the callers from visiting my boarders. Since I bought out my partner's share, I sleep like a baby, knowing things are in my own hands. Why, he gave me more grief than my young ladies ever have."

Lucy could not help liking Mrs. Pitt. She was a straightforward woman who, though tough as cowhide, was unusually benign for a woman of her calling. Under those quivering tides of tallow that rippled with each breath she drew, was a heart which, if not tender, was disarmingly sympathetic. "I'd say you were lucky, Mrs. Pitt. The weather plays havoc with our business, and I've heard some of your colleagues say the same."

"Who?" she demanded.

"Madame La Tour was saying just this morning—"

"That lazy French sow? She hasn't the slightest idea

how to run a successful house. It's the frosting does it, and she's too shiftless to tend the frosting. She'll be running cribs before long, that one."

Lucy nodded dumbly.

"Understand," Queen Rosie said, "the men come for the cake. It's the frosting that makes it extra sweet so they come back for more."

Lucy glanced over at French Jack and the other woman. They were deep in conversation over a length of silk braid. "I'm afraid I don't understand," she murmured, embarrassed.

"Quality, Pastora. The best food and drink. Beautiful surroundings. Music. Luxury most of these fellows have never known. My girls dress like royalty, and there's never a pout or frown on their faces. I train them to smile and listen and act interested in their gentlemen. At my place, a man gets more than he comes for. He gets to feel like a king."

"And the girls?" Lucy couldn't help asking. "What do they get?"

"Trouble and money," she answered brusquely. "If they're smart, they forget the trouble and keep the money."

Money, thought Lucy, the quintessential element by which this city and everyone in it functioned. She sat next to Henry Fearing on the sofa, listening to Albert's latest proposal. A fire danced on the hearth, punctuating the conversation with lively outbursts of crackling. The plan, as Albert conceived it, was nothing less than grandiose. He and Henry would open their own bank. They were skilled in the management of their own funds, so why shouldn't they be equally successful in the management of others'? Their reputation in financial circles was impeccable and surely would attract business. And since there was a great deal of money to be made in investments, why shouldn't they have a great deal more money to invest, bringing them even more abundant profits? Wells and Fargo, Wright, the Seligman brothers had all founded California banking houses. Eastern firms like Page and Bacon and Adams and Company had rushed to open local offices. Even the European Rothschilds had an agent in San Francisco. The city was growing as fast as men could make their way west. What better time to set sail than on a rising tide of population? Over the next few months, said Albert, they would gradually sell off all of their present investments on which they could make a profit, and their holdings in Missouri would be transferred in cash to the Page and Bacon branch here.

Lucy was overawed, listening to such talk of lofty figures and vast sums. Never, in her most extravagant fancies, could she have pictured herself here in the presence of two such powerful men, accepted into their confidence, a party to the creation of even greater power. A palpable thrill spread through her, like the sudden warmth of stepping from the shadows into blazing sunlight. Henry had been right. There was nothing at all wrong with power as long as you were the one to wield it. It occurred to her that Pa, good man though he was, might have been more than a little envious of such authority.

"Lucy?" Henry reached over and brushed her hair from her cheek. "You haven't made a sound. Have we put you to sleep?"

"Far from it. I'm all but struck dumb with wonder at the scheme. You make it sound so simple."

"And it is," Albert put in.

"Would you care to consider, quite impartially, mind you," Henry cautioned, "buying some shares in the bank? I daresay we might allow a few special friends to join our venture."

"Do you mean it? Henry, of course I would. I can't think of anyone whose judgment I trust more than yours and Albert's."

"It's at least four months away. We could open our doors in April, if all goes according to plan."

"Gentlemen, gentlemen," Polly Fearing chided as she entered the room, "do let's change the subject. One more word about this project of yours, and my ears will fall off. We asked Lucy here to celebrate her birthday, not to have a business meeting."

"Really, Polly," Lucy replied, "I'm enjoying myself. I've even decided to invest in the bank. Does it have a name?" she asked Henry.

"We hadn't come to that." He smiled. "Would you like to take a try at it?"

She thought. "Fearing and Fearing, of course."

"You can do better than that," Albert said. "Besides, you left out yourself and the other investors."

"Fearing and Company," Polly suggested.

"The Bay City Bank," Lucy said.

"The Bay City Bank," Albert repeated. "Henry, how does that strike you?"

"Very stylish. And with a definite appeal to civic pride. There isn't a greenhorn in San Francisco who doesn't want to be thought of as an old-timer. They want to be a part of the bay city, and they'll want to be a part of The Bay City Bank. I don't know which pleases me more, my dear, gazing at that pretty blonde head of yours or knowing what's inside it."

"Do let's get to the presents," Polly urged. She drew a small box from her skirt pocket. "Here, my dear. From Albert and Joe and myself. Joe sends apologies that he couldn't join us."

As Lucy opened the box, she caught her breath in pleasure. "Polly! It's much too grand a gift." She fingered the gold locket and chain, holding them up to shine in the lamplight.

"Nonsense. Do put it on."

"Here." Henry opened the clasp and circled the chain around her neck. "Let's have a look. Most attractive," he pronounced. "And now, my dear . . ." He reached into his coat. "My gift to you."

"What on earth is it?" She unfolded the paper in her hands and scanned it, puzzled.

"He wouldn't breathe a word of it to us," Polly said. "I'm burning with curiosity."

Lucy looked up at Henry, scarcely knowing what to say. "How did you ever do this? I'm flabbergasted! Such an expensive gesture. How can I accept it?"

"With a smile, my dear. It's yours."

"For pity's sake, what is it?" Albert demanded. "Aren't you going to let us enjoy it too?"

"The store." Lucy gazed at him dazedly, a smile spreading slowly over her face. "The deed to the store. Jack and I tried to buy it months ago, but the owner was adamant about not selling it. I can't imagine how you did this, Henry, but I shall be grateful to you forever for such a gift."

"Connections, my dear Lucy. All things are possible with the right connections."

243

"Have we a drop of wine, Polly?" Albert inquired. "I think this calls for a toast. To a woman of property."

Lucy savored the phrase. She spent more and more time entertaining the vision of herself as a person of affluence and authority. She tried on the image in her mind, as she might visualize a new gown. And each time she did, the idea seemed closer to the reality, until she found the fit quite comfortable and, indeed, altogether becoming to her. No longer did she feel intimidated on her weekly visits to the Express Building to deposit her funds. The banking department of the busy Wells Fargo office now seemed less a hallowed enigma than a familiar workaday establishment whose operations she understood as well as any of the austere clerks behind its dark wooden counter. Her blue eyes swept the room, taking in the business being transacted there, and she found herself looking forward to the day when she would stroll into The Bay City Bank, her bank, be greeted personally by Joe Mason and make her way to the counter, nodding graciously to the employees. The glow of Wells Fargo's polished brass weighing scales, the scratch of pens on ledgers, the clink of coins being counted, hinting of the vast, unseen riches of the place, all stirred in Lucy a heady sense of anticipation. It was within her power to become a woman of wealth, a force to be reckoned with. And having vicariously enjoyed such prestige, thanks to Henry and Albert Fearing, she became increasingly determined to acquire it for herself.

The change in her outlook did not go unnoticed. "Pastora," Jack teased her, "what are you going to do when there ain't no place higher to set your sights? I see you poking your nose into everybody's business. You ask the bookseller about his profits; you want to know the barber's rent; you talk pidgin to the China boys putting up new buildings, asking how much they're costing. Hell, you even got the brass to ask Queen Rosie how her business works. What are you fixing to do, lady, buy San Francisco?"

"Only a bit of it," Lucy replied airily. "And as for Mrs. Pitt, for your information her line of work turns out to be the most lucrative of all, short of the grog shops and gaming halls."

"I'll be damned if I can't hear you counting up sums in

244

your head twenty-four hours a day. What you going to do with all this money you're dreaming?"

"Who knows?" She laughed. "Perhaps buy a place in the country where the children can keep horses and ride. Wouldn't that be elegant? Isaac Woods, the banker from Adams and Company, was telling me he has a farm down on the peninsula, a pretty spread called Woodside Dairy. Doesn't that sound nice?"

"Seems to me you got awful big dreams for a little lady."

"Listen to me, Jack," she said, suddenly earnest. "I never knew before what it is to have the luxury of dreams. Everything I've ever done, I've done out of necessity. I had to make the best life I could for myself and the children. Well, what's happened is that the best has gotten better than I ever thought possible. I see opportunities I never conceived in my wildest fancies. And by heaven, I intend to use and enjoy them, or my name isn't Lucy Cordelia Curtis Bates."

He gazed at her a moment before he spoke. "Pastora," he said evenly, "not for anything in the world would I step in your way. I pity the fool who tries to stop you."

By the beginning of February, Henry and Albert had consolidated their wealth safely inside the granite walls of the Parrott Building which housed Page and Bacon. Worldly though they might be, both brothers were as eager as small boys to set about what Albert called "our greatest adventure." Talk was buzzing around that the Fearings were about to use their fortune to score an impressive *coup*. Shipping lines, perhaps, were their target. Hotels, thought some. No, said another report, they planned to take over the public coach lines and build a railroad on the peninsula.

"Such a flurry of gossip," Lucy said laughingly as she and the Fearings discussed these speculations. "I haven't heard anything like it since Honest Harry Meiggs slipped out of the bay on the wake of his worthless municipal warrants. People are on tenterhooks, waiting for your next move."

"No sense in showing our hand until the time is ripe," Albert told her.

"The city's awash with financial rumors," Henry said. "No use in stirring up more waves. In a few weeks The

245

Bay City Bank will present itself to the public as a *fait accompli.*"

"Some folks are saying that no investment is secure anymore." Lucy glanced from one brother to the other. "They say if Harry Meiggs couldn't make ends meet with his lumber and wharf and ships, nobody's safe. People are afraid to take risks."

Henry tamped his pipe. "A lot of businessmen were hurt by last year's decline, but that's history now. Poor Harry overextended himself. Given a month or two, the talk will die down."

Albert agreed. "The marketplace isn't that much different from a small hick town. When life goes along too quietly, folks start spreading rumors just to create a little diversion."

"Then there's nothing to worry about?"

Henry took her hand in his. "Lucy, rest that pretty head. When poor Harry bolted, it was as much a blow to the city's morale as its finances. What's needed to turn the tide is a show of faith, and that's what we'll give 'em." He knocked the bowl of his pipe against the table beside him for emphasis. "All you should be concerned with is whether we should attend the show at Maguire's theatre or the Metropolitan next week. You choose which."

Nothing pleased him more than introducing her to the amusements and experiences he took so readily for granted. Henry's world was a never-ending feast of delights, and Lucy was rapidly acquiring a taste for pleasures she had hardly known existed.

"You must have this, my dear." Henry turned from her and signaled the clerk in the china shop.

"But it's much too expensive!"

"It's an exquisite example of Sèvres. It deserves someone who'll appreciate it." He motioned to the tea set. The clerk nodded sagely and lifted it from its display case.

"Really, Henry, you mustn't be so extravagant. That tea set is money marching out of your bank."

"Don't take it so seriously, my dear." He laid a hand against her cheek and bent close to her, whispering, "I can make money, but I can't make Sèvres. If it pleases you, you shall have it."

"I shan't admire another thing, not so much as a round red apple, until the bank has opened. That's more important than anything else. I worry sometimes. People seem skittish about finances these days."

"Rubbish," he said cheerfully. "Don't you listen to a word of it."

Talk persisted that the business troubles rumored in the East might be spreading westward. But the East Coast was a world away, Lucy reasoned, and tales bred on the sea journey as prolifically as the rats in the holds of the ships that brought them dockside. Henry and Albert were far more schooled than she in such matters and so, as Henry had instructed, she paid scant attention to the prophets of doom. She had little use for the nay-sayers of the world. She'd learned from experience that an obstinate and, on occasion, ungrounded optimism was indispensable to making one's way in life. "I was not born," she told Jack, "to go about shrouded in gloom, like some of those fools."

"Pastora, maybe they're just cautious. You got a rash streak in you. You got to admit that."

"What of it? Without it, we couldn't be where we are today. You're hardly the one to lecture me on prudence, the way you gamble."

He waved the suggestion away with one hand. "Me, I pay a little for an evening's entertainment. I figure I come out even in the end. But I don't never risk big money. I'm a player, Pastora, not an idiot."

"And you think I am?" she shot back.

"Non. But I think you ain't yet wise enough to judge if Henry and Albert are doing the right thing at the right time."

"You're as dreary as those confounded rains, but I'll be hanged if I'll let you throw a wet blanket over my fires."

Lucy broke off as the door opened and a diminutive, coal-black figure stood shivering in a small puddle of rainwater. "What is it you want, child?"

The boy extracted an envelope from inside his threadbare jacket and held it out to her.

"For me? Mrs. Bates?"

He nodded solemnly.

She took it. "Wait a moment." She turned to the cash box.

"No, ma'am. The gen'man, he paid me."

She smiled. "Well, then, take a couple of pieces of toffee with you." She pressed the sweets into his hand.

"Thank y' kindly." He pocketed them quickly and was gone. Saint Valentine's Day. Look at this, Jack." She gaily flourished the lacy paper card painted with a small bouquet of forget-me-nots. "It seems I've an admirer."

"As if you didn't know who."

She opened the card and read the words written there in Henry's elegantly flowing script. At length, she looked up. "Sakes alive, the man's determined to make me his wife."

"You're blushing, Pastora." Jack grinned at her. "If you ask me, that's the one offer he's made that you *should* take up. You ain't going to do better, you know."

It was true that few men would let her have her head as Henry did. Moreover, he even respected what was inside it. He was a good man, and if he was slightly staid, he was still a thousand times more worthwhile than a flamboyant fly-away fellow like Caleb Bates. And what he lacked in ardor, he more than made up for in refinement and intellect. Lucy had grown increasingly attached to the Fearings, and as she had looked down at the watercolor bouquet of blue flowers on Henry's card, she realized that they were very much a part of her life now, and that she liked it that way.

"Henry, dear," she said with a laugh, "you should have seen that poor, shivering pickaninny when he arrived with your card this afternoon. The little thing was drenched. Such a pathetic messenger to bring me such a joyous proposal."

He hardly heard a word she was saying. His menu card lay unopened on the table in front of him. "As soon as The Bay City Bank is operating without a hitch, I'll be able to take some time away. What do you say to a trip to Saint Louis to meet the rest of the family? Polly can look after the children."

"You're way ahead of me, Henry. You must give me some time to broach the subject to Beth and Abel. And I'd have to find someone to help Jack while we're gone."

"When shall we break the news?"

She thought a moment. "Give me at least a week to find a suitable time to talk to the children. This is going to mean a big change for them."

"Today is Wednesday. At dinner, a week from Sunday. How does that sound?"

Lucy raised her wineglass. "A week from Sunday."

Whether it was wine or happiness, she didn't know, but she felt a pleasant flush of warmth and realized that she was smiling inanely at a total stranger across the room.

It was closing time at the store. Lucy locked the cash box in its drawer and shut the ledger. She glanced at the clock on the wall. Henry would be arriving in two hours to take her on their customary Saturday night outing at the theatre. If she hurried, there would be time to read the *Alta* before making supper for Beth and Abel. She extinguished the lamps and made her way to the door by the faint glow coming through the windows from the street lighting. "I'm sorry," she said as a woman bustled toward her in the February dusk, "we're closed."

"Lucy, it's me, Polly Fearing."

"Polly, dear, what on earth brings you out alone at this hour? Do come upstairs and have a cup of tea. It's too chilly to be standing out here."

"I mustn't. The gentlemen are meeting now at my house. Henry asked me to come to you right away to offer his apologies. He won't be able to go to the play tonight. There's some sort of crisis brewing." She drew her cape closer about her against the damp night air.

"Is it serious?"

"I don't know. The *Oregon* made port today with bad news. The eastern office of Page and Bacon has failed."

"Come inside," Lucy said as she unlocked the door and drew Polly into the shop. "What does that mean here in San Francisco?"

"Mr. Haight seems to think it won't mean anything, so long as people keep their wits about them."

"He's the head of the branch here. He ought to know."

"But Albert's not so sure reason will prevail. He says folks are restless as wild horses lately, what with all the silly rumors around."

"Can't Henry and Albert withdraw their funds until this blows over?"

"Mr. Haight has begged them not to. If the other depositors learned that such a large sum had been taken out, they'd probably panic. And both Albert and Henry feel duty-bound to help. Page and Bacon is in the family back East. They must do all they can for the company here."

Lucy peered at the woman's face in the pale light from

the gas lamp outside on the corner. "Polly, are you worried?"

She hesitated. "I'm not sure. I know so little about this sort of thing. Some of the other bankers have already arrived at the house. Isaac Woods is there, and William Sherman from Lucas, Turner and Company."

"Mr. Woods is a clever man, and Henry tells me Captain Sherman's judgment is very reliable. Don't be upset, Polly. I'm sure that, between them, the men will shore up Page and Bacon, if that's what's needed. Tell Henry I understand about this evening. He's not to give it a thought."

By Monday, it was apparent that Albert's fears had been well grounded. Word of Page and Bacon's failure spread quickly. The mood of the city was dark with apprehension. The *Alta* pointed out that the two banking houses were separate and that the failure in the East need have little effect here. But this appeal to reason went ignored. Public trust in the city's finances had been shaken by the Harry Meiggs scandal. Now, four months later, it appeared to be tottering. Lucy listened gravely to the rumblings. In the store, the streets, the marketplace, clusters of anxious people could talk of nothing else. Page and Bacon's eastern office had speculated heavily in a risky railroad venture and collapsed. A man could no longer put his faith in banks, much less his money.

"Jack, what do you think? Should we take everything out of Wells Fargo?"

"Have you talked with Henry?" he asked her.

"I haven't seen him. I expect he and Albert are too involved in this to think of anything else."

"They ain't alone. Ain't a one of us not feeling it. I say you and me, we hold fast. Wells Fargo ain't Page and Bacon."

"But already some folks are lining up outside the other banks, too."

By midweek, the lines were longer. What had begun as a trickle of worried depositors was threatening to become a flood. Then came an announcement from Page and Bacon in the *Chronicle*. " 'We must suspend,' " Lucy read. " 'We cannot raise coin on our bills. The coin is not in the country.' " She looked up at Jack. "It's gone," she said quietly. "What will happen now? Have you heard any word about the Fearings?"

"Only that they was working with the other bankers to keep things afloat. I'm going down to Wells Fargo. Biggs there is a friend. He'll give me the truth."

"I'm coming with you. Help me close up."

They could hear the clamor from Montgomery Street before they turned the corner. Two blocks south, the street became a maelstrom of humanity. From every direction, mobs surged toward the banking houses in a stampede to retrieve their money.

At the entrance to Adams and across the way at Wells Fargo stood guards with shotguns, holding back the angry throngs. A well-dressed woman, her face contorted with rage, tears streaming down her cheeks, was begging the guard at Adams to admit her ahead of the others. When he refused, she spat in his face. An old man clutching an empty basket leaned dazedly against the gray granite blocks of the Parrott Building, blood flowing from his nose and staining his grizzled beard with scarlet. A pair of toughs pushed Lucy roughly aside. "The vaults!" she heard one shout. "Go for the vaults!" He waved a funny sack in the air, like a battle flag.

Jack put a protective arm around her. "Let's go back. Ain't nothing we can do here now."

The heavy-set man beside him overheard and seized his arm. "The devil you say. I'll get my gold back if I have to use this on every one of them bastards at Adams." He brandished his pistol in Jack's face. "I crawled on my knees in half the rivers in California to get that stuff, and before I'm through, those bastards will crawl to me."

Jack turned from him without a reply. Stunned and silent, Lucy walked with him back to the locked store.

XIII

THE NEXT day, the city lay paralyzed. The Adams, Wright, Wells Fargo and Robinson banks had suspended payment and closed. Ugly crowds roamed the streets. It seemed the merest shift in the wind might whip them to havoc. Lucy and Jack drew the heavy iron shutters over the two shop windows and went home. Lucy stood gazing down from her view on the third floor, numbly watching the confusion in the street below.

Beth broke the silence. "Mama, why are those ladies crying? Are the men angry with them?"

"People are afraid. They show it in different ways."

Abel closed his book and rested his elbows on the dining table. "Mama, is my money from Castalia still at Wells Fargo?"

"Yes."

"How do we know they haven't spent it?"

"We must trust their good judgment. No bank wants to fail, son. I'm sure they're doing their best by us. Don't worry yourself about it."

"I'm eleven years old, Mama. I could go to work."

"At what? Catching rats for the grog shops? I won't have it."

"I was thinking I could be a newsboy."

"Do we need money, Mama?" Beth looked up at her, her dark eyes grave. "I still have Mrs. Pitt's ten-dollar piece."

Lucy stroked the child's head. "We'll survive. Wells Fargo is sure to pay some portion on the dollar. You let the grown-ups work things out. You children needn't fret."

252

Sunday services were somber. After the benediction, the parishioners walked silently from the church and straggled homeward, too preoccupied for conversation. Finally, Lucy could stand the suspense no longer. "Children," she told them, "stay inside until I return. Don't open the door for anyone. I'll be back as soon as possible."

She walked up the hill to Kearny and turned right, without stopping for those who raised their hats or nodded to their storekeeper. She paused only at Washington Street, where a ragged youngster was hawking a pile of newspapers nearly as big as himself. Lucy smiled at him, thinking of Abel, and bought the *Alta*. She sought the lee of a corner building and once out of the wind, turned the pages rapidly. Her breath caught in her throat at the sight of the announcement. "Wells, Fargo & Co. have completed a balance of their accounts this day . . ." She read on and suddenly, giddy with relief, found herself leaning against the side of the building, laughing and gasping at once. Wells Fargo was solid. She was safe.

At the corner of Pike Street was a large carriage, its driver loading two small well-worn valises into the boot. Queen Rosie Pitt stood beside it, clasping to her bosom a young woman whose bright coppery curls were held tightly in place by a Leghorn bonnet. She released the girl from her mighty embrace and saw her into the carriage. The driver snapped his reins, and the carriage moved away.

"Pastora." Queen Rosie occupied the full width of the walkway. "How are you faring?"

"Well, thank heavens. And you?"

"I've lost Iris. These girls, they don't stay put for long." She shook her head mournfully, her jowls waggling like a wattle. "Lord knows where I'll find another like her. A red-haired Jewess is as precious as a ruby. She can name her own price, that treasure."

"Mrs. Pitt," she said, impatient to be going, "I'm sure it's no cause for tears. Really."

Queen Rosie wheezed and fumbled at her clothing. "I must have left my handkerchief behind."

"Take mine." Lucy gave it to her. "You can return it another time."

Mrs. Pitt pressed it to her pudgy tear-stained cheeks. "It's just—everything. Everything at once. All slipping

253

away like water through your fingers. I was with Adams and Company," she said by way of explanation.

"Were you able to save anything?"

"Hardly a mite. Just when I was fixing to move to a bigger place, too. You can see it from here." Her hand shaking, she pointed toward a wide, stately brick building, its door and shutters painted green. "Ain't no way I could pay for the renovation now, not and keep a quality house at the same time, God help me."

"You have my sympathy, Mrs. Pitt. I wish you good luck." She circumvented the weeping woman and hurriedly made her way to the Fearings'.

The housekeeper, Octavia, opened the door.

"I've come unannounced, I know, but I must see Mr. Henry. Is he in?"

She led Lucy to the sitting room. "It's Miz' Bates, Mr. Henry."

Despite the overcast weather outside, the lamps in the sitting room stood unlit. The fire in the grate had dwindled to coals, and the room was chilly. In the gloom, Henry Fearing sat slumped forward on the sofa, his hands between his knees. He glanced up as Lucy's name was spoken. For a moment, he appeared confused. His face was ashy. Lucy struck a match and lit the lamp on the table beside him. "I hadn't heard from you. I was worried."

He looked up at her. His eyes were red with fatigue.

Lucy seated herself next to him and took his hand in hers. "Strange, isn't it," she said softly, "how misfortune lies in ambush behind all our brightest hopes. It was like that when my Ma and Pa and Willie died. Everything looked so rosy for us, and suddenly there was nothing and nobody left."

Henry cleared his throat. "It's never happened to me. Small things, minor calamities, but never anything like this. I don't know . . ." He bowed his head. "I don't seem able to cope."

"How bad is it?"

"There are those worse off. Isaac Woods has had to surrender everything to his creditors. He's ruined, left with only the clothes on his back."

"And you and Albert?"

"We have this house, but it's Albert's. There are some few investments we never could sell off. Almost worthless stuff. It didn't seem to matter then."

254

"And from Page and Bacon?"

"Scarcely anything. Perhaps enough to keep us going for a month, maybe two." He gazed blankly into the dark fireplace.

She held his hand tightly. "Henry, you're forgetting something. The store, Pastora and French, is yours. You bought the building."

"It was a gift to you."

"You paid for it. And if it belongs to me, then I have the right to make someone else a gift of it, too."

"No, I couldn't—"

"You're upset, Henry, but you're not an irrational man. Surely you'll accept your investment back, at least until you're solvent again. I thought we were friends. Wouldn't you accept the gesture if it came from Captain Sherman or one of your other friends?"

"I'm not irrational, but I'm not a beggar. I don't know." He rubbed his eyes wearily. "No." He stiffened suddenly and sat upright. "Never. Not from you. Not from a woman."

"But what's wrong with the store paying rent to you? We paid rent to the former owner, didn't we? It's yours," she repeated.

He would not hear of it. He rebuffed her arguments one by one.

"Where are Polly and Albert? I'm sure they'll be able to make you listen to reason."

"Albert's ill. Polly's upstairs with him."

"And Joe?"

"Asleep. He was exhausted."

"Henry," she said urgently, "don't refuse me out of pride. I thought we were too close for such a conceit to stand between us."

"I can't let you do it, Lucy. You've no estimate of your own situation. How do you know Wells Fargo will open its doors again?"

She unfolded the *Alta* and laid it on his lap. "See here. It says they'll open in only a few days."

He read the notice and drew a deep breath. "I'm glad for you."

"Henry, please, just promise me you'll consider my offer."

But she heard no more from him. When almost a week had passed and Henry's silence began to weigh on her,

Lucy set aside her pride and returned to the house on Stockton Street. If necessary, she would plead with this hard-headed, high-minded man whose stubborn dignity had touched her so deeply. They were, indeed, alike, she and Henry Fearing. He had been right in seeing in her a match for his own determination. They were a pair of mules, the two of them, but once joined, they'd move mountains together. She had only to make him see the sense of her suggestion.

"He's gone," Polly repeated, scanning Lucy's face to see if she had grasped her words.

Lucy stared at her without expression.

"Please," Polly said, leading her to a chair, "sit down."

After a moment she said, "Why, Polly? Why did he go? Why didn't he tell me?"

"He's too proud for his own good. He felt you had offered him charity. I told him he was wrong. Whatever money I have is Albert's, too. I told him you were only doing the same, married or not, but he wouldn't listen."

"Where did he go?"

"He didn't say. I'm not sure he cared. He just had to be gone from this place. Some men aren't able to accept defeat."

"But it would only have been temporary. He knew I'd help."

"He'd never have let you. Money's life's blood to Henry. He couldn't live like a leech. Albert's the more resilient. Henry's younger, and he's always been protected. Perhaps that wasn't for the best, finally, not when it hurts innocent people who care for him so much."

What Polly said was true. Lucy had felt more for Henry Fearing than she'd permitted herself to admit. She had thought, when she left Castalia, that she had locked a door behind her. But slowly, gently, Henry had coaxed that door ajar. Now, suddenly, it had been seized from her hands and slammed shut once more, leaving her alone outside of the inviting warmth she had glimpsed so briefly. She had allowed herself to care for Henry, and only now did she begin to comprehend how much. Perversely, it was her anger that enlightened her. She had cared for Henry, but he had cared more for his financial position. In the end, he had let it stand between them. Bitterly, she acknowledged that it was his loyalty to the bank

256

which had destroyed him. If only he had shown such a loyalty to her, she could have set things right again.

"Pastora," Jack told her, "you got dealt a bad hand."

"I'll survive," she said tersely. "Reed Pierce was the first to point that out to me."

"It ain't easy to be alone."

"I've been alone before."

"Me too, Pastora, but it ain't no pleasure. I'm sorry this happened. Henry was a good man."

"Stop talking about Henry," she said harshly. "He's gone, and I'll be damned if I'll waste my time brooding about it."

Jack glanced up at the vehemence of her words. He looked at her quizzically, saying nothing.

"For good or bad, my life is my own once more," she went on. "And I intend to do as I please with it, without having to depend on Henry or anyone else. He was a fool to leave. I could have helped him. Now, by God, I shall help myself, and if by chance Mister Henry Fearing ever returns, I guarantee you he'll be struck dumb by my proficiency."

"Lucy," Jack said quietly, "to hate ain't the opposite of love. Hate still cares."

"Go to the devil!" She drew in her breath sharply as the door to the shop opened and pretended to busy herself at her desk.

Jack nodded to Mrs. Pitt. "I'll be at the docks," he said as he left.

"Here you are." Queen Rosie took Lucy's linen handkerchief from her drawstring bag. "Freshly laundered and ironed. I'm sorry it took so long, but I've been trying to gather my wits about me."

"I'm glad to know someone has," Lucy replied tartly.

A resigned laugh rumbled from Mrs. Pitt. "Folks losing their heads left and right. Y'hear about Isaac Woods? Gone. Vanished. Looks like the poor sap got himself up as a woman and boarded an outbound ship. They found the Adams and Company books floating in the bay. Some of the pages missing, too."

Lucy sat down in the desk chair, shaking her head. "It seems there isn't anyone or anything left to depend on. I liked the man . . ."

"Here now, you're as glum as I was when you saw me

last. You cheered me up, you know. It's not often a lady like yourself would stop to speak to me in public."

"I'm happy to see you feeling better."

"The way I see it, I'll just have to work twice as hard —the girls too, if they want to stay in a fine place like mine. That grand house is still for sale, though Lord knows who'll buy. Ain't nobody buying these days and nobody giving credit."

"And businesses closing everywhere you look."

"Not mine, Pastora. Ain't no business like it. No matter how much I sell, there's more where that came from. How you going to beat that?"

"Could you wait a moment, Mrs. Pitt?" Lucy rose as an elderly lady entered with a younger facsimile of herself, obviously a daughter. She waited on them while Mrs. Pitt inspected several bolts of damask.

When they had gone, Mrs. Pitt pointed to a deep red bolt of cloth. "That's the stuff I wanted for my parlor sofas in the new place. Elegant, ain't it," she said sadly.

"Tell me something." Lucy seated herself once again at her desk. "If Adams hadn't failed, how much of a risk would you have been taking, moving into the larger building?"

"Oh, land!" Her laugh came again like muffled thunder. "None at all. I expect it's been the same since the beginning of time. Gentlemen want companions. Ain't nothing going to stop them, neither. Not even hard times like this. Sometimes they need the amusement even more when things are bad. And like I said, I ain't going to run out of what I sell."

"Tell me more," Lucy prodded her. "Can you give me a detailed estimate of your monthly cash outlay?" She dipped her pen in the inkwell.

Queen Rosie hesitated. She regarded Lucy with a mixture of confusion and skepticism.

"Please. A business with a guaranteed profit like yours is extraordinary."

"Well," Mrs. Pitt began uncertainly, "there's the rent, of course. Then there's fuel and food and liquor and linens. The percentage for the boarders, based on their work. The professor at the piano and the servants."

Lucy's pen scratched rapidly on the paper in front of her.

The wide brick house with its green door and shutters

was set back from Pike Street behind a low iron fence and a small, neatly plotted flower garden. Behind it, on Dupont Street, was a covered carriage entrance. It was a sizeable property, the main building itself extending almost all the way from one street to the other. The gentleman who showed Lucy through the warren of rooms pointed out its excellent possibilities as a rooming house. She nodded in agreement. "It's quite suitable. I'll give it some consideration."

The house sold for a good deal less than its worth. As for the required renovations, labor was cheap that summer. Even with the new gold strike on the Kern River, businesses continued to fail.

Though the profits of Pastora and French slackened during the months that followed, they were profits nonetheless. And the income from Mrs. Pitt's was as steady and substantial as she had promised. Lucy was developing more respect for Queen Rosie's judgment than for the opinions of those upright individuals who publicly held the portly madam in contempt, though their horses knew by habit the well-trodden way to her Dupont Street entrance. She had a new regard for the hard-headed madams of Pike Street and its environs, and they, in turn, sensing a certain shift in her sympathies, seemed pathetically eager to count as a friend this decent, hard-working widow with her two handsome children.

"What do you think Belle Cora gave me, Jack?" Lucy said. "Fifty dollars for the Orphans' Asylum! Won't Polly Fearing be thrilled?"

"Better you don't tell her it come from Charlie Cora's woman."

" 'Charlie Cora's woman,' why must you always call her that? Belle's a charming creature."

Jack grunted.

"Admit it, she's a beauty. Such lovely creamy skin and hazel eyes. You know you like brunettes, Jack," she teased, "and Belle's about the prettiest brunette around, except perhaps for Bethie."

"Lucy! Don't you go speaking about Belle and Bethie in the same sentence! What's happened to your senses? What will folks say if they know you got friends like Queen Rosie and Belle?"

"The devil take them all. What do I care for their opinions? Here comes Polly," she said, spying her through the window. "Now not a word about the money."

A smile spread over Polly's face as she gazed into the heavy box filled with gold coins. "I don't know how you did it. Over three hundred dollars, and in times like these."

"Generous friends," Lucy answered. "They knew it was for a good cause. Polly, please tell me, has there been any word of Henry?"

She shook her head. "I pray he's safe and well. I only regret that foolish pride of his that keeps him away."

"We all have our regrets," Lucy replied softly.

"You have nothing to be sorry for, Lucy."

"No. Perhaps I never made it clear to him how much he meant to me." She caught Jack looking at her and changed the subject. "Do come for tea on Sunday, Polly. Perhaps I'll have some more donations for you by then."

Jack did that often, Lucy realized as she ushered Polly to the door. Frequently she would turn around to speak to him and discover him staring at her again, studying her behind her back. It irritated her, and as she closed the door behind Polly she said quietly, "Jack, it makes me quite uncomfortable to feel I'm under constant observation. What interests you so?"

He shrugged.

"Why do I find you looking at me as though I were a stranger?"

"You've changed."

"I have? How?"

"I ain't sure." He shook his head thoughtfully. "You're here, same as always, but there's times I feel like you've moved away. Inside your head, you ain't where you used to be."

"And where, pray tell, do you think I am?"

"I don't know. Someplace out of range."

She gave him an exasperated look. "Out of range of what?"

"Where you was. Who you was."

"If I didn't know better, I'd say you'd been drinking."

He frowned as though vaguely troubled, then turned and went about his business in silence.

If anything, thought Lucy, it was Jack's behavior that was peculiar. He talked as though she had somehow strayed beyond his reach. It was nonsense, of course, nothing more than a quirk of his imagination. She chose to ignore it.

"That was some good pork roast, Pastora." Jack laid his napkin on the table.

His appetite, she observed, was unaffected by his notions about her behavior. "It was the least I could do, after you entertained the children all day," she replied.

"May I have another piece of cake, Mama?" Beth helped herself without waiting for a reply.

"Jack, will you take us to the theatre again next Saturday?" Abel asked him.

"Don't be rude, child—Listen!"

"It's the Big Six bell!" Abel leapt from his chair.

"Where do you think you're going?"

"Let me go see. Mama, please. Lillie Hitchcock's mother lets her go to all the fires."

"Lillie Hitchcock is the pet of Company Five. You are a young man who should be helping his sister clear the table."

"It's a big one," Jack said. "Hear all them bells."

"All right," Lucy relented, "but hurry back. It's nearly eight o'clock."

He returned just as Jack was leaving, trudging up the stairs, looking crestfallen. "There wasn't any fire."

"Why were the bells ringing?"

"There was a shooting down the street near the Blue Wing Saloon. Someone named Charlie Cora shot the marshal, General Richardson. Who are they, Mama?"

"Never mind. Jack," she said, "you know Charlie. Could he do that?"

"Don't ask me." He shrugged. "Maybe they was drunk. The general don't hold his liquor too good."

"Poor Mrs. Richardson. Poor Belle."

"They said they were going to lynch him," Abel continued. "Is there any more cake left?"

Though Lucy knew Charlie Cora only by sight, she followed his fate over the passing weeks with more than a casual interest. According to the newspapers, two days before the shooting, General and Mrs. Richardson had stalked out of the American Theatre in a huff after discovering that they were seated next to Cora, the gambler, and his mistress, the scarlet Belle. Presumably, the general and Charlie had made peace over drinks the follow-

261

ing night. But the next evening, walking together down the street, they'd had words again, and before anyone really knew what had happened, the general was dead and people were shouting for vengeance. Already there were rumors of reorganizing the old Vigilance Committee in the interests of justice and public safety.

Lucy was suspicious of this sudden epidemic of civic virtue. "People have been angry and restless since the bank panic," she told Polly Fearing. "They mutter about crime and corruption and blame the government or the rich or anyone else. Then something like this happens, and they focus all their rage on Charlie Cora. Who knows he wasn't trying to defend himself?"

"But the man's reputation—"

"Makes him an easy scapegoat. Charlie Cora's a gambler, and his woman's a madam. Believe me, Polly, if General Richardson had put a bullet through Charlie first, some way would be found to exonerate him."

"What's got you so fired up about defending this Cora fellow?"

"It's all the talk about another Vigilance Committee."

Polly frowned. "I don't like the sound of it any more than you do. When men take the law into their own hands, they're no better than the chaps they're after."

"Worse," said Lucy, "because there are more of them. Something happens to men when they become a mob. I know. I've seen it."

What she did not tell Polly was that these rumblings of rectitude gave her good cause for alarm. With the purchase of the property on Pike Street, Lucy had placed herself in a vulnerable position, and the popular vilification of Charlie Cora was, to her, not without its significance.

Despite the public furor, Belle rose a notch in Lucy's estimation. She spent every waking hour and every penny she possessed working for Charlie's release. "They say," Polly reported one day, "that woman's tried to bribe the jury." Perhaps it was true, but all that happened was that they failed to reach a verdict. Charlie Cora was held over for a second trial.

" 'Rejoice, Ye gamblers and harlots!' " Abel read from the pages of the *Bulletin*. "Why does it say that, Mama?"

"Because the editor is a sanctimonious windbag. He

thinks the world is divided between good and bad and fancies himself sitting at God's right hand. The man's a failed banker and an amateur editor."

"Why does he make you so angry?" Beth asked.

"Because he's a dangerous fool. The world isn't black and white. There's good in the worst of us and evil in the best. I long ago gave up passing judgment on others, and I shall expect the same generosity from you children."

"Criminals ought to be punished," Abel declared.

"By the law, not by public sentiment."

"Belle's a bad woman," Beth said soberly.

Lucy turned to her. "And what has she done to you that's so awful? As I recall, she once complimented you on your manners."

"But that's what everyone says about her."

"Listen to me, both of you. I don't give a fig for idle talk. Words are cheap. Live your life without hurting others, that's all I ask. And to blazes with what anyone says. Do you understand?"

They nodded in unison, two grave little faces bobbing. Only Abel seemed slightly puzzled at her outburst.

It was apparent that Abel was not only becoming a young man but a young man with ideas of his own. Though he kept his own counsel, he continued to read the vitriol published in the *Bulletin* by its editor, James King of William. He would listen to Lucy or Jack or Polly Fearing as they condemned the fanatics crying for another Vigilance Committee, his brown eyes glancing from face to face, without expression. Yet Lucy detected in him a certain chilly disdain for their views. How and when, she wondered, had he developed into such a rigid little moralist? She had tried to teach both children right from wrong but she had hardly expected Abel to seize upon her sermons like a determined dog clenching a bone in its teeth.

As silently unyielding as Abel was, so Beth was gay and tenderhearted. She was sociable, while he was studious. It must be his books, Lucy decided, that had fostered this slightly self-righteous streak. Never mind, he was already twelve, and in no time his thoughts would turn to courting young ladies. She devoutly hoped that day dawned before he became a pious little prig. Beth, on the other hand, would be a young woman in a few short years. She was already flighty as a butterfly, and Lucy wondered how on earth she would manage this dazzling, winsome creature who was, in her own way, just as head-strong as her brother.

"Well, Mama?" Abel stood at the top of the stairs, his arms akimbo.

"What sort of a greeting is that? Wash up. I'll have supper ready soon."

"Didn't you hear?" he said, a small note of defiance in his tone. "They shot James King of William."

"They what?" The fork fell from her hand onto the table. "Who did it?"

"The ex-convict, Casey."

"You said 'they.' "

He shrugged. "Casey's a crooked politician. They all wanted King dead. But he's still alive."

"Thank God."

"I thought you hated him."

"I disagree with him. What I hate is the prospect of a bunch of fanatics making a martyr of the man. His death would be all they'd need to turn this city into an armed camp."

It was. On Sunday morning at nine, she heard the bells begin to toll and watched from the window as grim-faced men marched past on their way to report for duty with the Vigilance Committee. She looked down at the procession in silence. They were said to be three thousand strong. Already they had been armed and drilled. She turned away. "Beth, tell Abel to hurry. You'll both be late to Sunday school."

Beth looked down guiltily. "He's gone, Mama. He left when you went into your bedroom to fetch your bonnet. He said they're going to storm the jail and get Cora and Casey."

She sat down and laid her bonnet in her lap.

"He said not to go after him," Beth added. "You wouldn't be safe."

"I'm not going. I'll wait here."

"Mama?" Beth touched her sleeve. "Why are you crying?"

Foolish as it seemed, she had thought Abel immune from that brutish lust for vengeance that crouched inside men, wanting only the excuse and the inducement to burst into wanton violence. But he was no different from

264

the others, this retiring, solemn-eyed child who had found it so easy to forget the past. Much of it was her fault, she knew. She had pressed him to forget, but there had been no choice. She wept with frustration and grief, knowing that she could not change him now.

"You made Mama cry," Beth told him accusingly when he finally returned.

He glanced at Lucy's swollen face. "I'm sorry," he mumbled. His cheeks were flushed with excitement. He strode around the room, his hands stuffed in his pockets, too worked up to sit down. "The bayonets!" he exclaimed. "Hundreds and hundreds of them gleaming in the air, and not a sound except for marching boots. The men formed a big open square in front of the jail and wheeled up a huge shiny brass cannon and trained it on the gates." He caught Lucy's expression and turned to Beth. "What crowds, Bethie! Thousands of people watching from the hills and the rooftops. I never heard such a hush. First they brought out Casey and then Charlie Cora—"

"No more," Lucy said quietly.

He looked at her for a moment, then turned and went into his room.

The day they buried James King of William, no business was conducted anywhere in the city. It seemed that scarcely a soul had bothered to heed the warnings of the handful of law-abiding men like the banker William Sherman, who opposed the Vigilance Committee. The tide had turned, and they were powerless against it. As the throngs joining in the funeral cortege crossed Sacramento Street, they could see, hanging motionless from the second story windows of Committee headquarters, the bodies of Jim Casey and Charlie Cora who had married Belle only hours before. Abel had gone to watch the procession, Lucy knew. She wondered how many more like it there would be and how many hangings would follow before he and the city lost their taste for blood.

Lucy hurried along the street. "Walk faster, Bethie. I've just this one errand to do and then I must relieve Jack at the store. I can't understand why you're so keen on coming with me to order a length of stovepipe." She took the child's hand as they turned onto Sacramento Street.

265

"Because I wanted to see Fort Gunnybags."

"Well!" Lucy stopped. "There it is, you foolish girl. You see, the Vigilance Committee has nothing but an old grain warehouse with a lot of sagging sandbags in front. It deserves that silly name." She skirted the head-high fortification, averting her eyes from the armed men standing guard on the roof.

"Wait." Beth tugged at her arm. "What's that?"

Lucy glanced toward the center of Davis Street. In the bright June sunshine, several workmen were hammering stair treads onto a high platform. She heard one of them curse and then laugh as he grasped a bruised thumb. Nearby, a man on a white horse sat surveying the construction. He was handsome, thought Lucy, fair-complected with a high, aristocratic forehead and a firm jaw. He had a full mouth which looked as though it might be quite appealing when smiling. But he gazed steadily at the structure, unsmiling, soothing his impatient mount.

"That, Bethie, is a scaffold for the hangings next Sunday. And the gentleman on the horse is Mr. William Coleman."

"He's the head of the Vigilance Committee? That man?"

Lucy nodded.

"But he looks like a nice man."

"They are all nice men." She turned away. "That's the pity."

Lucy grudgingly admitted to herself that the Committee had done some good. It had deported some unsavory characters, a few politicians among them, and demonstrated its powers of retribution sufficiently to discourage others. But in the months that followed, Lucy realized that it had done something else, too. It had changed the climate of the city. No matter that the Committee had at last disbanded toward autumn. The changes it had wrought remained. The simple fact was that the law mattered less. The people, having proven to themselves that they could take it into their own hands and manipulate it as they pleased, had lost respect for it. Sometimes Lucy would see Belle Cora, her fair skin paler than ever against her somber weeds, going about her errands with one of her Negro servants following behind to carry her parcels. What contempt she must feel, Lucy thought, for those sanctimonious citizens who glance away at the sight of her. But Lucy was not without her own degree of scorn for "the so-called law," as she put it. She had changed like everyone else. It seemed that now one was allowed to make one's own laws or to overlook existing ones to suit the occasion. The expeditious had triumphed over the orthodox. There was a certain heady freedom loosed in the city, and she was not immune to it.

"Look, Mama." Abel pointed to a brightly colored poster in the shoemaker's window. "That's for the new party, the Republicans."

"Mercy, the things you keep track of." She peered at the pictures of a bearded John Frémont and a clean-shaven William Dayton.

"Mr. Frémont wants to give women the vote. Would you vote, Mama?"

"If a cat had wings, would it fly? How do I know?"

"He wants to abolish slavery, too."

"And wreck the Union, most likely."

"When I grow up, I'm going to be in politics and do what's best for everyone."

"And when I grow up, I shall do everything in my power to prevent you from becoming a pompous charlatan like the rest of these sermonizers."

"I'm serious, Mama."

"So am I. There's not one of them worth the powder to send him up."

Abel followed the campaigns closely in the *Alta* and seemed pleased when Buchanan won, though Lucy didn't care a whit about who was president in far-away Washington. But she became increasingly aware that the boy, at thirteen, was an avid student of politics and that he was actually well informed on such matters.

"Why is it," she put it to him, "that over two years after the banking panic, things seem as bad as ever? Here it's eighteen fifty-seven, and still I see businesses floundering and closing to the left and right. Why can't your windy politicians do something about it?"

"It's not their fault. Too much money has been put into railroads, and crops have been poor this year. Gold production's dropped, too. There's no money circulating."

"I can see that for myself."

"Mama," Beth interrupted, "shall I wear the rose dress or the blue one to Martha Mason's party?"

"I was having a conversation with your brother."

"Boring stuff," Beth said.

"It's interesting," Abel protested.

"It is," said Lucy. Like Pa had said, there was fortune in the word misfortune. She had learned the truth of that statement firsthand after the bank panic. It occurred to her that the capricious hand of opportunity might once again be poised to knock. If that was the case, she intended to fling the door wide open.

XIV

LUCY RASED the gleaming brass knocker on the front door of the house on Pike Street. Out of habit, she glanced down the length of the street. As usual for a Sunday afternoon, it was empty and silent.

A towering, burly black man in servant's livery opened the door a few inches and peered outside, his eyes quickly taking in the street to north and south, as Lucy's had. "Aft'noon, Miz' Pastora." He bowed as he held the door open for her.

"Hello, Pompey. Mrs. Pitt is expecting me for tea."

"Yes'm." He led her past the empty ballroom, its glossy wood floor glowing warmly in the late afternoon sun that filtered through the lace curtains. Brass spitoons were positioned against the walls, and at the far end, between two windows, reposed Queen Rosie's pride and joy, her piano. "That case is mahogany clear through, not veneer, pure mahogany." So often had Mrs. Pitt made the comment, that Lucy repeated it to herself by rote as she passed.

Sundays at Mrs. Pitt's were quiet. Some of her girls went off with their men, some to gamble away their earnings and some stayed to do their sewing or mending and take afternoon tea. What the house might be like at other times, Lucy had no idea, since only at this time and on this day were her meetings with Queen Rosie conducted.

"Miz' Pitt'll be right along, ma'am."

"Thank you, Pompey."

Several of the girls were seated about the parlor, dressed so plainly now that they might easily have been mistaken for schoolgirls. Their simple attire was in

269

marked contrast to their sumptuous surroundings. A six-branched chandelier, gilded and hung with crystal droplets, presided over the room. A pair of matching sconces flanked the fireplace against ornate blue and red mock-India wallpaper. Queen Rosie's beloved red damask covered the three sofas and draped the windows. Here and there were several armchairs with seats upholstered in deep blue velvet. Tall lamps and silver trays with crystal decanters stood on the inlaid rosewood tables, and a Brussels carpet lay underfoot. Lucy was invariably impressed by the magnificence of Mrs. Pitt's establishment, in contrast to her own modest dwelling. The young ladies, however, seemed hardly to notice or care.

"Afternoon, Pastora," a chorus of voices greeted her.

"Hello, ladies." Lucy smiled. They were hardly ladies in any sense of the word. And not one of them appeared more than eighteen and most little over fifteen.

"Listen." A round-faced girl with brownish hair laid her darning in her lap. "It's Saint Mary's ringing the hour. When the wind's right, you can hear it from here." Her voice was soft and lilting.

"Dovey—is it?" Lucy had difficulty remembering their names. "Are you English?"

"Welsh, ma'am, but I've lived in London. How I miss those bells. That place sings with them. On the loneliest, wettest, darkest night, they make it cozy. The fog muffles the sound, and they chime so soft and friendly. Nobody's ever alone, it seems, so long as the bells ring."

"How beautiful it must be."

"A cesspit," said the one named Violet, not looking up from the hem she was clumsily sewing.

"If you'll hold your fingers higher on the needle, you'll find that easier," Lucy suggested.

Violet examined the hem with a disgusted look. "How the devil can a girl live when she don't even know how to sew or cook? I mended a buttonhole the other day that Big Etta said looked just like the hole in a buffalo's bottom."

"And she'd know," said another, giggling wickedly.

"Ladies!" Mrs. Pitt's voice reverberated from the hallway. "Put away your work and neatify for tea." The mountain of flesh waddled into the room and seated itself imperiously on a sofa. In her lap, she held a leather-bound ledger. "Violet," she commanded as Pompey set the tea tray by the hearth, "you'll pour today. I want no mistakes." She heaved a sigh. "If only I had a gold eagle for every boarder I've trained."

Lucy didn't doubt that she had at least that. But Queen Rosie, true to her word, maintained high standards. She insisted that a quality house exerted a civilizing influence on the male of the species. And as any woman well knew, there wasn't one of them who couldn't use the improvement. "You have another prospect for me, Mrs. Pitt?" Lucy asked.

"'Deed I do." She drummed her fingers on the ledger.

Despite the bad business year just past, or perhaps because of it, Lucy's investments were flourishing. With money scarce, a lady who wished to open her own parlor house had a hard time finding financial banking. Queen Rosie knew such ladies and knew which of them were trustworthy. Already she had produced a Miss Fulton who, in turn, had produced abundant profits for Lucy. "You're a generous woman, Mrs. Pitt," she said, accepting the tea Pompey brought her. "You don't seem at all concerned about competition."

"Hoo!" She laughed, spilling some liquid into her saucer. "Not with my reputation. For every one I let in, there's one turned away. Sylvie!" She wagged a finger at one of the girls. "Don't dip your biscuit! Do you remember," she asked Lucy, "that warehouse fire last week?"

"The champagne warehouse?"

"The very one. The gent who owned it was about to finance a lady from New Orleans in expanding her place. Now he ain't hardly got a dime for his own use. Ruined in a single night, poor fellow."

"How well do you know the lady?"

"Well enough. A square-shooter. No druggings and never a hint of the French Disease."

The girl, Sylvie, looked up reproachfully. *"Madame,* why is it always French?" she inquired. "It is the Spanish Pox, *non?* Give it back to them, *je vous en prie."*

Queen Rosie ignored her. "Pastora, you take a look at this." She handed her the book. "Judge for yourself."

"May I take it home with me?"

She nodded. "I'll tell Miss Corday to stop by the store in a few days."

271

"Miss Corday . . ." Dovey made a grimace. "That one's got eyes as cold as a cod."

Mrs. Pitt flashed her a look. "Mind your own business, Miss Mary Jane Catherine Thomas."

"Look, ma'am." Violet jumped up and displayed the ballgown she had been hemming. "For *soirée* night. Ain't it a beauty?" She flounced the green silk dress and executed a small dance step.

"I've three new boarders to introduce," Mrs. Pitt explained to Lucy. "I'll be having a *soirée* night for my better clients to meet the new lot."

"Music and dancing," Dovey piped gaily, "with all the real swells, judges and—"

"Silence!" boomed Mrs. Pitt. "With your loose mouth, you'll be getting seventy-five cents a turn in the cribs before you know it."

Lucy rose uneasily. "I'd best be on my way. Ladies." She nodded to the girls. "Thank you for tea, Mrs. Pitt. I'll be expecting Miss Corday."

True to Dovey's words, Miss Josie Corday's appearance was less than appealing. Her bleak, gray eyes held none of Mrs. Pitt's geniality. Her heavy brows grew together over the bridge of her nose, giving her face a stern, brooding look. A pronounced growth of mustache stippled her upper lip, and the scattering of dark hairs across her jaw suggested an imminent beard. This hirsute creature came to the store to retrieve her ledger, accompanied by two other persons—or, thought Lucy, perhaps more correctly one and a half. A diminutive, pale Negro servant stood obediently at her side. As Lucy held out the leather book for Miss Corday, he reached for it with his small childlike hands and clasped it under one arm without a word of bidding. He was scarcely three feet tall, with thin little pipestem legs and a thick trunk with a slightly protruding belly. Above his broad shoulders was a coffee-colored, freckled head with kinky auburn hair. Behind these two grotesques, the whiskered sea lion and her dwarf, stood a young girl of breathtaking beauty. She was as lovely as they were ugly. Petite and graceful, she was probably no more than fourteen, with a head of luxuriant black curls wreathing her fair face, limpid green eyes with long lashes, a saucy upturned nose and full, rosy lips.

Out of the corner of her eye, Lucy noticed Abel turn from his seat at her desk to gape at this unlikely trio.

"Your accounts are most impressive," Lucy told Miss Corday.

The woman stiffened perceptibly. "I pride myself on excellence, Mrs. Bates. I employ only Americans, English and Europeans."

"I'm sure we can reach some arrangement. Would it be convenient for you to call on me Sunday afternoon? My children will be in the country for the day with some friends."

She nodded curtly. "Peter? Fleur?" She beckoned the dwarf to follow her and placed an arm around the girl's shoulders, shepherding her to the carriage that waited outside.

"Mama . . ." Abel drew out the word with astonishment, "who were those queer people?"

"Weren't they, though?" She shook her head. "Miss Corday is a business acquaintance of mine."

"But who is Fleur?"

"From the way Miss Corday acted, I'd say her daughter, though it's hard to imagine she'd produce such a beauty."

Miss Corday's establishment was larger than either Mrs. Pitt's or Miss Fulton's. It bore the grand name of The Pacific Palace and boasted a continuous stream of patrons at all hours. Lucy, who received a weekly accounting from her investments, could not help but be amazed at the fortune to be made in such a venture. Though she was delighted with her profits, it was becoming increasingly evident that she could no longer cope single-handedly with both the bookkeeping of the store and the three other establishments.

"Your eyes are red, Pastora," Jack commented. "You get enough sleep?"

"Hardly. I've columns of figures burned into my brain."

He made a noncommittal sound.

"Where are the carved horn buttons? Did we receive the order?"

He extracted a box from the stack on the counter and handed it to her. "How long you think you can play at this game without getting into trouble?"

"Don't let's have this discussion again."

"What's happened to you? Ain't you got no shame no more?"

"Shame indeed. What use is that? Shame won't buy butter."

"What about respect?"

"Hogwash. I don't give a hang for that kind of respectability. People respect the dollar more than anything else, and in that manner I command all the respect I care for."

"Attention, maybe. Not respect. You know what you're acting like? Some wild crazy horse galloping ahead with no bridle, not looking left or right, just carried away with its own speed."

She didn't answer him.

"You go too far over the line, and you ain't going to get back so easy. The decent folks, hereabouts got long memories."

"My business affairs are private. There's been no talk, and you know it. Jack, where is Joe Mason these days? Still on the docks?"

"He picks up what work he can. Odd jobs mostly. Why?"

"If you see him, would you ask him to stop by?"

"You could tell Polly to send him."

"It might slip my mind. You mention it to him, would you?"

Joe seemed to be contemplating her proposal intently as she spoke, though Lucy couldn't tell from his face whether or not he followed her. She had explained herself as candidly as she knew how.

"You see," she went on, "I need someone who's both dependable and discreet. You would be paid by me. There's nothing reprehensible in that, unless, of course, your opinion of me has altered." She glanced at him but received no answer. "Look here, Joe, figures are figures, and books are books. I thought of you first because I was sure you'd find the money useful."

He frowned thoughtfully.

"Let me put it this way," she said. "A wine merchant's bookkeeper is responsible only for recording the correct figures. He's not held accountable for customers who imbibe too freely. The figures should be your only concern." Lucy leaned forward. "Well, haven't you anything to say?"

"I'm surprised," he finally replied. "That's all."

"These are strange times for all of us. I'm sure, after all that college educating, you never expected to be picking up odd chores on the waterfront. We do what we must to get ahead."

"I surely could use the money," he admitted.

"So. It's done. The ladies will deliver their receipts to me. You may collect them on Fridays and deposit them. You'll examine the weekly accounts they bring me. Now and then you'll compare the figures in their books with their grocers, wine sellers, laundrymen and the rest, just to make sure there are no errors or deceptions." She handed him Miss Fulton's ledger. "You might as well start with this."

Slowly, he reached for it and took it from her.

"*Sacré-bleu!*" Jack stepped inside the door and shook the rain from his hat. "How that stuff comes down out there! Me, I am going to build an ark if she don't stop soon. How's your Ma and Albert, Joe?"

"Well, thank you." He rose to leave.

"What you got there?" Jack asked, nodding at the book under Joe's arm.

"One of my ledgers," Lucy replied. "Good-bye, Joe." Lucy saw him to the door.

Jack waited until she had closed it. "What ledger? That ain't the sort we use here."

"It's another kind, that's all. Were you able to get any twill at the auctions?"

"Answer me, Pastora. Whose book you give to Joe?"

"It's no concern of yours. What about the twill?"

He slammed his palm down hard on the counter. "Damn you, woman! What have you done?"

"I asked him to do some bookkeeping for me. For *me*, do you understand? You know very well that family needs the money."

He stared at her across the counter. "Do you know what you're doing?" His voice was hard. "You and your sluts? You don't give a damn for nobody no more. You don't care that you corrupt Joe Mason or Jesus himself. You let your soul get eaten away with greed 'til there ain't no saving you."

"Rot! I suppose you never pocketed your profits with a smile on your face?"

"That's decent money for decent work!"

"Decent! I'm sick to death of that overworked word. You might as well be flaunting a bit of white cloth in your lapel like all those pillars of virtue who served with the Vigilance Committee. Do you know how many of those snow-white badges pass through Josie Corday's door?"

"No, and I don't give a damn. It's you I'm talking about. Let them all burn in hell. But you—" He shook his head in dismay. "Why you, Lucy?"

"Stop acting like a fool—"

"No!" he shouted. "It's you who's the fool! God knows what's become of you. You're as hard as that flint-eyed Corday."

"Mama?"

Abel stood in the doorway. How long he had been there, Lucy didn't know. Neither of them had heard him enter. He stood looking from her to Jack.

"Why are you shouting at each other?"

Jack took off his jacket and hung it on a peg.

"A small disagreement," Lucy answered quickly. "Where have you been, boy? You're soaked through."

"Out."

"I can see that for myself. Go upstairs and change into some dry clothes and light the stove. I'll be along presently."

They closed the store with scarcely a word to each other.

Lucy dished out supper for herself and the children. She sat at the table, absent-mindedly listening to Beth rattle on about her teacher's new sewing machine. Abel said nothing about the quarrel. He kept increasingly to himself these days and shied away from Lucy's inquiries. Perhaps it was difficult for him, being the only male among two women. Whatever it was, he was tight as a clam. That's what it's like, Lucy thought suddenly, they grow up and exclude you from their lives. But there was still time. "Bethie," she interrupted her, "would you like to have a sewing machine of your own?"

An amazed smile spread across her face.

"Your needlework is excellent. If it weren't, I wouldn't suggest it."

"Mother," Abel protested, "She's only eleven."

276

"Thank you, my little Spartan, I'm aware of that. But in my opinion, both my children deserve all the good things life has to offer."

If there was some disaffection between Lucy and Jack in the weeks following their argument, Abel's and Beth's company more than made up for it. What a joy it was, she often thought, to be able to indulge the children. Her own memories of childhood were mostly ones of constant toil and of Ma and Pa arguing over the farm. Once in a while, she would recall the good times with Willie or the tales Pa spun for them while the candlelight sent shadowy phantoms dancing across her quilt. It warmed Lucy to see that her own two children were as close as she and Willie had been. Night after night, Abel read aloud to Beth as she bent over her treasured sewing machine or embroidered a bit of trimming with her tiny, flawless stiches.

Perhaps Lucy was spoiling them, though she couldn't see what harm it would do Beth to try her hand at copying the fashions she pored over in *Godey's*. As for Abel, his proudest acquisition was his own small library, and books seemed to Lucy a worthy luxury. His shelves were lined with Pa's dog-eared volumes of Shakespeare, worn and shabby-looking next to his glossy new editions of Milton, Swift, Johnson, Dickens and the rest. He consumed books the way other children consumed sweets, greedily and with pleasure. His voice, as he read aloud, was full and clear. Sometimes Lucy, pausing to listen, her eyes still fixed on her newspaper, would wonder if he had indeed been serious about politics. He had a talent for spellbinding, there was no doubt of that. Even the driest of Bacon's *Essays* leapt to life as he read.

She saw less and less of Jack. As always, he was attentive to business, but he no longer lingered in the store to chat or came to share their meals. Twice Lucy had asked him to dine, explaining that it was the children's wish, but twice he had refused with vague excuses. The breach between the two of them grew irreparably wider. Neither was willing to budge an inch from his views. The determined strain in each of them that had brought them so far together now seemed to have divided them beyond hope. If either one had any regrets, they remained concealed. Lucy had precious little time to waste on contemplating Jack's pigheadedness. Between the children, the store and her investments, weeks seemed to glide away on the wind. Business at Pastora and French had never been better. The dainty Miss Fulton sent all of her young ladies to shop there, as did both Queen Rosie and Miss Corday. The gentlemen were not far behind, and the proper young ladies of the community, in constant rivalry with their tarnished sisters, followed in droves. Whatever Jack might think, Lucy's dealings were lining his pockets handsomely. They always had, she reflected—for all the appreciation he showed.

"Thank you, Peter." Lucy took Miss Corday's reticule from him and emptied the heavy gold coins into her desk drawer. "Miss Corday's not unwell, I hope."

"No, ma'am, jes' busy. Miss Fleur?" The dwarf stepped aside for her.

The girl came forward shyly and held out a gray felt riding hat. "Have you any black velvet ribbon, ma'am? Enough to trim the crown and make a bow under my chin?"

"Land, child, you don't want black. You're far too young and pretty." Lucy took the hat from her. "Hello there, son," she greeted Abel, "you look as if you'd run all the way home."

"Mama, it's coming! A man on horseback told me. The Butterfield Stage, all the way from Missouri! Please, let's go to see it."

"Keep calm, if you will. I'm helping Fleur. And you will please remove your cap indoors."

Abel flushed and tucked his cap under his arm. He smiled sheepishly at the girl. She seemed amused by his discomfort. He looked quickly downward, evading her eyes.

"We might use this bright blue," Lucy said, holding it against the brim of Fleur's hat. "Or a soft rose color. Look, here's a gray that's just a shade lighter than the hat."

Abel found his voice. "Martha Mason has a kitten that color."

The girl glanced at him.

This time he stood his ground. "Well, she does. It's called Misty."

Fleur looked at him in silence for a moment. Then she turned to Lucy. "I shall take the misty gray, ma'am."

278

Little Peter followed her out of the store, trailing her as closely as a dog guarding its pup.

"I'll wager that young lady cuts a fine figure on horseback," Lucy said, looking after them.

"She rides every Sunday."

"How on earth do you know that?"

He shrugged. "I know things."

"Don't you, though. And some of them are singularly curious. Now what's this about the stagecoach?"

He seemed to have forgotten momentarily. "Oh!" He glanced at the clock on the wall. "They say it's due before five. Mama, it's the first overland mail! Everyone's going to meet it."

"I suppose next you'll be wanting to tramp across the Sierras after Snowshoe Thompson on his mail route."

"Mama, listen to me. The rider said the mail left Saint Louis only a month ago today. One month!"

Lucy's eyes were on Abel, but her thoughts were suddenly far away. After a moment, she said softly, "My lands, a month to make that journey. Of course we'll go."

She stood among the expectant throng on Montgomery Street, the children at her side, scanning the teeming thoroughfare. "Are you sure it wll come from Market Street?"

Abel nodded, craning his head to see through the crush.

Anticipation played over the crowd, as perceptible as streamers of summer lightning flashing on the faces there. Lucy seized Beth's hand and squeezed it. "Bethie, can you imagine? It took your Mama five whole months to come cross-country. It was twelve years ago this very week that we arrived." Lucy felt the sharp, bittersweet invasion of memory. "A sorry-looking lot we were, ragged and bony, with the boots all but falling off our feet." She glanced down at Beth and caught her expression of forebearance. "I'm not exaggerating, Bethie." But there was no way the girl could possibly understand. To the children, Lucy's past was something so far removed across the chasm of years that, try as she might to illuminate it, it remained obscured, indistinguishable, little more than a will-o'-the-wisp.

All at once a roar went up from the crowd. The Butterfield Stage came wheeling around the corner of Market Street, its four horses lathered white and plunging ahead at full speed. The driver, crouching forward on his box, brought his horn to his lips and gave a jubilant blast. The resounding tumult was deafening. Hats flew into the air. Abel let out a whoop and hurled his cap as high as he could fling it. There goes the cap, Lucy thought. But she was as giddy as the rest, laughing one second, cheering the next. As the coach sped by toward the post office, the driver raised his battered hat aloft and waved it triumphantly. The coach clattered away, leaving a wake of dust and a street littered with headgear of every description. The elated mob swarmed over it heedlessly, occasionally taking a rambunctious kick, sending a topper or a slouch or a Chinaman's straw sailing merrily through the throng.

Beth tugged at Lucy's cape. "Look, Mama, there's Jack."

She made him out across the way, buying a copy of *L'Echo du Pacifique* from a newsboy.

"Who's the lady with him?" Beth asked.

"I wouldn't know." Lucy gazed at the stylishly dressed brunette. The woman laughed at something, tossing back her head, catching her bonnet just in time. She daintily repinned it in her hair, peering over Jack's shoulder at the newspaper. French, thought Lucy. Their women were uncommonly graceful. The lowest of them possessed a certain charm, even those *ingots* who'd been shipped here to rid France of some undesirables and coincidentally to furnish the city with a host of gaming hall dealers and cheap prostitutes. The French women had an elegance of bearing and a flirtatious wit that set them apart from their less worldly sisters. Not that Lucy was jealous, by any means. After all, how could anyone take seriously women of such unblushing frivolity? Surely Jack knew better than to fall prey to some *ingot* with an eye to her chief chance.

"What a handsome lady, Mama."

"Handsome is as handsome does, Bethie. Move along now."

Lucy began to wonder if Jack's peevishness wasn't somehow related to the woman. Perhaps he was merely acting like a lovesick pup. Perhaps he was so preoccupied with the pursuit of this coquette that his thoughts were far removed from the store. Whatever the cause, he was increasingly uncommunicative. He seemed to go about his business mechanically and with little enthusiasm. Lucy blamed the change on this seductive interloper, for want of an acceptable explanation.

"Abel," she scolded, "I asked you to clean the windows, not stand gawking at the passersby."

"Fleur and little Peter just went into the dressmaker's."

"The windows."

"Jack is waving good-bye to that dark-haired lady. She blew him a kiss."

"Where? Let me see." She peered out the window and retreated hastily as Jack approached.

"Who was that, Jack?" Lucy plucked idly at a bit of lint on her skirt.

"Who?"

"That woman. Isn't she the same one we saw you with a few weeks ago on Montgomery Street?"

"The lady is a friend."

"She has a name, I presume." Lucy busied herself at one of the displays.

"Madame Simone La Follette. The Brussels lace arrived, but less than we ordered."

"Rather a fashionable woman. A traveling actress, perhaps?"

"*Non,*" he replied sharply. "A widow lady."

"I'd hardly call those weeds. Obviously she's not mourning the late Monsieur La Follette."

"He's been dead since two years. You got any more questions?"

"Yes, as a matter of fact—"

"Mama," Abel interrupted, "I have to run. I forgot about loaning Fleur my book." He threw down his rag and made for the door.

"What book?"

"I said she could borrow it."

"Where is it?"

"I forgot to tell her I need it back!" He dashed out into the street, slamming the door behind him.

"Lucy." Jack placed his palms on the counter and fixed her with an even gaze. "Madame La Follette operates a lodging house."

"Does she? For young ladies?"

"Room and board for respectable folks. She has two

281

married daughters and she goes to Saint Mary's on Sundays. Does that satisfy you?"

"You must introduce us. Abel," she said as he returned. "Don't slam the door this time. Did you get your book?"

Jack watched him go. "Pastora, I believe that boy's very taken with the Corday girl. Maybe you better watch out for him."

"Ridiculous. Just because you're smitten with this La Follette woman doesn't mean the malady's sweeping the city. Fleur's very sweet, but she's at least a year older than Abel. Besides, her mother keeps a tight rein on her. When the poor child isn't cloistered, there's the dwarf dogging her every step."

"I don't wonder. Otherwise she might grow up like her Mama. But you mark me, keep an eye on the boy."

"He's too young for such thoughts."

"Passion's no respecter of age."

"Passion, indeed. What sort of drivel is that? Maybe if your mind were on your business affairs, you wouldn't entertain such nonsense."

"You telling me I ain't doing my job?"

"With your head in the clouds half the time. If that's the effect of passion, I pray it never overtakes me. Woolgathering's no friend of profit."

"You listen to me, Lucy." His voice was ominously quiet. "And you listen good. You're lucky I don't walk out and shut that door in your face. But I ain't leaving 'til I educate you. For a smart woman, you can be damn stupid. You're a passionate woman, Lucy Bates. Yes, you," he silenced her. "What you think gave you the drive and the will to survive when times were bad? And what made you leave Castalia and Reed, hey? What pushed you to succeed with Pastora and French here? Your passion, lady. But something's happened to it, and I ain't quite sure what. That fire, it becomes *quelque chose mauvaise et contraire*. It's turned on you, Lucy, by your own doing, you understand? It makes you hard like steel. You ain't no longer the woman I admired. It ain't easy for me to do business with a partner I don't respect."

She looked at him across the counter. "I notice," she said slowly, "that your respect for the dollar hasn't suffered any."

"And it ain't likely to."

"Am I to understand that you don't wish to be associated with me anymore?"

"You know what I'm talking about. You ain't got no need to traffic in whores. This store profits us plenty."

"Perhaps my sights are a bit higher than yours."

"They always were. But now you stoop in the gutter to satisfy your grand, high sights. Lady Lucy . . ." His eyes sought hers. "Have you got any idea how you disappoint me?"

"You're asking me to throw away a fortune. For what?"

"For you. You touch something filthy, the filth rubs off on you. That kind of money's tainted."

"I learned something a long time ago, my friend. It doesn't matter where money comes from, as long as it's there when you need it." She gave him the barest semblance of a smile. "Would it surprise you to know that Caleb Bates's legacy was tainted money? It was. As far as I know, every cent of it was stolen. Embezzled. What would you have expected me to do under the circumstances?"

He gazed at her as though he were not sure whether to believe her. "Things are different now."

"Indeed they are. All I cared about then was keeping body and soul together. Now I see what kind of life I can provide for me and the children, given enough money."

"But think, Pastora, at what cost?"

"The way I hear it, ten dollars the visit, twenty overnight."

He recoiled as though she had struck him. He stood back from the counter, staring at her. "It's too late," he said finally.

"If you say so. It's your decision."

"You can get yourself a new partner."

"No. I've enough money to buy your share. I'll hire someone to help me. Joe Mason knows the docks and auction houses. Perhaps I'll take him on full-time. I expect," she said drily, "you'll be my newest competitor."

He shook his head. "I don't think so." He looked suddenly very tired. "Maybe I move on again. This place ain't what it used to be."

XV

IT WAS the woman, of course, who had administered what Jack would have called the *coup de grâce*, Lucy reflected. Whatever differences existed between him and Lucy might have been resolved in time, had it not been for the advent of Madame La Follette. Jack had never been an unreasonable man, and Lucy had always been able, in due time, to make him see things her way. But at the first glimpse of the French woman, she had smelled trouble. There was no doubt in her mind that the intriguing Simone had used her wiles to separate her and Jack beyond redress. The La Follette woman had probably been jealous of an intimacy which did not even exist. How the stupid creature must have hated her. How she must have envied Lucy for her alliance with Jack and begrudged the hours he spent in her company. Simone had poisoned his mind against her and in so doing had destroyed their partnership. Lucy hoped she was satisfied. But perhaps Madame would view an unemployed carpenter in quite a different light than a prosperous merchant. Be it on their own heads. Lucy was through with them. She entertained the thought of changing the name of the store but decided against it. It was well known by now, and if the sight of it was nettlesome to Simone La Follette, Lucy would be quite pleased to let it fester. Nor was she about to turn away the "tainted" money Jack had so disdained.

"Good-bye, Miss Corday. Fleur, I know you'll be happy with the blue tarleton." Lucy opened the door for them and spied Belle Cora crossing the street. As Belle entered, her eyes met Josie Corday's and held them in a piercing gaze, hard and sharp as two glinting points of ice.

She glanced at Fleur and seemed about to speak, but Miss Corday seized Fleur by the shoulder and pushed her ahead of her out of the store.

"Your boy's becoming quite a little man," Belle told her. "I saw him standing in the upstairs window just now. How tall he is!"

"I'm afraid he'll tower over me in no time," Lucy said with a laugh. "Heaven knows how I shall keep the upper hand. My, but it's nice, Mrs. Cora, to see you getting out and around more."

"It's difficult sometimes," she confessed. "There are those whose faces I'd rather never see again."

"Josie Corday?"

She seemed surprised. "No. Why do you ask?"

"Perhaps I misunderstood. You seemed chilly toward her."

"Chilly indeed. She's the one with a hailstone for a heart."

"How so?"

"There are some things I can't condone. Business is business, and I'm all for it, but certain things are despicable."

"I've always found her to be fair-minded."

"She's a monster."

"That's a strong word, Mrs. Cora."

Belle shook her head. "Never mind. It's not something to be discussed. I'm in need of some black fringe for a bertha. What have you?"

Lucy and the children ate alone that night, as usual. If Abel and Beth missed Jack's occasional presence at the table, they said nothing about it. Lucy put away the supper things and carried her lamp to the table beside the rocking chair. Abel sat by the window, an open book on his lap, staring into the glassy darkness of the panes.

"Are you with us?" Lucy teased gently.

Beth looked up from her sewing machine. "What?"

"Not 'what,' dear. 'Beg pardon.' I was talking to your brother. Abel?"

"I was thinking, that's all."

"I should have known. By the way, Mrs. Cora commented today on how grown-up you were. She saw you watching her from the window."

"I wasn't watching her."

"I'll bet you weren't," put in Beth, her eyes on her sewing.

"What sort of language is that?" Lucy asked. "Bethie, why are you making such a face?"

Beth cranked furiously on her machine, giving no response.

"What's going on between you two?"

"Nothing," Abel replied hastily. He went to Beth's chair and clasped his arms around her shoulders.

What beautiful young people they are, Lucy thought, looking so alike though so very different. Beth raised her eyes from her work and turned to face Abel. The two of them exchanged glances. They were so close, this pair, that they could communicate without a word between them.

"Bethie," Abel said, "maybe you should ask Mama now."

"You ask. You're the elder."

"What on earth are you talking about?" Lucy demanded.

"Now you have to tell her, Abel."

"Mama—" He faltered.

Beth came to his aid. "We want you to allow us to do something. Don't be angry, please."

"Why would I be angry?"

"Because." Beth nudged Abel's arm.

"It won't hurt you to say yes, Mama. And it would make other people happy."

"Including yourselves, I presume. What is it?"

"French Jack invited Bethie and me to his wedding."

She drew a sharp breath. "Well. I don't suppose I'm surprised. That woman knew what she wanted from the start. When is this happy event?"

"May first. At Saint Mary's."

"You'll be bored, you know. The Catholics chant on in Latin for hours, and all on their knees. Very uncomfortable, I should imagine."

"May we go?" Beth pleaded. "Please? They're moving away to Canada right afterward."

It annoyed Lucy to feel the sense of loss that overtook her. She hadn't been sorry when they'd dissolved their partnership. Rather, she'd been relieved not to have him carping at her anymore. Why, then, should this news trouble her in the least? "Go," she said. "I guess you'll be wanting a new dress for the occasion, Bethie."

The girl smiled. "I'm making it now."

They were, she reflected, determined little creatures in their different ways. Beth, impetuous and perhaps a trifle spoiled; and Abel, dogged and persevering. They knew instinctively how to get the best of her, too. Beth by cajoling and winning smiles, Abel by patience and reasoning. Abel was the stronger of the two. Despite his bookishness, he possessed a character as sinewy as rawhide. He would be a force to reckon with one day. Beth was more volatile, with delicate sensibilities which made her at once vulnerable and appealing. Everyone, from Queen Rosie Pitt to her own brother, wanted to cosset and protect her.

The children seemed to sprout and flourish like a pair of supple saplings. One warm and cloudless day in September when Joe Mason exchanged vows with a jolly, dumpling-shaped German schoolteacher named Klara, Lucy heard the audible gasp that went through the congregation as Bethie, far outshining the bride, walked down the aisle in attendance. Throughout the ceremony, Abel's eyes rested on his sister, as though she were some new and exotic species that had found its way into the church. Her black hair was woven with pastel flowers, and her dress, of pearl-colored silk, had wide bows of pink ribbon at the flounces of the skirt and at her waist and collar. Her lips were bowed in a small smile, and her cheeks were flushed with excitement. Lucy glanced at Martha Mason, standing beside Beth. The girl fidgeted with Klara's bouquet and shifted self-consciously under the gaze of the guests. Not so Beth. She absorbed attention as though it were the food of life, and it seemed to Lucy, watching her, that she ripened under her very eyes.

At the reception after the wedding, Lucy found herself standing aside, observing the artless ease with which Beth charmed both young and old alike.

"Let me fill your punch cup." Polly joined her, fanning herself vigorously. "This hot weather makes for a mighty thirst. Tavie?" She handed the glass cup to the black woman presiding over the punch bowl. "Lucy, Albert heard from Henry this week," she said tentatively. "He's in Australia."

"Yes?"

Working for an importer. He's well, he says. I'd sooner he was here with us."

Lucy took a sip of punch and raised her cup to Joe as he passed. "Those two make a charming couple."

"I'd like to see *you* with a ring on your finger."

"I'm afraid I'm married to my business affairs, Polly."

"Joe says you're becoming a very wealthy woman. Investments in buildings and small businesses, nothing vast, but they all pay well. The city's healthy again, thank heavens." Lucy touched her cup to Polly's. "Prosperity," she said, "for us all."

"Joe told me you've been poring over pictures of houses in *Godey's*. Are you fixing to build? The way the children are blossoming, you could surely use a larger place."

"I've been looking at some land on Bush Street, out along the Western Addition. But," she hastened to add, "that's all far in the future. I expect it will cost dearly, and I aim to have the money safe in my pocket before the first spadeful of earth is turned."

"Come." Polly seized her arm. "Albert's going to start the toasts." She waved across the room to Martha, Beth and Klara's brother. "Gather 'round!"

Lucy scanned the guests, looking for Abel, but he was nowhere to be seen. "Bethie," she whispered, "where's your brother?"

"Isn't he here? He was standing by the door a moment ago."

"Where could he have gone?"

She shrugged. "You know how he is. He never tells me where he runs off to."

"Well, I won't have him being rude!"

"Hush, Mama. Joe's toasting Klara."

After the bride had gone to change clothes and just as the wedding carriage was brought around to the front door, Lucy caught sight of Abel slipping in from the kitchen. She waited until Joe and Klara had driven away before she reprimanded him. "What possessed you to leave the party like that? You were a member of the wedding. That's an honor and a duty, Abel, and your behavior was unforgivable."

"But no one missed me. I came right back."

"I missed you, and Lord knows how many others did. You'd better have a good excuse."

He looked at her evenly. "I haven't, Mama. Will you please forgive me?"

She felt the color rise in her cheeks. "Is that all you have to say?"

He nodded.

She knew there was no use in trying to wring any more from him. "You will write letters of apology to Mr. and Mrs. Fearing and to Joe and Klara. You will go to bed without supper, and tomorrow after Sunday services, you will clean the store from top to bottom until it passes my inspection. Discourtesy is a serious flaw in a gentleman. And by God, I intend to see you a proper gentlemen, if it takes the last breath I have in me!"

In the months that followed, Lucy began to wonder if there wasn't something troubling the boy. He seemed moody and erratic and absented himself for hours without explanation. Yet he never had any ailments or complaints. His schoolwork was exemplary, and he remained far ahead of the best of the pupils in his class. His teachers had recommended that he be sent to college in two years' time. Lucy noted with relief that the suggestion sparked his enthusiasm. It was difficult these days to move him to more than a monosyllabic response to anything at all. Bethie suffered most from this solitary independence of Abel's. Her brother's withdrawal had left her feeling forlorn and hurt and not a little jealous. She did her best to pretend not to care.

"Ach!" said Klara Mason. "You should see Martha and Bethie upstairs. I ask *'vas ist ein* taffy-pull,' and they give it to me to pull, too. Sticky! But it tastes plenty good. I tell them to clean up before Beth's mama closes the store. I don't tell you what it looks like up there now."

Lucy laughed. "Please don't! They wanted to make Christmas gifts for all of us. I expect we'll still be chewing taffy when Easter comes!"

"Easter," Klara replied dreamily. "Such a long time away. By Easter, I'll be fat like this," she said, clasping her hands wide in front of her belly.

"The time will pass quicker than you think. You'll have that baby in your arms before you know it." As the door opened, Lucy glanced at the customer who entered and said hastily, "Klara, will you look after things while I chat with Miss Fulton?" She drew Miss Fulton toward her desk at the back of the room. "Joe Mason's down at customs. I'll take care of you."

Miss Fulton waited until they were out of Klara's hearing before she spoke. "My laundry charges have gone up, Pastora. That Chinaman's turned bandit. I've looked for another, but it seems they've all raised their prices."

"Will it have much effect on the percentage of profits?"

"Not right now, but if costs continue to go up, I'll have to raise my prices."

"We'll deal with that if and when the occasion arises." She laid Miss Fulton's account book in her desk drawer, with her canvas sack of gold coins tucked beside it. "All's well otherwise?"

"I thank my stars. You heard about the ship fever?"

"Cholera?"

"Night before last, half a dozen men fell ill at The Pacific Palace."

Lucy glanced up quickly. "Miss Corday's? Are they sure it's cholera?"

"At first they thought it was food poisoning, but none of the girls took sick. Visiting Nicaraguans. A ship's captain and one of his officers, somebody from the government there and three merchants traveling with them. The ship's in quarantine."

"But what about Miss Corday's?"

"The Pacific Palace, too. The worst of it is, the doctors won't go." She gave a derisive snort. "Places like ours are good enough for this city's doctors so long as nobody's ill. Ain't that something to reckon on?"

"If those men die, The Pacific Palace is as good as dead, too." Josie Corday's establishment was not only the largest but the most profitable in San Francisco. "Is there no one to help?"

"My stable boy says a priest went in this morning with two nuns. Picture that! But who knows if they went for doctoring or laying out the dead."

"But those men needn't die! Not if they're treated soon enough. I know."

"Pastora? You know something I don't?"

"If they don't separate the sick men from the others in the house, they'll all fall ill."

290

"Of course. I hear they already quarantined the top floor for an infirmary."

"And is anything being done for the ailing men?"

She shrugged. "Ain't never heard of a priest bleeding nobody."

"Bleeding's old-fashioned rot. There's only one cure I ever knew to work. How am I to reach Miss Corday?"

"They ain't letting a soul in or out of there, 'cept the Papists. Maybe they reckon God'll protect those three."

"I must go. I can help."

"Pastora!" Miss Fulton cast a look over her shoulder toward Klara and lowered her voice. "Don't be a fool. You got a respectable name and two little ones to think of."

"I don't give a fig for public opinion. As for the children, no harm will come to me."

"Do this," she suggested. "Write down your magical cure, and I'll have the letter delivered to The Pacific Palace."

Lucy shook her head. "They'd never believe me. It's nothing but salty water." She caught the expression on Miss Fulton's face. "You see? You don't believe me either."

"Best you keep out of this. I ain't a stupid woman, Pastora. I know how much Miss Josie's place pays, but it ain't worth saving if it costs you your good name."

"And what kind of a name would I have if it were known I let six men die unnecessarily?"

"Land sakes, lady, ain't no one going to blame you."

Lucy found herself unable to sleep that night, except in short fitful spells from which she awoke feeling disturbed and unrefreshed. Once, in a dream, she saw the face of Celia Whiton, gaunt and wan and listless, her eyes dulled, her fire all but extinguished, waiting for death on an unfamiliar trail a thousand miles from anyplace like home. Lucy heard the wind shriek over their tents, rising in force and pitch until she sat up with a start, her hands clapped over her ears. She stared into the darkness a moment and sank back on her pillows, hearing only the sound of her own heart pounding.

Four times that morning she wrote the letter, and four times she tore it up. No matter how she tried to word it, it sounded written by either an addlebrained busybody or a reckless fanatic. The treatment was so absurdly simple that it was implausible. There was only one way to convince them.

"Klara, would you and Joe sleep here tonight with the children, if I'm not home? I might even be gone a few days. It's an emergency, or I wouldn't impose on you."

Klara looked bewildered. "But Friday will be Christmas Eve. What do I tell the children?"

"Tell them not to worry. If I'm not back, take them to Polly's for Christmas dinner, just as we'd planned." She took her cloak from the peg on the wall. "I doubt I'll be gone long, Klara. But if by chance I am, I know you and Joe can take care of everything."

Twice she almost turned back, recalling Miss Fulton's warning. But in her mind's eye. she saw Celia Whiton's face again and remembered watching Reed Pierce measure salt into the drinking water, thinking he might be a madman. But the four he had treated had lived. And without Celia, without Reed, she herself might never have endured. She was a rich woman in more ways than Wells Fargo could count. She had other accounts to settle. And though Celia and Reed would never know it, it was instinctively for them that she hurried down the windy street, her cloak askew, her hair blowing in disarray, her eyes fixed ahead of her as though afraid that the slightest interruption of her thoughts might tempt her from what she must do.

"No, madam," the constable insisted. "I got my orders. This place in quarantined."

"All I ask is a word with one of the people who are tending the sick. I could call out to them from here."

"I can't do nothing, lady. Sorry. My orders is to keep the neighborhood quiet and to see nobody goes in or out of the house."

As if to contradict him, the door of The Pacific Palace swung open. Little Peter emerged and stood at the top of the front steps, looking up and down the street.

"Peter!" Lucy cried. "I must speak to Miss Corday."

He looked surprised to see her and glanced at the policeman. The officer shook his head. Peter did the same, then turned at the sound of wagon wheels on the street and motioned to someone inside the house.

"Stand back," the constable directed her.

292

Two men jumped from the police wagon and walked halfway to the house. Down the steps came two of Miss Corday's servants, struggling with a furled and sagging sling of sheet, heavy with its dead weight. The policeman unfolded a canvas stretcher to receive the body, and Lucy watched them slide the stretcher onto the wagon-bed.

Suddenly Lucy turned and bolted for the door, past the startled officer and the servants trudging back up the steps. She flung herself through the doorway and into the dim recess of the hallway inside. She leaned against the heavy, carved bannister, trembling, trying to catch her breath to speak, but she could only nod to the startled, wide-eyed Negro who bolted the door behind her.

"Is it done, Weaver?" Miss Corday came from the parlor. Seeing Lucy, she waved the speechless servant away. "What in the name of God brings you here?"

"The men with ship fever. Take me to them. I can help."

"Have you lost your mind?"

"No. I know what I'm doing."

Josie Corday squinted, hard-eyed as a pawnbroker assaying a suspect gem. She gathered up her skirts and mounted the stairs, with Lucy close behind her. "You ain't leaving, you know. You got yourself trapped here now like the rest of us."

"I know that."

"You're a damned queer woman, Pastora."

It was chilly on the top floor of the house. Miss Corday led her down the narrow attic hall between the servants' cubicles. They were little more than cold, cheerless cells, few of them windowed, all of them dingy. The stench of illness and death pervaded the passageway. Josie Corday had spoken the truth—Lucy was a prisoner here, like it or not.

Miss Corday rapped on one of the doors. "Father Crowley, there's someone here to see you."

He was a ruddy-faced man with thinning gray hair. In one hand he held a rosary. Despite the chill, there were beads of perspiration on his forehead. He listened, a slight frown playing over his features, as Lucy spoke her piece.

"Don't think me mad," she begged him. "That was what I thought of it too, at first. I remember what Doctor

Pierce said. Folklore, he called it, but it worked. He said, 'the disease must be attacked at its very onset.' I recall his exact words, after all these years. We've not a minute to lose."

He studied her for a moment. "I don't see," he said slowly, "how it could hurt. I don't believe you're mad in the least. Pastora, is it?"

She nodded.

"You are either a very brave and misguided woman or you are the good Lord's answer to our prayers. Either way, you've shown great courage in coming here. Miss Corday, we need pitchers of water and all the salt in your pantry."

"I'll send Peter up with them." She hurried away.

"What may I do," Lucy asked the priest, "now that I'm here?"

"Sister Bridget and Sister Maria Teresa are disinfecting and fumigating the dead man's room. You might look in on the others. I'll stay with the captain for the moment. He's worst off."

She had forgotten how quickly the disease made skeletons of strong men. They lay in their cubicles, staring vacantly upward out of sunken eyes, with scarcely the strength left to blink. Their sheets were stained with watery vomit and excrement. Their breath reeked as badly as their bodies. Lucy had to check herself from retching.

"Pastora?" The young nun stood timidly in the doorway with a pile of linens. "Will you help me change this man's bed? I'm Sister Bridget."

Lucy caught Sister Bridget glancing at her covertly as they removed the filthy sheets and tucked fresh ones over the mattress. "Are you . . . employed here?" the nun asked her timidly.

"No. I'm a shopkeeper."

"Ah. But you're a Catholic woman?"

"No. Protestant."

Sister Bridget gave her a curious look and changed the subject. "So many to pray for . . ." She sighed. "The stricken men, the young ladies downstairs—"

"You pray for them?" Lucy lifted the sick man's head and held it as he sipped his salted water.

"We are all sinners, but we are all God's children. He waits only for us to return to His fold."

"Miss Corday and her girls too?"

She seemed surprised. "Certainly. God welcomes a repentant sinner like His own dear Son." She gathered up the fouled linens.

"What will you do with those?"

"Burn them. Father Crowley says there must be no contact between what the men have touched and those who are still healthy."

"Be careful yourself, Sister."

"And you. Sister Maria Teresa will wash the drinking cups twice a day. She'll be along any moment. She understands Spanish. Poor things," she said, gazing at the form on the bed, "so far from their own people."

Lucy lost track of time. Sometime after dark, she had no idea when, there was a knock at the door of the cubicle where she sat. "I must have nodded off," she apologized as the priest entered.

He set his lamp on the washstand. Lucy administered more liquid to the man lying listlessly on the bed. The lamplight tinged his ashen features with an exaggerated glow.

"What do you think?" Father Crowley asked.

"I see no change yet, but I remember it as being gradual."

"There's some food laid out for us in the last room on the right. If you'll stop in the one before it, you'll find soap and water to wash with."

Lucy could not imagine having an appetite, but when she caught the fragrance of the steaming tureen of soup and the basket of crusty brown biscuits, she realized how hungry she was. While they ate, Weaver and the dwarf, Peter, moved extra cots into one of the rooms. There was scarcely space to squeeze between them, but Lucy and the nuns slept as best they could, waking by turns to tend the men.

She wondered at the boundless vigor with which these churchly folk ministered to their ailing sinners. Lucy had never known anyone of their calling. She supposed she'd expected them to be an ethereal sort, abstracted, suspended in flight somewhere between heaven and earth by lofty theological meditations.

In fact, Father Crowley reminded her of one of the hardy Irish stevedores who worked the docks, though his speech was clearly that of an educated man. Sister Bridget, shy as she was, had the strength of a plowhorse, and the grandmotherly nun, Sister Maria Teresa, with her gnarled hands and wrinkled walnut face, seemed to Lucy like an ancient tree, bent now by the winds of years, but still staunch and flourishing.

Father Crowley organized the routine of the infirmary like a general waging hand-to-hand combat. Young Sister Bridget forgot no detail, however small, and tactfully reminded the others when fatigue rendered them forgetful.

Sometimes, in their delirium, the men spewed forth streams of curses. Lucy, though she had only a little Spanish, still caught enough of their meaning to blush. But Sister Maria Teresa would merely nod sympathetically, patting their hands, showing no trace of embarrassment. Only once, at a *"Madre de Dios,"* did Lucy see her raise her eyes heavenward and hastily cross herself.

They were a strange combination, these three, of sanctity and common sense. She had never met their like, and though the mysteries of the Roman faith were, to her thinking, so much claptrap, she couldn't help admiring them.

Lucy rose from the bedside and smoothed the covers over the sleeping captain. A shadow fell across the sheets, and she turned. She'd quite forgotten there was a window here. She went to it and looked out. The sky was bright blue. Fat, fluffy clouds seemed to hang motionless in the air, like white, cream-filled cats asleep on a blue carpet. How incongruous, such a high and wide glimpse of picture-perfect sky from this little cell. Somewhere beyond the roofs and hills, sun shimmered on the bay, ships were being unladed, people bustled about the marketplaces and laughing children swung in schoolyards. Lucy pushed hard at the sash and leaned out into the fresh air, drawing a deep, sweet draught of it.

"Pastora?" Sister Maria Teresa asked as she entered. "Is anything wrong?"

"No." Lucy pulled her head inside. "It's close in here, that's all. I needed a breath of air."

Sister Marie Teresa smiled tiredly. "Doing God's work is not always a tea party."

"Don't misunderstand me, Sister. I'm not doing God's work, only mine."

"As you wish."

"Sister, what day is this?" Lucy asked.

Her gray brows furrowed a moment. "Thursday. It's Thursday morning."

"Sister," she declared, "we've not lost one of them since we started the treatment. I believe we've won."

"Señor Garcia took a few steps this morning," the nun said hopefully. Bending over the captain, she touched her fingers to his neck and crooned softly to him in Spanish. "His pulse is strong, Pastora, and his color seems better this morning."

"Another day or two, and they should all be on their feet, though I expect it will be some time before they regain their strength." She watched Sister Maria Teresa stroke the captain's forehead. "You treat them as tenderly as babes, Sister."

"Señora, I am the eldest of nine and the only girl. I know from all my years that men are fragile souls, more so than women suspect. They need comforting. Sometimes," she said sadly, "they try to find it in a place like this."

That night, Father Crowley bowed his head over the small eating table and said grace. "Holy Father," he added, "we thank Thee not only for our evening meal but for Thy mercy and compassion on behalf of those whose lives You have saved. May their souls henceforth be dedicated to Thy good works. *In nomine Patris, Filii et Spiritus Sancti*, Amen."

Lucy glanced at the priest and the two sisters as they began their meal. Downstairs, a gaggle of prostitutes waited only for the word that would set them again to plying their trade. And here she sat, exhausted by days and nights that seemed to have comprised a lifetime, breaking bread with these three pious soldiers of Christ. Suddenly she felt the urge to laugh, to howl at the absurdity of it, startling the priest and nuns, waking the sick and puzzling the impatient whores two floors below. She clenched her fists tightly in her lap, trying to contain her hysteria. Finally the moment passed, and she was calm.

Sister Maria Teresa shook her awake and handed her a mug of strong, black coffee. *"Feliz Navidad*, Pastora. It's Christmas morning."

Lucy sat up. "Today? How are the men?"

"Coming along nicely. Father Crowley would like to speak with you."

He stood up from Señor Garcia's bedside when she appeared in the doorway and motioned her into the hall. "Miss Corday told me you have two children," he said as he joined her.

"Yes."

"Perhaps you'd like to be with them to celebrate our Lord's birthday."

"Yes?"

"Are you sure you won't need me?"

"The men are well on their way to recovery. We can tend them by ourselves. You turned the tide, Pastora. You did more than your share. Go home now. Bless you." He clasped both her hands in his for a moment. "You're a good woman."

"Don't overestimate me, Father. You'd be making a grave error." She summoned a faint smile, and turned to leave.

"Pastora," he called after her, "do burn your clothing and bathe before you go near the children. I'm quite sure there's no danger now, but one can't be too careful."

At the foot of the curved staircase, Lucy halted, her eyes momentarily dazzled by the sudden impact of light and color that flooded the parlor. Sun streamed through the silk-swagged windows and beamed brightly back from gilded mirrors. Red satin glowed like luminous coals. The whole room was suffused with radiance. Lucy's head throbbed, and she felt a fiery flush overtake her.

"Are you feeling all right, Mrs. Bates?"

She took a breath and, shading her eyes, saw young Fleur rise from a card table and approach the stairs. Miss Corday's boarders looked on in silence.

"I'm fine," she said unsteadily, "only a bit tired."

"The priest said the five of them will get well."

"Which ones?" asked a girl in a white cotton nightgown. "He never told us who died."

She realized that she did not even know the men's full names. "The captain and his mate, Señor Garcia, and the two called Hector and Ramon."

"Ramon!" The girl brightened. "He was yours, Fleur. It must have been Zoe's who died."

Lucy stared at Fleur.

298

The girl smiled. "The Father said you saved them."

The front door slammed and Josie Corday appeared. "They're leaving. The police are removing their man. We must disinfect and fumigate and stay closed for another week, but it's over." She noticed Lucy. "You're going?"

She nodded.

"Fleur, fetch Pastora's cloak." She took Lucy's arm and walked her to the door. "Just wait and see. In no time, business will be back to normal. A month, six weeks, and this will be forgotten."

"Miss Corday?"

"Yes?"

"I was under the impression that Fleur was your daughter."

"She is. Enjoy your Christmas dinner, Pastora."

Her house was empty. When she had bathed and changed, she took the newspaper-wrapped parcel of soiled clothing down to the alley behind the building and doused it with kerosene. In the dancing flames, she saw the scarlet splendor of Josie Corday's parlor and Fleur's image, ethereal and pale. As Lucy watched, the bundle of rags writhed and blackened and turned to ashes that fluttered delicately in the wind for a moment before they disintegrated.

The day was fair. The sky was dotted with only a few swiftly moving clouds, and a brisk ocean breeze quickened the air. By the time Lucy reached the Fearings', her fatigue had all but disappeared. Warmed by the sunshine, refreshed by the wind, her spirits revived. She raised the brass knocker and let it fall.

Joe Mason opened the door. "You're back. Is it safe for you to come in here?"

"Yes. The children?"

He stood aside as she entered. "They're in Martha's room, playing with her presents. Abel made a fearsome Herod at the church pageant, and Beth sang like the angel she was supposed to be."

"I'm sorry I wasn't there. I appreciate what you and Klara have done, Joe." She turned toward the sitting room.

He touched her arm. "They know."

299

"Who?"

"My mother and Albert."

"What do they know?"

"Where you were."

"How?"

He shook his head in futility. "Who knows how these things spread? Mother heard it Wednesday. Maybe the Corday woman's servants talked to the police. It's been in the newspapers. Your name wasn't mentioned until yesterday."

"Is that all?"

"No. Mother asked me how you found out and why you would go there."

"I went because I could help the sick."

"Perhaps you should explain that yourself. There have been outbreaks of cholera before, as Mother pointed out. It was The Pacific Palace that roused her curiosity."

Lucy glanced at him sharply. "You told her everything?"

"I had to. She and Albert were pressing me. I couldn't lie, not to them."

Lucy handed him her cloak and walked into the sitting room. "No, Albert," she raised a hand, "don't go up. Polly, let me have my say. I've no wish to embarrass either of you or to cause you any more trouble than I already have. I shan't set foot in this house again if I'm not welcome here."

Polly's usually placid face was strained. "Perhaps," she said quietly, "that would be for the best." She knotted her handkerchief around her fingers. "Lucy!" she cried suddenly, throwing the crumpled linen aside, "how could you betray us? Why would you involve Joe in such a vile business?"

"Joe has done nothing wrong. He has audited my account books. That is all. If columns of figures could corrupt, I daresay that Albert and Henry would have been doomed long ago. Don't be hard on the boy."

Albert rose. "I'll thank you not to try to obscure the issue by accusing me of venality. That is not the problem here, and your attempt to rationalize your actions only exposes your ruthlessness all the more. There are certain areas of interest that decent people avoid. The Chinese import their slaves by one ruse or another, yet I can not

300

condone those who would profit by them, whether first-hand or indirectly. This is much the same situation."

"You know very well how badly Joe needed a job!"

"And I'm sure your arguments were most seductive. But to Polly's and my thinking, he made a serious error of judgment. Perhaps our reduced circumstances served as his excuse. But you have none. Polly and I are deeply hurt that you've taken advantage of her son. That is the issue, and those are our feelings."

"Joe?" Lucy turned to him.

He spread his hands helplessly. "Albert, I never intended to hurt you or Mother. You must know that."

"Disappoint," Polly corrected. "You have disappointed us."

"Mrs. Bates," Joe said, "I've always felt I owed you a great deal. I'm sorry it's come to this."

"I daresay we all are," Albert responded.

"Everyone!" Klara's cheerful voice called from the next room. "Octavia says that dinner is almost—" Seeing Lucy, she hesitated in the doorway.

Polly stood up. "We must not spoil the children's Christmas dinner. Klara, please go fetch them."

Abel, Beth and Martha seemed oblivious of the waves of silence that fell repeatedly over the dining table, drowning all conversation, save for their sprightly accounts of the church pageant.

"I want Joe and Klara to stay on at the store," Lucy declared abruptly.

The children stopped talking. Abel's eyes went to Joe.

Joe glanced from Albert to Polly, but before any of them could speak, Lucy overrode them.

"There's a child on the way, and they need the money. I'll see to it Joe has no duties you'd find objectionable. Whatever you may think of me, I defy you to find fault with their working at Pastora and French. Albert?"

He stared pensively at the base of his wineglass, tapping his finger against the stem. At length, he looked up. "Polly, I have my own opinion. What do you think?"

She frowned uncertainly. "I don't know. My first response is that I want nothing to do with—" She paused, glancing at the children. ". . . the source of our disillusion." Polly gazed across the table at Lucy. "It has caused us great pain."

301

"I'm sorry, Polly. I'll abide by your wishes."

"I think it would be wise," Albert put in, "not to force sociability, under the circumstances."

"As you wish."

"But," he continued, "I believe Joe regrets the lapse of judgment that has caused our unhappiness. I doubt such a thing could happen again. Joe?"

"I give you my solemn word. I won't bring any dishonor on this house."

"It's still up to you, Polly," Albert prodded. "He's your son."

She yielded. "I cannot deny you decent employment, Joe, but I shan't find it a comfortable situation."

"I don't intend to impose on you," Lucy told her. "We'll take our leave directly after dinner."

Abel shifted uneasily on the carriage seat as they drew away from the Fearings' house. "Mama, why did Mrs. Fearing seem so sad?"

"Because she and I are at odds with each other. We cannot be friends anymore."

"But what about Martha?" Beth wanted to know.

"Martha has no quarrel with you. I expect things can be worked out. Driver," she called, "stop at the far corner ahead, please."

"Why did we come so far out Bush Street?" Abel asked. "It's deserted. There isn't anything to see here."

"But there is," Lucy countered. "Beth, take a look."

"There's a shed on that far hill and a barn."

"No. What do you see here, right beside the carriage?"

"Nothing."

The boarded walk along the unpaved street had buckled in places under the winter rains. It appeared unused and neglected. The land bordering on the walk was uncultivated, a snarl of overgrown vines and weeds. A faint footpath traversed it diagonally from the corner, disappearing into a thicket of dead brush. Lucy scanned the barren, windswept patch, suddenly filled with misgivings. But it was too late. "Children," she said, "this is my Christmas gift to you. Here is where we shall live one day. I shall build us a fine house on this land."

"Mama!" Beth was aghast. "Nobody will come 'way out here! We won't have any friends!"

"It does look a bit desolate now," she conceded, "but

302

you wait. I'm sure there'll be other folks moving out, too."

Abel surveyed the view in silence.

"You may go back now, driver."

The carriage jolted uncomfortably on the rutted street.

Abel turned his solemn dark eyes on Lucy. "I don't like this Christmas, Mama."

XVI

"IMAGINE!" QUEEN Rosie Pitt seemed genuinely amazed. "They say you made your pile importing girls to Castalia for the miners. As though you'd have known the first thing about the trade! I told them," she said, chuckling, "the little lady'd be a damned sight richer if that were true."

Lucy was aware that only the more absurd rumors reached her ears. But she was also aware of a palpable change toward her. The genteel customers of Pastora and French made a point of directing their inquiries to Klara or Joe, and those who could not evade her entirely looked upon her with a mixture of suspicion and distaste. The refined ladies of San Francisco might pattern their fashions after their sullied sisters, but there the affinity ended, and the lines were drawn. Lucy, to them, was a traitor to her class and her sex. They felt duped, hoodwinked by this clever little shopkeeper. The extent of their shock only magnified her sins in their eyes.

Lucy was no stranger to gossip, and knew that in time it would ebb, disappear and be forgotten. Until it did, she had no intention of drifting helplessly at its mercy. She willfully affected a bravado which, if not entirely comforting, gave her the satisfaction of knowing that it shocked and galled her enemies all the more. She wondered how these priggish creatures would take to the truth that their husbands and sons, fathers and brothers begot the profits of places like The Pacific Palace. Exposure, it appeared, was the crime. What was practiced surreptitiously was readily overlooked.

"She made her money in sheep, you know. That's the why of that name, Pastora."

Lucy halted in the street a few feet behind the two women gazing into the store window. One of them leaned forward, peering at the selection of lace displayed there. Her companion went on talking.

"I suppose that's why she's got no objection to making a fortune from rutting animals. There's nothing goes on in those places that she hasn't seen before and made money by."

Lucy brushed past them into the store. She slammed the door behind her. "How I loathe a woman with that sort of voice!"

Joe glanced up.

"One of those dreadful creatures who whinnies between titillation and abomination."

"Where?"

"Never mind. We'll be changing the name of the place, Joe. Let them think what they will of me, but I'll be hanged if they'll spoil my business. From now on, it will be Clay Dry Goods Company. At least they'll remember what street we're on. Will you have a new sign painted as soon as possible?"

"Do you think it will make a difference?"

"It will if I make myself scarce. Between keeping my books and planning for the new house, I'll have plenty to occupy my time."

"But Klara's not up to working a full day anymore, what with the baby coming."

"Hire someone new. You're in charge now. I shall raise your salary at the first of the month."

"Are you sure you want to do this?"

She sat down tiredly. "Joe, I'm hardly certain of anything. I keep thinking this fuss will go away, but it persists."

"I don't suppose," he said cautiously, "that you've considered divesting yourself of your other interests."

"I don't suppose I have! What difference would it make now? A brand doesn't wash off, Joe."

"But in time, they'd realize—"

"I'm sick and tired of waiting! And I refuse to court their favor. There's one thing I do know for certain, Joe, and it's that money shouts the loudest. Let them whisper all they want. Ultimately, I shall drown them out."

Lucy sat on the edge of Beth's bed, listening to her nightly prayers. The girl's black hair spilled over her pillow, lustrous in the glow of the lamplight. Lucy brushed a strand from Beth's throat and stroked her curls. When the last "amen" was said, she asked her, "Bethie, did you decide how you want to celebrate your birthday?"

"A theatre party. It's more grown-up."

"The theatre party it is. Invite as many as you like, but you must let me know by Wednesday so I can order the tickets in time."

"Mama, how old were you when you married Papa?"

"Sixteen. Why?"

"I'll be thirteen this birthday. That means in three years I can marry."

"Don't you dare! Whatever put that thought into your head? A young lady can have a grand time these days, going to parties and balls. Surely you wouldn't want to be tied down so soon."

"But it would be nice to have a man in the house, someone who belonged there, and he'd always be around when I needed him."

"You have your brother," she pointed out.

"What good is Abel? He's hardly ever home in the daytime. And at night, he's buried in his books. Besides, he's only fifteen."

Lucy tried to conceal her amusement. "How old a gentleman did you have in mind?"

She thought for a moment. "Someone Joe's age."

"Twenty-five? Goodness, that's a bit elderly, isn't it?"

"You said Papa was much older than you when you married."

"He was, but I'm not altogether sure that was a blessing."

"Then why did you marry him?"

"Because . . ." She paused thoughtfully. "I thought he wanted the same things I wanted. To leave that place and start a new life here together."

"And didn't he?"

Lucy stood up, smoothing her skirts. "Marriage is very complicated and full of discoveries. Your papa was a restless man. I'm not sure he could have stayed any place for long."

"I wouldn't like that. My husband will never leave me."

Lucy bent and kissed her on the forehead. "I'm sure he won't, dearest child."

306

Despite all she could do for the children, Lucy could not be their father. She could not satisfy Beth's longings nor offer an example for Abel to follow. The boy had to forge his own way to manhood without a star to guide him. Back in Castalia, Reed and White Russell and Jack had treated the children like their own. Lucy supposed Jack had been as close to a father as any Beth and Abel would ever know. She thought back and with a slight shock realized that she recalled hardly anything of Caleb Bates. In her memory, he remained only a tall shadow, a phantom whose children she had borne.

"Julia Harper is giving a party the same day as mine," Beth announced, angrily stabbing her embroidery needle in and out of the taut circle of linen. "It's not fair. She asked all the girls I wanted for guests."

"And she didn't invite you? That was rude of her."

"Julia Harper is a fat, smug cow. She thinks because her father is rich, she's some kind of royalty."

"What about Narcissa Brooks and Carrie Howe?"

"They're going to Julia's."

"Even Martha Mason?"

She nodded.

"Don't sulk, pet. They're not worth wearing a frown on your face. Besides, it's their loss. I'll tell you what. Instead of just going to the theatre, I'll take you and Abel to dinner, like a grown-up lady and gentleman dining out. That and the theatre, too. Would you like that?"

"Yes," she said, sounding not altogether mollified. "Mama," she asked, setting her embroidery hoop aside, "what's 'notorious'?"

"It means famous, after a fashion. Why?"

Abel came from his bedroom with an armload of books and his writing tablet.

"Narcissa Brooks's mother told her you were 'the notorious Pastora.' "

The boy slammed his books down on the table. "I hate that name!"

"Mind your manners!" Lucy flared. "And what's wrong with the name, may I ask?"

"It's the way they say it," he replied.

"Who?"

"People."

"I didn't think you were referring to talking horses. What, exactly, do you object to?"

"They say you have a bad name."

"I see," she said slowly. "And you've taken Pastora to be that bad name?"

He nodded uneasily, his eyes downcast.

"Son, look at me. That's better. Children, this is a difficult time for us all, but time always passes, and things change. I've told you before, words are only hot air that blows away and is forgotten. Try to be patient."

"I hate that name," he repeated.

"Now that the name of the store is changed, I doubt it'll be mentioned very much longer."

Beth gazed at her solemnly. "Why don't people like you anymore, Mama?"

"Never you mind. Your mother is at least as rich as the father of that fat cow, Julia Harper, and before I'm through, those wretched children will come fawning to you, if that's what you want. Give me time, that's all I ask."

But it was not that easy. Spring became summer, and still the cold stares did not thaw. Lucy raged in tight-lipped fury that a clique of pious hypocrites could wield such power over their lives. Her anger and impatience drove her to a frenzy of work. Reducing costs and increasing profits became an obsession. Miss Fulton, she decided, was becoming lazy and must be retired. She bought out her share of the house and installed a Miss Ware whom Belle Cora recommended. Lucy presided over her enterprises like a sharp-eyed hawk, swooping down and setting up a shrill flap until things were righted to her liking. "Land," Queen Rosie sighed, "we're only human, Pastora. I begin to think you're some sort of newfangled machine."

Sometimes Lucy caught the children staring at her as she bent over her books or her sheaf of plans for the house. Abel would gaze at her thoughtfully, his face empty of any expression, then return to his reading. In Beth's eyes, she saw something she could not quite name, something veiled and wary and resentful. Her glance became a sullen indictment, though not a word was spoken.

In July, Klara gave birth to a girl, Blanca, her *"kleine puppe,"* as she called the child. To Lucy's relief, Beth appropriated the tiny doll for her own adored plaything. She spent so much of her time at Klara's, fussing over Blanca that Lucy wondered if the poor babe knew which of them was her mother. Beth was home less and less, and Abel, even when he was home, seemed removed to some secluded inner sphere which no one was permitted to enter.

Lucy looked up from her mending. The afternoon sun poured through the open windows. Motes of dust swirled in its bright streams. The house was silent. She heard the distant sounds of children at play somewhere outside and glanced around the quiet room, startled by its stillness. A thought struck her, and she sewed rapidly, intently, trying to dispel it. But it persisted.

"I am losing my children," she said aloud, surprised at the invasion of her own voice. They were slipping away from her, locking their doors behind them, shutting her out. Their absence was as harsh as any confrontation. Despite the warmth, she shivered.

Lucy reached down and helped Beth into the carriage. "Where is your brother?"

The girl shrugged.

"Give me the courtesy of an answer, please."

"How would I know where he is?"

"I said an answer, not a question. Didn't you tell him we were leaving at two o'clock?"

"Yes."

"Where would he have gone?"

"He didn't tell me."

"Perhaps he went to the library and lost track of time."

"Not likely," Beth retorted.

"Why not?"

"It's too nice a day."

"Well, we can't keep the workmen waiting. We'll be on our way, driver." She turned back to Beth. "I don't understand that boy. I thought he was looking forward to this afternoon. I guess now you'll have the honor of breaking ground for the house."

"But I don't want to dirty my new dress!"

"Then you'll just have to do it cautiously, won't you," she replied, trying to conceal her annoyance. The girl was as prickly as a cactus. It seemed to Lucy that she was especially irritable where Abel was concerned. If Lucy

309

felt his aloofness keenly, poor Bethie probably suffered even more. "We must plan to do more things together," she announced, "the three of us. Outings on the bay, perhaps, or a day at the gardens."

Bethie gazed at the street ahead, saying nothing for the remainder of the ride.

Lucy spied Daniel Derby waiting at the corner of the property. The hot summer sun reflected on his bald pate. He mopped his bushy brows with a bright red handkerchief. Behind him, like a rag-tag squad of troops armed with picks and shovels, stood his Chinese crew. "Mr. Derby," she said, taking his hand as she stepped down from the carriage, "are we ready?"

"All laid out, ma'am. See there, those markers?"

Beth surveyed the outlines of the fountain. "It looks small."

Derby laughed and patted his rotund belly contentedly. "Don't you be deceived, Bethie. It always looks that way to the untrained eye. Where's the man of the house?"

"Beth will turn up the first spadeful. Shall we start?"

He motioned for one of the laborers to hand him a shovel. "Over here." He set it down at a boundary marker. "Mind you give it a good push with your pretty little foot," he said, placing Beth's hands on the shaft. "Now!"

She gave a small jab at the earth and stepped back quickly as though it might contaminate her. Lucy seized the shovel and with a vigorous thrust, turned up a clod of soil and sent it flying aside. "There. It's all yours now, Mr. Derby."

He clapped his hands, and the Chinese set to work in a flurry of digging. Dirt sailed into the air. Beth sneezed from the dust and daintily covered her nose and mouth with a handkerchief.

"I do think," Lucy said when they were once again in the carriage, "that you might have shown a bit more enthusiasm. You know how fond Mr. Derby is of you children."

"I felt silly with all those China boys staring at us. I don't see why we had to come. They could have started without us."

"I thought you and Abel were excited about the new house."

"He doesn't care. He doesn't give a hang about us or the house.'"

"How could you say such a thing?"

"It's true. He doesn't. He doesn't want to move out here."

"And what, may I ask, are his objections?"

"It's too far away."

"From what, his precious lending library? I'll buy him all the books he wants."

"No, Mama." Beth gave her a crooked little smile. "It's not his library. Why do you always assume he's off reading?"

"That's what he does at home."

"Maybe. But sometimes he just stares at the pages."

"Are you saying he pretends to read so he won't have to be bothered with us? Why are you smirking like that? It's most unappealing."

Beth looked at her scornfully. "You really don't know, do you? You're so busy with your books and figures and your money and your grand plans that you can't even see what's happening in front of your eyes. Abel and I are like sticks of furniture to you. As long as we're in our place in the house, you see just what you expect to see. You only care about Abel when he's not there."

"That's a lie!" She glanced at the driver's back and lowered her voice. "Everything I'm doing I do for you children."

Beth gave her a sharp, defiant glance. "No, Mama. You're the only one who cares about the house. Abel doesn't want to leave Clay Street." She held the gaze, waiting, knowing that somehow she had the upper hand.

"I don't understand."

"I told you, it's too far away."

"But from what?" Lucy shook her head, bewildered.

The small crooked smile played at Beth's lips. "Not 'what.' Who." There was a glint of triumph in her eyes. "From Fleur, of course. Didn't you know?"

Lucy scanned her face in helpless silence.

Beth nodded complacently. "He follows her everywhere."

Lucy grasped the seat of the carriage, the color draining from her face. "But Fleur is—"

"That ugly Corday woman's daughter, the one who comes to the store with the queer little darky."

"Dear God."

"Oh, Mama, don't take on so. I thought you knew he was infatuated with Fleur."

"You know very well I didn't! I never would have allowed such a thing to happen!"

"So you don't like her either. I despise her. All simpering smiles and dainty little mincing ways. She plays with Abel as though he were some kind of pet dog."

"Stop it!"

"I was only trying to tell you what was going on under your nose."

"I don't know what you're trying to do, but I don't like it. Keep your thoughts to yourself, young lady. I'll deal with your brother."

They did not speak for the rest of the trip home. Lucy gazed blankly out of the carriage, unmindful of the passing scene. How could she have been so insensible? What signs had she so carelessly overlooked? Abel had always seemed partial to Fleur, but the girl had such winning ways that Lucy herself had taken a liking to her. Why had it never occurred to her that Abel's interest might be something more? Why had she not admitted that he was fast becoming a man and granted him the possibility of such thoughts? Were all mothers naturally reluctant to recognize the first stirrings of manhood in their sons? Jack had foreseen this, she realized with a shock. And she had been so absorbed in her own cares that she had blinded herself to the obvious. It seemed unthinkable, this alliance, yet the more she dwelled on his unexplained absences and his silent moods, the more she faced the truth of it. She had so easily dismissed his behavior with one excuse or another, thinking him simply reserved and independent, that she had failed to understand him at all. It was her fault that this had happened, and it was up to her to right the situation before it was too late.

That evening, Lucy watched the children eating their supper. In Abel's place sat a quiet, taciturn young man, tall now for his age and lanky in that oddly disproportionate way of young boys. She studied him. His shoulders seemed not yet broad enough to accommodate such long arms. His neck seemed too slender for his head. The slight feathering of black above his lips was an intrusion on the otherwise smooth planes of his face. He seemed absorbed in the food on his plate, hardly bothering to look up or speak. Once or twice she saw Beth glance up slyly, looking from one to the other as though she were waiting for some spark to be struck between the two. She seemed to extract a perverse satisfaction from the silent tension. Lucy caught her eye with a warning stare. Beth merely shrugged innocently and turned her attentions back to the meal.

The girl, unlike Abel, was filling out with flawless grace and symmetry. She unfolded like a dark red rose, hinting of the voluptuous mysteries of nature. Lucy realized that at this precise moment, she was a witness to their metamorphosis. Right now, as they sat here eating their usual evening meal in the ordinary fashion, they were on the verge of coming into their own. They harbored the hopes and fears of strangers, secret from her, and moved inexorably into the forms of a man and woman whom she recognized yet did not know.

Lucy stopped him in the doorway the next morning. "Abel, wait a moment."

"You promised I could go to the library. Can't Beth help you with whatever it is?"

"Beth's gone to Klara's to tend Blanca. Sit down, please. I have to speak to you."

She pulled her chair close to his. "We must talk about Fleur."

He glanced quickly away.

"Don't be embarrassed. She's a very beautiful young lad. I don't blame you for finding her attractive. Son, does Miss Corday know that Fleur has been keeping company with you?"

Abel shook his head. "She thinks she goes out riding."

"I see."

He mumbled something she could not hear.

"Speak up, son."

"She told me her ma wouldn't approve."

"She's right, you know."

He looked up at her, his dark eyes filled with bewilderment. "But why, Mama? What's wrong with me?"

Lucy reached for his hand. "Not a thing. I expect," she told him gently, "that Miss Corday would prefer Fleur to make a match with someone older and more substantial."

"But I told Fleur I have two thousand dollars in the Wells Fargo Bank."

"And what did she say to that?"

He gazed at her for a moment, then looked away. "She wanted me to get it out so's we could go somewhere together. I said I couldn't."

Lucy prayed she sounded calm. "That would have been unwise of you both. Fleur's not happy where she is?"

"She says it's lonely. The other boarders come and go. You know how those girls are," he said, looking away from Lucy's gaze.

"Which girls?"

"The ones who work in those places. What would she have in common with girls like that?"

"I see. But there are gentleman callers."

"Mama," he said miserably, "Fleur hates those men. She despises them. You know what those men want."

She thought for a moment before she replied. "Someday soon you will be a man, and in your own way, you will want such things, too."

"Not like that, I won't! Pigs, that's what she calls them."

"Then what will she think when you grow up and have the same desires?"

"It wouldn't be anything like that. She's too good. Fleur is gentle, Mama, and shy and so very unhappy in that awful place."

"I know you want to help her, son, but Fleur is not your responsibility. She's still a girl, and she must obey her mother's wishes."

"But I can't—"

"Yes, you can. Perhaps the most difficult part of growing up is learning to do what is right." She hesitated. "I have not always succeeded at it myself. I begin to think I may have made some grave errors. But I shall do all I can to see that you don't. We mustn't go against Miss Corday's wishes. It's wrong for you and Fleur to be sneaking about behind people's backs. I'm asking you to stop seeing her."

"No."

"I'm ordering you, Abel. You must trust me. It's for your own good. I know more about such things than you."

"You don't! You can't know how I feel about her."

"Son, I respect your feelings, but they change nothing. You must do as I say."

He rose and stood as stiffly erect as a soldier at arms. He gazed down at her, unyielding.

314

"Please don't force me to go to Miss Corday," Lucy said gently. "I don't want to cause any trouble for Fleur."

"You wouldn't do that!"

"If I thought it was best for you, I would."

"Don't, Mama," he begged her.

"Then you must put a stop to it yourself. There is no other way." She rose and reached out to embrace him, but he stepped away. "Do it," she said.

Lucy shut the door behind her, removed her bonnet and placed it on the wall peg. "Where is he?" she asked.

Beth looked up from her stitchery. "Who?"

"Who. Your brother, of course."

"He went with Joe to the auction house. Mama, you act like a mother hen lately, always clucking about Abel. I declare, I think you favor him over me."

"Don't be foolish. I love both my children. It's just that Abel is going through a difficult time."

"Lovesick," she said scornfully, "mooning over *Mademoiselle La Fleur*."

"Mind your tongue. Perhaps if you'd show him a bit more understanding and sweetness, he wouldn't be so unhappy."

"It's not me he cares about. It's her."

Lucy turned to her. "Bethie. I believe you're jealous."

"Why should I be, just because we have no friends and not even my own brother wants to spend any time with me? Mama!" She flung her needlework aside. "What's happened to us? Why are we so alone? Even here at home I feel lonely. Abel shuts himself away, and you brood over your accounts, and no one comes to call, ever. We're outcasts, Mama! I loathe it here!"

"You refused to come look at the house with me today. The framing is up. You could have seen where your room will be."

"You aren't even listening to me!"

"I heard you." Lucy sat down wearily in her rocking chair.

"It's you, Mama. It's you people don't like. Ever since you went to Miss Corday's during the epidemic. Why?"

Lucy's head jerked up sharply. "You knew?"

"Mama," she said irritably, "it was in the papers, after all. If that priest said you were such a fine Christian woman, why does everyone avoid you?"

"I've told you. Rumors. Gossip."

"Then there must be something to them. What have you done?"

"It's none of your affair."

"No!" She leapt forward and grasped both arms of the rocker, thrusting her face close to Lucy's. "That's not true, not anymore. Whatever you've done has upset our lives. Don't you see, Mama? Abel and I are paying for what you did. We have no visitors. We're not invited anywhere. We're locked away here, hardly speaking to each other. You've made us prisoners, Mama. Do you like that?"

"Bethie, please, don't shout so. I promise you, in time—"

"No, Mama! No more promises! It's been months, and nothing's changed. I don't believe you anymore. I don't know what you've done, but I hate it! And I hate you for doing it!"

Abel stood in the doorway looking at them. "Beth?"

She faced him, still rigid with rage.

"Miss Josie Corday works for Mama. Mama owns her house and some others like it. Fleur told me."

"It's not true!" she cried. "Mama?"

Tears coursed down Lucy's face.

"Mama!" Beth seized her shoulders and shook her violently.

"Abel, Bethie—"

Abel went to his room without answering.

"How could you?" Beth shrilled, recoiling from her.

For a moment Lucy thought the girl was going to turn her back on her and walk away, but she lunged forward and brought the flat of her hand hard against Lucy's moist cheek. "Look what you've done to us all!"

Lucy lay in bed, sleepless. The stillness gnawed at her nerves. She turned again, fitfully, the bedclothes twisted uncomfortably about her. How had it come to this? She tried to sort out the jumble of thoughts that pressed into her mind, to make sense of what had happened. All her plans, all her efforts, had been for the children's sakes. She'd wanted them to have the opportunities she'd never known. She'd wanted nothing for herself. But here she felt a peculiar sense of discomfort, like a lump of something cold and nauseating inside her. She had been warned.

Time and again, Jack had tried to stop her. Why had she refused to listen?

Arrogance.

With a pang of recognition, she realized that the sensation she felt was her own shame. She despised Jack for having been right, but she despised herself more for having been so wrong. She had plunged ahead, oblivious of anyone else, brandishing the banner of the children's good as though it somehow sanctified her mission. The only person she had satisfied was herself. She had proven she could make a fortune and she had taken it for granted that it would make them happy. In fact, she had sacrificed their happiness to her own ambitions. Suddenly she remembered something Reed Pierce had said, something about the danger of not questioning oneself. He had warned her, too. He'd cautioned her that if she were ever sure she knew all the answers, she might well be a damned fool. The prophesy was fulfilled. She was a fool, damned even by her own children. She had lied to them, to Jack, to herself. She had tried to make them all believe she cared only for Abel and Beth, while they saw clearly that she was nothing more than a grasping woman bent on having her own way. She had alienated them all, even Polly and Albert Fearing. She had made trouble for Joe Mason. Her consuming ambition had poisoned everyone it had touched. She'd done the very thing that Pa had always condemned. She had traded her conscience for profit.

Trembling, she rose from the bed and wrapped a shawl about her shoulders. She went into the sitting room, lit a lamp and spread her account books before her on the table. . . .

"It's done," she told Joe two weeks later.

"Everything?"

"Banked. Mr. Biggs at Wells Fargo will advise me on some safe investments. Would you be good enough to deliver this letter to your mother when you see her?"

He pocketed the envelope. "It won't be easy for you. Nothing will change overnight."

"I know. I pray the children have enough patience and forgiveness."

"Mrs. Pitt was in the store today. She left this for you. For the new house, she said."

It was a small Berlin-work pillow of pink, scattered

with white roses. How Mrs. Pitt's swollen fingers could have stitched it, she couldn't imagine. Lucy traced the design with her hand. "Whatever you may think of her, Joe, she's not a bad sort at heart. I dread having to shun her."

Lucy sat alone on the grass with her newspaper, her back to the bright September sun. Her parasol lay unopened beside her. She spied a small troop of ants making its way across the linen picnic cloth toward the last crumbs of Bethie's cake. She shook the cloth and brushed them away with the black-bordered paper, then fanned herself with it for a moment before spreading it out again on her lap.

A sorry business, she thought, gazing at the headline, for men to be shooting at each other over words. She paused at the sound of Beth's laughter and smiled. A pair of flies droned lazily overhead and came to rest on a leaf at her feet. The rapping of hammers and the rasp of a saw were all that kept her from drowsing. She tried to concentrate on the newspaper. Where was the sense of it, a senator killed by a judge? She'd had no more regard for Senator Broderick than for the rest of his breed, but his death seemed to her pointless and deplorable. It appeared to matter not at all that dueling was against the law. Men swaggered to their deaths, pistol barrels glowing darkly in the first light of dawn, in dew-dampened glades and meadows where the birds sang on, innocent of matters like vanity and bravado. The futility of it, she thought, the sheer foolish pride that had brought these two civilized men, inflamed by oratory and political insults, to draw their weapons while a flock of spectators, their talmas wrapped close against the early morning cool like the great, folded wings of vultures, stood watching as if they were merely idlers at a rat and terrier fight. And now, after this carnival of bloodshed, the senator was dead. And for what? Judge Terry, monument of justice that he fancied himself, had simply proven once again that men could, and would, take the law into their own hands.

Lucy made no excuses for herself. In her own way, she had done the same thing. It had become too easy to be free. Here in this place of new beginnings, with its limitless possibilities, one answered only to oneself. And she, heady with her own independence, had strutted ahead as she pleased, without regard for anyone or anything else. In the long nights of silent contemplation when sleep eluded her, she had learned one thing above all. Such freedom extracted a higher price than she was willing to pay. She could no longer afford it. It had all but made enemies of her own son and daughter.

The social redemption of Lucy Bates, she reflected wryly, was scarcely an inviting prospect. For twelve years, ever since Caleb Bates had left, she'd been at liberty to go at large as she'd pleased, unconstrained by anyone else's restrictions or opinions. Now she must rein herself in, trotting and prancing decorously in step with the genteel matrons of San Francisco, who were, to her mind, mostly self-righteous prigs. But she would play out her part. She'd march to their rhythm and keep silent in the face of their narrow-minded views. She would dress with proper modesty, speak discreetly and endure all the suffocating niceties of convention, though the recognition of her own hypocrisy was sure to plague her, as galling as a burr under a saddle. To all aspects, she would prove a pillar of respectability. This she was obliged to do. But she was not obliged to surrender her soul to this whinnying, huffing herd. Let them have their appearances and their etiquette. She would present them willingly, for the safe of her children. But her soul, by God, remained her own.

"Mama? Are you daydreaming?" Beth scattered a handful of sawdust to the breeze. "Mr. Derby let me climb up the ladder to my room. You can see the water from where my window will be."

Lucy smiled at her enthusiasm. "We must choose some wallpaper."

"Blue and white. I want it to look like a part of the sky. With ruffled white curtains like clouds."

"Then that's what you shall have. Help me gather up the picnic things."

"Abel will be sorry he didn't come. His room looks down on the whole city."

Lucy tucked the folded linen cloth into her basket. "I want him to help in the store whenever he can. Joe's a model young man and a good example for him."

Joe placed the "Closed" sign in the window. Lucy locked her desk and gathered up her parasol and picnic basket. "You know the stock better than I, Joe. Have we any of that blue and white cotton left? The morning-glory print?"

"Not here." He took his jacket from its peg and slipped into it. "I can fetch some from the storeroom."

"There's no hurry. I thought Bethie might like it for her new room. This afternoon she actually seemed excited about moving. Things are changing for us, Joe. I'm sure of it."

"From what I hear, you acted in the nick of time. There's a scandal brewing around The Pacific Palace."

"Is it sickness?"

"Worse." He pocketed his keys and gave a last look around. "The Corday woman's dwarf got himself run down by a carriage today, right out there," he said, nodding toward the street. "Not more than two in the afternoon, and he could scarcely see where he was going. Abel and I ran out to help."

"Was he hurt?"

Joe shook his head. "He was half-seas-over, that's all, and weepy as a woman. Seems a pair of sots at Corday's decided they'd resume the Terry-Broderick duel last night. They were waving their pistols around in the alley behind the place. One of the girls tried to intervene and caught a bullet."

"How badly . . ."

"Bad enough. It struck her in the throat and killed her. You remember her, the little green-eyed beauty who shopped here. The dwarf was always hovering about her like—"

"No! Fleur? Abel heard this?" She darted for the door. "Joe, where is he?"

"He said he was going up to the storeroom to unpack some crates."

She raced to the storeroom and flung open the door. It slammed against the wall with a crash and shuddered. The new shipment of crates lay stacked in the center of the floor, unopened. "Abel?" She searched quickly about the high-piled bolts of cloth. "Abel!" she called, but the silent room swallowed up the sound. She ran outside and, catching up her skirts, dashed upstairs and burst into the sitting room. Beth leapt up, startled.

"Abel!" she cried frantically. "Where is he?" Without

waiting for an answer, she brushed past the bewildered girl and ran to his room.

"Mama! Mama! Mama!" Beth stood in the doorway, a look of terror on her face. "Mama, stop screaming! What's wrong? What's happened? Mama, don't shriek like that!"

In her hand, Lucy held his cap and his night shirt, the only things he had left behind.

XVII

SOMETIMES, IN the night, Beth would be awakened by stirrings on the other side of the partition that separated her own small room from Abel's. She would lie there, listening to Lucy's movements, knowing that beyond the thin wall her mother was once again poring over the remnants of his presence.

Lucy would stare down at the odds and ends of his washstand, a rock showing a fleck of gold that he'd found along the river in Castalia, his ink-encrusted pen, a school tablet with his laboriously copied Latin, a scrap of faded blue ribbon, perhaps once Fleur's, and a neatly arranged collection of newspaper clippings, mostly yellowed now. She had read them all, over and over, looking perhaps for a hint of his whereabouts, but they were only editorials and items of politics. She would sit on the edge of his cot and gaze at the single poster that decorated the room, a lurid broadside showing a galloping white steed ridden by a wild-eyed Indian, painted and feathered and brandishing his tomahawk between the words HENRY MILLER'S and TOBACCO. She rose then and went to his bookshelves, running her fingertips over the volumes there. Often, she took one down and leafed through its pages as if they might hold a clue to him. She replaced his books exactly as he had left them arranged. She reached for his cap lying atop the highest shelf, shook it free of imagined dust and held it clasped close to her chest, as though it were a part of him. After a while, the uselessness of the rite would intrude upon her. No memory, no touch of these remaining bits and pieces of his life would call him forth. It was then that Beth heard her close the door to his room and lock it, safeguarding all that remained of him. Lucy would make her way quietly to the sitting room, holding back her tears, let herself out the door and descend the stairs to the street.

Beth would stand at the window, her face half hidden by the thin white curtains. Through the mist, she looked down at the lone figure striding up and down the silent, empty street, her arms folded about her, the wetness of her cheeks shining clear and bright in the lamplight. Sometimes a keening reached Beth's ears, a low, fitful, intermittent wail. Beth remained there, keeping watch, until Lucy, chilled and spent, turned again toward the stairs below.

Mother and daughter made a pretense of their meals now, praising the food, urging another taste of this or that upon each other, as though neither noticed that the portions before them had scarcely been touched.

Covertly, Beth observed her mother across the breakfast table. The usually rounded contours of Lucy's face seemed, in a matter of days, to have dissolved. The well-defined planes of her cheekbones imparted a new severity to her appearance, and her straight, slender nose seemed conspicuously sharp in contrast to her puffed and reddened eyes.

"The newsboys," Lucy said suddenly. "I must inquire among the newsboys. Children seek out their own kind. Maybe one of them has seen him."

"Mama, I'm sure the authorities have asked in all the likely places. They promised you they'd do their best to find him. They know more about these things than we do."

"But how can we be sure? They haven't brought us any news, and it's been over a week. Perhaps I should try the waterfront again."

"Don't. Joe said it wasn't safe for you to go about alone there."

"I'll take him with me this time."

"Mama, Joe visits the wharves every day. You know very well he asks everyone he comes across."

"Customs agents. Importers. What would they know?"

"For my sake, Mama, please. If nobody recalled seeing him there before, you can't expect them to recollect him a week later. That's no place for you."

"And no place for a boy of fifteen, either," she said, thinking of the dingy, vermin-infested lodging houses clustered near the wharves, squalid and decadent as the beery vagrants that lounged about their doorways. She had closed her ears to the men's insults and coarse overtures. She had held her temper while they made sport of her in dank grog shops that stank invariably of sweat and smoke and stale liquor. She had sought out the crippled survivors of the sea, as they huddled listlessly on the sidewalks of the teeming streets, resting their backs against the buildings behind them, exposing their mangled stumps and sightless eyes to the warmth of the sun. She had approached the ship chandlers, the gaming hall-dealers, even the slovenly Chileno whores loitering about the street corners. Along the jetties, she had searched among the draymen and sailors, the Kanakas, the tattooed Maoris and the wizened salts hawking bits of scrimshaw. Past piles of cured hides, looming stacks of barrels and mountains of lumber, Lucy had made her way, dwarfed by the towering ships docked to either side. If a man wasn't reeling with drugs or drink, she stopped him, begging a moment of his time. She shouted above the clatter of horse-drawn wagons and handcarts, describing the boy, pleading for a chance recognition or a word of encouragement. No one remembered him. At last, she had leaned exhausted against one of the pilings at the far end of Meiggs' Wharf, looking out over the harbor. The light from the setting sun came and went, now dimmed by the onrushing fog, now reappearing. Beyond rose the dark outline of Alcatraz Island. Slowly the fog settled around it, obscuring its shores and swirling about its lowlands, until the topmost part of its fort was all that remained to be seen floating above the restless, churning mist. She had glanced away finally, and her eyes had caught her own reflection in the water below, the sprawling, disjointed image of a woman, writhing in the rippling waves that licked against the bleached wooden pilings.

"Mama?" Beth reached over and touched her arm. "You didn't hear me."

"I'm sorry, dear." She stirred her coffee absently. "What was it you said?"

"I want to change schools."

"You do? Why, Bethie?"

"Because . . . at my school everyone knows about you."

"I see."

"At a new school, people might not make the connection. Perhaps by the time they became acquainted with me and met you, everything would be forgotten."

She gazed across the table at the girl's earnest, hopeful face. "Oh, my darling child." Lucy shook her head in dismay. "What have I done? Of course you may do whatever you wish."

"I want to go to Miss Barlow's Female Seminary, Mama. But it's a private school," she cautioned, "and I don't know how much it costs to go there."

"I don't care. If money can buy you some peace of mind, the cost means nothing to me. I'll write to Miss Barlow right away, if you like."

Beth bounded up from the table and brought Lucy her pen and ink and paper. "Wait," she said. "I have the address in my room."

Lucy scanned the letter she had written and signed her name at the bottom. "There. I'll post it when I go to speak to the newsboys."

"I'll come with you."

"One of us should stay here, Bethie. In case someone brings word."

"Joe's downstairs. He'd see anyone who came by. Please, Mama. It's not right for you to spend your days roaming the streets by yourself. It only upsets you more. Let me keep you company."

Beth tried to affect a nonchalant air as they made their way through the streets and alleys, up and down the precipitous hills and along the sandy shore where children built sand palaces in the late September sun. She would pause to point out some sight to her mother or linger in front of a shop window, idly surveying its contents. Perhaps the passersby might think them merely out for a pleasant stroll. Perhaps they might not perceive that her mother's eyes were never still, that they moved about too rapidly, too restlessly, like those of a frantic, anxious animal. Maybe they wouldn't see the feverish flush on her cheeks and the taut, strained muscles of her neck or notice the oddly stiff, dogged pace she set.

It seemed to Beth that the fruitless hours of walking and searching and questioning only drove Lucy more relentlessly. Beth glanced at her warily, alarmed by this fervor that seemed indifferent to fatigue or discomfort. "Mama, stop. I have to rest. I've a blister on my heel." She leaned against the iron fence in front of a nearby house and unbuttoned her shoe.

"Let me see." Lucy knelt and examined the girl's raw, swollen heel. "It wants bathing. I suppose we must go home."

"Ladies." A shadow fell across them.

Lucy turned and stood up. "Your Royal Highness," she said, addressing the rumpled, darkly bearded figure.

He raised his walking stick in a stately salute. "Has there been any news of your boy, madam?"

She shook her head.

"I've made inquiries, you know," he said in his precise British accent, "as I travel about overseeing my affairs."

"That's very kind of you, Sir. Thank you."

He dismissed her gratitude with a regal wave of his hand. "Not at all. The well-being of my subjects is of great concern to me. Perhaps I shall issue a proclamation on your son's behalf. The *Bulletin* publishes all my official announcements, you know."

"I appreciate the gesture, Your Majesty," Lucy replied hastily, "but it isn't necessary. Bethie?" She took the girl's hand. "Are you ready?"

"And who," he inquired, "is this?"

"My daughter, Beth Bates. Bethie, show Emperor Norton a curtsy, if you please."

Beth looked at her mother, then back at the disheveled creature who fixed her in an imperious, expectant gaze. He sported a battered military cap set at a jaunty tilt, and beneath his unkempt beard was a soiled frock coat adorned with shabby epaulets and brass buttons, several of which dangled loosely at the ends of their threads. His brown trousers were frayed, his boots worn and dulled. He tapped the ground impatiently with his walking stick. Lucy gave Beth an admonishing nod. She made a perfunctory curtsy, her cheeks rosy with embarrassment.

"Ah, such a graceful young lady. It does one proud to have such lovely subjects. My dear," he proclaimed. "you're a fine specimen of this fair city. Look at it," he said, waving his stick grandly in the direction of the bay. "Was there ever a more pleasant domain? Constantinople."

"Sir?" Beth said, startled.

"I could have created Constantinople here on this bay. Perhaps I shall. With a great bridge reaching across it to the other side. A man with enough rice can make miracles."

Beth stared at him, dumfounded.

"Mark my words, girl. I've glorious plans for our nation."

"Yes, Sir."

"Rice," he said, raising his stick for emphasis, and with a curt nod he turned and strolled away.

"Mama!"

"I know, dear, but he's harmless. The poor man wasn't always like that. Come, let's be going."

"But how did he get that way?"

"He lost his fortune a few years back and never recovered. The birds!" she said suddenly and looked up angrily at the sky. "How I hate those birds!"

In the waning sunlight, flocks of swallows wheeled restively about the sky. They swooped and swirled in dusky waves, soaring upward with a great flapping of wings and hurtling down abruptly in dizzying dives, screeching as they came. Lucy grimaced and clapped her hands to her ears against the sound.

"But Mama, the swallows make a commotion every day at this time. They'll quiet down when the sun sets."

She took her hands from her ears and walked faster. "I despise them."

"Why?"

"Because," she snapped, "they saw him go. They know where he went."

"Mama!" Beth cried. "You're not talking sense."

"I hate them," she repeated. "They tell me that another day has ended and he's not returned."

Beth followed her home in silence.

Saturday morning, Beth left the house early with the excuse that Klara Mason had asked her to look after Blanca. As she closed the door, she gave a last glance at Lucy, who sat at the table poring over the mail. She was not sure she had done the right thing, stealing out yesterday, deceiving her mother, but it had seemed to her that she'd had no other choice. She'd turned to the only person she knew might help.

Polly Fearing, attired in a fashionable indigo walking-dress, sat gingerly poised on the edge of her chair, like a fragile blue vase precariously deposited there.

"Letters," Lucy gave a disconcerted wave at the paper-strewn table before her. "Acknowledgments of furniture orders for the new house. You know how it is," she continued vaguely, "so many things, details."

Tentatively Polly eased herself back in the chair. "I received the letter you sent by Joe a few weeks back."

"Yes. I wanted you to know how I felt about—"

"Never mind," Polly said gently.

"I wanted you to know that I realize what I'd done. To all of us. I felt I should tell you I was trying to remedy the situation."

"I understood. Lucy, I heard about Abel."

She froze. "You've word of him?"

"I'm afraid not. But Joe told me what happened."

"Oh."

"I know how you must be suffering, my dear."

"Polly!" She sprang up. "I haven't offered you anything! Tea? A cup of coffee? I've almost a whole lemon cake."

"Please, Lucy, sit down. Don't make a fuss on my account. I didn't come to be entertained. I came because I was concerned for you. I know Abel's running off must be terribly hard on you, but you mustn't let it get the better of you. You must take care of your health and try to make life as normal as possible for you and Beth. It wouldn't do for the boy to return and find you unwell. And think of Beth, Lucy. She's had the same shock. She needs you more than ever now. You must try to keep on an even keel for everybody's sake. Do you have any callers?"

"No."

"Then you must bring yourself to go visiting. Companionship can be a great comfort."

"I've no one who'd receive me. It seems I saw to that quite efficiently. Besides, somebody should be here in case he . . ."

"You could leave a note on the door. Lucy, please dine

with Albert and myself and Joe and Klara on Tuesday. It will do you good to forget your cares for a few hours."

"Does Albert know you're here?"

Polly nodded. "Please come. It would be a welcome change for Beth, I'm sure."

"I just don't know if—"

"For Beth. Please."

It was the baby, Blanca, who delivered them all from the initial discomfort that attended the gathering. By turns, they held and fondled her, stroking the pale gilding of down on her head, raising her high in the air to wave her little arms like a fledgling bird, exclaiming over her alert blue eyes and concentrating all their attentions upon this small, unwitting savior who dispelled their uneasiness.

"Albert," Polly observed, "she looks like such a mite in your arms. She all but disappears."

Blanca began to howl.

"Tiny but forceful. Klara?" He handed her the child.

"She is hungry." Klara crooned softly to the baby. "I take her upstairs."

Octavia appeared in the doorway. "Dinner is served, ma'am."

Polly rose. "As I recall, Beth," she said, taking her hand, "you especially like Tavie's apple dumplings. It wouldn't surprise me if she'd found time to make some. Tavie?"

The woman turned back with a knowing smile. "I can't say for sure, ma'am. Miss Beth, I'll just have to scout 'round out there. Could be they're hidin' someplace in my kitchen."

Beth consumed not one but two apple dumplings. Even Lucy mustered an appetite for Tavie's splendid dinner. "My word," she apologized, "I believe I gobbled like a billy goat, in spite of myself. I shall need the walk home to recover from all that good food."

"We'll come with you," Polly offered. "Albert, will you kindly fetch my wrap?"

"There's no need, Polly, really," Lucy replied.

"But it's a beautiful, warm evening, just right for a stroll. Martha," she instructed her daughter, "you stay here and finish your lessons. I'll have a look at them when I come home."

Reluctantly, the girl trudged up the stairs. Outside in

the night a firebell sounded. Martha paused as if to listen, but then she turned and, looking down at Polly, asked, "Mother, is Beth allowed to come here now any time she likes?"

Polly flushed. "Yes," she answered. "Now, no more chatter. See to your schoolwork."

Martha gave Beth a conspiratorial grin and bounded up the stairway.

They bade good-night to Joe and Klara at the corner of Jackson Street. "That Blanca's a sweet child," Lucy said. "Such a sunny disposition."

"Was I like that, Mama?" Beth wanted to know.

"Not always, I'm afraid. You were an insistent little thing with rather a lusty voice."

"And Abel?"

"Lucy," Polly interrupted, "have you met the Fiskes, John and Leanna? They're new in the city. A very attractive couple, to Albert's and my thinking. Isn't that so, Albert?"

"He's a most amiable sort," he agreed, "and Leanna plays the piano beautifully. Martha's taking lessons from her."

"You must meet them," Polly said. "I shall arrange it."

"Please—" Lucy stopped and put a hand on her arm. "Don't jeopardize yourselves on my account. My reputation—"

"They're new here. And Albert and I are quite capable of making our own decisions as to what's appropriate to a given time, if you recall."

Albert changed the subject. "On a night like this, there's something almost exotic about this place. Look," he said, pointing down to the edge of the bay where a low-lying fog had settled on the water and obscured the shoreline. The full moon illuminated the cottony white billows with a brightness that was startling. "Rather like being on a mountaintop, high above the clouds."

"Are there really mountains that high?" Beth asked. "So high that the clouds don't even reach the top?"

"Certainly." Albert took her hand as they rounded the corner onto Clay Street. "Why, in Europe—" He stopped as the clatter of a speeding carriage sounded behind them. "I say, it's a bit late for someone to be in such a rush. He's risking his horse, driving that recklessly at night."

"It's Daniel Derby," Lucy exclaimed as his stanhope came into view. "Mr. Derby! What's the hurry?"

"Lucy Bates? That you?" he called, smartly reining in his horse. He jumped from his seat and drew the snorting animal toward the sidewalk where they stood. "It's the house, Mrs. Bates—It's on fire."

"My new house?"

"The volunteers are there now, but she's a goner, Mrs. Bates. Those roof beams were catching like lucifers when I left."

"I must go."

"There's not a thing you can do," he warned.

Polly spoke up. "Albert and I will stay with Beth. Do what you must, Lucy."

"I want to go," cried Beth. "It's my house, too."

"No." Lucy stepped into the carriage. "Wait for me at home."

The fire glowed like a beacon ahead of them. As they neared it, Lucy could hear the roar and crackle of the flames and the loud, rhythmic chantey of the firemen as they manned their engines.

"Santa Anna's dead and gone,
Poor old Santa Anna!
Oh, we won our way at Monterey
And on the plains of Mexico.
Woe, Santa Anna!"

Daniel Derby stopped the carriage at a safe distance. Through the shimmering waves of heat, the skeleton of the building lay clearly illuminated by the flames rippling over it. The eaves, the window frames, the curved arches of the porch flared brightly against the night sky. The house groaned and hissed and spat like something alive as it was devoured. The blaze lapped greedily at the peak of the roof, despite the jets of water playing upon it. Sparks showered from the burning wood. The torch boys scampered to trample them out. As more patches of grass ignited, firemen rushed by with their shovels, heaving clods of earth over the fast-moving flames, their faces streaked with sweat and soot, looking like somberly painted Indians performing some arcane rite.

"Get back, boys!" came the shout. "She's going to fall!"

The volunteers scattered hastily as the charred timbers crumbled and gave way, one after another, toppling with a crash, sending up an explosion of sparks. Quickly, the men trained their hoses on the smoldering heaps of blackened lumber. Here and there a beam protruded grotesquely, like a dark, mangled limb. Above the ruins, the full moon hovered whitely among the splayed branches of a slender pine tree. Lucy stared at it vacantly for a moment, dazed and numbed. Suddenly she started, as though awakened. "The trees," she said quietly, glancing around her. "The four trees arrived."

"Brought from the wharf early this morning. We planted them in the afternoon." Derby brushed a cinder from his trouser leg and surveyed the scene. "Can't say as they make the place any prettier now. That one there looks to have got singed on one side."

"How did it start, do you know?"

Derby hailed one of the men. "Mate! The lady here owns this property. Could you spare us a moment?"

The man trotted toward the carriage, wiping the grime from his face with a shirtsleeve. "Ma'am." He doffed his hat. "Foreman Mooney, at your service."

"I wondered what had set it off."

"Vagrants, probably. Sometimes they camp in empty or unfinished buildings. It started inside, that's for certain. Most likely they lit a cook-fire, and it got away from them."

"Thank you. And please, thank the men for me."

"Yes, ma'am." Raising his hat to her, he donned it and ran back to his work.

Lucy looked after him. She gave a small, dry laugh. "Imagine. In the midst of a catastrophe, he thinks to remove his hat for a lady. Nothing left but ashes and gallantry." She looked about her. "And trees," she added. "I didn't realize how much I'd yearned to live once more on land where trees grow."

"It's late. We'd best be going. This night has been something of a blow to both of us." Derby snapped his reins.

As the carriage turned away, Lucy saw the torch boys standing along the slope of the street, waiting to guide the engines back to the firehouses. The dwindling light from the blaze reflected on their young faces. She gazed from one to another, taking in each of them as she passed by.

Derby gave them a salute. "Good lads," he said.

"I was looking to see if my son was among them. He admired firemen. They were his heroes."

"They did their best, ma'am."

"I shall send something 'round to the firehouses in the morning."

"No need to think about that now. You need a rest."

"No," she said abruptly. "Times like this, you don't lie down. The worse things are, the more you need to pick yourself up and go on. If I hadn't learned that long ago, I wouldn't be alive today."

Derby gave her a curious look.

"Well?" she challenged him. "When shall we begin to rebuild?"

"Mrs. Bates, this isn't the time for you to be making important decisions."

"That's for me to judge. I've started from nothing several times before in my life. Action is the best tonic for one's morale, Mr. Derby."

He shook his head slowly. "You do beat all, little lady. I expected you to be reaching for your smelling salts by now. What's come over you?"

"Necessity. I've no alternative. I can't afford to stop and brood over my troubles, not now. I need that house, you see. I need it to occupy my mind."

He gazed ahead thoughtfully, making soft clucking noises to his horse. "That site has to cool down before it can be cleared. There's the lumber to be ordered. Labor's getting harder to hire, what with people running off to that Washoe silver find over in Western Utah. Then, too, it's coming into the rainy season. That could hold up things."

"Mr. Derby. Daniel, if I may. I promised Bethie I'd give her a party in that house on her next birthday. That would be in February. I should like you and your wife to be there."

"That's only four months away," he protested.

"There's a substantial bonus waiting for you, if you can do it."

He didn't answer. He pursed his lips and nodded pensively up and down, calculating to himself.

"What do you think?"

"It's possible. Not that I can guarantee it, but I can try."

"That's all I ask."

"I have to say, Mrs. Bates—"

"Please. Lucy."

"Lucy, you are one plucky lady."

"I may be down, Daniel, but I'm not dead yet, and I don't intend to succumb for a long, long time."

Polly Fearing closed the window against the afternoon fog. "Anyone for another cup of tea?"

Leanna Fiske laid her cup and saucer on the tole tray. "With just a bit of milk." She smoothed her dark hair into place at the nape of her neck and turned back to Lucy. "Do go on. It sounds lovely."

"I'm not boring you?"

"Certainly not." She smiled, her slim, angular face softening with the gesture. "You were talking about the piano."

"In the drawing room. There will be Turkey carpets on the floor, a matched pair, and I shall take the red from them for the draperies and upholstery."

Polly chuckled. "I declare, I think there's a trace of the phoenix in you. You swooped up from those ashes and you haven't paused to light yet. It seems to me this house of yours grows grander every time I hear of it."

"But it does," she admitted candidly. "I've decided to make it the grandest house I can. I've worked hard for my money. It's time I enjoyed it."

"What sort of work do you do?" Leanna inquired.

Polly glanced up from the teapot.

"I've a dry goods store that's allowed me to make a few investments. Polly's boy, Joe, manages the store for me now, so I suppose you might call me a lady in retirement."

"I find that unlikely," Leanna said. "You don't seem the sort to enjoy idle solitude."

"A lady at liberty," Polly corrected, "but hardly at rest."

"Land, how could I be?" Lucy laughed. "There's so much to be done. Polly, did you speak to Octavia about her brother?"

"Septimus. He and his wife will arrive sometime after the first of the year. The woman's name is Biddy. Tavie

334

assures me she's a fine cook and housekeeper and Septimus has been both a stable hand and a manservant."

"Are you certain," Lucy said, lowering her voice, "that they're both freedmen? I shouldn't want to be involved in that sort of contraband."

"Mrs. Bates," Leanna Fiske spoke up sharply, "I should think it a privilege to help some poor black soul out of bondage."

"The Fiskes," Polly explained hastily, "are from New Hampshire. Leanna, Lucy hails from Missouri like my own dear Albert. I think you'll find it more comfortable in this city if you forgo the issue of slavery. There's a large Southern element in San Francisco, and were we all to be at each other's throats, there'd be chaos in the streets, not to mention here in this house. It's one of the few issues which Albert and I do not discuss. At any rate, Lucy," she continued, "Septimus and Biddy were made freedmen by their late owner's will. They'll be carrying a letter to that effect."

"If they're at all like Tavie, I know I'll be pleased. Leanna," she said as she turned to her, "you will consider taking on Beth as one of your music pupils, won't you? Since she entered Miss Barlow's she's developed quite an appetite for the feminine refinements. She's determined to learn to play the piano and to dance."

"I'd be delighted to teach her both."

"The dancing too? I was under the impression that New Englanders frowned on that sort of frivolity."

Leanna smiled. "It appears that we all have much to learn from each other."

Polly laid her cup and saucer on the tea tray. "The way the men are scampering off to the Washoe mines, young ladies may be hard put to find any dancing partners at all."

"It's another stampede," Lucy agreed. "Exactly like last time, except that now it's silver."

"They say the Ophir Diggings are the richest in history," Leanna marveled. "Do you think it's true?"

"We'll know soon enough," Polly told her. "This city reacts like a barometer to such things."

"For once," Lucy said, "I'll be quite content to observe the effects from a distance. You two could scarcely imagine how men are willing to suffer for their fantasies of a *bonanza*."

"What is that?" Leanna asked.

"The Mexicans use it in the diggings to mean a rich strike. If you ask me, news of a *bonanza* is usually more rumor than reality. These finds sound more inviting than they actually are. I've seen Western Utah, and not for all the riches in the world would I be willing to gaze upon that godforsaken, barren tract again."

But others, it appeared, had no such misgivings. As men streamed eagerly over the mountains to the north in that fall of eighteen fifty-nine, a backwash of silver sluiced southward to be absorbed by the Mosheimer smelting works and thence by the city's treasuries. A bright array of bullion bars, lustrous and tempting, gleamed in the window of Alsop and Company's banking house. Washoe ore was bringing in two to five thousand dollars the ton. Moreover, the stuff kept coming. It seemed there was no end to the rich veins that streaked the mountains and canyons of Western Utah.

"We lost the fellow who was going to carve the newel posts," Daniel Derby reported to Lucy. "He decided he'd rather carve silver out of Sun Mountain. But one of the China boys can do the job, I think. I gave him a sketch, and he seemed to grasp the idea."

They walked slowly over the grounds. Here and there, blackened patches scarred the earth, reminders of the fire. "I should like the planting done as soon as possible," she told him. "In front, on either side of the entrance, the white azaleas, and along this side of the house, below the covered porch, we should alternate the iris and the hummingbird flowers."

Derby jotted her instructions in a well-worn notebook. "You don't want anything under those pines. Nothing's going to grow there."

"No. The graveled walks should cut across the lawn and circle the trees. See." She paced a pattern of lines between the house and the trees, stopping at the half-finished carriage house on the far corner of the property.

"You ought to have some kind of hedge here. Never can tell when someone will buy that land and build behind you."

"Myrtle. It grows high enough. There should be a screen of it along the rear boundary."

"Seems to me you've thought of everything."

"Not I. Klara Mason. Horticulture is her hobby. She assures me all these things will grow here."

Despite Daniel Derby's initial qualms, the house rose again rapidly. On the ground floor were the drawing room, dining room, kitchen and pantry, a library and a sitting room with a wide window seat in the bay that faced the street. Behind these, adjacent to the kitchen, were two servant's rooms. The second story boasted four bed chambers, a nursery and, for Lucy, a small dressing room. There was even a spacious, windowed bathroom at the end of the upstairs hall.

As she went from room to room, making notations to herself as to chandeliers and sconces, draperies and curtains, carpets, wallpaper, upholstery and linens, she envisaged the house as it might one day be, filled with Beth's and Abel's families, the children, her grandsons and granddaughters, laughing in the nursery, sliding down the glowing mahogany bannister, sitting in their high chairs in the large, sunny dining room. As she oversaw the paneling and painting and papering of each room, she saw also, in her mind's eye, that it was not simply a house but a way of life she sought to build, her future and the future of her children.

Already the dark green shutters had been hung outside each window against the white-painted clapboard walls. A low white fence surrounded the property on all sides, and within it, the newly seeded lawn, the trees and flowers and shrubs awaited the first autumn rains.

In warehouses by the wharves, the consignments of furniture piled up. There were two japanned lowboys for Lucy's bedroom, a grandfather clock from Boston, a mahogany highboy from Philadelphia, a slant-topped cherrywood desk, rosewood tables, sofas, bedsteads, benches and chairs. As the first carpets were laid on the glossy floor, a steady procession of vans and carts began to draw up to the door.

"Such elegance!" Polly Fearing exclaimed, as she paused to catch her reflection in the gilt-framed oval mirror on the stair landing.

Lucy stepped aside as two workmen passed with Beth's dressing table. "Gentlemen, that goes under the north window in the blue room."

"How will you cope with such a big place until Septimus and Biddy arrive?" Polly wondered.

"Rather haphazardly, I should imagine," Lucy answered cheerfully. "But I'll have time to learn what's needed for the kitchen and the rest of the housekeeping."

"It's clouding up." Polly glanced toward the open front door below, its space partially blocked by the advent of Beth's piano. "I hope they get everything in before it rains. My dear," she said, kissing Lucy on the cheek, "I wish you great happiness here. It's a splendid establishment, and I know you'll enjoy it."

It was that, Lucy thought, gazing out of the rainwashed window of their lodgings over Clay Street. The house was everything she had intended it to be, roomy yet hospitable, luxurious yet practical. She stared at her image in the pane, wondering why tonight, at the last, she suddenly dreaded leaving these small lodgings. She turned away and went to Abel's room, bare now of all his possessions. She herself had stocked his bookshelves in the new house, arranging the volumes precisely as he had left them here. She looked around at the empty space. It seemed hollow and impersonal. "He was here," she said quietly. "You may deny it, but he was here."

"Mama?"

"Bethie. You startled me."

"Were you speaking to someone?"

"No." She thought for a moment. "It's just that it seems as though we are abandoning him, leaving him behind us."

Beth reached out a hand to her. "Please, come help me finish my packing."

Lucy glanced once more around the vacant room. Tears stung her eyes. Quickly, she brushed them away and took a deep breath. "I'm coming," she said and clasped Beth's outstretched hand.

XVIII

LEANNA FISKE seated herself at the piano and tentatively struck a chord. She smiled to herself and nodded approval at the sound. "Gather 'round, everyone!" she called. "Let's have a sing." She opened the pocket-sized copy of *Put's Golden Songster* that lay on the music rack and glanced at the pages. "John," she asked her husband, "would you kindly bring me my spectacles?"

"In a moment." John Fiske deftly fanned a hand of playing cards onto the tabletop, all diamonds, all in sequence. The youngsters gathered about him murmured in amazement.

"How is it done?" Beth wanted to know.

"Like the others I've shown you, sleight of hand. Easy as butter melts in the sun." He rose and went to fetch Leanna's handbag. "A lesson to you, boys and girls. A fellow can deal you most any hand he wants."

"Show me how," Beth insisted. "After all, it's my birthday."

"Never," he said, laughing. "A lady's dangerous enough without a deck of cards in her hand. Come to the piano."

"Wait for me!" Martha Mason squirmed impatiently on her chair.

"Only a moment more," promised Mr. Mills, the silhouette-cutter, as he snipped swiftly across his sheet of black paper. "There," he proclaimed, raising his voice over the music. He held the silhouette in front of the lamplight.

"Wonderful!" Polly exclaimed delightedly. "It's her, right down to that little upturn at the end of the nose."

With a flourish, Mr. Mills slipped it into a folded piece of heavy white paper and presented it to Polly.

"I believe," Lucy told him, "that's the last of them. I'm glad you could come. You've been most entertaining. Septimus!" she summoned the black man from the dining room across the hall. "Would you please bring me the envelope I left on my desk in the library? It's for Mr. Mills. Come," she took his arm, "I'll see you to the door."

When he had left, she stood for a moment in the hallway, listening to the voices from the drawing room. Beth's party was a success, no doubt of it. The girls from Miss Barlow's, chattering like chicks, had been led on a tour of the house by Beth, exclaiming in shy wonder over the size and opulence of the place but mostly over the fact that there was a room set aside for the sole purpose of bathing. "Grand," said one, bending to run her fingers over the carpet on the floor, "just like a queen would have in a palace."

Lucy couldn't help but smile, knowing how sweetly the words fell on Beth's ears. The girl was determined to show off the fashionable refinements of the establishment, as though it were a reflection of her own respectability. Her schoolmates were suitably impressed.

The Fearings had come with Martha, Joe and Klara. Daniel Derby and his wife, Susan, had brought their son, Walter, who'd joined the small group of boys, mostly brothers of Beth's classmates, in tongue-tied bashfulness that vanished summarily when Biddy's lavish spread appeared on the table. John Fiske, towering and brawny, had held them all spellbound, performing adroit card tricks with his incongruously large, powerful hands, and Mr. Mills, hired for the occasion, had provided each of the young guests with a souvenir of the festivities.

Lucy walked through the dining room, past the sideboard where Henry Fearing's Sèvres tea set reposed in solitary elegance. In the pantry, Septimus and Biddy were washing the remnants of the feast from the blue and white china that had been delivered from Shreve and Company only the week before. "Thank you both," she told them. "I realize a party of twenty-one was rather a large order, but it went very well, I think."

"Ain't hardly enough left to feed a lone mouse," Biddy chirped proudly, holding a freshly dried glass up to the light. Septimus nodded soberly in agreement. Biddy was the talker of the two, spry and vigorous and cheerfully impatient with Septimus, who was deliberate and diligent and, it seemed, perpetually solemn. He had sad, deep-set eyes, a long face with a lantern jaw and a slight stoop to his shoulders that gave the impression that he bore some ponderous burden in tacit tolerance.

In the drawing room, Leanna was providing the guests with a fast-paced round of musical chairs. Polly gasped and fanned herself with her hand as she lost her place and joined Albert and Daniel Derby by the fireplace. "I say it's a good thing they've voted to split California," Albert was telling him. "There's not much to the southern half that anyone would want anyhow. We here up north have all the wealth. Southern California's little more than a parasite, living off the rest of us."

John Fiske tapped his fingers thoughtfully against the marble mantel where a pair of painted plaster lambs drowsed on their pedestals. "It won't go through," he contended. "Congress is too concerned with the matter of secession to take up the subject."

"But surely no secession is imminent," Lucy protested.

"I wouldn't be certain of that," John cautioned.

"Is it true, Albert?" Polly looked at him worriedly.

He shook his head sadly. "I wish it weren't, my dear, but the situation looks darker as time goes on."

Young Walter Derby let out a victorious whoop as he won the game from Klara, the last remaining player. Leanna played a few bars of a triumphal march and, closing the lid over the piano keys, rose from her seat.

Lucy went to her and took Leanna's hands in hers. "How kind of you to have played for us. You made the party ever so festive. I hope it didn't tire you."

"Never. It's a pleasure for me, especially to see the young people enjoying themselves. John and I haven't been blessed——"

"I daresay it's time for us to go," her husband broke in. "Lucy, I'm glad to have met you at last."

"You'll both come again, I hope, for a less strenuous evening. Excuse me," she said, hearing the doorknocker. "That's probably someone calling for one of the children."

The parents, Lucy noted, had come in pairs to collect their offspring. They'd stood in the hall, affecting a non-

341

chalant air though their eyes strayed repeatedly to the rooms beyond, taking in all they could glimpse, like surveyors appraising the value of a newly discovered and remarkably rich tract. Their ill-concealed fascination with her home gave Lucy a wry satisfaction. "Do call again," she told each of the ladies sweetly, fixing them with a keen and knowing gaze. To her surprise, some said they would be delighted, and even those who seemed ill at ease at the invitation did not decline it outright.

Daniel and Susan Derby were the last to leave, thrusting the reluctant Walter ahead of them out the door. Lucy leaned against the carved mahogany paneling as she closed it behind them. "Goodness," she said to Beth, "that Walter's a nice boy, but he's a handful of energy. I don't know how Susan copes with him."

Beth shrugged. "He's common."

"Vulgar? Was he rude?"

"No, just common. I suppose it's to be expected. After all, his father works with his hands."

"Indeed!" Lucy grasped her arm and steered her toward the staircase. "For your information, my queenly daughter, your own father worked with his hands to build the first home you ever knew. I shouldn't be looking down on the Derbys because Daniel built this one."

"Papa's cabin was years ago. This is a different world."

"Even so, the only other person hereabouts with regal airs is Emperor Norton, and he's mad as a coot."

"I'm not putting on airs, Mama," she replied coolly. "I just mean to be select. I shan't only be received in polite society." She halted on the landing and turned to face Lucy. "I intend to be polite society."

Lucy gazed after her in silence as she continued up the stairway. For a moment, she considered dashing after her, seizing her by the shoulders and shaking the highflown notions from her head. But she had only herself to blame if Beth was rebounding with a vengeance from her excursion to Coventry. She heard the sound of Beth's bedroom door being closed and mounted the stairs. " 'They have sown the wind,' " she said resignedly, " 'and they shall reap the whirlwind.' "

Lucy laid her newspaper on the dining table, glanced at it again and turned the page face down on the brightly polished surface. She placed her spoon on the plate beneath her half-finished dish of dessert. "I believe I'll have my tea now, Septimus."

"Yes'm." He disappeared into the pantry.

"What will Biddy say?" Beth chided. "You didn't do justice to her baked custard."

"I lost my appetite."

"Because of something in the paper?" She reached over and unfolded it in front of her.

"Don't," Lucy said quickly. "It's not fit reading for the table."

Beth paid no heed. When she had finished, she put the newspaper down beside her place and gave it a shove with her fist, sending it skimming across the table to the far end. "Where is Humboldt Bay, Mama?"

"To the north, somewhere above Meiggsville."

"Why would they want to kill Indians for no reason?"

"Why indeed," she said flatly. "Another Vigilance Committee wreaking its own brand of havoc."

"Slaughtering babies and squaws? It says they murdered almost two hundred. They hacked little children to pieces with axes—"

"Please, don't. I know what it says."

"Mama." Beth reached toward her and took her hand. "I understand."

"No." She shook her head sorrowfully. "You couldn't."

"Don't be foolish, Mama." Beth's tone was gentle. She held Lucy's hand tighter.

"You couldn't possibly know."

"Why? Because I was only a baby then? I know what you're thinking. You read something like that and it makes you afraid for him. Mama, Abel has been my brother for as long as I can remember, but he remembers back before then. Surely you didn't think he hadn't confided in me."

She looked across the table. "I had no idea."

"You mustn't be upset by this, Mama. What's past is past. Abel might as well be our own flesh and blood by now. He's one of us."

"Sometimes, when I hear of those things—" She broke off, making a small motion toward the folded newspaper. "I wonder if that's such a fine thing to be. One of us."

"Never mind," she said sharply, "it's safer. Mama, I swear to you, he'll be all right. You know how clever he is."

"I wish I could believe that." Lucy stared off at the lamplight above the sideboard. "When I was a child, there were always tales about domesticated creatures running off and returning to the wilds."

"Mama! Really!" Beth sprang up, her face taut with anger. "How could you?" She gave her chair a violent push, slamming it against the table. "Listen to me, Mama!" she cried, pounding her fist down on the back of the chair. "As long as you live, don't you dare say another stupid, insensitive word about Abel, or I'll—" She stopped short as Septimus entered, carrying the tea.

When he had gone, Lucy raised a hand to stay her. "Dear girl, forgive me. I didn't think what I was saying." She took her head ruefully. "It's been so long. There isn't any kind of awful thought that hasn't crowded its way into my head by now."

"Well, if I were you, I should discount them. That sort of worrying is absurd. It's unfair to Abel, and it makes me feel sick to my stomach to have you thinking such crazy things."

Lucy gave her a small, contrite smile. "You're right, of course." She looked at Beth thoughtfully. "I suppose there comes a time when parents find their children's counsel wiser than their own. You're growing up so fast, Bethie," she said wistfully.

"Oh, now, Mama." Beth came to her and kissed her cheek. "I daresay," she continued lightly as she walked away, "that you've a lesson or two left in your book to teach me."

"Indeed I do!" Lucy called after her. "You neglected to fold your napkin!" How on earth, she wondered to herself, did I come by this amazing, complex creature? Neither child nor woman, frivolous and flighty, yet wise and wordly, all at the same time. What a marvel she is, Lucy thought, and such a beauty too. She couldn't imagine what might become of this phenomenon that was her daughter, but she knew without a doubt it would be interesting to watch.

Lucy sat at her desk in the library, writing her grocery lists. Outside the window, the skies were overcast and threatening rain. She paused and lifting the glass chimney from the lamp beside her, struck a match and lit it.

"Ma'am?"

"Septimus. I didn't hear you come in."

"There's a gen'man to see you. From the police, ma'am."

The chimney fell from her hand and broke on the floor. Septimus dropped to his knees and began to collect the shattered pieces. "Later," she said unsteadily. "Take the gentleman to the drawing room, please. I'll be there shortly." She drew a deep breath, clasped her hands across her chest and closed her eyes for a moment, trying to compose herself.

He stood at the tall front window, cautiously fingering the fringe on the ruby velvet drapery. Seeing Lucy, he dropped it, embarrassed.

"My son——" she began.

"We think not, ma'am," he replied quickly. "But a boy of his age and general description. From what you've told us, this boy is not quite tall enough to be Master Abel, but you'd best have a look."

She sank into a chair. "He's dead."

He nodded. "Found near Fort Point. Most likely off a ship. I've a carriage waiting outside."

"Thank you, but I'd prefer to have my man, Septimus, accompany me. We'll follow you in my brougham. Give me a moment to fetch a wrap."

She held tightly to the black man's arm as the cloth was pulled back, her breath caught in her throat. The boy's face was bloated and waxy, as though the sea had washed the color from him. She felt herself begin to gag and turned away, shaking her head.

The policeman handed her a phial of smelling salts. "I'm sorry you had to go through that, ma'am. We were almost sure it wasn't your boy, but we've had no other inquiries, and no one's come to claim him, so we thought there might be a slim chance . . ."

"What will become of him?"

"The city takes care of such things."

He had looked young, Lucy thought as she rode homeward. Younger perhaps than Abel, so white and callow and vulnerable. A nameless lad, some mother's child, drifting alone and lost on the frigid waves and washed ashore like so much flotsam. Lucy laid her head back against the carriage seat and gazed out of the window. "Septimus!" she called suddenly. "Stop here, please."

He helped her down to the street. Lucy looked up at the facade of the church. She had never been inside Saint Mary's, and who knew if the boy had been a Catholic or a Protestant or anything at all. But Saint Mary's doors were open, and it would suffice.

She seated herself in one of the front pews, facing the tiers of candles that flickered before the altar, and bowed her head.

As she left, she paused in the doorway to slip some coins into the alms box there. A fine, misty rain had begun to fall. She wrapped her mohair mantle close about her and stepped outside. "We'll be going home now, Septimus."

He nodded and helped her into the brougham. As he mounted the driver's box, there was a knock at the side of the carriage. "Ma'am? Pastora, is that yourself?"

She peered out. "Septimus! Hold up a moment!" Lucy opened the door. "Father Crowley, how good to see you again. Do step in out of the rain. May we drive you somewhere?"

He hesitated a moment. Then, reaching in back of him, he gave a tug. From behind the dark folds of his cassock, he withdrew a slight, spindly, yellow-skinned girl. Her black hair was braided in an untidy plait, and she blinked her almond-shaped eyes uncertainly, as though dismayed by the sight of the tall, shining carriage. She wore rumpled blue pantaloons, a small jacket and a pair of threadbare cloth slippers through which her toes protruded.

"For pity's sake, Father. What have you there?"

"For pity's sake, indeed, Pastora." He held the girl firmly by the shoulders as she attempted to slip to safety behind the screen of his voluminous robe. "May we?" He boosted the terrified girl into the carriage and seated himself facing Lucy. The girl cowered beside him. "I bought her."

"You what?"

"From the ragpicker, Li Fu. He says she's his daughter, Lin, though I expect that's just a handy tale. They bring these children in by whatever ruse they can. He was haggling with another Chinaman over the price of her, right out there in the open on Dupont *gaai*."

Hearing the Chinese word, the girl gave him a quick glance, then burrowed further into the corner of the carriage.

Lucy looked over at the frightened child. "How old is she?"

"Ten. Li Fu wanted four hundred for her. When I stepped in, he changed his tune. Said she was a good-for-nothing 'big foot.' Too thin, he said, like a wet cat. His buyer disappeared into the throng. That kind doesn't want attention. I offered him three hundred, and he took it."

"You paid him three hundred dollars for her? Father, how on earth—"

"Not exactly. I had ninety on me from some charity gifts. By that time we'd drawn quite a crowd, and Li Fu was looking over his shoulder for the police."

"But what will you do with her?"

"That's why I came 'round to Saint Mary's. I thought someone here might have heard of a parishioner in need of a servant."

"Isn't she too young?"

"Rather that, Pastora, than to stand exposing her body from the window of a crib. Within a few years, she'd be diseased and useless and locked in some dark, hillside cave to be allowed to die. They don't often see the light of their twentieth year, these creatures."

Lucy gazed at the small figure huddled on the opposite seat. The girl glanced up furtively, caught her look and hurriedly lowered her eyes. A condemned child, apprehended and afraid. But still a child, Lucy thought, like all the other waifs that came to these shores by one means or another. "Septimus!" she called, opening the carriage door. "Take us to Doctor Vanderhoef's on Kearny. Then I shall want to come back up to Sacramento Street to find the laundryman, Wong. Father," she said as she pulled the door shut, "I believe I can spare ninety dollars."

Doctor Vanderhoef brought the silent, wide-eyed Li Lin into the vestibule where Lucy and Father Crowley waited. "Well," he began reluctantly, "the little thing needs nourishment, but it seems relatively healthy otherwise. I still think you're making a mistake, Lucy. As your family physician I feel I have a right to speak out."

"Thank you, Martin. I appreciate your concern. But tell me only one thing. Is it true the Chinese carry peculiar infections?"

"Some do, no doubt. In all honesty, I see no sign of

347

sickness in this one. I was merely thinking of the effect upon your family. What will Beth make of this?"

"I couldn't say. I'm not yet sure what to make of it myself, but my mind is made up."

"Then you'll excuse me if I ask you to go now before my next patient arrives. It might not look well for this little creature to be in the office. You understand." He dismissed them with a nod. "I'd best go wash."

"Tong yan gaai," Father Crowley said, glancing out of the carriage window at the teeming thoroughfare, "the Chinese Street."

Both sides of Sacramento Street were lined with flimsy wooden buildings, some with overhanging balconies decked with red and yellow paper lanterns or long, narrow, cloth banners that dripped rainwater steadily on the passersby beneath. Rows of open food stalls were festooned with sheaves of herbs and swags of dried fish, stiff-finned, open-mouthed, their skins bronzed and glistening. Flocks of trussed fowl, roasted brown, hung headless by the legs above a jumble of straw baskets filled with odd-looking greens. Crates of exotic fruits and vegetables cluttered the sidewalks, and sacks of rice lay stacked in the shelter of the doorways, out of the weather, like hastily erected parapets. Despite the drizzle, the public scribes and fortune tellers plied their trades at small tables under cover of the balconies. On the walls behind them, paper posters, damp and curling at the edges, advertised their services in broad-brushed characters. Here and there stood tall, forbidding gates in bizarre open work patterns, hinting of the alien life within. Some few entrances were flanked by huge, fierce effigies in gaudily colored armor, staring fiendishly from wild, painted eyes. Others were little more than planked holes dug out of the narrow, dark gaps between buildings, leading to sunless caverns where families congregated like moles in their underground diggings.

Slowly the carriage made its way through the noisy throng. Lucy pressed her handkerchief daintily to her nose. "I'm afraid," she apologized to Father Crowley. "I shall never become used to either the sounds or the odors, no matter how many times I pass through this place." She glanced out the window at the clusters of yellow faces upturned to stare at the elegant vehicle in their midst. Moon-

348

faced women, eardrops dangling, their hair in elaborate knots, gabbled in wonder. Small boys in skullcaps stopped their games to gape silently. Men in dark tunics and loose trousers with their single braids dangling beneath their hats gazed expressionlessly at the intruders. A rotund chap, his high rank proclaimed by his silk gown and vest, gave them a cursory look, then beckoned with his long-nailed fingers to the pair of porters trailing him, their trays of wares balanced on their heads. The porters, looking neither left nor right, followed dutifully. Behind them, an elderly man, stooped by his years, plodded along under the weight of a towering, intricately fashioned bamboo kitchen, complete with tureens and dishes. In a thin, high-pitched voice, he hawked his bill of fare as he went, his cumbersome load swaying precariously from side to side.

Septimus drew up in front of the green wooden door of Wong's establishment and dismounted from his seat. Ignoring the whining entreaties of a toothless beggar, he made his way to the door and knocked. A woman opened it and stepped quickly back a pace at the sight of the black man there.

"Wong," he said. "Miz' Bates wants to see him."

"Wong Ah Ji!" she shrilled and ducked inside.

The Chinaman came out to the carriage and sat in the seat beside Lucy, averting his eyes from the girl. He listened in silence until Lucy had finished her explanation. He shook his head curtly. "No good, missee."

"Wong," Father Crowley put in, "would you have the child sold into slavery?"

He scowled and gave Li Lin a look of disgust. "What you pay for this nothing?"

"Never mind," Lucy retorted sharply. "Do as I ask, please. Tell the child I shall take her to my home. She will be fed and looked after. She will be expected to help about the house. She'll be shown what to do."

Wong looked at Lucy for a moment. Then abruptly, he turned to face the girl, spitting out a strident volley of sound.

Startled, Li Lin blinked and nodded timidly. Her brown eyes filled with tears.

Father Crowley glanced uneasily at Lucy.

"Wong," she interrupted him, "why is she crying? What did you say to her?"

"I tell this worthless person, do like missee say, or missee feed her to dogs."

"How dare you! Tell her it's not so!"

Wong gazed at her evenly, unmoved.

"If you don't, I shall tell everyone that Wong does bad work. He cheats. He steals from his customers."

He grunted angrily and made a curt utterance without bothering to look in the direction of the petrified girl.

Lucy reached over and wiped the tears from her cheeks. Li Lin seemed relieved. She took a deep breath and wiped her nose on her sleeve. "No, child!" Lucy thrust her handkerchief into her hands and helped her blow her nose.

"I think that will be all, Wong. Thank you." Father Crowley opened the door.

Wong gave them a last look as he got out and scurried away, sputtering irritably to the gaggle of curious onlookers that had surrounded the carriage.

"I gather," Lucy said dryly, "that Wong does not approve."

"He may not be alone," Father Crowley warned. "There's not much sympathy spent on the heathen souls in our city."

"You seem to be an exception, Father."

"Ah, well, in the matter of a child—" He left off, smiling sheepishly. " 'Suffer the little children to come unto me,' " he said. "How could I take that not to mean all of them?"

Lucy laughed suddenly. "Father, I believe nothing you could do or say could surprise me in the least."

"Nor you, Pastora." He grinned. "We do have our odd adventures, don't we?"

"Mama!" Beth flung Lucy's bedroom door wide, sending it clattering against the wall.

Lucy jumped. "I didn't hear you knock," she said pointedly, addressing Beth's reflection in the mirror above her dressing table.

"What is going on in this house? There's a Chinee in the pantry wearing one of my old dresses and eating the gingerbread Biddy baked for me!"

"Her clothes were ragged," she said matter-of-factly, "and she was hungry."

"And our house is a haven for every stray dog and cat on the streets?"

"She's a child," Lucy corrected, turning to face her.

"A Chinee."

"Sit down, Beth. I said," she enunciated, "sit down."

Beth seated herself, stiff-backed, on the edge of Lucy's black and gold Hitchcock rocker. She grasped the curved arms tightly, as though to restrain herself from springing back up.

"The girl's name is Li Lin. She'll be helping Biddy and Septimus with the housework."

"In my clothes?" The chair lurched forward, and she steadied herself.

"You've no use for what you've outgrown. Those things only go to the ragpicker after we've removed the trimmings. Why should you object?"

Beth ignored the question. "She's too young to be any use around the house."

"Nonsense. We can always use another pair of hands in a place this large."

"And another mouth to feed? Mama, the Chinee don't even eat like us. They live on those queer things that make Sacramento Street smell to high heaven. Do you want our home smelling like some heathen hovel?"

"She's eating the gingerbread, isn't she? She'll eat whatever we serve."

"Well, I heard Biddy telling Septimus that she won't have that creature sitting at their table in the kitchen. It's not wholesome. Biddy says she's not to be allowed near the cooking, either."

"Very well, then. Let Septimus see how he likes carrying trays upstairs to the nursery."

Beth bounded up from the chair. "You want him to wait on that wretched creature?" She marched angrily to the fireplace and spun around to face her.

"I doubt he'll do it for long. Best to say nothing and let Septimus and Biddy come around of their own accord."

"I don't understand you!" Beth stamped her foot hard on the floor.

"That," Lucy answered evenly, "is not necessary. I am the mistress of this house, and I give the orders here."

"But Mama," she wailed, "what will my friends think when they find out we have one of those heathens living under our roof?"

351

"It's not unheard of. People employ Chinese servants these days."

"You call that a servant?"

"I should think it the most tactful term for all concerned."

"How long is she going to stay?"

"Beth," Lucy told her impatiently, "for reasons of my own, I have brought Li Lin to live here. She will work for her keep. She will stay as long as the arrangement seems suitable."

"Well, I say it's not suitable!"

"You, my dear," she replied with an edge to her voice, "do not have a say in the matter. You have not presented a single persuasive argument against her presence here. Wearing your cast-off clothing and eating a bite of your gingerbread are not sufficient grounds for turning her out."

"Then explain to me what grounds you had for bringing her here in the first place!"

"She's so young . . ." Lucy began and faltered. "There are children out there—" She looked away. "Never mind," she said brusquely.

Beth studied her in silence for a moment. "Mama," she warned, "don't think you can replace Abel with any old stray from the streets. You feel guilty because he ran away, and now you bring some homeless heathen into our house to salve your conscience. It won't work. You can't go searching the city for waifs. This is our home, not an asylum."

"Beth." Lucy held up a hand to quiet her. "Perhaps there's truth in what you say, but I didn't seek out the girl. The situation presented itself, you might say. There didn't appear to be an alternative. In good conscience, I couldn't do otherwise."

"So now," she said flatly, "we are saddled with Li Lin."

"You needn't think of it that way. She's my responsibility."

"Yes, but how am I to explain her?" She moved to the window beside the fireplace and stared pensively at the sheets of rain cascading down the panes.

Lucy removed the pins from her hair, shook it loose from its coils and began to brush it with long, firm, methodical strokes, as though the gesture of neatness might

352

somehow set everything in order. In the mirror, she saw Beth turn to look at her.

"I suppose," Beth said slowly, "I could say that she's my servant. That would account for her age. You said she'd be helping around the house, didn't you? So it's not really a lie."

"Well, I guess not, but . . ."

"Then that's the explanation. She's my own personal maid."

"Bethie, this has been a very trying day for me." Lucy laid down her hairbrush. "Please try to be accommodating."

"Never mind, Mama." She walked to the door. "It's all right. Now I know what to say."

Gradually, Septimus and Biddy relented, though Biddy maintained a pose of apprehensive sufferance, staring covertly at the girl as if at any moment she might commit some barbarous act that would disrupt the peaceful routine of the household. Septimus looked on Li Lin with his sad, weary gaze, as though she were simply the latest addition to the infinite load that was his lot to bear. Only Wong, the laundry man, refused to yield. He would make his deliveries, hissing and muttering his disapproval, then, stuffing the soiled wash into his baskets, take leave with a pitiless stare of contempt for the bewildered girl.

Beth, for all her enterprise in explaining Li Lin's presence, had neglected to consider the practical difficulties of transforming a bashful child with no command of English into an accomplished lady's maid. Out of necessity and via exasperation, she became Li Lin's tutor. To Lucy's vast, though secret amusement, the obedient girl allowed herself to be taken under Beth's wing and, hungry for approval, hovered close by her side, awaiting her slightest direction.

"No, no." Beth seized Li Lin's hands. "Not the buttons. The sash. There." She placed her hands on the ribbons at her waist.

Li Lin frowned and looked abashed.

"Sakes alive, Mama, she doesn't even know how to tie a bow!"

Lucy glanced up from her sewing. "Mercy. I guess you'll have to teach her. Here." She laid down the nightdress she was hemming. "Let me help. Turn around, Beth." She took the ribbons in hand. "Watch me, Lin."

She nodded gravely. "Yes, missee."

"Now," Lucy said, when she had twice demonstrated the procedure, "you try it. That's right. No—" She caught her hand. "This one goes over. See?"

Li Lin grinned. "Missybet, see?"

Beth eyed her reflection in the mirror on the sitting room wall. "Good, Lin. Can you do it again?"

The girl pursed her lips and gave the sash a tug. Very slowly, her face screwed tight with concentration, she made first one bow, then, delighted, another. "Good, Missybet?"

"Good, Lin. What do you think, Mama? Shall I wear this for the dancing lessons Friday? Mrs. Fiske says there are two new boys coming."

"It's lovely, dear." She returned to her sewing table. "Lin, would you ask Septimus to bring the tea now?"

Li Lin glanced quickly at Beth for sanction.

"Tea, Lin."

"Yes, Missybet." She scampered away into the dining room.

On alternate Fridays Leanna Fiske held her dancing classes in the drawing room. At first there had been only a handful of girls, gingerly imitating the steps Leanna showed them. But news of the classes, not to mention Biddy's cakes and cookies and lemon punch, had rapidly attracted more young people, so that there were now a dozen girls and nearly as many boys, all holding each other circumspectly at arm's length, diligently bobbing in rhythm to the sounds of the piano. Beth gloried in being the hostess for these occasions, magnanimously pressing the refreshments upon her young guests until it was a wonder they could maneuver about the floor at all, their stomachs awash with punch and sweets. Li Lin observed these rites from the hall chair that faced the drawing room door. She sat quietly, her hands in her lap, gazing across the way to where flushed-faced girls, giggling breathlessly, romped in a schottische or whirled in a waltz with self-conscious, perspiring boys who feigned forbearance. Lucy, seeing her there, wondered what she made of this strange ritual which she studied silently, her dark, almond

354

eyes fixed upon Beth as she gaily executed her promenades and curtsies.

The dancing class spawned spelling bees and quilting parties and, one warm day in March, an ice-cream party on the porch. Beth flourished in her new-found social arena, and Lucy, for her part, found it impossible to refuse the girl any diversion she desired. She herself had never enjoyed such pastimes. It filled her with pleasure to hear the high-spirited chatter and laughter that swelled through the house, and Li Lin, always at Beth's beck and call, bounced about as buoyantly as a rubber ball, fetching and carrying for her young mistress.

Beth wore her hair in the newest fashion, parted in the center, rolled under high at the nape of her neck and pulled into a soft, round cushion in the middle. She was becoming quite the young woman, her bosom well-formed above her tiny waist and her carriage erect and graceful. She was not above practicing the gentle art of flirting on the boys who came to call, though young as they were, her efforts went largely unnoticed.

With the move to Bush Street, Lucy's past appeared to have been laid aside, locked behind, it seemed, in the old lodgings that had confined them in their exile. It was Beth, of course, who had occasioned the change. Some few ladies, mothers of her friends, had already taken it upon themselves to call on Lucy. They inspected her cautiously, reservedly, over the rims of their teacups and thawing finally under her deliberate charm, pronounced her home "splendid," her daughter "exquisite," and herself "most entertaining." Lucy totted up these compliments as scrupulously as though they were figures in a ledger, calculating the value of the sum as her present social currency. In time, she reckoned her capital sufficient to afford a little modest speculation. It was, by chance, Father Crowley who presented the initial opportunity for Lucy to put her prestige to the test.

"Ladies . . ." She tapped her spoon against the side of her empty cup. "Please let me help you to more tea before the Father speaks his piece. Septimus, would you pass the cakes again?"

Septimus moved among the guests, dispensing Biddy's Jenny Lind Cake, spice loaf and, especially for Polly Fearing, her favorite cream cakes.

"This spice loaf is delicious," Ada Brock said. Ada looked not unlike a spice loaf herself with her plump little shape, cinnamon hair and round, dark, currant eyes. She licked the crumbs daintily from her fingers. "What do you suppose is her secret?"

"I believe she puts in a measure of wine. Septimus?"

"Madeira, ma'am."

"The Knight sisters, Amanda and Verity, pale and fragile-looking as the china plates in their laps, glanced at each other in wordless consternation. They were temperance-minded.

"But of course," Lucy put in quickly, "the alcohol evaporates in the baking."

The sisters looked relieved but chose slices of Jenny Lind Cake.

Amy Winslow declined another cup of tea, patting her sleek coil of chestnut hair as though by chance a single strand might have escaped. It wouldn't dare, Lucy thought. Nothing about Amy Winslow remotely suggested such abandon. She sat imperiously upright in her chair, statuesque, her handsome features apparently hewn from the same rose-colored marble that framed the fireplace beside her. Cool, perpetually unruffled, she regarded Lucy always with that wary appraisal which one beautiful woman accords to another without for a moment relinquishing her own rank. "Such a pretty tea set," she observed. "Sèvres, isn't it, Lucy?" she added, thus announcing herself, at the least, her peer in matters of taste.

"Yes, it is." Lucy handed Jane Gallagher's cup and saucer back to her, noting that poor Jane, who was hopelessly short-sighted, squinted and peered at the tea set and seemed disappointed to find that it was simply china. "Jane, dear," Lucy suggested, "let Septimus move your chair closer to Leanna Fiske so that we can give Father Crowley a little space to speak. Father?"

He laid his plate on the table beside him and rose, running his hand across his thinning gray hair and nervously clearing his throat. "Ah, ladies——" he began, looking ill at ease before their upturned faces. Suddenly he laughed at his own discomfort and shifted his feet abruptly in what might have passed for a skittish jig. "Bless you all," he said with a wide smile, "for responding to Mrs. Bates's invitation by your presence. I confess, I'm quite out of my element, not only at a tea party but in the concern that brings me among you." He paused as if to marshal his thoughts. "We have, in this city, an orphans' asylum for youngsters without families. Because they have no parents, these children are adoptable. Often, they are placed with local families. But in my peregrinations, as I do the Lord's work, I've encountered a problem that's out of my bailiwick. That problem, ladies, is the number of waifs roaming about this affluent city, ill-fed, poorly clothed and prey to its sinister side. The children I speak of are not orphans. Some are runaways. Others have homes, if they can be called that, where drunkenness and licentiousness prevail. There's many a man, alas, lying dead to the world in a grog shop while his motherless young ones are crying with hunger. Some of these fellows fall victim to crimps and are shanghaied. It may be years before they return. In other cases, we have the children of the women who walk the streets, youngsters innocent as lambs, who are neglected by their profligate mothers." He stopped and glanced among the listeners to gauge his effect. "These poor little children," he continued, his brogue caressing the words, "sleep in saloons, in gambling halls, in doorways and in open stairwells where the rats prowl at large. And if, by a stroke of fortune, these vermin don't abuse them, there are two-legged vermin all too willing."

"Excuse me," Amy Winslow interrupted. "Are you saying there's no Catholic charity to help these children?"

"Nor Protestant either."

"I suspect," Polly Fearing said reflectively, "that it's not a problem to be assigned willy-nilly to Protestants or Catholics or anyone in particular."

"This is our city," Lucy said. "In fact, we *are* this city because we are its people. If the city's riches and pleasures are ours, its poverty and suffering must be ours also."

"Now see here . . ." Verity Knight fluttered a hand timidly in the air. "To pamper the poor is to rob them of their enterprise. It merely creates a class of indigents."

"Oh, hush," snapped her sister, Amanda. "We're discussing children."

Verity ignored her. "They'd have to be taught skills and trades."

"That," said Father Crowley, "is precisely the sort of thing I'd hoped to hear. These youngsters, wretched as

357

they are, can be salvaged. And what is our future, if it isn't our youth?"

"Exactly what did you have in mind?" Ada Brock wanted to know.

"A shelter," Jane Gallagher answered for him.

He nodded. "Lodging, food, clothing, adequate supervision."

"They can attend the public schools, can't they?" Leanna Fiske inquired.

"Yes, indeed."

"So," Amy Winslow declared, "you want us, in particular, to assume this burden."

"No, ma'am," he corrected her. "I wanted to bring the dilemma to the attention of some wise and warm-hearted Christian ladies, in hopes that they'd have some constructive ideas."

"With all due respect, Father," Polly said, "ideas don't feed and clothe. Some action must be taken."

Father Crowley glanced innocently around the room.

"There is nothing that you, personally, can do?" Amy persisted.

"I'm afraid my duties are clearly prescribed. On rare occasions," he said, glancing meaningfully at Lucy, "I venture beyond bounds when there appears to be no moral alternative. That's how I came to be here today."

Leanna opened her handbag. "I believe this calls for paper and pencil. Now, Father, shall we begin at the beginning?"

Father Crowley waited until all of them had left. "Well, Pastora, it looks like we lit a fire under those fashionable flounces. What do you say?"

She laughed. "You did it. You all but shamed them to action. I think Polly had an excellent thought in suggesting that Bethie and Martha and their friends might help. It will do the children good to realize there are others less fortunate than they."

"And you made a fine choice of a name. The Good Shepherd Home, and yourself a shepherdess."

"My children don't like the name Pastora."

"No? I should think they'd be proud of their mother. You're a feeling woman, Pastora, and not afraid to follow your heart."

"I regret to tell you that I'm also headstrong. My own selfish pride has caused a lot of sorrow on occasion."

He dismissed her with a wave. "I trust those days are dead and gone. What good is the past if not for learning our lessons?"

She gave him a quizzical look.

"One hears a bit of this and that," he said lightly. "It's a small city, after all."

"I see. Well, Father, it appears that today you have been instrumental in my social redemption. Might I persuade you to stay for supper to celebrate?"

"A celebration, is it?" he teased, his blue eyes merry. "With perhaps a taste of *spiritus frumenti* for the observance?"

"Follow me, Father."

"I can not help myself," Lucy was saying to Leanna Fiske. "I have a special place in my heart for those stray children. I suppose, in a way, I'm trying to strike a bargain with God to care for my own lost child. Li Lin," she called, spying her in the hallway, "did you tell Beth she's late for her piano lesson?"

Lin poked her head timidly around the door. "Yes'm. Missybet coming. She sleep too much." With that, she disappeared.

"What a delicate little thing she is," Leanna observed.

"She reminds me of a shy, bright-eyed creature of the forest, a young squirrel, perhaps. Oh dear," she said, hearing the grandfather clock chime the quarter hour, "I'm so sorry Beth overslept. I gather Naomi Brock's party last night was a grand success. Bethie? Is that you?"

"Yes, Mama," she answered from the dining room.

"I told Septimus to serve you on a tray in here. He's already cleared the table."

As she buttered the last piece of her corn muffin, Beth asked, "Mama, whereabouts is Milledgeville, Georgia?"

"I wouldn't know exactly. Why do you ask?"

"There were some Georgia people at Naomi's. My, but their gentlemen are gallant."

"That's enough party talk for now. I'll leave you two to get on with the lesson." She rose and took Beth's tray.

"Mama, I invited Naomi and two of the young men to tea this afternoon."

"You might have asked my permission, Beth. Biddy has enough to do without sudden tea parties."

"Oh, she won't mind, Mama. There'll only be four of us."

Ada and Solomon Brock's daughter, Naomi, was two years older than Beth, but her slight stature and reticent ways gave her the appearance of being younger. She spoke with a faint lisp which, though nearly imperceptible and altogether pleasant to the ear, kept her in a perpetual state of rosy-cheeked embarrassment. Naomi was always a bit disconcerted, one of those people who, though trimly attired, seemed in constant danger of coming apart at the seams. If the bow at her collar didn't slip loose, her sash came undone, or her bracelets became caught in the lace cuffs of her dress. Her brown hair, seemingly possessing a life of its own, was forever springing free from the neatly crocheted net around it. Lucy couldn't help liking this sweetly comical flustered girl who had become Beth's closest confidante.

The two young men were of another stripe entirely. Courtly and self-confident, their manners polished to an impressive dazzle, they seemed as at ease in a strange drawing room as they might be at home or at a picnic or, Lucy fancied, on the pitching deck of a ship at sea. The elder one, Boyd Stevens, was the son of the owner of the Pioneer Iron Works, south of the docks. He'd returned from the University of Georgia, bringing his cousin who had decided of late that his education lay in traveling rather than studying. Nicholas Stevens was tall, with fair skin, curly reddish-blonde hair and a marked cleft in his chin, which gave some distinction to his otherwise bland features. Lucy noticed, as she greeted Beth's trio of guests, that he had a way of smiling spontaneously whenever he was addressed. He grinned automatically, as though complimented by the attention, and replied politely, smiling still, in a pronounced Georgia drawl that reminded her of the syrupy flow of molasses from a jug.

From her chair in the sitting room she listened to the sounds of the young people across the hall, singing as Naomi played the piano.

"Oh, do you remember sweet Betsey from Pike . . ."

As the last chorus died out, Naomi launched into the beautiful, melancholy "Old Folks at Home." The Stevens boys, Lucy thought, were probably Secesh, like so many Southern families these days. She found herself wondering suddenly what it might be like if secession actually became a fact. The Georgian, Nick, would be a foreigner or, worse, if it came to war, an enemy of the Union. She found the idea almost inconceivable. Surely no one the likes of the affable young man in her drawing room could raise a rifle against a Northern boy, the spit of himself, ingenuous and green, his whole manhood ahead of him.

She found herself gazing into his hazel eyes as he bade her good-bye, searching foolishly for a trace of belligerence there, but he merely gave her his customary smile and thanked her for her hospitality.

"Mama, may we go out to Land's End after church tomorrow? Nick hasn't seen the sea lions."

"Papa will let us have the brougham," Boyd assured her. "We'll have the young ladies home before sundown."

"Please, Mama."

"If Naomi's mother agrees," she said. "But you mayn't leave until after Sunday dinner is done."

"Half-past two, then?" Nick asked Beth.

She looked at Lucy.

"Only if you bring a note of approval from Mrs. Brock, Nicholas."

"Do get it now, Naomi." Beth led them to the door. "I'll be dressed and ready at half-past two."

Lucy smiled indulgently at Beth, who sat curled in the window seat of the sitting room, the glow of the excursion still fresh on her cheeks. "I'm glad to hear the ships and sea lions obliged with such a picturesque parade. I take it Nicholas wasn't disappointed."

"He told me he's thinking of staying for a while, working in his Uncle Dabney Stevens's office at the Iron Works."

"Really? Then he must like it here."

"Mama, you should hear him talk about New Rosedale."

"What is that?" she inquired, intent on her darning.

"His family's plantation. It's somewhere between Milledgeville and Atlanta. They raise cotton there. They have kennels and barns and coops and stables." She took a breath. "And gardens and a smokehouse and laundry house and scores of slaves to work it all. Imagine!"

"It sounds very grand. How old is Nick Stevens?"

"Nineteen last month. Mama, what should I wear to the

361

theatre next Saturday? He says the young ladies back home are all very fashionable."

"I'm sure anything you choose will be quite suitable."

"I don't want to look suitable. I want to look glamorous."

Lucy laughed in spite of herself. "My dear child, you're only fourteen, and it's just an outing with the boys and Boyd's parents. You don't want to look like one of the costumed ladies on the stage."

"You do like him, don't you, Mama?"

"Is it so important? They both seem like nice young men."

"But Nick is handsome and he's not like the other boys I know. He's so refined and courtly."

"And grown up."

"He's a real gentleman, Mama, and I believe he likes me."

Lucy laid her needlework aside. "Then, Beth, you'd be wise not to let him see how much that pleases you. Gentlemen don't appreciate young ladies who fall into their laps as easily as fruit drops off a tree. And remember, dear, though he's the first caller to pay you court, he won't be the last. You're still very young. There are many more gentlemen quite as nice as he."

Despite Lucy's admonition, Beth passed her days in a transport of delight over Nick Stevens's attentions. She was clearly flattered to command the interest of this cultivated young man, five years her senior, who, if he was not yet worldly, was patently wealthy, patrician and unfailingly gallant. Lucy suspected that his appeal relied in no small measure upon his elaborate tales of life at New Rosedale, which nourished Beth's penchant for splendor like manna from above.

"And there's jessamine," he was telling her, "twining around the pillars of the verandas in front. It smells so sweet that the scent fills the house. Outside Ma's and Pa's window, there's a big magnolia with blooms the size of dinner plates."

"How many are in your family, Nick?" Lucy inquired, helping him to another serving of roasted duck.

"There's my brother, Gwinnett. We call him Gwin. He's reading law. My older sisters, Regina and Lydia, married brothers from Charleston and moved away. I had a younger sister, Caroline, but she was killed last year in a fall from her horse."

"Nick, tell Mama about the ballroom."

"It was built when Lydia and Regina were still at home. We've had some fine parties there. Last time, Ma had half a dozen flowering dogwoods brought in, and the ladies all wore white dresses to match. Pa said he didn't care if he never went to heaven because he'd already seen it."

Lucy cast a glance at Beth, whose food lay ignored on her plate. The girl gazed at Nick in rapt attention as he described the festive doings at New Rosedale, where life seemed to be a constant, carefree cycle of balls, picnics, fish fries and hunting sprees. "Tell me," Lucy said, "is there much talk of secession there?"

He turned to her with his disarming smile. "I'd expect so, ma'am, what with this being an election year. Like Henry Clay said a few months back, if the Republicans win, it will signal the end of the Union."

"But surely there'll be no open hostilities."

"It's not likely, ma'am. It's only a matter of preserving our constitutional states' rights. These are prosperous times for all of us, north, south, east and west. There'd have to be a lot of hard thinking before folks would tamper with success."

"Nick," Beth interrupted, "do save some room for dessert. Biddy always makes meringues for Sunday dinner."

He laid down his knife and fork. "My Pa says the Northern bankers have invested too heavily in the South not to protect their interests."

Lucy raised the small glass bell beside her place and rang for Septimus to clear for dessert. He gave a look of displeasure at Beth's full plate and glanced reprovingly at Nick, who, accustomed as he was to the attendance of servants, failed to heed his presence. As Septimus reached the pantry door, he suddenly stopped short and stood still, listening.

"It was the doorknocker, Septimus, though I can't imagine who'd be so thoughtless as to intrude at an hour when everyone's eating Sunday dinner."

He emerged from the pantry and trudged past them into the hall, frowning. After a few moments, he returned.

"A pair of gen'men, Miz' Bates, in the drawin' room."

She stiffened. "From the police?"

"Not from the looks of 'em, ma'am. They's workin' men, mos' likely."

"Forgive me," she said to Nick as she rose. "I'll settle this at once. Do go on with your dessert."

A tall, silver-haired man stood with his back to the room, contemplating the painted plaster lambs that reposed above the fireplace. He was dressed in shabby canvas trousers and a flannel shirt and carried in his hand a battered slouch hat that attested to hard times past.

"Sir?"

As he turned, she noticed that he wore a spruce white neckerchief, an oddly punctilious touch, considering his appearance.

"May I ask your business here?"

He looked to the far end of the room where the door lay open to the library beyond. His companion stood quietly in the shadow of the lintel.

"It's a fine house, Mama."

XIX

HER OUTCRY brought Beth, Nick and Septimus running from the other room. She collapsed into a chair, trembling uncontrollably.

"Brandy," Nick ordered Setptimus. "Hurry."

Beth was in tears, her head pressed close against Abel's chest.

"Bethie, calm down." He patted her shoulders. "Mama? Are you all right?"

She looked at him and nodded, her eyes glistening. She made a move to rise.

"Easy, there, ma'am." The older man took her arm. "Give yourself a moment's rest."

"Nick." Beth reached out to him. "Come here. Meet my brother, Abel."

He gave Abel a wide smile. "I thought as much. Do you always cause such a stir among the ladies?" He took the brandy glass from Septimus and handed it to Lucy.

"Come," she said, setting down the glass. "There's food waiting on the table. You must have something to eat. Septimus, will you see what Biddy has left in the kitchen?"

Lucy watched the boy eat, her eyes fastened on him as though the disappearance of baked apples and meringues was, at his hands, a miraculous feat.

"Well, Seth?" Abel laid down his napkin and turned to the man beside him. "It's a far cry from murphies fried in salt pork, wouldn't you say?"

"What are murphies?" Beth wanted to know.

"Why, potatoes, you goose," Nick answered. " 'Cept it's not a word a lady would use."

365

"Abel? Mr. Slade? Will you have coffee or tea?" She gave Septimus their orders, and when the cups had been filled, she pushed her chair back from the table. "Tell me everything now. From the beginning."

Abel stirred his coffee, gazing down at the whorls made by his spoon. "You know why I left."

"Yes."

"Why was that?" Nick inquired.

"Not now," Beth told him.

"I meant to go to Castalia. I don't know why. I thought I'd work my way toward there on one of the riverboats, but when I got aboard, it seemed all the passengers were men on their way to Western Utah. They said there was enough silver in the Washoe country for any able-bodied fellow to make his fortune."

"And did you?" Beth interrupted. "Did you make your fortune?"

He gave her a wry grin. "Not quite."

Seth Slade spoke up. "It's rough country, Mrs. Bates. The most desolate land I ever hope to see. Nothing but barren mountains and arid, rocky hills with scarcely the solace of a single shadow to fend off the damnable sun. Only a lizard could thrive there."

"You needn't tell me, Mr. Slade. I've trudged across that wretched terrain on my own two feet."

"And what water there is," Abel continued, "tastes so foul you can barely get it down."

"How well I remember. Go on."

"Up Gold Canyon, below Sun Mountain, is the Ophir Diggings. Between them and Six-Mile Canyon, there's blue stuff all over the place. Silver. And men staking claims right and left."

"Virginia Town, they call it now," Seth explained.

"And that's where you've been living?"

Abel laughed. "If you call it that. I was working a claim with a pair of Irishmen, sleeping in a sage brush lean-to, until one of those devilish Washoe zephyrs demolished it just before the snows began. When Seth took me into his shack, I was living in a five-foot hole in the ground. There's a lot of us survived that way."

Nick shook his head incredulously. "Like a pack of miserable Indians."

Seth broke the silence that followed. "Exactly. Isn't that right, my boy?"

"The Diggers are no fools, not if they endure those winters." Abel matched Nick's smile with his own.

"He was a sorry sight, Mrs. Bates," Seth said. "Not that any of us was a fashion plate."

Her attention was on Abel. "And then?"

"The winter storms came. We told tall stories and gambled. After we ran out of food, we had mule meat. There was no feed for the animals anyhow. Most of them had to be shot or turned loose in the snow. Some of our fellows froze to death, too. Others went from dropsy of the chest. The two Irishmen I worked for were lost in the last avalanche. When Seth and I left, there were still snow squalls coming up every now and then."

"Mrs. Bates," Seth put in, "allow me to reassure you that the boy's good character is intact. It wasn't all tall tales and gambling. I had the pleasure of tutoring this young fellow over the winter months. Time passed a great deal faster, thanks to his company."

"You've been very kind to my son, Mr. Slade. I appreciate that."

"Sounds to me," Nick said, "like Washoe's no place for a civilized man."

Seth cocked his head to one side and regarded him with a trace of a smile. "There's a mixed cast of players, as you might expect. Judge Terry, the gentleman who dispatched Senator Broderick, is there. As a matter of fact, he's the leader of the Secesh boys."

Lucy glanced at Abel's companion. There was no malice in his blue eyes. He seemed merely quietly amused. He had a pleasant face with a strong jaw, a straight, prominent nose and high forehead. Despite his white hair, he was, she guessed, no more than a few years her senior. He sat tall and erect, as coolly detached as a silver birch, bending occasionally to the gusts of conversation that fanned about the table.

"To hear Henry Comstock tell it," Abel was saying, "you'd think he'd not only discovered the vein but planted it there in the first place with his own almighty hand."

"Comstock's a blow hard," Seth said. "He's trying to take sole credit for the strike, though he knows about half as much as most of the Mexican foremen working the digs."

"Mr. Slade," Lucy interrupted, "I owe you a great debt for bringing my son home."

"Well," he said, glancing at Abel, "there's a time for everything. It was time to come back down below."

"Down below?"

"To San Francisco."

"I see." She smiled. "The least I can do is to invite you to a proper meal after all you've been through these past months. Will you dine with us on Friday evening?"

"I'd consider it a pleasure, ma'am, to—" He broke off as Li Lin emerged silently from the pantry, tiptoeing shyly around the table as though she might, with luck, merge into the wallpaper as she passed.

"Who have we here?" Abel asked.

Lucy caught Lin's hand. "Her name is Li Lin."

"She's my personal maid," Beth announced.

Seth raised his eyebrows. "Well, well . . ."

Abel chuckled. "Ah, Miss Elizabeth Bates, the Duchess of Bush Street, I presume."

Beth flushed and looked away.

"Lin has come to live with us," Lucy said. She introduced the child, who curtsied obediently, averting her eyes from the strangers. "You may go now, Lin."

"It seems," Abel told Lucy when the guests had departed and Beth had gone to bed, "that there have been a lot of changes in my absence. Hanged if Bethie hasn't turned into a stunner. What do you make of her beau?"

"Money, position and manners."

"Just her piece of pie."

"But a loafer, I fear. He talks vaguely about working for his Uncle Dabney at the Pioneer Iron Works, but I've yet to see him make a move in that direction."

"Was I imagining things, or did he seem a little chilly?" He stifled a yawn.

Lucy rose and took the lamp from the table beside her. "Pay it no mind. Nick is used to commanding Beth's undivided attention. Come. It's late, and you must be tired." She led the way through the hall, stopping abruptly at the foot of the stairs. "Tomorrow, when I wake, I'll be afraid it was all a dream."

He kissed her cheek. "No, Mama. I'm back. It was Seth who insisted."

"What sort of a man is Seth Slade?" she asked as they mounted the stairs.

"What can I say to that? A good man. Educated. Traveled. He and his partner have a claim in Six-Mile Canyon."

"He's a distinguished-looking fellow," she observed. "That is, if you make allowances for his get-up."

Abel gave her a curious glance and started to reply but evidently thought better of it. "Good-night, Mama. I'll see you at breakfast. Truly," he smiled, "I will."

Lucy took in the ten places set at the dinner table and noted that the last of the guests had finished eating. "You must forgive me," she told them, "but on this occasion I can't find it in me to permit the gentlemen to take their brandy and cigars in the drawing room while we ladies chat in the sitting room. I don't want to miss hearing more of my son's experiences. Shall we go together?"

Father Crowley rose and pulled out her chair. Nick and Beth led the way, succeeded by Klara and then Joe, who flung an arm around Abel's shoulders and gave him a brotherly squeeze. Polly Fearing remained seated, waiting for Albert. He was deep in conversation with Seth, a technical discussion about refining ore which Lucy had long since dismissed as too difficult to follow. Seth Slade, she observed, had lost no time in tailoring his appearance to the fashions here "down below." From the shine on his boots to his haircut, he was attired like a true gentleman of the city. He wore his new frock coat and trousers and white linen shirt as though accustomed to such refinements. A gold watch chain adorned his silk waistcoat, purchased, she suspected, to complete the picture. She wondered, slightly amused, whether or not there was a watch attached.

"Water seepage is the problem," Abel was explaining to Joe when Lucy entered the drawing room. "If it weren't for that, there wouldn't be so many cave-ins."

"*Ach,* but what a hard life it is there," Klara sympathized.

"But there were good times before the snows came. Gaming and prize fights. Hey, Joe, you should have been there the time Brownie Burns went fourteen rounds against Levi Marsh. What a *soirée* we put on afterwards. Seth," he said as the older man came into the room, "if I recall rightly, you stood on a table and sang every verse of 'You Never Miss Your Sainted Mother Until She's Dead and Gone to Heaven.' "

Lucy laughed in spite of the fact that Seth was her guest. "I apologize," she said quickly.

"If you heard my singing voice, ma'am, you'd know it's I who should be apologizing."

"And there was dancing, too," Abel continued, "at Dutch Nick's Saloon on Saturday nights."

"With ladies?" Beth inquired.

"Three white women and a Paiute princess."

"Mrs. Bates," Nick said, "didn't Bethie tell me your husband was killed by the Paiutes?"

"He was, yes."

"Young man," Father Crowley addressed Abel, "have you heard about the good works your mother has done in your absence?"

"The waifs' home? Aunt Polly told me."

"The ladies are doing a splendid job. A few more weeks of fund-raising, and they'll be able to negotiate for the house they've found on Green Street."

Albert Fearing reached into his pocket and withdrew several coins. He handed them to Lucy. "You're the treasurer, I believe."

"Albert, really, you've been more than generous already."

"You must allow me to make a contribution," Seth said, "for the privilege of your son's company and the privilege of making his mother's acquaintance."

"Please," she answered, not wanting to embarrass him, "you've brought me enough of a gift." She opened the small, inlaid box on the table next to her and dropped Albert's coins inside.

"But I insist." He walked to the table and opened the box.

"We must be going, Joe," Klara reminded him. "Tomorrow you have to be early at the store." She rose and took his hand.

Polly paused at the front door as she was leaving. "My dear," she told Lucy, "I'm so happy for you."

"And I," Albert echoed, pressing her hand in his. "Father Crowley, if you're ready, we'll drive you home."

"May I walk with Nick to his carriage, Mama?" Beth asked.

"Yes, but don't be long."

"Mrs. Bates." Seth Slade stood beside her, hat in hand. "Would you do me the honor of dining with me at *L'Onde* tomorrow evening?"

"That's kind of you, but I—"

"It would be my pleasure."

"But isn't *L'Onde* a bit . . . grand?"

He smiled. "Please say yes. I should like to discuss the matter of Abel's future."

"His future?"

He nodded. "Tomorrow. Shall we say half past seven?" With a slight bow, he departed.

Lucy brushed a scattering of cigar ashes from the table-top as Septimus cleared away the brandy glasses. "Abel," she called in the direction of the hall, "what's this about your future that Mr. Slade wants to discuss?"

He came to the doorway. "Seth's taken an interest in me. He's a smart man, Mama."

"We shall see. Help me douse the lights, will you?" She caught sight of the inlaid box and opened it. "Great heavens!"

"What is it?" Abel looked over her shoulder.

"Your friend gave us five twenty-dollar gold pieces! See, here's Albert's thirty dollars, and there's a hundred more! Can Seth afford such an extravagant gesture?"

Abel laughed. "Land sakes, Mama, of course! Seth owns the better part of the Slade and Daggett. The take from that mine's over a thousand a day. Besides, Seth's a lawyer. Last year alone, he made fifty thousand dollars just straightening out tangled claims."

Lucy smiled sheepishly and shook her head in wonderment. "As I live and breathe."

"What did you think he was, Mama, a vagabond?"

"I had no idea. Where does he hail from? Where are his people?"

"Concord, Massachusetts. I don't know anything about his folks, but he's not married."

Lucy carried the box into the hall. Abel caught up with her.

"Did you hear what I said, Mama? He's not married."

"That's no concern of ours, is it? There's a fine line between information and gossip, my dear, and I'd advise you to stop short of it always."

"Yes, Mama," he replied, suppressing a smile.

Seth Slade stood in the drawing room, running his fingers lightly over the back of the red velvet sofa. Seeing Lucy, he bowed. "You make a handsome picture, ma'am."

"Thank you kindly." As Septimus helped her into her

cloak, she saw Seth scanning the room, his eyes lighting here and there upon its furnishings, as though he had not noticed them before. "Are you looking for something?"

"Am I? No, ma'am."

"You seemed to be glancing about."

"I was observing your fondness for red."

"I find it very cheerful."

"And luxurious."

"That, too."

He took her arm as they walked to the door. "An interesting color, red, if you stop to think of it. The color of sovereigns and sinners, noble and notorious at the same time."

"Are you suggesting," she said archly, descending the front steps to the gravel path, "that I'm courting aristocracy or iniquity?"

"Not at all." He helped her into the carriage. "But you must admit red does suggest the gay life."

She looked at him sharply. "You mean a parlor house."

He nodded, smiling, and settled into the seat behind her. He flicked the reins and turned the carriage toward town.

"And how would you know about such things, Mr. Slade?"

"Oh, a gentleman picks up that sort of information."

"Tell me," she said lightly, as though changing the subject, "has my son told you much about me?"

"He has. I know a great deal about you, Mrs. Bates. But please," he said, turning to her, "that was not the source of my observation. I was only making conversation. I had no intention of bringing up the past. Please don't take offense, ma'am."

"If you are not offended by my past, I shan't be offended by what you say. Is that fair?"

"Most generous, ma'am."

"But still," she persisted, "you disapprove of my choice of red."

"No, ma'am, that's not my affair." His eyes were on the road ahead. "But you surely did use a lot of it."

"You're telling me that my drawing room looks like a parlor house?"

He chuckled. "I'll be damned if it doesn't."

She drew her cloak closer about her. "Well, Mr. Slade, you don't mince words, do you?"

He grinned. "How many grand houses have you seen in your lifetime, if I may ask?"

"Why—" She paused. Suddenly she laughed. "None. Not a one. Fancy houses perhaps, but not grand ones."

"I thought not. You're an enterprising lady from all I hear. I'm sure you'll take my remarks in the spirit in which they're given."

"Is it advice you're handing me, Mr. Slade?"

"Something like that." He clucked softly to his horse. "Why'd you build so far from town?"

"Two reasons," she said bluntly. "I wanted to put certain places behind me, and the land was cheap. Given time, I'm sure the city will come to me."

"You're an outspoken lady, too. I admire that. May I take the liberty of calling you Lucy?"

She was not at all sure what to make of Seth Slade. He'd twitted her about her house and made it clear that he was privy to her past, yet he had done so without reproof, in fact, amiably. He was a prospector, a roving gambler like the rest of that breed, yet cultivated and courteous. She found herself watching him intently as he ordered their dinner, speaking to the waiter fluently in French.

"Abel tells me you've traveled a lot, Mr. Slade. Have you been to France?"

"I lived a year in Paris. My father was with our government there."

"What is it like, Paris?"

"A wedding cake. Ornate, rich, full of spice. Its only drawback is that it's teeming with cutthroat French."

She laughed. "And is your family still there?"

"They're dead. My father long gone, and my mother and sister lost to typhoid. I suppose if I hadn't been away at college, it would have claimed me, too." He paused momentarily. "Lucy, that brings me to what I wanted to discuss with you."

"I'm afraid I don't follow you."

He refilled their wineglasses, turning the bottle expertly with a twist of his wrist so that not a drop fell on the white damask tablecloth. Something in the smoothness of the gesture put Lucy on her guard. Seth Slade was a man of many facets, she thought quickly, and she still knew very little about him. While his candor was refreshing, she wondered just how much of what he said was true. Often as not, a man who made his fortune overnight was apt, just as quickly, to make a past to suit his fancy. Caleb Bates had been such a man. And now Seth Slade, his pale blue eyes startling against his tanned face, was looking at her across the table, a smile of unknown origin playing at his lips. "Well," she said warily, "do you intend to explain yourself?"

"I've been giving some deep thought to Abel's education."

"Oh." Lucy relaxed slightly. "Is that all? He did tell me you were an excellent tutor. I thank you for your efforts."

He rotated the stem of his wineglass between his thumb and forefinger. "I have taken the liberty," he continued slowly, "of writing to Harvard College, my *alma mater*, on his behalf."

"Harvard? But that's in Massachusetts!"

He nodded. "In two or three weeks' time, I'll be leaving for the East Coast to settle some business affairs. I'd like to take the boy with me. I've alerted the College that I intend to bring him to Cambridge for an interview."

Lucy felt a flush rising in her cheeks. "I'm afraid," she said evenly, "that I cannot permit it. However well-meaning your intentions may be, Abel belongs with his family."

"It's what he wants."

"He is sixteen years old!" Quickly, she glanced around the crowded room and lowered her voice. "He's not old enough to make such decisions."

"You know as well as I that he's very mature for his age. He has a good head on his shoulders, Lucy."

Her hands were shaking. She slipped them under the table. "You have brought my son home to me, Mr. Slade, only to tell me you intend to spirit him away again. I find myself wondering why you would do such a cruel thing and I also find myself wondering what sort of coaxing and persuasion you've employed to entice him away from his home and family."

Seth started to reply, but she went on, her voice trembling with anger.

"How dare you? How dare you presume to stand between a mother and her son?"

"Please." He raised both hands in protest. "I'm not an ogre, Lucy. It was my understanding that you had always intended the boy should go to college."

374

"For your information, there's a college being organized right now in Oakland."

"Lucy," he said gently, "I couldn't think more of Abel if he were my own son. I beg you, let me take him to talk with the people at Harvard."

"And have him swallowed up behind its walls for God knows how many years?"

"We are not at odds, Lucy, no matter how things appear. I'm sure we both want what's best for him."

"As his mother, that's for me to judge."

"Then I should warn you," he told her, "that I feel quite as strongly about this as you do."

"You could at least allow him another year before pressing him to make such a decision."

"I don't believe there's time," he said somberly. "In my opinion, the country may be at war before another year passes. The journey might be impossible. Lucy, how could you possibly justify denying him the best education available?"

She glared at him in wordless fury.

"He's an extraordinarily brilliant young man, not to mention persevering. He has a fine future ahead of him. It's time he prepared for it."

"Under no circumstances will I spend so much as a single dime to send my son away into some sort of educational exile."

"That's not necessary. The boy has made a little money in the mines, and I'd be happy to make up the balance of the costs."

She held his gaze for a moment. The color had gone from her face. "I see. You've contrived to leave me no choice."

"My dear." Seth rose and came to her, bending down beside her chair. A waiter appeared, frowning solicitously, but Seth waved him away. "No one is conspiring to hurt you, least of all, Abel. Let him enjoy this opportunity."

"He will be lost to me forever."

"No." He grasped her hands in his, refusing to let her pull away. "He knew you'd be afraid of that. He said, 'Tell Mama I give her my solemn promise to come back to stay.' You have my word, too, Lucy."

"And what," she asked him dully, "is your word worth, Mr. Slade?"

"Trust me."

She glanced at him.

"Take a chance on me, Lucy. You won't be sorry. I've never yet made a vow I didn't honor."

"You cut out a part of my heart and you ask me to believe that it's safe in your hands?"

"If that's how you see it, yes."

The May sun, golden with the promise of summer, shone down on the fields and hills surrounding the lone dwelling on that part of Bush Street. Wildflowers bloomed on the grassy slopes to either side, and below the covered porch of the house, the azalea and iris had begun to show tight pale green buds. Though it was cool in the shade of the porch, Beth was fanning herself. The young ladies of New Rosedale, to hear Nick tell it, when not engaged in dancing or stitchery occupied themselves largely with much fanning on the veranda. Beth, Lucy noticed, had been quick to take the cue.

"I still think it's hateful!" Beth fanned herself more rapidly. "It's not fair, Abel. You've not been home a month and you're setting off again tomorrow, leaving Mama and me all alone."

Abel tilted his chair back and propped his feet up on the porch railing. "You're not alone, Bethie, and you know it."

"Must we suffer through this again?" Lucy said irritably. "Each of us knows how the others feel."

"I'll write," he promised. "With the new Pony Express mail, the letters should take less than a month to arrive."

Beth pouted prettily. "If I know you, you won't want to spend five dollars the ounce too often. We'll be lucky to hear from you once a year."

"How do you know Harvard will accept me?" he asked her slyly. "Maybe I'm too much of a hick for those fancy Easterners."

"Northerners," Nick corrected him, stretching languidly. " 'Pon my soul, Abel, I'll be hanged if I understand why you'd choose a school that lets darkies apply. What sense is there in taking a monkey out of the jungle and trying to teach him Greek?"

Beth giggled behind her fan.

Abel gave him a sanguine smile. "Careful, now. If one of those monkeys can graduate from Harvard when you ain't even finished your second year at Georgia, where does that leave you?"

Seth, sitting on the railing at the corner of the porch, hummed quietly to himself as he tamped his pipe.

"Why, my friend," Nick countered smoothly, "that just proves, don't it, that the standards at Athens are superior to Cambridge?"

"Do stop," Lucy said. "Can't we talk about something else?"

"You heard, I suppose," Nick said to no one in particular, "about the Paiutes burning Williams' Station? Isn't that right near Sun Mountain, where you were?"

Seth nodded. "I heard. Five men and a woman and child killed."

"Maybe that Paiute princess of yours was doing a war dance and not a polka like you thought."

"Abel," Lucy said abruptly, "did Wong bring back the last of your clean shirts?"

"They're in my trunk, Mama. I'm all packed."

She wished the thought of his going did not depress her so. Already she felt an emptiness within her, as though it were not he, but some part of herself that was slipping away. Tomorrow, the steamer *Sierra Alta* would sail out of the Golden Gate, heading south to the Isthmus, diminishing in the distance until the ever-present sea mists engulfed and obliterated it, leaving only a thin plume of smoke to disappear quickly in the ocean breeze.

Lucy had forced herself to maintain a cordial attitude toward Seth Slade, if only for Abel's sake. It was apparent that his affection for the boy was genuine, so she could not fault him on that count. Still, she remained resentful and suspicious of this man who hd come between them, dangling the plum of a fine education in front of Abel, knowing it was just the nourishment he craved. In truth, she would have felt a good deal more comfortable if her feelings toward Seth were not so confusingly mixed. Despite her distrust, there was nothing to suggest that he was not exactly as he appeared, decent and kind, refined and affluent. Given another set of circumstances, she might even have liked him.

Lucy glanced toward Seth, who was explaining their planned route to Beth. The pillar at the corner of the porch where he sat had begun to cast its long, dark silhouette across the green-painted floor between them. She stared into the stream of shadow, wishing against all hope that the gloom of evening would never come.

In the weeks that followed Abel's departure, Lucy plunged herself into a tumult of activity. Not a day was allowed to pass without some purposeful pursuit. Not an empty hour was permitted to remind her of the vacancy he had left.

She exhorted and goaded and badgered on behalf of the Good Shepherd Home, until it was hard to tell whether she achieved cooperation by consent or capitulation. With the deed to the premises signed, it was she who undertook the refurbishing, while Polly and Leanna visited the sheriff, the police and the local hospitals to advise them of its existence. Amanda and Verity Knight were in charge of engaging the small staff, determined that, as Verity put it, "indigent ladies of high moral principles and diligence" were to be chosen. The scarcity of such paragons was, it appeared, something of an eye-opener to the good sisters, but with much clucking of their tongues, they persevered and triumphed. Ada Brock, Jane Gallagher and Father Crowley served as the admissions committee. Poor Ada, whose heart was as soft and sweet as custard, emerged red-eyed from these meetings, unable to shake off the woes of the waifs who were referred to them.

With fourteen children, aged three to twelve, the Good Shepherd Home opened its doors. Beth, Martha, Naomi and their friends each spent one afternoon a week organizing games, teaching handcrafts and helping the children with their lessons. Beth had prevailed upon Nick and Boyd Stevens to round up some young men to befriend the boys who boarded there. In spite of Lucy's misgivings that they might quickly lose interest, the young people acquitted themselves admirably. The *Alta* and the *Bulletin* praised the civic-minded undertaking, both of them noting that it had been initiated by Mrs. Caleb Bates who, as one of them recalled, "Achieved distinction through her selfless compassion in the cholera outbreak of 1858." That, Lucy thought, was a reminder she could well do without. She waited apprehensively for repercussions, but none came. The stain was gone. Her slate was wiped clean, and the future hers for the making.

"Ho, there!" Nick poked his head around the door to

the drawing room. "Mrs. Bates, I declare!" He laughed, seeing her teetering atop the stepladder which Li Lin held firmly in place. "It looks like the refurbishing bug bit you good. Is this an epidemic? First the Good Shepherd and now Bush Street?"

"Be a dear, Nick, and hand me the yardstick, will you?" She took it from him and measured the width of the window. "I've decided," she said, descending the ladder, "this room could do with a bit more light. They say you never know a house 'til you've lived in it a while. I'm thinking it's a little too dark in here." She folded a swatch of pale, silvery-green damask under her arm and jotted her measurements on a piece of paper. "Lin, please tell Bethie that Mr. Stevens is here."

Li Lin trotted off toward the stairs. Lucy folded the stepladder and motioned Nick to a chair. "We had a letter from Abel this morning, from New Orleans. They had a safe journey, but he said the weather was almost intolerably hot and the insects fierce as cannibals."

"They must have reached New York by now."

"God willing. Beth tells me you're starting work for your Uncle Dabney next week."

He grinned. "Pa wrote me. Gave me a lecture. Either find work or come home."

"But aren't you lonesome for New Rosedale after such a long absence?"

Her question went unanswered as Beth flew into the room, cloak in hand. "I'm ready, Nick. We won't be late, Mama. It's only a tea party."

"Be on your way," she told them. "You'll find me in the library when you return. I have to read through Joe's ledgers from the store."

Fortunately for Beth, Nick occupied so much of her spare time that she scarcely had a moment to miss her brother. Nick, it appeared, had staked his claim on her and was digging in to stay. There was no doubt in Lucy's mind that he was flattered by Beth's affections, though she wondered how long it would be before he found such adoration cloying. To Beth, he was faultless, ideal, above the slightest criticism.

It worried Lucy to think the girl might be courting folly, but her admonitions fell on deaf ears. The idea of being the belle of New Rosedale was too tempting for someone with Beth's aspirations. The danger was, on the one hand, that she might suffer a grave disappointment and, on the other, that she might eventually achieve her dream and leave San Francisco behind her. The likelihood of secession, or even war, made this latter possibility even more disturbing to Lucy. Either way, it seemed to her that Beth was aiming for trouble, but she could not find it in her to deny the girl the pleasure of his companionship. In fact, Lucy herself enjoyed Nick's presence. He was no bother, really. He was pleasant and courteous and occasionally quite amusing, and she liked having a young man in the house to help fill the void Abel had left behind.

"We received another letter, Nick." Beth buttered her biscuit. "They were in New York City on their way to Cambridge. Abel said Seth took him to all the fancy places and to Barnum's Museum and bought him a lot of new clothes at a place called Brook's."

Lucy frowned. "Sheer extravagance. His clothing was in perfect order when he left here."

"But Mama, perhaps the styles in the East are different."

"San Francisco is a very fashionable city. How different could they be? Anyway, that's not Seth's responsibility."

"New Englanders are stubborn as mules, ma'am," Nick told her with a twinkle in his eyes. "They're great ones for taking charge and insisting on having their way."

"Indeed," she retorted crisply. "I've been called a mule myself, more than once. Seth Slade will have to learn that I control the affairs of this family, not he."

Nick changed the subject. "Hanged if I didn't see a sight today, coming back from the office. Right at the corner of California and Kearny streets there was a bootblack, a white man he was, kneeling down, polishing some darky's shoes. Can you beat that? Makes you wonder what this world's coming to, don't it?"

"Come now, Nick. This isn't Georgia. In this city—" Lucy broke off as Septimus came to remove the soup plates. "Septimus, you may close the windows now that it's dark outside."

"No, please," Beth interrupted. "The smell of the fresh

paint from the drawing room is revolting, Mama. I'd sooner be chilly."

"As you wish. Septimus, would you be good enough to ask Li Lin to fetch my shawl?"

"Yes'm. Miss Beth?"

"Mine too, please. Honestly, Mama, if it's not the painters, it's the drapers underfoot. I'm tired of entertaining in that tiny sitting room. Aren't you ever going to be finished with your decorating?"

"Soon," she said.

The new Brussels carpet had been her first purchase. It was pale green and dusty rose, and she had been at some pains to find a wallpaper to suit it. She had settled on one with a background of the same green and a fanciful pattern of white, plumelike leaves. It had seemed a shame to mask the woodwork with white paint, but she had to admit the room looked less overpowering now. The sofa and two small chairs had been newly covered with rosy velvet to catch the color of the carpet and the marble fireplace, while the other upholstery and the window draperies were of the silver-green damask she had found.

With some satisfaction, she placed Queen Rosie Pitt's pink and white needlework pillow in the big wing chair, where it looked very nice indeed. The room seemed larger than it had before; and though not as imposing, it was altogether charming, rather like a lush corner in some inviting garden. For all her complaints, Bethie was delighted with the transformation and proceeded to have several new dresses made to compliment the room. She was, Lucy thought, the fairest flower of all, and not in the least oblivious of the fact.

" 'Pon my soul." Nick stood in the drawing room doorway, looking from Beth to Lucy. "If you two ladies aren't a pleasure for the eyes." He joined Beth on the sofa. "Evening, beauty. Mrs. Bates, that's a most becoming gown you have on, if I may say so."

"Thank you, Nick." Lucy smoothed the crinoline-puffed skirt of her dress somewhat self-consciously. It was a color she had never worn before, a sandy, silk moiré that matched her blonde hair. Draped across her bosom were three tiers of lustrous, chocolate-brown passementerie, caught in tasseled clusters on her sleeves. Her waist she reflected with permissable pride, looked almost as slim as Beth's, set off as it was by her wide, billowing skirts.

"Mama's dining with Seth Slade. He sent a message this morning, saying he'd come back."

"Why, Beth Bates," Nick chided her, "don't you go tattling on your Mama."

"But it's so. And his messenger brought a letter from Abel, too. Read it to Nick, Mama."

"Yes," he said. "What's the news?"

Lucy reached into her reticule and withdrew the folded envelope. She opened the pages in her lap and began to read.

August 6, 1860

Dearest Mama and Bethie,

I confess that my first glimpse of this place overawed me. Not that Cambridge isn't pretty. There's a bright blue river running by and wide, green fields and many streets lined with handsome houses, all shaded by beautiful elms, old ones from the size of them. But the university was a sobering sight. It is made up of a number of staid-looking brick buildings without much ornament, as though to say there is no license for indulgence or nonsense in this place. Even the courtyards and halls are hushed. Learning is a serious business here. I felt very timid before my interviews began, but Seth buoyed me up with good cheer and encouragement.

The gentlemen of Harvard are much like their buildings, but though they are quite austere and their examinations were minute, I found most of them very receptive. It appears I need to improve my Greek, but all in all, they seemed to approve of me. If it had not been for Seth's tutelage, I am sure I would have failed their scrutiny.

As you can see from the address below, I am lodged with a Mr. and Mrs. Alvah Mountford. Mr. Mountford practices law across the river in Boston, and the family has three daughters. The middle one I judge to be Bethie's age. The Mountfords have made me very comfortable and treat me as one of their own. Mr. Mountford was at Harvard with Seth and is well known to him, so I am not cast among total strangers, Mama.

I shall write again as soon as I become used to my new surroundings. Meanwhile, I think of you both often, and you are never far from my mind. I know you were unhappy to have me leave, but I feel there is much to be gained here and that Seth has done our family a great service through his efforts on my behalf. I ask you both to receive him with the same warmth you would show to me.

Ever your loving son and brother.

Abel

Nick gave Beth's hand a squeeze. "I'd say he sounds mighty content. Seems like there's no reason for either of you to fret. The time will pass before you know it."

"Mercy!" Beth exclaimed. "The time! We must be going. Lin?" she called. "Where is Naomi Brock's birthday gift?"

"Here, Missybet." Lin emerged from the hallway bearing a blue satin pincushion adorned with a scarlet ribbon. "You like my bow?"

"It's beautiful," Lucy answered her, rising to see Beth and Nick to the door. "Don't forget to give Naomi my best wishes," she told them.

Nick opened the door and gave a start. He laughed sheepishly. "Mr. Slade, good evening, sir."

Seth's hand was still poised to knock. He looked equally startled. "Am I interrupting?"

"The children were just leaving." Lucy stepped aside. "Do come in."

He handed his hat to Lin and followed Lucy into the drawing room.

"I suppose I should begin by thanking you for all you've done for Abel." She seated herself across from him. "He seems very pleased with Cambridge. He appears to be in good spirits."

"We had a grand journey. He opened my eyes to things I'd long ago taken for granted. The young are a tonic, especially when they're as keen and enthusiastic as he. You've a lot to be proud of in that boy, Lucy. He's made of good stuff."

"He's always been his own man, even as a child. I can only claim credit for a small part of him."

"You're wrong. We both know how different his life would have been without your influence."

"He appears," she said guardedly, "to have taken you into his confidence."

"Months ago. You needn't be concerned. The past is of no importance now, and his future is very bright indeed."

She stood up, "May I offer you something to drink? I've some excellent Spanish sherry in the library."

"That would suit me just right."

He took the glass she brought him and raised it to her with a look of sly amusement. "May I compliment you on such a tasteful drawing room?"

"Do you like it?" She brushed an unseen speck from her skirts. "I was of a mind to make it lighter."

"It's a most attractive setting for a most attractive lady." He withdrew a small package from his coat pocket and, reaching across to her, laid it in her lap.

"What is this?"

"A memento of our trip, if you will."

"Really, this isn't necessary. You've no reason to bring me a gift."

"That's not so. You gave me the gift of your trust. I assure you, my gift is not so precious as that."

She opened the lid of the box and removed the square of cotton inside. She looked up at Seth, speechless.

"Aren't you going to put it on? It will look very becoming on that dress."

"Great heavens," she breathed, "I never saw jewels like this." She took the brooch gingerly in one hand and ran her fingers over it. At the top was a single huge pearl, round and circled with glittering diamonds. Beneath it hung a second pearl, easily the size of the first, but shaped like a perfect teardrop. The brooch glowed against her skin as though it emitted a brilliance of its own. "I've never laid eyes on anything so magnificent. Wherever did you find it?"

"In New York City. In Mr. Charles Tiffany's store on Broadway, to be exact. He assured me it's an exceptionally fine piece."

"I should say. But Seth, I can't wear this. It would hardly be correct to accept such a gift from a gentleman I don't know well."

384

"I told you. It's a poor trade for your trust. If anyone inquires, you can say you received it in an exchange."

She laughed. "They'll think I exchanged my virtue!"

"Come now," he teased her, "if that were the case, you'd have a fistful of them!"

Lucy rose and went to the mirror that hung above the piano. "I'm afraid you're much too late. I'm well past my maiden years by now." She peered into the glass, adjusting the brooch. "There. How does that look?"

"Very suitable. May I fetch your cloak?"

"It's on the chair in the hall." She followed him, glancing down at the shining jewels on her bodice. "I am not sure I can carry off all this splendor. I shall feel quite uneasy being goggled at."

"What rot," he said amiably. "You know you'll love it. I never yet met a lady who didn't revel in attention." He opened the door and motioned her out.

"And I suppose you've known a large number of ladies in your time?"

"No more than my share." He assisted her into the carriage and seated himself beside her.

Lucy reached beneath her cloak and fingered the brooch. Warily, she inquired, "And is it your habit to dispense such expensive gifts to them?"

Seth laughed. "Oh, come, my girl, can't you drop your guard for five minutes?"

"I beg your pardon?"

"Loosen up, girl. Enjoy yourself."

"I'm hardly a girl."

"No? Perhaps you might be, if you'd let yourself. What is it? Do I seem such a dangerous character?"

"I don't know. I'm not sure."

He gave her a curious glance. "Why?"

"Because . . . you're rather overpowering. I give you credit for your honorable intentions, but the fact remains that you swept into my home without notice and rode roughshod over my feelings."

"Only because I wanted the best for that boy. Did I do anything so inexcusable?"

"No."

"Yet something about me still bothers you."

She gazed ahead at the darkened, empty street. Finally, she said, "I don't know what it is you expect for all your generosity."

"Ah." He thought for a moment. "Just the pleasure of it, I suppose. And what does any man want, anyway? A little pleasure, a little peace and his good health. For pity's sake, Lucy, relax. I'm not such a menace." He looked at her. "Smile, can't you? You looked very beautiful smiling into the mirror back there, toying with your brooch."

"Now you flatter me."

Seth pulled the reins up sharply. The carriage halted. He turned to her. "I've little use for flattery, Lucy. It's not my way. I was quite sincere just now. You may either accept the compliment with polite thanks or, if you're convinced that I harbor some sinister design, I shall set your mind at ease by turning this carriage around and taking you home. The choice is yours. I'd looked forward to a pleasant evening, not a duel of words. Which will it be?"

She felt her face grow hot. "Forgive me," she said quietly. "I've been quite rude."

"That you have." He snapped the reins. "At least, praise God, you're honest."

XX

THERE WAS no logical reason, Lucy told herself, why she should feel the slightest degree flustered in Seth Slade's company.

To all appearances, there was nothing in his bearing or character that was not pleasing or even, were she the sort inclined to magnification, admirable. He lived modestly, she knew, in a hotel nearby his office. Like so many other gentlemen of means, he seemed to spend a good deal of time talking business in the hospitable atmosphere of the Bank Exchange Saloon on Washington and Montgomery. Though he kept his dealings to himself, Lucy gathered that the Slade and Daggett Mine was only one among a number of his interests. He was a man who neither announced his triumphs nor protested his trials. Once, in a rare moment of reflection on the day's affairs, he smiled pensively and said to her, "The wheel turns, Lucy dear. That's all any fellow has to remember. The wheel is never still. It comes 'round again and again." She did not press him to explain. Seth's reserve was part of his self-reliance, and she respected that. In turn, he honored her pursuits. He made no attempt to pry into the affairs of the store or to influence her investments or to intervene in the seemingly endless challenges of operating the Good Shepherd Home. He was, however, hardly disinterested in her. He sought out her company more and more as the weeks passed. There were gifts of flowers and books and, wonder of wonders, a stereoscopic viewer that brought the icy cataract of Niagara Falls plummeting into an explosion of mist inches from her eyes.

Sometimes, Lucy would pause inadvertently in the

midst of brushing her hair or doing her mending to wonder why Seth Slade chose to seek out her companionship when surely he could have his pick of younger and prettier women. She was almost thirty-two years old, no girl certainly. Gazing into the glass above her dressing table, she observed that the golden, corn-silk hair of her youth had faded now. Here and there strands of silver brightened her temples. Her blue eyes were clear, and her cheeks still kept a rosy tinge, though time had worn its fine trails above her cheekbones and beside her mouth. It was, she supposed, what might be termed a "handsome" face, no longer pretty and never what she'd thought of as beautiful. Still, it was pleasing enough for a woman of her years. And while most of the women Lucy knew had ripened into matronly figures, she had remained slender, even girlish. Lucy was neither vain nor foolish enough, however, to think that Seth Slade was drawn to her looks alone. When she thought about it, which she did more often than she cared to admit, she realized that Seth had sought out someone as self-sufficient as he. He had a certain confidence in her. To tell the truth, she had a certain confidence in him, too. She supposed no harm could come of that.

Lucy glanced up sharply as a log in the fireplace broke, sending a surge of sparks darting up the flue. She laid her reading aside and turned up the lamp on the table beside her. The November days were short, and the nights increasingly chilly. She stoked the fire and put on another log. From the hall came voices and the sound of the front door closing. Nick strode into the drawing room, gave her a curt greeting and stood staring sourly down at the blaze on the hearth.

"Where's your smile, Nick?" she inquired pleasantly. "It's not like you to be out of sorts."

"I'm late."

"What of it? Bethie's always late."

"The town's a madhouse. Streets filled with masses of fools carrying torches and shouting and chanting like lunatics. Bonfires every which way. We'll be lucky if the whole city doesn't catch and burn to the ground."

"What in the name of heaven has happened?"

"You didn't hear?" He stuffed his fists in his pockets

388

as though to govern himself. "It's Lincoln. The Republicans won the election."

"What does that mean?" she asked quietly.

"War."

"But you've always said—"

"Things are different now. With Lincoln president, there's no recourse but secession."

"That's a big step, Nick. One or two states, perhaps, if the hotheads have their way, but surely there'll be no shooting."

"Hear me, Mrs. Bates. It's inevitable. While I'm standing here, the die is being cast."

Beth interrupted them. "Here I am," she announced, pirouetting prettily in the doorway to display her new frock. "Well, what do you think? Nick, what's wrong? You don't like it?"

"It's fine, I guess."

Beth looked crestfallen.

"Mr. Lincoln has become president," Lucy told her. "Nick feels that's a bad omen."

"You would too," he said, "if you saw those so-called patriots lighting their bonfires down in the town."

"I'm surprised you didn't stay to watch," Beth replied tartly. "I thought you'd taken a liking to fires. And," she added pointedly, "the sort of people who enjoy them."

"What sort is that?" he wanted to know.

She shrugged. "I was thinking of people like Lillie Hitchcock."

"Lillie's Secesh. She wouldn't lower herself to be among that crowd."

"I just wondered. You know how queer she is about fires."

"Bethie," Lucy cautioned, "you're sounding quite unkind. As I remember, Lillie Hitchcock has been the pet of Company Five since she was a child. When Abel was younger, he was green-eyed with envy, watching her ride by with the firemen."

"We'd best be going," Nick said. "Boyd and Naomi are waiting for us at her house."

"As you wish." Beth turned and disappeared into the hall.

Lucy caught Nick's sleeve as he passed. "Promise me you won't go near the mobs tonight, not even out of curiosity. I don't want either of you in any danger."

389

"Yes'm. The young ladies will be safe. Don't you worry."

Nevertheless, Lucy sat up in bed, reading, until she heard Beth come home. She wrapped a shawl over her shoulders, padded across the hallway and tapped at Beth's door. "May I come in?"

Beth sat on the edge of the bed, her eyes red-rimmed and swollen.

"Dearest, what is it?" Lucy put an arm around her and drew her close.

"Everything."

"Surely not everything. What things?"

"They're going to war, Nick and Boyd."

"Such nonsense. There is no war. You're allowing a lot of loose talk to upset you."

"There will be. Everyone says so."

"Everyone, indeed. Two proud young men with Southern sympathies. How are they to know what's in the minds of people older and wiser than they?"

"Lillie Hitchcock asked Nick to escort her to a dance last week. He never told me. I heard from someone else that he was there."

"But tonight he was with you."

"He talked about her. He said she's amusing. She talks about politics. Her father's a friend of Jefferson Davis, she says."

"I detect a good measure of jealousy, Beth. It won't do to have Nick see that you're jealous of Lillie Hitchcock."

"He laughed at me," she said miserably. "He thought it was funny."

"Probably only because it was absurd."

"Mama, I swear to you I won't let her have him! He's mine!"

"Stop this at once. You're behaving like a little fool. Nick isn't the only fine fish in the sea."

"He's mine," she repeated, rubbing the tears from her cheeks, "and she's trying to take him away. She's invited him to Sunday dinner."

"Perhaps only to talk about the political situation. It's not strange for the Secesh to want to gather their wits about them now. It's quite possible she's not even interested in him as a beau."

"I won't let it happen, Mama."

390

"It's out of your hands, I'm afraid. Nick is free to do as he pleases. But you'd be wise to curb your jealousy, Bethie. It's not attractive. If you want to attract a gentleman, you must be on your best behavior."

Beth buried her face in her hands, sobbing. "I hope she dies."

"Enough." Lucy rose. "You're working your way toward hysteria, and I won't have it. Get some sleep. Your head will be clearer in the morning. And mind, you, do as I say. There are more young ladies than Lillie Hitchcock out there in the world, and if you choose to compete with them, you'll have to be at your best." She closed the bedroom door and crossed the dark hall. She paused a moment, still hearing the sound of Beth's crying. "Poor lamb," she said quietly.

The pale December sunlight slanted down through the slats of the porch railing, spreading sharp patterns of dark and light like a striped carpet before the open front door. Lucy waited while Father Crowley took his leave of Seth in the drawing room.

"Ah, Pastora," the father said, contentedly patting his belly, as he came to the door, "that was a splendid feast. Would you be so kind as to thank Biddy for me?" He took Lucy's hands in his. "I wish you all the blessings of this joyful season, Pastora."

"And a happy Christmas to you, too, Father." She waved as he went down the steps, cassock flapping in the breeze.

Seth sat by the fire, filling his pipe as she rejoined him. "Pastora . . ." He looked across at her and smiled as she took a chair. "The name amuses me."

"The children detest it. To them it smacks of notoriety."

"I thought it came from your Castalia days."

"It does. But they don't remember that."

"Nevertheless, I like it. Speaking of the children, where did Beth go? She disappeared the moment dinner ended."

"I expect," Lucy said dourly, "that she's in her room sulking over Nick. That young man is tormenting her. I'm not sure it's deliberate, but the results are the same."

"Running hot and cold is he?" Seth laughed softly and shook his head. "Young love. Spooning and sobbing."

"She's much too wrought up over Nick. I wish to God she weren't such an impetuous girl."

"She'll simmer down."

"No, Seth. Bethie's spoiled, and that's largely my fault." Her eyes were solemn with concern. "She means to have her way, and Nick is no exception."

"Then you're in for a patch of stormy weather, I fear. I'm sorry I shan't be here to see you through it."

"And I'm sorry you won't share Christmas with us. How bad is the situation in the mines?"

"From all reports, the shafts are flooded and the hoists and mills ruined. I'm afraid the weather in Washoe is justly famous for extremes. As soon as I'm sure the Slade and Daggett will recover, I'll be back. I've a boat to meet early next month."

"You're sailing?"

"No, no. A business associate is arriving, coming all the way from Germany. I must be here to welcome him."

"I declare, you're the most industrious man I ever met. You're like a juggler with six balls in the air at once."

"And this one," he said mysteriously, "is very special. It may not land for several years."

"Are you teasing me? Should I try to guess?"

"No. I expect you'll be there to see it."

"You do?" She looked surprised.

Seth dropped the subject. He reached into his pocket and pulled out a little white box. "Would you be good enough to take this?"

"Not another present!"

"Not exactly. Just keep it for me until I come back. Then you may either hold onto it or return it to me, as you please. Go ahead," he invited her, "open it."

She raised the lid. Inside, resting on a cushion of blue velvet, lay a single, small circlet of gold.

Seth raised a hand. "No. Don't say anything. Not now. You're an independent woman, Lucy. Only an idiot would try to press you. Take your time. The choice has to be yours."

For a moment, she couldn't reply. "Seth," she said cautiously, "we scarcely know each other."

"Nonsense. Are you anything other than what I already see and know? As for myself," he said, spreading

392

his arms wide to either side of his chair, "this is all of me. I've nothing up my sleeves. If what you perceive suits you, I'm a fortunate fellow. If not . . ." He paused to relight his pipe, "then I'll be deprived of a fine companion. Such are the risks."

"I'm not sure the Lord meant me for marriage," she said hesitantly. "My grooms have a way of disappearing."

He reached over and took her hand. "Not I. You may depend on it."

"My late husband, Caleb Bates . . ." She paused, searching awkwardly for the words. "I don't know how to say this, but he was not a man of much sympathy or tenderness, if you understand me."

"You're telling me the marriage bed was not a pleasant place for you."

She nodded.

"I shan't harm you, Lucy." He gazed down at her hand and brushed her fingertips with his. "You're trembling. Relax, my dear." He touched the hollow of her palm, slowly tracing each of the fine lines there. She said nothing, feeling only his light caress against her skin. He lifted her hand to his lips and gently kissed the smooth mounds and furrows of her palm. He pressed her fingers to his lips. After a moment, he tenderly closed her hand and laid it against the folds of her skirt. They looked at each other in silence. "Now," he said, "you know all there is to know." He rose. "I'm afraid I must be on my way."

When he had gone, she stood for a long time by the window, staring out over the porch to the empty street beyond. A mantle of fog was moving inland. She watched it settle over the hill. The pearly iridescent mist was irradiated by a veiled sun. It shone and swirled like the last traces of a dissolving rainbow, now pale yellow, now pink and finally, as the sun vanished behind it, dull and gray. There was not a sound, inside or out, to disrupt the quiet. Yet, as Lucy watched the writhing clouds of fog, a tumult of thoughts and feelings disturbed the tranquillity. Like the mist beyond the windowpanes, her mind meandered and churned and turned back upon itself in hazy whorls.

She did not need a husband, nor did she wish to learn to need one. After Henry Fearing had decamped, she had sworn never to be dependent upon anyone. No man would make himself indispensable to her. No man would hold her heart for ransom. Her life, as it was, was full. She was not at a loss for company. And yet, she wondered, what if she were to turn Seth away? Seth Slade was a prize catch for any woman, if that mattered. There were, she knew, social advantages to being married, but she had never pined to be a part of the city's aristocracy, that self-satisfied band, fond of boiled shirts and bowing that, like as not, a scant ten years ago had been scrambling after nuggets in the mud or jumping another fellow's claim. No, she reassured herself again, she did not need a husband.

But as she turned from the window, she realized with a sudden pang that Christmas was not going to be as cheerful without Seth. He had only just left, yet already she missed knowing that his knock would sound at the door tonight as it did almost every night. "Damn," she said quietly. A surge of resentment overtook her. Seth Slade had somehow insinuated his way into her life and now, to compound the transgression, had come to her with an offer of marriage. She thought of the way he had gained Abel's confidence, then dangled the offer of a Harvard education before him. Seth Slade might as well be the devil himself, smooth-talking and smiling, enticing them with his temptations. For a moment, she hated him. Then she remembered something French Jack once said. She heard his voice clearly. "To hate ain't the opposite of love. Hate still cares." She shook her head furiously as though to rid it of the thought, but the echo refused to leave. "Damn," she repeated. "What has this man done?"

She made no mention of Seth's proposal to Beth. The poor child was in a state over Nick's attentions to Lillie Hitchcock. The news would only aggravate this obsession of hers to possess him. Then too, Lucy was at a loss to answer the obvious question Beth would put to her. She swung like a pendulum between the two alternatives, trying vainly to sort out her thoughts, not knowing what reply she would give Seth when that time came.

"Well, Septimus." Lucy folded her newspaper as he set the steaming bowl of oatmeal before her. "I'm afraid the fat's in the fire."

"Ma'am?"

"The news." She tapped the paper with her finger. "South Carolina has voted to secede from the Union."

"Shall I leave Miss Bethie's cereal?"

"Put it at her place. Li Lin went to fetch her. Septimus, do you realize what this news means?"

"No, ma'am."

"There's likely to be a war over the issue of slavery."

"Yes'm." He nodded and disappeared into the kitchen.

There was no way of knowing what he felt. His sad eyes revealed nothing. Whatever his thoughts might be, he rarely communicated them. Sometimes his impassivity irritated Lucy, but she couldn't help respecting that streak of mute, stubborn reserve in him.

Beth took her place at the table and snapped open her napkin with a sharp twist of her wrist. "Guess what, Mama? I heard Lillie Hitchcook lit up a cigar on a dare and smoked it, right in front of a roomful of people."

"Christopher Columbus heard the world was flat. I've no patience for gossip, Beth. You know that."

"Whose side are you on, Mama? Sometimes you act as if you don't give a hang what happens to Nick and me."

"I care what happens to you."

"You've never liked him," she pouted, poking irritably at the mound of oatmeal in front of her. "Admit it."

"That's not so. I have my reservations, but I don't dislike Nick."

She pounced like a cat on a sparrow. "What reservations?"

"Nick's only nineteen. I know he affects maturity, but—"

"You think he's affected?"

"Occasionally he strikes me as a bit pompous."

"How would you know?" she retorted. "You weren't raised among genteel people."

Lucy laid her spoon on her place. "My dear girl," she said evenly, "how wrong you are to accept manners as character. They are not one and the same. A man can have one without the other."

"How dare you say he has no character!"

"I didn't. You weren't listening. Nick is young, and so are you. You both have much to learn. Character comes with years."

"And you think I'll feel differently about him when I'm older? I won't, Mama."

"Time will tell."

"You're playing the waiting game, aren't you? You know very well that if there's a war he'll be the first to go, and you're sitting there praying that he'll leave me and I'll forget all about him. How can you be so cruel, Mama?"

"Excuse me." Lucy rose. "I've better things to do than to listen to such unpleasantness. I'll be in the library. I expect your apology before another hour has passed."

Many an evening now elapsed, Lucy noticed, without Nick's stopping by to call. Beth's face looked taut and pinched, as though she suffered a constant toothache. The pervasive gloom of the winter rains only darkened her mood. Lucy's attempts to raise her spirits led nowhere. Frustrated, irritated, beset by her own uncertainties, Lucy withdrew from comment. They skirted each other warily, like a pair of strange curs. Mealtimes passed in virtual silence, save when one of Abel's letters provided a neutral territory for conversation. Only Li Lin, cheery as a cricket, seemed oblivious to the pall that hung over the household. When Beth snapped at her, she merely looked apologetic and set about her tasks with renewed effort. She fetched the water for Beth's bath, rubbed her dry, and meticulously arranged her hair in intricate rolls and curls, lacing it with ribbons or flowers for occasions like Leanna's dancing parties.

The dances at the house on Bush Street attracted more young people than ever. Lucy was relieved to note that Nick still turned up as usual every other Friday, if only because his presence greatly improved Beth's disposition. But the improvements seldom lasted long.

"Lin?" Lucy spied her in the hall, helping Septimus hand out cloaks and umbrellas to the departing guests. "Where is Beth? She should be saying her good-byes."

Lin shook her head mournfully and glanced toward the ceiling as though it might be in danger of falling upon them all.

Lucy found Beth upstairs in her room, stalking back and forth in a storm of rage. She threw off her dancing slippers and tore at the ribbons in her hair. "Childish, he said! Nick said it's childish to waste time with parties when the country's on the brink of war."

Lucy picked up the ribbons from the floor and flung

them angrily on the bed. "I'm sick and tired of your hanging on Nick's words as though they were gospel! And what the devil does he want to fight a war for, anyway, if it's not to defend his precious New Rosedale with its fancy balls and parties? Answer me that!"

"I'm not having any more dances." She wriggled out of her petticoats and sent them flying with a kick.

"Fine," Lucy said grimly. "I shall have Lin bring your supper to your room. I prefer to spend my evening in peace."

Lucy went downstairs to break the news to Leanna. "Some of the young men are stirring up the girls with all this war talk. Perhaps we'd best stop for a while until it blows over."

Leanna seemed genuinely disappointed. "But don't you think it's just the time for diversion? If these young people from Union and Secesh families can laugh and dance together, isn't that an object lesson for them all?"

"It's Bethie's decision. She's the hostess, after all." Lucy gave the woman's hand a sympathetic squeeze. "Leanna!" Her tone brightened suddenly. "How would you like to teach me to dance instead?"

"You?"

"I've always wanted to learn."

"But Lucy, how? You'd need a partner."

Lucy glanced beyond her to the dining room, where Septimus was clearing away the last of the refreshments. "I believe," she replied with an odd little smile, "that could be arranged."

Beth's reaction, as expected, was one of horror. "Mama, it's scandalous! What would people say if they saw you prancing about with one of the servants? And a Negro, too! You're making a spectacle of yourself!"

"Only in the privacy of my own home, unless," she challenged, "you intend to spread it about."

"Never!"

It actually was a bit of a spectacle, Lucy had to admit. Septimus acquiesced to his new role with his customary stoicism, betraying none of the amusement he must have felt at her clumsy attempts to learn the steps Leanna showed them. He matched Lucy's curtsies with low, respectful bows and held her decorously at arms' length as they moved, his face grave with concentration. Occasionally, Li Lin would peek around the doorway to watch and then flee, a hand clapped to her mouth to suppress her giggles. "Let them all laugh, Septimus," Lucy said airily, nodding her head to Leanna's tempo. "You're doing me a favor, and I appreciate it."

"Yes, ma'am, and," he caught his breath, "one-two-three, turn!" He whirled her deftly around.

"When Seth returns," Lucy called to Leanna, "I shall have a dance. Do you suppose Father Crowley would come?"

"Does an Irishman jig?"

"I shall hire musicians. We'll make a grand evening of it."

"And 'round again, ma'am," Septimus told her, steering her adroitly about the floor.

"When is Seth due?" Leanna inquired.

"I wish I knew."

When Leanna had gone, Lucy found herself, as she did so often lately, standing at her bedroom window, watching the sun set behind the incoming fog. The silvered sky glowed with the last rays of light, and the hills stretching below her to the sea grew soft and indistinct under the shroud of the onrushing mist. It was an hour full of change and mystery and expectation, hushed and singular. The fog drew close around the house, secluding it, and her, from the land beneath. Here and there, faint lights glowed through the mist, hinting of life in the shadows far beyond. Lucy opened the window and felt the cool dampness against her skin. She shivered, not from chill but from some peculiar sense of anticipation that seemed borne on the nightly fog. When she could no longer make out anything in the enveloping darkness, she lowered the sash and turned away.

Septimus came into the sitting room. "A message, ma'am, just delivered."

She held it up to the sunlight from the bay window and read it. "He's back," she said. Her hands shook as she folded the paper.

Beth looked up from her knitting. "Who?"

"Seth. Is the messenger waiting for a reply, Septimus?"

"Yes'm."

She went to her desk in the library. Afterwards, she tried to remember what she had written, but her mind was blank. Seven o'clock, he had said, tonight.

Lucy heard the sound of the front doorknocker over the seventh stroke of the grandfather clock. She looked quickly into the mirror above her dressing table, staring at the image there as though waiting for it to speak, but it gave no hint of a response. She turned away and went downstairs to Seth.

He was standing by the piano, filling his pipe. He looked up as she entered. "Lucy, what's wrong?"

"Nothing, nothing at all."

He came to her and took her face in his hands. "My dear, you look like a frightened filly scenting smoke. Here," he said, leading her to the sofa and drawing her down beside him. "Are you all right?"

She nodded.

"But something is bothering you."

She raised her eyes to his. "You win."

"No." He shook his head. "No, not like that. I'm not the victor coming for his spoils, Lucy. It's not owning you I'm after. I beg you, my dear, only to share. Whatever life holds, I'm asking you to share with me. Don't come to me like this. Are your feelings so contradictory?"

"You're a fine man, Seth, and if I were not to accept you, I'd probably curse myself for a fool forever. I won't lie to you. The idea scares me, but all the great blessings of my life have come from doing things I feared."

"Then it's marriage you're afraid of, not me." He sighed. "Well, I suppose that's fortunate. Look at me, Lucy." He raised her chin. "I've not been married before. I'm a stranger in that land myself. Shall we help each other on this expedition? Let's take it a day at a time, my girl. God knows, anyone can be happy for a single day. What do you say? Are we partners?"

She glanced away. "Partners."

"Lord, woman, but you're a skittish one. If ever a body needed gentleness, it's you. All things considered, I can't think highly of your Mr. Bates."

"I want to forget about him."

"And so you shall."

The house was quiet now when they returned from dinner. The others were long asleep. Lucy sat on the sofa, Seth's arm around her. Together, out of words at last, they watched the fire dwindle in the hearth. It was peaceful, sitting close, sharing the hush of late evening. Gradually it occurred to Lucy that the room, even the house, seemed larger to her than before. A foolish thought, yet she knew it was true. Her future had expanded. The doors she had once shut were opening again, and beyond them lay the new expanse of her life, unfamiliar and untried, yet shining in the darkness like a beacon welcoming her to a breadth of possibilities. She smiled drowsily and laid her head on Seth's shoulder.

"Sleepy?" he asked.

"A little."

"I'd best be leaving. I've an early meeting tomorrow with that German fellow who just arrived."

"Your new associate?"

"Hugo Schmidt."

"And you still won't tell me anything about him."

"Only that we'll be going to Saint Helena on Monday."

"Saint Helena? What's in Saint Helena?"

He chuckled. "Prospects."

"Ore?"

"No. I'm getting out of the mining game."

She sat up. "But Seth, you told me yourself that the Slade and Daggett was a *bonanza*."

"So it is, but I can't manage it from here, and I've no taste for life in Washoe. Besides, a Paiute crone swore it would be the death of me."

"Now you're joking."

"She did. They say she's a seer. 'The blue sand will kill you,' those were her words."

"More likely the Paiutes just wish the lot of you would go away and leave them in peace. Surely you didn't take her seriously."

"Hardly. But I've had an offer for my share. I'm taking that seriously. How does a quarter of a million sound to you?"

Lucy gasped. "Dollars?"

"It's worth a good deal more than that, I expect, once they solve the flooding problems, but it's not a bad return on an investment of five thousand, wouldn't you say?"

"Dear God, we'll be so rich!"

He laughed. "Does that make you happy?"

She thought for a moment. "Once it would have. Isn't it peculiar how things change."

He stood and brought her to her feet. "I'm a wealthy man, Lucy, but damned if the expression on your face

400

doesn't make it all worth more than the money." He laid his hand on her cheek and bent to kiss her.

For a moment she stood stiffly still. It had been so long since she had known the embrace of a man's arms and the urging of his mouth against her own. She felt the strength of Seth's body and breathed the scent of his skin, masculine and unfamiliar. His warmth enveloped her like the surge of a gentle wave, and she felt herself swept along, her defenses melting, her form yielding to his, borne against her will on the undercurrent between them. She pulled back, her face flushed.

"Why did you do that?" he asked.

"You frightened me."

"No." He held her lightly by the shoulders and looked down at her. "It's yourself that frightens you. Stop holding yourself on such a tight rein, Lucy. Trust me."

"I'm afraid."

"In time, then. I can wait. Good night, my dear."

"Will I see you before you leave for Saint Helena? Come for dinner Sunday, Seth, please."

"I'll be here. Sleep well, Lucy."

But sleep eluded her. She lay awake staring at the slivers of moonlight that slipped through the curtains and streaked the ceiling overhead. Her head reeled with feelings that refused to let her rest. Desire and fear, longing and resentment jarred the silence of the room. Again and again, guilt intruded, too, as she reproached herself for her anxiety. By any reasoning, she should be the happiest woman in the world. Seth was right. Only her own emotions stood in the way. She was charging the sins of the past against him, when he was no part of them. Whatever pain she had suffered with Caleb Bates or Reed Pierce or Henry Fearing had no business intruding on the present. She hated them, even Reed, for stealing her happiness away so that she could not share it with Seth now when it meant so much to him. Finally, she reached for her robe at the foot of the bed, wrapped it about her and went to the window. The sky was growing light. Some distance away, on the other side of Bush Street, a gang of Chinese workmen warmed their hands over a small fire. She looked on as they gathered up shovels and picks and set to digging along the boundary markers strung across the vacant lot. There would be

401

neighbors soon. She watched as the workmen labored, the piles of earth grew higher and the hollow grew deeper.

"Bury the dead," she said suddenly, aloud, surprised at the bitterness in her voice. "Dig, damn you. Dig."

Seth arrived early for Sunday dinner. As Lucy came into the drawing room, he turned from the mantel and raised a glass to her. "I helped myself to some whiskey. I trust you don't mind."

She dismissed him with a wave. "Biddy wanted to know if we wanted gravy with the roast. What on earth is that bottle doing on the mantel?"

"I brought it for you. A souvenir of the Slade and Daggett." He handed it to her.

"My but it's heavy!"

"Come to the window."

Lucy rotated the glass bottle in her hands. "I've never seen anything quite like it," she mused, tilting it this way and that to catch the sunlight. It contained a strange dark blue sand that continually changed color as she moved it. Sometimes it was indigo, then greenish, now black, then violet. "It's beautiful. Like the colors of a butterfly's wings. What is it?"

"Almost pure silver."

"Mercy! No wonder it's so heavy. Does it lie in the ground just like this?"

"Sometimes. Most of the time it has to be hacked out and put through the mills."

"May I keep this?"

"Of course."

She placed the bottle on the table beside the wing chair. "There. Does that suit you? Seth," she said, motioning him to be seated, "I was thinking. There are so many things we haven't discussed. This house, for instance."

"Where we'll live?"

"Yes."

"Wherever you wish. It's your decision."

"I'd like to stay here, if you think you'd be comfortable. There's plenty of space. You've never been upstairs. Let me show you."

She led him up to the second floor, first to the nursery. "I had in mind that this would be a place for my grandchildren one day." She pulled the draperies apart, filling the room with light. "See, it has a dressing room there and closets in the passageway to my bedroom."

"In there?"

She hesitated. "Come."

"A most inviting room." Seth went to the rocker beside her fireplace and sat down. He glanced around. "Very comfortable indeed."

Lucy blushed. "Perhaps we ought to go back down. Dinner will be ready." She opened the door. "Are you coming?"

"Yes." He paused by the window. "I just wanted another look."

"Mother?" Beth stood in her doorway, gazing across the hall at the two of them as they emerged from Lucy's room.

"I was showing Seth the house," Lucy replied quickly. "That's Lin's room, down there," she told him, "and the one between hers and Beth's belongs to Abel."

Beth gave them a curious look and started down the stairs.

"You haven't told her," he said, holding Lucy back at the top of the stairs.

"Not yet," she answered guiltily. "But I've written to Abel."

"Why are you afraid to tell her?"

"Because I believe that child wants to marry Nick Stevens. She's too young, Seth, and I don't want to add fuel to her fires."

"She has to know sooner or later."

"Seth," she said slowly, "couldn't we just go off and be married without a lot of ceremony? It might make things easier."

"For you, too, is that it?"

"Yes."

He kissed her lightly. "Then that's what we'll do, as soon as I return from Saint Helena. Hanged if I'll let you stall me off and fidget yourself into a stew."

"I wouldn't do any such thing!"

"No? My dear, you act like a small child quivering at the edge of a stream, the water looking colder to you with every passing minute."

"I don't!"

"You do. And by God, you'll take the plunge, even if I have to give you a shove." Seth put his arm around her

403

and led her down the stairs. "The water," he whispered in her ear, "is actually running very warm."

He was gone longer than either of them had expected. Lucy received three letters, the first informing her that he was staying at the home of a Doctor Crane near Saint Helena. She replied quickly, wanting to know if he were ill, but his answer reassured her that Crane was merely his host and "a man with similar interests." What those interests were, she couldn't fathom. Seth knew nothing about medicine, of that she was sure.

From what he wrote, it appeared that an oddly mixed group of gentlemen had suddenly turned their attentions toward the town in the little valley to the north. The German newspaperman, Charles Krug, and his wife had a fine spread of some five hundred acres. A spread of what? she wondered. Grain, perhaps, but she couldn't imagine Seth Slade as either a farmer or a miller. A Frenchman named Pellet was lodged with Doctor Crane, and a Hungarian named Haraszthy was visiting the Krugs. The businessman, Sam Brannan, had come up from San Francisco to open a hotel near the Indian hot springs. Lucy read the names over again, adding those of Seth and the newly-arrived Herr Hugo Schmidt. They made a curious lot. Try as she might, she couldn't figure out what had attracted them to Saint Helena and the Napa Valley.

Seth's last letter arrived in mid-February.

My Pastora,
My work here has only started, but it is well organized under Herr Schmidt's capable direction. I shall be in the city on the twenty-fifth and needn't return here until April, if all goes well. Make whatever plans you please, as I am feeling particularly indulgent toward this hard-won, stubborn woman who has thrown caution to the winds at last, and dares to become my wife. I bless you for waiting for me, dear Lucy, and look forward to starting our journey together without further delay. I promise you, upon my honor, more smiles than tears . . .

The house had been cleaned from top to bottom. The woodwork, the mirrors, the silver shone. Biddy, Septimus

404

and Li Lin scuttled about the kitchen like industrious ants. The carpet from the drawing room lay rolled in the hall closet. The lamps were lit, and scores of flickering candles had been placed about the downstairs rooms to add to the brilliance. Flowers bloomed on the tables, and garlands of leaves decked the fireplaces and circled the bannister leading to the second floor.

Hurriedly, Lucy stepped into her satin dancing slippers. She turned toward the mirror. "My land," she breathed, taking in the spectacle of the woman before her.

Li Lin had woven a coronet of pink ribbons in her hair to match the silk of her gown. Her shoulders were bare. The low scoop of her bodice revealed the rounded hint of her breasts above gathered tiers of tulle that banded her bosom and widened into bowed sleeves above her elbows. Below her tiny, corseted waist billowed three layers of skirt, each edged with flounces of puckered tulle drawn into scallops by velvet bows like those at her sleeves.

She stared unabashed at the elegant figure in the glass. She took Seth's pearl brooch from her dressing table and pinned it to her bodice. Then she added the pearl earbobs he had given her that afternoon. She stepped back and looked again. This exquisitely arrayed woman, resplendent in diamonds and pearls, was none other than herself. She glanced down at the gold band on her finger, moving her hand to catch the reflection of the lamplight against it. These hands had pulled turnips, boiled soap, gathered buffalo chips and shorn sheep. Now they were smooth and white, the nails buffed to a shine. Catching her image again in the mirror, she spun giddily around and laughed aloud. A knock sounded at the door, and she clasped her hand to her mouth like a child caught in some covert mischief.

"Mama?" Beth poked her head in. "Are you alone? I thought I heard—" She broke off and opened the door wide. "Merciful heavens, Mama! You're beautiful! Look at you!"

Lucy blushed and smoothed her skirts. "Honestly? Do you think so?"

Beth shook her head in wonder, a smile spreading over her face. "You look like genuine royalty."

"Did the musicians arrive?"

"Yes, and Seth's here, Mama. He asked me to tell you. He's downstairs, and he has a valise with him. Is he going away again?"

"Why don't you bring him up, and we can talk about it."

"Up here? To your bedroom?"

"Yes."

Seth came up the stairs followed closely by Beth. As he reached Lucy's doorway, he halted. Lucy stood in the center of the room, not moving. Slowly, he set down his bag and came to her.

"My God," he said quietly, "I've married a beauty." He kissed her and stepped back to look at her again.

Beth glanced from one to the other.

"Come in and sit down, Bethie. Seth and I have something to tell you."

"I heard," she said dazedly. "I heard what Seth said."

He went to her and embraced her. "Beth, your mother and I were married this morning. I want the news to make you as happy as we are."

Beth's eyes brimmed with tears. "I don't know what to say."

He laid his finger against her lips. "Don't say anything. It's our secret, until the announcement. Only the three of us know."

Beth nodded solemnly. Then, abruptly, she bolted past him and flung her arms around Lucy. "Mama, Mama, I never even dreamt it!"

Seth smiled. "Neither did your Mama, for a while. She took some persuading."

"Will you live here with us?" Beth wanted to know.

"He will," Lucy told her.

"Seth, are you my father now?"

"Only if you want me to be. I don't expect to be called 'Papa,' if that's what you mean."

Beth giggled. "I don't think I could. I'm too used to 'Seth.' "

"We must hurry," Lucy said. "The guests will be arriving."

XXI

WITH A flourish, the four musicians struck up another waltz. Naomi Brock, flushed and ecstatic, danced in Boyd Stevens's arms, tendrils of hair flying and a dew of perspiration on her upper lip. Despite her pretty gown and the ribbons that bobbed among her curls, she looked to Lucy like a beloved rag doll, frazzled and limp, whose limbs might at any moment fly to the four corners of the room. "That dear girl!" Lucy laughed as Seth swung her around. "I often wonder what holds her together."

"I'd a sight rather have her than the marble Mrs. Winslow."

"Amy's not a bad sort, once you know her."

"Just look at the woman." He turned her toward the front of the room where Amy and Warren Winslow were waltzing. "That smile carved on her face and her eyes so wide you'd think she'd just sat on a tack. Listen to me, wife. Never trust anyone, man or woman, who smiles with his eyes wide open."

"Who said that, your Paiute crone with her prophesies?"

"Seth Slade, the seer of Bush Street."

"Indeed. And does he foretell when we'll make our announcement?"

"That's up to you, my love."

"Seth," Lucy said, lowering her voice, "I've never given a ball before. I've not the faintest idea how such things are done."

"From the look of it, no one would guess. I suggest we tell them when we adjourn for midnight supper."

"Seth, will you look at Verity Knight tripping about

407

like the Queen of the May with Father Crowley? And I thought her such a prig. You don't suppose she actually sampled the wine, do you?"

"More likely it's a tribute to the Father's Irish charm. Her sister seems quite taken with Asa Hudson, though."

Lucy glanced toward the fireplace, where Amanda Knight stood fanning herself, her eyes glowing bright with merriment above the silken arc of her fan as Asa Hudson bent close to whisper something in her ear. "What does your friend Mr. Hudson do for a living, Seth?"

"A little of this, a little of that. Much like me. Right now, he's waiting to hear if Theodore Judah can wring some government money out of Washington for a railroad."

"And what will he do if Mr. Judah succeeds?"

"Just what we'll all do. Buy land. Where the railroads go, people go. Towns and farms and ranches spring up wherever there's decent transportation."

"Is that why you went to the Napa Valley?"

"Aha!" He gave her a knowing smile. "You're still trying to ferret out my secret, are you? Not a chance. And don't expect me to talk in my sleep, either."

Her cheeks reddened. "I must take a rest. All this whirling about has me dizzy."

Seth led her into the library. Beth and Nick were seated on the sofa. Daniel Derby stood by the desk, with his wife, Susan, poised nervously in the chair beside him.

"It's a crime," Daniel was saying. "Any way you look at it, it's a crime."

"'Pends where your sympathies lie," Nick replied, smiling.

"That's rot, young man, pure and simple."

Susan laid a hand on Daniel's arm and made a soft, clucking sound.

"Well, it is," Daniel persisted. "Robbing a federal mint is against the law."

"Maybe there's folks who think there are more important issues at stake than breaking a single law."

"Are you telling me that you Secesh boys condone throwing law to the winds like a pack of freebooting anarchists?"

"We are in San Francisco, aren't we?" Seth broke in. "Seems to me that if the Secesh rob a mint in New Or-

408

leans, there's not anything we can do about it, one way or another."

Daniel frowned. "It's the principle."

Susan rose. "Daniel dear, do let's dance. The music is going to waste out there." She led him into the drawing room.

Jane Gallagher bustled through the library doorway, her husband in tow. "Lucy, it's a grand party. Michael and I are having such a good time."

Her husband mopped his forehead and sat down. "This woman of mine would waltz me into the grave if she had her way."

Jane extracted her spectacles from her reticule and set them on the tip of her nose. "Oh, it's you over there, Bethie. And Nicholas. Michael dearest, these are two of the young people who help us at the Good Shepherd Home."

"Excellent work," he pronounced, nodding. "Martha Mason and her beau were just telling me about the job you young folks do."

Jane smiled approvingly. "And Doctor Vanderhoef and Sarah were saying that their daughter wants to give drrawing lessons at the Home, if we'll have her."

"Have her?" Lucy laughed. "If I'd known, I'd have carried her there in my own arms! I'll speak to the Vanderhoefs later."

Nick stood up. "If you all will excuse us, I've a powerful thirst."

Lucy caught Beth's arm as they passed and drew her aside. "Nick appears a bit flushed, Bethie. I hope he hasn't had too much wine."

"Really, Mama. Nick's a gentleman. He's quite used to parties and balls. He can take care of himself."

"Nevertheless, I shouldn't like to have any political arguments this evening."

"Mr. Derby started it! He said the Secessionists who robbed the New Orleans Mint were nothing but common criminals!"

"All the same, look after Nick, please. He and Boyd tend to be a little hotheaded at times."

"Oh, Mama." She grimaced and swept after Nick, irritably tossing her skirts.

"My dear," Seth said, "shall we go for another turn around the floor? It's almost time to stop for supper."

He watched her face with obvious pleasure as they moved in time to the music. "You dance beautifully, my Pastora, did you know that?"

"Thanks to Leanna and poor, patient Septimus." She waved at Leanna and John Fiske as they passed. "Is it time yet, Seth?"

He paused and took his watch from his waistcoat. "I think so. Come."

They stood before the fireplace. Lucy smiled nervously and smoothed the hair at her temples. Seth raised an arm, and the music broke off, dwindling raggedly into silence. All eyes were on the two of them. Seth turned to her.

"No," she said quietly. "You do it."

"My friends—No," he corrected himself, "our friends, your lovely hostess and I have an announcement to make."

A murmur of anticipation swept the room.

Seth spoke louder. "This morning, at eleven o'clock, Lucy and I became man and wife."

"Hurrah!" Joe Mason burst out. Klara looked embarrassed and plucked at his sleeve.

"Hurrah indeed!" called Father Crowley, followed by a chorus of cheers and applause.

"Wonderful!" Ada and Solomon Brock pressed forward to shake their hands. Ada whispered to Lucy, "I believe Boyd will ask for our Naomi's hand any day now. How I love weddings!"

Lucy laughed and chatted breathlessly amid the tumult of blessings and congratulations. Seth bent to kiss her cheek. "Looks like we've made a lot of folks happy. Shall we lead the way to the dining room?"

"As I live and breathe," Lucy said, surveying the gathering around the table, "don't look now, but Septimus is actually smiling!"

His ebony skin glowing in the warmth of the lights, Septimus presided over the feast, beaming proudly as he served. At his side was Octavia, borrowed from the Fearings for the occasion, while in the kitchen, Li Lin assisted Biddy in sending forth her cornucopia of poached trout, duck with olives, veal cutlets, peas and rice with mushrooms. For dessert there were molds of blancmange, garnished with raisins and nuts, and platters of little cakes. The champagne bottles popped throughout the meal, invariably causing some of the ladies to start and the men to laugh at their discomposure. The toasting began, with Albert Fearing and then John Fiske and Joe Mason drinking to the bride and groom, their toasts solemn and humorous by turns. Next, Father Crowley raised his glass. "May our Holy Father in heaven bless you both. May all the saints preserve you, and," he added with a grin, "may the devil get himself lost looking for this house!"

Asa Hudson's voice rose above the cheering. "I propose a toast to the new man of this house, as fine a gentleman as ever graced this city, who's had the good judgment and better still, the good luck, to lay claim to one of its fairest treasures."

Lucy laughed self-consciously and curtsied in his direction. Nick stood by the sideboard, an open champagne bottle in his hand. He lifted it in salute and filled his glass.

Seth cleared his throat. "Dear friends, I'm a man with a lot to celebrate this evening." He slipped his arm around Lucy's waist. "My splendid wife, your warm wishes and last, but not least," he said, turning to catch Beth's eye, "the best pair of children any fellow could wish." His voice faltered. "To my new family."

Impulsively, Lucy embraced him. For a moment they held each other close, unaware of the others.

"May you know health, happiness and peace, all of your days," Doctor Vanderhoef said quietly.

"Peace," someone echoed.

"And peace throughout this great land of ours!" proclaimed Daniel Derby.

"Well said," came the response.

"Justice," Albert Fearing added softly. "There must be justice."

"Don't expect justice from the Black Republicans," Solomon Brock told him bitterly. "They'd steal a man's lawful rights quicker 'n a dip would make off with your poke down in Finn Alley."

"Now, now, gentlemen," Seth intervened, "let's lift our glasses in the spirit of fellowship, shall we?"

A palpable wave of relief flowed through the room. Jane Gallagher giggled nervously.

"Tarnation!" Nick slammed his palm down hard on the top of the sideboard. "If we're going to drink a toast, let's drink to that great crusader for justice, Mr. Jefferson Davis! To Davis! To the C.S.A.! To the gallant Knights of the Golden—"

With the swiftness of a striking rattler, Albert Fearing lunged through the crowd and grabbed his arm, all but throwing him off his feet. Nick's glass flew aside, scattering champagne as it went, and smashed on the floor at Doctor Vanderhoef's feet. Klara Mason cried out and tried to rub the champagne from her eyes. Warren Winslow dabbed at Amy's stained gown with his handkerchief. Albert, thrusting Nick ahead of him, made his way toward the sitting room. Nick looked dazed. His face was blank, save for a bemused grin that seemed fixed in place.

From the rear of the room came the unmistakable bass voice of John Fiske.

"My country, 'tis of thee,
Sweet land of liberty, Of thee I sing . . ."

Some joined him. Others, like Boyd Stevens and Solomon Brock, attempted to hoot them down. Lucy glanced helplessly over the chaos. Beth was weeping in Naomi's arms. Joe Mason was trying to soothe Polly Fearing.

"Please!" Seth's voice rang out. "Ladies and gentlemen! Let us bring the evening to a close with a short prayer. Father Crowley," he said, motioning Lucy back to clear a space for the priest, "if you would do the honors."

Father Crowley stared at the floor in thought for a moment. Then he raised his head and turned slowly, looking around the room, fixing upon each and every face with his keen-eyed gaze. "Merciful Father in heaven," he began, "grant us Thine infinite wisdom and patience in times of stress. Help us to forge our swords into plowshares and our anger into compassion, that we may cultivate peace here on earth. *In nomine Patris, Filii et Spiritus Sancti*. Amen."

As the last of the guests departed, Lucy leaned back against the heavy front door. The grandfather clock struck two. She pushed a fallen wisp of hair from her face.

"Poor dear." Seth put his hands on her shoulders. "It turned into a bit of an ordeal, didn't it?"

She nodded numbly.

He took her in his arms and brought her to him. "I'm afraid Nick was in his cups. Some of the others, too."

412

"Seth, there's one thing I don't understand. What was it that Nick said that caused Albert to go at him like that? They're both Secesh, aren't they?"

"Nick started to say something he shouldn't have."

"But what?"

"Something about the Knights of the Golden Circle. It's a secret group of the Secesh."

"What do they do?"

"I don't know, my dear. Word has it they're a militant bunch who'd like to deliver California to the Confederacy."

"Is Nick a part of it?"

He sighed tiredly. "It's possible. Perhaps Albert is, too. Who knows?"

Lucy shook her head. "I'm not sure of knowing anything anymore. I hate the thought of the Union being destroyed, but I was raised in Missouri, and I understand how these people feel."

Seth laid a finger to her lips. "Hush. It's not our quarrel, is it? Let's forget about it for now. It's time you and I turned in, my girl. It's been a long day."

When Lucy awoke, she lay quietly unmoving, still suffused with the warm comfort of sleep. Drowsily, she became conscious of the sound of Seth's breathing close by her pillow. She turned toward him, suddenly aware of the rumpled sheets against her naked skin. She felt her face flush at the thought of sleeping without her shimmy, her nude body pressed so close to his. She had bared herself to him, timid and hesitant as a virgin, anxious to douse the lights, to wrap herself in the safe shroud of darkness. But he would not allow her.

He had looked down at her, stroking the blonde hair fanned out against her pillow and bent to kiss her mouth. She had felt her heart hammer so thunderously that she feared Seth would hear it, too, and be as embarrassed as she was. If he did, he gave no sign. His hands traveled across her smooth shoulders and down to cup her breasts. He had held them ever so gently, circling her nipples lightly with his thumbs. A rush of unfamiliar sensations overwhelmed her. She stiffened uneasily. Seth spoke tenderly in her ear as he moved his hand downward to touch the soft mound between her thighs. He lowered his mouth to her breast. The heat of her body was so warm that she failed to protest when he brushed aside the sheets. He gazed at her, taking in her nakedness, exploring the hills and valleys beneath him with slow, deliberate enjoyment. Her breath came faster, and she found herself straining toward him hungrily, eager for the feel of his mouth and hands. When he entered her, she moaned, a long, low sound of pleasure. "Yes," he had said, "yes, yes," and speaking softly, he had reassured her and encouraged her.

She had never known that a woman could feel such things as he brought forth in her. Gasping, she gave herself over to his movements and caresses, thrashing against the sheets, past all control or care. When at last they lay breathlessly together, out of strength, their arms around each other, she moved her head to the hollow of his shoulder and brushed her lips over his warm flesh, murmuring endearments until she knew from his breathing that he was asleep.

Seth stirred and rolled over. He opened his eyes and found her gazing at him. He reached out and touched her cheek, brushing the tousled hair from her face. "Did you sleep well?"

She nodded.

"Why so quiet?"

"I was thinking about last night."

"You're blushing."

"I feel . . . a little indecent. Good women shouldn't enjoy such things. I don't know what made me behave the way I did."

"Lord, woman!" He laughed. "Don't apologize! That's puritanical hogwash. I can assure you that the good women of France, among others, enjoy every moment with their men, and God has yet to smite them for it."

"But what would people think?"

"Silly girl, it won't show on your face. Here, give me a kiss."

As their mouths met, she felt his hand graze her body. "Seth—" She broke from him. "Now? In the daylight?"

"Now and then and dark or light," he said as he drew her to him. "We've only just begun."

It was their secret, the pleasure that lay behind the closed doors of their upstairs room. Sometimes, Lucy found herself thinking about those moments in the midst of her tasks and she would glance up quickly, her cheeks

414

red, reproaching herself for such carnal wanderings. But it pleased Seth to arouse her passions, and he pleased her in ways she had never dreamed possible. Sometimes, they just lay quietly entwined, sharing the sweet, elemental animal warmth of each others' bodies. In the night, they slept touching always, reaching out an arm, a foot, for contact. There was between them something that defied definition, some primitive connection that not even the deepest slumber could thwart.

Lucy passed her days oblivious to the bleak chill of spring. Eager as a girl, she awaited Seth's return each evening. He would come bearing bits of news gleaned from the Bank Exchange, sometimes with a bouquet or a gift, always with high spirits and a hearty embrace. Surely, she thought, no two people had ever taken such delight in each other's company. Their joy was contagious. Septimus smiled routinely, and Biddy outdid herself to spoil the man of the house. Li Lin whirled through her chores like a gaily spinning top, and even Bethie seemed happier.

Abel was doing well at Harvard, she learned, sitting over breakfast with his latest letter. He had attended a Union rally with the Mountfords. The Massachusetts winter was "as cold as Simon Legree's heart," he said, "but I'm told there will be an early spring." Lucy smiled as she folded his letter. By now he had received word that she and Seth were married. No matter how harsh the cold, that news would warm him.

Seth stirred his morning coffee thoughtfully, folded the *Alta* and handed it to Septimus.

Septimus laid the paper beside Lucy's plate at the other end of the table.

"I expect Beth will be down shortly," she told him. "Would you ask Biddy to keep her breakfast warm, please?"

"Yes'm."

Lucy scanned the newspaper. She glanced up, frowning. "Did you see that President Lincoln has ordered reinforcements sent to that fort in Charleston?"

"Yes."

"But the people of Charleston wanted the Union garrison withdrawn. Won't this just antagonize them? I'm beginning to think Nick was right when he said the die was cast. Seth, tell me the truth. Is there no way of escaping a war?"

"Damned if I can see how it can be averted, short of a miracle."

"Such profanity, and so early in the morning."

"War is a profanity."

"I'm sure Nick thinks his cause is sacred."

"Holy wars, my dear, have wrought more havoc than Satan."

"Hush," Lucy warned, "Beth's coming."

Beth kissed them both and sat down, stifling a yawn.

"You were late last night, Bethie. I heard Septimus let you in at a quarter to eleven. You promised to be home by ten."

"It was a special evening, Mama. I'm sorry."

"And what was so special about it?"

"Boyd asked Naomi's parents for her hand. They're to be married next month."

"Well," Seth said, "you don't seem very pleased. I thought they were your friends."

She shrugged. "Naomi won't have time to be my friend anymore. She'll be a married lady with a husband."

"Don't talk nonsense, dear," Lucy told her. "Naomi is very fond of you."

"I wish I were getting married," she said petulantly. "It seems I'm the only one who isn't."

"There's plenty of time for that," Seth assured her.

"And if there's a war? Mama, if Nick were going away to fight, you'd allow us to be married first, wouldn't you?"

Lucy looked helplessly across the table at Seth.

"Beth," he said, "Naomi and Boyd are older than you and Nick. War or no war, you two have plenty of time."

"Bethie, let's not get into this discussion again, please. It's too early in the day for arguments."

Beth sank into sullen silence. Seth stood and laid his napkin on the table.

"Time to be off, Pastora. I have to make arrangements to go back to Saint Helena in a couple of weeks." He put his arm around her waist as she walked him to the door.

"Will you be gone long?"

"A month, perhaps."

"Oh, Seth, no. What's so important that it would keep you away for a month?"

"About thirty-five acres of hillside, my love. And that," he added with a smile, "is all you'll get out of me for now."

She missed him even more than she had anticipated she would. Sometimes in the night, half-asleep, she would reach out for him, only to find the empty sheets cold against her skin and wake with a sharp pang of loneliness.

Despite the warm April days and a constant round of parties and receptions for Naomi and Boyd, Beth was glum. Nick preached so fervently about the Confederacy, the cause and a man's duty, that it all but set Lucy's teeth on edge. Green and guileless, he spouted his noble sentiments with the innocent cheek of a schoolboy spoiling for a scuffle. Lucy wished Seth were here to contradict his high-flown notions. He knew more about such things than she.

Septimus stood at the foot of the stairs as Lucy came down. He held out the newspaper. "I'm not a readin' man, ma'am, but Biddy was out front with the fruit peddler, Wah Ming, when the paper come. She done read it to me."

Lucy stared down at the three rows of thick, black lettering on the front page of the *Alta*. "Attack on Fort Sumter!" read the first. "Surrender of Major Anderson!" And then, "Civil War Commenced."

"I shan't be wanting any breakfast. Only some coffee."

"Yes'm," he nodded dolefully and turned away.

She sat at her desk, a single lamp glowing beside her in the darkened room, her pen scratching swiftly at the paper in front of her. "The city has been in turmoil since the news," she wrote Seth. "Crowds gathering, most of them in front of the newspaper offices, desperate for more information. There is much shouting of slogans from both sides, and underneath all the noise, a general restlessness. I sense a great sadness, too, among many people, to think that after only eighty-five years the glorious design of our country appears doomed to failure." She paused and pressed the blotting pad to her lines. "Bethie has been made ill by all of this. She has had difficulty keeping her food down for the past two days and suffers from spells of vertigo. How glad I am to know you will be coming home soon. We are gloomy here and in need of your support and cheer. I heard only today that Washington is being fortified against attack, but perhaps this is another rumor. There are so many now. Please, my dearest, do hurry back as soon as you can . . ."

When she had folded and sealed the letter, she took the lamp and went upstairs. Outside Beth's door, she paused. She opened it a crack. The girl was sleeping peacefully, the moonlight casting a white splash on her coverlet. Lucy closed the door softly and went to bed.

The news seemed to grow more depressing with each passing day, with reports of troop movements, shipping blockades and bloody slave insurrections. There were mass meetings and public demonstrations. Friends became enemies. Polly Fearing came to the house in tears because Joe had called Albert a traitor to his face. She was torn between her son and husband, and Lucy was at a loss to comfort her.

Beth's indisposition continued to plague her, though she was well enough to go with Nick to the first summer concert at the Willows. Still, it worried Lucy that her complaint refused to disappear. Poor Bethie, she reflected, such a delicate, highly strung creature, always so sensitive to the slightest disturbance. Yet, when the attacks passed, she appeared in the bloom of health. Nick was courting her more ardently than ever, despite the war news, or perhaps because of it. He had taken it upon himself to pose for a photograph which he ceremoniously presented to Beth, in case, he said, he was called to his duty. He fancied himself a man of the world, now that he spouted his Secesh doctrine with such inflated authority. And Bethie's spirits, despite the dark dispatches from the East, soared in his company. The contradiction baffled Lucy. One moment the girl was weak and nauseated and the next she was begging to be allowed to go to the theatre with Nick. She had no temperature, Lucy noted with relief. Nonetheless, the spells had persisted, and she had decided to call in Doctor Vanderhoef. Perhaps he could prescribe a tonic for Beth's nerves.

Though Lucy was puzzled by Beth's malaise, she understood the distress in the Fearing household all to well, she thought, standing for a moment in front of the windows of the Clay Street Dry Goods Company. "Joe," she called out as she entered, "that's a fine idea of Klara's, to make the window arrangement all of one color. Do you suppose we could have a different color each week? It might be very arresting."

"Sure enough." He rose from the desk. "How did the ledger look to you?"

She handed it to him. "Very good indeed. You're a fine businessman, Joe."

"Mrs. Slade, if you ever want to sell, Klara and I would sure like to buy the place for our own. We've enough saved for a partial payment, and you know I'd be good for the rest."

She looked surprised. "Why, Joe, I'd never considered it. I wouldn't even know what kind of price to ask."

"But you would entertain the idea?"

She thought for a moment. "I'd have to take up the matter with Mr. Biggs at Wells Fargo. He advises me on such things. But I didn't come here to discuss business, Joe."

"No?"

"Joe, you must make peace with your stepfather. I respect your sympathies and I'm not asking you to compromise your principles. Just to apologize for having spoken out so heedlessly. This breach between you and Albert has upset your mother terribly."

His eyes were hard. "He is a traitor. All I did was speak the truth."

"No," she said gently, "what you spoke was only your opinion. Joe, think what a pickle we'd all be in if we went about airing our sentiments indiscriminately. Why, half the people I know would stop talking to me if they knew what I thought of them sometimes. All I'm asking is that you employ a bit of tact."

"Hypocrisy, you mean. You, of all people, counseling hypocrisy." He shook his head. "I wouldn't have believed it of you."

Lucy gave him a wry smile. "Joe, dear, it's hardly hypocrisy when Albert is quite aware of your feelings. I can't believe you're not magnanimous enough to extend the olive branch. It's not for Albert's sake, remember. It's for your mother. Show a little tolerance, Joe. It would be a gallant gesture on your part."

"Did Mother put you up to this?"

"She did not. But I can't bear to see her in such misery, not when you could so easily set things right."

He glanced away guiltily. "I didn't know it had upset her that much."

"Well, now you do. I trust your judgment. I know you'll act responsibly."

Joe gave an embarrassed laugh. "I haven't had such a stern dressing-down since they found out I was keeping the books for Queen Rosie's and Miss Fulton's and Josie Corday's."

" 'Touché,' as French Jack would say." Lucy kissed his cheek. "I must be on my way. I'm expecting a visit from Doctor Vanderhoef. And Joe, I will ask Mr. Biggs what he thinks about selling the store."

Lucy ushered the doctor up to see Beth and retired to the sitting room to wait. Li Lin sat gazing out of the bay window, elbows propped on the sill, her chin cupped in her hands. "Missee," she said, her back to Lucy, "you think Missybet will be all right?"

"Of course I do," Lucy assured her.

"It's been more than a month she's been sickly, missee."

"Slightly over three weeks, on and off."

She wriggled around on the cushions of the window seat. "No, ma'am," her eyes were downcast, "more like five. Missybet make me promise at first I don't tell."

Lucy looked up sharply. "What are you saying?"

"Missybet afraid you make her stay home," she replied contritely, "so she don't tell you until you find out, but she was ill many days before you know."

"Good grief, child, why didn't you say something?"

"I promise—"

"Yes, yes," she interrupted irritably, "but you were not acting in her best interests, Lin. Hush now. The doctor's coming downstairs." Lucy stood to greet him. "Martin, Lin has just told me something you should know."

He raised a hand. "In a moment. Lin, would you ask Septimus to fetch us some brandy? Run along now, please."

"Martin—"

"Sit down, Lucy." He walked to the fireplace and put both hands on the mantel. He leaned against it tiredly.

"How serious is it?"

He took a moment to think. Then he stood erect and walked over to her chair. "Not at all serious and very serious, depending on how one looks at it. The girl's in the family way, Lucy."

She stared at him. The color drained from her face. "No," she said hoarsely, "no, my God, it can't be——"

"Stay calm. There's not a thing you can do. I know it's a shock, and I know it's a most distressing situation, but there's no use getting yourself worked up over it."

"Martin," she said weakly, "Bethie's only fifteen."

"And a very healthy young woman. We can be glad of that."

"How did she take the news?"

"Ah, Septimus," he said, "there you are." He took the tray from him and set it down. "That will be all, thank you." He poured some brandy into a glass and handed it to her. "Lucy, it would appear that Beth is not altogether naive. According to her, she wanted this."

The glass shook in her hand as she drank. She set it down unsteadily on the table.

"She feels Nick will do the chivalrous thing."

She drew a deep breath and rose from her chair. "Thank you, Martin. I'll see you to the door. It seems I have something to discuss with my daughter."

No sooner had the doctor left than Lucy went upstairs and flung open Beth's bedroom door, her face flushed with rage. "How could you?" she cried. "You willful, brazen little brat! You've gone and ruined your life over that foolish boy! How could you be so stupid?"

Beth attempted to feign indifference. "But Mama," she began, then stopped to blink away the tears that belied her bravado. "Mama, he will marry me. I know he will."

"That's not the point," she snapped. "You're both too young even to know what you've gotten yourselves into. Good God, Bethie, if you'd do something so damnably irresponsible, how can you think yourself responsible enough to marry and raise a child? Answer me that!"

Sobbing, she wiped at her cheeks with the bedsheets.

"Lord," Lucy murmured, "how I wish Seth were here to give that boy a piece of his mind. Beth, does Nick know?"

She shook her head.

"I shall send him a note at once."

Lucy wrote two notes, one to Nick and another to Seth. When Septimus had left with them in hand, she sank into the chair at her desk, her head buried in her hands, weeping softly. She looked up, distraught, when she became aware of Lin's presence at her side.

"Missee, what's wrong? Is Missybet going to die?"

"Oh, child, no." She pressed her handkerchief to her swollen eyes. "Come here." Luey put her arms around her. "Missybet's going to have a baby."

Lin drew back with a look of wonder. "Now?"

"No, dear. Not for a while yet. Just before Christmas, Doctor Vanderhoef says."

"How long is that?"

"Several months."

A smile spread over the girl's face. "A boy baby. That is the best kind. Missybet will have a most honorable boy baby."

Lucy shook her head in dismay. "Honorable is not quite the right word, I'm afraid. Why don't you go upstairs now and see if Beth wants anything. That's a good girl."

With a sigh, Lucy closed the top of her desk. "Oh, Seth," she said aloud to the empty room, "you would know what to say to him. I only pray he's the gentleman Bethie thinks he is."

Septimus glanced at the cup and saucer on the table beside Lucy's chair. He frowned. "Tea's gone cold, Miz' Slade."

She looked up from the *Alta*. "I'd forgotten it was there."

"You want me to fetch you some hot?"

"No, thank you. It'll be supper-time soon. I'll wait."

"You feelin' poorly, ma'am? You ain't touched Biddy's gingerbread."

"I'm sorry," she murmured, her gaze returning to the newspaper. She looked again at the words printed there. "News of May 8," she read, "Declaration of War by the Southern Confederacy." It had begun, almost two weeks ago now. While the city had gone about its business, basking in the brilliant sun, warmed by balmy breezes, the bay shining under the cloudless skies, the news had been snaking westward, like some vile effluvium, spreading its poison as it came. "Here." She handed the paper to Septimus. "I don't want to read anymore."

He folded it and set it on the tray with her tea things, then paused at the sound of the doorknocker. "That'd be

Mr. Nick, mos' likely. He did say he'd come by after work. It's about that time, ain't it?"

"Take the tray with you, please. I want to be alone with him."

Nick strode into the room, ruddy-cheeked with excitement. "Afternoon, ma'am," He gave a hasty bow and went to the fireplace, pacing back and forth in front of the hearth like a restless colt, eager to race. "Sorry I'm late. Boyd and I had to talk with Uncle Dabney. I expect you heard the news."

"Yes."

"We're going, ma'am, Boyd and me, just as soon as we can book passage."

"You are going nowhere!" she said, startled by the force of her voice. "You have pressing obligations to attend to first. You'll not be leaving until you've done your duty here."

Nick looked at her in blank bewilderment.

"You read my letter?"

He nodded uncertainly.

"I said it was a matter of utmost importance to us both." Lucy clasped her hands tightly together to keep them from trembling. "It also involves Beth."

"Yes'm," he said, looking thoroughly confused.

"Nicholas, Beth is going to have a baby. She is carrying your child. Have you anything to say to that?"

He gaped at her, speechless. Quickly, his eyes darted away, avoiding hers.

"Answer me."

"Ma'am—" He spread his hands helplessly. "What can I say?"

"You can tell me what you intend to do about it. You brought about this unfortunate situation."

"It just—happened," he said feebly.

"Oh, it did," she mocked him. "Rather like being struck by lightning, was it? No fault of yours, I suppose."

He stared down at his boots.

Lucy rose and stood facing him. "Look at me, you foolish young man! You have played fast and loose with all our lives, including your own and that unborn child's. And you come here night after night, ranting about responsibility and duty and the honor of your precious Confederacy. Words, Nick, words! Well, the time for words is past. Are you or are you not a man of responsibility, duty and honor? Or are you so carried away with your exalted cause that you ride roughshod over everything and everyone else, as though they were dirt under your shiny, brown boots?"

"Ma'am," he protested, "you know that's not true. You know how I feel about Beth."

"Prove it."

He swallowed hard. "Yes, ma'am."

"Go on, Nick," she challenged him. "Don't stop now."

"We'd best be married."

"Indeed. And soon. I've written to Seth to come home at once. He'll want to speak with your Uncle Dabney, I expect. Meanwhile, not a word of this predicament is to escape this house. Do you understand me?"

"Yes'm." His voice was subdued. "I s'pose I ought to see Beth, oughtn't I? I mean, to ask her properly and all."

"Go into the sitting room. I'll send her downstairs."

She watched after him as he walked across the hall. Only God knows, she thought, what this folly will lead to. They were rash and headstrong, both of them, Nick brandishing his new manhood like an unwieldy broadsword and Beth, haughty, ambitious and possessive, determined only to win at this game she was playing. For all their affectations, they were nothing more than a pair of stupid, ignorant, spoiled children, unprepared for the consequences of their actions. Lucy felt a surge of pity for them. Never mind, she told herself, it's too late for that, too.

XXII

THE RITES had been performed with a minimum of ceremony. The two families had assembled in the Bush Street drawing room, stiffly polite, eying each other uncomfortably. Poor Naomi, newly married herself, wept openly throughout the proceedings, holding tight to Boyd's hand as though she might somehow be able to forcibly stay his departure for the East. During the wedding feast that followed, an air of stilted cordiality pervaded the dining room. The toasts were formal and perfunctory, fruitless attempts, Lucy thought, to dispel the disgrace that hung over the table like an unmentionable odor.

That morning, she had taken Beth aside before the guests arrived and led her into the library, closing the door behind them.

"Bethie, there's the matter of a wedding gift to be settled. I've no idea what you may expect from Nick's parents, the situation being what it is. As for myself, you know very well how I feel about what's happened."

"Yes, Mama."

"What's done is done. I intend to make you the same gift that I would have if your marriage had taken place under more auspicious circumstances. I thought five thousand dollars an appropriate sum."

"Oh, Mama!" Beth threw her arms around Lucy's neck. "Thank you! Thank you five thousand times!"

"My dear," she said, smiling, "as someone told me when I married your father, 'it's a fortunate woman with a dot of her own money.' I pray you never need to spend it, but it's yours for security's sake."

"I understand, Mama."

"Go along now and fetch your nosegay. Nick and the others will be arriving soon."

Beth's nosegay now reposed in a silver vase in the drawing room. Lucy paused as she passed by and fingered the cascade of pink silk ribbons that formed a shining swirl on the rosewood tabletop.

Seth came up behind her and put his hands on her shoulders. "What are you thinking?"

"How strange I felt this evening, watching those two go up the stairs to bed together. It seemed so wrong. They're still only children in my eyes."

"But on Monday, that boy leaves to fight a war."

"Oh, Seth—" She turned and buried her head in his shoulder. "He's so young. What if—"

"Hush. Worry accomplishes nothing except to torment the worrier. The matter is out of our hands. Let's make the next few days as happy as we can. What do you say we take the young folks to The Willows on Sunday?"

"Perhaps they'd rather be alone."

But Beth and Nick went along eagerly. "What a grand idea," Beth called gaily, raising her voice over the music in the air. "Mama, we haven't had an outing together in years, and it's such fun here." She watched as Nick took his bowling ball in hand and sent it unerringly down the alley, toppling the last remaining pins. "Bravo!" She clapped delightedly. "How many is that?"

Seth mopped his brow. "Nick's taken four out of five. I concede defeat, my boy. Shall we get a glass of punch?"

The park was thronged. Under the lacy shade of the trees, people paused to savor their refreshments, watching the children sailing toy boats in the stream below. A band of little girls, skirts flying, played tag among the willows, darting in and out of the overhanging greenery like small wood-nymphs. Couples, hand in hand, drifted toward the concert grounds, lured by the sound of a Strauss polka. Above the lilting tune, vendors noisily hawked their wares and a trio of whooping boys rolled their hoops, rushing after them through the crowds, pausing abruptly to observe the troupe of acrobats that leapt and somersaulted on a patch of grass nearby.

Lucy sipped her punch, gazing at the passersby. Men, dressed in their Sunday best, doffing their hats, bowing, greeting each other; ladies in bright spring dresses, the sun shining on their silk parasols, smiling and laughing and chatting. Like fragments in a kaleidoscope they came together, passed and moved to form new mosaics of color. How strange, she reflected, to think that we happy folk are a people at war. She knew that not far away, the military was reinforcing Fort Point, lest the city be invaded from the sea. She glanced quickly at Beth and Nick, wondering if they shared her thoughts, but they were a million miles removed, gazing into each other's eyes, oblivious of the crowds around them.

Seth set down his empty glass. "What will it be next? How about a go at target-shooting?"

"I'd best warn you," Nick told him genially, "I'm even better with a gun than a bowling ball." First Seth and then Nick took turns with the pistols the concessionaire gave them. "Mercy!" Beth took her hands from her ears as Nick laid down his pistol. "You weren't boasting. Look, Mama, all right in the center of the target."

"Ladies," Seth said, "would you care to try your luck?"

"Oh, land," Beth objected, "it wouldn't be proper."

"Nonsense," Lucy retorted. "It was your own father who taught me to shoot, and a good thing, too, in those days. May I, Seth?"

The concessionaire gave Seth a wary glance and reluctantly handed her the pistol. He retreated several steps to safety. Lucy raised the gun and sighted down the barrel. With a mixture of embarrassment and awe, Beth looked on as she squeezed the trigger and fired.

The concessionaire heaved a sigh of relief. "Not bad at all, ma'am, for a lady."

Seth eyed her with mock alarm. "Looks like I'd better watch my step. You never told me you knew how to shoot."

"Mama, did you actually ever have to use a gun?"

"No, dear, and I trust I never shall." Out of the corner of her eye, she saw Nick's smile fade. "Come," she said, "let's go listen to the concert, shall we?"

It was late. Beth and Nick had retired upstairs. Lucy looked up from her book as Seth came into the drawing room. "Seth?" She peered past the lamplight. "What have you there?"

"My Colt. I've been thinking. Since both of us know

how to use it, it might be wise to keep it where it's handy."

"Whatever for? It's a dangerous thing to have lying about."

"These are dangerous times. No one knows what's going to happen here. There are rumors of secret military drills among the Secesh. If they try to take over the city—"

"I'd surely let them take it, rather than use that gun."

"Lucy, I'd feel safer knowing that if I'm away on business you'd have the means to protect yourself."

"As you wish, but do put it out of sight, please." She motioned toward the table where Seth's bottle of Slade and Daggett silver stood. "That drawer's empty. Remind me to tell Septimus it's there. He'd be scared out of his wits if he stumbled across it."

Seth shut the drawer. "It's after eleven. Shall we go to bed?"

She closed her book. "I don't know that I could sleep. I keep thinking about tomorrow."

"Nick's mind is made up."

"Yes, but—"

"But nothing. We can't stop him. He's seen to his responsibility to Beth, and now he must leave." He reached for her hand. "Let's get some rest. It won't be easy for any of us."

Long after Nick had gone, Lucy would come upon Beth standing alone in the sitting room as she had that morning, looking after Nick as he waved from Dabney Stevens's carriage. He had refused to let her accompany him and Boyd down to the bay. "It's better this way. I shouldn't want you having a faint spell in those crowds. Stay here where you'll be looked after." He had gone then, striding jauntily down the walk to the street, hoisting his baggage into the carriage, pausing only once to look back and wave at the figure in the bay window.

After Nick's first letter, from Panama, the weeks passed with no word from him. "Don't be alarmed," Seth consoled Beth. "With the state of affairs as it is, you mustn't expect to hear from him with any regularity. It's nothing to fret about."

Each morning, Beth scanned the "War News" column on the front page of the *Alta*, as though it provided some tenuous link between her and Nick. It was filled with the unfamiliar names of faraway places like Fairfax, Fort Pickens and Manassas Junction. After a while, she abandoned the practice. "The *Alta* is prejudiced in favor of the Union, anyhow," she said, shrugging. "Who knows if what they print is true?"

As the days lengthened into summer, Beth gave up her duties at the Good Shepherd Home. Her condition was becoming evident. She occupied her time with needlework and reading or playing cards with Li Lin in the cool shade of the porch. It was not a life which suited her. "Mama" she pouted, "I feel like an exile."

"You made your own bed," Lucy replied. "You must lie in it now, and don't complain."

"I'm bored. Sometimes I even wish I were back at school."

"Naomi is coming to tea today, isn't she? That will be company for you."

"Naomi's bored, too. It's not fair that married ladies can't go to parties and balls."

"In your condition, you're not going anywhere."

"Naomi's jealous. She wishes she were going to have Boyd's baby."

Lucy glanced up. "You didn't tell her when you were expecting, did you"

She shook her head. "But they'll all know, when it happens."

"Let's not think about that." Lucy gazed at Bethie, who was bent over her needlework. Abruptly, she rose and moved her chair to catch the sunlight on her newspaper. "More Fighting in Missouri," the headline read. It was impossible to imagine the placid fields of her memory violated by cannon-fire and hoarse commands and the cries of men falling wounded on the fragrant, sun-warmed grass. The sounds of summer she remembered only as sweet and peaceful, the melodies of birds, the lazy hum of insects and the clear peal of the dinner bell summoning Pa and Willie from their work.

But the skirmishes continued in Missouri, and late in August, the *Alta* triumphantly reported that the Union had avenged its loss at Bull Run with a victory at Springfield. "Our Loss 200 Killed and 700 Wounded and Double that Amount for the Enemy."

How Lucy wondered, can one be expected to rejoice

when we are our own enemy? Whether the news was good for one side of the other, it meant, in human terms, only pain and death. The names, the places, the numbers of dead and wounded merged and blurred in her mind. She was conscious only of a dull, relentless ache and the memory of the bloody body of the Indian boy Mr. Bates had shot on the trail. She saw him still, his eyes open, looking startled, his life gushing from the nape of his neck.

"Lucy, dear."

She looked up at the sound of Seth's voice. It was late in the afternoon, and Bethie had long since gone inside, leaving Lucy alone on the porch.

"You seemed very far away."

"I was."

"I received a letter from Abel today. It was sent to my office."

"Why there?" she asked, puzzled. "He knows how much I love to hear from him."

"Because he wanted my opinion as a man. I expect that also he didn't want to upset you."

"He's not ill, is he, Seth?"

"He's fine. He's happy with his summer job in Alvah Mountford's office, but he wanted to know if I thought he should return to Harvard this fall or enlist in the Union—"

"No!" she cried. "He can't! It's dreadful enough that we should be so worried over Nick! I couldn't stand knowing that Abel had gone to war, too. The two of them, fighting against each other?"

"Stay calm, my dear. I already dispatched my reply. I took the liberty of expressly forbidding him to consider any such thing. My tone may have been a bit harsh, but I wasn't taking any chances. He said he'd abide by my advice, so I expect that's the last of it."

"Thank God."

Seth took his watch from his waistcoat and glanced at it. "I'd best go pack for Saint Helena before suppertime. I'll be leaving early in the morning."

"I'll do it."

"Good." He slipped an arm around her waist as she rose to go inside. "I was hoping you'd say that. You know what a mess I always make of it."

His arm still around her, they went together to their room, where Lucy set about packing his valise. "I begin

430

to think," she said, "that you've a pretty lady hidden up there in Napa Valley. Otherwise, why would you travel there in the midst of summer? It must be fearfully hot."

"You're not seriously jealous, are you?"

"Almost."

He smiled. "I suppose I should be flattered that you think my energy so boundless. What makes you think I'd want a mistress?"

She paused a moment. "Variety?"

Seth laid a hand on her cheek. "My dear, I'm married to a very complicated woman who constantly surprises me. I've all the variety I can handle right here." He kissed her gently. "Shall we take a short nap before Septimus calls us to supper?"

"Will you tell me about your interest in Saint Helena?"

He laughed aloud. "Ah, back to that, are we? The phantom mistress. Well, my dear, she's quite beautiful. An outrageous whim on my part perhaps, but then again, maybe not. In any event, as soon as the weather cools and I'm sure that she's ready to receive you, we'll go up there together."

"And then I'll find out what you've been doing all these months?"

"You will. Now come here and let me set your mind at rest."

In the last week of September, despite the ban on correspondence between the rebel South and the Union, Beth received a letter from Nick. It had been written from Savannah but mailed in a second envelope, readdressed in an unfamiliar hand, from Baltimore. He and Boyd, he wrote, had secured passage from Panama on a British ship. The captain, well greased with California gold, had skirted the blockade and sent them off in the longboat, under cover of darkness, to one of the small islands along the coast. From there, "by luck, ingenuity and a stretch on shanks' mare," as Nick put it, they had made their way northward to Savannah. Boyd had gone off to join the Army at once, but Nick was on his way to New Rosedale for a few days before enlisting.

"And what else does he say?" Lucy wanted to know.

"It's private, Mama."

She glanced up, then shook her head apologetically. "Of course. I didn't mean to pry, dear."

Long after the letter arrived, it still lay on the table beside Beth's bed, becoming soft and limp with handling. The sight of those pages, now soiled with fingerprints, the creases all but worn through from folding and unfolding, filled Lucy with an uncomfortable combination of pity and anger. He had left Beth dishonored and with child, to pore forlornly over a few flimsy sheets of paper in the solitude of her room. Though she damned herself for her doubts, Lucy wondered sometimes whether it had actually been the noble cause of the South that called Nick home or whether he had grown tired of San Francisco and Bethie and found a handy way to escape his obligations. But there was no way of knowing, she reflected, not until the War was over. Whichever was true, the one answer would come too slowly and the other too soon.

"Mama?" Beth called from the sitting room. "Is that you?"

"Yes, Bethie." Lucy removed her bonnet and laid it on the hall chair.

"Look, Mama." Beth held up the tiny rose-of-Sharon quilt she was sewing. "It's almost finished. Isn't it sweet? Where did you go this afternoon?"

"To the Good Shepherd and then to the store. I wanted one last look around before I turned the keys over to Joe and Klara."

"Wasn't it spookish being all alone there on a Sunday afternoon?"

Lucy sat down in the window seat and gazed absently through the glass into the deepening twilight. "I wanted to be alone with my thoughs. So much of my life was tied up in that store. There were spooks, to be sure. French Jack, Queen Rosie and her girls, you children—such a lot of memories."

"I was glad to leave that place. Life here is ever so much nicer."

"It is, I suppose, but I was proud of that store."

"You worked like a common drudge, always slaving to make it succeed. You even made Abel and me work sometimes."

"I hear the voice of Mrs. Nicholas Stevens of New Rosedale plantation, if I'm not mistaken. Listen to me, Bethie. Don't look down on anyone who does an honest

432

day's labor. Your grandfather worked the land, and your father built the cabin you were born in."

"Oh, Mama," she said wearily, "don't let's have that tiresome recital again." She looked up from her quilting. "Speaking of Papa, I guess Nick wouldn't mind my telling you that we were thinking of naming the baby Caleb, if it's a boy. Caleb Bates Stevens."

"Don't."

Beth looked startled.

"I just meant—" Lucy groped for the words. "Since you never really knew your father, it might be more appropriate to choose something else. I should think," she advised her cautiously, "that Nick's parents might find it flattering to have the child carry one of their family names. It would be a wiser choice, Bethie, seeing as you've come into that family under a bit of a cloud. You need all the good will you can muster."

"If it's a girl, we're going to name it after Nick's mama anyway. Her maiden name was Sue Lacey Calvert. What do you think of Sue Lacey Stevens?"

"Very pretty indeed. Why not Calvert for a boy?"

"Calvert." She brightened. "And we could call him Cal for short! Mama, that's a good name." She broke off and sighed. "If only I could write to Nick. Even if I could get a letter through, I wouldn't know where to send it."

"These are hard times, dear, I know, but the War can't last forever." She went to Beth and kissed her cheek. "I must go freshen up. Seth's due home in time for supper."

"Hot as Hades, it was," Seth said, slicing into his melon. "And the dust was something fierce. Even the greenery looked dulled and brownish. We'd best wait until after the first rain to take our holiday."

"May I go too?" Beth wanted to know.

Seth shook his head. "Not this time, Bethie. I've arranged a surprise for your mother."

"And I cannot imagine what it could be," Lucy said, smiling at Seth across the table.

"A farm," Beth suggested.

"Seth, you wouldn't. If there's one thing I don't want to be, it's a farmer's wife. I saw enough of that life as a child."

"Why, my dear, I think you'd look quite lovely pulling up beets in that peach-colored silk you're wearing. Don't you, Bethie?"

Beth gave him a mischievous glance. "And with her diamonds flashing in the sun. Think what a handsome picture you'd make, Mama."

"You're as balmy as Emperor Norton, both of you," she retorted good-naturedly. "Anyhow, I've left my working days behind me, and good riddance, I say."

Seth laid down his spoon. "You did Joe and Klara quite a favor in selling them the store."

"Not really. They were willing to meet my price. It was fair for both sides."

"Has Joe made peace with Albert yet?"

"Yes, though I gather there's still some tension between them. Polly and Martha came to call last week. Seth, did you know that your friend, Asa Hudson, told Albert that you and he had each bought fifty shares of railroad stock? Albert says the Central Pacific is just another pipe dream." dream."

"I disagree. In fact, if the opportunity arises, I plan to buy more."

"A railroad over the Sierra Nevadas? It would be nothing short of a miracle. Who's behind this scheme?"

"Theodore Judah, the fellow who built the Sacramento line up to Negro Bar a few years back. The others are businessmen—lawyers, mining men, a pair of hardware dealers and a jeweler. There's a dry-goods merchant in it, too. And Stanford, the grocer, who'll likely be the next governor." He caught the look on her face. "Now, Lucy, don't be a doubting Thomas."

"A rather unlikely bunch to build a railroad. Seth, there's been talk for years of trying to put a line over those mountains. What makes you think this attempt will pan out?"

"The War. Congress will have to support the project. The Union needs the mineral wealth we have in the West. Mark my words, my dear, if we can link up with the eastern railroads, Central Pacific stock will be a *bonanza*."

Lucy smiled at him. "You're an inveterate gambler, Seth Slade. What is it, the excitement?"

"Naturally." He smiled back. "Why should a fellow settle for faro when there are bigger games to play?"

"Seth," Beth asked him, "if there's a chance to make a big profit from railroad stock, shouldn't I take some of my wedding money and—"

"Merciful heavens, no!" Lucy interrupted. "One gambler in the family is quite enough."

"But Mama, you took your chances. The sheep, the two stores."

"I did those things out of necessity. If I'd known then all that I know now, I'd never have dared."

"Your Mama's right, Beth. It's easier to lose than win."

"I declare, Seth," Lucy said quietly when Beth had left the table, "I wish that girl didn't have such a craving for wealth. She seems to think it's the answer to everything. Money or none, life is rarely easy. I'm afraid she's not up to coping with the knocks when they come along. It's my fault for spoiling her."

"Don't fret." He pushed back his chair and rose. "She'll grow up fast, motherhood is upon her."

Yet Lucy remained concerned. Beth was still a flighty child, full of fancies. To hear her talk, week in and week out, the baby might as well be little more than a novel possession, a toy, a doll for her to play with and fondle and dress up.

Seth peered out of the bedroom window for a glimpse of the dawning day. "Don't look now, Pastora, but I'll wager it showers before noon."

Lucy came to his side, still pinning up her hair, and looked out. "Does that mean it will have rained up in Saint Helena?"

"Very possibly."

"Do you really think it's safe to leave Bethie with Septimus and Biddy and Li Lin?"

"Certainly Septimus and Biddy are fully capable of coping with any situation that arises." He buttoned his waistcoat and took his watch and chain from their stand on the lowboy.

"But what about an emergency? How would we get word?"

"Biddy can write. What's wrong, Lucy? I thought you were looking forward to the trip."

"I am," she said reluctantly. "It's just that I've never taken a holiday before."

"Never?" Seth donned his coat. "Then it's about time, say I."

Lucy smoothed her hair and gave a last glance into the mirror. She saw Seth's reflection there, smiling at her.

"I declare, Seth Slade, I believe you're determined to turn me into a hedonist."

"What an attractive prospect." He bent to kiss the back of her neck. "Now, no more shilly-shallying, my girl. That boat's not going to wait for us."

Lucy stood on the deck of the ferry in the early morning sun, one hand holding her bonnet fast against the cool wind that scudded across the water. Seth looked up at the sky, shading his eyes. "Wild geese. Listen." The birds sailed overhead, calling plaintively. "They're coming south early this year. That means a hard winter."

"It will be a hard winter anyway, what with Abel still gone and Nick off to war."

"I thought we were going to try to forget about our cares for a few days."

"We are," she promised. She looked out over the bay and smiled to herself. "Seth, do you know, the first time I ever saw the ocean, I was just about here? I remember being astonished that it didn't crash and roar in some sort of wild, blustery tempest the way it always did in my Pa's tall stories." She laughed. "How naive I must have been. And to think that was less than eight years ago. How things have changed."

Time and again, that thought echoed in her mind as the stage rumbled northward from the landing at Benecia. Where there had once been only a vast expanse of vacant terrain, untenanted save for the deer, coyotes and rabbits, there were now neat farmhouses and tilled fields. Herds of cattle drowsed and ruminated behind miles of encompassing fences. Only the occasional hawk wheeling overhead defied the domestication below. The faint tracery of game tracks had yielded to broad, well-rutted roads plied by wagons and carriages and lone riders who slowed to hail the stage, then raced ahead for the honor of announcing its arrival, leaving behind dense billows of brown dust.

The stage wound its way over and around the rolling pasturelands until, gradually, the road began to level out and the gentle contours of the landscape gave way to bolder forms. Here the terrain was defined by contrasts. Ahead stretched the flat valley floor, an unbroken plain marked by a patchwork of farms and orchards. In the distance, to left and right, rose craggy heights topped with forests. It looked to Lucy as though whatever power had shaped the narrow valley had made a path as smooth as the stroke of a titan's thumbprint, pushing the earth haphazardly aside, leaving that range of jagged ridges in its wake.

The temperature in the valley was perceptibly warmer. Lucy opened her fan. The other passengers, all gentlemen, waved their hats fitfully back and forth in front of their perspiring faces.

"We're approaching the town of Napa," Seth told her. "Give a look."

It was an agreeable place, she observed. Here and there among the sprucely painted shops and homes, the Stars and Stripes hung from a porch beam, a pole or a window sash. It was a neat, proud little town, not at all like the hodge podge of a Castalia or Volcano or Hangtown where strangers came to make their pile and decamped for the next strike without a backward glance. It was a modest village, to be sure, yet its straight streets and tidy garden plots and well-kept homes bespoke the plucky self-respect of folks who had come here intending to stay forever, through good times and bad. Lucy had never seen a town like this, yet, oddly, it seemed both friendly and familiar. Intuitively, she knew what it was. "Seth," she said, turning to him, "it's an American town, isn't it."

"Yes indeed. Not unlike a lot of the villages back East."

She gazed out of the window. "Land, if you could have seen Saint Luke's Plains. A handful of shabby buildings that always looked like they'd been dropped there by accident." She laughed. "In those days, I thought Saint Joseph was a real town. It wasn't. It was a carnival with noble intentions." She paused a moment, remembering. "I wonder what it's like now."

"Beggin' your pardon, ma'am." The gentleman on the opposite seat ceased fanning himself with his hat and leaned forward. "I couldn't help but hearin'. Saint Joe's a *city*, ma'am." He emphasized the word with reverence. "A real fine city."

"A city." She shook her head, smiling. "I suppose I should have expected that."

"What is that scent in the air?" she asked.

He inhaled a deep breath and looked pleased. "What does it smell like to you?"

Lucy wrinkled her nose. "I don't quite know. It's very pungent but not at all unpleasant. It reminds me of something, yet I can't think what."

"Wine," answered one of the other passengers. "It's the smell of the pomace."

"What is that?"

"The refuse of the grape crush after the must is pressed out." The man caught her puzzled look and explained. "The must is the juice for fermentation. That's the tail end of the harvest in the air. See?" He pointed out the window. "There's the vineyard it's coming from."

Off to the right of them, a small road led to a barnlike, redwood building. A pair of long, open-bed farm wagons lay untended outside, their teams tethered to a post. Beyond stretched fields striped with rows of low grapevines, their stubby, gnarled trunks somehow grotesquely beautiful beneath the umbrellas of silvery green leaves. "Mercy, but it's a pretty sight, isn't it, Seth?" Lucy looked back at the vineyard as they passed it. "It must take a lot of workers to harvest a place that size, but I suppose there's plenty of Indian labor hereabouts."

"Indians?" The other man glanced at her incredulously, then chuckled. "You're having a little joke, of course."

"But I wasn't."

Seth laid a hand on her arm. "There are very few left in these parts. Disease. The white man. The usual," he said gently. "Those that remain keep to themselves, well away from the farms and ranches."

"But Seth, there were whole tribes of them living in places like this. How could they just disappear? And who works the fields?"

"Chinese, mostly. They don't shirk hard labor and they don't complain. They're satisfied with ten or twelve dollars a month and a roof over their heads. Here, now, we're coming into Saint Helena. Gather up your things."

Lucy alighted from the stage and looked around her. The pretty village of Saint Helena might as well have sprung from the pages of a sketchbook. It lay in the midst of the bucolic valley bounded by its far hills, their harshness softened and blurred now by the heat haze that shimmered upward from the plain. Both sides of the street were lined with trim buildings, presided over by leafy oaks and a cloudless blue sky and, to the north, the looming heights of Mount Saint Helena. It was the mountain, she realized, that gave the town its quaintness. Dwarfed by the steep, rocky peak in the distance, it seemed a place in miniature, a bustling, hospitable, toy town invented to delight some lucky child. Passersby stopped to observe the arrival of the stage, smiling, waving, calling out greetings to friends and strangers alike.

"Hallo!" Seth hailed a short, stocky man emerging from a store with an armload of packages. *"Guten tag, Herr Schmidt.* Do come meet my wife."

Herr Schmidt looked flustered and glanced about for a place to lay his parcels. Propping them carefully against a hitchingpost, he came forward, brushing assiduously at his coatfront with both hands as though to polish himself for the presentation. Save for the coat, Lucy observed, he was dressed like a farmer. Yet his short, dark hair and neatly-shaped muttonchop whiskers were more the mark of a gentleman. An odd combination, she thought, as he gave her a courtly bow and turned to shake Seth's hand.

"I trust everything is in order for Mrs. Slade's arrival?"

"Ja, ja. Some few last things—" He gestured toward his purchases. "If you will be so kind as to wait a moment. I bring the carriage and fetch your bags. My lady." He nodded to Lucy and went to gather up his packages.

Lucy took in a deep breath as the carriage rolled along the open countryside. "My, but the air here is dry. It's so light that it makes me feel as buoyant as a butterfly."

"It's a tonic," Seth agreed. "That's one of the reasons Sam Branann built his hotel up here. Between the climate and the hot springs, he's hoping to attract a lot of visitors."

Lucy peered through the trees at a towering wood stucture that hovered over the road. "Do stop a moment, Herr Schmidt. Will you look at the size of the water wheel up there on that mill? It must be at least four stories high! What an industrious little valley this is."

"Doctor Bale's place," Seth told her, "but we mustn't waste time. The sun will be setting soon. Let's go, Herr Schmidt."

"The place we're staying, is it far?" she asked.

"Only a little farther," Seth assured her, "but I want you to have a good look around while there's still enough light."

Toward its northern end, the valley narrowed in places. The road ran close to the hills on the western side.

The sun slanted down through thickets of manzanita, madrone and oak and, higher up, tall stands of fir. At a signal from Seth, Herr Schmidt slowed their pace. "Now," Seth directed Lucy, "close your eyes until I tell you to open them."

She felt the carriage move on for a way; then it turned up a slight incline and halted.

"We're here."

Lucy opened her eyes. Ahead lay a narrow lane, cleared out of the dense brush and trees. It wound up the hill above them and disappeared into the woods. At its foot, along the roadside, were two cairns of boulders to mark its entrance. A sturdy post rose above the pile of rocks to the right, and nailed to it was a redwood shingle bearing the words "Pastora Vineyard" in neatly painted white lettering. An arrow beneath pointed up the hill.

Lucy stared at it, shaking her head from side to side as a smile spread over her face. "Your mistress," she said finally, "a vineyard."

"Our vineyard," he corrected her, as the carriage started up the drive.

Lucy reached for his hand and held it. "You always were a gambling man, my love."

"Herr Schmidt thinks we've a winning enterprise. Isn't that so, my friend?"

He nodded emphatically. "*Ja.* Four, five years, my lady, you wait and see."

"That long?"

"Wine is not oats. Wine is art."

"Herr Schmidt has the best of credentials. His family has been producing wine in Germany for generations. Look there—" Seth pointed off into the underbrush.

A lone doe, tawny against a clump of green ferns, stood frozen, staring at them with large, startled eyes. As they drew abreast of her, she turned and loped gracefully away, melting into the foliage.

The drive followed a narrow, rippling stream. The boughs of the trees overhead formed a canopy over the carriage as it passed beneath. Sunlight filtered down through the leaves, dappling the earth like handfuls of gold coins strewn along the way. As they rose above the valley, the air grew cooler. The stream passed from sight, leaving them in silence save for the sound of the carriage and the fuss of a handful of agitated birds that kept apace of them, fluttering from branch to branch, scolding them for their intrusion.

Abruptly, they emerged from the twilight of the lane into a wide, sunlit clearing. Herr Schmidt reined in the horses. Lucy blinked in the glare and shaded her eyes with her hand.

"Well?" Seth said.

"It's a mirage," she said slowly.

On the far side of the clearing stood a large, square single-story cottage. An arched veranda across the front and a high, mansard roof gave it an oddly stately look, set as it was amid the dense woods to either side. Its freshly painted exterior sparkled like new snow. The gray front door, between two pairs of windows, lay slightly ajar.

"Chang!" Seth called out. "Are you there?"

The door swung wide, and a short, spindly Chinese dashed toward the carriage, his braid bobbing and his slippered feet churning up a small cyclone of dust as he came. He drew himself up short beside them and, folding his arms, bowed ceremoniously.

"Chang, meet the lady of the house, Mrs. Slade."

"Missee." He bowed again.

Lucy smiled and nodded to him. "I'm delighted to meet you, Chang."

The face beneath the black skullcap was narrow, with high, sharp cheekbones. His lips curved upward in the suggestion of a smile, though his eyes looked pensive. A studious face, Lucy thought, but of what age she couldn't decide. He was too self-possessed to be a young man and too energetic to be old.

"Missee would like tea?"

"Later, Chang," Seth told him. "I want to show Mrs. Slade around first. You may take the baggage inside."

Herr Schmidt stepped down from the carriage and held out his hand for Lucy. "Mind!" he said loudly. "You be careful with those bags, you hear, Chang?"

Lucy suppressed a smile. Herr Schmidt was one of those men who spoke to lesser mortals as though their station in life confirmed them as deaf or slow-witted or both.

"Now," Herr Schmidt said, wringing his hands with anticipation, "we three take a little walk, yes?"

He strode across the clearing, followed by Seth and Lucy arm-in-arm. He paused, waiting for them, in front of a long, low, barrackslike structure made of redwood siding. At each end a tin stovepipe rose from the roof. Along the side were several tiny windows hung with thin cotton. "The bunkhouse for the workers. The door is on the other side so as not to face your house, my lady."

"How thoughtful."

"I thank you." Herr Schmidt made a small, proud bow. "If you will now come over here." He marched across a rutted trail to a spacious redwood shed built into the brush-covered hillside. With a grunt, he pulled open its wide doors and motioned them inside. "The presshouse, my lady."

Lucy peered into the dim recess of the shed and made out a large, round object on a low platform. "Do my eyes deceive me," she asked, stepping closer, "or does it look like a big washtub?"

Herr Schmidt looked crestfallen. "A crushing-tub," he gently corrected her. "See here, at the bottom, the juice-tub for the must."

"Ah."

"And then," Seth put in, "off it goes to the fermentation barrels."

"And where are they?" she inquired.

Seth laughed. "Now, now, we're years ahead of ourselves as it is."

"The vines." Herr Schmidt glanced at Lucy. "You don't mind walking some more?"

Beyond the shed and the bunkhouse, the trail cut through the undergrowth and curved around the foot of the hill. Above it rose another, wider slope. As far as Lucy's eyes could see, ranks of small, squat vines dotted the terrain, gently undulating ribbons of planting that followed the contours of the hill. In the distance, two Chinese knelt on their haunches, tying small cloth streamers to a wire between two posts.

"To discourage the rabbits and deer and the like," Herr Schmidt explained. "They are our worst enemies."

"You don't have to tell Mrs. Slade," Seth replied. "She's a farm girl herself."

Herr Schmidt gave Lucy a surprised look. "*Ja?*"

"Yes indeed. And if the animals aren't enemy enough, there's always the frost and the drought."

"We've the stream and two fine wells," Seth assured her. "As for frost, that's the beauty of this place. The frost tends to settle in the valley, pushing the warmer air upward. We're quite well protected."

Lucy surveyed the tiers of vines stretching off toward the setting sun. "Seth, how big is the vineyard, all told?"

"It runs around the hill there and down onto a lower slope. We've a little over twenty acres planted. Enough to be self-sustaining, once we begin to harvest in full."

"Twenty acres," she said admiringly, "all tilled and planted and tended. But Seth, surely you have more than those two workers over yonder."

"The others are in the caves."

"Caves?"

"We'll save them for tomorrow. Come, it's growing dark. Chang will brew us some tea. Herr Schmidt, will you join us?"

"Thank you, no. I must look in on the workers and then go to my quarters to finish a letter to my dear wife. I'll join you at the sound of the supper gong."

"Herr Schmidt's room is attached to the stable," Seth told Lucy, "on the other side of the house, by the caves."

"I do hope it's comfortable," she volunteered, following Herr Schmidt along the dusky trail.

"Oh, yes, my lady." His tone softened. "I am hoping my Anna will soon join me."

When they reached the cottage, he bowed once again to Lucy and walked on. A soft glow illuminated the veranda, and through the windows she could see the shadowy form of Chang as he moved about, lighting the lamps.

Seth put an arm around her shoulders. "It's nothing as grand as Bush Street, but it has three bedrooms, small and simple, a serviceable kitchen and a good-sized room for sitting and dining."

"Oh, Seth," she said quietly, "this whole day has seemed such an improbable adventure for me. I can scarcely believe this place is really ours."

He cupped her face in his hands and kissed her. "Listen," he said, drawing away, "I hear the coolies coming from work. It wouldn't do to have them catch us in a sporting pose." Decorously, he gave her his arm. " 'My lady,' as Herr Schmidt would say. . . ."

443

XXIII

THE COTTAGE was quiet, save for the rustling of papers as Seth sat at the table, reading the reports and letters Herr Schmidt had given him. Chang, who had proven himself an admirable cook, had retired to the bunkhouse, Lucy emerged from the kitchen and set her lamp on the table. "It's spotless. The man cleans as well as he cooks. Wherever did you find him, Seth?"

He jotted a notation on one of the sheets in front of him and gathered them into a pile. "I stole him," he said, pushing his chair away from the table. "His cousin, who works for Asa Hudson, said Chang was unhappy with his employer. I arranged a meeting through Asa's man and whisked Chang off to Saint Helena before he had a chance to change his mind."

"How long had you planned all this?"

"I began reading about wine making in Washoe. I don't know why, except that a fellow gave me the books when we were snowbound. After Abel and I came down below, I made some inquiries and then spent a few days up here looking around. The more I learned from people like Doctor Crane and Monsieur Pellet and Krug and Haraszthy, the more I was convinced that wine could be one of California's great agricultural resources. I bought the land then and there. As soon as I returned from taking Abel to Harvard, I put my plans into action."

"And these other men, are their vineyards doing well?"

"Last year's yield at the Krug place was over eight thousand gallons."

Lucy leaned over his chair and clasped her arms

around his shoulders. "I love seeing you this way," she said, laying her cheek against his head. "You're as young and eager as a colt when you talk about it."

"Make no mistake, my love. It's still a risk."

She slipped into the chair beside his. "For a lawyer, you're a very romantic man, do you know that? What other sort of fellow would go chasing after silver mines and phantom railroads, much less do something as fanciful as this?"

"But not without a good deal of research, I assure you. I'll tell you a curious thing, though," he said thoughtfully. "It's unlike any other investment I've ever made. There is an element of it that appeals to one's sentiments." He fingered the cold bowl of his pipe and laid it down. "Maybe it's because I never sired any children of my own. Then again, perhaps it's nothing but egotism."

Lucy laid her hand over his. "Tell me."

It was a moment before he spoke. Quietly, he said, "The thought that someday, after I'm gone, this place will survive me. That these same vines will still be bringing forth fruit. That somewhere people will be drinking wine from these grapes. Or is it just mortal foolishness to want to leave a legacy that's alive?"

She drew his hand to her lips and kissed it. "I love you very much, my husband. And you could never be a fool, even if you tried."

They sat in silence for a moment. Then Seth rose and laid his papers and pen and inkpot on the window sill. He glanced around the sparsely furnished room. "We could use a shelf or two. There's still a lot to be done to make the place liveable."

"One of my old Turkey carpets would fit this room. And I believe Polly said she has an old sofa stored in her attic. It won't take much. I'll make a list tomorrow."

Lucy sat at the table late the next morning, jotting down the items they needed for the cottage. More linens, perhaps a small table and a rocking chair. Another lamp or two. A shaving stand for Seth and a dressing table for her. She paused, listening to the rapid rhythm of Chang's chopping knife as he prepared the noon meal.

"Ho, there!" Seth threw open the door and came in, unloading two heavy, leather saddlebags. They sank to the floor with a jingle. "Hear that? Music for Chinese ears."

"Isn't it dangerous for you to bring the pay from town all alone?"

"The only bandit in these parts is the fellow who deals cards at the saloon. What have you been doing all morning?"

"I've been educating myself. Herr Schmidt brought me some reading about your Golden Chasselas grapes. He offered to show me the caves, but I said I'd wait for you."

"The workers will be coming up to the bunkhouse shortly to collect their wages and eat. As soon as I've paid them, we'll take a look. I'll tell Chang to keep our dinner waiting."

Lucy stood in the shade of the veranda, observing the ritual of the monthly payday. Across the drive, next to the bunkhouse, a ragged line of coolies stood stoically in place, facing Seth and Herr Schmidt. A more oddly clad band she couldn't have imagined. They looked for all the world as though they had scrambled blindly in a rag-picker's heap, donning whatever they could snatch. Black braids protruded from slouch hats above padded Chinese jackets, with western-style trousers brushing cloth-slippered feet. Some wore skullcaps or wide straw hats with ill-fitting Occidental woolen coats, their pantaloons tucked into leather boots and occasionally, absurdly, a neckerchief knotted at the throat.

On the ground beside Seth lay the coin-filled saddle-bags, gold to the right, silver to the left. Herr Schmidt paced back and forth like a commander in front of his troops, peering at the roster in his hand, reading off the alien syllables at the top of his voice lest any of his herd be so obtuse as not to recognize his own name. As they stepped forward, one at a time, he leaned over Seth's shoulder and quietly murmured the amount due. Seth reached into his bags and counted the coins into the man's out-stretched palm. Sometimes one of the workers would address them. "Boss" to Herr Schmidt, "Mistah" to Seth. But most merely nodded and retreated to the line, clutching their pay tightly in their fists.

"Where did you find such a motley lot?" Lucy asked as Seth escorted her down the sloping trail at the far side of the house.

"Don't underestimate them. They're as fine a bunch of laborers as I've ever seen. Herr Schmidt hired them out of Sacramento. If you think they worked hard on the

446

planting, wait until you see what's ahead of you. We didn't know what we were getting into here, just that we needed a cellar of sorts."

"Why must you have a cellar?"

"If the wine isn't protected from the temperature changes outside, it's ruined. Goes sour. The earth and the rocks insulate it and keep the temperature fairly constant. Look there, Lucy."

At the foot of the hill beside the stable building, the brush had been cleared away, exposing bare soil. A high, arched opening, almost wide enough for a wagon, had been dug into the earth. Around it, the slope itself had been cut back, presenting a wall of rock on either side of the entrance.

"But it looks immense!" she exclaimed. "When you mentioned caves, I thought of some small burrow that an animal might make."

"Stay here while I fetch a lantern from the stable."

Lucy looked into the yawning cavern, unable to discern anything in the pitch-black darkness within.

"Here we are. Hold onto my arm so you don't stumble. There may be rocks on the floor."

It was cool inside. The lantern light bobbed eerily against the rough stone passage. Their footsteps rasped hollowly as they made their way into a wide underground chamber.

"This is the largest room," Seth said, his words echoing from the walls. "The fermentation barrels will be in here. Then, when the time is right, the new wine will be racked, drawn off to fresh casks to clarify it. Follow me." He led her deeper into the darkness, through a narrow tunnel. "This will all be storage. It's unfinished as yet. We can only go a bit farther."

Lucy moved after him in silent amazement. She reached out to touch the ruggedly hewn walls, pocked with scars of the coolies' picks. "It's gritty. It feels like pumice," she said, rubbing her fingers against the blackish rock.

"Much the same. Some kind of volcanic ash. The digging ends here, as you can see."

Ahead lay a welter of picks and shovels and woven baskets, some partly filled with rubble from the excavation.

"How much longer will it be?"

"Someday I'd like to see a thousand feet in here. We'll hollow it out as it's needed. Pretty impressive, what Hong Hing-wing and his men have done, isn't it?"

"If you'll forgive a lapse of propriety, my dear, it's just about the damndest thing I ever did see."

Seth laughed. "Well put, Pastora. How do you feel about the place that bears your name?"

"Proud," she answered without hesitation. "You never cease to astound me."

"Don't forget to give credit to Herr Schmidt. He's the expert. He works like a Trojan. And Hong Wo and his boys toil in here like industrious moles."

"Who is this Hong Hing-wing?" she asked as they stepped out into the sunlight.

"The head coolie. You saw him in the pay line. The tallest fellow, wearing the blue neckerchief."

She shook her head, "There were so many of them. It's going to take me some time to get used to all this."

"We've the rest of our lives, my love."

Later, when Seth's work was done and the day had ripened into plum-colored twilight, they walked together, hand in hand, along the trail to the vine-covered hills. A half-moon hovered above the treetops on the heights, casting a wan light over the dusky lowlands beyond.

"How peaceful it is," Lucy said softly. "We might as well be the only two people on earth. I'd thought myself a city-dweller after all this time, but I guess there's a part of me that will always belong to the country."

Seth kissed her lightly on the forehead. "I suspected as much. I wouldn't have brought you here if I'd thought you wouldn't love this valley as much as I do. It's hardly the spot for someone like your mincing Amy Winslow or the highfalutin' Knight sisters."

"Oh, Seth," she said, "why are you so hard on those poor women?"

"God save me from strait-laced ladies. They're all polish and no passion. Give me a woman who can be touched by a spread of land and a little moonlight."

"I didn't realize you disliked them so."

"I've seen too many of those bloodless prigs," he said, slipping an arm around her waist, "and so have you. They made your life miserable once, and they'll do it again."

"You're talking about Beth."

448

"Most of those people are your friends, but there are some I wouldn't trust as far as I could chuck a China clipper. Behind that self-righteous civility, they're a gaggle of unfeeling, small-minded women who'd trip all over each other for the joy of casting the first stone."

"I daresay that has as much to do with my past as Bethie's indiscretion."

"Either way, there'll be no avoiding a scandal once the talk starts."

"You've been thinking about this, haven't you?"

"For longer than you know. We're both aware that Bethie is a delicate, thin-skinned girl. She's going to have a difficult adjustment to make, as it is, without being the object of a lot of gossip."

"I know. It's been on my mind, too, but I didn't want to burden you with my worries."

"Our worries. I feel as strongly about Beth as if she were my own. Lucy, that's one of the reasons I hurried to make the house ready up here."

She looked up at him. "Seth? Are you saying what I think you are?"

"She's still in a condition to travel, isn't she? It's not a difficult journey. If she were to come here a few weeks before the child is due, she could stay until a month or so after the proper time and return to the city with no one the wiser."

"But what if there were complications?"

"There's a doctor in town."

They turned and walked back toward the house. After a moment, Lucy spoke. "I was a fool, you know. I had no idea of the kind of man you were when I agreed to marry you. I don't believe I ever fully understood until now what a fortunate woman I am."

"Then you'll do it?"

She stopped and clasped him close to her. "Bless you, my love. Of course I will."

Preceded by the freight wagons, Lucy, Beth and Li Lin journeyed to Saint Helena. Septimus and Biddy remained behind in the Bush Street house to look after Seth.

Herr Schmidt was waiting with the carriage. As the ladies disembarked from the stage, he doffed his hat with a flourish and bowed in his stiff, punctilious way first to

449

Lucy, then to Beth. At the sight of the twelve-year-old Lin in petticoats and poplin and carrying her own little reticule, the poor man halted in mid-gesture as though paralyzed. He stood there, pitched forward frozen, looking as if he might topple to the ground at any second.

"Ah!" He caught himself and stood upright, his fingers playing nervously over the brim of his hat. He glanced from Lucy to Beth.

Lucy was at pains to keep a straight face. "Li Lin is Mrs. Stevens's maid, Herr Schmidt."

"*Ach, so!*" Recovering his composure, he granted Lin the trace of a nod. "And now to the carriage, my lady."

Above the valley, the November sky was a deep, vivid blue, washed clear by a spate of recent rain. In the Krug Vineyard, the leaves had turned scarlet on the vines, and the wild mustard now grew rampant among the orderly rows of planting.

As the carriage turned up the drive to the house, Beth caught sight of the painted sign with its legend, "Pastora Vineyard." She pursed her lips but made no comment.

In response to a shout from Herr Schmidt, Chang darted from the cottage to meet them, wearing a broad smile of welcome. Glimpsing Lin, his smile quivered slightly though it remained fixed politely in place. He sucked in his breath with a short, sibilant sound. As the girl stepped down from the carriage, he raised his eyes from the trunks he was unloading and stared without expression at the shoes, the dress, the hair neatly braided and coiled at the nape of her neck. After a moment's hesitation, he said something in Chinese.

Lin answered him, chirping brightly as a bird, and went to fetch her small valise from the pile of luggage.

She is a betwixt-and-between child, Lucy thought suddenly, looking after her. She is neither one of us nor one of them any longer.

Chang appeared to like the girl. At least, he pressed her into service around the cottage to help him with the meals and a few light chores. But sometimes, when the coolies passed the veranda where Beth and Lin played at dominoes for hours on end, Lucy would see on some of their faces the same pitiless scorn she had seen on the face of Wong, the laundryman. Others ignored Lin's presence entirely, probably not knowing what to make of this odd hybrid in their midst. A few, including Herr Schmidt, accorded her occasional crumbs of reluctant courtesy. But Lin seemed not to notice or care. As always, she devoted herself to Beth, and when the rains began in their full winter force, pouring down for days at a time, confining them to the cottage, it was Lin who buoyed their spirits with a continual round of songs and needlework and games. Indeed, Lucy thought, it was Lin who made their imprisonment bearable. The rains had isolated the valley from all but sporadic news of the outside world. Occasionally, in the rare intervals between storms Lucy would receive a packet of letters from Abel and Seth, accompanied by back issues of the *Alta* and some parcels for the household, a side of bacon, perhaps, or some jars of preserves.

"Seth is going to try to join us for Christmas," she told Beth, glancing up from one of his letters.

"I hope he's a strong swimmer," Beth answered glumly, not looking up from her playing cards. "Lin, do turn up the lamp. I can barely see."

Lucy scanned the pile of newspapers in her lap. "Rebels Falling Back on the Line of the Potomac," read one. She laid it face down on the carpet at her feet. Since the telegraph connection six weeks ago, the *Alta* had displayed on its front page a daily reminder of this latest triumph, a sensational illustration of jagged bolts of electricity flashing across the globe and the bold black letters "By Overland Telegraph." It was, to Lucy's thinking, little short of a miracle that news wired from the East by noon now reached San Francisco before nine the same morning, racing time and winning, to all intents and purposes, by over three hours. The thousands of miles between the two coasts, half of which she had walked on her own two feet, seemed suddenly to have contracted as simply as a man might compress the length of a spyglass, sliding its sections together to fit compactly into his pocket No longer was the War a world away. The news sped westward over the wires with startling immediacy, destroying once and for all the delusion of tranquillity that had comfortingly tempered the truth.

There had been no more letters from Nick. No word of his whereabouts or welfare. He might as well have vanished into the air like a wisp of gunsmoke over the battlefields. Lucy glanced at Beth over the top of her newspaper. The girl shifted her weight awkwardly in her chair, cradling her protruding belly in her arms. The woman's body seemed so at odds with her child's face that Lucy, despite herself, found the spectacle grotesque. The evidence of Bethie's offense now offended her also, gross, flagrant and inescapable. She wished the wretched event would hurry up, if only to spare her the sight. At least, she thought, there's some scant comfort in knowing the girl is legally married and not the victim of a deceiver like Caleb Bates. What a naïve little fool she had been to let him turn her head with his tall tales and promises. She had been nothing more to him than an accessory to his escape beyond the Line. She had served him well. They had made a plausible pair, Mr. and Mrs. Caleb Bates. At last, he had paid for his misdeeds at the hands of the Paiutes. The truth had died with him, as far as she was concerned, and Bethie need never know any of it. Bethie was Mrs. Nicholas Stevens now, and Lucy alone knew that that was the first lawful name she'd ever had.

The storms continued, as heavy and unrelenting as any Lucy could remember. They were captives in the cottage. Conversation gave way to vacuums of silence broken only by the constant tattoo on the roof, the click of ivory dominoes and the creak of Lucy's rocker. The roads in and out of the valley were almost impassable. The lowlands were under water. Cattle were starving or drowned and acre upon acre of crops destroyed. Herr Schmidt and his coolies, wet to the skin, struggled to keep the hillside and its vines from washing away into the valley below. Daily they labored at erecting low dikes and digging a series of trenches above and around the vineyard. And daily their work was eroded or inundated, forcing them to begin all over again, drenched and shivering, racing time and the muddy torrents that sluiced continuously down the slopes.

Lucy began to worry about Beth. Suppose her time came and something went amiss? They were helpless. The weather held them in its thrall. The roads were barely safe for a carriage, much less for a traveler in Bethie's condition.

Chang, trailed by a pair of packhorses, succeeded in making his way to town for provisions. He returned, hours late, rain-slicked, his black braid dripping, looking like a half-drowned muskrat.

"Bless you, Chang," Lucy said as he brought in the last

of the sacks and parcels. "At least we shan't starve. Go put on some dry clothes. I'll brew a pot of tea."

Teeth chattering, he waved her words aside.

She laid a hand on his arm. "At once, Chang. I won't have you perishing for your loyalty. Go." She shooed him out the door and opened the moist packet of mail he had brought. The newspapers were soaked and scarcely legible. Sacramento was flooded. The Sonoma Valley to the west and the mining towns to the east fared no better. From the soggy pages of the *Alta*, Lucy extracted a single letter from Seth.

"He's leaving today," she said, as Beth appeared in the doorway. "I pray he can get through, though heaven knows how long it will take him."

"Mama."

"Yes, dear?" She scanned the rest of the letter and folded it. "Bethie? What is it? You look pale as a ghost."

"I think it's happening, Mama."

Lucy's hands began to tremble. She laid the letter on the table. "Come. Get out of those clothes and into your shimmy. You'll be more comfortable. Best to lie down and conserve your strength."

Through the night, Lucy sat by her bed. The pains came only sporadically, rousing them both from their nodding. When morning came, Lin tiptoed in with Lucy's breakfast, looking timid and frightened.

"Missybet? You all right? You hungry?"

Beth clenched her jaws and let out a cry. She grasped Lucy's hand and held it.

"Don't look so worried, Lin. Missybet will be fine. She's not hungry just now. Go help Chang with his chores, please."

It was a long labor. Not until afternoon did the pains occur with any frequency. Beth's strength was flagging. She whimpered wearily as another spasm overtook her. Ashen and hollow-eyed, she gritted her teeth and clutched the bedpost tightly with both hands, tossing her head violently from side to side.

Lucy mopped the perspiration from her forehead. "It won't be much longer."

"Mama!" she gasped. "I can't stand it!"

"Yes, you can. Now try to breathe slowly and deeply."

As the throes seized her again and again, it was all Lucy

could do to bear the sight of her suffering. She thrashed like a tormented animal, shrieking, clawing at the bedsheets, begging aloud for God to ease her pain.

Lucy opened the door a crack. "Lin," she called, "the baby is coming now. Have Chang warm some water to wash it, and bring me the pile of linens."

It was a boy. Beth took him listlessly in her arms, almost too tired to care, but as his tiny fingers brushed her cheek, she smiled faintly and said his name.

"Calvert Stevens."

The baby began to bawl loudly.

"I know, I know," she whispered softly, "you've had a hard day, too."

Lucy closed the bedroom door behind her and leaned weakly against it. Lin and Chang stood in the narrow hall, silent and anxious.

"Missybet has a fine, healthy son."

Chang beamed and scurried away. Lin bounced excitedly up and down on her toes, giggling with relief.

"You may go in for a moment, but don't stay long."

Lucy sank into the rocking chair and closed her eyes.

With a start, she sat up. It was almost dark. The rain had stopped. She could hear voices outside. She flung open the front door. "Herr Schmidt, is that you? I've news!"

"Pastora?" Seth strode out of the dusk, followed by Herr Schmidt. "Is it Beth?" he asked, doffing his oilskins as he hurried to her.

She reached out and took his hands in hers. "I delivered us a grandson this afternoon."

For a moment he looked down at her in silence, his eyes brimming. With a choked sound, he embraced her and held her tightly half weeping and half laughing.

"*Das ist wunderbar!*" Herr Schmidt clapped his hands. "In my quarters I have some wine. Wine I bring from the Rhine Valley to the Napa Valley, in case I need a taste of home. I fetch it. Tonight we drink a toast!" He bounded down the steps from the veranda and trotted off, splashing his way down the muddy path.

Lucy went inside and lit the lamps. Seth emerged from Bethie's room, a proud grin on his face. "That's the smallest person I ever saw. No bigger than a Sunday roast. What a fine gift for Christmas!"

454

"Mercy, I'd quite forgotten it was Christmas Eve."

"You look exhausted, my dear." He cupped her chin in his hand and brushed a stray curl from her cheek. "Was it rough going?"

She nodded. "It took almost a full day. Poor Bethie."

"The weaker sex indeed. Ah, Herr Schmidt," he said as the door opened, "how good of you to share your wine with us. Chang!" he called. "Bring us four glasses—no, six! You and Lin must come, too."

They gathered about Beth's bed. The baby dozed peacefully at her side. With great ceremony, Herr Schmidt poured the honey-colored liquid into their glasses, allowing a splash each for Chang and Lin. He lifted the wine to his nostrils and breathed in the aroma. "Ah," he murmured, *Sommer und Sonnenschein.*"

"Bethie," Seth said, "the toast is yours."

Beth eased herself upright against the pillows. She stared down into her glass. "To Calvert Stevens," she said quietly, "whose Papa would be very proud of him." Quickly, before the tears could come, she took a gulp of wine.

Later that night, Lucy woke, aroused by the rain drumming once again on the roof overhead. She lay still in the darkness, thinking about the baby, this tiny boy, her grandchild. What a distinguished-sounding name he had. Calvert Stevens. She whispered it to herself. Calvert Stevens, a child born to wealth and position. Land, but how remarkable that seemed. What would Ma and Pa have made of this little patrician, scion of New Rosedale and the city of San Francisco? He was a child born to luxury. Wine and dancing parties, steamships and servants, gaslights and telegraphs. And war, she thought—one mustn't forget the War. Should the Union perish, he might grow up in a divided land, never knowing the kind of fierce pride that had inspired men to venture across its wilderness as Pa had, assured that the entire length and breadth of it was theirs for the taking. Then, all things had seemed possible. But perhaps, Lucy told herself, she was merely feeling wistful. A new generation had been born today, an omen of her own mortality. With age, the scope of possibilities diminished, constricting year by year, finally as cramped and close as the winding-sheet itself. Silently, she chided herself for feeling so melancholy when Calvert's birth should only be a source of happiness.

"Pastora?" Seth spoke softly.

"Yes?"

"Did the storm wake you?"

"I've been thinking."

"About the baby?"

"And other things. I'm feeling a bit sad and old."

"Ah, now." He turned and took her in his arms. "Old, is it? What nonsense." He slipped his hand under her chemise. "You don't feel old to me, my girl. You're as firm and smooth as I last remember. And just as spry, I'll wager. I know just the remedy for your spirits."

"For shame," she reproached him. "You won't even allow me a little midnight melancholy. Why did I marry such a lickerish fellow?"

"To keep you young. Hush now," he said as he covered her mouth with his.

Afterwards, she lay there beside him, pressed to his sleeping form, wondering that his touch could so renew her. He was tender and warm and vigorous, and he aroused her until she felt as though every inch of her being was afire with sensation. At no other time did she feel as alive and sentient as when Seth made love to her. She laid her head against his chest and slept.

In the weeks following Calvert's arrival, the storms continued almost incessantly. Seth returned to San Francisco on the first day of the new year, eighteen sixty-two. On the third day, the town of Napa was inundated. The nearby river surged over its banks, coursing through the streets. The valley was cut off. There was no travel in or out, no mail, no telegraph. Doggedly, Herr Schmidt and his workers tended their system of dikes and channels. Each day that passed without the young vines breaking loose from the saturated soil signified another small triumph.

Finally, after almost a month of rain, the heavens cleared. The sun shone down on the moist and glistening earth with a brilliance that seemed blinding after the weeks of constant gloom. With the first shipments of goods came news. Most of California was devastated. As far south as Los Angeles, whole towns had been washed away. Sonora had endured over six feet of rain in the past two months. The legislature had been forced to move from Sacramento to San Francisco, swept from the capitol by the floods there. Reports of death and destruction filled the pages of the *Alta*. Lucy shook her head in awe at the toll the storms had taken. At least seventy lives lost, she read. "This record," said the *Alta*, "must embrace white men alone, for Chinese have been drowned by the hundreds. In Yuba alone there were at least fifty; in Placer County one hundred and fifty according to the *Courier;* and intelligent Chinamen say the number of their countrymen destroyed in the state by the December floods alone was about five hundred."

War news, however, was scarce. In places like the Sacramento Valley miles of telegraph poles lay submerged and useless beneath the deluge.

Herr Schmidt finally gave in to fatigue. The poor man, Lucy noticed, could barely keep his eyes open for his evening meals. Only the sight of the baby, Cal, seemed to rouse him from his weary daze. He held the infant and rocked him, singing softly to him in German, stroking the fine golden hair on his head. Lucy smiled at the sight of the burly wine-master, prattling affectionately to the uncomprehending child.

"Do let me take him from you now," she said. "I know how tired you are."

"In a moment, my lady, in a moment." He stroked the baby's cheek with his fingertip. "Tomorrow maybe I rest. The coolies will be having their holiday."

Lin looked up from her needlework. "It's the Chinese New Year, Chang says. Missee, why do you not celebrate the same New Year as the Chinese?"

"I really don't know, dear."

"Chang says our people have celebrated more than seventeen thousand years."

"*Ach*," said Herr Schmidt, "that is what you call folklore. Tales. Superstitious fables."

"How do you know?" Lin asked.

Lucy rose from her chair. "It's growing late. Put Cal to bed, please, Lin. Bethie and I will fold up the sewing. Herr Schmidt, I wish you a good night's sleep."

Lucy bolted from the snug warmth of her covers, her ears ringing. "Merciful heavens!" she exclaimed, whipping the quilt from the bed and throwing it over her. Barefoot, she dashed into the hall, the bedroom door clattering against the wall behind her. Bethie stood in the open doorway to her room, cradling a wailing Cal, as a volley of crackling explosions ruptured the silence.

"It's the heathen Chinee, Mama!" Beth shouted over the din. "They nearly frightened the life out of Cal."

"For pity's sake!" Lucy leaned against the doorjamb, her heart pounding. "This isn't Sacramento Street, after all."

"It might as well be." Beth clasped the baby close to her bosom and covered his exposed ear with her palm.

Lucy winced as another salvo of blasts rang out. She went to the front window and brushed aside the curtains.

In the circular drive below the house, the coolies had gathered, padded in layers of clothing against the morning chill. In the midst of them, ribbons of firecrackers sputtered and burst, writhing on the damp earth like fat, red snakes. Occasionally, one of the men would rush forward bearing a single, ominously large yellow tube, its fuse lit, and drop it to the ground, dashing back just in time before its powder blew with a resounding roar, sending aloft a plume of sparks and smoke.

On the veranda, clad only in her chemise and a shawl, a delighted Li Lin was watching the celebration, clapping her hands with glee at the racket and jumping for joy at each loud explosion that rent the air.

Lucy threw open the door and seized her by the arm. "How dare you expose yourself in your nightclothes?" she rebuked her, realizing as she spoke that she herself was wearing only a shimmy and quilt. "Chang!" she cried, trying to make herself heard over the uproar. "Chang, come at once!"

With obvious reluctance, Chang detached himself from the group and trotted toward the cottage, as Herr Schmidt emerged from the path at the edge of the clearing, still stuffing his nightshirt into his trousers, looking like the stunned victim of some unforeseen disaster.

"Herr Schmidt!" Lucy called, waving him toward the house. "It's quite all right. It's their custom. They do this sort of thing each year in San Francisco."

"*Tim-ding faat-choi.*" Chang saluted her as he entered. "Happy New Year. The Year of the Dog, missee."

"Indeed. Any poor dog would have fled cowering for cover by now. You may start breakfast, please."

Herr Schmidt's face was as white as his nightshirt.

"Mein Gott!" he breathed, heaving himself into a chair. "I thought perhaps it was Indians attacking."

"Not in these parts," Lucy assured him. "I'm sorry your rest was disturbed. It's all quite harmless, really, just a lot of noise. Will you excuse us while we dress for breakfast?"

As they sat at breakfast, Herr Schmidt addressed Lin over a heaping spoonful of boiled eggs. "Young woman, why must the Chinese blast their way into the new year?"

"It's the custom, sir."

"In my country, we ring church bells. A beautiful sound in the cold winter night."

Beth laughed. "You must admit, you'll have a grand story to write to Frau Schmidt."

He shook his head in dismay. "First the floods and now this barbaric deviltry. I'm afraid my Anna will think twice about coming to California."

"Ah, now," Lucy said, "it's all in the telling, isn't it? I'm sure you can make it sound very colorful. As for the rains, I daresay we'll see the end of them shortly."

She wished she had not been so quick to predict their passing. With each successive downpour, Herr Schmidt would fix her with a sad, reproachful gaze, his eyebrows raised in silent inquiry. "Soon, soon," she would say, praying that this time, at least, she might be proven correct.

Lucy began to count the days until the last week of March, when young Calvert Stevens could show his face in San Francisco without disgrace. Obligingly, he had been a small baby and thus served the deception well. He was alert and good-natured and helped the gray days pass more quickly, though Lucy longed to be with Seth once again. Business and bad weather kept him in the city. He wrote daily, as she did, but the mail came through only in the brief respites between rains. Out of ennui, Beth had taken to reading whatever newspapers reached them, but the persistent reports of Rebel losses only made her moody and snappish. Fort Henry had fallen. Savannah had surrendered to Commodore Dupont. White flags flew at Nashville. After an interruption of almost two weeks, the telegraph chattered to life again, only to announce the Federal occupation of Manassas. Bethie took to her room, pleading a headache.

"Dearest girl," Lucy stroked Beth's hair as she sat in bed nursing the baby, "you mustn't let the news upset you. It's not good for you. It will sour your milk."

"I can't help it, Mama. What's to become of us? I worry so for Nick. Sometimes I see him in my dreams, and when I try to cry out a warning to him, it's always the same. He smiles and waves and nods, and no matter how loudly I shout, he never hears me."

"My poor child. Wait until we're back on Bush Street. You'll have your friends to entertain and your piano and lots of things to do. You'll see, a little diversion will alleviate the worries and nightmares. I expect we'll all be happy to leave here after such a hard winter."

"You wouldn't have had to come at all if it weren't for Cal and me."

"It was for the best."

Beth looked up at her with a rueful smile. "I love you, Mama. I'm sorry for some of the wicked things I've said and done. I know I've made you unhappy."

"That's all in the past." She bent to kiss her head. "I've learned for myself that guilt is only useful if it saves you from making a misstep. Once that moment has passed, however, it's best not to dwell on it. Life demands that we live in the present, Bethie. The past is a teacher, not a jailer."

XXIV

Despite the cheerful prospect of returning home to Duan Street after an exile of nearly five months, Lucy felt a certain sadness at leaving the cozy cottage on the hill. It was a part of her now, this house where her first grandchild had been born. And in the weeks that Herr Schmidt and his crew had labored to save the vineyard from destruction, she had come to worry over it and cherish it as he did. As a gesture of gratitude to the coolies, she had asked Chang to prepare a list of delicacies to be sent up from the city for the men to share. She felt a bit sorry for Herr Schmidt, abandoned now to the sole company of his heathens whom he continued to eye as warily as a man burdened with a pack of undomesticated hounds.

"Never you mind, my lady," he said, helping her into the carriage. "This week I dine at the Krug place. German food, German talk. Just like home."

"My husband knows what a heroic struggle you've waged up here, Herr Schmidt, and I intend to make it clear to him that he wouldn't have a vineyard at all by now if it hadn't been for your efforts."

"I thank you, my lady." He stepped into the driver's seat and took the reins from Chang.

Chang peered into the carriage at the baby asleep in Beth's arms. "Boy and Missybet, you come back soon," he ordered them soberly.

As they rounded the curve of the drive and began the decent to the valley below, he called after them in Chinese.

Lucy turned to Lin.

461

"A wish for a safe journey, missee, and thank you for the gifts of food."

As soon as they were settled at home, Lucy dispatched Septimus and Lin to the Chinese shops of Sacramento Street with Chang's list. Septimus toted the parcels into the kitchen, his nose well elevated above the pungent odors that emanated from them. He gave Lucy a dubious glance.

"Set them on the table, and I'll see to packing them."

"Not on my table!" Biddy cried. "Sakes, ma'am, you want your supper tastin' like Chinee slop?"

"Now, Biddy, it's perfectly good food, I'm sure. Perhaps not to our tastes, but it won't defile your table."

"Hmph!" She waved Septimus away, seized a pile of towels and spread them over the tabletop. "All right, set that stuff down. Mind you, I ain't touchin' them things, not whilst I have dough to knead with these hands."

"Go back to your baking. Lin can help me. Septimus, I'll want you to take this down to the freight office right away, so don't unhitch the horses."

Seth poured his evening glass of whiskey and raised it to Lucy with an amused look. "The queen of the kitchen has had her feathers ruffled. I took Biddy a fine goose that Asa Hudson sent us, and there she was, clucking about, angry as a wet hen. Seems you sang Chang's praises a bit too loud for her ears."

"Mercy, I didn't intend to hurt Biddy's feelings."

"Never mind. I smoothed things over. Where's Bethie?"

"She went out with Septimus. She wanted to stop at Naomi's on the way home. Naomi left a note that she'd heard from Boyd."

Beth was back well before supper. She joined them in the drawing room. "The letter was written over three months ago," she reported. "From somewhere in Virginia. I can't remember the name of the place."

"But how did it get here?" Lucy asked.

"By ship from Panama, in the hands of the captain."

"Received from a blockade-runner probably," Seth said. "But Boyd, he's well?"

Beth gave a wan smile. "As well as can be expected. He said sometimes they marched so long in the winter cold that he could scarcely feel his feet under him. He's learned to sleep on frozen ground as if it were a feather bed."

"He's telling the truth, you know," Lucy said gently. "I've done the same."

"But the food, Mama. It's beans and salt meat and sometimes some stringy beef. And," she said with a grimace, "there are weevils in the biscuits."

Lucy shuddered and closed her eyes against the picture.

"Mama, Naomi is organizing knitting bees to make stockings for the Confederate soldiers. May we have one here next week? I can't stray too far from Cal, and I would so like to have company."

"But how are the stockings to reach the soldiers?"

"Blockade-runners, just like Seth said."

Lucy glanced at him.

He frowned thoughtfully, contemplating the bowl of his pipe. "The truth of it is, we live in a divided house. But as long as you're making stockings and not bullets, I can't find it in my conscience to object."

"Amy Winslow and Leanna Fiske are knitting for the Union," Lucy informed him. "Polly Fearing told me, though she can't join them because of Albert."

"A knitting war, is it?" He chuckled. "The Union ladies racing the Secesh? I can see it now. Feverish bands of women perspiring over their wool, hair tousled, fingers flying, racing each other to heel and toe amid a clacking of needles. For all we know, the contest may be decided right here in the parlors of San Francisco."

Beth rose from her chair. "It's hardly a cause for levity."

Seth went to her and gave her a hug. "These days we need all the laughs we can scavenge. Don't be afraid to drink your draught with a little sugar, Bethie. And as for your knitting circle, the young ladies are welcome any time."

The War had sprawned a tumult of social activity, though the outnumbered Secesh tended to be discreet about their gatherings. Most of the festivities of the Union sympathizers were held for the benefit of the Sanitary Commission. Thousands upon thousands of dollars flowed eastward to provide food, relief and medical care for the soldiers. Not a week passed without a gala auction, a fair or a theatrical benefit for the Commission. By tacit agreement with Beth, Seth and Lucy did their part, though sometimes, in the midst of the gaiety when Lucy found herself looking out over the jovial whirl, the men with their dapper, snow-white shirts and shining boots and the ladies resplendent in patriotic silks of red, white and blue, she felt a sudden treasonous pang of conscience and prayed that somewhere in the South at that very moment, a woman the spit of herself was dancing on behalf of Nick.

The city continued to swell with the multitude of refugees arriving from the beseiged states to the east. New hotels and houses rose as quickly as hammer and trowel could meet board and brick. Commerce was exuberant, despite the rising prices. Business at the Clay Street store had never been better, Klara told Lucy when she stopped by the Bush Street house one day. "But *ach*, the cost of cotton! Who could imagine it would ever be so dear?"

"The cost of nearly everything," Lucy agreed. "Seth says the skippers are the cause of most of it. They're risking capture by Rebel privateers, so they feel entitled to a higher price for their shipments."

Klara shook her head sadly. "How long, how long?"

"Hush. Here come Bethie and Blanca."

Blanca toddled into the room, tightly clutching Beth's hand. Almost three now, she was demure and dainty, with straight flaxen hair and cheeks so rosy they might have been berry-stained.

"Did you put the baby to bed?" Lucy asked her.

"Yes, ma'am." She rubbed her eyes with her small fists.

Klara rose. "It's time for Blanca's nap, too. We must be going. Blanca, would you like to have a baby of your own to play with?"

"Now?"

"Not now. Soon."

"Klara," Beth asked, "do you mean it? When will it be?"

"In October." She smiled. "Joe is hoping for a boy this time."

"Poor thing," Beth said when Klara had gone. "I dearly love Cal, but I'm not sure I ever want to go through that again."

"You'll change your mind. Nature has a way of helping us women forget."

"Afternoon ladies!" Seth called from the doorway, as he doffed his hat and sent it skimming through the air to land, as it inevitably did, upright on the hall chair.

"I didn't hear you come in." Lucy kissed his cheek. "You're home early."

"That's because Asa Hudson has invited us to a Mozart recital this evening. He wants the three of us to join him."

"Seth, how wonderful!" Beth clapped her hands. "Oh, Mama," she said, looking crestfallen, "I can't, can I, what with the baby and all?"

"If you feed him just before we leave, I'm sure he'll sleep for a few hours. I don't see any harm in it."

"It seems like years since I had an evening out. Land sakes, I must find something to wear!" She sped past them up the stairs to her room.

For Beth to be denied her beloved society was as perverse as forbidding a bird to fly. Her face was incandescent with joy as she took her seat in the hall. Asa Hudson, Lucy noticed with some amusement, made a point of treating Bethie as though she were his peer. Childless and a widower, he had always displayed a certain avuncular fondness for the girl. Now, courtly and gallant, he sought out her opinion on the musical selections, quite as though she were a lady of his own middle years.

"Well?" he whispered to Beth, "did you like the sonata?"

"I thought the left hand a bit weak on the keyboard."

"Ah." He nodded sagely. "Being a pianist, you would know more than I. The only thing these hands can play is *vingt-et-un*."

He was a charming man, Lucy thought, with a singular facility for accommodating himself to the moment. Whether he was discussing the War news with her or business with Seth or passing the time of day with the likes of Amanda Knight, his talk, his tone, even his mien, shifted to suit the occasion as effortlessly as a chameleon changed coloring. He would, she decided, have made a superb salesman, the sort of fellow who could successfully peddle pork among the flock of Temple Emanu-El. Whatever he turned his hand to, it seemed fated to make a profit for him.

"Is he just lucky," Lucy asked Seth over breakfast the next morning, "or very clever?"

465

"Very clever indeed."

"Why hasn't he taken himself another wife, I wonder."

"He has. A wife, mistress and preoccupation."

"His work? Making money?"

Seth nodded. "What do you think of this?" he inquired, sending the *Alta* skating across the table to her place. "The lower left corner."

" 'Petition to Congress to pass a Pacific Railroad Bill,' " she read. She scanned the four paragraphs. "It's signed 'Many Citizens.' You and Asa?"

"Among others."

"And will it pass this time?"

"Unless I miss my guess."

"I should think the government would be calling up all its men and materials for the War."

"My dear, the North has a virtually limitless supply of men and steel. That's its great advantage in the long run."

Lucy held up a hand. "Is that someone at the front door?"

"I'm gettin' it, ma'am," Septimus said from the hall.

Moments later, he returned bearing a visiting card on a small silver tray. "Hiram S. Berry, Esquire, Attorney-at-law," she read. It bore a Washington Street address. Lucy gave Seth a bewildered glance.

"Well, what the devil, show the fellow in, Septimus, and bring another cup and saucer."

"He asked to see Miz' Slade."

"No matter," she told him. "Whatever he has to say, he can tell us both."

She was not sure whether Hiram Berry actually nodded to them as he looked from one to the other, since his head moved constantly, as though he were either nervous or had a tremor. He was a short, thickly built man with an unruly, drooping ivory mustache and a florid complexion. He stood at one of the dining-room chairs, holding the back of it with both hands, like someone about to make a speech.

"Do sit down, Mr. Berry," Seth invited him.

He eased himself into the chair. "It's, um, a matter of some delicacy," he said, addressing his reflection in the mahogany tabletop.

"Then you'd best be out with it."

He cleared his throat. "It concerns the last will and

466

testament of Bertha Rosemary Pitt. I sent you a letter ma'am, but I received no reply."

"But who is—" Lucy stopped short. "My land, you don't mean Queen Rosie, do you?"

"The same. Deceased over a month now. I sent you a letter," he repeated.

"It must have been in one of the packets of mail that were lost in the floods," Seth told her.

"I'm so sorry, Mr. Berry," Lucy said. "I was genuinely fond of the woman."

"And she of you, ma'am. She spoke of you with great respect, said you always treated her like a real lady."

Seth glanced from Lucy to Hiram Berry and back. "Would one of you care to explain?"

Mr. Berry coughed and put his handkerchief to his lips.

"Seth, Queen Rosie was the proprietress of a grand parlor-house on Pike Street." She drew a deep breath. "In fact, I owned the property. I bought it for her soon after the bank run. At the time," she said lamely, "it seemed a wise investment."

Seth regarded her across the table, the hint of a smile at the corners of his mouth. "As an investment," he replied smoothly, "I'm sure it was wise."

"Though not prudent, I'm afraid."

"That's your affair, my dear, not mine."

"Mr. Berry, how did she die?"

"Her heart gave out. It was quick and merciful."

"She was an honest woman and a kind one, an exceptional lady for her trade."

"Yes, ma'am. Which brings me to the business I came to discuss. She directed that her belongings be sold, everything converted to cash. And the money . . ." He paused, fixing Lucy with an apprehensive gaze. "Well, that's yours to dispense."

"Mine!" she said, aghast. "Dear God, whatever did she do that for?"

"For the waifs' home, ma'am, The Good Shepherd. She said, 'You tell Pastora,' begging your pardon, ma'am, 'tell Pastora what to do and she'll do it. She knows how much I love little children.' "

"She did," Lucy said dazedly. "It's true."

"Well, my dear," Seth said, smiling broadly, "I'd say you have an embarrassment of riches on your hands. What kind of bequest are we talking about, Mr. Berry?"

"Ah, about seventy thousand dollars," he murmured, swallowing hard.

"Great heavens!" Lucy exclaimed.

"It was you, my dear, who saw the profit in such an enterprise." Seth's eyes were twinkling with amusement. "What do you plan to do about this pretty predicament?"

Lucy held her head high. "Exactly as Queen Rosie wanted me to." She frowned fleetingly. "Though I do wish I could think of some way to explain such a sum to Father Crowley and the ladies."

"If I may suggest, ma'am, nobody will know it's not your own generosity."

"That wouldn't be right," Lucy told him. "I cannot take credit for someone else's good works."

"An anonymous donor," Seth suggested. "A lady who has gone from the city, leaving a token of affection for it behind her, in your hands."

"Will it work?" she asked.

"Of course." Seth rose from the table. "There's no one to know but ourselves. I trust you'll see to the details, sir."

Lucy stood in the hall, looking after the departed Hiram Berry. "I hardly know what to say, Seth."

He slipped an arm around her waist. "Your chickens have come home to roost, my love. You know, there always was an altogether appealing trace of the strumpet in you."

She flushed deep red. "Seth Slade! How could you say such a thing?"

"And who is in a better position to know?"

"Mama? Seth?" Beth came down the stairs with Cal in her arms. "Did someone just leave? I saw a gentleman from my window."

Lucy looked up at Seth.

For a moment he let her stand there, enjoying her quandary. "Yes, yes," he relented finally, "a business crony, Bethie. Fellow by the name of Berry."

"Oh." She lost interest. "I'll be on the veranda, if you want me, rocking Cal."

Once Queen Rosie's largesse was deposited in the Good Shepherd account at Wells Fargo, there remained only the matter of Lucy's reporting the windfall to the ladies and Father Crowley. She waited until the meeting had come to its end before she made the announcement, carefully repeating Seth's words exactly. There was an outbreak of applause and chatter. Lucy thought she detected a slyly quizzical look on Father Crowley's face and a slight purse to Polly Fearing's lips as she clapped her hands, but perhaps it was merely a passing pang of conscience or her imagination at work. No matter, it was done. The ladies gathered up their things and prepared to leave.

Ada Brock, Naomi's mother, took Lucy aside. "Has there been any word from Nick?"

Lucy glanced quickly around her. Talk about the War was not permitted at their meetings because of divided loyalties. "No. What about Boyd?"

"Nothing. You heard about Pittsburgh Landing."

"Yes."

Ada shook her head sorrowfully. "It's beyond imagining. Over twenty thousand men killed or wounded in a single encounter? How could it be?"

Lucy had no answer.

"We're so worried for Boyd."

Polly Fearing overheard and came to them. She laid a hand on Ada's arm. "It's madness," she said sympathetically. "You have your principles, Ada, and I have mine, but all the same, it's madness. The world's turned upside-down. Time was when my Albert and his brother, Henry were fast friends with William Sherman." She glanced at Lucy for confirmation. "A fine, peace-loving man, William Sherman, a banker. He tried to prevent that awful run on Page and Bacon, and when the Vigilance Committee formed, he was one of the few men brave enough to oppose it." She sighed. "Now, his name cannot be mentioned in our home. What have things come to?' she asked plaintively and turned away.

Ada followed her to the door in silence.

What Polly said was true. Almost nothing made sense in the spectral presence of the War. The spring days lengthened into summer, fair and balmy, fraudulently serene, resplendent with blossoming trees and flowers. Well-dressed, well-fed men and women filled the sunny streets, took their picnics at the cliffs and beaches or promenaded in the pleasant parks and gardens. It seemed to Lucy as if they were all players reciting their expected lines, making the expected gestures, going about their business absurdly oblivious of what was happening beyond the blinding brilliance of their brightly illuminated stage. New Orleans surrendered. Jane Gallagher held a ball for Michael's fiftieth birthday. Yorktown fell. Wah Ming, the fruit vender, brought the first strawberries of the season. Vicksburg was beseiged. Asa Hudson came to dinner.

"Lucy?"

She glanced up from her plate at the sound of Seth's voice.

"Mama," Beth said, "didn't you hear what Mr. Hudson asked Seth?"

"Uncle Asa to you, Bethie," Asa told her. "I was just saying, Lucy, that a pair of gentlemen from Sacramento recently asked me if I thought my friend, Seth Slade, might ever be interested in representing California in the Senate."

"Good grief, what did you tell them?"

"That I'd never discussed politics with Seth. Not precisely the truth, but I thought it the more judicious reply."

Seth folded his napkin. "They've sent you on a fishing expedition, have they?"

"It was all quite casual. I had the impression they were thinking well into the future. Now that the Railroad Bill has passed Congress, we'll need men in Washington who are sympathetic to the railroad interests."

"Not according to Emperor Norton," Seth said. "I ran into him on my way home this evening. Said he'd written President Lincoln not to sign the Railroad Bill. Says it's more important to build a bridge over the Golden Gate first."

"Oh, Seth," Lucy interrupted, "be serious."

"It wouldn't do, my dear, to appear too hungry when, in fact, I'm not. Asa, you may tell those fellows I've never given it any thought. Now I shall. I think that answer is sufficient for the moment."

Lucy contemplated the prospect often in the days that followed, wondering how she would feel if the situation actually presented itself. Senator Slade. The title had a stately cadence. She'd never given a fig for politics or politicians, but Seth was different. He was a man of honor and a man of action. What a thrill it might be to live in Washington, to travel, to be in the very hub of the circles of power. Seth did not broach the subject, so Lucy

470

let it drop, though she did mention it in one of her letters to Abel, since he was so interested in politics.

With the War-caused interruptions in the Overland Mail, correspondence between the two coasts was fitful. Weeks passed without a word from Abel; then, suddenly, a long-delayed pile of letters would arrive all at once. Reading through them, Lucy wondered now and again if she didn't detect a nascent hint of condescension toward the world west of Cambridge, Massachusetts. "The best minds in the country," he wrote, were there. "If only you could see the vast libraries in these homes," Lucy read, "and the fine paintings." The theatre, the concerts, the lectures were all, according to him, superlative. Mr. Emerson himself often came to dine at the Mountfords'. "The table-talk," Abel said, "glides easily from Pliny the Elder to Plato and back to Bacon without a break or hesitation, much less a single opaque stare of ignorance. The ladies, even the younger among them, seem almost as familiar with intellectual concerns as the gentlemen. They are not only well-schooled in such subjects but have teethed, fed and been raised on them since birth, by virtue of the conversations that continually surround them in these homes." Lucy felt a twinge of jealousy toward the hallowed and luminous precincts of the Alvah Mountfords.

"Ah, now," Seth reassured her when she voiced her feelings over dinner one evening, "Abel's just lapping it all up like an eager pup. It's nothing more than enthusiasm." He glanced toward Beth's usual place at the dining table. "Isn't Bethie eating supper?"

"Lin took a tray upstairs for her. The news of the attack on Charleston upset her. Nick's sisters, Regina and Lydia, live there."

"I'd forgotten. You don't seem any too cheerful yourself, my love."

"It's this awful bloody War. And seeing Bethie worry so. And another summer ahead without Abel."

"Blue enough, are you?" He put down his knife and fork. "What do you say to a trip up to the vineyard before the weather gets too hot? Shall we invite Asa to come along? He's jolly good company. How about it, my girl, a little change of scene?"

The mere sight of the valley, so green after the rains

of winter and gaudy with poppies, clover and lupine, was a tonic to her spirits. As Herr Schmidt guided the carriage up the drive beside the rushing stream, Lucy felt the sudden joy of homecoming. This shady land, this glade, these hills were theirs, hers and Seth's. The slopes were alive with lush new growth, exuberant and full of promise. Here, all good things seemed possible.

After supper that first night, Asa pushed his chair back from the table and raised his brandy glass. "To the Pastora Vineyard, my friends. This valley is as lovely a spot as I've ever seen. I wouldn't blame Seth for having bought this place for the sheer beauty of it, and to blazes with making it pay."

Lucy laughed. "Now, Asa, you know Seth better than that. Always a gambler, but never a spendthrift. One of these days, he and Herr Schmidt will be drinking your health with wine from these same hills, just wait and see."

"Seth," he asked, "how much of a return are you expecting to reap?"

"With slightly over twenty acres in cultivation and roughly four hundred vines to the acre, we should eventually harvest about four tons per acre. At a rate of a hundred and fifty gallons the ton, we can hope for twelve thousand gallons a year."

Asa let out a low whistle.

"Eventually," Herr Schmidt emphasized. "It will be many harvests before we reach the maximum. Nature will not be hurried, Mr. Hudson."

"And what sort of stuff will it be?"

"A dry white," Seth told him. "A good, respectable table wine, with a bit of luck and a lot of Herr Schmidt's wizardry."

"No. No magic." Herr Schmidt tapped his forehead. "In here, I have the knowledge, the experience, the intuition."

"First thing tomorrow, Asa, Lucy and I will show you around."

"Splendid." He drained his glass and stood up. "If I may, I'll slip into the kitchen now to thank Chang for this feast. I'll see you at breakfast."

It was still cool as they walked down the path past the bunkhouse. In the distance, the thin patches of morning mist that still hovered over the valley were rapidly dissolving in the sunlight. The coolies were already on the slopes, squatting among the rows of greenery, busy at their labors.

"Hong Hing-wing!" Seth hailed the head coolie, who scrambled to his feet with a respectful bow. "Good work," he said, smiling. "The place looks fine." Seth gestured in a wide arc, taking in the hillside.

"Yes, mistah." Hong nodded rapidly, returning his smile. "See—" He pointed toward the slim new tendrils branching out from the vine beside him, beaming proudly.

"Yes, indeed." Seth clapped him on the shoulder. "Go on." He waved a hand. "We shan't disturb you."

Hong Hing-wing knelt down and examined the recent growth. His calloused hands touched the pale green leaves and shoots with practiced gentleness. Deftly, he pruned away the weaker suckers and tied the hardy canes to the redwood stake beside each vine.

"When will you see the first grapes?" Asa inquired.

"There should be a good scattering of them next season, but they'll have to be removed. These first few years, all the nourishment has to go to strengthen the vines."

"That sun is getting hot." Lucy fanned herself. "Do let's show Asa the caves, Seth."

"Phenomenal," Asa commented as they emerged from the dark corridors and stepped out into the daylight once again. "What's that building going up next to the stable?"

"A three-room cottage for the Schmidts," Seth replied. "Frau Schmidt is expected in September."

"And poor Herr Schmidt is worried half to death to have her sailing while there's a war on. Come," Lucy said, "Chang's made some lemonade. It will be cooler on the veranda."

Chang served them and withdrew, leaving the men to their business talk, with Lucy sitting quietly nearby. Finally, Asa set down his glass and, shading his eyes, looked out over the porch, watching the coolies troop back from the slopes for their noon meal. "They're a diligent race, those Chinee," he said admiringly. "You have to grant them that."

"Speak for yourself," Lucy chided him. "You two

473

have hardly glanced up from your maps and charts all morning."

Thoughtfully, Seth tapped a finger on the folded map in his lap. "Give a look here, Asa. What about this area?"

"It's at the top of my list."

"And the title deeds?"

He chuckled. "Who knows? Some are registered, but a lot of that land is still in *Californio* hands. There's almost no way of unearthing those Mexican and Spanish records, if indeed they ever existed."

Lucy peered over Seth's shoulder. "It looks to me as if you're planning to buy up every foot of available land in the Sacramento Valley. Wouldn't it be easier just to bid for the area along the railroad right-of-way?"

"Not as easy as it sounds," Seth answered. "The government has awarded alternate sections of land to the railroad on either side of the promised route all along the way, and a good portion of it is nothing but mountain and desert. No, my girl, with Sacramento the western terminus, that area will soar in value. The Homestead Act and the War have sent a lot of folks heading westward. My guess is that some of them will keep coming until they reach California, and by then, the railroad will be bringing even more."

"But if that's the case, I should think the owners would be determined to hang onto their land."

"For a while, perhaps," Asa told her. "But the thought of profit is contagious. Once a few of them start boasting about the prices they've gotten for their holdings, the rest will be easy. Most of those *Californios* stand to receive sums of money they can't even count. They'll be thrilled beyond their humble dreams to sell off their land. It's largely a question of timing."

"And you and Seth intend to be there at the right time."

"Indeed we do."

Throughout that summer and into the fall, Seth and Asa traveled from San Francisco to Sacramento half a dozen times between them. They were men after Pa's own heart, Lucy thought. "Buy land," Pa had always said, "buy land." By the time work commenced on the Central Pacific early in January of eighteen sixty-three,

474

Seth's and Asa's holdings would have astonished even a visionary like Pa.

"Aren't you two concerned that you might be putting all your eggs in one basket?" Lucy asked Seth, as she glanced into the mirror above her dressing table and adjusted her earbobs.

"I've an egg or two left hatching on the nest, my dear." He buttoned his silk wasitcoat. "You needn't worry."

"But everything you do seems tied to the railroad. First the stock, then the land, and now you tell me you've subscribed for more stock. What if the venture fails?"

"But it won't," he replied cheerfully, donning his coat. "Besides, a lady wearing diamonds and pearls and a blue silk ball-gown is far too distracting for talk of business. Hurry along, now. Septimus will be waiting downstairs with the carriage."

Lucy rose and picked up her reticule from the table. "I'm ready. Do I pass muster?"

"You look lovely, my Pastora. I intend to dance your toes off, if you'll allow it."

"The Sanitary Commission is welcome to my toes, so long as their ball helps those poor devils in the field. Tell Septimus I'll be along as soon as I say good night to Cal and Beth."

Patriotic fervor, it appeared, had prevailed over a steady drizzle of rain that slicked the cobblestones and trickled down the window panes outside the ballroom. From across the thronged room, Lucy spied Asa making his way toward them, dodging the swirl of skirts and coattails that whipped about the dancing floor.

"Congratulations!" She laughed. "For a moment I was afraid you were going to be swept away."

"As was I. Now that I've risked life and limb to get here, I wonder if you'd spare me Seth's company for a short while. There are some gentlemen present from the state legislature that I want him to meet."

"Now, Asa," Seth replied good-naturedly, "I'm beginning to feel like a prize steer, the way you parade me in front of those fellows."

"These are important men, Seth. They're eager to meet this chap they've heard so much about. They want to invite you to dine with them while they're in town. Lucy, my dear, you don't mind, do you?"

"Of course not. There's Klara Mason." She waved a greeting. "You'll find me chatting with her, unless some gentleman comes along and waltzes me away."

"Do keep me company," she told Klara. "I've scarcely seen you all year, what with our trips back and forth to the vineyard. Where is Joe?"

"In the far corner, I think, dancing with the widow Gibbs. *Ja*, there."

Lucy made out Joe's blonde thatch above that of his pewter-haired partner. "And you, Klara, how are you feeling these days?"

She smiled sadly. "Some days good, some bad. He was such a little baby, and we had him for such a short time, not even eight months. I still see that tiny coffin in my dreams."

"I know how you feel." Lucy took her hand. "I lost one of my own. Bethie's twin."

"But you had a son already. That is what hurts me. Joe wanted a boy so badly."

Lucy changed the subject. "You've been most kind in writing to Frau Schmidt so often this past year. Herr Schmidt told Seth how much she appreciates all your advice."

"*Ach*, the poor woman is so bewildered. In a strange country, not used to its ways, and she with hardly a word of English. She was so disappointed to find that her husband's friend, Krug, was married to an American."

"Your letters have been a great help to her."

"When you told me that she and her husband were alone up there among a pack of Chinamen—Ah, here comes Joe." She beckoned him toward the corner where they sat.

At his side was a stout woman resplendent in plumcolored silk and glittering with onyx. In spite of her wreath of gray hair, Lucy judged her to be no older than herself. There was in her full, round face something vaguely familiar, though perhaps it was simply the similarity of their ages and circumstances.

Joe bent to kiss Lucy's cheek. "Do you know Mrs. Gibbs? She's just moved here from Auburn. Ma'am, may I present Mrs. Seth Slade."

"I'm delighted to meet you." Lucy held out her hand.

After a moment's hesitation, Mrs. Gibbs extended her hand. Their eyes met. As Lucy glanced away, she saw the woman's other arm hanging at her side, withered and stunted. Lucy looked up again slowly. Above the perfunctory semblance of a smile, Nelly One-arm gazed at her with the wary scrutiny of a duelist sighting down his barrel.

Lucy found her voice. "From Auburn, did you say?"

"My husband passed his last months there."

"Do sit down," Klara said, motioning them to a pair of vacant chairs beside Lucy.

Mrs. Gibbs seated herself next to her. "I've heard a good deal about you, Mrs. Slade. Just the other day, someone was speaking of your son. A handsome, dark-complected young man, I'm told, and very bright." Her eyes challenged Lucy. "You must be proud to have such a fine boy."

Nelly knew. Castalia had been too small a town for secrets, just as Lucy had feared. "I am equally proud," she said evenly, "of both my children."

"But you're right about Abel," Joe told the woman. "He's as smart as they come. Gone off to Harvard College, he has."

"You don't say." Nelly opened her fan and fluttered it daintily at her bosom.

"My dear!" Seth hailed Lucy from the outskirts of the crowd. "Shall we have a dance?" He came to them and kissed Klara. "Hallo, there, my boy." He shook Joe's hand heartily.

Lucy rose. "Seth, allow me to introduce Mrs. Gibbs. She's new to the city."

Seth bowed. "I trust you find it to your liking, ma'am."

"I do indeed. I was just having a most pleasant conversation with your wife about young Abel. An exceptional boy, from all I hear."

"He is that. And now, if you'll excuse us—" He smiled. Taking Lucy's arm, he led her toward the dancing floor. "That was a nice compliment."

"It was not a compliment, Seth," Lucy said quietly. "She was striking a bargain."

He gave her an odd look.

"She was threatening me. And Abel too. What you heard was blackmail. Walk me to the refreshment table, and I'll tell you about our Mrs. Gibbs."

He drew thoughtfully on his pipe as she spoke.

". . . And now, evidently Abner's dead, and she's come

477

here to play the rich and respectable dowager. Seth, tell me you don't think she'd stoop so low as to spread stories about Abel."

"She won't, as long as she's sure of your silence."

"I suppose I shall have to toady up to her to reassure her." She gave a grim smile. "Stupid woman. If she knew more about me, she'd realize I'd be the last person to want to rake up anyone's past. My own is none too sterling."

"I shall make a point of asking her to dance and telling her how charming you found her. That ought to set her mind at rest."

Lucy took his hands in hers. "My dearest, how did I ever make do before you came alone? Does it annoy you, always rescuing me and the children from one scrape or another?"

"There's no greater appreciation than being thought indispensable, my love."

"You are, you know," she said softly. "Sometimes that frightens me."

"Great heavens, woman, you are in a dark mood. How can you be glum in the midst of all this gaiety?"

"I don't know." She hesitated. "Sometimes it rings so hollow. We prance about at parties and balls as though there were nothing amiss in the world, while every day hundreds of women like myself see their husbands and sons sacrificed to the cause." She grimaced. "How I hate that phrase, 'the cause.' It's so chaste and sanitary and smug. When I think how I would feel to lose you—"

"Stop it." Seth took her by the shoulders. "This isn't like you, Lucy."

She looked up at him, her eyes brimming. "Until I met you, I never really knew what a risk it was to love a man."

"Listen to me, Lucy, and don't ever forget what I say. Seize every bit of happiness that falls to you and enjoy it without guilt and without apology. The wheel turns soon enough, my girl, and the bad times come when you least expect them." He handed her his handkerchief. "Fretting about the future only sours the present. Let tomorrow be. Come now, let's dance."

She wondered, afterward, if it had been a premonition, some inexplicable sense of foreboding that had intruded upon the festivities to warn her of bad tidings.

Two days after the ball, Beth at last received a letter from Nick, a crumpled envelope, one corner torn, the penciled address smudged and barely legible. Nick's brother, Gwin, was dead.

"How did he die?"

"All he said was 'killed near Fredericksburg some weeks ago.' "

"And Nick's sisters?" Lucy asked her.

"Evacuated from Charleston and gone inland to stay with friends. He said there's no use trying to tell me what it's like. Sometimes when there's a quiet night, he wonders about me and the baby."

"When was the letter written?"

"The end of June." Beth glanced down at the folded pages in her lap. "On the road north to Pennsylvania."

"Bethie!"

"I know, Mama. But he didn't mention Gettysburg by name. He could have been going somewhere else," she said, "couldn't he?"

XXV

"BETHIE," LUCY called from the library, "come let me have a look at you before you go." She closed her book at the sight of her. "Land, what a pretty dress. Do turn around."

The violet velvet of her dress and the sleek coils of jet-black hair set off Beth's creamy skin to perfection. What a stunner she is, Lucy thought, sloe-eyed and long-lashed, the full lips parted expectantly, waiting for a word of approval. "Yes," Lucy said.

"Yes?"

She gave a disconcerted laugh. "I was thinking how beautiful you are, my darling daughter. Violet suits you. What's the occasion this afternoon?"

"Martha Mason's eighteenth birthday. Mrs. Morse is giving her a tea."

"Is that the mother of the boy Polly told me about? She said Martha had a serious suitor."

Beth made a face. "Nathan Morse. He's in the grain business with his father."

"That sounds perfectly respectable. Why the grimace?"

"He's dull. Naomi says if Martha marries him, it's only because she doesn't want to bother to change the initials embroidered on her underclothing. Where's Septimus? He's supposed to drive me."

"He went to post some letters. He ought to be back any time."

Beth glanced at the book on Lucy's lap, tilting her head to see the title on its spine. *Poems?*

"By Mr. Emerson. It's one of the books Abel sent me."

"For pity's sake, doesn't he know we have bookshops

480

here? He'll end up a pauper, the way he sends books all the way from Cambridge."

"I get the distinct impression that he feels he's doing missionary work among the Philistines." She sighed. "Nevertheless, I intend to have at least a nodding acquaintance with these idols of his by the time he comes home. I'll be hanged if I'll stand in the shadow of those Mountford ladies."

Beth gave a derisive laugh. "I wouldn't let him have the satisfaction."

"There's Septimus now. Run along, Bethie, and give Martha a kiss for me."

Lucy opened her book and glanced down at the page. From upstairs came the sound of little Cal's voice, shrilling merrily at some diversion of Li Lin's. Lucy looked upward, smiling. Always, in all her dreams and hopes for this house, she had heard the treble of childish laughter, the sound of Beth's and Abel's children at play. She sat there for a moment, basking in her contentment, watching the afternoon sunlight trickling down the library wall like a splash of molten gold.

"Miz' Slade! Miz' Slade! Come quick!" Septimus was shouting. "It's Miss Bethie! She's took ill!"

Lucy threw the book on the desk and ran from the room. "Where is she?"

"Out front. She was walkin' to the carriage, readin' her letter, and—"

"Never mind. Give me a hand."

At the sight of her, Lucy let out a cry. Beth lay by the side of the street, beneath the open door of the carriage, fallen like a heap of crushed violet petals limply stirring in the wind. But it was only the movement of the breeze playing at her skirts. She was unconscious, the color drained from her flesh. Lucy cradled her in her arms, frantically stroking her face. "Bethie, Bethie, what's happened?"

"Let me, ma'am." Septimus bent down and slid his arms under Beth's body. Tenderly he lifted her.

"Take her into the sitting room, Septimus, to the window seat. I'll fetch the smelling salts."

Lucy raised Beth's head from the cushions and held the phial to her nostrils. "In the name of God, Septimus, what happened out there?"

"Like I told you, she jes' made an awful sound and fell. The letter—"

"What letter? Where is it?"

He looked bewildered. "Maybe the wind took it?"

"Find it! Go after it!" she said, as Beth gasped and moaned faintly. "Go!" she cried, "the wretched thing must be out there somewhere. Bethie? Can you hear me?" Gently, she massaged the girl's temples. "My dearest, what is it?"

Beth's eyelids fluttered and opened. Her gaze was scalded with pain. Hot tears trickled down her face, wetting Lucy's fingertips. Lucy drew out her handkerchief and pressed it to her.

"It's Nick," Beth whispered, the words half lost in a sob.

"Tell me."

Her voice trembled. "He was wounded and taken prisoner."

Lucy clasped Beth's hands in hers and held them tightly. "Wounded how? Where is he?"

"I don't know . . ." She shook her head. "Yes, now I remember. He's in the United States Army Hospital in Chester, Pennsylvania. But he didn't say what had happened to him. Or maybe it was in the letter, I didn't finish it. Where is it?"

"Septimus went looking for it. He thinks it was blown away when you fell."

"Oh, Mama," she cried.

"Yes, yes," she murmured, taking the girl into her arms and holding her close, "weep, my darling. Get it all out. And then, just think how fortunate you are that he was spared. He's safe now, out of the War. Wounds heal, Bethie. At least now you know where he is. In spite of everything, there's still so much to be thankful for." Lucy stroked her hair and rocked her as she wept, until, at length, Beth drew apart from her.

"I want to go to Cal."

"Of course, dear." Lucy helped her up.

"Ma'am." Septimus stood in the doorway, shaking his head in futility. "Ain't no letter anywheres you look. Only the good Lord knows where she's got to. I'm sorry, Miss Beth, but she's blowed away. Gone."

"It's all right, Septimus," Lucy told him. "You tried. Bethie, now that you know where Nick is, you can write to him yourself. Lie down now and rest. I'll send a note to Martha, explaining why you missed her tea."

"Ma'am," Septimus said, "I near forgot. There's a letter come for you, too." He withdrew the envelope from his pocket and handed it to her. "You want me to stay here whilst you read it?" he asked apprehensively.

"No." She smiled, looking at the writing on the envelope. "It's only from Mister Abel. But thank you, Septimus."

Lucy sat in the window seat, gazing down at Abel's meticulous hand, his letters marching erectly across the pages, like stalwart ranks of soldiers, determined and firm in their purpose. His stubbornness shows in his penmanship, she thought sourly. She held the letter up to the waning light from the window and read it over again for the fourth or fifth time. She had lost count.

"President Hill of Harvard and Mr. Mountford both agree . . ."

"Pastora?" Seth's voice rose over the sound of the front door closing.

"In here."

"Great days, woman, why are you hiding alone in the shadows like a praire dog in a hole?" He lit a lamp, then glanced at her. "Lucy, what's wrong?"

"There's mixed news and bad news. Take your pick."

Seth went to her and sat down, slipping an arm around her. "Better break the worst to me."

"Nick's been wounded and captured. We don't know the details because Bethie collapsed on the street in a faint and the damnable letter blew away. All we know is that he's in a Union Army hospital in Pennsylvania."

"Praise God he's alive," he said quietly. "How is she taking it?"

"Last time I looked in on her, she'd cried herself to sleep. Seth . . ." She handed him Abel's letter. "Have a look at this."

He read it slowly, then folded the pages and gave it back to her. "It means he'd be gone at least another two years."

"At least! Why 'at least'?"

"He graduates next spring, and if he remains there to attend the law school—"

"Which he's determined to do—"

"That's a two-year course of studies, sometimes longer, depending on whether or not he pursues some special field. Lucy, I know how you must feel."

"It would give me great pleasure to knock President Hill's and Alvah Mountford's heads together for encouraging this."

"Obviously they wouldn't have, if they didn't think he had the stuff."

"I know," she said resignedly. "We have no choice but to agree, and Abel knows it, too. Even if we didn't, what could we do? What with Bethie and the baby here and all the problems of traveling in the midst of a war, we can't even attend his graduation, much less swoop down on Cambridge and snatch him away."

"You wouldn't do that anyway. He's making something of himself, that boy. You're going to be very proud of him, Lucy."

"If I ever set eyes on him again. He begins to sound like a stranger to me even now, full of intellectual airs and flaunting refinement like a two-bit harlot."

"I can understand your being angry, but don't be angry with Abel. I'm the one who started all this in the first place. Blame me."

Lucy glanced up at him sharply. "Believe me, I do. The devil of it is that I both hate you and love you for it at the same time. I despise having my feelings pulled this way and that."

"You've had a bad day, my dear. Let me fetch you a glass of sherry for your nerves." He took out his watch and looked at it. "It's almost suppertime. Perhaps Beth would like to join us. Let's put this law school business out of our minds and concentrate on cheering her up."

Beth's face was puffy from weeping and sleep when she joined them. Seth handed her a glass of sherry and raised his own. "To Nick's speedy recovery and homecoming."

"He isn't coming home," she said disconsolately. "He's a prisoner."

Lucy reached over and took her hand. "No misery lasts forever, dear."

"Perhaps he'll be exchanged," Seth suggested.

"But that would only mean he'd be back in the South. I want him here. I want to see for myself that he's all right."

"In time, Bethie," Seth told her, "in time."

Lucy changed the subject. "Beth, how do you feel about Cal's birthday party? Shall we go through with it as we intended?"

"You must," Seth said. "Our sorrows shouldn't interfere with the pleasures of an innocent child."

"Yes," Lucy agreed, "and after all, it's his first real birthday celebration. He was too young to understand last year, but now that he'll be two, it will mean something to him. You must start planning, Bethie."

Beth looked from Lucy to Seth. "You're telling me I should try to keep my thoughts occupied with other things."

"Bethie," Seth addressed her firmly, "it won't do Nick a dime's worth of good for you to torture yourself. I don't give a hang what you find to occupy your mind. That is," he added, giving her an encouraging grin, "so long as it's lawful and decent. All I care about is seeing you get through your days without suffering. Shall we make a pledge to present a cheerful facade? God knows this house needs brightening."

Cal knelt on the drawing room carpet, oblivious of the fact that he was the center of attention. He clapped his hands with glee as Blanca Mason yanked the string on the top she had brought him, sending it reeling across the marble hearth to rest finally at Asa Hudson's feet. Cal scrambled up and ran to Asa, his arms outstretched. Asa scooped him into his lap and placed the top in his small, chunky hands. "Now, Cal, aren't you going to open your other presents? Blanca, my pet, fetch me that parcel on the table next to Father Crowley." Asa gave the boy a hug and jounced him on his knees. "Trot, trot to Boston and trot, trot to Lynn . . ."

Cal squealed delightedly, knowing what was coming.

"Watch out, little one, you don't fall—in!" Asa spread his knees wide, sliding Cal toward the floor, catching him just in time.

Beth laughed. "Uncle Asa, you're the last man in the world I'd expect to hear reciting nursery rhymes."

"I'll have you know," he said, fixing her with a glare of mock offense, "that I was once a rather adorable child myself. Granted, not as adorable as this lad, but I was quite the darling in my day."

"A likely tale," Seth retorted genially. He raised the decanter in his hand. "Anyone running dry? Polly? Albert?"

Albert Fearing held up his glass. "Go on, Cal. Open your Uncle Asa's gift. Then you may have ours."

Asa cut the string with his penknife, and Cal tore at the wrappings impatiently. "Mama," he crowed, "a drum, a drum!"

Beth clapped her hands to her ears. "Uncle Asa, how could you?"

"Ah, but it's not just any drum." He tapped his fingertips on the painted tin surface. "Watch, Cal." Asa reached into his pocket and withdrew a gold coin. He placed it in the boy's hand. "Put it in the slot. That's the boy. Hear it rattle? Every time you put a coin in, the drum will make a different noise."

"Leave it to you, Asa," Lucy said, "to set the boy on the path of capitalism. Here, Cal, give me the drum and go see what Aunt Polly and Uncle Albert and Martha have brought you."

"And Nathan," Martha took her fiancé's hand. "It's from Nathan, too."

Alas, Lucy thought, Nathan was indeed as colorless as Bethie had described him. He was curiously staid and fusty for such a young man and seemed at a loss in the face of their frivolity.

"Joe, look at that! What a clever thing." Klara Mason watched as Cal, his face grave with concentration, cranked the toy Albert had given him. As he turned the handle, a pair of loose-jointed acrobats, suspended between two posts, somersaulted wildly about, their wooden limbs flying through the air. Li Lin jumped off her chair and ran to Cal's side for a closer look.

Cal placed the toy in her lap.

What a sweet child he is, Lucy reflected, an amiable and generous cherub of a boy, with his thick, golden curls and fair skin. He had Nick's coloring, down to the hazel eyes, though Bethie showed in the shape of his features. What a handsome young man he would be one day. Lucy caught sight of Joe Mason's face, intently gazing at the boy with a look of melancholy so painful that her breath caught in her throat.

"Now, my lad," Father Crowley called across the room

to Cal, "you come here and sit on an old man's knee. Let's see what I have hidden behind these robes."

"More presents?" Cal asked Beth, his eyes wide with amazement.

"More presents."

"Ah," said Polly Fearing, "the innocent wonder of childhood. What a tonic for the spirits."

"Ma'am," Septimus addressed Lucy from the doorway. "Biddy says dinner's ready when you are."

"We've only a few more gifts to open, Septimus. It won't take long."

"Yes'm." He lingered there, a proud, patriarchal smile on his face, watching Cal unwrap the priest's gift.

It was a brightly painted toy ark. Father Crowley lifted the roof, and Cal peered inside.

"Ooh." He scooped up a handful of carved animals.

"Father," Beth said, "how very sweet of you."

"And a gentle reminder," Lucy put in, "to teach the boy his Scripture. Wherever did you find such a charming gift, Father?"

"The work of a penitent soul, Pastora. A poor sot of a seaman made it while trying to distract himself from the demon rum. His hands shook like a halyard in a gale, though you'd never guess it from the workmanship." He set Cal on the floor. "Now, I must be on my way."

"I'm sorry you won't stay for dinner." Lucy rose. "Septimus, will you hitch up the carriage and drive the Father back? Lin and Biddy can do the serving."

Father Crowley brushed the suggestion aside. "No, no. I'll walk part way and then catch the street railway. The exercise will do me good. Stay where you are, Pastora. I'll see myself to the door. Ladies and gentlemen," he said, giving them a wave, "blessings on you all."

"Now," Naomi Stevens spoke up, "I believe it's my turn." She proferred a white-wrapped package to Cal.

Naomi looked tense, Lucy thought. The weeks and months without word from Boyd were beginning to tell on her. Which was worse, she wondered, knowing nothing or knowing, like Beth, that your husband lay wounded and a prisoner-of-war? Quickly, she caught herself and gave Naomi a cheerful smile.

"Hanged if it isn't Dan'l Boone himself!" Seth exclaimed. "Let me have a look, son." He held the doll at

487

arm's length for inspection. "The coonskin cap, the buck-skins, even a pair of little moccasins."

"Septimus," Beth asked, "would you bring those last two gifts from the library?"

From Beth there was a red wooden cart, painted with blue letters. One side read "Calvert" and the other "Stevens." Cal hauled it happily around the room, loading it with his new toys.

"And ours, Septimus," Lucy told him.

Cal dropped the handle of the cart with a clatter and let out a joyful squeal at the sight of the tall, brown-and-white rocking horse with its leather bridle and shining stirrups. He grasped the horsehair mane as Septimus set him upon it. Taking the reins, he whooped with pleasure as he lurched to and fro.

Nathan Morse, Martha's beau, at last allowed himself the extravagance of a smile.

"Come now," Lucy said, "we mustn't keep Biddy waiting any longer."

Seth lifted the protesting boy from his mount and set him on his shoulders. "You may ride all you like tomorrow. Right now, it's into your highchair for dinner."

Asa took Naomi and Beth on each arm. "Ladies, I wonder if I could interest you in coming to the theatre with me next week. That is, if you don't mind having such an elderly escort."

Lucy smiled. Asa had gone out of his way to buoy Beth's spirits since the news about Nick. He had taken her and Cal on outings. He brought books to Bethie and trinkets to the boy and romped on all fours after him, making ferocious sounds that sent the scampering child into peals of skittish laughter. He had all but become a member of the family, taking Beth and Cal under his wing and boosting the spirits of the household considerably.

"Seth," Joe Mason inquired, taking his place at the table, "how's your vineyard coming along?"

"Herr Schmidt's a little concerned about the sparse rainfall. So far this season there's scarcely been enough to moisten the ground.

"The poor man," Beth said with a laugh. "Last year he was all but washed away, and now he's talking about the possibility of having to irrigate by hand if things don't improve."

"What will you do about the vineyard," Joe asked, "if you go off to Washington?"

Seth glanced up, surprised. "Washington?"

Joe looked around the table. "Have I spoken out of turn? I'd heard some talk that you were being considered for the Senate."

"I guess it's no secret," Asa said affably. "The Sacramento bunch thinks very highly of our host."

"But nothing's come to the boil yet," Seth put in. "I've a meeting with Governor Low next month. I should know more after that."

Lucy noticed that Naomi, Beth and Albert had pointedly withdrawn from the discussion. Martha met her gaze with an uneasy look.

"I know so little about politics," Martha apologized.

Lucy took the cue. "Then we shan't discuss them. After all, this is a party, not a conference. You must tell us about your wedding plans, Martha."

As the girl spoke, Lucy nodded occasionally and glanced now and then at Nathan, who seemed resigned to the arrangements, less a participant than an accessory. Still, anything was preferable to awakening the antagonisms that lay so shallowly beneath the flow of conversation. These days, Lucy thought, one was forced to make one's way so gingerly through any gathering that mixed Secesh and Union, that one might as well be fording a perilous river strewn with slippery rocks. Regardless of the festivities, she always found herself, at the last, exhausted and relieved to have reached shore without a mishap.

The house was quiet. Septimus padded about the dining room, wiping the last cake crumbs from the table. Lucy rubbed her eyes wearily and picked up Cal's Dan'l Boone doll from the hearth where he had abandoned it. She stood by the firelight, fingering the buckskin fringe.

Seth came in from the library with a glass of whiskey. "Tired?"

"A bit. It's a strain. I guess we're all prisoners of the War, in a way."

"It went well, though I do think Joe tends to bait Albert once in a while. Come and sit down, my dear." He moved to make a place for her next to him on the sofa. "What have you there?"

489

"The doll." She looked down at it. "It reminds me of someone I knew. The clothes, the moccasins, even the leather face. He looked like that." She laid the toy on the table beside her. "He was Abel's father, Luther Moore. It's been sixteen years since Luther died, yet it might as well be a century. Watching Cal this evening, it occurred to me that this year had flown by me. The months are blurred. They've darted by as swiftly as hummingbirds. I sense them passing, yet it seems I can't catch them and hold them in sight."

"When I was a boy, a single summer seemed forever. I suppose it's all a matter of growing older." He took her hand in his. "I have a small present for you, my dear."

"For me?"

"It's a little something to make you smile." He rose. "I have to go out to the carriage house. I'll be back in a moment."

"Seth?" Lucy looked up as he returned bearing two large, burlap-wrapped bundles.

"Roses for my girl. This way, you shall always have flowers, year after year. I thought we'd plant them by the porch."

Smiling, she touched the thorny stems. "What color will they be?"

"White."

"My favorite roses. You knew that."

"They're climbers. With luck, they'll grow up the porch pillars and perfume the whole house."

"I want them under our bedroom window."

"Wherever you wish, my dear." Seth kissed her. "We shall plant them together tomorrow."

Lucy took his hand in hers. For a moment, they sat in silence, their fingers locked, looking into each other's eyes. Then, without a word, they rose and went upstairs.

It was an unusually dry winter, marked by fair and unseasonably warm days. Lucy looked out over the railing of the veranda to where Cal played contentedly with Lin in the shade of a pine tree. From where she sat, she could see Seth's rosebushes soaking up the afternoon sun and the watering she had just given them. She took pleasure in tending her flowers and shrubs, even in the weeding and watering and pruning. There was something

490

deeply satisfying in the work. Oddly, she found more joy in the doing than in the results of her chores. Perhaps that was what had kept Pa going, year after year, despite the crops that failed. Poor though he was, he had left her a legacy more durable than any fortune. He had encouraged her to sow hopes. He had willed her his stubborn determination and his love of the land. Even here, in the city, it was not the grand theatres and halls or the splendid new mansions on Rincon Hill that touched a chord in her. Rather, it was the full, sinuous shape of the hills themselves, the sight of the low-lying sandspits, the harsh rocks and cliffs and the misted heights across the bay that stirred her. Always, it was the land.

She was alone on the porch. Bethie was at the Good Shepherd, teaching her needlework class, and Seth was in the drawing room, meeting with half a dozen bankers and businessmen from San Jose, whom Asa had brought to call. From the open windows, she could hear the low chirring of their conversation. These meetings had occurred more frequently with the passing weeks. Though Seth was usually reticent about his affairs, Lucy could tell that the increasing enthusiasm on his behalf had struck a spark in him. The possibility of going to Washington seemed more real now than ever. Lucy glanced over the lawn, the shrubs, the hedges and trees and felt a sudden prescient pang of homesickness.

Lucy was restless after Seth and Asa set off for Sacramento. She found it difficult to concentrate on the business of the household. They were to be gone only a matter of days, but even so Seth's absence seemed to have left her in a sort of suspended animation, unable to see ahead or to plan or even to imagine what their future might hold. Their lives hung in the balance, until the legislature gave or refused its encouragement. There was no way to sense which direction the wind might blow. For the moment, Lucy was in the doldrums, at the mercy of an inertia that was both unaccustomed and unsettling. Not since she had cast her lot with Caleb Bates had her own fate depended so completely on someone else's. It was, she thought ruefully, the single aspect of marriage which clashed with her temperament. Not that she begrudged Seth his prospects. Nothing would make her prouder than to see him honored with the rank and esteem he so richly deserved. Yet how different things would be. They had always been partners, she and Seth. She wondered how she might feel as a mere accessory to his career, living vicariously through his pursuits, playing the modest, subordinate wife, compliant and decorous. She regarded the niceties of etiquette much as she regarded displays of affection. They were gestures to be freely and generously given out of the truth of one's feelings, not payments to be made upon demand. Silently, she damned that stubborn, rebellious streak in herself that longed to revolt against the strictures of propriety. The devil take it. She had toed the mark before, for Beth's and Abel's sakes, and she would do the same for Seth. If the fates were determined to contrive a proper lady from this flesh and blood, she would suffer the consequences with a dutiful smile, and Seth would never be the wiser. Whatever happened, it was his happiness and tranquillity that mattered most to her, for the blunt truth remained that, equals or not, they were one, and any distress of his was hers also.

Lucy sat in the library, unable to concentrate on the book in her lap. Seth was due back by nightfall. She listened to the grandfather clock strike the half hour and closed her book with an impatient slap.

Septimus tapped at the open door. "You've a caller, ma'am."

Lucy took the visiting card from him, read it and looked up slowly. "She's here?"

"In the sittin' room. I put her in there because Miss Bethie's practicin' at her piano in the big room. Biddy's got the kettle on for tea. You want me to set the tray for two?"

"No," she replied sharply. After a moment, she relented. "Yes, hang it all, go ahead, Septimus, but tell Biddy not to go to any bother."

Nelly One-arm had made herself comfortable in the bay window seat. Lucy remained standing. "To what do I owe the honor of this visit, Nelly?"

"Eleanor. I prefer Eleanor."

"As you wish."

"It's a nice home you have here."

"We like it."

"I've just bought the Sanborn place on Rincon Hill."

Lucy's surprise showed, in spite of herself. "Indeed. A

rather grand establishment for a lone woman. Abner must have done very well."

"I believe you know the folks who live next door to the Sanborn house. Their name is Winslow."

"Amy and Warren. Yes, I know them."

"She's been right neighborly. A very gracious lady."

Lucy smiled wryly at the picture of Amy Winslow welcoming Nelly One-arm to Rincon Hill.

"She mentioned she knew you. She said you were the one who'd founded the waifs' home where she does her charity work."

"She gives me too much credit. There were a number of us who saw the need for such a place."

"She said she sees you quite often, at the meetings of the ladies of the Good Shepherd."

"Ah, there you are, Septimus," Lucy said as he entered with the tea tray. "Set it there, if you will. I'll call if I need anything."

"Mrs. Winslow also told me your boy's going to take up the law."

"Do you take milk and sugar in your tea?"

"Just a bit of milk. You must be pleased with the way he's advanced himself."

"Molasses cake?" Lucy handed her the teacup and saucer and waited while Nelly selected a particularly large portion of cake.

Nelly took a bite and licked the crumbs from her fingertips. "The law is such a dignified and respectable profession, don't you think?" She didn't wait for a reply. "A lawyer's reputation is so important. His background has to be immaculate, everything aboveboard, if you follow me."

Lucy set her cup and saucer down with a clatter. "You may stop prancing about like a trained bear, Nelly. I see your fangs quite clearly. Come to the point."

"Ah, well . . ." She smiled smugly into her teacup. "One good turn deserves another, as they say."

"Just what sort of a good turn did you have in mind?"

"It's difficult, you know, moving to a new place, not knowing many folks there. Being admitted to society—"

"At last." Lucy laid her napkin on the tea tray. "I should have seen it before. Rincon Hill, Amy Winslow, the Good Shepherd. It's all quite plain to me now, thank you."

493

"The ladies' society of the Good Shepherd Home is highly thought of."

"And what will you be wanting next," Lucy retorted, "a pound of flesh?"

Nelly's dark eyes were as hard as two jet beads. "You already know what I want. It's not much to ask, considering . . ."

"Suppose," Lucy said evenly, "you were to do your worst. Why would anyone believe your gossip? People hereabouts know Abel better than they know you."

"There are others who know. When I left Castalia, there were still your friends there, White Russell and Celia Beal."

"Celia would never harm Abel, nor me either, for that matter."

"She's a senile woman who rattles on about the past, and White Russell's a bitter old man who talks too much when he's in his cups. The story's made the rounds often enough. You know as well as I do that even an empty rumor can scotch a reputation, let alone one with the ring of truth to it."

"Frankly, Nelly, I don't care a hang whether or not you join the ladies of the Good Shepherd, if you're willing to give your money and your time. The only issue that matters to me is my son's future."

"Then you'll see to it that—"

"I didn't say that. How am I to know you won't come sniffing about for some other favor?"

"Like Abner used to say, 'I've never dealt from the bottom of the deck. I lay my cards out fair and square.'"

"You expect me to take your word that this will be the last of it?"

"The way I see it, you don't have a choice. But you have my word, if it counts for anything to you."

Lucy stood up. "I expect full value for my transactions."

Nelly rose and faced her. "You always did, as I recall."

"You neglected to mention Doctor Pierce. I want to know what became of Reed."

Nelly gazed at her complacently. "I was waiting for you to ask. The woman finally gave up the ghost, almost three years ago now. Not a week later, that old Indian of Pierce's, Captain Wally, he died too. The doctor just packed his things and closed up his place without a good-

494

bye to anyone. Folks said he went back to his people in Virginia. You never had any word of him?"

"It wouldn't have mattered," she said quietly. "Times change. People change. I was only curious. I believe your cape is in the hall."

Nelly donned her cloak and drew it about her. "It's been a most agreeable afternoon. I look forward to seeing more of you and, of course, the other ladies." She gave Lucy a full-toothed smile.

At the sight of Beth emerging from the drawing room, the lupine smile disappeared. "Your daughter?" she said hesitantly.

"This is Mrs. Gibbs, Beth."

"Yes," Nelly said quickly, "I believe we might have met once or twice when you were a small child." She searched Beth's face for a glimmer of recognition. "But I can see," she continued smoothly, "that it was much too long ago for you to remember."

"I'm sorry, ma'am."

"Don't be," Lucy told her. "Believe me, it's quite all right."

"Mama, is Seth coming home tonight?"

"He's supposed to arrive in time for supper. At any rate, that was his intention. If you'll excuse us, I'll show Mrs. Gibbs to the door."

"Lucy, my dear, you must call me Eleanor."

"Eleanor." She enunciated each syllable with ill-concealed reluctance.

"That poor woman," Beth said, looking after her. "How sad to have been born misshapen like that. She must feel so helpless."

Lucy made a derisive noise. "Mrs. Gibbs is as helpless as a hungry coyote."

"You don't like her?"

"I make it my business to tolerate her." She paused, listening. "It's someone on the porch. You don't suppose she's come back, do you?" With a sigh, Lucy opened the door. "Seth!"

"Don't look so surprised, my dear. I live here." He took off his hat and tossed it on the hall chair.

"Mama thought you were someone else."

"Yes." He turned to Lucy. "I saw the widow Gibbs getting into her carriage. What was she after?"

"She wants me to give her a leg up into local society."

"Wonderful," he said drily. "I can think of few things more amusing than to see those hidebound ladies clasp her to their bosoms."

"Seth." Lucy laid a hand on his arm. "You must have news." She gave Beth a meaningful look, and the girl tactfully headed for the stairs.

"Yes." He extracted his pipe and tobacco pouch from his pocket. "I have news of a sort."

Lucy followed him into the drawing room and seated herself on the sofa opposite his chair. "Land sakes, Seth, don't keep me in suspense like this."

"I've decided against it."

"What?"

He tamped his brier abstractedly.

"But I thought your mind was made up. What with all the support and encouragement you've received—"

"I had a long talk with Governor Low."

"And he dissuaded you? How could he? On what grounds? He ought to know how well you'd serve the state. Everyone else seems to agree that you'd be a great asset in the senate. How could one man change your mind, even if he is the governor?"

Seth drew on his pipe and pitched his spent match into the ash-bed on the hearth. "The governor brought up certain issues and considerations that he felt I'd overlooked. He was very persuasive. I saw the sense in what he said."

"And what's that?" Lucy shook her head in bewilderment. "What on earth were his arguments?"

"Political opinions," he said tiredly, rubbing a hand across his eyes, "internecine elements."

"I don't understand this, Seth. Does his word carry so much weight? I thought senators were chosen by the state legislature. Why, for months now all those gentlemen from up and down California have—"

"Lucy," he said brusquely, "I've made my decision."

She looked at him in silence for a moment. Quietly, she asked, "How does Asa feel about this?"

"He's disappointed. He's irritated. I think he liked being the power behind the proposed throne. He enjoys all that strategy and plotting and subtlety. It's his game."

"Did he attend your meeting with the governor?"

Seth nodded and rose from his chair. "My dear, it's been a very long day. I've been up since before dawn. If

496

you'll forgive me, I think I'll forgo supper and go to bed early."

She frowned. "Seth, aren't you feeling well?"

"I could use some rest, that's all."

"Shall I have Septimus bring a tray up to you?"

He dismissed the suggestion with a wave. "I'm not hungry."

"Perhaps later . . ."

"Perhaps." He turned from her, taking his hat from the chair in the hallway, and made his way upstairs.

He did not wake when she came to bed. In the morning, when she woke, he had already dressed and gone down to breakfast. Lucy came to the table as he was folding his napkin and pushing back his chair. He stood up and kissed her on the forehead.

"You're leaving so early?" she asked.

"I've been away most of the week. There's work piled up at the office."

"Why don't you ask Asa to join us this evening?"

"I believe he said something about going to a concert. We'd best make it another time."

"Whatever you say, my love." Lucy sat down and glanced at the newspaper beside her place. When she heard Seth close the front door, she pushed it aside, unread.

To be truthful, she was somewhat relieved that their lives would not be uprooted by a move to Washington. Still, it might have been an adventure. What puzzled her was the oddly abrupt, impassive way Seth had dismissed the idea after giving it so much of his time and thought. It wasn't like him to take up anything without pursuing it to its limits. When Seth bothered to devote his efforts to something, he saw it through, patiently and determinedly, to its very end. Yet a single meeting with Governor Low had completely reversed his thinking.

It was several days before she found a moment alone with Asa Hudson. Lucy watched him chatting with John and Leanna Fiske across the Winslows' drawing room. When he moved aside to put out his after-dinner cigar, she approached him.

He turned and started.

"I didn't mean to creep up on you, Asa."

"A most pleasant surprise, Pastora."

497

She gave him a curious look. "You never called me that before."

"No? I must have picked it up from Seth. You're not offended, are you?"

"No. But don't let Bethie hear you use it. My children abhor that name."

"And why is that?"

"Ah, well," she said, "you know how it is with children. They can be peevish about the most insignificant things. By the way, Seth told me about your meeting with the governor."

Asa seemed taken aback. "He did?"

"Do let's find a place to sit down."

He followed her to a damask-covered bench in front of the fireplace. "And what did he say?"

"He was vague about it, but I gathered the governor put forth some political considerations that changed his mind."

"Quite so. Nothing for a woman to trouble her pretty head about." Asa took his watch from his waistcoat pocket, opened it and glanced at the dial.

"Am I keeping you from something?"

"Beg pardon?" He replaced the watch. "No, no, of course not."

"Seth seemed reluctant to talk about the matter."

Asa put his palms down on the bench and hunched forward, staring absently at the other guests. "I didn't know you were interested in politics."

"I'm not. I'm interested in Seth."

"He made his choice. It's not my place to discuss Seth's decisions."

"I've never known you to be shy about discussing your railroad investments or your land purchases or even this senatorial business."

Asa sighed. "Lucy, you're putting me in an awkward position. Moreover, I'd never thought you the kind of wife who solicits information behind her husband's back."

She stiffened. After a moment's pause, she apologized. "You're right, Asa. I didn't mean it to sound that way, but you're right. It's just that what happens to Seth matters a great deal to me, and in this case I'm in the dark about what happened."

Asa smiled. "He changed his mind. It's that simple.

498

Surely you don't think that's strictly a feminine prerogative."

"There you are!" Seth came toward them, bearing two glasses of brandy. "What are you two talking about?"

"You," she said.

"Don't get up, Asa," Seth told him, "not on my account."

"It's late and I must be leaving." He bowed to Lucy. "Seth," he said, nodding farewell, "you've quite a wife there."

"Why do you suppose he said that?" Lucy asked Seth. "It sounded like a compliment."

"It's almost exactly the phrase I use when I'm forced to compliment some poor woman on her wretchedly ugly baby. 'That's quite a baby,' I say, 'that's quite a baby.'"

"A bit thin-skinned tonight, aren't you? Come on, Lucy, you know how highly Asa thinks of you. Don't carp about his choice of words, my dear." He drained his brandy glass and set it down. "Perhaps it's time we bade our host and hostess good night."

XXVI

IT MIGHT as well have never happened. The months of meetings and conferences, the planning, the hours that Seth and Asa had spent huddled together in deep discussion had been shrugged off and discarded, like the tenuous shreds of a dream left to disintegrate in the daylight. No mention was made of the senate again.

Seth was now concerned about the infinitesimal progress of the railroad, which had been beset by delays and interruptions. Already people were calling it "the Dutch Flat swindle," though at the rate it was going, it seemed hardly certain even to reach Dutch Flat, much less the eastern slope of the Sierras beyond. The prevailing pessimism was gleefully fueled by everyone who stood to lose by the success of the Central Pacific. The Pacific Mail line, Wells Fargo and the Overland Stage Company were awash in crocodile tears over its prospective failure. Rumors ran rampant. The Central Pacific was insolvent. Work was at a standstill. Construction crews were being dismissed. Seth and Asa, in the opinion of Albert Fearing, had simply thrown good money after bad. Albert had no way of knowing, of course, just how heavily they had invested in the Sacramento Valley in expectation of the railroad's completion. This they kept to themselves.

As winter turned into spring, it seemed to Lucy that Seth was increasingly preoccupied. He was quieter than usual, and there was a dogged set to his jaw and a tension about his mouth that belied his customary optimism.

"The Central Pacific will pull out of this rut. This year, next year maybe, but they'll do it."

Lucy laid a hand on his arm. "If they can't—"

500

He cut her off. "They will."

"Seth, what about the land?"

"What about it?"

"If the railroad were to fail."

"It wouldn't be worth dust."

"It's still good farmland."

"So? Washoe's full of silver, but without the miners to dig it out, what's it worth? It's immigrants we need, settlers, legions of them. They're the only way of making our investments pay off."

"They'll come," she declared, "with or without the Central Pacific. It might take a bit longer, but they'll come."

"Meanwhile, our capital is tied up in a lot of fallow acreage."

"Seth," she said cautiously, "I have a good deal of money of my own, and if ever—"

He squeezed her hand. "Bless you, my dear, but the situation hasn't yet come to that. I trust it won't."

"You always said we were partners."

"And so we are." He smiled. "Pretty clever of me to have taken a rich wife, don't you think?"

"I only meant that with so much of your money bound up in that land and the railroad and the vineyard, all these things that take so long to reap a profit, perhaps it might make you rest easier to know that whatever I have is yours to use as you see fit."

"The vineyard . . ." He frowned. "Who would have believed after last year's storms that we'd have so little rain this season? It's as though the heavens had poured it all out at once and run dry. I'm going up next week to have a look at the place."

"Take me."

"But I'll only be staying a day or two."

"Please. Don't refuse me. It's not fair that I should only share the good times. Don't rebuff me or exclude me just because things go wrong." She touched his cheek with her fingertips and turned his face to hers. "Do you know how I'd feel, Seth, to think that you knew so little of me that you'd treat me like some frail, quivering lily?"

He seemed surprised. "Have I done that? Lucy, I only mean to spare you from distress."

"At the price of allowing it to come between us? No, thank you. I'd sooner welcome adversity with open arms than have it separate us. And where's the justice in your always taking on my problems, if I'm not allowed to share the burden of yours?"

Seth shook his head thoughtfully and gave her a faint smile. "Never argue with a lady, I say, especially if she's making sense. But what's all this to do with going up to the vineyard?"

"I was beginning to feel excluded. I didn't like the sensation."

He bent to kiss her. "As you wish, my love." He cupped her face in his hands. "Champagne or ship's biscuit, whichever fate serves up, we'll take together. But remember," he warned, "t'was you insisted."

"I declare, Seth Slade!" A note of irritation crept into her voice. "You sound quite patronizing. You know very well I'm not a coward and I'm not fragile. I sometimes think you men fancy your wives dependent just so you can feel you control them." Her cheeks were flushed now. "Hang it all, I do need you. I do rely on you. But I'm not some kind of parasite, clinging to you for dear life. I'm sturdy as an ox,. and I'm asking to shoulder my part of the yoke, that's all. I should think any sane man would vastly prefer that arrangement."

"Are we having an argument?"

"Yes!"

He ran a hand through his hair, shaking his head. "I'll be damned if I know why."

"Because I don't want to be shut out of your life!"

"Damn it all, woman!" he roared. "You aren't! What the devil do you want? Afternoons at the Bank Exchange Saloon with me and my business cronies? What in God's name is bothering you?"

"I don't know," she said, suddenly quiet. "It was just a feeling I had."

"You're imagining things."

"Mama? Seth?" Beth stood in the doorway. "Is something wrong?"

"No," Lucy replied quickly.

"Your Mama and I were having a heated discussion."

"It's about Abel, isn't it."

"Abel? Why would you say that?"

She glanced uncertainly from one to the other. "I thought it was about the letter that came today. Mama's right about Abel, Seth. He writes as though we were ignorant peasants and he was up there on Mount Olympus with the rest of the gods, talking down to us. 'Selina Mountford, the Pallas Athena of Brattle Street.'" Beth grimaced. "Nauseating!"

Lucy laughed in spite of herself. "Ah, yes, the exalted Mountfords."

"My dear," Seth put in, "they're merely a decent, God-fearing family."

"Of shining intellects and splendid trappings," Lucy added. "The reek of their refinement perfumes his letters."

"He's a snob," Beth said.

Lucy glanced at her. "You're hardly the one, Bethie, to go casting the first stone on that account."

"Perhaps if I wrote to Alvah Mountford—"

"Oh, Seth, no," Lucy told him. "It's not the Mountfords' fault. Abel has always had a streak of arrogance that's tough as gristle. It used to irritate me no end when he was a child. Now I think he's the one who'll suffer most from it. It will just make it all the more difficult for him to learn life's lessons."

"And meanwhile," Beth said tartly, "we're forced to listen to him preach the gospel according to the Mountfords."

"Poor Luther Moore would rise from the grave if he knew how that boy puts on airs. In fact," Lucy declared, "I believe I shall mention that when I write. The jolt might shake some sense into him."

Beth smiled wickedly. "If Miss Selina Mountford, the Pallas Athena of Brattle Street, knew—"

"That's enough, Bethie," Seth cut her short.

"He does seem quite taken with her," Lucy said thoughtfully.

"I wonder," Beth mused, "if he's told her about Fleur, Miss Corday's daughter. How do you suppose the aristocratic Miss Mountford would feel about that episode?"

Seth rose. "Bethie," he said slowly, "I hear the voice of a busybody in this room. Abel's flirtations are not your concern, my dear. Your place in life is to be his sister. You'd do well to remember that."

For a moment she stood looking at him with a strange, sullen stare. Abruptly, she turned and walked away.

Lucy grasped Seth's arm. "What's gotten into that girl?"

503

"An all too proprietary interest in her brother's affairs, from the sound of it. Now, where were we?"

She looked away. "I've quite forgotten."

"And so have I."

Despite their quarrel, Seth seemed pleased to have her company on the journey to Saint Helena. It was always a pleasant trip, though they both noticed that the usually verdant hills of May were already stippled with the arid, sunburnt signs of summer. The sparse rainfall had left its mark everywhere in the valley. The splashing brook that ran along the drive to the cottage had been reduced to an inaudible trickle, and the surrounding thickets of dry brush rustled and chafed in the wind like leaves of tissue paper.

Herr Schmidt and his workers had constructed a weir across the streambed to collect a portion of the flow. The coolies, buckets suspended from their shoulder-poles, plodded impassively back and forth from the banks to the hillside, patiently irrigating the vines by hand. Herr Schmidt looked tired, Lucy thought, and Frau Schmidt's face seemed drawn with care.

Frau Schmidt was a little, birdlike woman, in all respects a sparrow. She was brown-haired and brown-eyed and fluttery in her movements, with a small, reedy voice and a way of shying away after she had spoken, as if she had startled herself by daring to let out a peep. She smiled and nodded agreeably when addressed, though her English was scant and gestures served her better. She seemed in awe of Chang, who presided over the main house like the stern captain of a ship on which she was a reluctant passenger. She gave him a wide berth on her visits there and ate her meals in silence, averting her eyes from this exotic being who laid such curiously tasty collations in front of her.

In the vineyard, the fruit buds had begun to appear on the vines, minute grapelike bunches of green half-hidden among the leaves.

Lucky knelt and examined a cluster of the infinitesimal, round buds. "Herr Schmidt, what will become of the vines if this drought persists?"

He bent down beside her. "I will tell you a secret, my lady," he whispered solemnly. "Vines must suffer to produce fine wine. This is something that the great wine-masters have learned over the centuries."

" 'Adversity builds character,' my Pa used to say. You make your vines sound almost human."

He nodded. "They are not so different from us as you might think. A man, he comes from a certain stock, he inherits a certain character, yes? Then, the way he is raised and nourished, the place he lives, his circumstances, his experiences, all these act upon his character to make him an individual. It is the same with wine. You see that hill across the valley? If today I were to plant this very Golden Chasselas strain over there, the wine would not be the same as from these vines. An expert could taste the difference. Wines are like people, my lady, some good, some bad, but no two alike."

"I understand better now what my husband said about the vineyard being a living legacy. He likened it to having children."

"Ja," he replied softly, *"ja."* Abruptly, he rose, embarrassed by his sentimentality. The dinner gong sounded. Herr Schmidt gave Lucy his arm, as Hong Hing-wing and his men began to straggle past them toward the bunkhouse for the noon meal.

"The baby, Cal, he is well?" he asked as they walked down the sloping path to the house. "And Mrs. Stevens?"

"Cal is walking and talking. He has the energy of a steam-engine, I'm afraid. I expect my husband told you that Mr. Stevens was wounded and taken prisoner."

"Yes, my lady. You have my sympathy."

"He was an officer with the Henry Volunteers at Gettysburg and took a minié ball in the leg. Beth received a letter from him a few weeks ago, saying that he'd been moved from his hospital to the prison at Point Lookout, Maryland."

"Then he is at least well enough to travel."

"We'd hoped he might be exchanged, but now that there's no more exchanging of prisoners, I'm afraid he'll be at Point Lookout for the duration of the War."

"Ach, my lady, such a sad affair, your War." He changed the subject. "And how is your friend, Mr. Hudson, may I inquire?"

"We've not seen much of him lately. I expect his business dealings require most of his time."

"But is he not Mr. Slade's partner?"

"In a few ventures, yes. Some railroad investments, some land in the Sacramento Valley."

"*Ja*, this I know." He fell silent until they had almost reached the cottage. In front of the presshouse, he halted and turned to her. "He is an honest fellow, Asa Hudson, yes?"

Lucy gave him a puzzled look. "Yes, I should say so. Why do you ask?"

"My lady, perhaps I should not mention this at all." He hesitated and cleared his throat nervously. "I would not mention it to your husband, since he might take offense at me for bearing tales. He would be quite within his rights, I assure you, my lady."

"Herr Schmidt, if you've something to say, please say it."

"I thought perhaps you would know if there was any truth in what I have heard."

"Unless I know what it is," she replied, "I can't tell you."

He frowned and looked uncertain. Then he shook his head apologetically. *"Nein,"* he said decisively. "I regret that I was about to repeat an idle rumor. Forgive me, my lady. It was a lapse of discretion on my part."

"You are forgiven. Come now, let's move along or it will be Chang who won't forgive us."

When Seth returned from walking the Schmidts to their bungalow after supper, Lucy broached the subject of Herr Schmidt's odd remarks to her. "Seth, did Herr Schmidt say anything to you about Asa?"

Seth looked up, surprised, over the pipe he was lighting. He drew on it for a moment. "No. What the devil would he have to say about Asa?"

"I don't know. That's what's so curious. He inquired about him today, in a rather oblique way. He seemed concerned about some sort of gossip. He wanted to know if I thought Asa was honest. I said he was, of course."

"That's strange. Herr Schmidt hardly knows him. The one time Asa visited here, I had the impression they liked each other."

"I don't think Herr Schmidt was speaking for himself. He said something about an idle rumor. It was obvious he didn't want to trouble you with whatever it was. He seemed to think you'd resent his intruding in your affairs."

"Which I would. It's not his place to inquire into Asa's and my dealings, especially if he comes bearing gossip."

She thought for a moment before she answered him.

"Seth, it's not like Herr Schmidt to carry tales. I don't think he would have brought up the subject if he weren't concerned that there might be some truth in it."

He sighed tiredly. "My dear girl, it's altogether too late to sit here speculating on some trifle. If the man has something to say to me, let him do it straightforwardly or keep it to himself."

It was not until they were aboard the ferry, crossing the bay toward home, that Lucy thought of it again.

"No," Seth told her, "Herr Schmidt never brought it up. I gave him ample opportunity, too. I mentioned how often Asa spoke of the vineyard and the beauty of the place."

"What cause would anyone have to spread rumors about Asa?"

Seth laughed aloud. "Since when has gossip depended upon an actual cause? If anything, I should say that Asa's probably the object of some envy. He's successful. He's rich. And he answers to no man but himself."

"You're describing yourself, too, Seth."

He glanced at her. "I am all too well aware of that, my dear, believe me." Abruptly, he walked away toward one of the benches in the stern of the boat.

Lucy stood at the railing, looking after him. Despite the fair sky overhead and the fresh ocean breeze that made pennants of the ribbons on her bonnet, she felt an oddly stifling sensation, as though the air were close and heavy with some oppressive damp. It was not Herr Schmidt's behavior that troubled her. That was all but forgotten, as she stared out over the blue expanse of the bay. No, it was something else, something as subtle as the slightest shift in the wind, bringing with it the faint odor of some dark vapor, its source still obscured beyond the horizon.

But once they were settled at home again, Lucy wondered if the sensation had merely been a product of her imagination. On its surface, life in the Bush Street house seemed as placid as a millpond undisturbed by so much as the splash of a bullfrog. Well, almost, Lucy thought. A single frog presented itself, beady-eyed, heavy-chinned and unlovely, in the person of Eleanor Gibbs. Her lavish generosity to the Good Shepherd Home had won her the admiration and favor of the ladies' circle. At least some of Abner's lucre was going to a good cause. Always, Nelly inquired after Abel, lest Lucy fail to heed the whisper of the Damoclean sword being honed to a razor-edge.

"Eleanor." Lucy caught up with her at the door, as Father Crowley and the ladies were departing. "Nelly, if I may," she said, fixing her with a sweet smile, "don't leave just yet. I'd like a word with you."

Nelly followed her back into the drawing room.

"Septimus, you may finish clearing away the tea things later." Lucy dismissed him with a nod and waited until she heard the pantry door close behind him.

"Hang it all, Nelly!" she burst out. "I'm tired of your veiled threats and allusions. I refuse to allow you to irritate me anymore. You have what you want. Now, once and for all, leave my son out of this! You're a stupid woman, do you know that? You can't project your thoughts any farther than the nose on your face. Think, woman. If I were to regale the ladies with the truth of Nelly Gibbs, I'd be ostracized, too! Had you never considered that? You've put us both in the same boat, don't you see?"

"And you," Nelly retorted, "sit there with your nose in the air like something in the boat stinks to high heaven! Lady, I have a long memory. You always were a smug, self-righteous little baggage. Don't think I've forgotten how you lowered yourself to come to my wedding like you was attending some sideshow and Abner and me was a couple of dancing bears you could throw tidbits to."

"That's a lie! I came because you yourself invited me. It seemed the decent thing to do."

"Decent!" She spat the word through closed teeth. "Ain't you grand to make such a big sacrifice on the altar of decency. How does your halo fit, lady?"

"It wasn't any sacrifice, Nelly," she said evenly. "You're quite mistaken."

"No? There wasn't a woman in that village who'd so much as give me a nod of her head. Are you going to tell me you were different from the others?"

"I treated you fairly in my store."

Nelly made a derisive sound. "At the profit you were taking in, you would have served the devil himself, smiling all the while."

"Nelly, you've misunderstood me from the start. It's true," Lucy went on, "I never would have courted your friendship, given the difference in our—" she hesitated

508

"—our callings. But it was not my intention to treat you with contempt. It's not my place to stand in judgment, Nelly. And I never thought it was. If you'll excuse my candor, a harlot's life is a miserable lot, in my opinion. Not for all the gold in California would I be so abused. I always felt—"

"Keep your pity. I came there to make my pile, like everyone else."

"It wasn't pity I felt, Nelly," Lucy said quietly. "When I looked at you and Velvet Annie and the others, I felt lucky. That's all. It was my good fortune to have my wool to sell and my store of goods. Without them, I'd have had to sell myself in marriage to the first man who asked, and I'd already done that. I'd sold myself to a stranger for a waybill west. I was too young and green at the time to know what I had done."

Nelly regarded her impassively across the space that separated them. "I was young and green once." Quickly, her eyes scanned Lucy's face for a sign of skepticism. After a moment, she went on. "We lived in Boston, close by the waterfront. My Ma, she was sickly. Always in her bed. Pa was a drayman, but he never could hold a job. He was a sot. Ma sewed for a living. Me, I wasn't ever going to be any use, what with only one good arm." She gave Lucy a tentative glance, then shrugged. "One night Pa was drunk in a tavern, and I asked some of the other men to help me fetch him home. There was one, the captain of a merchant vessel he was, who said he'd carry him back if I'd ship out with him. The others laughed. They knew he was in his cups. I was all of sixteen, and here was this handsome devil offering to take me away from there and show me the world."

"And you went?"

She nodded. "Brazil, Chile, Panama, all the way 'round. He cut me adrift in Panama. Tired of me, I guess. But there were plenty of men like him in the saloons there. They were glad of a whore who spoke English. A hot, stinking sewer, Panama. California seemed like heaven after five years in that place." She paused, remembering. "In Castalia there were American women like myself, women like I'd known back home. But it was too late for me. I was what I was, and they'd have none of me." Her eyes met Lucy's. "Do you know how quick I would have given up all my hard-earned gold just to be one of them?"

"But now you are, Nelly. And if you'd lay the past to rest, you'd be far more likeable."

"It ain't that easy." She winced. "I have to watch my language and speak like a proper lady. I have to hold a teacup like I was used to polite society."

Lucy laughed. "With the exception of Amy Winslow and the Knight sisters, I doubt there's a one of us that came from money or polite society. Leanna's Pa was a failed musician who dreamt of selling the pieces he composed. Polly was born on a farm, like me. And Jane Gallagher's folks kept a louse-ridden lodginghouse for sailors, back in New York. That's one of the beauties of California, to my mind. There aren't a lot of yesterdays. People here live in the present and take you as they find you. There's a lot to be said for a short memory."

"Pastora?" Seth's voice came from the hall. "Whose carriage have we out front?"

"Pastora," Nelly said. "They still call you that."

Lucy rose and went to welcome him. Seth kissed her cheek and glancing past her, caught sight of Nelly One-arm seated on the sofa. He gave her a perfunctory bow. "Mrs. Gibbs, good afternoon."

"Almost evening, Mr. Slade. What with the days so much longer this time of year, I quite lost track of time. I'll be leaving now."

At the front door, she halted and turned to Lucy. "Tell me something. Would you have introduced me to your lady friends if I hadn't brought up the boy's past?"

Lucy hesitated a moment before she replied. "No," she admitted, "I wouldn't have."

"An honest answer," Nelly commented drily. "So I've got no reason to believe you weren't being honest about everything else. If I misjudged you before, I apologize. A woman like me, like I was, she gets all too accustomed to being treated like a leper. Whores have feelings, too. Did you ever think of that?"

"Believe me, I understand very well. I sincerely hope, Nelly, that we need never discuss any of this again." Lucy held open the door for her.

At the top of the steps, Nelly stopped. "About your boy . . ."

"Yes?"

"It's forgotten."

Seth poured himself a glass of whiskey and raised it to

Luey as she entered. "Your health, my dear. What does the widow Gibbs want for her silence now?"

Lucy smiled pensively. "Nothing. The account is closed, I believe."

"How did you manage that?"

"I'm not altogether sure. I think she and I understand each other now, though I doubt we could ever be friends."

"I've some good news of my own, Pastora. President Lincoln has amended the Railroad Act. That means there'll be an infusion of capital coming into the project. The Central Pacific can proceed at full steam."

"But what about the laborers they had to dismiss? Father Crowley told me a lot of men are refusing to sign up again, and others are quitting after only a month or two."

"White men. But there's an inexhaustible supply of Chinamen willing to do the job."

Lucy gave him an incredulous look. "Those little people? Why, hardly any of them weighs a pound more than I do. How can they be expected to pull a man's weight on a railroad?"

"What they lack in size and heft, they make up in energy and industriousness."

She laughed. "I'd like to see the looks on the faces of those strapping Irish workers of the Union Pacific, when they catch sight of the Lilliputians coming to meet them from the western end." She put her hand to his cheek. "Seth, I'm glad things have taken a turn for the better. You've seemed so preoccupied these past few months."

After supper they sat together on the porch. The air was still warm with the heat of the day, and the twilight crept at its slow summer pace over the hills. The white roses Seth had given her glowed in the shadows like phosphorescence, and the crickets chirred rhythmically in the gathering darkness. Lucy reached out and clasped Seth's hand. She tried to recall just how long it had been since she'd felt such contentment between them. Before the last trip to the valley, before Seth's journey to Sacramento— almost six months, she realized. Whatever it was that had so troubled him seemed at last to have faded away, leaving them close together under this clear, starry sky with its promise of a fair tomorrow.

"Bethie," Lucy told her, "I'm glad you decided to come up here to the vineyard with us. A change of scenery is always a tonic." She brushed a fine coating of grit from the porch table and laid down her mending. "Mercy, but this drought has made things dusty. Even the leaves seem to have lost their color. Where did Cal and Lin disappear to?"

"They're playing hide-and-seek in the caves."

"Chang is making lemonade. Perhaps you should fetch them now so the treat won't spoil Cal's supper."

As Beth went down the steps, Lucy caught sight of Herr Schmidt and waved. Mopping the perspiration from his forehead, he paused for a moment on the path in front of the presshouse and gazed at it, as though by wishing alone he might fill it with baskets of grapes and overflowing troughs of juice.

"Herr Schmidt," Lucy called, "do come up here and rest in the shade for a moment. Seth ought to be back from town shortly."

"How kind of you, my lady." He stuffed his handkerchief into his breast pocket and glanced down at the soil on his hands. "*Ach,* but I am hardly presentable."

" 'That's clean dirt,' my Pa used to say, 'straight from the good earth.' " She motioned him to the chair beside her. "Do join me."

He sat down with a weary sigh. "We struck a boulder, digging the new well. One whole day spent getting it out of the way."

"And one day nearer water," she consoled him. "By the way, I've been meaning to ask you something."

"Yes, my lady?"

"What on earth was it that had you so concerned about Asa Hudson a few months back?"

He looked embarrassed and stared down at his dirt-encrusted boots. "Foolishness. A tale told by a silly woman."

"A woman?"

"A friend of Frau Krug's, who was staying with her."

"And this lady knew Asa?"

"*Nein,*" he said sheepishly. "She had never even met the man. It was a story about her husband, a lawyer in Sacramento. She wanted me to believe that some men had come to him saying that Asa Hudson and Seth Slade had cheated them out of their land. I'm sorry, my lady. I should never have allowed her to say such a thing. I told her she was wrong to connect Mr. Slade's name with a tale like that."

512

"Obviously they had no grounds for their complaint, or we would have heard about it."

"Please forgive me. I should like to forget that I was so gullible. I had no business asking you about Mr. Hudson."

"I daresay that Sacramento lawyer was talking out of jealousy. He probably wishes he'd bought the land himself. Consider the matter forgotten, Herr Schmidt. Ah, Chang," she said as he came outside, "set the tray here. Bethie, Cal, Lin!" She waved to the trio in the clearing. "Fresh lemonade!"

Herr Schmidt rose and stepped aside for Beth. "Tell me," he said, returning to his chair as she sat down, "your husband's health, it is improved?"

"I—" Beth hesitated. "I'm not sure. For a time, he seemed quite optimistic. Then his mood changed. I don't know why. Perhaps it's just the internment." She looked down at Cal, who sat on the floor of the veranda playing at cat's cradle with Lin, and she fell silent, the lines of her young face suddenly etched deep with desolation.

He shook his head sympathetically. "Such a long war. But I am told it cannot last much longer. This time next year, *mit Gottes Wille,* Calvert, your papa will be here with us."

"Papa?" Cal looked up at him. "Papa's in the picture."

"That's right, Cal," Beth told him, "that's your papa in the picture." She turned to Herr Schmidt with a wistful smile. "My husband posed for Bradley and Rulofson before he left. I keep the photograph with me always, in a drawer by my bed. Would you like to see it?"

When Beth returned, Herr Schmidt had Cal seated on his lap. He waved his open palms in front of the child and then, with a deft flourish, produced a bright silver dime from behind the mystified boy's left ear.

"Do it again!" Cal cried, bouncing with delight.

"Another time," Herr Schmidt promised, pressing the coin into his hand.

"You put that into your Uncle Asa's drum-bank when we go home," Beth instructed him, handing the leather-bound photograph to Herr Schmidt. "Lin, take Cal inside now and wash his face and hands, please. They're sticky from the lemonade."

Herr Schmidt studied the face in the picture. At length he glanced up at Beth. "A fine young gentleman," he declared. "I see his face in the boy."

"May I?" Lucy asked him. "I haven't looked at it for a long time."

She stared down at Nick's face, young and bland, remarkable only for the familiar cleft in his chin. His eyes looked patiently into the camera box, while the trace of a tolerant smile played at his lips. How self-confident he appeared, standing straight and tall between the pillars painted on the canvas background, one hand resting lightly on the back of a chair. His coat was open, and the white of his shirt and the shining silk of his waistcoat and tie seemed almost luminous. The photograph, Lucy realized, had captured exactly what he was, an aristocratic, elegant, proud young man, permitting himself the indulgence of a portrait for his sweetheart.

That glimpse of his image as she'd sat there in the shade of the porch on that warm October afternoon remained engraved on Lucy's mind, as though somehow the photographer had distilled from him the essence of his youthful character and preserved it, immune from time and tribulation, in such a way as to make the picture itself more true of him that her own blurred memories. Long afterward, she still saw the self-assured stance, the permissive, slightly humorous expression, the immaculately fashionable appearance he presented. These existed. Beside them, all thoughts of him seemed nothing more than flimsy fabrications that faded with the sputtering of a log on the hearth, a footfall in the hall or the clouds of evening mist that blew in from the bay.

General Sherman's troops entered Milledgeville on November the twenty-third. Behind them, on the route from smoldering Atlanta, lay New Rosedale. The Rebs were in full flight before the advancing Union Army, the *Alta* reported. And Sherman's men, as they pressed onward, "were laying waste the country." Bridges, lumber stocks, railroad depots, foundries and even homes met the unsparing torch. Alongside the grim accounts of devastation appeared cheery advertisements offering "Holiday Presents for Everbody."

What kind of Christmas would it be, Lucy wondered, for the homeless innocents left in the blackened wake of William Sherman's march toward Savannah? And at New Rosedale, if by God's mercy it still survived, would the crowded dining room table groan, as Nick had once told them it did, complaining under the weight of the huge hams as they were carved and served to the cousins and aunts and uncles gathered in celebration of the birth of the Prince of Peace?

In truth, she could envisage only a scant cluster of men and women, shadow-colored in their black and purple mourning, silent and heavy-hearted, their eyes tarnished with despair. Once, peace had seemed paramount, but what toll had the Union march exacted from her grandson's future, from Beth's and Nick's? There was, as yet, no way of knowing. They must all, of necessity, cling to hope. Life must go on as usual, as if by willing themselves serene and invulnerable, they could somehow extend that protection to New Rosedale.

Lucy stood at the bedroom window, looking out over the city, as a chill ocean wind drove pale tides of mist inland through the channels between the hills. The January sun shone whitely through the fog, glinting like an empty porcelain dinner plate. Below, in the street, a solitary carriage passed by, silent and ghostly, its sound muffled. She jumped, startled, as Seth entered.

"My dear, I didn't mean to frighten you. I was sitting in the library just now, wondering where you were. It's mighty quiet for a Saturday afternoon. Where are Bethie and Cal?"

"They went to Naomi's. They'll be back before we leave for the theatre."

"I told Asa to come by for a drink and a bite to eat first. We'll go together in his carriage. What were you doing up here all alone?"

"Thinking."

"Of what?"

"About what I should wear to the theatre," she told him.

He indulged her the lie. "You know I fancy the pearl-colored silk you wore to the Vanderhoefs' New Year party."

"Then I shall be happy to oblige you. Let me fetch it from the wardrobe and give it to Lin to freshen."

Asa and Seth rose, glasses in hand, to salute her as she entered the drawing room.

"How lovely you look," Asa commented.

"A reflection of Seth's good taste, my dear Asa. It was he who chose the gown. Do sit down, please. I hope I haven't interrupted you."

515

"I was just telling Seth he's lucky he's not still in the silvermining game, what with the way that market has fallen off these past six months."

Seth brought Lucy a glass of sherry. "I hope you're not feeling the pinch too painfully, Asa."

He shrugged. "These fluctuations are inevitable when a lot of speculators flood the marketplace. Silver stocks will go up again eventually, as soon as cooler heads prevail."

Seth took the bottle of Slade and Daggett ore from the table beside his chair and rotated it in his hands. Its dark iridescence glowed in the lamplight like the coals of some cold, unearthly fire.

Lucy smiled at Asa. "Did you know a Paiute seeress warned Seth away from mining? She said silver would be the death of him. Don't look so skeptical." She laughed. "She did."

"Yes? Well, I wish she'd been around to warn me away from the stock exchange. Here's to your wise Paiute." Asa drained his glass and set it aside. "We'd best be starting to the theatre, if we don't want to get caught in the throng and miss the curtain. The Keans are bound to draw a big crowd."

The Opera House, as Asa had prediced, was sold out. Mrs. Kean, to Lucy's thinking, was a bit too full-blown to play a convincing Ophelia, but Mr. Kean, despite his years, acted the mad Dane with such power and intensity that scarcely a rustle or cough escaped from his rapt audience.

It was close in the theatre, and Lucy was glad of the gust of fresh air as the doors opened and they rose, still applauding, from their seats.

"Bravo!" Seth exclaimed. "What a fine performance."

"True," Asa agreed, "but Adah Isaacs Menken is more to my tastes."

"Come now, Asa," Lucy objected, "She can't hold a candle to the Keans."

"Ah, but she cuts a handsome figure."

Seth draped Lucy's cloak about her shoulders. "According to Asa, the shapelier the leading lady, the more diverting the drama."

"I'll step outside," Asa told them, "and see if I can locate my coachman in this mob. It looks as if it's beginning to rain. You two stay here until I find the carriage."

"It's nice to see Asa again," Lucy said, looking after him. "He hasn't been coming by as often as he used to."

"Perhaps he's——" Seth broke off. "What's that? What's happening out there?"

From the street came a woman's sharp scream and the sound of men shouting, their hoarse cries indistinguishable in the confusion. In the doorway, there was a sudden spasm of activity. Several people, women mostly, came rushing headlong back through the exiting crowd.

Seth jostled a path toward the exit. Lucy hung close behind, fearful of losing sight of him in the throng.

"I saw him!" a woman cried out.

Lucy glanced in the direction of the voice. A pale girl, her eyes wide with panic and her cloak askew, stood trembling against a wall. Quickly, Lucy turned away. As she and Seth reached the arched brick doorway, she craned her neck for a glimpse outside, but the press of people spilling onto Washington Street and the glare from the tier of gaslamps overhead made it all but impossible to make out anything beyond.

"Stay back! Get back now!" A burly police officer, his arms widespread, motioned the bystanders out of his way. Beyond him, in the street, two constables crouched over the writhing, disheveled form of a man who lay face-down on the rain-slicked pavement. As they fastened their handcuffs about his wrists, he raised his head and shouted at the top of his lungs. *"Marrano sinvergüenza!"* One of the constables cuffed him sharply. But again, with the frenzy of a captured animal, he lifted his head and bayed out in Spanish, *"Ladrón!"*

"Great God!" Seth grasped Lucy's hand and dove through the crowd.

On the far side of Washington Street, Asa Hudson, stunned and ashen, stood slumped against the door of his carriage. His coachman, Julian, stood over him, holding Asa's left arm aloft, tightly clasped in his ebony hands. The white cuff of Asa's shirt was stained with scarlet.

"Let me through," a man called out. "I'm a doctor."

Seth and Lucy stepped aside for him. Motioning Julian away, the doctor seized Asa's arm. He shook Asa's coat loose and let it fall. With his pocketknife, he cut away the left sleeve of his shirt. The doctor plucked his handkerchief from his pocket and wrapped it around Asa's forearm. "I'll need another to stanch the flow. It's a deep gash."

Seth handed it to him. "Asa, what happened?"

517

He shook his head dazedly. "A man—It happened so fast I didn't even see his face."

"But why?" Lucy asked. "Why would anyone do such a thing?"

"He came hurtling toward me. All I remember is raising my arm to ward him off."

A cry went up from the crowd as the police pulled Asa's assailant to his feet and dragged him, protesting, to the waiting wagon. As they pushed him inside, he turned and shouted over his shoulder.

"Embustero sucio!"

"Ladies and gentlemen!" the burly officer cried out as he made his way to the carriage. "The excitement is over. Go along now." He touched Asa's shoulder. "Sir, would you come with me? We'll need a statement from you as to what happened here."

"Good Lord, man," Seth retorted, "can't you see he needs medical attention first?"

"Mr. Slade. Sir." The officer touched his cap deferentially. "I didn't see it was you. This gentleman's a friend of yours?"

"He is."

"We'll see to it that he receives proper care, sir."

"It's all right," Asa said. "Julian," he told his driver, "take the Slades home. Then you may call for me at police headquarters."

"We'll come with you," Seth said.

Asa smiled weakly. "This doesn't concern you. Please. I'll be quite all right."

"Asa," Lucy objected, "we can't leave you like this. Let us follow you in the carriage with Julian and wait for you."

"As you wish." He took the officer's arm. "It appears," he said, summoning an unsteady laugh, "that tonight's drama was not confined to the stage."

Julian opened the door of the carriage and helped Lucy in. Seth seated himself beside her.

She reached out and took his hand. Her own were trembling. "Seth, I don't understand. That man, attacking Asa like that. And shouting. He kept shouting about something."

Seth gazed ahead into the darkness. "A shameless swine, he called him. A thief and a liar."

XXVII

Lucy had insisted that Asa come home with them. At first he demurred, saying he was quite well enough to return to his rooms at the Occidental Hotel, but it was obvious that the experience had left him badly shaken. Seth and Lucy prevailed upon him to stay the night in Abel's room.

"That young fellow seemed utterly irrational," Seth told her as they prepared for bed.

"You saw him?"

"No. He was in an adjoining room. Asa looked in for a moment, just long enough to tell the police he couldn't positively identify him. Nevertheless, they have him red-handed. I could hear him raving on in Spanish before they took him to the lock-up. Something about his poor old father, from what I could understand."

"He didn't offer any motive for attacking Asa?"

"The police said he seemed to have a whole litany of grievances against the world. Who knows if they're real or imaginary? He was ranting like a maniac, from what they told me."

Lucy slid between the sheets as Seth doused the lamp. "What a ghastly evening."

"Indeed. Poor Asa." Seth chuckled drily in the darkness. "He didn't even enjoy the play all that much."

In the morning, Lucy awoke abruptly from a disturbing dream. She blinked her eyes against the light, trying simultaneously to absorb the reassuring presence of morning and to hold onto the fragments of the nightmare. She was curious as to why such an absurd dream could possibly upset her. They had been in a boat, she

519

and Seth, one of the steamers that plied the rivers. They sat in the bow while a group of Germans were enjoying a picnic in the stern. The Germans, Herr Schmidt among them, were drinking a dark, crimson wine. Seth and Lucy called out a greeting to Herr Schmidt. As he turned, they could see that he was drunk. He gazed at them without expression and said something in German that caused the others to stare at them. It began to shower, and as she and Seth dashed for cover, she looked back to see the Germans, their faces wet with rain, still looking after them.

A silly, senseless nightmare, she thought, unable to make head or tail of it. She rose and dressed quietly so as not to wake Seth.

Septimus took a tray up to Asa, but he would have none of it and insisted on joining them at the breakfast table.

"A day's rest," he said, "that's all I need, and I can have that in my own rooms without being an inconvenience."

"Stay," Cal begged him, tugging at his trouser leg.

"At least until this evening," Lucy said. "Then if you're sure you're feeling well, Septimus can drive you back to your hotel."

"Ah, well," he acquiesced, "I know when I'm outnumbered."

"Such a dreadful incident," Beth said, "and in the middle of a public street."

"Why did the man want to hurt Uncle Asa?" Cal asked.

"Nobody knows," Seth told him. "The man was upset. He wasn't thinking clearly."

"Enough, enough," Asa said. "Cal, didn't you tell me you had some toy soldiers you were going to show me?" He pushed his chair back from the table and knelt down on the floor. "Come. I'll give you a pick-a-back ride upstairs to the nursery, if you'll show me your army."

"Seth," Beth asked as they left the dining room, "do you think the man might have been drunk?"

"I don't know. He was shouting epithets, none of them flattering. He might well have been."

Suddenly Lucy remembered the dream. She glanced at the stairwell, waiting until Asa and Cal had turned the corner. "Seth, he called Asa a liar and a cheat. Wasn't that what he said?"

"Yes. Why?"

"I was reminded of that queer business with Herr Schmidt."

"What was that?" Beth wanted to know.

"Nothing to concern yourself with, Bethie. It was something he meant to tell Seth. Run along now, darling, and let's all try to forget this nasty episode, shall we?" Lucy looked after her as she went upstairs. "Seth," she began. "I may be an awful fool for telling you this, but that was what Herr Schmidt wanted to say to you."

"I don't follow you, my dear."

"As near as I can remember it, there was a woman visiting the Krugs who said that Asa and you had cheated people out of their land. Herr Schmidt defended you, but then he came to me and asked if I thought Asa was honest. Later, he was very apologetic about it. He said it was nothing but a rumor."

"But how did it start? Who was this woman?"

"The wife of a lawyer in Sacramento. She said some men had brought their grievances to him."

"That's news to me. I've not heard any complaints from any Sacramento lawyer. Of course, Asa spent a good deal more time there than I did. He completed a lot of the final transactions on his own."

"But you saw the deeds, didn't you?"

"Most of them. Here now, Lucy, I'd have no reason to examine any papers that Asa said were in good order."

"Where are they?"

"Don't you think you're carrying this rumor a bit far? They're in the safe in my office." He frowned suddenly. "What is it?"

"That young man. I overheard him say his father had lost his home. And I recall now that the police said he wasn't a local fellow. He came from somewhere upriver."

"Near Sacramento."

Seth let out a deep breath. "It's sheer foolishness, I suppose, but it wouldn't hurt to have a look at those papers, just to settle the matter. God forgive me for even bothering. I wouldn't want Asa to be insulted. When a partnership's based on trust, you don't go spying on your partner's work behind his back."

"But the rumor concerned you, too. You have a right to prove it's untrue."

521

"Still, it's a distasteful business, any way you look at it. At least," he declared, "it will all be put to rest by dinnertime."

The noon meal came and went without Seth. Asa retired for a nap. The skies had cleared, and Bethie, Cal and Lin sat outside on the porch, while Lucy repaired to the sitting room to do her mending. She glanced up as the grandfather clock in the hall struck three.

"Grandpa Seth, look at me!" Cal cried. "Watch me!"

Lucy looked out the bay window. Seth paused on the path to watch the boy somersault unsteadily over the grass. He patted Cal's blonde curls approvingly and walked toward the house.

"What kept you?" she called out when she heard the front door close behind him. "We held off eating dinner for half an hour, but we couldn't wait any longer. Are you hungry? I told Biddy to save you something."

He stood in the doorway to the sitting room, his hat in his hand.

Without moving her eyes from his face, she laid her mending aside. Quietly, she asked, "How bad is it?"

His voice was a monotone. "I don't know." He walked to the window seat and sat down, slumped forward, his hands on his knees.

Lucy got up from her chair and went to sit beside him. "Is it the deeds?"

He nodded. "Almost a third of them are missing from the safe. I don't know whether Asa ever put them there at all or whether he's removed them. We'd agreed they'd all be kept in the same place, so I naturally assumed the whole lot were there. I added up those in the safe against the number of transactions I knew we'd made, and . . ." He fell silent, shaking his head.

"Perhaps there's a very logical explanation. Why don't you ask Asa?"

"There's more. I went down to the jail and spoke to Ramon Gonzales."

"Is he the man—"

"Yes." Seth pressed his lips together. The muscles of his jaw tensed. After a moment, he took a breath and went on. "His story is that Asa gave his parents a sum of money with the understanding that it was only a partial payment for their land and that there would be two sub-

522

sequent payments of slightly smaller sums. In fact, as I recall, a number of our deals were written that way. The Gonzales fellow's parents can't read or write and they either hadn't the money or the sense to bring in a lawyer. They took the papers to a cousin who read them and said they seemed to be in order. But they never received the full purchase price they were led to expect."

Lucy frowned, puzzled. "But haven't they a copy of the agreement?"

"Damn." Seth slapped his kneecap angrily. "That's the devil of it. When they finally took their papers to a lawyer, the only sum specified was what they'd already received."

"Seth? Are you saying that someone substituted false documents for the ones you and Asa agreed on?"

"I'm not, not until I see them with my own eyes. But that's what Ramon Gonzales says. If the parents are illiterate, how would they know the difference until someone told them?"

"What are you going to do?"

"I'm going to have a talk with Asa. If that doesn't give me any satisfaction, I'll go upriver and start asking questions."

"Assuming," she said cautiously, "that Asa played some part in this, what reason would he have? I thought he was a wealthy man."

Seth rubbed his eyes tiredly. "He's a speculator, my dear, a gambler like myself. I'm fairly conservative. Asa is more inclined to take risks. It's possible he overextended himself in one area and fell short in another. Perhaps he has every intention of seeing that these people eventually get their full payment—"

"But for the time being, they've been victimized."

"And so have I. Those were our mutal funds. And it's more than the money, Lucy. If what Gonzales says is true, my partner, my friend, has robbed me of my good name. In the business world, that's worth more to a man than cash. Seth sighed. "Good God, I pray that Gonzales fellow is thoroughly insane."

"Did he seem rational when you spoke to him?"

"I say, you two." Asa appeared in the doorway. "This house is as quiet as a tomb. I thought you'd gone out and left me to amuse myself as best I could. Seth, my friend, you missed a fine dinner. Where's Cal? I promised him I'd kick his ball around the lawn with him."

Seth rose. "Asa, we've important business to discuss. Let's go into the library where we'll have some privacy. Excuse us, Lucy."

She sat there, unable to continue her mending. Occasionally she heard their voices rise, then fall and fade away again. Silence hung over the house like a heavy thundercloud, interrupted only by these distant rumblings and the steady, dispassionate ticking of the hall clock.

At last, she heard the sound of the library door opening. They were walking slowly, saying nothing. Seth paused before the door to the sitting rom and cast her a look. He was white-faced, and his gaze was pained.

Asa glanced at Lucy. "I'm leaving," he said tonelessly.

She went to them. "Asa—"

"I'll be going now. Thank you for your hospitality."

She looked from one to the other. "What happened?"

"Later," Seth told her. "But it's just as I feared."

"Oh, Asa!" Impulsively, she laid a hand on his arm. "How could you? You're our friend! How could you disappoint us like this? Deceiving those poor people, deceiving Seth who trusted you, tarnishing his good name."

Asa pulled back, flushed with anger. "Damn it, woman, you should be the last one to accuse me of that!"

"Stop it!" Seth's voice was harsh.

"I've had all the sanctimonious sermons I want from either of you. And you, Lucy Slade—or Pastora, as it were—have no right blaming me for blackening your husband's name. You saw to that well enough yourself."

"Asa," she cried, "what are you talking about?"

"Caesar's wife," he retorted bitterly, "Caesar's wife."

"That's enough, Asa!"

For a moment, Lucy thought Seth was going to strike him. She thrust out her hand between them. "No. If I've done Seth wrong, Asa, I want to know it. What do you mean, 'Caesar's wife'?"

"Lucy, please—"

Asa overrode Seth's protest. "Plutarch, wasn't it, who said 'Caesar's wife ought to be above suspicion'? Except that the last time I heard those words spoken, they were coming from Governor Low. A senator's wife, he said, ought to be modeled after Caesar's. You let us run a

524

merry chase, didn't you, Pastora?" Asa's face was florid with rage. "How was I to know what you were before I came to San Francisco? And the others who supported your husband for the senate, men from San Jose and Monterey and Sacramento, how were they to know? There must only have been a handful who remembered, sitting there, biding their time, waiting for the whole endeavor to come falling down on us like a house of cards, while they groomed their own man for the job. Be thankful, lady, that Governor Low has a long memory for details."

"In heaven's name," she gasped, "I never—"

"In heaven's name," he mocked her, "you with your bawdy houses and your whores! Who are you to tell me—"

Seth lunged at him. Asa dodged the blow, stumbling toward the door.

"Don't, Seth! He can't fight back. He's injured." Lucy grasped Seth by the shoulders to stay him.

For a moment, the two men stood staring at each other wordlessly. Then Asa turned and walked out of the house.

Lucy cast a stricken look at Seth and ran into the drawing room, her cheeks wet with tears.

She felt a hand on her shoulder, but she could not bear to face him.

"It's no use weeping now. What's done is done. Take my handkerchief."

"Oh God," she murmured miserably. "It was I who ruined your chances. Asa's right. I'm no better than he. We've both dishonored your name. How could I have been so stupid as to overlook the possibility? I should at least have thought to warn you. It never even occurred to me . . ."

"Nor to me." He sat down beside her. "Don't think I haven't asked myself a hundred times how I could have blundered ahead so naively. Believe it or not, the matter never came up until my meeting with Governor Low. I realize now that most of the chaps who supported me were relatively new to the city or came from other places in the state. Perhaps a few might once have heard the rumors and either forgotten or failed to make the connection between Lucy Bates and Mrs. Seth Slade. Lord knows, Joe Mason was aware of it, and Albert Fearing, too, and neither one seems to have given it a second thought."

"How can you possibly forgive me?"

"Not just you, my dear. How can I forgive my own negligence? I was careless. I allowed the prospect of the senate to dazzle me and blind me to everything but my own ambitions." He took her hands in his. "Lucy, what you did before we met never mattered to me. It was a closed book. I've known you only as the woman I wanted for my wife. How could I believe anyone would stoop to using the woman I love against me? But," he went on, taking a deep breath, "someone would have, inevitably. What a political innocent I was. On that account alone, I'm not fit to serve government. It's just as well I found that out before I'd gone in over my head."

"That's not true. You would have made a great senator, if it weren't for me. Dear God, Seth, what have I done? I've blighted your hopes and soiled the name of the finest man I've ever known. I wonder you can stand the sight of me. How you must despise me."

"My dear, the greater fault is mine. I knew all there was to know about you, yet when the prize was dangled in front of me, I leapt for it greedily without giving a thought to those facts. A man is responsible for what he knows, Lucy. I acted irresponsibly, and I took a number of good, well-intentioned men along with me in my folly. I bear the blame for that. A wiser man would have rejected their overtures from the first."

She shook her head disconsolately. "The truth is, you married someone whose very presence in your life holds you back from becoming all that you should rightfully be." She turned away. "You'd be better off if I were dead."

"In heaven's name, woman!" Seth seized her and brought her to him. "What would possess you to say such a thing?"

Her eyes brimmed. "I only wish I'd never caused—"

He put his finger to her lips. "And I wish I were the man you believed me to be. Let's not dwell on our shortcomings anymore. I've had a bellyfull of disappointments today, and I daresay you have, too."

"I have something more to say, Seth." Her voice was low. "I've disappointed you more than you know. I was never completely honest with you. May God forgive me. I am not what you thought." She hesitated. "I was never a widow. I was never married. It's time you knew the whole truth of me."

"What are you saying, woman?"

"Just that." She was trembling. "I never told anyone."

"But who the devil was Caleb Bates, if he wasn't your husband? Not a figment of the imagination, surely."

"No. He existed, but he wasn't my husband, Seth. He was already married. I found it out after he died." She glanced away. "He wasn't even Caleb Bates."

"Go on."

"His same was Benjamin Collier. He had a wife and three daughters."

"How do you know this?"

"I saw them. In a daguerreotype. It was in our wagon. He said it was a picture of his brother's widow and her children. I can still remember the woman's expression, so shy and anxious. She was inclined to fits of melancholy, I think. He once implied he'd had to contend with a mad-woman."

"Lucy, I don't understand—"

"I saw the picture again. After he was killed, I dug up a parcel he'd buried. It was there, wrapped in an oilskin packet, along with a newspaper article that told how a man named Benjamin Collier had taken over two thousand dollars from a bank where he'd worked. He'd disappeared, it said, leaving his wife and three daughters behind. Then I remembered that a stranger in Saint Joseph had called him by that name."

"You're sure Bates and Collier were the same man?" She nodded.

"Do the children know?"

"No."

He turned her face to his. "Lucy, why did you never tell me this? Why did you feel you had to keep it to yourself all these years? Surely you knew it wouldn't make any difference to me. You were very young, and—"

"Seth, there was more than four hundred dollars in that parcel."

He looked at her in silence for a moment. "Stolen money."

"I kept it. I pretended he'd left it with me when he went away. I used it to buy a flock of sheep. The store in Castalia, the place on Clay Street, the investments I made—none of them would have been possible without that money."

527

"I see."

"Every bit of my success came from that money." Her voice caught in her throat. "I'm sorry, Seth."

Seth reached out and drew her to him, holding her close. "Here now, why are you weeping? What was so wrong in what you did? Were you supposed to leave it there to be discovered by some Indian or prospector? Any sane person would have done the same. As I see it, you were damned lucky to find it when you needed it."

"It was more than that. I was ashamed."

He pressed his handkerchief to her cheeks. "Of what, my dearest girl?"

"Of having been deceived and used. I was part of his disguise. That's all I was to him."

"Lucy, Asa used me and deceived me. It's not a pleasant feeling, but there's nothing to be ashamed of if you weren't a willing party to it."

"But all this time you thought I'd earned my success myself."

"And you did. Nobody else accomplished those things. What's the difference whether the man gave you his money for safekeeping or whether you stumbled upon it yourself? It's what you did with it that makes you extraordinary. I daresay few women would have been so enterprising. Most of them would have spent it on the necessities of life and gone through it in no time."

"You're not disappointed in me?"

"I am. But only because you didn't trust me enough to tell me this long ago."

"I try never to think of it."

"Ah, Lucy." Seth smiled and shook his head. "For an intelligent lady, you can be mighty foolish sometimes. In God's name, woman, are there any more bodies buried in this family? We've been married nearly four years. Can't you trust me by now?"

"There's nothing more to tell. I swear it, my love." She raised his hand to her lips and kissed it.

"Then set your mind at ease. Bates is dead and gone. Only you and I know about this."

"It's strange," she said, suddenly pensive, "but I sometimes think deception is contagious. Caleb Bates deceived me, and in turn, I've deceived Beth."

"It wouldn't do her any good to know."

"And what about Abel? We are all party to that deception. From the moment we met, you praised my honesty, yet it seems to me that my life is a tangle of subtleties."

Seth rose and knocked the ashes from his pipe against the hearth fender. "Whatever it is, my dear," he said fervently, "it's damned interesting. I'll never die of boredom, that's certain."

She dried her cheeks with his handkerchief and gave it to him. "What's to be done about Asa, Seth?"

"We'll dissolve our partnership, of course."

"Won't you have to take him to court, to clear your name?"

"I doubt that I'd have much ammunition, save for my word against his, and it would cause a public scandal, regardless of the outcome. In plain words, my dear, my reputation is hanging by a thread right now, and I shouldn't want to see it frayed to the breaking point."

"But won't it all come to light anyway, when the people he cheated start complaining to the authorities?"

"Asa is extremely clever," he said bitterly. "There's no evidence. He's certain of that. And how much credence would the authorities give to a bunch of illiterate *Californios*? They'd probably be secretly delighted to see the wretched lot of them thrown off their land and driven back to Mexico."

Lucy glanced at him, appalled. "Seth, are you telling me you're going to let him get away with this?"

"Vengeance is the Lord's business, not mine. What's important is that I vindicate myself by making restitution to the families he swindled."

"But how?"

"How? By going up there and locating them. By paying them off."

"By yourself? Rightfully, Asa is responsible for half of whatever they're owed."

"Asa, my dear, simply hasn't the money. He's even in arrears at his hotel. He's overextended himself beyond my worst fears." Seth took a deep breath. "I believe I could use a glass of whiskey. Excuse me."

When he returned, Lucy asked him, "What will happen to Ramon Gonzalcs?"

He frowned. "I suppose he'll be tried and convicted. The fact is, he assaulted Asa, and he'll have to take the consequences." He set his glass on the mantel and stared

529

into the unlit fireplace. "Hiram Berry," he said suddenly. He turned to Lucy. "He's one of the best criminal lawyers in the city."

"Hiram Berry? That peculiar little man who came to me about Queen Rosie's will? He seemed as meek and timid as a rabbit. And why would a criminal lawyer be writing wills and chasing down heirs?"

He allowed himself a wry smile. "Because, my dear, your Queen Rosie's trade made it necessary for her to have a man like Berry at her beck and call. I looked into his background after he came here that day. Evidently your rabbit turns into a tiger in the courtroom. I believe I'll track down Mr. Berry first thing Monday morning and see if I can make it worth his while to defend Gonzales."

"But Seth," she said cautiously, "won't it come out at the trial that you were associated with Asa in this business?"

"All the more reason to have Gonzales's lawyer in my pay. Look here, Lucy. If I see to it that Gonzales's parents get their money and I hire a lawyer to defend him, surely that would take the edge off of any grudge Gonzales has against me. Besides, I'm pretty sure he believed me when I told him I knew nothing of Asa's manipulations. He could see how disturbed I was to have learned those papers were missing."

She went to him, and he put his arms around her. "What a terrible twenty-four hours," she said. "I feel as though I'd been struck."

"My poor girl." He rested his cheek on her hair. "So many illusions shattered by a single blow."

Lucy looked up at him. "I've always loved you for not holding my past against me. You know very well I'm incapable of not forgiving whatever mistakes you've made. I only pray I can regain the love you once entrusted to me.

"You can't." He saw the look of hurt on her face and kissed her. "Because I couldn't love you any more than I do now."

In the night, lying close beside him, Lucy tried to sort out her feelings. There would never be any way she could repair the damage she had done to Seth's career. He was bound to a wife whose ill fame surfaced when least expected. What fools we are, she reflected, not to see farther than our own fingertips, not to understand that our actions are never without consequence. The slightest deed, like the merest motion of a hand in water, sent out an inevitable, ever-widening wave, lost perhaps to the eye, even to memory, until it broke against some distant bank, laden with the jumbled flotsam and jetsam of its journey.

Seth stirred and, still asleep, slippped his arm around her hip. This good man. Lucy thought, so distressed by his own failings and so forgiving of hers. She found his hand and slept at last.

"Pastora?" Seth called from the hall.

"In here. I'm in the library, doing the household accounts." Lucy closed her ledger as he bent to kiss her cheek. "How was your day?"

"A mixed bag." He sat down on the sofa and began to fill his pipe. "It started out well enough. Hiram Berry will take the case. We can rest assured that Gonzales will have the best possible defense. As for my meeting with Asa," he added, tamping his tobacco down forcefully, "it was strained, to put it mildly. But he's accepted my offer to buy his share of our partnership. And at least now I know what's owed his victims." He frowned and struck a match on the sole of his boot.

"Is it a great deal of money?"

"Not to someone who has it." He drew on his pipe, his brows still furrowed in thought. "The problem is," he went on, tossing the spent match into the wastebasket at her feet, "at present, I'm richer on paper than in pocket."

Lucy pushed her chair back from the desk. "By how much do you fall short?"

"Over thirty thousand, including what I'll have to pay Asa."

"And what about Mr. Berry's fee?"

"Ah, yes, there's that, too." He shook his head in annoyance. "Just one more thing to consider."

"What will you do, Seth? Could you sell off some of the land that you and Asa bought and make up the difference that way?"

"Yes, but it wouldn't be wise. With every mile of track laid by the Central Pacific, the value of that land increases. I'd be a fool to let it go before the transcontinental railroad is operating. No, my dear, I expect the solution is to borrow the cash at the best rate of interest I can negotiate. But before I come to that, I'm going up to the Sacramento Valley to start doling out whatever I can afford. If I at least prove my intention to pay, perhaps that will forestall any further threat of scandal. I'll be leaving in the morning."

"I'll see you to the boat. I've business with Mr. Biggs at Wells Fargo tomorrow. You will write, won't you, to let me know where you're staying and how long?"

He wrote to her almost immediately from his usual hotel on J Street in Sacramento. Lucy copied the address from his letter and went out to the kitchen, where Biddy was salting a fragrant stew while Septimus polished the serving pieces. "The silver will have to wait, Septimus. I need you to do an errand for me before closing time at Wells Fargo." She laid the folded paper on the table. "Deliver this to Mr. Biggs, please."

"Yes'm." Septimus wiped his hands clean. "That's all? No message?"

"No. He already knows what to do with it." She bent over Biddy's kettle and breathed in the aroma. "I don't suppose you're going to tell me what's in there that smells so delicious."

"Little bit this, little bit that," Biddy replied airily, "jes' the what t' eat for an Irishman."

"I do believe that Father Crowley dines here more on your account than mine. Take care," Lucy said with a smile. "For all we know, he may want to convert you and carry you away."

"Hoo!" Biddy threw up her hands in mock horror. "None of them spookish candles and foreign singsong for me. No, ma'am." She shook her head vehemently. "I'll take my religion pure and simple. Anybody 'round here gets converted, it'll be Father Crowley himself. Ain't a man livin' who can't be reached through his belly."

Biddy had a point, Lucy thought, watching Father Crowley ladle out his third portion of stew. "I'm sorry Seth isn't here, Father. He always enjoys your company so much. You're a welcome relief from the usual business and social obligations."

"And you from my sots and whores, Pastora."

She blinked, then laughed aloud. "I daresay I'll never get used to such candor from a man of the cloth."

"If I can't recognize a sinner, how am I to save one?

By the way, I dined at Mrs. Gibbs's home after our last meeting of the Good Shepherd group."

Lucy's face was without expression. "And?"

"We had a long talk. She told me how she first met you."

"Yes," she said cautiously, "we were both living in Castalia at the time."

"Working at your disparate trades, as I understand it."

"You could say that."

"She intends to take instructions in the Faith. She wanted my advice."

"Heavens! Are you serious?"

"Indeed. And so is she. I expect she'll make a jolly good Catholic. There's none so devout as the reformed sinner."

Lucy shook her head in amazement. "I declare, first she climbs her way into society and then she climbs her way into heaven."

Father Crowley cast her an admonishing look over the bowl of his spoon. "Now, now, Pastora, unless you're certain of your own place among the angels, you've no right to criticize."

"Forgive me. You're quite correct. In fact," she said thoughtfully, "I rather prefer not knowing if I shall be received in heaven. All due respect, Father, but your absolution seems too easy to me. I prefer to tussle with Old Nick single-handedly each time he creeps up on me. I don't always win, mind you, but when I do, I know the victory is my own and I'm stronger for the next battle."

" 'Stubborn and independent,' that's what Seth calls you." He patted his lips with his napkin. "Speaking of Old Nick, what have you heard from young Nicholas? And where's Beth? I was expecting to see her here tonight."

"She's spending the evening with Naomi. They're both very concerned about the turn the War has taken."

"With good reason. The Rebs are going under, no mistaking it now. And Nick?"

Lucy paused a moment before she spoke. "It's hard to tell. Each letter seems different from the last. At one time he seems hopeful, and the next he's confused and melancholy. He says his wounds have healed as well as can be expected, though he still has some discomfort. I wish I knew what it was that troubles him so."

Father Crowley smiled sympathetically. "I expect it's the rigors of prison life. Tell me, Abel is well?"

"Courting the goddess of justice and Miss Selina Mountford with equal fervor. I pray neither lady is siren enough to keep him away forever."

"Not a chance. He and Beth are Californians, born and bred. There's not a state in the Union, nor the South either, that has the excitement of this place. They'd be bored to distraction anywhere else."

"I do hope you're right," she said worriedly. "Abel seems to think we're a poor second to the intellects of Cambridge, and Bethie has her heart set on being the mistress of New Rosedale one day."

"Mark my words, you've nothing to fear. Your grandchildren will be playing within these walls and chasing about your vineyard."

"If it survives. This winter has brought us another year of drought. A lot of the *rancheros* are leaving the valley because of the poor crops. I pray our wells hold out."

"And I shall do the same, Pastora. When will you have your first harvest?"

"Next year, God willing."

"I look forward to the time I see bottles of your own vintage on this table."

"No more than I, Father." She gazed down the length of the dark mahogany tabletop, trying for a moment to imagine that day. In her mind's eye, she saw Bethie and Nick laughing with Cal. Abel, in his usual chair sat erect and tall, solemn as always, the very image of the earnest young lawyer. In Seth's place—But here she stopped for strangely he was absent. But this was foolishness, nothing more than the present truth intruding on her reverie. Still, the vision bothered her. Whenever Seth was away, she missed him more keenly than she liked to acknowledge. It was as though some essential part of her was lacking, some cog or lever without which she did not fully function. She busied herself. She went through the expected motions, but without Seth, they were merely that. Only when he returned did she feel once more complete, restored by the simple fact of his presence.

Seth brushed the dust of the journey from his hat and tossed it onto the hall chair as she emerged from the library. He held her close and kissed her. "Thank you, my dearest."

"You received the money?"

"Yes. Biggs sent it to my hotel, as you'd told him to." He cupped her face in his hands and looked down at her, smiling. It was a moment before he spoke again. "I'm sorry you had to raid your own coffers."

"Seth, what's mine is yours. I couldn't have you borrowing when I had money to spare. What good is it to me if I can't use it to give my husband a little peace of mind?" She took his hand and led him into the drawing room. "Were you able to square your accounts with those people?"

"Every last one of them, thanks to you. Now, have you a glass of whiskey to spare a weary traveler?"

She brought it to him and sat beside him. "I'm so glad you're back and that this wretched business is over and done with."

"A messy, unpalatable affair, my dear," he said with an expression of distaste. "Humble pie is not to my liking, but I hope I've convinced those poor folks I had no part in Asa's schemes. I have the papers he gave them. They aren't the original ones we'd drafted. He rewrote them for his own purposes and substituted his version. All of which proves that a gambler in dire straits is nothing more than a cornered animal. Survival is everything, and damn the means."

"Seth, I chanced upon Hiram Berry in Montgomery Street. He says he may want you to testify on Gonzales's behalf."

"I'll call on Berry in the morning. The sooner I see the last of this, the happier I'll be."

Septimus appeared in the doorway. He nodded to Seth. "Welcome home, Mr. Slade. Ma'am," he addressed Lucy, "Miz' Naomi's here to see Miss Beth. You know if she's about?"

"She's upstairs, Septimus. I wasn't aware she was expecting anyone, but I'll fetch her."

"I'll do it," Seth said. "I want to change out of these dusty clothes."

Lucy went into the sitting room where Naomi was waiting. "Hello, my dear. I'll keep you company 'til Bethie comes down."

"Thank you, Mrs. Slade. I'm sorry to intrude like this." She removed her gloves, dropped one and bent to retrieve it, knocking her bonnet askew in the process.

Poor Naomi, Lucy thought; try as she might, never all of a piece. "Have you heard from Boyd?"

"Yes'm." She fumbled with the cuff of her dress and withdrew a crumpled envelope. "Oh, Mrs. Slade—"

"Naomi, is Boyd all right?"

"Yes'm, only—"

"Cousin!" Beth ran to kiss her cheek. "What a nice surprise. Does this mean you've heard from Boyd after so long?"

Naomi nodded miserably.

"He's all right," Lucy said quickly. "Naomi, what's the matter?"

She handed the letter to Beth. "It's New Rosedale." Her eyes filled with tears. "I'm sorry, Bethie."

Beth paled. Her hands trembled as she unfolded the letter and spread it in her lap.

"What happened, Naomi?" Lucy asked her.

"Boyd was in Atlanta, ma'am, when it fell. His arm was broken, and he was mending there. When he heard that General Sherman had gotten through to Milledgeville, he became worried about Nick's folks."

"'I was dodging Yankees,' Beth read aloud, 'lest they decide to make sport of me, seeing I was not in condition to fight back.'" She fell silent and read on. A tear spilled on the page. She took out her handkerchief and blotted the paper dry. When she was through, she handed the letter to Lucy.

"May I, Naomi?" Lucy asked.

Naomi nodded and went to Beth. She knelt on the floor before her chair and took Beth's hands in hers.

. . . It was dusk, and I could smell the stench of something burnt even before I made out the silhouettes of the three chimneys against the night sky. Chimneys and a mass of black rubble are all that remain of one of the noblest homes in Georgia. As I walked about, looking for signs of life, I heard some darkies singing somewhere beyond the smokehouse. Field hands, they were, at a cook-fire. I introduced myself, not knowing what kind of a reception to expect, but they were only a handful of confused black folks making a meal of a watery soup which they kindly shared with me. The Yankees stripped the place of food, they said. The smokehouse, the chicken coops, the corn and grain bins, the root cellar—they raided them all. They even dug up Aunt Sue's flower beds, looking for silver and valuables.

One of the household servants must have betrayed her, because they suddenly left the gardens (this is according to a graybeard named Ham) and went straight for the kennels where the stuff was buried under the dirt floor. They shot the dogs, even though Ham told them they were harmless pets and not trackers. The Yankees had lanterns in the kennel, the better to see what they were doing. Somehow it caught fire, and the blaze spread to the house. Calm as anything, they just went about loading their loot onto their wagons and animals and rode off without a backward glance.

My dear aunt and uncle departed the following dawn with two of the servants, but I do not know where they are now. Those poor black folks that remained for me to find were as bewildered and lost as children alone in a forest. God knows what will become of them, or any of us, for that matter. As I write, Sherman's men are still marching toward the sea, with more tales of looting and burning in their wake.

My dearest wife . . .

The rest of the letter was meant for Naomi's eyes alone. Lucy folded it and laid it on the table. "Bethie, I don't know what to say—"

"Don't say anything, Mama," she replied bitterly. "You're the one who kept praising William Sherman, as I recall. 'A good man,' you said, 'a fine man.' As long as I live, I never want to hear that name again. Now please leave us alone, Mama. I know where your sympathies lie in this War, and I want to be with my own kind."

Lucy flushed as if she had been slapped. "Bethie, my feelings about the War are only to wish it over. How dare you accuse me of being unsympathetic? I care nothing for the victories and defeats these men inflict upon each other, save when they touch the ones I love. Your future is the only thing that matters to me now."

"I have none."

"Oh, Beth," Naomi cried, "don't say that."

"Naomi's right," Lucy told her. "Of course you have a

future. Perhaps New Rosedale will be rebuilt. Don't confuse tragedies with endings, Bethie. Only death is final. Tragedies are a part of life." She rose and kissed both girls. "Naomi, dear, thank you for bringing the news yourself. You're a good friend."

Lucy ascended the stairs slowly. She could hear Beth sobbing and Naomi's soft voice trying to soothe her. How long had it been since good news knocked upon the door of this house? She tried to remember. The past two years a series of misfortunes. First flood, then drought. Nick wounded and captured. Asa's deception and Seth's financial troubles. And now this. "How long, Lord, how long?" she murmured.

"Missee?" Lin stood at the top of the staircase, holding Cal's chubby hand. "You spoke?"

"Only to myself, Lin." She knelt and took the boy into her arms, holding him close and stroking his curly head.

He tilted his face up to hers. "Grandmama, are you crying?"

"My eyes are tired, dear, that's all."

"If you let them go to sleep, they won't be tired anymore."

"You're quite right. Perhaps I shall take a nap before supper. Lin, don't go downstairs just now. Missybet wants some privacy for the moment. You and Cal stay in the nursery until Septimus calls us down to eat."

Lin helped her to her feet. "Missee, is something wrong?"

"Mister Nick's parents have lost their home. It was burned in the War."

"I am sorry, missee." She frowned and shook her head. "So much unhappiness. Maybe you better go to a fortune teller."

"A what?"

"A fortune teller," she repeated soberly. "There are many good ones on Dupont *gaai*. Shall I go for you? I will ask him when the gods will bring good fortune to the house where I live."

Lucy smiled and patted her cheek. "Do as you wish, my dear. Thank you for the thought."

The conversation slipped her mind until, several days later, Lin knocked timidly at the door of the sitting room where Lucy was darning.

538

"Missee," she whispered, "I may come in?"

"Certainly. What is it?"

She scampered to Lucy's chair. "The fortune teller. You know what he tells me?"

Lucy held the eye of her needle up to the light and threaded it. "Oh, dear!" She laughed. "Don't tell me you actually still believe in that nonsense."

"But missee," she argued, "this man tells me long ago Missybet going to have a boy baby. He tells me Mister Nick will be sick from the War."

Lucy glanced up. "Is that so?"

She nodded solemnly. "He is very wise. And now," she added, a smile spreading over her face, "he tells me there is no sadness in this house. The bad times blow away like fog, and there is sunshine. The house is happy. There is another sadness, but it is far away. We see it, he says, but it is not near this house."

"And how much did this information cost?"

"Two bits."

"I shall repay you, since you went on my behalf, but you mustn't be throwing away money on superstitions, Lin. If you ask me, at two bits a visit, the fortune tellers are the only ones sure of good fortune."

Seth received the news with a chuckle. "We've a Chinese guardian angel, is that it? Well, one can't be choosy. I'll accept good news from any quarter these days. Gonzales goes to trial tomorrow. Let's see how right Lin's soothsayer proves on that matter."

The courtroom smelled of varnished wood and wet wool. It was raining outside, and the air in the building was humid and heavy. Hiram Berry, true to Seth's word had set upon Asa with the feline cunning of a tiger, now skirting him obliquely, now lunging forward to attack, tearing his testimony apart with swift, sure slashes.

At first, Asa had adroitly evaded his thrusts. Summoning all of his protean charm, he dodged and parried with such subtlety that Lucy, as much as she despised the sight of him, found her gaze fixed upon his face as he spoke. If she had ever doubted the full measure of his knavery, his testimony disabused her, once and for all. But at the last, he was no match for Hiram Berry. The fox, exhausted and cowed, fell prey to the tiger.

She felt herself tense as Seth stepped into the witness

box. She could see how angry he was. His body was rigid with suppressed indignation. He bit off his words like a snapping cur, and his eyes, ice-blue and hard, stared at Asa with a look that chilled her.

The last witness was the young man's father. Silver-haired and weathered, stooped from years of labor, he shuffled to the witness box dressed in a nearly-new suit that had obviously been borrowed from a man taller and larger than he. He spoke haltingly and with a heavy accent, nervously wringing his gnarled and calloused hands. Tears of gratitude glistened on his leathery cheeks as he told of Seth seeking him out and making amends for Asa's deception. Stepping down, he started to return to his seat, then paused and went to Seth. He grasped Seth's hand in his and tried to speak, but the words caught in his throat. Trembling, the old man bent his face to Seth's and kissed his cheek.

As they left the courtroom, Seth took her arm and steered a wide path between them and Asa Hudson. Neither of them looked at him.

"It went well," Seth said finally, opening the door for her. "Gonzales will be punished, of course, but I expect Hiram will fetch him a lighter sentence than he would have received without our help."

"Poor old Señor Gonzales. To think anyone could be so low as to victimize that elderly, defenseless man—"

"Enough," he said. "Let's not dwell on it, please."

Whether by augury or coincidence, Lin's seer appeared to have earned his two bits. The newspaper contained only the brief statement that "Mr. Seth Slade of this city testified as a witness on behalf of the defendant."

That part of it, at least was over. In the weeks that followed, Seth met with Asa in stilted, painful sessions to dissolve what remained of their partnership. The strain showed on Seth. "Soon," Lucy comforted him, "it will all be a thing of the past. Aren't you the one who's always telling me how the wheel turns?"

He smiled tiredly. "And what makes you so stubbornly cheerful this evening?"

"A jolly letter from Abel about how well he's doing in school. He's third in his class, he says. And not a single smug reference to the holy cities of Cambridge and Boston or the sainted Selina Mountford."

"Ah, that stuff nettles you, doesn't it? Don't fret so

about the boy. I daresay his professors are working the hide off him. Law school is a humbling experience, my dear, and I doubt he has much time to spare from his studies."

"That would suit me perfectly," she said tartly. "I didn't ship him off to Cambridge for a degree in snobbery."

"No," he agreed with a sly grin, "for that, he could have stayed home and listened to Bethie. Have you seen those drawings she's been making?"

"Designs for another mansion for New Rosedale. It's a harmless enough preoccupation, though her plans make the Occidental Hotel look like a chicken coop."

"It'll never be built, you know."

"Bethie's design? Of course not. But if it makes her happy to draw—"

"No. None of those great plantation houses will rise again. Without slave labor, they'd be impossible. After this war is over, it will be years before the South recovers. It may not even happen in our lifetime. I'm afraid Bethie's dreams will have to be trimmed to fit the truth. But for the moment, at least they give her some solace. Now, my girl, how about a breath of fresh air? Shall we take a stroll in the garden before supper?"

Despite the drought, the first signs of approaching spring had begun to appear. The slim, green-sheathed buds of the iris showed on their stalks like fingers pointing upward toward the roses that climbed the columns of the porch. The azalea bushes were lush with new foliage, and acacias bloomed on the far gardens that dotted the hillsides. The days grew perceptibly warmer, and the raw winds of winter gave way to temperate breezes that sent flocks of white clouds crossing overhead like fat sheep grazing in a sky-blue field.

Lucy woke to the sound of bells. She donned a robe over her chemise and went to open the curtains. Seth stirred. "Is it a fire?" he asked sleepily.

She peered outside. "The morning mist hasn't burnt off yet. I can't see anything."

Septimus was waiting for them as they came downstairs for breakfast. He sprang from the hall chair and rushed forward, his usual equanimity abandoned. "Wah Ming—" he began, gesturing toward the front door. "He say it's done, it's—" His tongue tripped over his words and he spluttered helplessly.

"The fruit vendor? What about Wah Ming?"

He seized a breath. "The War! Wah Ming tol' me it's over! He got the news down below, in town. There's bells ringin' and flags flyin' and folks shootin' off guns!"

"Oh God," Lucy gasped. Her eyes swam with tears. "Bethie!" she cried, "come quickly! Cal, Cal," she called up the stairwell, "Papa's coming home!"

He came clattering down the stairs, tripping at the bottom and falling into her outstretched arms. Lucy hugged him tightly to her bosom, crying and laughing all at once.

"Mama?" Beth paused on the staircase. "Is it true?"

"It's over, my darling. At last."

Beth sat on the stairs, her face buried in her hands.

Cal wriggled free from Lucy's embrace. "If Papa's coming home, why is everybody crying?"

Seth pressed his handkerchief to his glistening eyes. He crouched next to the child. "Because, my boy," he said, lifting him to his shoulders, "crying is all a body can do when his feelings are too powerful for words." He rose, carrying Cal, and the boy stretched his arms high.

"I can touch heaven!" he shouted happily.

"Yes." Lucy laughed. "Of course you can. Today, all miracles are possible."

XXVIII

THERE WERE salutes, the gunfire at last aimed harmlessly skyward, bursting over the hills and the bay, followed by a stillness in which a thousand flags flapped and snapped in the wind and bunting rustled at the windows, balconies and rooftops where it had appeared overnight, a profusion of red, white and blue blooming forth miraculously from barren fields of glass and iron and shingle.

But like blossoms blighted by a sudden, deadly frost, the colors faded all too quickly to dark and somber swags of black. The bright promise of that day was extinguished, and the city lay draped in dismal mourning. The president was dead, assassinated. The anguish and rage would not be contained. In an eruption of fury, mobs attacked the offices of half a dozen newspapers lately sympathetic to the Southern cause, hurling type from shattered windows, sending broken furniture crashing to the street below and wrecking the presses. When the convulsion subsided, an oppressive quiet returned to the streets. The very air seemed heavy with sorrow. Flags drooped at half-staff, stirring only when the listless breeze sighed briefly and fell still again. It was as though the blow had knocked the breath out of nature itself. In the silence, the cannons of Fort Alcatraz thundered their final tribute over the waters of the bay, echoed from Fort Point, Black Point, Angel Island and the decks of the warships in the harbor. The bells of every church and firehouse joined in a melancholy dirge, and the rhythm of muffled drums resounded from the closed and shuttered buildings lining the downtown streets.

Lucy stared numbly at the newspaper. "Friday, April

28, 1865," it read. "Booth Tracked and Killed." She felt nothing. It was beyond the power of vengeance to redeem a country from its sorrow. Only time could heal. From the hallway, she heard Septimus greeting Seth. She glanced through the drawing room door at the grandfather clock.

"You're home early," she said as he came in.

"I felt a bit weary. Odd how something like this affects one physically. I stopped by the Bank Exchange for a drink on the way. Rumor there has it that Asa Hudson has left the city for good. I heard he moved to Los Angeles."

"Good riddance. The mere thought of him still makes me feel betrayed and angry."

"He wasn't a malicious fellow, my dear. Simply weak."

"To my thinking, weakness is just as great a menace as evil. They do equally as much damage."

"What do you say we change the subject? Where's Bethie?"

"Gone to Albert's and Polly's. They're giving a tea for the young people. It's Martha's husband's birthday."

"Nathan Morse? A wake would be more appropriate."

"A young man of utterly measurable charm, I'm afraid. I can't think why Martha married such a stick."

"Damn," Seth brought his hand down hard on his knee. "Damn, but I'm tired of gloom." He stood up suddenly. "Come on, Pastora, let's go upstairs and change clothes. We'll hitch up the carriage and go out to dine. Oysters and champagne, that's the prescription I need."

"Do you think it's right to enjoy ourselves in public, so soon after Mr. Lincoln's death? I wouldn't want to be disrespectful."

"I hope and pray, my dear, that when I go to my reward, it won't be a signal for you to deny yourself whatever joys remain in this world. I daresay our late, beloved president wouldn't begrudge us an evening out. We'll drink a toast to his memory, if that will soothe your conscience."

"But Biddy's already preparing supper."

"Can't it keep? Now who's a stick? What's got into you?"

She smiled. "Nothing. Perhaps I'm growing old and set in my ways."

Seth took her hand and brought her to her feet. "You know my cure for that, my dear."

"You are a shameful man, Seth Slade. It's only five o'clock in the afternoon!"

He laughed and caught her around the waist. "So late? We haven't a moment to waste!"

Lucy wondered if other married people were as happy as they. Sometimes she would glance covertly at the faces of other couples, but only rarely did she glimpse between them that smile of secret sharing that revealed a hint of the fires within. And when she did, she would look quickly away, embarrassed, as though she had intruded upon some intimate intercourse not meant for public eyes. Still, it warmed her to think there might be others as fortunate as they. There was power in the kind of love she and Seth shared. Whatever blows fate dealt them seemed always to rebound from the invisible, resilent sinew that united them. If only Bethie and Abel could find such joy and contentment in marriage.

Almost every morning now, Cal would ask, "Is Papa coming home today?"

"Poor dear," Lucy said to Beth, "I'm afraid we did him a disservice in raising his hopes. At the age of three, it's difficult to comprehend that some things require time and patience."

But soon he lost interest, inquiring only rarely and then not at all. It was not surprising. How could the child be expected to long for a father he had never known? All that Cal knew of Nick was his photograph, a stack of letters he couldn't read and the changes of mood that news of him, good or bad, wrought upon the grown-ups.

For almost four years, the temper of the household had responded like a weathervane to the slightest breath of news about Nick. Now, after the excitement of the surrender, it seemed oddly becalmed and static. It was a deceptive calm, Lucy reflected, born of suspense rather than tranquillity.

Finally, in June, the announcement came. President Johnson had ordered the release of all Confederate prisoners-of-war. Bethie wept with joy. Lucy, noting Cal's bewilderment, couldn't help but laugh and hug him and promise, "Someday you'll remember all this and you will understand."

545

At last they heard from Nick. His telegraph message read: "Exchanged at City Point, Virginia. Will visit family at Regina's in Charleston. Letters follow. Nick."

Beth was disappointed. "Naomi says Boyd's already on his way home. He'll be here by the end of August."

"But Bethie," Lucy told her, "Boyd's parents live in San Francisco. It's only natural for Nick to want to spend some time with his folks, after all they've been through. They have to decide what to do about New Rosedale."

"I should be there," she argued. "After all, I'm a Stevens now."

"You're not their blood and you hail from a state of the Union. Exercise some tact, my dear. Wait until Nick knows what his plans are."

"But it's my life, too! And Cal's. It's not fair for Nick to leave us sitting here while he has a gala family reunion."

"Beth." Seth folded his newspaper and laid it on his knees. "I don't think you fully comprehend the conditions in the South. It's no place for you and Cal just now. I am sure Nick has your best interests at heart."

"You must learn to obey your husband's wishes without carping, Bethie."

"Excellent advice, my dear wife." Seth smiled at her.

Beth bounded up impatiently from her chair. "I know what I'll do. I'll have Septimus drive me downtown and I shall buy the fanciest, prettiest silks that Joe and Klara have in stock and then I shall have a dress made for his homecoming." She went into the hall. "Lin!" she called upstairs. "Look after Cal. I'm going out."

"Ah, well," Seth said to Lucy, "who can blame her for being impatient?"

"She's spoiled, Seth. She thinks only of herself. Tell me, what do you suppose Nick will do?"

He paused to light his pipe. At length, he said, "Nick is lazy. A hero, yes, but lazy nonetheless. His brother, Gwin, would have been the one to take over New Rosedale when the time came. He was the eldest, and from all reports he was ambitious and hard-working. Nick could have lived quite handsomely, enjoying his hunts and balls and parties, while Gwin bore the responsibilities of the place."

"And now?"

"Who knows? He's been through a dreadful initiation

546

by fire. And fire either strengthens or destroys a substance. Either way, he's no longer the same young man who left here." _

"You're saying he'll be a stranger."

"In many ways, I expect he will be."

The warm, dry weeks of summer passed without further word from Nick. Seth, returned from a trip to the vineyard, reported that the valley was burnt brown, a virtual wasteland. Their wells were holding out, though Herr Schmidt doubted they could last much longer. Unless the coming winter brought plentiful rain, there would be no first harvest next year, nor any year. All the planning, all the labor would be for nothing. Lucy understood now how Pa must have felt to see his dreams blighted. She understood his frustration and rage in the face of forces that rendered him powerless. Nightly, she prayed for the season ahead, for the vines and fruit that meant so much to Seth. His living legacy he'd called them. For that reason alone, she prayed, they must not be allowed to die.

How eager everyone was to forget the War and the sympathies that had divided them, Lucy thought. It seemed now like nothing more than a prolonged nightmare, from which they had awakened and found their lives untouched. In a place like this, far away from the battlefields, it was not difficult to dismiss the bitterness that had separated people like Ada and Solomon Brock from her and Seth. It was a good thing, she supposed, amity being preferable to enmity. Yet in its own way, it was just another dream. Here in this blessedly safe city, they were free to leave the past behind as effortlessly as a child closed his story book and opened another, transporting himself in his imagination from one illusion to the next. But what it was like to be there, where Nick was, she could not conceive.

Beth did not show Nick's letters to Lucy and Seth. It was plain to see they saddened her. His father, she told them, had suffered a seizure that had paralyzed his left side, and his mother had dark spells of melancholia. She sat by her husband's bedside, weeping for hours at a time in inexpressible, mute misery. Nick's sister Regina was the only one in the family whose home remained unscathed. Nick's parents, along with his sister Lydia and her family, were crowded together there, war-weary, discouraged and uncertain.

"Nick says he's going to New Rosedale, Mama. He wants to see it for himself before they decide what to do."

"A very sensible idea."

"Pray, Mama. Pray that he wants to rebuild it."

"That might be difficult, Bethie. We don't know the family's financial situation. The plantation has been ruined. They've no slaves now to farm it. And Confederate dollars are hardly worth the paper they're printed on."

"But you rebuilt this house when it burned."

"In quite different circumstances. Beth, you must resign yourself to the possibility that it's a lost cause. That way of life is gone forever, Seth says."

"Mama, don't say that! How can you be so heartless? You know how much it means to Nick and me."

"My dear girl, cruelty is the furthest thing from my mind. Dreams are fragile, Bethie. All it takes to shatter them is a moment's truth, and right now Nick is closer to the truth than we are."

She had tried her best to prepare Beth, but when his next letter came, the girl took it to her room and lay there sobbing until she retched. Finally, Lin and Lucy undressed her and put her to bed. Lucy didn't have to ask what he had written.

"Papa's coming home," Cal announced soberly at breakfast the next morning.

"Sometime, Cal. Sometime," Seth told him.

"Soon," he insisted, poking his spoon into his oatmeal.

"Darling boy," Lucy said, "I know it's difficult, but try to be patient."

"No!" He banged his spoon against the side of the bowl. "Papa's coming soon. Mama says he's on his way."

Seth glanced across the table at Lucy.

"I don't know," she said flustered. "Bethie was in no condition to talk last night. Cal, when did Mama tell you this?"

"When I got dressed. Papa's going to come on a big boat."

"It's true." Beth stood in the doorway to the dining room. Her face was pale, and there were dark hollows under her eyes.

Seth rose and pulled out her chair. "That's the best piece of news we've had in months."

"He's never going back. There's nothing there for him anymore, he said. His Pa wants to sell the land."

"Beth," Lucy said gently, "I know how disappointed you are, but there's nothing you can do about it. Try to see the bright side, my dear. Nick's on his way back here. You'll be together at last."

"He wasn't like anyone else," she said slowly, the tears coming to her eyes. "He was different. He was special. He was genteel and aristocratic. He had a grand plantation, and—"

"For God's sake, Beth," Seth interrupted irritably, "don't talk about him as though he were dead. Which did you marry, anyway, Nick or New Rosedale?"

Before she could answer, Lucy spoke up. "He's been through a great deal, Bethie. I'm sure the loss pains him even more than it hurts you. He'll need all the sympathy and comfort and cheer you can muster. He must make a new life now. He'll need your support. So much depends upon you."

"Spunk, my girl," Seth told her. "No backward glances from here on. Remember the lesson of Lot's wife. Besides, after all Nick's endured, I'll be damned if I'll see his homecoming turned into a wake. Do I make myself clear?"

She nodded.

"Damn!" Cal said gleefully.

"That, my boy, is my word, not yours. Don't use it. Eat your breakfast, please. Beth," Seth asked her, "when will he arrive?"

"He said he was leaving right away. That was over a month ago."

"But my dear," Lucy said, "he could be here in as little as three weeks' time!"

"Soon," Cal promised.

"Yes, indeed, my boy," Seth agreed. "Septimus!" he called in the direction of the kitchen.

"Sir?" Septimus appeared with the coffepot and filled Beth's cup.

"We'll have a bottle of champagne with our Sunday dinner, Septimus. We've something to celebrate. Mister Nick's on his way back to us."

"Yes, sir," Septimus said. "Miss Beth, it sure will be good to see you smilin'."

If she was not yet smiling, Lucy thought, at least Beth

549

had regained her composure by the time they sat down to the noon meal. Seth bowed his head.

"Dear Lord, this day we are especially grateful to You for protecting Nicholas Stevens, for his recovery from his wounds and for his imminent reunion with this family. We pray for his safe passage and speedy arrival. For these and all Thine other blessings, past, present and future, we thank Thee. Amen."

"Amen," Cal repeated.

Seth took the champagne bottle from the table and opened it. The cork gave a loud pop, and Cal squealed with surprise. Lucy, watching his face, smiled at the innocent, childish delight that sent him into giggles as Seth struggled to suppress the foam. Suddenly Cal's face froze, spread wide in a laugh that became a shriek. The house shook. The windows rattled ominously. The dishes on the table bounced and slid and clattered together.

"Under the table!" Seth yelled.

Beth seized Cal from his chair as they scrambled to safety. For a moment, the motion stopped. Then came a series of wrenching jolts. Lucy could hear the sound of glass shattering. The walls creaked. A piece of plaster bounced down the door jamb and broke on the threshold. From the other rooms came the noise of sliding furniture and of objects tumbling to the floor. Cal screamed in terror, long after the movement ceased.

Lucy caught her breath. "There now, Cal. It's over. Don't cry."

Beth stroked the boy's face. "It was an earthquake, dear. It's gone now. See, it didn't hurt you, did it?"

In the dim light beneath the sheltering table, Lucy made out Seth's form crouched on the floor at the far end. "Oh, no." In spite of herself, she began to laugh. In one hand he still held the champagne bottle and in the other, his half-filled glass, intact.

"Not a drop spilled!" he called out triumphantly, rising to his feet.

Lucy shook with laughter as she emerged from under the table. "Congratulations, my love. Thank God I married a man with a cool head and a steady hand."

"I'll go have a look at the damage. Lucy, you'd better see to Biddy and Lin and Septimus. Come on, Cal." He held out a hand to the boy. "Let's see what got bounced about."

550

Lucy found Biddy kneeling in prayer, clutching tightly to the back of a kitchen chair, while Septimus was dazedly mopping up the remains of a bowl of applesauce. Lin, visibly trembling, appeared rooted where she stood, not daring to move from the pantry doorway.

"It's quite all right. Here, Biddy," Lucy said as she helped her to her feet, "don't take on so. These things happen now and then. It's not Judgment Day, only an earthquake. Lin, don't just stand there. Give Biddy a hand. Come now, everyone," she ordered, giving the words more authority than she felt, "dinner will proceed as soon as possible. Let's get on with it."

One wall of Beth's room revealed a long, diagonal crack, and in the library below, books had been thrown from the shelves and lay scattered about the floor and the furniture in a haphazard litter. The looking glass on the stairway had broken, and the two plaster lambs that had rested on the mantel in the drawing room were now an indistinguishable jumble of fragments. Seth had counted three broken window panes and several places where the ceilings would need repair, but on the whole, the house had fared well.

Downtown, the effects were far worse. Water and gas pipes had ruptured. Walls had split and fallen, and City Hall was badly damaged. Despite some injuries, no one had been killed. For that, at least, they could all be grateful.

As it had before, the city picked itself up, dusted itself off and went about its business. Lucy, overseeing the repairs to the house, could not help but remember the earlier quake, when they had lived above the Clay Street store. They had owned so little, had so few possessions, that a dustpan and a broom had sufficed to clean up. How long ago that seemed, a lifetime away, yet it was only eleven years, to the month. Time had slipped by so fast, and trying to hold onto a single day was as futile as trying to grasp a handful of the sea. Lucy watched Beth bowed over her needlework in the seat of the bay window. She was a woman now, in the full bloom of her extravagant, voluptuous beauty. Her hair shone like polished onyx surrounding the pale ivory of her skin. Her full mouth, slightly pouted in a faint, humorous expression of scorn, hinted at a willingness to tease. Her dark eyes were framed by long, thick lashes, and the glow of color on her cheeks accentuated the striking contrasts in her coloring.

Each day now, Beth took her new lavender silk dress from the wardrobe and laid it across her bed. Twice, though she had yet to wear it, she'd insisted that Lin iron its lace bertha and beribboned sleeves. Beth seemed, at last, to betray some anticipation at the prospect of Nick's return. New Rosedale had ceased to be a topic of discussion.

"Mama," Beth said without looking up from her work, "you're staring at me again."

"I was admiring the way you look, my dear. I was thinking how lovely Nick will find you. He's a fortunate young man to have such a pretty wife waiting for him."

She held her embroidery hoop at arm's length and surveyed her stitchery. "Mama," she said thoughtfully, laying the work aside, "sometimes it scares me. It's been such a long time since Nick and I were together. We'll hardly know what to say to each other."

"I shouldn't worry about that, if I were you."

"But I've changed so much since he left. I'm grown up now. I have a child. I'm not the same person he married."

"That's one of the great adventures of marriage, Bethie. Think how monotonous it would be to live with someone who remained exactly the same, forever fixed in his ways. I'd sooner keep house with a log. At least I'd have the pleasure of watching moss grow on it."

"But you and Seth haven't changed."

"You're wrong. We've grown together, like a pair of trees planted so close that the branches interwine and become joined. In many ways, we support and protect each other. We're stronger for that unity. I think that if anything were to happen—"

"Pastora?" Seth called from the hall. "Are you ready to leave? Ah, here you are," he said, coming into the sitting room, hat in hand. "Did I interrupt anything?"

"Mama was explaining marriage to me."

He raised his brows. "Really? Then perhaps she'll be so kind as to explain it to me."

"Never!" Lucy laughed, rising from her chair. "That would remove all the mystery. Bethie, dear, I'm going to the Good Shepherd to look over the budgets while Seth's at the bootmaker's. We should be home by six."

"Come along, my love." Seth put his arm around Lucy's shoulders. "I've no intention of letting you dodge the issue so slickly. I expect a full revelation of the secrets of marriage. I'm all ears."

Lucy paused in the doorway. "I forgot one thing, Bethie," she said, turning back. "A sense of humor is essential."

The air grew cool on the ride home, though the sun still shone brightly above a low-lying mist that scudded through the narrows of the Golden Gate and settled over the harbor behind them. Septimus reined in the horses before the carriage-house, and Seth alighted, his new boots tucked under his arm. He held out his hand for Lucy.

In the middle of the lawn, Lin was pushing Cal on the rope swing that hung from the largest bough of the pine tree there.

"Lin, dear," Lucy called, "what's Cal doing out so late? It's high time he was washing up for supper."

The boy leapt from the still-moving swing and sped to Lucy, throwing his arms around her and burying his face in her skirts. He began to sob.

Lin ran to them. "Missee," her voice was low, "it's Mister Nick."

"He's here?" Seth's face broke into a wide grin.

"Yes, sir." Lin hesitated. "Cal, he starts to cry. I bring him out here, so nobody hears."

"But Lin," Lucy asked, "what's the matter with the child?"

"Oh, Missee—" Lin looked up at her, her grave eyes filling with tears. She shook her head, wordlessly.

"Where are they?" Seth wanted to know.

"In the drawing room."

Lucy pried the weeping boy's hands from her. "Take him in the back door, Lin, and go upstairs until suppertime. Seth," she said, grasping his arm as they walked toward the house, "I'm afraid."

"Hallo!" Seth shouted as he opened the door. "Is it true? Nick, my boy, you're home?"

They sat close together on the sofa, Beth clasping both his hands in hers, her back to Lucy and Seth as they entered. Over her shoulder, Lucy caught sight of his face. "Oh, Nick," she and Seth said in unison. "Nick," she repeated, "how good it is to see you."

She noticed immediately how greatly his face had changed. The boyish roundness was gone from his cheeks. The bland contours of youth had been pared away, revealing the pronounced, angular planes of maturity, emphasized by the deep cleft in his chin. He smiled only briefly. That look of cheeky self-assurance, so familiar from his photograph, had vanished. There was a new hardness to his gaze, and lines of weariness were etched beneath his eyes.

"You've returned a man," Seth said quietly.

"Almost." He put his hand on the arm of the sofa and rose.

Beth turned to them. Her face was white. As she moved, from behind her billowing skirts, a pair of crutches clattered to the floor.

"Almost," he said again, "though I wouldn't say entirely." He grasped the mantel to steady himself. "Would you?"

Slowly, Lucy raised her eyes from his truncated trouser-leg. "Oh, God. Nick, I'm so sorry."

"So am I," he replied, his face without expression.

Seth cleared his throat and gathering up the crutches from the floor, handed them to Nick. He put his hand on his shoulder and looked into his eyes in silence for a moment. "My son," he said finally, his voice unsteady, "we're very glad to have you back. Nothing can diminish that." Seth gave him a smile. "This calls for a drink, don't you think?" He didn't wait for Nick's answer. He turned away, the smile fading from his face. "I'll be with you all in a moment," he said, and he went to lay his new pair of boots on the chair in the hallway.

XXIX

LUCY TRIED to avert her eyes from the awful evidence of Nick's mutilation. She taught herself, as time went on, to fix her gaze always upon his face, despite the marks of strain and bitterness that she discerned there. Lucy wondered if Beth would ever fully recover from the shock. The girl went through her days like a sleepwalker. All her customary liveliness and gaiety had vanished at the sight of him. In her eyes was a stunned, stricken look of anguish, as though she had suffered a savage blow from a source that she neither perceived nor understood. Only Cal, his initial horror past, accepted Nick's condition without flinching. Blessed by the natural, artless resilience of his child's mind, he simply took it for granted. He would climb upon Nick's lap, full of innocent curiosity, and ply him with questions that none of the others, out of delicacy or dismay, would have dared to utter.

"Papa, when you were a prisoner, did they lock you in a castle?"

Nick gave him a wry smile. "No, Calvert, only in a tent camp."

"Couldn't you escape? In the storybooks—"

"I didn't have any storybooks to tell me how. At any rate, I couldn't have hopped very far, not like this. Jump down now, son. Your weight's a bit much on my stump." He lifted the boy to the floor.

"Does it hurt? Do you want your medicine?"

"Not yet. Bethie, is the newspaper lying about?"

She rose from the piano bench. "I'll get it."

"No." He reached for his crutches. "I can get it myself. Where is it?"

555

"In the library. On Mama's desk."

Lucy closed her book. Beth went back to the piano, absently practicing her scales. The front door slammed shut, and Lucy heard the sound of Seth whistling to himself in the hall.

"Ladies and gentlemen," he announced cheerfully, "I call your attention to the weather outside."

"Rain!" Lucy sprang from her chair and stood at the front window, watching the large, heavy drops splash against the glass and stream downward to spill over the sill onto the parched ground below. "Oh, Seth, I pray it's pouring up in the valley."

"I could have told you it would rain." Nick settled himself once again on the sofa with the paper. "My wound always warns me ahead of time."

"Are you very uncomfortable?" Beth asked him. "Let me put some pillows—"

"Stay where you are, Bethie. I'm quite capable of taking care of myself, thank you."

"I saw your Uncle Dabney this afternoon at the Bank Exchange," Seth told him. "He's as eager as ever for you to join him and Boyd at the Iron Works. Says he'll keep the position open until you're ready."

" 'Open' indeed. Of course he can keep it open. It doesn't exist. You know as well as I do that he and Boyd can manage the place themselves. His charity has a reek to it that makes me want to retch."

"If we may put your delicate sensibilities aside for a moment," Seth said quietly, "a job is what one makes of it. You're a bright young fellow, Nick. I daresay you'd make a valuable contribution to your Uncle Dabney's business. And from all he's said, he feels the same way."

"Perhaps," Lucy suggested, "Nick would like some time to make up his mind. After all, there's no reason to rush into anything. A little holiday might do wonders for us all. Seth, what about a trip up to the vineyard? It's so beautiful there after the first fall rains."

"Do you feel up to it, my boy?"

"I'm as good now as I ever shall be. Besides, I'm curious to see the place, after hearing so much about it."

"Then let's the four of us plan to leave on Saturday."

"Me too!" Cal cried.

"Not this time, darling," Beth told him. "Your mama and papa want to be by themselves for a bit."

"That's not fair!" He pounded his small fist on the floor. "You never play with me since Papa came home!"

"That's enough, Calvert." Nick threw him a warning glance. "If you don't behave, you'll be sent upstairs."

"I say," Seth exclaimed, "perhaps you two would like to go up to Saint Helena without us old folks."

"No," Nick replied quickly. "I'm looking forward to having you show me around the place and explain its workings."

"But Herr Schmidt can do that," Beth said.

"I don't want to take Herr Schmidt away from his duties," he told her. "And it would be more entertaining for the four of us to go together."

Beth flushed and returned to her music.

They took the steamer as far as Suscol and then, as a lark, they boarded the new railway to Napa, where Herr Schmidt met them.

Despite the journey, Nick insisted upon seeing the vineyard, the out-buildings and the caves before nightfall. At supper, he ate little, pleading fatigue and discomfort, and fell asleep in his chair as soon as the meal was over.

Lucy lay in bed, close beside Seth, her hand in his. The cottage was quiet, save for the tattoo of a fresh rainstorm on the roof. Outside, on the vine-covered slopes, the thirsty earth was soaking in the moisture. Already the new growth of wild mustard on the hillside and in the valley below hinted at deliverance from the drought.

"Pastora," he whispered, "are you awake?"

"I was listening to that lovely sound overhead," she murmured, laying her face against his shoulder.

"I hope it wasn't a mistake, thinking Nick would be ready to travel again so soon. He looked ashen by the time he went to bed."

"He was very eager to come. Seth, does it strike you that he doesn't seem to want to be alone with Bethie, not even for an hour?"

"I daresay it will take them both some time to get used to each other again."

"She tries so hard to please him."

"He doesn't want her sympathy, my dear."

"But what does he expect?"

"I don't know." Seth sighed. "I don't think he knows,

557

either. Give him a while, Lucy. It's a difficult adjustment for us all."

By mid-morning the skies had cleared. Sunlight the color of pale, golden wine poured over the landscape, drenching the valley and trickling through the underbrush on the hills in thin, shining streams that shimmered wetly with the movement of the leaves overhead. Out behind the house, Chang was preparing a barbecued piglet for dinner. The savory scent of the roasting meat filled the air around the veranda. Nick brushed away a fly that had alighted on one of his dominoes. "Your turn, Bethie." He leaned back in his chair and stretched. "How much do you pay your coolies?" he inquired.

Lucy looked up from her reading. "You'd have to ask Seth."

"Not much, I'll wager."

"I believe their wages are very reasonable."

"Some smart fellow ought to ship a boatload of them to Savannah. If ever a place wanted for cheap workers now, it's the South."

"But surely you have all those freed slaves eager to earn a living."

He gave a dry chuckle. "Hell, they're much too grand now to stoop in the fields for the white boss. Ain't a one of them doesn't think he's going to be independently wealthy."

"But Nick," Beth said, "you could be the one. You could make a fortune supplying Chinese workers for the cotton fields."

"Ah, well," he said, dismissing the idea, "it was a thought." Despite the midday warmth, he shivered.

Lucy noticed, as he reached for his crutches, that his hands were trembling. "Nick, are you feeling well?"

"I will, soon as I have my medicine."

Beth rose and went to open the door for him.

"Damn it, Bethie," he said tiredly, "let me do for myself, won't you?"

"You should, you know," Lucy told her when he was out of earshot. "You mustn't make him feel any more of a cripple than he already does." She closed her book. "Listen. I hear horses on the lane. Seth's back. Run and fetch Herr Schmidt, Bethie. He's in the caves with Hong." Lucy went to the railing of the veranda, waiting to catch a glimpse of the cooper's wagons.

Rounding the corner of the drive, Seth reined in his horse and raised his hat triumphantly. Behind him came the two wagons, creaking to a halt with their cargo of iron-staved casks bumping hollowly against each other as the procession stopped.

Lucy ran from the porch, as Beth and Herr Schmidt, followed by Hong Hing-wing and his men, converged upon the wagons. Herr Schmidt rubbed his hands together with pleasure at the sight of the barrels.

Seth clapped him jovially on the shoulder. "Next year, my friend. Next year they'll be full up."

"*Mit Gottes Wille*," Herr Schmidt murmured. "Hong," he ordered, pointing toward the largest of the casks, "we begin with the fermentation barrels."

As the draymen unlashed the ropes that secured their loads, the first of the huge barrels rolled to the ground with a resounding thump. Hong Hing-wing called out a command and gestured toward the caves. The coolies pushed the cask across the drive, sending it bouncing and rumbling ahead of them along the pathway.

Nick joined them. "Why the two sizes?"

"The larger ones are the fermentation barrels. When the wine is fermented, it's racked, drawn off to smaller casks to clarify it and allow it to age."

"How long does the whole thing take?"

"From harvest to table?" Herr Schmidt fingered his whiskers. "That we have to wait to know. Maybe seven, eight months, but that is a guess at this point."

"We shan't interfere with your work," Seth said. "You and Frau Schmidt are joining us for the barbecue, aren't you?"

"*Ja, ja,* with pleasure."

"Then perhaps you'll come early, and we'll drink a toast to christen our fine barrels."

Seth refreshed Herr Schmidt's whiskey glass. "Nick, my boy, how about you?"

Nick held out his glass. "Don't mind if I do. I still like the taste, though it seems to have lost its effect on me."

"Has it, now?" Seth raised his eyebrows. "I'd like to learn that trick myself." He took a deep breath. "Hang it all, Chang is making me hungry as a bear with that aroma."

"*Ha.*" Herr Schmidt laughed. "Me also."

"I think," Nick said quietly, "that was the thing that I hated most. The stench. Filthy bodies and stinking wounds. You can't imagine what it's like to smell your own flesh rotting away."

"Nick," Seth spoke to him gently, "this is not the time or the place."

Beth looked about to faint. Lucy reached over and took her hand. Herr Schmidt cleared his throat and swallowed a gulp of whiskey, while Frau Schmidt glanced worriedly from one to another of them.

"Perhaps," Seth told Nick, "that stuff's affecting you more than you thought."

"It's not. Ladies," he said, nodding to the three of them, "I regret the impropriety, but I assure you I'm not drunk. Behold." He rose, leaving his crutches behind, and stood erect on his one leg, his hands folded atop his head.

"Nick, please," Lucy begged him, "sit down."

Chang rapped at the doorjamb and stepped out onto the porch. "Dinner, Missee."

With palpable relief, they filed into the house and seated themselves at the table. Frau Schmidt, silent until now, made a polite attempt to converse in her awkward English. She turned to Nick, beside her. "In your War, you have many young friends from California?".

"Nick's not a Californian, Frau Schmidt," Beth informed her. "He's a Georgian."

"Ah," she said, though it was clear the distinction eluded her.

Herr Schmidt addressed her in German.

"Ah," she repeated, nodding this time. "Georgia, *ja*."

"I met but one soul from these parts, save for Boyd and myself. An older gentleman he was, a doctor from Fredericksburg who was looking after a wounded comrade of mine."

Seth handed him a plate heaped with steaming slices of pork. "Help yourself to the peas and rice, my boy. We're very informal here."

"From Fredericksburg?" Beth asked. "I thought you said he was a Californian."

"I gather he was for a time." Nick passed the serving bowl to Frau Schmidt. "Wore a gold nugget on his watch chain. A goodly sized chunk, bigger than my thumbnail. He plucked it out of a river with his own hands, he said.

Lucy smiled. "He must have been one of the lucky ones who caught the gold fever early. Those who came later worked a lot harder than that for their take, believe me."

"Mercy, yes," Beth put in. "I remember hardly anything from those days, but I do recall how the hydraulickers terrified me. Their noise was ferocious, and they made the riverbanks crumble away like so much sawdust. Abel used to tease me, saying if I didn't do as he liked, he'd tell them to turn their hoses on me."

"Dear God!" Lucy laughed. "He didn't! What a naughty child."

"Herr Schmidt," Nick asked, "would you be so kind as to pass the bread this way?"

"It's a pleasure to see you with such a keen appetite, my boy," Seth told him.

Nick glanced up for a moment, taking in the ample spread upon the table. His eyes seemed far away. "So much," he said softly. "So much good food . . ." He fell silent and bowed his head toward his plate.

"I wonder," Lucy spoke up quickly, "what's become of Castalia. According to Eleanor Gibbs—"

"That's the place." Nick looked up. "Castalia. Named after the place where the muses drank. Doctor Pierce told me."

Lucy felt the color drain from her cheeks. Her hand shook as she laid down her fork, and her voice was unsteady as she spoke. "Nick, was that Doctor Reed Pierce?"

"Yes'm, I believe that was his name."

"But Nick!" Beth cried. "He was our friend. He lived in a gloomy cabin with a sick lady and an Indian helper. Isn't that right, Mama?"

It was a moment before she spoke again. "Nick, tell me," she asked quietly, "how was he?"

Nick buttered his bread. "Not well, I'm afraid. Overworked, tired. There weren't enough doctors to go 'round. I heard some time later that he'd passed away from pneumonia."

Lucy grasped the tabletop and rose. "If you'd all be kind enough to excuse me for a moment."

Seth rapped lightly on the door to their room and opened it. He sat beside her on the bed. "Here," he said, handing her his handkerchief, "yours is a goner." He slipped an arm around her shoulders. "You must have loved him very much."

She nodded.

"I'm sorry, my dear."

"He was . . ." she faltered. "He was so kind. Such a sad, good man. We needed each other, I think. If he'd been free, I suppose we would have married."

"Forgive me for being selfish, but I'm glad things worked out as they did."

"Oh, Seth." She glanced up at him. "Don't misjudge me. I'm glad, too. It's just that he once meant so very much to me."

"I understand." He brushed an eyelash from her face.

"We were never, he and I—"

Seth laid a finger on her lips. "That's none of my affair. I'm only happy that you had the companionship of a good man at a time when you needed it. And I'm sorry his death pains you." He stood up. "I'll tell the others we'll proceed with dinner."

"No," she said, taking his hand. "Wait. I'm coming." She patted her eyes dry. "I want to be with you." Rising, she kissed him gently on the cheek. "Thank you, my dearest."

Lucy could not now imagine a life for herself any different from the one she had. Yet there had been a time long ago, when, awake or asleep, all her reflections and reveries had revolved around Reed Pierce; invisible, secret worlds whirling dizzily in orbit about his vital warmth. Then, she realized, the tension between concealment and exposure, between the pleasure of forbidden thoughts and the pain of undeniable truth, had only heightened her sensibilities. There was no ache so acute, no enchantment so intense as that found within the confines of a hopeless love. Its very hopelessness enhanced it. It was fragile, evanescent, and in consequence it was infinitely precious and affecting. Never could it be exposed to the subtle corrosions of the commonplace. Never would it become habitual or stale. It burned forever, its brightness undiminished, like the light from a far galaxy.

Looking back, she neither regretted nor lamented that love. It had revealed to her, for the first time in her life, the feelings a man and a woman might have for each other. It had hinted at the fulfillment that she had found so many years later with Seth. It had driven her to San

Francisco, to the wealth and position and contentment that she now enjoyed. It was a part of the fabric of her life, a slender, brilliant band still as pure and untarnished as the gold of Castalia.

It was nearly Christmas before Nick acquiesced to joining the Pioneer Iron Works. In the preceding weeks, he had blown alternately hot and cold, relaxed and optimistic one moment, and irritable and depressed the next. He had vehemently refused to partake in their Thanksgiving dinner. "A damnable Yankee invention," he labeled it.

"Nick," Seth argued, "the observance has nothing to do with politics."

"It was enacted by Abe Lincoln. I'll have none of it." He and Beth and Cal spent the day with Boyd and Naomi.

But finally, settled in his new position, he seemed perceptibly calmer and less volatile. Perhaps the demands of his work took his thoughts away from his anguish. Perhaps the simple pride of bringing home his weekly salary helped to restore his confidence in himself. Whatever the case, by Christmas, the spirits of the household were lighter than Lucy remembered them having been for years. Awakened by Cal, the family assembled in the drawing room where Septimus was kindling the morning fire, barely able to reach past the profusion of brightly wrapped parcels that lay scattered about the hearth.

Seth looked around. "Where's Biddy? We can't begin until she's here. Lin, run and tell her to come out of the kitchen."

"Merry Christmas!" Biddy crowed cheerfully as she hurried into the room, bearing a large basket.

"What's in there?" Cal asked, hopping up and down with anticipation.

"As if you didn't know, child. What do Biddy and Septimus make for you folks every year?"

"Turkish delight!" He peered into the basket and withdrew a small package tied with white string.

"Put that back, Calvert," Beth instructed him. "You know you must wait until after prayers."

Seth bowed his head and began. At the sound of his "Amen," Cal dipped eagerly into Biddy's basket, passing the packets of sweets among them.

"Not one bite now, you hear?" Biddy told him. "Don't you dare spoil my beautiful big breakfast."

For Septimus, there was a new waistcoat and for Biddy a pair of filigreed tortoise-shell combs. Beth cried out with pleasure at the sight of the gold earbobs Nick had given her. Lin, beaming, stroked the velvet trimming on her green woolen mantle and, after much persuasion, put it on and pirouetted about for them, giggling shyly.

"Cal," Lucy said, "do let me see what your Uncle Abel has sent you. Bring it here."

From the sturdy wooden crate, he withdrew an exquisitely carved little side-wheeler, no more than a foot in length.

"That's a beauty," Seth remarked, examining its tiny pennants and the coiled anchor chain of knotted black silk. "See here, the lifeboats even swung loose."

"Next year," Lucy promised the boy, "your Uncle Abel will be here with us."

"What does he look like?"

"He's tall and handsome, with shiny black hair and large, dark eyes," Beth told him.

Nick chuckled. "Hanged if that doesn't sound like one of the carriage horses."

Out of the corner of her eye, Lucy saw the color rise in Beth's cheeks and the slight movement in her lap as her hands balled into fists. It struck her as curious that the remark should annoy her so.

Seth excused himself and was gone for a moment. When he returned, he carried a huge, polished leather trunk, and from each arm hung a pair of matching valises.

"Sakes alive, Seth." Nick laughed. "Are you leaving us?"

"Oh, Seth," Lucy said, running her hand over the smooth surface of the trunk, "how handsome."

"There are three more trunks to come, my dear. A lady should travel in style. We've passage booked for Boston, leaving the last day of March—in plenty of time to attend Abel's graduation from the law school. Nick, Bethie, you'll be in charge of the house."

"You did it!" Lucy threw her arms about him. "Land, but I look forward to going."

"No more than I look forward to showing you the East, my love, not to mention showing off my wife a bit."

564

"Mama," Beth said, "you must go dressed in the latest fashions."

"Don't worry, I plan to make it evident to the Mountford ladies that San Francisco is quite as stylish as Cambridge."

"I shouldn't fret about that," Nick told her. "From Abel's letters, they sound like a flock of sober puritan pigeons. You'll knock those dull, gray birds right off their perches."

"Why, thank you, Nick. What a nice compliment."

"Now, Biddy," Seth said, "where's that spread you promised?"

"On the way, Mister Seth." She jumped up, patting the new combs in her hair. "Just you give me a few minutes."

Seth surveyed the welter of paper and boxes and ribbons. "Bethie, give me a hand in cleaning up this debris. Calvert, take your presents up to your room, please. You too, Lin."

"This place looks as though it had been struck by an earthquake," Lucy said, winding the wrinkled lengths of ribbon around her hand. "Bethie, dear, put these in the drawer of that table for now. Lin can iron them later."

"The drawer's locked."

"The key is under that bottle of Slade and Daggett ore."

Beth opened the drawer. "Mama, there's a pistol in here!"

"So there is. I'd quite forgotten."

"Has it always been there?"

"Just as a precaution," Seth replied. "Make sure you lock it up."

Nick patted the pockets of his coat abstractedly. "I must have left my tobacco pouch upstairs."

"I'll fetch it," Lucy offered. "I'm taking up an armload of gifts."

"No, no." He rose. "I can't remember where I left it. I'll go."

She ascended the stairs with deliberate slowness, mindful of his crutches tapping behind her.

"Breakfast is served," Septimus announced from the hall below.

"Lin! Cal!" Lucy called. "Time for breakfast."

"Coming." Cal's voice answered from Beth's and Nick's room.

"Calvert?" Lucy stopped in the doorway. "What are you doing in there?"

"Nothing."

"Well, get down off that chair. You've no business playing at your father's shaving stand."

"Cal!" Nick swung past her, lurching as he seized the boy around the waist. Nick's crutches fell away, and the two, father and son, toppled backward onto the bed. Nick sat up, shaking Cal's wrist. His hold was so tight that the child's hand lost its color. "Let me have that! Damn you, boy, give it to me!"

Cal opened his fist, and a small box flew across the room, striking Beth's dressing table. Its contents scattered. Like a shower of hailstones, the white pills rolled about the floor.

Cal began to cry. "I wanted to take medicine like you, Papa."

Nick grasped his shoulders roughly. The boy winced in pain. "Did you?" Nick demanded. "Did you take any medicine?"

Cal shook his head.

"Tell me the truth!"

"Nick!" Lucy cried. "Don't strike him!"

"I didn't, Papa! I didn't! Honest!"

"Please, Nick, you're hurting him."

"Not half as much as he could be hurt."

"Calvert," Lucy said, "get down on the floor and pick up every single one of your Papa's pills."

Nick shoved him off the bed. "If I ever catch you alone in this room again, boy, I'll whip the hide off you!"

"Nick, I'm sure he's learned his lesson. There's no need to be so harsh."

"The devil you say!" he retorted. His face was white with fury. "Do you want him to suffer like me?"

"I don't understand what—"

"Never mind. Be good enough to close the door. I want a word with my son. We'll be down presently."

Cal's eyes were dry by the time he came to the table, but Lucy, glancing covertly at Nick, was still unsettled by the ferocity of his anger. To be sure, Cal had done something wrong, even dangerous, but she found it difficult to reconcile the child's misdeed with the brutality of Nick's response. She had glimpsed, in his eyes, the visceral panic of an animal at bay, lashing out wildly in terror and rage. She wondered suddenly what scars he bore that were not so conspicuous as those they saw.

"Seth," Lucy asked him that evening when they were alone, "do you think there's anything wrong with Nick, besides the obvious?"

He scraped the dottle from his pipe and blew into it tentatively. "Why do you ask?"

"He became enraged with Cal this morning. I've never seen such fury in anyone."

"Lucy," he said, pocketing his pipe, "Nick has every right to be angry."

"For a moment I was afraid he'd injure the boy."

"I expect it's not easy for Nick to govern his feelings. Self-discipline never was his forte. Besides, we really don't know what he went through in the War; he so rarely discusses it. I daresay his rage will dissipate eventually. In the meantime, we must try to be patient with him."

"All the same, it frightened me."

Seth doused the lamp. "It'll do you good, my girl, to get away from your cares and worries. The journey to Massachusetts won't come a day too soon."

Lucy set out immediately to amass a suitable wardrobe for the trip. There were lists to be made of gloves, shoes, slippers and bonnets, of costumes for all occasions—traveling, visiting, walking, dinner and evening dresses. She consulted Seth about the weather in Cambridge and pored over *Godey's* pages for hours on end with Beth. Lucy had never had occasion to indulge herself in such a grand style. She was determined that Seth would be proud of her. Abel, too. As for the Mountford ladies and their lot, they stood to learn a thing or two about the worldly refinements of San Francisco.

From Joe's and Klara's Clay Street store came yard upon yard of goods; enough, Seth observed, to rig a brigantine. There were linens and poplins, tarletons and tulles and silks in a profusion of moirés, taffetas, grenadines and reps. There were trimmings of lace, ribbons, and plumes, of braiding, cord and tassels. In Sacramento Street, thanks to Lin, she found a Chinese woman who embroidered in a hand so fine that one could scarcely make out the individual stitches.

"It looks," Nick told her, "like Christmas is going to last 'til spring this year."

"Parasols!" Beth cried. "Heavens, Mama, we haven't done a thing about parasols to match your outdoor costumes."

"They're on my list. Do you think a camel's hair sacque would be appropriate for the sea voyage?"

"Fastened with a satin bow," Beth suggested, "with matching bows at the sleeves."

"My word, are you two still at it?" Seth said as he came into the sitting room. "I doubt such planning went into Scott's Anaconda—no offense, Nick."

"None taken."

Seth kissed Lucy's cheek and glanced down at the tissue-filled box at her feet. "I see the dressmaker's called again, or has she finally moved in with us?"

Beth laughed. "She might as well. Mama, show Seth."

Lucy held up the ivory silk evening dress with its intricate edging of scallops and rosettes. "Isn't it beautiful?"

"Is that a train I see?"

"The very latest fashion."

"I'll take your word for it, my dear. Come, Nick, let's us men adjourn for a whiskey before supper."

Nick reached for the crutches beside him on the windowseat. "Who's that?" he asked, peering through the curtains to the street. He parted them and looked out.

"Is someone coming?"

"I guess not." He dropped the curtains. "He turned and walked away. I could have sworn he was standing there looking at this house."

"Perhaps he was admiring Mama's garden."

"More likely he was a tramp, from the sight of him."

"Maybe the poor fellow wanted work."

"In that case," said Seth, "let him look elsewhere. You two are shortly going to be in charge of this place. Don't let your sympathies get the best of you. I don't want to come home and find this house has turned into an annex of the Good Shepherd."

If Lucy had any doubts about leaving, they were dispelled by Beth's eagerness to take her place as the lady of the house. "Mama," she confided as Nick and Seth left the room, "it will be such good practice for me. One day, we'll have a home of our own. Sometimes," she added wistfully, "I wish we were there already, but you know how Nick feels about using my money. He wants to wait until he can pay for it himself."

"You know you're welcome here forever, as far as Seth and I are concerned. I don't much like the idea of having you far away. I'd especially miss having Cal around."

"We wouldn't be far away," she promised. "Nick says he'll never go back East again. This is our home."

Three days before their departure, Lucy's wardrobe for the journey was completed, down to the last cambric handkerchiefs embroidered to match her dresses. Beth surveyed the array of clothes laid out in the nursery. "Goodness, Mama, it's a wonder Lin can find her way to bed through all this." She ran her fingers over the cherry-colored silk of a dressing gown. "Everything is so pretty. It looks like a bride's trousseau."

"It's the problem of packing that concerns me now," Lucy replied. The four large trunks, once so capacious to her eye, now seemed scarcely capable of holding everything. She drew in a deep breath. "Well, I'd best begin somewhere," she said, picking up a pair of parasols. "I shan't be using these two on the voyage, so they can go in the bottom of one of the trunks."

"Do you want me to stay to help you?"

"No, dear, run along to the Good Shepherd. Say my good-byes for me there and tell them I shall write."

It was a slow process. Not since she had left Missouri had she undertaken such a long journey, and then, she reflected, the preparations had hardly been like this. Dried beans, bran and molasses had given way to silks, bustles and lace. Instead of skillets and shovels, she now traveled with jewels and fans. It was a far cry from the wagon train, but she found herself filled with the same anticipation she had felt that bygone spring, so long ago, in the hurly-burly of Saint Joseph, when California was yet a dream.

"No!" Lin's voice came angrily from the stairs. "Never, never! You are a naughty boy, Cal. You play no more outside today. You go to your room."

Lucy went into the upstairs hall. Cal, his mouth drawn into a pout, stood with his little arms akimbo, defying Lin. "What's the matter here?" Lucy asked her.

"I come inside to fetch my shawl, and when I go out, Calvert is talking to a strange man at the front gate."

"You know very well, Cal, that you're never to speak

with strangers, even if they address you first. What did the man want?"

"Nothing."

"Nothing? What did he say?"

Cal chewed at his lower lip. Reluctantly, he answered, "He asked if that was my swing on the tree."

"That's all?"

"He asked me what my name was. He asked me what my Mama's name was. He wanted to know if she was home."

"You told him?"

He nodded.

"And what did he say to that?"

"Nothing. Lin took me away."

"As well she should have. Lin's right, Calvert. Now go play in your room until suppertime. And don't let me hear of your doing this again."

"Yes, ma'am." Head down, he shuffled grudgingly into his room.

"And don't slam the door!"

"I declare," Lucy told Seth when the boy was bedded down for the night, "that child never used to misbehave. Now it seems you can't turn your back on him for a minute without his getting into trouble."

"Perhaps it's attention he wants. I expect he's a little jealous at having to share Bethie with Nick after having her to himself for almost four years. But just think," he added with a smile, "come Saturday morning, you'll sail away and leave all your worries behind you."

She reached across the sofa and took his hand. "I'm as giddy as a girl." She laughed softly. "I can hardly wait to steam through the Golden Gate. It's not just the idea of seeing Abel. I want to see everything. Panama, the Atlantic, Boston, all the places I've only heard and read about. Is Concord far from Cambridge?"

"Not at all."

"Then you'll show me where you were born."

"The very house."

"And the places you played and studied and went to Sunday school?"

"Everything, my love," he promised, pressing her hand. "Will you join me in a brandy?"

"I think not. I'll try to pack a few more things before bed." She rose and kissed him on the forehead. "Don't be

570

long, my dearest. Nick and Bethie will be late at the theatre. Lin's going to wait up for them."

Lucy held her new blue grenadine mantle at arm's length, admiring the dressmaker's handiwork. She slipped it on over the saffron silk she was wearing and stepped back several paces from the small looking glass that hung in the nursery. She wondered if she should include the saffron dress in her packing. It looked very handsome with the blue mantle. But no, she would need fresh clothing on her return, and it was best left behind. She laid the mantle on Lin's bed and, lining it carefully with tissue, folded it and put it in the open trunk beneath the mirror. Suddenly she glanced up from the trunk, seeing her own puzzled expression in the glass. "What on earth—"

She stepped out into the hall. From below, came the sound of Seth's voice commingled with someone else's. It was not Nick's, she could tell, though she couldn't make out the words. They were both speaking at once, arguing, from the sound of it. Good Lord, she thought, it couldn't be Asa Hudson, could it?

"You have no right!" Seth said loudly.

"Every right in the world!"

Seth lowered his voice to a conciliatory tone, and their sounds faded away toward another room.

"Seth?" Lucy called. "Who is it?" She waited a moment for his answer, but he had not heard her. Taking her skirts in hand, she descended the stairs.

"It's not money I want!" came the angry words. "It's too late for that. Money can't help me now." It wasn't Asa, Lucy realized. "And there's no sense in trying to get rid of me. I'll only come back." Something in the voice suddenly chilled her with terror, though she didn't know why.

"She's suffered a great shock lately," Lucy heard Seth say as she approached the door to the drawing room. "In heaven's name, man, at least give us—"

"Sweet Jesus." Lucy reached blindly for the doorjamb to steady herself. Her knees buckled as dizziness and nausea engulfed her.

Seth ran to her side and caught her. He half-led, half-carried her to the wing chair.

She pressed her hands to her face, gasping for breath.

At length, her head still reeling, she raised her gaze once more to the ravaged specter of Caleb Bates.

His bloodshot eyes assessed her without expression. His hair, blanched by the years, hung unkempt and unruly about his bloated face. His skin was mottled with florid patches. He swayed slightly in his chair, and she realized that he was very drunk.

"We thought—"

"I know what you thought," he told her. His tongue was thick from alcohol. "I'm here to see my daughter."

"No! You can't!"

"The devil you say. It took me long enough to find her." He reached for Seth's brandy glass on the table and emptied it.

For some reason, the sight of him appropriating Seth's liquor filled her with rage.

"Give us time," Seth said, "Let us at least prepare her."

"I don't have time to give. I'm a gone coon, don't you understand? I'm dying, and I want to see my daughter before it's too late."

"Beth has been through too much recently." Lucy's voice was as sharp as an icicle. "I won't allow you to subject her to this."

"It's not for you to decide, Lucy Bates, is it?"

"Bates," she spat. " 'What was your name in the States? Was it Jackson or Johnson or Bates?' " She threw the old, familiar rhyme at him, her eyes bright with defiance. "It was never Bates, was it, Mr. Collier?"

He grasped the arm of his chair unsteadily. "How the devil—"

"Never mind," Seth told him. "It doesn't matter how."

"You've no claim to Beth," Lucy said. "You deserted us."

His gaze grew glassy as the brandy took effect. "I meant to come back," he said dully. "I did. I started out with the Stewart party, but we met a fellow on the trail who recognized me. I cut away in the night and went down to Monterey."

"Why didn't you return to Castalia?" Seth demanded.

He shook his head as though he were trying to clear it. "He knew. The fellow knew I'd been living there. Then the Mexican War broke out, and I enlisted. By the time I got back, in . . ." He paused, groping for the date. " 'Forty-nine, it was, I stopped in Sonora. Struck it rich, I

572

did. After that, there was the Mariposa digs. I made another pile. I was going to come back rich."

"You never came back at all," Lucy said, surprised at her lack of emotion.

"I heard Castalia was all staked out. There were new places." He pressed his fingers to his eyes, trying to remember. Lucy saw that his hands shook. "Ah, it's only a lot of names. Money made, money spent. By the time I got back to Castalia, you'd gone. There was nothing for me there. Then came the Kern River strike . . ."

Seth cast Lucy a warning glance and tapped his finger against his watch chain. "We can discuss this later. Meanwhile, you must leave. You have to give us time—"

"No!" He seized both arms of the chair and started to push himslf up but he lost his balance and fell back. "No. I'm here, and here I'll stay."

"Please," Lucy begged, "if you have any feelings for Beth at all—"

"Don't argue with me, woman." He brushed her words aside with a back-handed wave that sent the brandy glass toppling from the table.

"See here," Seth said angrily, "if you won't listen to reason, I'll summon the police and have you arrested for trespassing."

He gave Seth a wan, hard smile. "The Chinee let me in, didn't she?"

"You forced your way past her. Damn it, Bates or Collier or whatever your name is, you cannot stay here. Get out!"

He shrugged and rose from the chair, this time successfully. "It's not so cold I can't wait on the porch."

"No!" Seth seized him by the lapels. With a single, swift movement, Bates brought his fist upward between Seth's arms and struck him on the jaw. Seth lurched backward a step. Lucy cried out and ran to him. Bates staggered and steadied himself on the table beside him.

Seth pulled away from Lucy and lunged for him.

Bates grasped the first object his fingers closed upon. Like the infernal light from some darkly glinting comet, Lucy saw the bottle of silver streak over his head in a wide arc as he brought it down with all his force against Seth's skull.

He fell without a sound as the fragments of glass and metal smashed and scattered about him on the marble hearth. Lucy darted toward him, but Bates shoved her aside with a savage thrust. She stumbled and fell, screaming Seth's name.

"Get up, man," Bates commanded him thickly. He stood over him, looking dazedly down at the blood that gushed from his temple and flowed in a widening river of crimson across the hearth. "For pity's sake, man," Bates cried out, his voice hoarse, "get up." He bent over and shook Seth by the shoulders. Slowly, he dropped to his knees and touched his fingers to Seth's throat. "My God," he whispered. He swayed groggily and gripped the hearth fender for support. After a moment, he rose and turned.

She raised the pistol and fired.

His head jerked back. He tottered and grabbed wildly at the air to either side of him as he slid slowly to the floor. His jaw was slack and his mouth open. He was making sounds from deep in his gullet like a dog about to be sick.

The pistol fell with a clatter into the open drawer beside her. Her arms outstretched, Lucy went to Seth. Kneeling, she lifted his head tenderly into her lap and bent to kiss his lips. She took her handkerchief from her sleeve and tried to clean the blood from his face. She smoothed the hair back from his forehead and clasped his lifeless hand in hers, touching her lips to his fingers. At last, she laid it down and looked up. Lin stood at the doorway, staring into the room in mute horror.

"Wake Septimus," Lucy murmured, "and tell him to fetch the police." And then, uncontrollably, she began to shriek.

XXX

THEY FOUND her there, still sitting on the hearth, rocking back and forth over him. Hoarse from screaming, her voice all but lost, she emitted small, mewing sounds, unintelligible fragments of the words formed by her swollen lips.

"Miz' Slade. Ma'am." Septimus wiped his eyes with his fists.

Two policemen stood on either side of Septimus. In the hallway beyond, two others waited with Biddy. One of the men cleared his throat and held out his hand to Lucy. She shook her head.

"Please, ma'am. Let me make you comfortable in a chair."

"No!" she whispered. With the hem of her saffron silk dress, she gently tried to wipe the dark stains from Seth's hair.

The two men raised her whimpering in protest. Her dress clung to the dried blood that lay spilled across the rose-colored marble of the hearth and made an ugly tearing sound as they brought her to her feet. They carried her to a chair. She attempted to rise and go to Seth, but Septimus laid both hands on her shoulders and held her there. "You stay put. Mister Seth ain't hurtin'. Ain't nothin' you can do for him that the good Lord ain't already doin'."

"Where's the girl?" one of the men asked him. "You said she saw what happened."

"Upstairs," Biddy called tearfully. "She's upstairs with the child."

575

"And what's your name?" He took out a notebook. Biddy, trying to control her tears, choked on her reply.

"That's Biddy. She's my wife," Septimus answered for her.

"Neither of you witnessed this?" He glanced down at the pistol in the open drawer.

"No, sir. We'd gone to bed."

"Biddy, if you please, send the young lady downstairs." He turned to Lucy. "Mrs. Slade, try to tell me what took place."

Lucy seemed not to have heard.

"Did you or your husband know this man?"

Involuntarily, she shuddered. Her teeth began to chatter.

"Easy, now." He put a hand on her arm. "Septimus, are there any spirits about? Can you fetch the lady some brandy?"

He nodded and disappeared into the library.

"Officer Trumbull."

The policeman glanced up as one of his men led Li Lin into the room. He frowned. "Nobody told me she was a Chinee." He motioned Lin to a chair. "Mrs. Slade, try again, please. Did you know the man?"

Lucy looked at him blankly.

Trumbull sighed and addressed Lin. "Girl, who was he? Did he say what business he had here?"

Lin's eyes were on Lucy.

He waved his hand in front of her. "Savvy English?"

Lin's lower lip began to tremble. She let out a sob and looked quickly away.

Trumbull made a sound of disgust. "Ah, being a Chinee, it doesn't much matter, I'm afraid. Burr," he ordered one of his men, "take a look in the fellow's pockets." He took the brandy glass that Septimus brought and held it to Lucy's lips. The strong smell made her choke, and she gagged on the liquid.

Burr rose from Bates's body. "Not much on him, sir. A few dollars and a hotel key."

"Which hotel?"

"The What Cheer House."

"All right, men, cover them up. We've seen all there is to see." He took Seth's pistol and put it into his pocket.

There was a commotion in the hall. "Mama!" Beth ran into the room and stopped short, frozen at the sight. "In

576

the name of God!" she cried. She stared aghast as the policemen lifted the two canvas-shrouded forms. "Mama, you're covered with blood! Are you hurt?"

Lucy shook her head. As they bore Seth past her, she groped frantically for the canvas, trying to pull it from him. With a guttural cry, she pitched forward onto the floor.

Septimus and Officer Trumbull carried her to the sofa. Beth knelt beside her, stroking her hand.

Nick approached them unsteadily on his crutches, his face ashen. "What's happened here?" His voice was low and strained, as though he were trying to keep from shouting. "I'm Mrs. Slade's son-in-law, and the young lady is my wife, Mrs. Stevens."

"Officer Duncan Trumbull, sir, at your service. As near as we know, a man forced his way into the house, had an argument with Mr. Slade and struck him a fatal blow. Mrs. Slade shot and killed the intruder. But all this is according to Septimus here, who somehow got the story from the Chinese girl."

"Lin?" Nick went to her. "Is this true?"

She nodded.

"Lin," Beth said suddenly, "where's Cal?"

"He's safe," Septimus told her. "Biddy's up in his room with him. He don't know what's gone on."

"But who was the man?" Nick asked.

"We'll find out," Trumbull assured him. "The girl doesn't seem to know, and Mrs. Slade is in a state of shock right now. She hasn't been able to answer any of the questions I've put to her."

"She must be taken upstairs to rest," Nick said. "Obviously she's in no condition to help you now."

Trumbull hesitated only a moment. "Burr, you and Septimus carry the lady to her room. Mr. Stevens, I'd like you and your wife to have a look at the intruder to see if you can identify him."

Lin rose from her chair tentatively, looking from Nick to Officer Trumbull. When neither responded, she slipped quietly from the room and followed Lucy up the stairs.

All that night, Lin stayed with her, refusing to retire to her bed in the nursery. She sat in the rocker at the foot of Lucy's bed, alternately dozing and staring silently into the distance, lost in her own thoughts.

Lucy forced herself to remain awake. She would not

yield to sleep. She would not allow this day, the last day of Seth's life, to be extinguished. She sat rigidly upright on her pillows, her hands clenched tightly, as though she could somehow hold fast to all that was dear to her, denying the inevitable finality of his death. When the dawn came, she began to weep.

Lin went to wake and dress Cal. After a time, Beth appeared with a tray of coffee and rolls. Lucy waved it aside. Beth sat on the edge of the bed. "At least you were with him, Mama. He didn't die alone—"

"You little fool, we all die alone."

Beth flinched but said nothing.

"I want Nick to fetch Hiram Berry and bring him here at once. You'll find his address in the notebook on my desk in the library."

"Mama, please tell me what happened. Who was that man?"

"Do as I say. And hurry."

"It's not yet eight o'clock, Mama."

"Damn you!" Lucy flung the covers aside. "I'll tell Nick myself!"

"No." Beth held up a hand. "Stay here. I'll do it. Please, Mama, you must save your strength."

She lay back and closed her eyes for a moment.

"Missee?" Lin peered through the half-open door from the hall. "Cal, he wants to see you. It's all right I let him?"

"Yes. Bring him in."

He approached the bed hesitantly. "Aren't you feeling well, Grandmama?"

"No dear," she murmured stroking his curls, "I'm not."

"I wanted to make sure you were here."

"You did?"

"Papa said Grandpa Seth went to live with the angels. Grandmama, why did he go? Didn't he like it here with us anymore?"

Lucy blinked back the tears. "Grandpa Seth's love is always with us. Nobody can take it away. But he had to leave because God called him."

"Will God send him back?"

"Not for a long time." She swallowed hard. "Run along now. I'm staying right here; don't you worry."

It was almost ten before Hiram Berry arrived and was

ushered upstairs by Beth. Lucy drew her dressing gown about her and motioned him into the room.

"Ma'am, I am most distressed—"

"Sit down, Mr. Berry. Bethie, leave us alone, please. Close the door after you."

"Such a terrible, terrible loss. He will be missed, Mrs. Slade, by everyone who knew him."

"Mr. Berry, I want to retain your services."

He pursed his lips and gazed at her, nodding thoughtfully. He cleared his throat. "I'd be honored to serve you in any way I can, ma'am but I am rather confused about the events that occurred here last evening. Mr. Stevens was unable to enlighten me beyond the elementary facts."

Lucy shifted uncomfortably against her pillows.

"You move with difficulty, ma'am. Are you in pain? Shall I call Mrs. Stevens?"

"Mr. Berry, there is no medicine in this house, nor anywhere else for that matter, that could help me now."

"Ah . . ." He fingered his mustache self-consciously. "Of course, of course. I quite understand. Now," he went on gingerly, "if you would please tell me in detail exactly what occurred."

"I must be certain that what I say is kept in confidence between us."

"You're assured of that, ma'am, both legally and upon my honor."

"Make yourself comfortable, Mr. Berry. It's a long story."

Several times, as she spoke, he closed his eyes, then opened them abruptly to pose a question. He sat with his hands splayed, drumming his fingertips together.

Lucy paused, choking back the sobs that rose in her throat. He leaned forward and gave her his handkerchief. "Take your time, ma'am."

She tried to compose herself. "I took the key from the table as quietly as I could and unlocked the drawer where the pistol was. He—Mr. Bates—stood up and turned—"

"And this man, Bates or Collier, he appeared then to be going to attack you? Under those circumstances, your action would be justifiable."

She took several deep breaths. "I don't think he knew what he was going to do next."

"But he might well have turned on you. You had no way of knowing."

"Mr. Berry . . ." She clasped her hands tightly in her lap. "I appreciate your intentions, but you must know the truth. Understand me clearly. It was not myself nor even my daughter I was thinking of. I killed Caleb Bates because he murdered my husband."

His expression betrayed nothing. "My dear lady," he said finally, "it is possible that you might have to choose between truth and prudence. I implore you to consider the ramifications of each, before you commit yourself. There is sufficient latitude in the facts to construct an excellent argument for self-defense. As your lawyer, I would advise you to accept that license, though I would not attempt to coerce you, if your conscience forbade it. Weigh the consequences, I beg you."

"You're suggesting that I bed down with a lie."

"Perhaps, if it comes to that. It might be preferable to bedding down with the vermin one finds in prison. I fail to see the benefits of incarceration either for you, your family or the public at large. But," he went on, slapping his palm down firmly on the arm of his chair, "this is all quite hypothetical as yet. Is there anything else I should know?"

"Yes. Li Lin, the Chinese girl who lives with us. I think she saw me fire the pistol. I believe she was standing behind me. I know she must have heard everything. She was just across the hall in the sitting room when we were arguing."

"Then she also knows that the intruder was actually Mrs. Stevens's father."

"Lin is very devoted to this family, Mr. Berry. I don't believe she would willingly reveal anything that might hurt any of us."

"Legally, she's irrelevant to the case. I was merely concerned that she might speak out of turn and complicate matters."

"Irrelevant?"

"The testimony of a Chinese is not admissible in any legal action involving a white person."

"I see. Then you needn't worry about her talking out of turn. Lin is absolutely trustworthy."

He stood up and went to the window, his hands folded behind him, and stood staring out at the hills beyond. At length, he spoke. "Mrs. Slade, if you want my advice, which it appears you do, it would be to present yourself as quickly as possible to the district attorney. Tell him everything that happened last night, up to the point of your unlocking the drawer and Mr. Bates or Collier rising from the hearth. At that time, I shall make it clear that you had every reason to fear that your own life was in danger. Was the key to the drawer still in its lock when the police arrived?"

"Yes. I'd left it there."

"Then they have no way of knowing the drawer was not unlocked at some earlier time in the evening. If that were so, it would have been quite natural for you to have seized the weapon to protect yourself, without any premeditation whatsoever. Mrs. Slade, the district attorney has it within his discretion to decide whether or not to bring charges against anyone. No one may challenge his decision. If he concludes that the killing should be excused as justifiable homicide on the grounds of self-defense, you would be spared the ordeal of a trial. It would be to your advantage to seek him out immediately as an expression of your wish to cooperate with the authorities." He turned to her. "Have you made your choice?"

She fingered her wedding band, turning it around and around on her hand. After a time, she glanced up. "I will do what I think my husband would wish me to do for the sake of our family. If you will excuse me, Mr. Berry, I'll dress now and go with you to the district attorney's office."

He nodded and went to the door.

"Mr. Berry."

"Yes?"

"It was Mr. Bates who taught me how to shoot a pistol. At Fort Bridger, many years ago."

"Yes'm." He let himself out and shut the door.

She dressed and went downstairs. Nick, Beth and Hiram Berry were waiting for her in the drawing room.

"No!" Lucy stood in the doorway, staring at the bare floor and the cleanly washed marble on the hearth. "You have removed every trace of what was done to him!"

"Mama, the carpet was badly stained. It wouldn't have been right to let Cal see . . ."

"Yes," she said weakly. "I understand."

Septimus entered the room. "Miz' Slade, Officer Trumbull is at the front door."

"Send him in," Hiram Berry told him. "Do sit down, Mrs. Slade." He motioned her to his chair. "Sir," he greeted Trumbull, "I am Hiram Berry, Mrs. Slade's lawyer. You are just in time to follow us down to the district attorney's office."

Trumbull nodded a greeting to Lucy. "Mrs. Slade, before you go anywhere, I would like to ask all of you if the name B. B. Collier is familiar to you?"

Lucy's heart began to pound violently. She held herself erect in her chair, afraid to move.

"Is that the man?" Nick asked.

"It was, yes. We found his name on his hotel registration and on some personal effects in his room. Have any of you ever heard of a B. B. Collier?"

Berry glanced at each of them. "Evidently not. As I understand it, sir, the man forced his way into this house demanding to see his child. Mr. and Mrs. Slade told him that his child, if indeed there was such a child was not here. He became enraged and—" He cut himself off with a wave of his hand. "But you can hear Mrs. Slade's own account in the district attorney's office. Let's not subject the lady to having to relive the incident more than is necessary. Ma'am, if you're ready."

Lucy rose, steadying herself on the chair.

Berry seemed to have an afterthought. "Mrs. Stevens, would you send Lin along with us? Have her bring a phial of smelling salts, if you will. Just in case," he said to Officer Trumbull. "You understand."

The clock in the anteroom read half-past two as they left the district attorney's office. Lucy wondered if it was correct. She had lost track of time, and though she had not eaten anything all day, she was not hungry. Lin ran ahead of them and held open the heavy door. Lucy, escorted on either side by Hiram Berry and Officer Trumbull, stepped out onto the street. She winced as the brisk March air stung her face.

"Are you all right, ma'am?" Trumbull inquired solicitously.

She nodded, averting her eyes from the harsh, unsparing sunlight that glared down on the busy thoroughfare. The street sounds assailed her ears. The touch of the wind against her skin was excruciating. She felt suddenly flayed, as though the flesh had been stripped from her and the

582

usually benign breeze were chafing against raw, open wounds. She felt only pain, outside and inside; deep within, her grief lay like a cold, sharp stone bruising her soul. The shock was wearing off, she knew, exposing her to agonizing truth.

She leaned back in her carriage seat, her eyes closed, praying for the strength to bear her anguish. But what right, she thought, have I to pray? If it weren't for her, Seth would be alive. He had given her the only real happiness she had ever known, and she had seen him destroyed. There would be no more peace for her on this earth, knowing that she had sown the seeds of his destruction. Killing Caleb Bates had not avenged his death. It had only compounded her torment. Now nothing could undo what she had done. She was condemned to a purgatory of grief and guilt that she had brought upon herself. It hardly seemed to matter whether she escaped imprisonment or not. She would never again be free.

"Lin," Hiram Berry said softly, leaning forward on his seat, "do you understand everything you heard?"

She glanced quickly at Lucy, then back to him. "Yes, sir."

"The police don't know that Mr. Collier was Beth's father. He used another name when Beth was born."

"I know." She gazed at her hands folded in her lap. "He tells me he is Caleb Bates, come to see Missybet. I tell him she's not home. He pushes me away. Then," she said, beginning to weep quietly, "I heard."

"Oh, Lin!" Lucy brushed the tears from her cheeks with her fingertips. "Don't cry, I beg you. I am so sorry you had to be a part of this. God help me for entrapping you in a lie."

"It's for Missybet. No good for her to know everything. Already there is too much sadness."

Berry leaned back, apparently satisfied. "We should hear of the district attorney's decision within a matter of days, ma'am, but my impression is that things went well. The fact that you and Mr. Slade are socially prominent and well-respected is very much in your favor—"

"Some people have long memories, Mr. Berry. I was not always in such favor."

"Your charity is celebrated, ma'am. I guarantee you it has sufficiently eclipsed the past—"

"Were it not for my past, my husband might have fulfilled his dream of serving California in the senate. I wrecked that dream, Mr. Berry. He brought me joy and love and contentment. I repaid him with disappointment and death."

He cleared his throat uncomfortably. "Ma'am, I know how you must feel."

"Do you?"

"I believe Mr. Slade would condone your actions today."

"We'll never know." She gazed at him without expression.

She repeated the wretched tale, as she knew she must, to Beth and Nick. Her voice was flat, and the words lay heavy on her tongue like a thick, distasteful scum. Waves of nausea overcame her, and she barely finished her account before she had to bolt from the sitting room to retch. She crouched over the porch railing, gasping for breath, as dry heaves convulsed her.

"In the name of heaven, Nick!" Beth cried, "tell Septimus to help me get her to bed."

Lucy brushed her away and stood up. "No. It's over. Bring me a towel and some brandy to rinse my mouth."

Beth led her into the house. "You must rest, Mama. Go upstairs now."

"I can't. There's too much to be done."

"Nick and I can see to the funeral arrangements."

"No! It is the last thing I shall ever be able to do for him!"

"At least let us help."

"You must go to the telegraph office, Bethie. I have to let Abel know we aren't coming."

"But what will you tell him?"

"Please . . ." She pressed her hands to her aching temples. "Let me think."

Lucy could not bring herself to tell Abel what had happened, only that their trip was now impossible and that she would write him to explain.

With Beth and Nick at her side, she executed the preparations for the funeral, all but recoiling from the unctuous solicitude of the preacher, new to their parish, who so lugubriously deplored the loss of a parishioner he had met only once.

"How dare he presume to share our grief," she muttered as he left the house.

"He meant well, Mama."

Nick made a wry smile. "God spare us all from the tactless blunders of the well-meaning."

"Mama, you're pale as ashes. Lin said you didn't sleep at all last night, and you haven't eaten a morsel today. It wouldn't do for you to be too ill to attend the services."

"Don't badger me, Bethie. I must keep busy."

Despite Lucy's protests, Beth sent for Doctor Vanderhoef.

"My dear." He laid his bag beside her bed and took her hands in his. "We are all deeply sorry. What a horrible experience you've been through."

"Not 'through,' Martin. It's not over. It will never be over."

"Let's let the good Lord in His infinite wisdom attend to that. Meanwhile, you must take care of yourself. Seth would insist upon it." He opened his bag and withdrew a small bottle of brownish liquid.

"What is that?" she asked as he measured it into the water glass on the table.

"A sleeping draught. It will allow you to get some rest."

"I don't want to sleep, Martin. I don't want to dream."

"Lucy, do as I say. I'm not leaving here until you swallow it."

If she dreamt, she was blessed with forgetfulness. She awakened slowly, through a soporific haze, numbly aware, from the angle of the sunlight on her covers, that it was late in the day. She stretched slightly, reaching out to the sheets beside her. They were cold against her skin.

With the force of a tidal wave, memory surged over her, flooding her with anguish. Lucy pulled aside the covers and ran to the dressing room. She threw open the door to Seth's wardrobe and buried her face in his clothing. The rough, familiar wool of his coats caressed her cheeks, and the scent of him filled her nostrils.

Lin opened the door from the adjoining nursery and saw her sitting there on the floor, holding his clothes in her arms. Without a word, she passed into Lucy's room and brought her a robe. Gently, she took Seth's things from her and led her back into the bedroom, where she

585

seated her at the dressing table. Picking up Lucy's hair-brush, she began to stroke it through her hair.

The mirror on the stair landing lay covered under a shroud, and the pictures were turned to the walls. On the front door, a crepe bow marked the mourning house.

Lucy sat at her desk. "My dearest son," she wrote. "Our Seth is dead. Forgive me, I beg you, for not setting down the circumstances, but I cannot bear to repeat them once again. The enclosed account, from the *Alta*, is an accurate one. Do not come home upon receipt of this letter," she continued. "I implore you to stay in Cambridge for your graduation. It would be Seth's wish. It is mine also. I am sending you Wells Fargo bills of exchange for one thousand dollars. This was to be our gift to you in admiration of all you have accomplished. Seth was very proud of you, my son, as am I. My only regret is that we cannot share your happy graduation day. Meanwhile, I long to see you. Your loving Mother."

Beth tapped lightly at the open door. "Mama, Father Crowley is here."

Lucy folded the letter and sealed it. "Send him in."

"Pastora." He embraced her.

Her eyes filled with tears. "Seth liked to call me that."

"You'd rather I didn't?"

"No, of course you may. I'm proud of it, if only because it pleased him. Sit down, Father."

"You look tired, my dear."

"We've been inundated by friends and acquaintances coming to pay their respects. Present company excluded, I find the ritual exhausting."

"They only wish to comfort you."

"Indeed." Lucy gazed absently out the window beside her desk. "What can anyone know of someone else's sorrow? All their well-intentioned regrets and lamentations ring hollow in my ears. There is no comfort for me, Father. There never will be."

"I quite agree with you."

She glanced at him, startled.

"God can heal, my dear, but it's up to you to accept His mercy. If you refuse—"

"Father Crowley, I killed a man."

"I know."

"And you can forgive that?"

586

"It is not for me to forgive. God alone can forgive. I am merely an agent of the Lord, but as such, let me remind you that as much as He may despise the sin, He also loves the penitent."

Her voice was low. "I have sinned greatly, Father. The burden of my sins is almost insupportable. Perhaps God could forgive me. I don't know. But I do know that I can never forgive myself."

He rose and laid a hand on her shoulder. "I hope your Christian charity is not confined to your good deeds for others, Pastora. You might do well to exercise some of it on your own behalf. Don't hesitate to call upon me for help."

She had steeled herself for the funeral, for the preacher's sonorous condolences, for the hands that reached out to her in sympathy and the compassionate eyes that followed her exit from the church. Back at the house, she moved dazedly among the guests, her head throbbing. She felt oddly removed, as though not even these dear, familiar friends could breach the grief that sequestered her.

Polly and Albert Fearing were among the last to leave. Albert's face was drawn, and he limped badly from gout. Polly took Lucy's hands in hers and held them tightly. "Are you sure you don't want us to come to Saint Helena with you for the burial?"

"Quite sure, Polly. But it's good of you to ask."

Albert kissed her cheek. "Our thoughts will be with you, my dear."

Lucy watched as Polly helped him down the steps to the front walk.

"Ma'am." Hiram Berry touched her sleeve.

"Thank you for coming, Mr. Berry."

"I've been waiting to have a word alone with you." He gestured toward the sitting room. "May we?"

She seated herself in the bay window and waited while he closed the door and took a chair.

"I saw the district attorney this morning, just before I came to the funeral. He has declined to bring charges against you." Berry looked at her expectantly.

"Thank you."

"That's the last of it, ma'am. The matter is closed. You're free of it."

She shook her head. "No. I shall never be free. I have

587

shackled myself to a lie. I am bound to drag it about with me for the rest of my life."

"I regret that the news does not lighten your burden."

"Forgive me, Mr. Berry. I am most grateful for your help. Without you, I—"

He raised a hand and stood up. "Don't mention it, ma'am. I was glad to be of assistance."

"I'll see you out."

"There's no need." He paused at the door. "Mrs. Slade, I still believe that your husband would have wished us to do exactly as we did."

She appeared not to have heard him. "We had only five years together. That was all, Mr. Berry. Only five years."

They buried him atop the vineyard's highest hill, overlooking the rows of vines that traced the gentle curves of its slope. Lucy, Nick and Beth stood together. A few feet away, Herr Schmidt, his head bowed, stood holding his wife's hand as they listened to the words of the minister summoned from Saint Helena. Behind the Schmidts, at a respectful distance, were Chang, Hong and the other coolies, their faces solemn, their oddly assorted hats clasped deferentially in front of them. A slight breeze blew over the vineyard. The young leaves, pale and silvery against the green wood of the new canes, quivered restlessly. Wildflowers bobbed on the nearby slopes, and in the valley below farmers went about their daily chores in the verdant patchwork of their fields.

They walked back toward the house in silence, leaving Hong Hing-wing and his men to close the grave. At length, Beth spoke. "It's a fine day, Mama. As pretty as can be. Seth would like being here on a day like today."

"Bury me beside him, Bethie."

"What, Mama?"

"When my time comes, I want to be laid to rest here with Seth, not in some city cemetery, away from the man and the land I love. Promise me, Bethie."

"I promise, Mama."

Lucy sat alone on the veranda, taking in the sights and sounds of the spring afternoon as if it were somehow imperative that not a single detail of this day should slip away, unrecorded, from her memory. Through the open window, she could hear Beth and Nick in conversation inside and the chink of crockery and cutlery as Chang set the table for supper. The trees had ceased their stirring. The woods about the house lay still, as though the setting sun were spiriting with it all vitality and movement. The day was ending. Soon the light and life of it would disappear and perish. Lucy drew her shawl close about her. Already the green of the leaves and the contours of the trees were becoming indistinguishable, devoured by shadows. Color and form melted into blackness. In the dark void, a single bird sang four clear, sharp notes and fell silent. The air grew cold with the evening damp. Lucy rose and went into the house. She washed her hands, and after folding the towel on the washstand beside the bed she bent to turn down the sheets.

Nick paused in the hallway and glanced through the open door. "What are you doing?"

"Before supper, I always—" She stopped.

"You always turn down Seth's side of the bed for him. I know."

"I wasn't thinking."

"It's like my ghost leg. Sometimes I could swear I feel my toes tingling or a cramp in my calf, and without thinking I go to shake my leg. Strange, isn't it, how the impulse survives the loss." He gave her a sympathetic smile that faded to a look of pain. "Bethie," he called, "where the devil did you put my toilet case? I can't find it anywhere in our room."

"It must be there," she called back. "You said you put it in the bag."

A strange expression came over his face, and he paled so suddenly that Lucy wondered if he was going to be ill. "Nick—"

"Damn you, Bethie!" he cried. "I said I'd put it *on the bed*. I left it there for you to pack."

Beth appeared in the hall. "I guess it's still in San Francisco," she said sheepishly. "I misunderstood you."

His lips were white. "I've got to have it."

"Really, Nick," Lucy told him, "it's of no consequence if you don't shave for a day. No one will think worse of you."

"My medicine is in that case."

"Darling," Beth asked him worriedly, "are you in pain?"

"I will be, if I don't have it. I must go back tonight."

"Tonight?" Lucy gave him a puzzled frown. "You can't, Nick. By the time you'd reach Suscol, the last boat would be long gone. There's no way to get back to the city until tomorrow."

"I must. I could take the carriage."

"Nick," Beth said, "you're not making any sense. Where would you rest and water the horses in the middle of the night? You don't even know the roads. And what would you do when you reached the bay? Swim? There won't be a ferry 'til morning. I'm sorry about the medicine, my dear, but surely—"

Nick cut her off. "Do you have any Gilman's Elixir?" he asked Lucy.

"No."

"McLean's Cordial? Goodall's Soothing Syrup?"

"I've a bottle of Goodall's, but it's back at Bush Street."

"Oh, God," he muttered.

"Missee," Chang called from the end of the hall, "all ready supper."

"I don't want anything to eat," Nick said, turning away.

Beth caught his arm. "Please, my dearest, what can I do for you? This is all my fault—"

"Nothing. You can't do anything. Leave me alone, Bethie. Tell me," he asked Lucy, "is the bed in the spare room made up?"

"Yes. Why?"

"I want to sleep alone tonight."

"Nick," Beth begged him, "don't shut me out. If you're in pain, I want to help you."

"No." He swung away with a hard thrust of his crutches.

Beth stared after him, but Lucy laid a hand on her arm. "Don't. Let him be. Do as he says, Bethie. Perhaps he doesn't want you to see him suffer."

Beth glanced after him, looking bewildered, hurt and anxious. "Mama, I don't understand this."

"Nick wants to be alone now. You're his wife and you must abide by his wishes."

Nick's voice interrupted them from the spare room. "Send Chang in," he called out. "I must speak to him."

"Would you like him to bring you a tray?" Beth asked.

"I told you. I don't want any food. Just send Chang."

Lucy and Beth were seated at the table. Chang returned from Nick's room and looked from one to the other. The trace of a frown creased his forehead and vanished.

"Chang," Beth asked, "what did Mister Nick want?"

He shook his head vehemently. "Nothing. Nothing I got."

In the night, unable to sleep, Lucy rose and went to the window. She drew aside the curtain. A bright half-moon rocked on the gently swaying bough of a tree. Pale, ghostly fingers of light splayed across the bedroom floor, reaching out and retracting in rhythm with the movement of the breeze.

Nick's plight still puzzled her. Before retiring, she had knocked at his door and found him sitting on the bed, still dressed, reading a book. He had dismissed her as though he hadn't a care in the world. Yet earlier, in the hallway, she had seen in his face the same animal panic she had glimpsed before, when Cal had been caught playing with his pills. She stared up at the moon, as if it might illuminate the dark confusion that disturbed her. The clock in the other room struck three. Lucy tried to sort her thoughts, fanning them out in her mind like a hand of playing cards. Nick's odd behavior, the medicine, Cal and Chang. But they refused to follow any suit. What had he wanted from the Chinaman? She froze, drawn abruptly out of her thoughts by a movement on the veranda. She stepped to one side to get a clearer view through the window.

Nick stood on the porch. In spite of the fact that he was fully clothed, he was shivering in the night air. He laid his crutches down and seated himself in a chair. He grasped its wooden arms and rocked back and forth, overcome by a protracted fit of yawning. When it had ceased, he slumped forward, covering his face with his hands. Suddenly, he sprang from the chair and lunged for the porch pillar, seizing it between his hands, holding it for dear life, lurching wildly from side to side like some mad Samson trying to bring the roof down upon himself. He raised his face to the moonlight, taking in great gulps of air and shuddering.

Lucy threw on her dressing gown and a shawl and grabbed the blanket from her bed.

"Nick," she whispered as she opened the door.

He started at the sound of her voice. "Go back inside. It's chilly out here—"

"I brought you a blanket."

He took it from her and wrapped it about him as he sagged back into his chair.

Lucy sat down beside him. "Tell me only one thing, Nick, and tell me the truth. It's not your leg that ails you, is it?"

He glanced away without replying.

She took his hand. His skin was cold to the touch. "Chang was the key. I asked myself how a Chinaman might have helped. I have lived a long time, Nick. One hears of such things. It's not your leg that torments you. It's want of your medicine, isn't it?"

He nodded. Another spasm of yawning seized him. Lucy waited until it had abated.

"How long have you been taking opium?"

"Since they amputated my leg."

"And you cannot quit it?"

"I tried. Twice. When they first stopped the medication, I fell sick. I thought I would go mad with the illness, until they told me what was wrong and dosed me. Then, after a few months, I felt strong enough to try to stop gradually." He pressed his palms to his eyes and rubbed them fitfully. "It was no use. I lied. I bribed. I stole it when I had to. There's no way I can live without it now. Not anymore." He shivered and clutched the blanket about him.

"You can't stay out here, Nick. Come inside where you'll be more comfortable."

He looked at her for a long moment, then shook his head in despair. "It won't matter. You don't understand. You can't know what it feels like to have your body want to burst out of its skin." He trembled convulsively in his chair and fell still. A renewed fit of yawning overtook him. "I must get back to the city," he mumbled.

"Mama? Nick?" Beth stood in the doorway. "What are you doing out here in the dark?"

Nick looked to Lucy. Despite the overhanging shadow of the porch, she could see the fear in his eyes. She held his glance for a moment, then answered. "His leg is paining him, Bethie. We were chatting, I couldn't sleep either."

"But it's too chilly to be out."

"I needed a breath of air." Lucy stood up. "We were just about to come inside. Fetch a lamp, will you, Bethie? The moon's gone behind a cloud." She waited a second, then whispered, "It's not for me to tell her, Nick. I will keep the confidence, but you can't go on living like this. You must promise me you'll try again to stop."

"Yes," he said quickly, "yes, but not now. Not right away. Give me time. For God's sake," he begged her, "give me time."

XXXI

THE NEXT morning, Nick appeared to be exhausted from the rigors of the night. He dozed almost the entire way home, waking only to foggily navigate his way from the carriage to the railway and then to the steamer. As they neared the city, Beth glanced at his sleeping face cushioned against the shawl she had thrown over the top of his seat. She smiled.

"He looks so young when he's asleep," she whispered to Lucy. "All the pain disappears from his face."

Lucy looked across at Nick. He might be taken for Cal's older brother. They had the same complexion, the same fair halo of curls and, in repose, the same cherubic expression. She gazed at him in silence for a long time. This fallen angel, she thought, frail and corrupted. Now she understood the fear and hatred she had seen in him. He feared and hated himself. In spite of the pity she felt for Nick, her greatest concern was for Beth and Cal. She was even more afraid for them than for Nick.

"Sakes alive," Beth said as the boat's whistle sounded, "I believe he could sleep through an earthquake."

"He's making up for the rest he missed last night."

Beth shook him lightly by the shoulders. "Nick, we're almost home. We'll be docking shortly."

He nodded drowsily and yawned.

"You've slept the whole trip," she told him. "You didn't even wake when some noisy children were chasing each other about the deck."

He glanced up, blinking in the bright sunlight. "It's a trick I picked up in the War," he murmured, closing his lids.

"Do try to stay awake until we reach the house," Beth said.

But he could not. Once in the carriage, he again dozed off.

"Nick." Lucy jostled his arm. "We're here."

As Septimus helped Beth out, Nick rubbed his eyes with his knuckles. "Thank God," he said.

"Is the sleeping a part of it?" Lucy asked softly.

He nodded and rose from his seat.

In the hall, she stood looking after him as he made his way upstairs. "Nick!" she cried suddenly. "Wait! Don't!"

He pretended not to have heard.

She ran to the bottom of the stairs and called up to him. "Nick, please! Think about it first, I beg you!"

"Mama?" Beth leaned over the upstairs balustrade, her arm around Cal. "What's the matter?"

Lucy hesitated a moment. "Nothing."

Beth frowned. "What's going on between you two? I don't like secrets."

"Neither do I. Perhaps you'd best speak to Nick."

Lucy hung up her cloak and went into the kitchen. Biddy was shaking a freshly baked cake onto the cooling rack. She wiped her hands and put her arms around Lucy.

"Welcome back, Miz' Slade. You holdin' up all right?" Biddy held her at arms' length, studying her face. "You look a little peaked to me. You go set yourself down, and I'll have Septimus bring you some tea and a bit of this lemon cake."

"I'm afraid I haven't much of an appetite, Biddy."

"Nonsense. You got to eat. What would Mister Seth say if I didn't see to it you took care of yourself? You do like I tell you now, and let me set the tea tray."

Unable to summon the will to argue, Lucy allowed Biddy her way. Now, swallowing the last cold drops of tea in her cup, she laid it down and glanced out of the sitting room window. A carriage passed by on the street outside. She watched it stop at the house across the way. The gentlemen of the house alighted and walked up the path. The door opened, and he went inside.

How many afternoons had she waited in this same room for Seth, keeping watch to greet him as he arrived home from a day's work? She had thought nothing of it then. Yet now, seeing the ritual from afar, it seemed in all its simplicity to be something infinitely precious. The anticipation, the reunion and the companionship, once such commonplace elements of their daily life, were prizes beyond reckoning, luxuries she had taken for granted. Across the street, the lamps were being lit in the downstairs rooms. Fortunate people, she thought, I pray you know how blessed you are.

"Mama," Beth said as she came in and settled herself next to Lucy, "why didn't you want Nick to take his medicine?"

"Is that what he said?"

"He said you thought he should stop using it. What possessed you to tell him that? You're not a doctor. He needs that medicine."

"Did he tell you why he needs it?"

"He didn't have to. It's for his leg, of course."

"Where is he now?"

"Resting. He'll be down for supper."

"Let's talk about it then, shall we?" As an afterthought, she added, "Tell Lin to serve Cal in the nursery."

Lucy scanned Nick's face as he seated himself at the supper table. "You're feeling better, I see."

He nodded and unfolded his napkin.

"I shan't break my word to you, Nick, but Bethie already knows I disapprove of your dosing yourself with those pills. Perhaps you should take this opportunity to tell her why."

"Ah, another time, another time. We've just got home, and—"

"I don't understand any of this," Beth said petulantly. "You both act as though you're hiding something. Whispering in the middle of the night and arguing about the silly medicine. I ask Nick, and he says, 'Your mother doesn't like it.' I ask you, Mama, and you say, 'We'll talk about it later.' How much later? And what is there to talk about, anyway? Nick can take care of himself."

"I believe he can, Bethie. I wish he would."

"What's that supposed to mean? Why are you speaking in riddles?"

"Nick . . ." Lucy laid down her soup spoon and gazed across the table at him. "Please trust me when I say that I am pressing this matter for your own good. Secrets fester, Nick. They're poisonous. You must believe me."

596

He looked at her in silence. Abruptly, he glanced away and shrugged. "You're making a fuss over nothing. It's of no consequence, really. It doesn't affect my health or my work or our marriage, so long as . . ."

"So long as what, Nick?" Lucy demanded.

"You know."

"But I don't know!" Beth cried. "In God's name, what is this all about?"

"As long as I take the pills," he explained, "I'm fine."

"Beth is convinced that you need them because your wound bothers you."

"Sometimes it does."

"Mama, that medicine is necessary for Nick. You know very well he has to have it for his pain."

"Nick?" Lucy fixed him with a steady gaze. "Is that the truth?"

His eyes met hers, bitter and resentful. "You won't let go of it, will you?"

"No. For your own good, Nick, I won't."

His hand shook slightly as he pushed away his plate. "Bethie, it's true I need the pills. But only for now. I'll stop taking them one of these days, I promise. It's not just on account of my leg, you see. It's more than that." He looked down at the table. "It's gotten to where I need the medicine for its own sake."

She frowned, puzzled. "I don't follow you. What's in those pills?"

"Opium," he muttered. "The more you take, the more you need."

"Nick, what do you mean?"

"He means, Bethie, that using opium becomes a habit. He's not his own man anymore. He's a slave to those pills."

"But that's ridiculous!" Beth's voice grew shrill. "Anyone with a shred of character can break a foolish habit. Isn't that so, Nick?"

"Yes. Yes, of course it is. It takes time, that's all."

"But why?"

"It brings on a sickness, Bethie," Lucy told her gently.

Nick glanced up sharply at Lucy. "I don't want her seeing me that way. You don't know what it's like."

"I believe," she replied, "that the vows you made said 'in sickness and in health.'"

"I'll go away somewhere when the time comes."

"No, you won't," Beth said. Her voice was calm. "Whatever you have to go through, I'll help you."

He smiled suddenly, a disarming, self-conscious grin. "You're a good girl, Bethie. Bless you. But we needn't go on about this tonight, need we? It's getting late, and we're tired. Another time, we can—"

"Nick," Lucy interrupted him, "do you know what I see? I see a cornered animal, frightened and angry, dodging this way and that to evade the inevitable. Is that the way you want to live?"

"Damn it!" He slammed his hand down hard on the tabletop. "What's the matter with the way I've been living? I do my job. I care for my wife and child. I don't make any trouble in this house. Why the devil can't everyone let well enough alone?"

"But Nick," Beth said, "surely you don't want to be bound to taking opium for the rest of your life. That's unnatural. No matter what you say, nothing could be worse than not being your own master. That stuff doesn't own you. You have the mettle to do anything you please. Look how courageous you were in the war—"

"Please, Bethie, don't." He raised a hand to quiet her.

"You're strong, Nick," she persisted. "Mama's wrong, I know it. You're not afraid of being ill. Why, in no time at all, you'd be feeling fit again and you'd never have to give a moment's thought to this whole silly business."

"It's not that easy. I'd have to take time away from the office. You don't realize what—"

"Nick," Lucy broke in, "I'm sure your Uncle Dabney would understand if I told him I needed you here at home just now. He wouldn't have to be told the whole story."

"For God's sake, can't we change the subject? Why do we have to discuss it this very minute?"

"Is there ever going to be any better time?" she asked. "Abel will be home soon. I want a happy, healthy family under this roof."

"I'm as healthy as I'll ever be. There's no reason—"

"Nick." Beth cut him off. She reached across the table and took his hand in hers. "Do it for me," she said softly. "If you didn't, I'd always wonder why. If you did, I'd know that everything I've always believed about you is true—that you're strong and gallant and not a slave to anything or anyone. Please, Nick, I beg you."

"You're like a pair of hounds, you two, yelping and snapping, trying to chase a possum up a tree."

"You didn't answer Beth."

He glanced from one to the other. He looked suddenly young, vulnerable and anxious. He gave a curt laugh and spread his hands. "Why not?" he said airily. "If it will make peace between us and keep you both from pestering me, why not? Let me have a night's rest, that's all."

"You must tell me what to expect," said Beth. "I must know how to help you."

"I will, Bethie. Eat now. The food is getting cold."

Late that night, Lucy heard his crutches on the stairs. As she lay in bed, she could hear him moving fitfully about the downstairs rooms. Despite his show of bravado, she knew he was afraid.

They kept Cal away from him, lest the boy be frightened by his father's agony. The restlessness, yawning and drowsiness that Lucy had seen in Saint Helena had in no way prepared her for the symptoms that ensued after his first full day of abstinence. Nick awoke from a deep slumber in a state of frenzied agitation. Abrupt, violent bursts of energy overtook him. He thrashed against his pillows like a wounded beast in the mindless torment of its death throes. Suddenly, he leapt from the bed and dragged himself to a chair, heaving himself rapidly to and fro, and his arms clasped about his chest. "Oh, God," he muttered, "my skin is crawling."

Beth glanced at Lucy, wide-eyed with fear.

"We must stay calm. Nick, would it help you to eat something?"

"No! No food!" A fit of sneezing seized him.

Beth put her hands on his shoulders and began to knead his muscles. "Mama, his skin is cold. I can feel it through his nightshirt."

Lucy took his hand. He shook with chills, and his arms were prickly with goose-flesh. "Blankets," she said and went to fetch them from the linen shelf in the hall.

As the hours passed, Beth grew more worried. When Lucy knocked on their bedroom door, Beth stepped out into the hall and whispered, "It's getting worse, Mama. His skin is cold and clammy, and he can't stop his teeth from chattering. He insists on pacing about the room on his crutches, but he trembles so badly that I am afraid he'll fall."

"Go have something to eat, Bethie. I'll stay with him for a while."

"Get out," he said as Lucy entered. "Leave me alone."

The pain and humiliation of his look stung her more deeply than his words. "No, Nick. You'll not be left by yourself."

"Does it give you pleasure to watch this?"

"Don't talk foolishness."

"You don't trust me, is that it?"

"Get back into bed, Nick. You're in no condition to be moving around."

"No." He pulled away as she touched his arm. "Let me be."

"How long will this last?"

"Forever."

Indeed, it seemed as though his suffering only increased as day gave way to night. His tremors worsened. His complexion was ashen, and he developed a marked tic on the left side of his face. He vacillated between chills and sudden spasms of heavy perspiration. By morning, he had vomited himself dry.

"Mama," Beth said, drawing Lucy aside, "perhaps we ought to send for Doctor Vanderhoef. Nick has dreadful cramps. He's in a great deal of pain."

She went to his bedside. "Where does it hurt?"

"Here," he said dully, laying his hand on his abdomen. "Please, it will pass. I know it will. Just let me out of this room. I feel as if I'm in captivity again. In the name of all that's merciful, let me get out of here."

"You're ill. You mustn't go anywhere."

"I beg you, just allow me to go down to the library. Anywhere, so long as I'm not shut up like this. After two years in a Yankee prison, it's more than I can bear."

Lucy looked at Beth. "What about Cal?"

"I could have Biddy pack a picnic for him and Lin. Septimus could take them out for the day."

"Do it, then."

As soon as Cal had left the house, Nick made his way unsteadily downstairs with both of the women beside him. He settled himself on the sofa in the library. He closed his eyes and winced, holding his side.

"Another cramp?"

He nodded. "Bethie, I could use some pillows."

"I'll bring them."

"Is there anything I can do?" Lucy asked.

"A cup of tea, I think. I'm dried out from retching."

The tea appeared to have helped him. As the afternoon passed, his shivering abated, and the color returned to his face. He was warm enough to discard his blankets, and his spirits were considerably improved. "What a nuisance I've been to you both." He smiled tiredly. "God knows, I'm sorry to have put you through all that."

Lucy gave his hand a reassuring squeeze. "I'm glad you're feeling better."

Beth began to weep.

"Don't, Bethie," Nick told her. "It's over."

"It's not that. I'm so relieved. It's been . . ."

"Come sit by me," he said, slipping his arm around her as she joined him.

Beth laid her head against his shoulder. Tenderly, he stroked her hair.

Lucy left them there together and mounted the stairs. Exhausted, she stretched out across her bed, not bothering to loosen her clothing. "Seth," she sighed, "Seth . . ." and she fell asleep.

By evening, the past three days seemed nothing more than a nightmare, its power for horror diminished by the presence of the lamplight and the familiar sights and scents of the supper table. Beth, pale and fatigued though she was, gazed at Nick with such unabashed affection that he looked away, embarrassed. "I'm sorry," he said again. "I never wanted you to see me like that."

"Don't apologize," Lucy told him. "We're very proud of you, Nick. You battled for your self-respect and you won. That's nothing to be sorry for."

"What's self-respect?" Cal wanted to know.

"It's when you know you've done something right, something good," Lucy heard herself replying. And, she thought suddenly, it is something lost to me beyond all recall.

Nick's illness, despite the distress it had caused, had served to distract her from her own anguish. Now, the crisis past, the demons it had held at bay returned to haunt her. She tired easily under the weight of her grief, and the inescapable affliction of her guilt burned in her like a draught of some bitter, corrosive liquid. Though the household had returned to an even tenor, its very normalcy seemed to Lucy a cruel irony. The April sun shone brightly through the window panes, illuminating the glossy floors and the polished mahogany furniture. Lucy glanced about the drawing room at the marble, crystal and gilt that surrounded her. She ran her fingers over the rose-velvet upholstery of her chair. For all this luxury, she reflected, it is a wasteland. It is barren, arid, its sun too harsh, its landscape offering no relief to this traveler. Her days were like desert-crossings broken only by nightfall and sleep. She grew to dread the dawn and the pain it brought. "In time," people said, "in time." But some miseries, like Nick's wounds, were beyond remedy.

"Mama, what are you gazing at?"

"What is it, dear?"

"I asked what you were looking at. You were staring into the fireplace. Are you cold? Shall I light the fire?"

"No, Bethie. Thank you."

Nick laid his newspaper on the sofa. "Hanged if this country isn't set upon its own ruin. This Civil Rights Act is going to flood the polls with hordes of ignorant Chinese and black men. It's an open invitation to corruption. Where did those boneheads in Congress get the idea that the accident of being born on this soil should confer the privileges of citizenship? Even President Johnson opposed it. At least, praise God, they excluded the Indians or we'd likely have half-naked savages whooping their way to the voting booths."

"I wish Abel were here."

Lucy glanced up quickly toward Beth.

She looked flustered. "I only meant that I wish he were here because it would cheer you up, Mama."

"You know your mama wants him to graduate. Anyhow, he'll be back before summer's over." Nick folded his paper and rose. "I left my book in the library."

"While you're there, Nick," Lucy said, "see if Biddy's shopping list is on my desk. I seem to have mislaid it."

"Mama, that's not like you," Beth chided. "You can always put your finger on everything."

"Not lately, I'm afraid." It was true. Lucy found it difficult to concentrate these days or even to remember the most commonplace details of the household routine. She felt a peculiar sense of dissipation, as though, like a piece of tumbleweed, she blew before the wind, lacking all volition and sense of direction. Sometimes the sensation frightened her. She had always endeavored to be the mistress of her own fate, yet now she felt powerless, uprooted at the mercy of phantom gusts that left her disturbed and disorganized. Seth had been her ballast, and without his reassuring presence she was adrift, meandering without purpose through this span of days unmarked by boundaries or destinations. But it was not only the loss of Seth that had cast her to the winds. She had mortgaged herself to deceit, and in so doing had forfeited an indefinable part of her life. She had somehow lost charge of that inmost self she had always taken so readily for granted.

If anything steadied her, it was the presence of Bethie, Nick and Cal. She longed for Abel's return. Whatever meaning her life might have now came from the children. It was part of growing old, she supposed. One's children became the guardians of one's fate.

They tried their best to divert her over the summer months, and she felt obliged not to rebuff their good intentions. They insisted on her going with them to Woodward's Gardens, which were lately the talk of the city. Mr. Woodward, proprietor of the What Cheer House, had decided to allow the public to enjoy his hitherto private Eden on Mission Street. What a curious place it was. Ostriches strutted about the man-made hillocks, staring back unconcerned at visitors who stopped to gawk at the strange, gangling birds. People strolled in wonder among the acres of lushly planted trees and shrubs each marked with its identifying tag. Occasionally, one of the resident menagerie, a docile gazelle perhaps would emerge from the bushes to confront the passersby.

"I begin to suspect," Nick said drily, "that they are even more amused by our presence than we are by theirs."

"What do you think of it, Mama?" Beth asked. "Did you ever see such tidy lawns and splendid flower beds? And the conservatory! All those rare, tropical specimens! My, but he's collected such beautiful things here."

"I don't quite know," Lucy mused absently watching as a pair of seals cavorted on the rocks in their pool. "I'm not sure what to make of it."

Mr. Woodward was a collector, it appeared, of almost anything collectible. There were displays of sculpture and paintings of Indian crafts, of fossils, shells, coins and minerals. He had amassed an assortment of animals, some living, others stuffed and mounted. What he could not acquire, he created, like the landscape with its ponds and moss-covered boulders. He had laid out serpentine paths and erected little bridges here and there over the water and, as a gesture to the public, added amusements like swings, toy boats and a bandstand for concerts.

"I guess he wants to make people happy," Lucy said, though for some reason, Mr. Woodward's efforts left her with a trace of melancholy. Apparently, he had meant to create a place of wonders and pleasures, as if godlike, he could furnish the delights of Paradise rediscovered. There was something almost wistful in his magnificent undertaking, for it struck her that only a man to whom Paradise seemed forever lost would devote his life and his fortune to trying to create a facsimile of it. Was he, like Lucy, someone fallen from grace by his own hand? Were there others, perhaps hundreds or even thousands of them, going about their daily lives unrecognized, unknown except to God and their consciences?

Beth and Nick went often to Woodward's Gardens that summer of sixty-six, yet Lucy had no wish to revisit the place. It was, to her, a monument to regret, and she had her fill of that, both awake and dreaming.

Herr Schmidt, overcoming his characteristic caution, wrote from Saint Helena that the vineyard showed promise of a fine harvest. There had been a goodly flowering of buds and a spell of dry, warm weather to set the crop. The fruit was beginning to mature. "Do try, my lady, to come here, if only for a few days, so that you may share this miracle of nature with us," he wrote. But Lucy could not bring herself to go. Sometimes, in her sleep, she still heard the rasping of the coolies' shovels behind her as she had walked down the hill that balmy day, leaving Seth behind forever.

Despite her reluctance to go, the fate of the vineyard now mattered more than ever to her. Its success would be the culmination of Seth's dreams and efforts. The progress of the Central Pacific, too, became increasingly important. It seemed somehow essential that all of Seth's visions should become realities, as though their fulfillment would reaffirm his existence and testify to his wisdom.

After more than three years, the railroad had at last reached Dutch Flat, and work had commenced on the Summit Tunnel. By slow degrees, the forbidding mountain yielded to the Chinese laborers who picked away at its obdurate granite, advancing at the rate of some eight inches a day. The immensity of the endeavor stirred her sentiments. To Lucy, there was something infinitely touching and admirable in the magnitude of men's dreams. She thought of her father, who had hacked a farm out of the wilderness; of the gold-seekers with their visions of Golconda; and of daft Emperor Norton with his fancies of a great span across the bay. She understood what so many others failed to see; that the promise of profit was less a reason than an excuse for men to express that most secret part of themselves. Wealth might dwindle and success pall, but a man's dreams could sustain him. There were, she decided, the dreamers and the plodders, those who either lacked imagination or the courage to dare. Sometimes she caught herself feeling sorry for Nick, not so much because his wounds circumscribed him but because he lacked that splendid, irrational spark that had the power to illuminate the common hours of a man's existence. Abel, on the other hand, had always been a striver, reaching out for some unseen objective, yearning to excel. Perhaps, thought Lucy, dreamers are born, not made.

Abel's room was prepared for him. The odor of fresh paint permeated the upstairs hall. The curtains hung crisply starched at his windows. The pillows and mattress had been aired and his bed linens laundered and ironed. Often, when Lucy awoke in the night, she would tiptoe quietly into his room, set her lamp on the table and sit for a while on the edge of his bed, trying to imagine what he would be like now. Had he grown much taller, she wondered. Was he bearded or clean-shaven, his voice booming or soft, his manner retiring or aggressive?

Joe Mason was delighted when she stopped at the store to tell him of Abel's imminent return. "I'll wager I'm almost as eager to see him as you are," he said. "What are his plans, once he's home?"

Lucy glanced across the counter toward the back of the store, where Klara was measuring some goods for Eleanor Gibbs. "He wrote in his last letter that Mr. Mountford was recommending him for a position here in the office of Simon Waite. It seems Mr. Waite is an old friend of Alvah Mountford."

Nelly nodded her approval to Klara. "Simon Waite?" she said, approaching Lucy. "Simon takes care of all my legal affairs. My late husband made a number of investments, and I of course understand nothing of such things," she said, giving Joe a disarmingly helpless look. "Amy and Warren Winslow sent me to Simon. He's Warren's lawyer, too."

Joe grinned at Lucy. "A pair of fine endorsements, if you ask me."

Klara handed Nelly her parcel. "Abel, a lawyer. How pleased you must be, Lucy."

"Yes indeed," Nelly echoed as Joe opened the door for her, "a most gentlemanly profession. If you've finished with your purchases, Lucy, perhaps you'll let me have a word with you." They walked a few steps down the street, until they were past the store window. Nelly paused and turned to Lucy. "Will he remember me?"

"I expect he will."

"It might be best for us to meet as though for the first time."

"Nelly, let me assure you that Abel is neither indiscreet nor unworldly. He's quite aware of the value of a short memory, believe me."

"Your word is good enough for me, Pastora."

"My children don't like that name. I wish you'd not use it in their presence."

"They don't? Why not? I should think they'd be proud of all you've made of yourself."

"They are prouder of some things than others. I'd be obliged if you'd not call me Pastora in front of Abel or Beth."

Nelly smiled. "It seems you and me are always striking bargains."

"So it does. Good day to you, Eleanor."

That evening was warm. The heat of the August sun still hung about the house, despite a light, dry breeze. Lucy donned a robe over her chemise and went into Abel's room. She stood at his window, looking out at the gibbous moon that glowed like a shiny silver finial on the spire of the pine tree. The night was fogless and starlit. Her eyes sought out the familiar constellations. Once, long ago, she and Willie had become lost on their way home, and Pa, finding them cold and afraid, had shown them how to make their way by the stars. It had seemed to her then that grown-ups possessed the answer to every question and the solution to every problem and that their lives must be gloriously uncomplicated. How omniscient adults appeared to children. And adults, loath to tarnish that innocent admiration, concealed from them the galling disillusionment that came with years. There were no certainties, only probabilities. There were no answers, only questions. And she, Lucy realized, was less sure of herself than she had ever been. There seemed no wayposts to guide her anymore. The constellations no longer consoled her.

She started and turned. Beth stood in the doorway, barefooted and tousled, her robe clasped about her, rubbing her eyes sleepily.

"I didn't mean to frighten you, Mama," she apologized, stifling a yawn. "I heard you come in here and I wondered if anything was wrong."

"I was only looking around. Remind me to pick some flowers, Bethie, to put on his table. How does the room look to you? Do you think he'll like it? Will he find everything he needs?"

"Everything but his fancy friends, I expect."

"I'll put his Emerson books beside his bed."

"Oh, Mama, I was making a joke."

"I shan't have him comparing us unfavorably with the Mountfords."

Beth gave her a resigned smile. "I'll fetch the Emerson books. I was going downstairs anyway, to tell Nick to come up."

"It's late. I thought he'd gone to bed."

"He likes to put on his dressing gown and read for a while without keeping me awake. I daresay he's lost track of the time. Sleep well, Mama. And stop worrying about Abel, will you?"

Lucy slipped beneath the covers of her bed and closed her eyes. Drowsily, she stirred at the sound of voices wondering whether she had lain there only a moment or had dropped off and then awakened at the noise. Beth and Nick were quarreling loudly in the library, apparently unmindedful that the row was audible upstairs. With a sigh, she rose and reached for her robe.

"Nick, Bethie," she called softly, leaning over the bannister, "do lower your voices."

There was a momentary silence, and then she heard Beth weeping. Nick said something, but Beth didn't reply. Lucy turned back toward her room.

"Mama," Beth cried from the bottom of the stairs. Her voice choked on a sob. "Mama, he lied to us."

Lucy descended the stairs, her fingers pressed to her lips. "Hush," she whispered. At the sight of Beth's anguished face, she felt suddenly heavy with dread. "Dearest, what is it?" She put her arms around the girl and drew her close.

"He's been deceiving us all along. He never stopped taking those awful pills."

Lucy stiffened. "Come. We can't stand here in the hall for everyone to hear us." She put her arm around Beth's shoulders and led her back into the library.

Nick looked up as they entered, then glanced away. He pressed his hands to his ears and shook his head. "I don't want to hear any more."

Lucy closed the door. "Is it true?"

Beth wiped her tears on the sleeve of her robe. "He hid them behind the books on that shelf. They were there all along. That's why he wanted us to bring him down here that day."

On the floor, beneath a space in the neat rows of volumes, two books lay where they had fallen. Lucy picked them up. "Nick," she asked quietly, "why?"

He gave her a look of searing bitterness. "You don't understand. There's no other way."

"You betrayed our trust in you!" Beth accused him. "How could you do such a thing to Mother and me?"

"Do you call it trust to follow me down here and come sneaking up behind me?"

"That was not her intent, Nick. You're mistaken."

"It doesn't matter," Beth said. "After this, I shall never be able to trust you again, so long as you live."

"Nor I you. No man wants a wife spying on him."

"Stop this," Lucy demanded, "both of you."

"It's too late," Beth replied dully.

"Give me the pills, Nick."

"It's no good, Mama. He'll only get more."

Lucy reached for the small, white box on the table beside him. Swiftly, he grasped her wrist and spun her away.

"How dare you treat my mother roughly!" Beth seized his shoulders and shook him furiously. "After everything she's done for you!"

"I don't want favors! Not hers or yours or anyone else's!"

"And where would you be without them?" she shouted.

He took hold of her arms and shoved her from him.

"Don't touch me! Do you understand? Don't ever touch me again!"

"Please," Lucy begged them, "don't bellow so. It's late. Nothing can be solved at this hour. You're only disrupting everyone's sleep and creating a scandal with all this brawling. Go to bed now. In the morning—"

"I'm sleeping in Abel's room," Beth said.

"Bethie, dear," Lucy told her tiredly, "that's no way to—"

"You heard me. And unlike some people, I mean what I say. I'm sleeping in Abel's room," she repeated.

"Then go, damn it," Nick retorted.

Beth looked at him as though she were going to speak. Abruptly, she turned her back to him and left the room.

Lucy gazed helplessly at Nick. "In heaven's name, what's to be done?"

"Nothing. Leave me alone. I'll be up presently."

In the morning, when she came to the breakfast table, he was already gone. Lin brought Lucy's coffee from the kitchen.

"Where is Septimus?" Lucy asked her.

"He took Mister Nick to work."

"So early? Did he at least have something to eat before he left?"

Lin shook her head. "He said he'd get something on the way. Missee?"

"What is it, Lin?"

"I don't like it when Missybet is unhappy. Last night—"

"Nobody can be happy all the time, Lin. Married people have their differences like everybody else. Let's forget about last night, shall we?"

She nodded soberly and disappeared into the kitchen.

Lucy glanced up from her needlework as the clock

struck eleven. Poor Bethie, she thought, she must have lain awake most of the night. Already she had missed breakfast, and unless she awakened shortly, she'd be late for noonday dinner. Lucy put aside her sewing and went upstairs. She tapped lightly at the door to Abel's room. "Bethie? It's Mama, dear." She opened the door. "It's time to get up."

Beth stirred. Slowly, she sat up, staring vacantly at the faint hint of light beyond the curtained windows. She pressed her palms to her eyes. "What's to become of us, Mama?" she asked softly. "What's to become of our marriage?"

Lucy sat down beside her on the bed. "Some things take a lot of forgiving, Bethie. We have to stretch ourselved to do it, but at the same time we grow. Your being angry at Nick won't help anything."

"He failed us, Mama. He deliberately deceived us."

"He failed himself, and that's even worse. His deceit wasn't malicious. He only wanted us to believe he'd done the right thing. He was ashamed that he'd failed. He's to be pitied, Bethie, not despised. We must give him another chance."

"He's destroyed my faith in him, Mama."

"It can be restored, given time and change. Life is long, my dear. Don't be so quick to think things are final. It's going to be difficult, I'll grant you. In a way, it will be just as hard for you as for Nick. He must overcome his addiction to opium, and you must overcome your mistrust. If you will only help and support each other, you'll find the struggle can bring you closer together." She took Beth's hand in hers. "I beg you, for you own sakes and Cal's, to make the effort."

"How can you pardon him so easily, after the way he treated you and the ungrateful things he said?"

"Because I want you both to be happy." Lucy paused a moment. "And because there isn't one of us who doesn't need forgiving for one thing or another." She rose. "Come, now. It's almost time for dinner." Lucy went to the window and parted the curtains. "It's a beautiful day, Bethie, and—" She broke off with a frown. "Whose carriage is that? Are you expecting anyone?"

"No. Is it Nick? Perhaps Boyd has driven him home for dinner." She glanced out the window, tying her robe about her. "That's not Boyd's."

The driver alighted and opened the door. A tall, slim man stepped down, attired in a dark suit and carrying a pearl-gray cloak over his arm. He turned back toward the open door, his hand outstretched. From the dim interior of the carriage emerged a fair, slightly built woman dressed in deep blue, with a large, plumed hat that all but obscured her face from view.

"Who are those people?" Lucy asked irritably.

"Never mind. They probably have the wrong address. Septimus will tend to them." She went to fetch her slippers.

"Bethie, come here."

"What is it? What are they doing?" Beth peered over Lucy's shoulder. "Dear God," she breathed, "it's him. Mama, it's Abel!"

"But he wasn't due 'til next week!"

"It's Abel, Mama, and he's brought a lady with him!"

XXXII

ABEL FLUNG his arms around Lucy and hugged her tightly. At length, he retreated a step and gazed at her. He threw back his head and roared with laughter. His eyes were crinkled with merriment, and his teeth shone white against his olive skin. His voice was hearty and deep. "Mama, dear, you look as if you'd seen a spook," he said, still laughing.

"I can hardly believe my eyes, that's all. You said you'd arrive the week of the twentieth."

"We wanted to surprise you." He stepped aside and drew the woman to him, his arm around her slender waist. "Mama, this is your daughter-in-law, Selina."

Lucy's eyes filled with tears. She clasped Selina's hand in hers. After a moment, she found her voice. "My dear, welcome to our home. Welcome to our hearts."

"I'm honored to meet you, Mrs. Slade," she said, giving Lucy a warm smile.

Lucy returned her smile, shaking her head in wonderment. "Forgive me. I realize I'm gaping but I never expected . . ."

"It's quite all right. I warned Abel that it might be a shock to you."

"It's nigh unto impossible not to stare at her, Mama. Isn't she a beauty?"

Selina blushed and cast him an admonishing look.

She reminded Lucy of a crystal prism. She was so tall and slim, so fair of face and hair as to appear almost translucent. Her features had a striking sharpness to them. Her patrician nose, the planes of her cheeks and forehead, the point of her chin, all seemed to have been cut and polished to a fine edge. The emerald brilliance of her eyes, flashed with animation as she spoke, and she possessed a high-pitched voice that fell on the ears with such clarity of sound as to compel immediate attention.

Abel stepped into the hallway. "Septimus!" he called. "We need a hand with some baggage."

Lucy took Selina's arm and led her inside. "Beth will be down in a moment. Cal is up in the nursery, but he'll join us for dinner. Mercy, I must tell Biddy there will be two more at table."

Septimus halted in the dining room doorway, glancing uncertainly at the newcomers. Slowly, an astonished grin spread over his face. "Why, Mister Abel," he said, his voice rising with jubilation, "if you ain't a sight!"

Abel grasped his hand and shook it warmly. "Septimus, this lady is my wife."

"Ma'am." He bowed.

"Hello, Septimus. I'm pleased to meet you."

"Septimus," Lucy told him, "send Biddy into the drawing room when you've brought the baggage in. And tell Lin to put fresh linens on Mister Abel's bed. Selina, let me take your pretty bonnet. Make yourself comfortable, dear."

With a deft motion, Abel tossed his hat onto the hall chair. For a moment, Lucy's breath caught in her throat; the gesture was so like Seth. She felt a sudden pang of longing, wishing he were here now to welcome this handsome young man he had so readily taken for his son. "Come," she said, showing them into the drawing room.

Abel looked about him, as though eager to take in every familiar object. "Where are the lambs that used to be on the mantel?"

"They were casualties of the last earthquake, I'm afraid."

"Earthquake?" Selina looked alarmed.

"Nothing worse than a shake or two," Lucy assured her. "Abel why don't you fetch us each a glass of sherry? You'll find everything in the library. Bring one for Bethie, too."

"I very much regret," Selina said kindly, "that we arrive at a time of mourning. I hope it doesn't add to your burdens."

"No, my dear. I can't remember when my spirits have

received such a needed lift. My only regret is that you and Seth never had the pleasure of meeting."

"I feel I know you both quite well, from all Abel has told me."

"Hello." Beth paused in the doorway. "I'm Elizabeth Stevens. And you must be."

"Selina Mount—" She broke off. "Bates," she corrected herself.

As Selina rose to greet her, Beth came into the room and kissed her cheek. "I thought as much. My congratulations and best wishes. Do call me Beth. Everyone does. There you are!" she cried as Abel came in bearing the tray of glasses. "You're a scamp, do you know it? How like you to make up your mind to surprise us." He set the tray down, and she ran to him, laughing as they embraced.

"Look at you, for heaven's sake," he exclaimed. "Mama, we have the two most beautiful women in America right here in this room. Bethie, you were never lovelier. Where's Nick?"

"He's at his office."

With a cry, Biddy bustled into the room, wringing her apron excitedly in her hands. "Sakes alive, Mister Abel! What good news this is!"

"Biddy, say hello to my wife, if you will." He glanced with pride at Selina.

"Miz' Abel, welcome to San Francisco." She frowned slightly. "Are my eyes playin' tricks, or do you look a trifle pale? It's the food on them ships, I'll wager. No matter, I'll put the roses back in your cheeks in no time. Miz' Slade, I'd best carve up that fresh ham and save our chicken for a pie. You're just lucky," she scolded Abel genially, "that I've a nice, big corn puddin' in the oven and a sponge cake coolin' on the sill. Shame on you for not giving me notice so's I could make somethin' special."

"I'd say it's fortunate you're too big to spank," Beth teased him, "or Biddy'd take you over her knee."

"I apologize, Biddy. Am I forgiven?"

"Oh, now," she said, embarrassed, "ain't no harm done. I've even got some of those pickled peaches you like."

"Hey!" said Abel, spying Cal in the hall. "Is that my nephew? Come here, boy, and let me have a look at you."

Cal hung back timidly, edging behind Biddy's skirts. She reached for his hand and thrust him forward. "Mind

614

your manners, Calvert. S'cuse me, now. I'll be goin' back to my kitchen."

Beth beckoned to the boy. "Darling, this is your Uncle Abel. He sent you that beautiful little steamboat for Christmas. Now you can thank him in person."

Cal stuck out his hand in Abel's direction, all the while staring bashfully down at the floor. Abel took his hand and shook it.

"Thank you for the boat, sir."

Abel cupped the child's chin tenderly in his hand and tilted his face upward to meet his gaze. "That's a good boy." He smiled. "I guess lots of people have already told you how much you look like your Papa."

Cal nodded solemnly.

Gently, Abel took him by the shoulders and turned him toward Selina. "This is your Aunt Selina, Cal."

"Well, Calvert?" Beth prompted him. "How do you greet a lady?"

He made a stiff, self-conscious bow and darted to Beth's side.

"Very good, Calvert," Lucy told him. "Selina, you've met almost the entire household. Where's Lin, Cal?"

"Making up the bed." He wriggled onto Beth's lap.

Abel raised his sherry glass. "To you, Mama."

"To our family being together again," Beth said.

"To you and Selina, my son. May your marriage be as full of joy and contentment as Seth's and mine." She sipped her sherry quickly, blinking back the tears.

Selina halted, her glass halfway to her lips, looking toward the doorway.

Lin stood uncertainly in the hall. She caught sight of Abel and broke into a broad grin.

"Selina," Lucy said, "this is Li Lin."

Selina gave Abel a bewildered look and sought a place to set her glass.

"Welcome home, sir."

"Thank you," Abel replied. "And will you welcome my wife, too?"

Lin advanced a few steps toward Selina and curtsied. "Welcome, Mrs. Brother." She looked up, flustered as Abel, Beth and Lucy burst into laughter. "I have made a mistake?"

"No, not at all," Abel assured her. "You're a clever girl. That's a fine name."

"How nice to meet you, Li," Selina said.

"Lin," Lucy corrected her. "The Chinese put the surname first."

"How curious." Selina smiled and said, "Lin, then."

Beth lifted Cal off her lap. "Run along with Lin and wash up for dinner."

"I expect," Lucy said to Abel, "that you two might like to refresh yourselves before we sit down at table. Why don't you show Selina upstairs?"

He took Selina's hand and led her into the hall. "Abel," Lucy heard Selina whisper, "does the Chinese girl live here? In this house?"

"Well, Mama," Beth said when they were out of earshot, "what do you think of her?"

"She's beautiful, that's obvious. I suppose it will take us all a while to get to know each other. It must be difficult for her, coming into a new family."

As they filed into the dining room, Lucy touched Abel's arm. "You'll be sitting there, at the head of the table."

"Mama?"

"You're my son and the rightful heir to that place."

"As you wish, Mama." He looked around the room. "Nothing's changed. I'm glad."

"*Eigner Herd ist goldes Werth,*" Selina said. "German," she explained, seeing Beth's puzzled expression. "It means 'One's own hearth has golden worth.' "

"You speak German!" Lucy said. "Won't the Schmidts be delighted."

"And French and Latin," Abel added proudly.

"Who are the Schmidts?" Selina asked.

"Herr Schmidt is the winemaster of our vineyard," Lucy told her. "His wife speaks very little English."

"Tell me, Mother," Abel inquired, "what are the prospects for the harvest?"

"Excellent, according to Herr Schmidt."

"You haven't been up there to see for yourself?"

"Not since—No."

"But we must go up for the harvest," he insisted. "After all these years of hearing about the place, I wouldn't miss it for anything. I don't believe Seth ever wrote me a single letter without telling me about the progress and the problems of the vineyard. Outside of the family, it was the closest to his heart."

"It was," Lucy said softly.

"Then it's settled. Seth would want us all to be there, I know. And I want Selina to see as much of California as I can show her before I begin practicing."

"Practicing law?" Beth asked.

He laughed. "Of course, silly. I've a meeting with Simon Waite week after next. With luck, he'll find a place for me in his office."

"Father recommended Abel to Mr. Waite," Selina told Lucy.

"He has a fine reputation," Lucy replied. "I'm grateful to your father for having such confidence in Abel."

Beth shook her head. "It's hard to believe that the same young man who went sneaking off to a hanging is ready to practice law."

"A hanging?" Selina laid down her fork, aghast.

"That was a long time ago, Bethie," Lucy admonished her. "We've no such things as vigilantes anymore."

"I should hope not," Selina said.

"I wasn't thinking of the Vigilance Committee, Mama. I was thinking of the Indian girl, back in Castalia."

For a moment, Lucy's and Abel's eyes met. Abruptly, she said, "Beth, that's quite enough of such a sordid subject. Selina, dear, do let me help you to another slice of ham."

"Thank you. Abel has told me about the work you've done for the Good Shepherd Home. I hope I shall be allowed to do my part, too. It seems such a worthwhile endeavor."

"It is," Lucy replied, "though I confess I've not done my full share lately."

"Mama tires easily," Beth said.

"Perhaps Selina can take over some of your duties," Abel suggested.

"Do your children have a reading club?" Selina wanted to know. "I should think it very important that they be introduced to good literature. *Tu es quod legis.*"

"You are what you read," Abel translated.

"Indeed," Lucy said. "They do receive lessons, but I don't think anyone has brought up the idea of a reading club."

"In Cambridge, we always had them, even as small children."

"After dinner, I shall show you the library. I hope you'll find it as comfortable as your own."

"And then, my dear, I'll show you about the city," Abel told her.

"I should like to have a nap first."

"Of course," Lucy said. "I daresay you've both been up since dawn. Do give the poor girl a rest, Abel. The sun sets late these days, and you'll have plenty of time left to show Selina around before evening."

It was nearly seven, Lucy noted, hearing the grandfather clock in the hall chime the quarter-hour. She glanced up at Beth, who was seated at the piano, her hands resting idly on the keys as she gazed out of the drawing room window. "Did Nick tell Septimus when to expect him this evening?"

Beth shook her head. "He only told him that he'd get a ride home with Boyd."

"We must wait supper, if necessary. It wouldn't look right to—" She broke off at the sound of Selina's voice on the stairs.

Abel ushered Selina into the room. With a sibilant rustling of silk she seated herself and smoothed the white lace fichu about her shoulders.

"You look very lovely, my dear," Lucy told her, "but you mustn't think you have to dress for supper every night."

"It's no trouble. We always do it at home."

"This is your home now," Abel reminded her.

"Tell me," Lucy asked, "did you enjoy your drive around the city?"

"Very much. I had no idea it was so small. One hears so much of San Francisco that I suppose I had expected its size to match its reputation."

"It's really just a spit of land that extends into the bay," Abel explained. "It was even smaller before they filled in a portion of the harbor to extend the business district."

"There seems to be an uncommon amount of sand or dust in the air."

"Sand," Lucy replied. "We are built on sand hills. Is the Massachusetts shore so different?"

Abel smiled. "The New England coast is rocky and wooded and green, Mama. I sometimes think that everything sturdy and durable in the Yankee character comes from having its roots in that rugged terrain."

"By contrast, San Francisco seems—" Selina searched for the right word. "Impermanent."

"Exempla sunt odiosa," Abel said to her.

"What's that supposed to mean?" Beth asked.

"Comparisons are odious."

"Couldn't you have said that in the first place?" She rose from the piano bench. "Here comes Nick." She glanced apprehensively at Lucy.

"Do go meet him, dear, and tell him what a grand surprise we have for him." She waited until Beth had left the room. "Try not to remark on Nick's disablement. He resents any show of pity."

"I understand, Mama."

Nick wore a broad grin as he entered. "As I live and breathe! Not only is he back, but he's brought us a bride. Ma'am," he said, attempting a bow for Selina's benefit, "you're by far the prettiest Yankee these eyes ever lit upon. But then, that's hardly compliment enough, since most I've seen were in uniform."

Selina smiled. "It appears that all the rumors I've heard about the gallantry of Southern gentlemen are true."

"Miz' Slade," Septimus announced, "supper is served."

"Mama?" Abel offered Lucy his arm.

"I believe," Beth declared, laying her hand on his other arm, "that I shall insist on your escorting me, too, just because it's been so long since we three were together."

Nick chose to disregard the slight. "Sister-in-law," he said to Selina, "I'd be quick to give you my arm, if I could spare it. Consider it offered, if you will. May I have the honor?"

"Mais certainement. C'est mon plaisir."

"What a tiny creature you are, Mama," Abel remarked. "In all my memories of you, I saw you ever so much larger than life."

She laughed. "Is that so? I expect that's part of growing up. Selina, dear, you sit here at my right. Nick, you're at my left beside Bethie."

Nick glanced at Abel as he took his place at the head of the table, but he made no comment.

"Abel," Lucy said, "remind me to show you the crates of books in the carriage house. They're all of Seth's law library, and you must have them."

"Mama's even prouder of you than she lets on," Beth told him.

"I never could have done any of it without you, Mama."

"How difficult it must have been for you," Selina said to Lucy, "raising two children all by yourself in a little cabin in the wilderness, surrounded by Indians."

"I hardly thought of Castalia as a wilderness. Besides, within a few years it became a thriving village. And I assure you that the Indians were a most amicable lot."

"Still, I doubt I'd have your courage. One can't know, can one what savage instincts they possess or what sort of dreadful rituals they might practice against the white settlers."

"Indeed," Beth said, a small smile playing at her lips, "who can fathom the savage soul? If, that is, they have souls at all. Abel, you're the one with all the education, so you tell me. Do you think Indians have souls? Can they distinguish right from wrong? Do they feel remorse for being devious or deceitful, I wonder?"

Lucy spoke up sharply. "That's enough, Beth. If your memory were better, you'd know how foolish you sound. They were gentle, generous people," she told Selina "without a trace of selfishness or greed. They believed in sharing all that nature provided. Unfortunately, their innocence made them victims of everything petty and grasping in the character of their so-called betters."

Beth looked down at her plate. "I'm sorry. Mama's right, Selina. I was only teasing."

"Are there Indians around these parts?"

Lucy shook her head. "Hardly any to speak of."

"Never you mind, Selina," Nick said jovially, "we've plenty of other curiosities to pique your interest. Why, there's Woodward's Gardens and the sea lions by the Cliff House, just to name two. Have you ever seen a sea lion?"

"I've never even heard of one. Are you joking with me?"

"Not at all," Abel assured her. "They're grandly whiskered brutes that weigh as much as a quarter of a ton and frolic about the shore as comically as kittens."

"We must take a picnic to the cliffs on Saturday," Nick said. "Think of it, Bethie, the four of us can have such good times going on outings and to the theatre and concerts together."

Nick's tone was ebullient. Lucy realized he was almost giddy with relief at Abel's and Selina's presence. With their arrival, he was spared any further confrontations for the time being. But he was deluding himself if he thought the matter settled. How long would it be, she wondered, before Abel or Selina sensed something unpleasant in the wind? She glanced around the table. Nick was behaving as though he were master of the revels, presiding over their reunion. He bantered with Abel and twitted Selina for her Yankee accent. Selina blushed prettily and appeared not to mind. She was quite accustomed to being the focus of attention, Lucy decided. Abel laughed readily at Nick's sallies and glanced adoringly at Selina as though to reassure her that they were all in good fun. Lucy looked at him thoughtfully, trying to see in this elegant young man with his cultivated ways some trace of the primitive child who had once squatted by a riverbank, twining baskets of reeds. He had Luther Moore's height and bearing. The planes of his face, like Luther's, were sharply hewn. Of the Indian woman, there remained only the fullness of her lips and the dark, penetrating gaze which even now, as he laughed, retained the enigmatic gravity of her look. Beth, she noticed, had scarcely touched her supper. She toyed abstractedly with the food on her plate, paying little attention to the high spirits of the others.

"Bethie," Lucy said, "I think it would be nice for Selina to meet our friends, especially some of the young people. Perhaps you and I could organize a reception."

"But Mama, we're still in mourning."

"It would be a small gathering, a tea perhaps. Seth would want us to do it, I'm sure."

Beth seized the idea, as Lucy had known she would. Nothing pleased Bethie more than to busy herself with matters of society. "We must have it outdoors," she announced. "A lawn party would be quite the thing. With the weather so balmy and the days still long it would be so nice to be outside. How many do you think we should invite, Mama?"

"Under the circumstances, we'd best limit the list to our closest friends."

The next morning, Beth was in perceptibly higher spirits. She tapped at the open door to the library where Lucy was working at her desk. "Here." Lucy handed Beth the stack of envelopes. "Have Septimus deliver them."

Beth glanced through the pile. "The Winslows, the Fiskes, the Gallaghers, Father Crowley, Mrs. Gibbs—"

She looked up, surprised. "I thought you didn't care for Mrs. Gibbs."

"All the other ladies of the Good Shepherd group are invited. The omission would be too obvious."

"If you say so. The Vanderhoefs," she continued, "the Fearings, the Derbys. Oh, Mama. The Derbys? Must you be so democratic? I know Mr. Derby has made a lot of money building houses, but that hardly makes him a gentleman. What will Selina think?"

"Don't tell her."

"I shan't have to. She'll know when she sees his hands."

"The Derbys are invited. That's that."

Beth grimaced. "As long as they don't bring that dreary son of theirs. The Brocks," she went on, "and Naomi and Boyd. Selina will like them, I think. Martha and Nathan Morse—" She sighed. "Well, we can't very well avoid having poor Nathan. Joe and Klara Mason. Uncle Dabney Stevens and Aunt Rose, of course. And the Knight sisters. Mama, you forgot Hiram Berry."

"I didn't forget him. I thought Mr. Berry's presence would be a reminder of . . . of less pleasant things."

"Shouldn't we invite Simon Waite, now that Abel's going to work for him?"

"I think not. We don't know the gentleman, and it might look as though Abel were trying to curry favor."

"Oh, Mama, I do so want it to be a beautiful party," she said wistfully. "It seems so long since we had a happy occasion in this house. And I want Selina to see that San Francisco people are quite as nice as those back East."

"These are our friends, Beth, whether or not Selina likes them."

"Still, I want everything to be perfect."

Flower-decked tables dotted the lawn, draped with white damask cloths that stirred languidly in the breeze. The gentlemen, at ease in their light summer clothing and straw panamas, savored Biddy's rum punch, while the ladies, their faces framed by parasols, favored the tea or lemonade. Cal darted about, playing hide-and-seek with Blanca Mason under the tablecloths, and Septimus, his face aglow with perspiration, presided over the sumptuous spread of refreshments.

"My dear boy," Warren Winslow said, pumping Abel's

hand enthusiastically, "I hear Simon Waite has taken you into his office. You couldn't ask for a better opportunity."

"Yes, sir. It's a great piece of luck."

"Not so, Abel. Believe me, Simon doesn't dole out favors. If he wants you, it's because he thinks you have the stuff to be a first-rate lawyer. He'll drive you like a drayhorse but no harder than he drives himself. You'll work hard, my boy, but you'll go far if you follow Simon's example."

"Mr. Waite is an old friend of my father," Selina put in. "It was Father's idea that Abel should meet him."

"Was it? And a good one, too. Father Crowley," Warren said, stepping aside as the priest joined them, "have you met this lovely bride?"

"Indeed I have." He raised his glass of punch to Selina. "To your health and happiness. Warren, your wife is trying to catch your eye, I think."

Warren acknowledged Amy's wave with a nod and excused himself.

"Well, Abel, how does it feel to be home again?"

"Splendid, Father. I'd missed all these familiar faces more than I'd realized."

"It will do your mother a world of good, having you here. You're just what she needs for her spirits."

"We shan't be living here indefinitely," Selina told him. "Once Abel is established in his profession, we shall find a home of our own."

"Nearby, I trust. Lucy needs her family close about her, now that she's lost Seth." He reached out and caught Lin's hand as she passed. "Whoa, there, my girl. You look as pretty as a lotus flower in that white dress. You're becoming quite the young lady. How old are you now, Lin?"

"Almost seventeen, sir."

He shook his head. "Has it been that long? I must be losing track of time. Confound it, you make me feel like an old man."

"It is a fine thing to be old, Father. Years bring the gift of wisdom with them."

"They do, do they? Then I've plenty to look forward to. Don't let me keep you. I must fetch a cup of tea for Polly Fearing."

Selina watched as he made his way through the guests to the refreshment table. "He seems just like anyone else, doesn't he?"

Abel gave her a curious look. "Why shouldn't he?"

"It's only that I've never met one of them before."

"One of them?"

"A priest. How does he happen to be here?"

"He's a dear friend of Mother. He came to her for help in founding the waifs' home. Father Crowley is responsible for our having Lin with us, too. He took her away from a ragpicker who was trying to sell her."

"Sell her?"

"Unfortunately, there's an illicit trade in importing young Chinese girls for immoral purposes."

"Here? In San Francisco? Abel, that's disgusting! And still it goes on?"

"There are efforts to block it, but the Chinese find devious ways around them. Lin was fortunate."

Selina glanced across the crowded lawn to where Lin stood talking to Klara Mason, holding Cal and Blanca by the hands. "I don't fully understand. Lin seems to be on speaking terms with everyone here. Is she to be treated as a servant or as a member of the family?"

"She's a bit of both, actually."

Selina frowned. "You don't find it difficult to reconcile the two? And how is one to accept a heathen as part of the family?"

Abel laughed at her consternation. "Lin's quite civilized, I assure you."

"You know very well what I mean. Someone with that background—"

"My dear, you're in California now. We're a young state with a short history. Background is not a paramount concern hereabouts. We live in the present. One's actions are the only basis for moral judgment."

"You can't dismiss heredity just like that," she countered.

"I can. I do."

"Then we are in disagreement."

Abel took her hand and squeezed it. "You'll learn," he told her. "I expect it all seems very different and strange, but you'll get used to our ways."

"Selina," Beth called, "do come and meet Doctor Vanderhoef and Mrs. Gibbs. Abel, you mustn't keep her all to yourself."

"Mrs. Gibbs." Abel bowed. "Mother has spoken to me about you."

Nelly looked at him uncertainly.

"I believe she said you were a client of Simon Waite's."

"Ah, yes . . . My congratulations on your new position. I presume this beautiful lady is Mrs. Bates." She extended her left hand in greeting.

Puzzled, Selina glanced at Nelly's other arm, then quickly averted her eyes and shook her proffered hand.

"Selina, may I present Doctor Vanderhoef?" Abel smiled as the doctor put an arm around his shoulders. "Doctor, Bethie tells me you've been most attentive to Mama since her ordeal. We're all very grateful to you."

"She's a remarkable lady," he answered, his eyes searching out Lucy. He watched her for a moment as she sat talking to Dabney Stevens. "She's looking rather thin, to my eyes. I wish she'd put on a bit of weight."

"Then I wasn't mistaken," Abel said. "She seemed very small to me, very slight. But she was quick to blame it on my having been away and grown."

Beth shook her head. "Mama hasn't looked herself since Seth died, Abel. The sadness still gnaws at her."

"I'll go have a talk with her," Doctor Vanderhoef said. "Excuse me, will you? Selina, my dear, I'm delighted to have met you."

"Martin," Lucy greeted him, "how good to see you. You know Nick's Uncle Dabney, I believe."

"Indeed." The doctor shook his hand. "I understand that Boyd and Naomi are going to make you a grandfather before long. You must be very pleased. Would you mind, Dabney, if I borrowed this lady for a few minutes?"

"I certainly would," he said smiling as he rose, "but I shan't deny you the honor. Here, take my chair."

The doctor seated himself and took out his pipe. "Do you object?" he asked Lucy.

"Not at all. Seth smoked a pipe. I like the aroma because it reminds me of him."

"Lucy, how are you feeling these days? I'm inquiring as your physician, not simply to make polite conversation."

Lucy sighed and shook her head. "Weary, Martin. I'd thought my strength would return to me as the months passed, but it hasn't. I try not to let the children know how easily I tire. I want them around me. I find their presence a comfort."

"Then you must conserve your energy. I want you to

625

take a nap every afternoon." He reached into his pocket and withdrew a notebook and pencil. "Here." He wrote something and handed her the slip of paper. "Any good apothecary sells this tonic. Take it three times a day, before meals."

"I will, Martin. Thank you. Martin—" She hesitated. "May I speak to you in complete confidence?"

"Of course. Need you ask?"

Lucy glanced across the lawn to where Nick stood chatting with his cousin Boyd and Martha Morse. "We have a serious problem, Martin. Abel and Selina know nothing about it. Neither Beth nor I can cope with it, I'm afraid. We need your help."

"What is it, Lucy? Tell me."

When she had finished, he leaned back in his chair, gazing off at Nick, his brow creased in thought.

"Nick insists there's no harm to it. I don't know whether to believe him or not."

He took a deep breath. "There's no physical harm, so far as I know, though I have my reservations about opium because of the problems that can arise when the drug is discontinued. Then too, prolonged use of opium requires the user to keep increasing his dosage in order to maintain its effects. Generally speaking, I regard that sort of dependency as unwholesome, if not unhealthful. I will say, without qualification, that the dependency must exact a stiff toll from his mental condition."

"And from his marriage, too, Martin. Beth has lost a great deal of respect for him. She thinks his character weak."

"I daresay his own self-respect is rather precarious."

"Can't something be done?"

"Yes. It's possible he might be weaned away from the drug by steadily reduced doses, combined with the use of a placebo. But the process would take several weeks, and he would still have to endure the same symptoms. Abel and Selina don't know, you say?"

"No. Only Bethie and myself. Martin, if his self-respect is already precarious, surely the fewer people who know, the better."

"You're right." He watched the smoke from his pipe rise and disappear in the air. "I could take him under my wing, Lucy. Sarah and I are alone in the house, what with our daughter gone East to visit her grandparents. He could have Deborah's room."

"It would be an imposition, Martin. I can't ask you to—"

"You didn't ask. I suggested it. That way he'd be under my supervision, and no one need be the wiser. But as I told you, it might take several weeks, maybe even a month or so."

"We're going to Saint Helena in ten days. We'd planned to stay at least a month. Dabney has given Nick a holiday from his office so that he can be with us to oversee our first harvest."

"Is it necessary for Nick to be there?"

"Not really. It was intended more as a family excursion."

"All right." He stood up, clamping his pipe firmly between his teeth. "Let me speak to Sarah. She'll not say a word to anyone, I assure you. Then I'll have a talk with Nick."

"I think Bethie should be present, too. He must be made to understand what he's doing to their marriage."

"Agreed."

"Martin—" Lucy grasped his hand before he could move away. "I am forever in your debt for this."

"Let's pray we meet with success."

She watched him wend his way through the guests in search of Sarah. He caught sight of her at the corner of the porch and beckoned her to him. Beyond, on the front walk, a bearded figure, walking stick in hand, ambled toward the party. He paused for a moment, scanning the crowd, then marched resolutely in the direction of the refreshment table. "Merciful heavens," Lucy murmured, spying the gold fringe of his epaulets. She glanced hastily around. Father Crowley was standing nearby, talking to Daniel Derby. "Father, Daniel!" She motioned to them.

"Yes, Lucy?"

"It's Emperor Norton! What shall we do?"

"Do you want me to heave him out?" Daniel asked.

"No, I don't want to make a fuss and spoil the day."

"Let me take care of him," Father Crowley offered.

"I'll go with you," she said. "Dear me, what will Selina think?"

Emperor Norton turned as Father Crowley laid a hand on his arm. "Sir?" he inquired imperiously.

"Your Royal Highness. Father Patrick Crowley, at

your service. And this is the lady of the house, Mrs. Slade."

"We've met," she said, eying the heaping plate of sweets in his hand.

Behind the table, Septimus stood stricken with consternation as His Majesty continued to pile his plate with cookies, sandwiches and slices of cake. A rustle of whispers spread through the assembled guests.

"May I suggest, Sir," Lucy said quickly, "that Your Majesty might enjoy taking some refreshments home. Septimus, fetch me a basket from the kitchen and line it with a clean napkin, if you will."

"In the meantime, do have a glass of lemonade." Father Crowley handed it to him. "To what do we owe the honor of this visit?"

"I like to see my subjects having a fine time," he replied, waving his walking stick grandly in the direction of the others, unmindful of their stares. "There I was, taking my constitutional, when I heard the sound of merry voices. It does one's heart good to be among happy people, given all the sorrows that beset this mortal flesh."

Lucy smiled sympathetically.

"And what, may I ask, is the occasion for these festivities?"

She felt her cheeks flush and caught Father Crowley's amused look. "It's a reception, Sir, for my son and his new wife."

"And where are they?"

Abel came forward, a twinkle in his eye. He bowed. "Abel Bates, Your Royal Highness. And this lady," he said, stepping aside, "is my bride."

Selina glanced helplessly from Abel to Emperor Norton. With the swift, fluttering gesture of a startled swan, she gave a summary curtsy, her wide eyes fixed on the disheveled interloper.

"My best wishes to you both," he proclaimed, raising his glass in a toast. "A handsome pair," he told Lucy. "You must be proud indeed."

"Oh, I am, Sir," she assured him. "Won't you take a seat while Septimus and I make up a nice parcel of sweets for you?"

"Don't mind if I do." He allowed Father Crowley to lead him to a chair in the shade of a tree.

"Mama!" Beth touched her elbow. "How mortifying!"

"He means no harm. He's only a poor, lonesome creature who heard the sounds of the party and wanted to be a part of it." She took the basket from Septimus and began to load it with food.

"Beth." Doctor Vanderhoef approached them with Nick at his side. "May I have a word with you in the sitting room?"

"Go along," Lucy told her.

Selina's high, clear voice rose above the others. "Do you mean that he simply expects to be received?"

"And is," Abel answered.

"But he's a madman!"

"He wasn't always. He was a successful fellow who lost his fortune speculating on the rice market. The calamity unsettled his mind."

"And people blithely indulge him this absurd fantasy?"

"I suppose," Abel said thoughtfully, "that having known him before, folks understand that it could just as well have happened to them. There's a lot of people hereabouts who've suffered financial reverses at one time or another. Their minds were strong enough to withstand them. His wasn't. I guess they're grateful for their own sanity and glad to oblige someone less fortunate."

"But how utterly demeaning to take part in the conceits of a lunatic!"

"Selina," Lucy called, turning from the table. "Do be a dear and take this basket to Emperor Norton. Then you and Abel can offer to escort him to the gate. I suspect he'll take that as a compliment and go quite readily on his way."

Lucy watched as Selina walked toward him, holding the basket at arms' length. What a peculiar family the Mountfords must be, she thought, to stuff their heads with theories of probity and virtue and then, like misers, to spend not a jot of their abundance in practice.

Selina laughed uncertainly as she led the Emperor to the gate. *"Quelle sottise, mes amis, n'est-ce pas?"*

XXXIII

THE AIR in Saint Helena was warm and dry. Flurries of dust rose in their wake as Herr Schmidt, with Abel at his side, led the way along the trail past the bunkhouse. As they neared the curve of the path, Lucy saw Abel's steps quicken. With long, eager strides, he turned the corner of the hill, Herr Schmidt hurrying to keep up with him. Beth, Selina and Lucy maintained their own leisurely pace some distance behind, walking slowly in the afternoon heat, their parasols shielding them from the sun that shone down from a clear, glass-blue sky. As they rounded the bend, they saw Abel halt at the sight of the vineyard. Before him, the verdant tracery of vines rose and dipped along the slopes, branches heavy with fruit and leaves fluttering in the warm wind like a vast multitude of silver-green butterflies about to take flight. Slowly, he removed his hat. He stood there, motionless, gazing silently over the luxuriant hills as though he had quite forgotten the presence of the others.

"But what tiny little grapes!" Selina exclaimed, cupping a bunch in her gloved hand.

"Wines grapes, ma'am," Herr Schmidt replied. "Not so large as grapes for eating."

Abel turned. "Mama." He reached toward Lucy, and as she came to him he took her hand in his. "It's everything Seth said. Everything he dreamed it could be. Do you know," he said softly, "I'd all but forgotten what it feels like to be a part of the land, to know that you belong to it and it to you. Then, just now, when I came 'round the curve and saw all of this, it came back to me. I remembered the hills and glens of Castalia, the spring, the rocks, the river. I remembered everything about the place and how much I felt connected with it in some odd, visceral way that I never recognized then or understood. What a shock it was to have it return to me so suddenly."

"It's not odd, son. It's something bred in the bone. My Pa had it, and so did yours. Bethie, on the other hand, is like my Ma. She could never understand it." Lucy looked up at him, smiling. "It's mystical, that kind of bond with the land. There's no sense trying to explain it."

"Come along, you two," Beth called to them. "I want Selina and Abel to see the caves."

Abel lingered for a moment, his eyes taking in the expanse of fruit-laden vines. He looked out over the valley and the distant heights on the far side. "Good God," he murmured, "how beautiful it is."

"Abel," said Selina, "are you coming?"

"I'll catch up with you." Hat in hand, he climbed slowly toward the crest of the hill where a solitary marble tablet, stark and white against the greenery, marked Seth's grave.

Herr Schmidt paused at the mouth of the caves to light a lantern. As they stepped into the cool, murky interior, Selina glanced about in wonder. "It's like a trip to the underworld."

Beth and Selina walked close behind Herr Schmidt but Lucy hung back, waiting for her eyes to adjust to the dimness. For a moment, until she made out the rugged walls of the cavern, the two young women, in their silks of purple and blue, seemed to float against the boundless darkness, like petals bobbing on the fathomless waters of a black pond.

Abel appeared at her side. He reached out to touch the rough-hewn rock. "It's amazing. What a task it must have been to hollow out these tunnels."

"Quite so," Herr Schmidt said. "Now, if you will follow me." He led them past the fermentation barrels that loomed in the shadows, waiting to be filled. Beyond, where the vault narrowed, lanterns glowed in the gloom, their light playing on the faces of Hong Hing-wing and his men as they fitted wide shelves along the passageway. As Herr Schmidt and the others approached, the coolies broke off their sawing and sanding and hammering. Hong reached for a broom and swept aside the shavings and sawdust in their path. Seeing Lucy, he doffed his skull-cap. "Missee," he greeted her, bowing.

"It's good to see you again, Hong. Abel, this is Hong Hing-wing. He's the workers' head man. And this young gentleman, Hong, is my son, Mr. Bates. He and his wife have joined us for the harvest."

Hong bowed, and his men followed suit. "Welcome," he said.

"Hong, you've done a remarkable job here," Abel said.

"So." Hong grinned broadly and spoke in rapid Chinese to the workers who smiled and nodded animatedly in Abel's direction.

"We will not keep you from your work any longer," Herr Schmidt announced loudly, his voice reverberating from the walls.

"Tell me," Lucy asked him as they made their way back toward the bright, daylit archway, "can you estimate what sort of harvest it will be?"

"Good, my lady. All through the valley, this is a fine year. The weather has blessed us. I regret that Mr. Stevens is not here also, to share in our good fortune."

"At the last moment he had to stay behind," Beth told him. "He was needed at his office."

"I think it quite unfair of his uncle," Selina said. "It's not right of him to go back on his promise."

"It was imperative that he stay," Beth replied. "Don't blame Uncle Dabney."

"My dear," Abel said, taking Selina's arm, "from what I hear of Simon Waite, I'll soon be in Nick's shoes. This may be the last holiday we'll have together in a long time."

"My son has been taken into an excellent law office," Lucy told Herr Schmidt. "He'll begin work as soon as we return to the city."

"A fine career for a gentleman. I wish you success and satisfaction."

"Thank you, sir. You and your wife are joining us for supper this evening, aren't you?"

"We are. With your indulgence, I would like to acquaint you with the records of the vineyard. Ledgers, correspondence . . ."

"I want to learn all there is to know, Herr Schmidt. I intend to see this place become everything my stepfather intended it to be."

In the evening, Frau Schmidt joined them, listening in shy silence to their lively speculations about the harvest, nodding enthusiastically each time her husband glanced her way.

"Do sit by me," Selina invited her as they went to the supper table.

"*Danke schön*. Thank you." She took her place a trifle apprehensively. "I am sorry. My English is not so good," she apologized to Selina. "I do my best."

"*Das beste ist gut genug, Frau Schmidt.*"

"*Sie sprechen Deutsch!*" she chirped in astonishment.

"And French and Latin, to boot," Abel boasted.

Selina smiled self-consciously. "What a delicious aroma," she said as Chang set his steaming bowls on the table. "What is it, Mother Slade?"

Lucy laughed as she ladled out the portions. "Actually, I don't know. It appears to be slivers of pork or chicken in a sauce of some sort with greens. I learned long ago not to question Chang's magic."

Selina glanced dubiously at the helping on her plate.

"Are there no Chinese in Cambridge?" Beth inquired.

"I don't believe I've ever seen any."

"Nor I," Frau Schmidt told Beth. "Before I came here, never." She took a forkful of food "*Das ist sehr gut,*" she said to Selina.

Lucy watched as Selina took a tentative taste and nodded agreement with obvious relief. The Mountfords, she decided, were very sure of themselves and of nothing else. She was reminded of the New Englanders who had descended upon the gold-diggings, determined to make California the Massachusetts of the Pacific. And now Selina had descended upon their family, determined to—what? To make Abel over in the image of the Mountfords? That, she thought, will happen only over my dead body.

In the days that followed, Herr Schmidt, often as not accompanied by Abel, made his daily rounds of the vineyard, examining the grapes with patient expectation, watchful against the invasion of the bees and birds attracted to the ripening fruit. "Such a critical time," he would murmur gazing paternally over the vines. "Nothing must happen now to spoil our harvest."

Below the hills, some of the valley vineyards had already begun to pick and crush. The odor of the pomace, sweet and winey, filled the breeze. Selina, sitting on the veranda with Lucy, fanned the air rapidly. "I do wish the wind would shift."

Lucy inhaled deeply and smiled. "I like the scent. It puts me in mind of everything good and bountiful in nature."

"Abel tells me you were born on a farm."

"I was. But it was a long way from here. In Missouri."

"He said your parents died when you were young and that you had to work for your keep."

"That's true."

"You had no other family? No grandparents?"

"I never knew them."

"How sad. That seems so strange to me. Back home, we have large, close families, and everyone knows his ancestry. Mama has embroidered our family tree in crewel work. It hangs over the fireplace in the library. There's a great security, I think, in having a sense of one's origins."

"Selina," she said, "you must not expect California to be like Massachusetts, or Californians to be like New Englanders. If you do you'll miss all that's so special and colorful and unique to this place. I'm sure it's as different from Cambridge as peaches from pears, yet one can develop an appreciation of both."

"You're right, Mother Slade. Forgive my nostalgia, if you will." She rose. "It must be nearly noon. I believe I'll freshen up for dinner."

The heat of the late September sun remained, though the sun itself had long since disappeared behind the trees on the hill above the caves. Lucy heard the sound of Abel's footfall on the veranda outside. Despite the heat, his pace was brisk.

"Well, ladies," he announced as he entered. "Herr Schmidt says the picking starts day after tomorrow."

In the morning, the fermentation barrels were brought from the caves to the presshouse. Hong Wo and his men traveled back and forth all day from the wells, water buckets on their shoulder-poles, giving each piece of equipment a last washing-down. Against the wall of the bunk house, twin pillars of stacked wicker baskets lay in

634

readiness. Suddenly, the long, monotonous months of waiting were forgotten. Even the warm, restless breeze seemed feverish with expectation.

Though the evening brought relief from the heat, Lucy found it difficult to sleep. She dozed fitfully, not so much immersed in sleep as floating upon it, aware of the approaching dawn as the clock in the other room chimed the passing hours. At five, she rose and put on her dressing-gown and slippers.

"Mama!" Abel looked up from his breakfast. "What are you doing out of bed?"

"You said the picking would begin before sunup. I couldn't rest, knowing it was starting. Sheer foolishness on my part, I suppose. Thank you, Chang," she said as he poured her coffee.

"Poor Herr Schmidt." Abel smiled. "I doubt he slept a wink. Late last night, I found him in the press-house, armed with his must-scale and his acid-scale, eager as a chemistry student to use his shiny instruments. Bethie!" he exclaimed, seeing her in the doorway. "What rouses you at this hour?"

"I heard Mama stirring," she said, yawning. "Anyway, we've all waited so long for this day that I didn't want to miss any of it."

"Hush," Abel said, lowering his voice. "We mustn't wake Selina." He pushed his chair back from the table and donned his coat. "I'll see you both later."

"Abel," Lucy asked him, "before you go would you be good enough to lead us in a short prayer?"

He paused for a moment, then bowed his head and spoke. "Heavenly Father, who has seen fit to give us these gifts of nature, bless them to our use as we prepare to harvest them. Bless our labors, too, that we may bring forth a vintage deserving of the toil and hopes we have invested. We thank you. And," he added, "we thank you for Seth who gave us this dream to share. Amen."

Like an abrupt, brisk change in the wind, the haste of harvest-time swept over the vineyard. The workers, making their way among the rows of vines under Hong Hingwing's command, filled basket after basket with the dense, tight clusters of green grapes and carried them to the waiting wagons that rolled back and forth from the presshouse, where the fruit was spilled into the separators to be removed from its stalks. With each turn of the crank, a hail of grapes fell into the receiving tubs below. Next, the fruit was poured into the crushing tub. Braced on the footboards at either side, two coolies battered a steady rhythm against the bottom of the tub with long wooden pestles. Beneath them lay the wide juice tub, slowly filling with liquid from above.

Lucy stood at a distance from the open doors of the presshouse, not wishing to intrude. Speed and efficiency were imperative. Not so much as a single basket of a day's pick must go uncrushed before nightfall. The aroma of must and pomace perfumed the air. She felt heady with the scent and the excitement. The sight of the barrels being filled and fitted with their fermentation tubes seemed suddenly to make the process complete, though it was far from that. Still, it meant that the earth had yielded up its miracle. And now, in these barrels, young wine would be born.

"How will you know," Selina asked Abel, "when the juice has fermented?"

"I won't, but Herr Schmidt will. The days following the harvest are as crucial as the harvest days themselves. Herr Schmidt tells me that a white wine like ours is even more sensitive to temperature than a red. He'll be watching over the fermentation process day and night. When the time is exactly right, the young wine will be drawn off into the aging casks." He rose from his chair and stretched. "I'd best get all the sleep I can for a day or two. When the racking begins, I want to work alongside Herr Schmidt."

"Racking?" Selina asked.

"Drawing off the wine," Lucy told her.

"Mercy, but it seems complicated. Mama made dandelion wine once, and I don't remember it being half so ticklish."

Abel bent to kiss her forehead. "My dear, this is a far cry from making a few bottles of dandelion wine. There are over three thousand gallons out there awaiting our attention."

"Herr Schmidt told me that's a jolly good yield for our first year," Beth added. "Within five years, '*mit Gottes Wille*,' as he says, it could be as high as twelve thousand."

"But what will you do with it all?" Selina wanted to know.

636

"Sell it, of course," Lucy said. "Seth always intended that the vineyard should pay for itself."

"But that would make us tradesfolk!"

"Selina," Beth said, barely concealing her irritation, "rest assured, you won't be asked to go from house to house peddling wine with Mama's name on the label."

"Mama," Abel said with a grin, "won't you be pleased, though, seeing your name on our wine."

"Only if the vintage comes up to our expectations. Anyhow, I thought you despised that name."

"Pastora?" Beth said, seeming surprised. Catching sight of Lucy's even gaze, she looked away, embarrassed. "Well, once, perhaps, a long time ago. But," she added quickly, "if the wine's any good, I expect we'll all be proud of it."

"Where does the name come from?" Selina inquired.

"It's Spanish for 'shepherdess,'" Abel explained. "When Mama was farming sheep, the Mexicans called her that."

Selina regarded Lucy with a curious expression. "You're a remarkable woman, Mother Slade. From what Abel tole me, I thought you used to be a shopkeeper."

"That, too," Lucy answered cheerfully, "though my father would quite agree with your distaste for tradespeople. Still, one does what one must. Your family was never in trade, I take it."

Selina shook her head vehemently. "The first Mountford, Joshua, was a clergyman. He came to America in sixteen thirty-six."

"Then he wasn't on the Mayflower?" Beth asked, her eyes wide with innocence.

"That was my mother's side of the family."

"Oh."

"I'm going to get some sleep," Abel announced. "These past few days have all but worn me out. Selina?"

"I'll join you. Good night, Mother Slade. Beth."

Beth waited until she heard the door to Abel's room close. "Mama, can't Abel see how conceited she is?"

"Now, Bethie, be generous. Give her time. I think Selina's a bit put off by the differences between here and her home. Perhaps she's even a little frightened by all the strangeness. She's not yet used to us. After all, the Mountfords are a very illustrious family."

"So are we!"

637

"I trust," Lucy said, rising, "that you'll remember this conversation the next time you're tempted to put on airs. You're not entirely blameless in that regard, Bethie, so keep it in mind." Lucy kissed her cheek. "I'm tired, too, my dear. I believe I'll go to bed."

"Good night. And Mama," she called after her, "I think Pastora is a fine name. We're truly proud of you, Mama, Abel and I."

Despite her weariness, sleep would not come. Once, Lucy reflected, Beth's words would have filled her with joy, but now they fell hollowly upon her ears. She had deceived the children. She had chosen to live a lie, and the truth, bitter and unpalatable, curdled even the sweetest triumphs. Good fortune derided her, and moments of happiness turned into irony. Such was the price of deception.

"Mother Slade," Selina said, coming onto the veranda the next morning, "you've been looking a bit pale lately. Are you feeling well?"

"I'm fine, dear. Where did Bethie go? I haven't seen her since breakfast."

"She's in the caves again. Ever since Herr Schmidt began racking the wine, she and Abel can't seem to tear themselves from his side."

"It's their vineyard, too, my dear. And yours, for that matter. One day they'll be in charge here. It's good for them to learn every phase of its operation."

"Beth too? I can't think why she'd want to spend her time in those dank caves, learning how to make wine. It's hardly an occupation for a lady."

"Here in California, Selina, it is quite permissible for a lady to turn her hand to business. Our laws affirm that right. There's many a woman, myself included, who owes her fortune to that license. It may appear unseemly to you, but to me it seems a blessing. Ah," she said, relieved to change the subject, "here comes Bethie now. Darling," she said, as Beth followed her into the house.

"What is it, Mama?"

"I received a letter from Doctor Vanderhoef. Chang brought it from town this morning."

"Is Nick all right?"

"Yes, dear. The doctor feels he's getting better every day, though he did say that Nick's self-confidence is very shaky. He seems afraid to trust his ability to stay away from the drug. When we get home, we must do all we can to bolster his faith in himself."

"I'm almost afraid to go back, Mama. When we left, Nick and I were at swords' points. It was nearly unbearable for us to be alone together."

"Then you must begin again with a clean slate."

"You make that sound so easy. It's not."

"We're leaving next weak, Bethie. I suggest you use the time 'til then to practice forgiving and forgetting. I see no alternative, if you value your marriage."

At the sound of their voices in the hall, Nick appeared on the stairs. "Welcome home!" he shouted cheerfully. "How was the harvest?"

"A great success," Abel told him. "I wish you'd been there with us."

"How are you, Nick?" Lucy asked, her eyes searching his face.

"Better than I've been in years." He kissed Beth's cheek.

Beth relaxed perceptibly. "Where's Cal?"

"Upstairs in the nursery. I've a surprise waiting for you all. Come into the drawing room."

"Champagne!" Selina cried delightedly. "How nice!"

"What's the special occasion?" Abel asked.

"Whatever you wish it to be," Nick answered, smiling at Beth.

Beth slipped her arms about his waist and hugged him. She glanced up into his face, her eyes moist. "I'm so happy."

"So am I, Bethie. Abel, will you do the honors?"

Abel opened the champagne and poured it into the glasses on the tray.

" 'Fill every glass,' " Selina said gaily, " 'for wine inspires us and fires us with courage, love and joy.' "

"What a lovely sentiment," Lucy remarked.

"It's from John Gay's *The Beggar's Opera,* written in seventeen twenty-eight."

"Isn't she a marvel?" Abel said with a proud smile. "I bless my luck in marrying a woman of such beauty and intelligence."

Lucy raised her glass. "To health and happiness."

"And to the wine we left behind," Abel added.

Nick set his glass on the table. "You sound as though you enjoyed yourself."

"Every moment. Why, just to wake in the morning and walk that land, just to see the valley and the hillsides so green and productive—I can't explain the pleasure it gave me."

"You don't have to. I felt that way once. But that was long ago and someplace else," he said brusquely. "Now you're the fortunate one."

"It's my intention," Lucy told Nick, "that the vineyard should belong to the whole family. I want you and Selina to feel at home there, too."

"Of course, of course." He changed the subject. "By the way, I bought five tickets for *The Jealous Wife* at the Opera House tomorrow evening. I thought we'd all dine out together and go to the theatre."

"That's dear of you, Nick," Lucy said, "but I hope you can dispose of my ticket. I don't feel quite up to staying out so late. Will you forgive me?"

"Are you sure you won't come?"

"I am, but you children go and have a good time."

That fall and winter, it seemed to Lucy that the four of them, Abel, Selina, Beth and Nick, were inseparable. Despite Nick's work and Abel's long hours in Simon Waite's office, there was always a party, a play or a concert to keep them coming and going. Selina spent a good part of her days conducting her reading club at the Good Shepherd Home and tutoring several of the waifs in French— the usefulness of which Lucy found debatable. But Selina shrugged off her doubts. *"C'est quelque chose pour passer le temps."*

"Beg pardon, my dear?"

"Something to pass the time, Mother Slade, that's all."

Lucy glanced at the book in Selina's lap. It, too, was in French. *"Les Misérables,"* she pronounced as best she could.

"By Victor Hugo. You've not read any of his works?"

"I'm afraid not." Lucy returned her gaze to her newspaper. The construction of the Central Pacific had shuddered to halt in the Sierras, benumbed by snow and ice. Some said that even if the line were ever completed, it might only be able to operate six or seven months a year, depending on the weather. The prospects were discouraging, but then, perhaps it was only the winter rains that made her feel so dispirited. Cal had taken cold and was fretful and feverish, and she herself felt a bit rheumy. She pressed the back of her hand to her forehead and found it hot. Her eyes smarted. She folded the paper and rose from her chair. "I believe I'll lie down until supper," she told Selina. "I think I may have caught Calvert's cold."

Selina laid her book aside. "I'll bring you some sassafras tea."

"Thank you, dear. I'd appreciate that."

Cal recovered within a few days, his complaint forgotten, his boyish energy as irrepressible as ever. Lucy's indisposition lingered on for a week, then two. Her impatience gave way to resignation. "Ah, well, Cal is young yet. I am not. I expect age makes these little maladies harder to shake off."

"Nonsense, Mother Slade," Selina told her. "It's this vile winter weather, I'm sure of it. Between the nasty chill of the fogs and the continual downpours, it's a wonder we're not all ailing. Such prolonged dampness is most unwholesome."

"Fetch me a fresh handkerchief, would you? You'll find one in the top drawer of that chest. You're an angel to be so helpful." Lucy sniffed moistly and pressed the clean white linen to her nose. "But you mustn't think you have to keep me constant company. You have your own affairs to look after, and I'm quite content to lie here and drowse or read."

"Oh, dear!" Selina's eyes widened. "Mother Slade, do stay still. You're bleeding."

"I am?" Lucy looked at the bright red stains on the handkerchief. "It's nothing but a nosebleed. It will stop in a moment."

"I'll fetch some cotton." Selina hurried away. "Here," she said as she returned to Lucy's bedside, "use this." She tore off a small piece of cotton and rolled it between her palms. "Put this wad under your upper lip. Sometimes that helps. And tilt your head back."

Lucy swallowed, tasting blood. Of all the messy inconveniences, she thought. She glanced up at Selina, a picture of perfection, as always, with every golden hair in place, her dress immaculate. Lucy felt a surge of vanity. How utterly wretched she must look. The absurdity of the thought made her want to laugh, but the trickle of blood in her throat caused her to gag.

"Mama? Selina? What are you two—" Beth halted in the doorway. "What's wrong?"

"Mother Slade has a nosebleed. I'd thought that it would have stopped by now but it hasn't." Selina gave Beth a worried look.

"How bad is it?"

"It seems to be abating, but it's been over half an hour since it began."

"I'll have Septimus fetch Doctor Vanderhoef."

Lucy raised a hand in protest, but Beth was gone.

"I'll get some more cotton," Selina said. "Don't move."

It was ridiculous, of course, to call on Martin Vanderhoef for something as trivial as a nosebleed. Lucy felt all the more sheepish when, by the time he arrived, it had stopped entirely. "We brought you out on a wild-goose chase, Martin." She smiled tiredly. "I'm sorry. Bethie shouldn't have bothered you."

He dismissed her words with a wave of his hand. "Now that I'm here, let me have a look at you. Open your mouth, if you will." He frowned slightly. "Sore throat, is it?"

"I've had a spell of catarrh, nothing serious."

He examined her, despite her protests. Finally, he rose, slipping his stethoscope into his bag. "How long has it been since I last saw you?"

"About five months. Why?"

"Are you still feeling fatigued?"

"A bit," she admitted, "but I'll be up and around in no time."

"You're looking rather pale, Lucy. Try taking some beef tea every day. That ought to put the color back in your cheeks."

"I will, Martin. My apologies for having inconvenienced you."

It was late. Lucy closed her book and rested her head against her pillows. From the drawing room below came the sound of Beth's piano, the slow, sweet strains of Foster's "Beautiful Dreamer." Lucy hummed quietly to herself. A tap at the door brought her upright in bed.

"Mama," Abel said, "may I come in?"

642

"Of course. I thought you and Selina were downstairs."

"Selina is. She's having a game of dominoes with Nick. You gave her quite a start this afternoon. Are you feeling better?"

"Yes." She patted the coverlet. "Come sit by me. Tell me about your work and Mr. Waite. You know I'm interested in what you're doing." She took his hand in hers as he sat down.

"Mama, Selina is quite miserable here."

Lucy glanced at him. He looked grave and confused. "In our house, do you mean? Then you must find a home of your own at once. Perhaps a small suite of rooms in—"

"No," he interrupted her. "It's not our house, Mama. I meant that she doesn't feel at home in San Francisco. Sometimes, in the night, I wake and find her weeping. She misses the East and her family something fierce. I don't know what to do, Mama."

Lucy took a deep breath. "Does she want you to go back to Massachusetts?"

"She'd never ask me to do that. She knows I belong here."

"And you? Are you so sure you belong here? Mind you, I want you here." She pressed his hand tightly. "But God forbid that you should resent having to stay on my account. None of us would be happy under those circumstances. I warn you, though, I would use every argument I could to dissuade you from going. That's selfish of me, perhaps, but I must be candid with you."

"No, Mama. I'm not going to leave again. There's no other place for me but California. I know that now. But I understand how Selina feels. I felt it too, when I was in Cambridge—a reassuring sense of the fitness of things. The traditions and the conventions that those people have give their lives an orderliness, Mama, a sort of equilibrium they can rely on. She was comfortable there, certain of who she was and what was expected of her. She's at a loss in San Francisco. The novelty of this place and the liberties we exercise frighten her, I think."

"Then you must give her time. She's only been here a few months. After a while, she'll grow used to our ways and more sure of herself."

"Sometimes," he said thoughtfully, "I wonder if I did her a disservice in asking her to marry me. Back there, it seemed our interests were so alike."

643

"I expect they were, dear. For a while, you became a part of the Mountford family. Don't worry. Selina will become part of ours." She gave him an encouraging smile.

He rose, hearing Selina's voice on the stairs. "Please keep this to yourself, Mama. I wouldn't want Bethie and Nick to know. They seem so happy together."

She looked after him as he left the room. How little we really know of each other, she thought. Despite our closeness, we are each sequestered in our own secret sorrows. Sometimes an attitude or a gesture hinted at what lay beneath the surface. When Abel spoke of the vineyard, Lucy would catch a glimpse of the smoldering resentment in Nick's eyes as he glanced away. And when Nick complained of aching in his ghost leg, Beth grew nervous, her face tense, her voice on edge, fearful of what he might do to allay the pain. Selina, oblivious of these things, found refuge from her homesickness in her books, as though by burrowing deeply into their pages she might be transported to the familiar surroundings of the Mountford library, so far away. Abel would gaze at her in silence for minutes at a time, troubled by the distance that separated them despite her nearness. Finally, he would speak, his tone solicitous, his words endearing, and Selina would look up, her eyelashes fluttering like someone awakened suddenly from a dream, and for a moment she would seem startled to see them all there.

No sooner had Lucy recovered from her illness than Beth became unwell. She was suffering from headaches and nausea and had difficulty keeping her food down. "At least," Lucy said, laying her palm on Beth's forehead, "there's no fever. Perhaps it's only something you ate. Is there anything I can do to make you more comfortable, dear?"

"Thank you, Mama, no. I'll just have to wait until it passes, I guess. Are you going shopping today?"

"Yes. Why?"

"Perhaps you'd take Lin along. I'm sure Selina wouldn't mind looking after Cal for a few hours. Ask Lin to fetch some of her Chinese herbs from Sacramento Street. Her teas are settling to the stomach. Oh, and we're all out of Goodall's Soothing Syrup. Would you please buy a bottle for Nick?"

"Goodall's?"

"This rainy weather bothers his leg."

"Bethie, doesn't Goodall's contain laudanum?"

"What of it?"

"Laudanum is a tincture of opium."

"I know, but Nick says there isn't enough in it to affect a gnat. Anyway, he only takes it now and then. Land sakes, Mama, it's mild enough to give to Cal when he has a cough. As long as Nick doesn't resort to those dreadful pills, there's nothing to be concerned about."

Nevertheless, Lucy felt uneasy. She took Nick aside after dinner. "Perhaps, Nick, you ought to ask Doctor Vanderhoef to recommend something else."

"There's no need for you to worry," he said, smiling reassuringly. "I've licked the problem. I can take that stuff or leave it alone. It's only a matter of moderation. A dram or two of Goodall's can't hurt me. It eases the pain, that's all."

"What are you two whispering about?" said Selina, coming into the sitting room. "Nick, play a game of *écarté* with me. Abel's in the library, poring over some work for Mr. Waite, and Beth's gone upstairs to lie down. I'm ever so bored."

"Always ready to help a lady in distress," he replied genially. "Get out the cards. I'm on my way. I declare," he whispered to Lucy as Selina withdrew, "sometimes I think Selina could find a way to be bored in the middle of an earthquake."

"Or at least say she was," Lucy replied with a laugh. "Go along. I'll look in on Bethie on my way to bed."

As the weeks passed, fair days began to outnumber stormy ones, a sure sign of approaching spring. From the window in the library where she sat, Lucy could see the bright green stippling of new growth that topped the myrtle hedge. Selina sat with Cal on a blanket on the lawn, armed with a slate and chalk to teach the boy to write his name. "We were always tutored at home as small children," she'd told Beth. "Papa thought the early years of schooling altogether inadequate. And so they were. When my sisters and I finally did go to school, we were well ahead of all our classmates." For the time being, Beth allowed the Mountford superiority to prevail.

"There you are, Mama. I was wondering where you'd disappeared to." Beth came into the library, carrying her mending basket. "May I join you?"

645

"Certainly, dear. Do sit down."

Beth folded her hands in her lap. She stared down at them for a moment, then glanced up at Lucy. "Mama, Nick and I have been talking about finding another place to live."

Lucy looked startled. "Why? And where, Bethie? You aren't thinking of leaving San Francisco, are you?"

"Oh, no, Mama. We'll be nearby, I promise. It's just that . . ."

Lucy gave a small sigh of relief. "You don't have to tell me. I know how difficult it is for Nick sometimes. I see the way he watches Abel kicking Cal's ball about the lawn or playing tag with the boy and his friends, and I think how sad it must make him, not to be able to run about with his own son. And when Abel speaks about the vineyard, it only makes the loss of New Rosedale all the more painful for Nick. I don't blame him for—"

"Mama," Beth interrupted, "it's not that. It has nothing to do with Abel or anyone else." She smiled slowly. "I'm going to have another baby, Mama. I'm two months along."

XXXIV

In the garden, the iris and azalea were putting out buds. Along the shore of the bay, a few hardy swimmers tested the waters, still cold despite the warm sun and a mild breeze that stirred among the acacia trees on the surrounding hills, causing them to loose a fine, golden rain of blossoms.

Lucy sat on the porch, gazing out over the green lawn. Ever since she'd been a girl, back in Missouri, springtime had been like a tonic that quickened her blood and heightened her sensibilities. The April air, honeyed by the faint, delicate scent of wildflowers, had seemed to her to be as heady as wine. Yet now, try as she might, she could summon no response to the burgeoning signs of spring all around her. Neither the freshness of the breeze nor the promise of the season moved her. She felt curiously hollow, as though her passion for life had all but seeped away, spilled in the tears she still shed for Seth, along in her room at night. For a while, she sat there rocking slowly back and forth in her chair, disconcerted by her own indifference, waiting for the song of a bird or the patterns of light on the lawn to strike some sweet, familiar chord in her. After a time, she rose and went inside.

"It's quite discouraging," Beth said as she seated herself at the supper table. "Selina and I saw such a pretty little house on Green Street today. It would be perfect for Nick and me and the children, but the people who live there aren't sure they want to sell it."

"It was lovely," Selina agreed, "very plain, but with dentils under the cornice and above each window to give it some distinction."

Lucy looked at her blankly.

"A simple, classic architectural ornamentation in the style of the Greeks."

Abel gazed at Selina with open admiration. "My dear, you never cease to amaze me."

Selina made a small, impatient gesture, an almost imperceptible flick of her fingertips. "I don't mind helping you look for a place to live, Beth, though I must say I'll miss your company when you move. It will seem quite dull without you and Nick here."

"You'll have Mother and me," Abel reassured her.

"No thank you, Septimus," Selina said as he proffered her the serving bowl.

Septimus dished a dollop of apple jelly onto Cal's plate.

"What do you say, Calvert?" Selina asked him.

"Merci, Septimus." He looked toward Selina and grinned proudly.

"Sakes alive, boy," Nick said, "what else has your Aunt Selina been teaching you?"

He took a breath, then hesitated, his brow furrowed. Selina gave him a nod of encouragement.

"Bonjour. Je m'appelle Calvert Stevens."

"Bravo!" Nick exclaimed.

Beth glanced at Lucy with a slightly pained expression.

"They're never too young to learn," Selina went on gaily. "My little group at the waifs' home is making remarkable strides in French."

Lucy laid down her fork. "I'm going to quit my work at the Good Shepherd."

Beth broke the silence that followed. "Mama? You're not serious?"

"I am. I've already sent a letter to Father Crowley."

"But why, Mother Slade? Your name is synonymous with the waifs' home."

"I'm sure it will continue to thrive without me. I've given it my best, and now I feel it's just a bit more than I can cope with. I haven't the energy I used to. There are lots of younger people like yourselves to take my place."

"It won't be the same," Beth said. "The children know that you and Father Crowley are responsible for the place. They all but worship the two of you."

"It's true," Selina told Abel. "You ought to see how

648

they tag along after her in the halls. Some of them reach out to touch her sleeve, as though she were some sort of talisman."

"I've made my decision, my dears," Lucy said quietly. "That's all there is to it."

Father Crowley, like the others, was reluctant to accept her resignation, but Lucy stood firm. "Don't try to wring blood from this old turnip," she chided him. "I mean what I say. I haven't the strength these days to spread myself too thin."

"You couldn't simply curtail your activities?"

"Show me a little pity, old friend. I'm not doing this on a whim. It's not that I want to quit, Father. I feel I have to."

"You know best," he said with a sigh. He frowned abruptly. "But you must do one last thing for me. Will you come by on Sunday afternoon and explain the ordering system to the new cook?"

"It's perfectly simple. Amy Winslow can do it."

"All due respect to Amy, but she's inclined to be a trifle imperious. Knowing Mrs. O'Malley, she might well decamp in a huff, before she'd cooked so much as a pot of porridge. Do it as a favor to me, Lucy. Then you'll be leaving the place ship-shape."

"All right." She smiled suddenly and added, "but I warn you, this is the last time I'll let your Irish charm get the better of me. Is that understood?"

At the last minute, Beth and Selina said they wanted to go along with her to the Good Shepherd. "You're welcome to come, but I shan't be staying long," Lucy told them.

"It's a beautiful day," Selina said, "just right for a little drive."

"And I have to fetch a knitting pattern I left there on Wednesday."

"I can get it for you," Lucy replied.

"You wouldn't know where to look. Besides, Selina's right. The weather's too nice to stay indoors."

As they neared the waifs' home, Beth glanced out of the carriage. "Hardly a cloud in the sky," she observed. "But look! Look there, Mama, above the church steeple. It's the most enormous hawk I've ever seen! Do you think it could be an eagle?"

649

"Where?" Selina demanded excitedly, craning her neck to peer out. "Oh, yes. My word, what a monstrous bird!"

"Where is it?" Lucy asked. "I only see a flock of gulls."

"It's directly overhead now," Beth said, pointing skyward. "See there?"

"The sun's too bright. I can't find it." Lucy squinted, searching the sky.

Suddenly a burst of noise erupted. Beth and Selina broke into laughter at Lucy's startled expression. As they drew abreast of the Good Shepherd Home, she saw that on the porch and steps and spilling over the grass behind its fence were fully fifty smiling people, waving and cheering her arrival. The children, now thirteen girls and sixteen boys, leapt up and down, giggling and jostling each other gleefully at the look of amazement on Lucy's face as she alighted. The girls, wearing snowy, starched pinafores over their dresses, each carried a red rose. The boys, most in knickerbockers and white shirts, a few proudly attired in long trousers and jackets and bow-knotted ties, stood behind them. At the rear were assembled all of the ladies of the Good Shepherd alliance, the staff and, grinning broadly, Father Crowley. He made his way through the crowd and came to her, his arms spread wide in welcome.

"We diverted her attention," Beth said with a pleased laugh. "She was taken completely by surprise."

He took Lucy's arm. "Come along. The children are impatient to begin. They've been practicing their little pieces for two weeks, ever since I received your letter."

There were songs, *tableaux vivants* and recitations, and speeches by Father Crowley, Amy Winslow and two of the children. One was a pale, grave lad with the sad eyes of someone who had lived long and seen much. The other was a merry, black-haired girl whose tongue tripped over her words in her enthusiasm, causing her to blush to her roots.

Lucy, her arms full of roses, sat in the center of the front row of chairs, occasionally pressing her handkerchief to her eyes. Finally, the girls and boys filed before her to say their good-byes. Most of them she knew by name. Some she had known since they were scarcely able to walk, when they had come to the home as ragged, hollow-eyed toddlers, their skin spotted with sores, their bodies so starved that they had vomited up the food they gulped down so voraciously. She looked into each face, now and then stroked a child's cheek. When the procession had passed, Beth rose and took the small parcel that Verity Knight handed to her.

"For you, Mama, from the young ladies. All the girls contributed to it, even the littlest ones. We held their hands and guided their fingers."

It was a sampler, brightly embroidered with sprigs of flowers. In the center, carefully cross-stitched, were the words:

Lucy Slade
Our Pastora
from the children
of the Good Shepherd Home
1860-1867

Before Lucy could speak, Father Crowley stepped forward, carrying a large, blue-painted tinware chest. Around all four sides, interlaced in yellow, were repeated the initials L.S. And on the top, the doll-like figure of a woman with a shepherd's crook lay surrounded by small, gray, woolly creatures which, were it not for their hooves, might have been mistaken for fat, lop-eared puppies. Lucy laughed and hugged it to her.

"The boys wanted to do something, too," Father Crowley told her. "This was their idea."

"I shall treasure them both," she told them, standing. "Just as I shall treasure my memories of this place, of you children and especially of this day. Bless you."

When the last drop of lemonade had been drunk and the cake platters held only a scattering of crumbs, Father Crowley led her to her carriage, followed by a gaggle of children. "Sure and now you didn't think we'd let this occasion pass without a celebration, did you?"

"It never occurred to me," she said, her eyes moist. She reached out to tousle the heads of the children nearest her. "Don't be a stranger, Father. I shall want to know how this flock is faring. Bring me news now and then, won't you?"

"It's a promise, Pastora." He helped her into the carriage.

She leaned forward in her seat, still holding his hand.

"It's not me they should be thanking, Father. None of this would have happened, if it weren't for you."

"That's not so. I only saw the need. You provided the answer. You gathered the ladies together. You coaxed and badgered the funds out of people's pockets. You've been the driving force behind this place from the start. We'll miss you, Pastora."

Selina handed her a fresh handkerchief.

"I'm sorry—" Lucy's voice broke.

"Come, children, let's have a song!" Jane Gallagher called from the porch.

Softly, the pale, solemn boy who had spoken earlier began to sing.

"What shall we do with a drunken sailor;
What shall we do with a drunken sailor?"

"It was such a peculiar choice," Beth was telling Nick. "It was so oddly comical that even Mama burst out laughing. Somehow the day didn't seem sad anymore, after that."

"It wasn't sad," Lucy corrected her. "It was touching, that's all."

Nick reached for his crutches and rose. "I believe I'll go fetch me my nightly cigar."

"Have one of mine," Abel offered, reaching into his breast pocket.

Nick waved it aside. "Yours are a bit strong for my taste. I've some of my own upstairs."

"I'll get it," Beth said. "I'm going up to kiss Cal good night. Where are they?"

Nick glanced at her sharply. "Bethie, I said I would go." He waited until Beth reached the stairs, then followed.

Abel returned to his reading. The room was silent, save for the sound of Selina turning the pages of the newspaper. At length, with a sigh, she laid the paper aside. "There is absolutely nothing worth seeing at the theatre."

Abel looked up. "What about *East Lynne* or *Camille?*"

"Not again," she said tiredly.

"Is there no Shakespeare at the Opera House?"

"Only a second-rate company doing *Macbeth.*"

"Perhaps we could go to a minstrel show," he suggested.

"You know I don't like minstrel shows. I find them extremely vulgar."

"Well, then," he said amiably, "we'll just have to wait until—"

"No!"

The three of them started at the sound of Beth's cry from the upstairs hall.

"No!" she repeated, her voice rising to a scream. "Nick, don't! You can't! Give them to me!"

Abel leapt from his chair.

"Stay where you are," Lucy told him.

"What's the matter?" Selina demanded worriedly.

"Damn you!" Nick shouted. "Let go!"

Abel made a move toward the door, but Lucy grasped his arm. "It's not your affair. Keep out of it."

"Liar!" Beth screamed. "You lied to me! You've been lying all along!"

They heard the sharp sound of a slap, and then Cal's voice, small and frightened.

"Papa, Mama, why are you fighting?"

"Give them to me!" Beth shrieked. "Can't you see what you're doing to us?"

"Get away from me, woman!" he yelled. "Keep your hands off of me!"

"I won't let you do this!"

They heard a dull, thudding noise against the wall of the hall overhead. Cal began to wail. There was scuffling in the hallway and the sound of Nick's voice spewing out a stream of curses.

"I've had enough," Abel said, brushing past Lucy. She jumped up after him, with Selina close behind. As they reached the bottom of the stairs, Beth stood poised on the top, her back to them, a fist raised high above her head. Her other hand groped for the bannister behind her. Then, as Nick lunged for her fist, she drew back toward the stairs, swaying unsteadily. She reached out to either side. Nick's cigar-case dropped from her hand and fell at Lucy's feet. With a gasp, Beth lost her balance and pitched sidelong down the flight of stairs, snatching at the air as she tumbled, silent as a stone, her body rolling over and over toward Abel's outstretched arms as he ran to catch her. Nick stared down at them, aghast. Cal began to scream.

"Mama, Mama, Mama!"

"Bethie, darling . . ." Abel took her face in his hands. "Are you all right?"

She emitted a sound, half sob, half moan. Abel cradled her in his arms. Lin appeared in the hall above, her white nightgown ghostly in the dim light as she knelt down and embraced the weeping child. She murmured gently to him and taking his hand, led him toward his room.

Lucy leaned over Beth. "Dearest girl, are you hurt?"

"Give her a minute, Mama," Abel said. "She's had the wind knocked out of her."

Slowly, Nick descended the stairs. "Bethie, I—"

"No," she whispered. "Get away from me."

He flinched. "I'm sorry, Bethie. It was an accident."

"It was an accident," Lucy retorted bitterly, "that never would have happened if it weren't for you."

"May I have my cigar-case?"

Lucy glanced down at her hand, realizing that she must have picked up the case without thinking. She turned from him and opened it. Inside lay a single cigar and four white pills. She removed the pills. "Take it."

"You know what I want."

"You'll have to find it elsewhere. You'll not be getting it from me."

He looked at her in silence for a moment. Without a word, he went down the stairs, averting his eyes from Selina who stood at the newel post, her face white. As the front door closed behind him, Beth grimaced with pain.

"Oh, God," she whimpered, "how it hurts."

"I'll take her to her room." Abel lifted her into his arms.

"Merciful heavens," said Selina, seeing the dark stain on the stair-carpet. "She's hemorrhaging."

"Find Septimus," Lucy told her. "Send him for Doctor Vanderhoef."

"The baby," Beth whispered. "Not the baby. Please."

Selina and Abel were waiting in the drawing room when Lucy came down with the doctor. She walked him to the door, and when he had left she went to them. "Beth's resting. He gave her something to make her sleep."

"And the baby?"

"She's miscarried. It was the fall."

"In the name of God," Selina said, "how could Nick

654

endanger his wife and child for the sake of a few pills?"

Lucy glanced at her.

"She knows, Mama. I told Selina everything that you told me upstairs."

Lucy sagged into a chair, exhausted. "He can't help himself. It's hopeless. We thought he was over his addiction, but it has too strong a hold on him. Beth thinks he keeps the drug in his office and brings home only the dose he'll need." She shook her head. "Bethie and I have done our best to help him quit, and Doctor Vanderhoef has done everything he could possibly do."

Selina shuddered. "What a vile, sordid situation. To think of poor Beth being married to an opium fiend."

"Really, Selina," Abel said, "you don't have to make it sound worse than it is."

"I'm not. That's what he is. That's what those degenerates are called."

"Labels won't solve anything, Selina." Abel rubbed his eyes wearily. "I'll take Nick aside tomorrow and have a talk with him."

Nick was not at breakfast the next morning. "He didn't come home," Lucy told Abel. "God only knows where he spent the night."

"I'll go to his office. How is Bethie?"

"Weak. She needs to stay in bed for several days. Selina is having breakfast with her upstairs."

"Mama, Selina is very distressed."

"We're all distressed, Abel."

"Selina's never been exposed to anything like this. She's always been insulated from the seamy side of life. To find this sort of thing happening here in this house, so close at hand, has upset her terribly."

"What do you expect me to do about it?" Lucy snapped. "Right now, I'm more concerned about Beth. Selina will have to adjust to the existence of human frailties. Not everyone is as impeccable as the divine Mountfords."

"You don't have to be sarcastic, Mama. Selina is my wife. I don't like to see her disturbed."

"I'm sorry, dear," she said quickly. "This is a difficult situation for all of us. Please do everything you can to help Nick. I don't know how much more of this Beth can endure. It's destroying her trust in him. It's destroying their marriage. I beg you, Abel, try to make him regain his senses."

"I'll try. I can't bear the thought of his hurting Bethie so. She doesn't deserve such misery."

Selina said nothing more about the events of the previous evening. She seemed disinclined to make conversation. All morning, she busied herself fitfully with her embroidery, her books, her mending, tiring quickly of each in turn. She moved restlessly from room to room, first the drawing room, then the library, then the sitting room, as though there were no place in the house where she was comfortable. "If you'll not be using the carriage, Mother Slade," she said finally, "I'd like to do a bit of shopping this afternoon."

"Go ahead, my dear," Lucy replied, relieved at the prospect of a few hours alone. She sat in the bay window, the newspaper unread in her lap as she stared vacantly out at the street. It seemed to her that ever since Seth's death, there had been no peace in this house. She wondered if it might, in some obscure way, be her own doing. Had she set some awful force in motion that night, some spirit that afflicted them all? Too many sores lay festering beneath the surface of their lives, making it impossible to enjoy any sense of tranquillity. No wonder she was always tired. She closed her eyes and leaned back against the cushions of the window seat.

The slamming of the front door awoke her. "Abel? Is that you?"

"It's I, Mother Slade." Selina's cheeks were flushed. She removed her hat and flung it on a chair. "I have just had a dreadful experience."

"My dear, what happened? Shall I fetch you a glass of sherry to calm your nerves?"

"No, thank you. I was at the milliner's on Powell Street. A young woman came in, and as we were both trying on hats she struck up a conversation. She asked me where I had found the ribbons for a bonnet I was wearing. I told her I'd bought them from Klara Mason, and since I was on my way to the Clay Street store I offered to drive her there. She came along, bought the ribbons and thanked me. And then," Selina went on, "when I left Joe and Klara, I saw her, bold as a—as exactly what she was, standing on the street corner, handing her visiting cards to a pair of men!"

Lucy suppressed a smile. "Selina, dear, you put quite a fright into me. There's no need to be so perturbed. The young lady didn't—"

"She was not a lady!"

"But surely she behaved in a ladylike manner, or you wouldn't have offered her a ride."

"She brazenly took advantage of my good nature. She compromised me! She played me for a fool!"

"Nobody else is the wiser, dear. Don't make such a fuss over a trifle."

"But to think that a woman like that would dare to impose on a lady! I've never even laid eyes on her kind before!"

"I'm sure such women exist in Cambridge, too."

"If they do, they know their place. They wouldn't presume to enter a shop patronized by gentlewomen."

Lucy glanced out the window. "Here's Abel," she said, grateful to see him as he alighted from Simon Waite's carriage.

"You mustn't tell him."

"Your secret is quite safe with me, Selina. Abel," she called as he opened the door, "did you find Nick? Did you talk with him?"

"I did." He kissed Selina on the cheek.

"And?"

He sat down, shaking his head. "It was a strained conversation, at best. He insists that the drug has no ill effects whatsoever, that only the lack of it causes him suffering. He says if it weren't for you and Bethie plaguing him, there would be no problem at all."

"But Abel," Lucy said, "what of his own self-respect? Has he given himself up entirely to this vice?"

"I'm only repeating what he said, Mama. If you ask me, what I heard were the pathetic excuses of a desperate man who's resigned to failure. I felt sorry for him. Unfortunately, it must have showed, because he became acrimonious. He accused me of siding with Bethie only because we were flesh and blood. He said I had no right condemning him, when I'd spent the War safely in Cambridge enjoying myself."

"Did he at least ask how Bethie was?"

"Yes. He was very concerned. I told him to come home."

"You didn't!" Selina exclaimed.

"I did. What good does it do for him to stay away? Calvert needs his father, and in spite of everything Bethie's still his wife."

"You tried," Lucy said wearily. "We've all tried. And now, what we can't change we must learn to live with."

But that was not as easy as it sounded. The tension in the house was palpable. Cal began to feel the strain, too. He developed a chronic stomachache and had bouts of diarrhea, though the doctor was at a loss to find what was wrong with him. Nick's presence in the house was perfunctory. He ate there, he dressed there, he slept there—without, Lucy suspected, any conjugal felicity. Often as not, he rode off in a hired carriage as soon as the evening meal was over, returning in the small hours of the morning, long after Beth and the others had retired. On Saturdays and Sundays, he rose late and absented himself quickly, sometimes with a wry quip about "going off to fight the tiger," though his genial smile was no longer in evidence.

If indeed he did go off to gamble, Beth seemed not to care. She appeared relieved when the door closed after him and was nervous and taciturn when he was at home. Selina, though she could not avoid him, made no effort to conceal her disapproval. Only Lucy and Abel attempted a semblance of affection toward Nick, for all the good it did. He plainly resented the bonds that tied him to the house on Bush Street, though Beth, understandably refused to move elsewhere.

May came, bringing benign breezes, bright sunshine and blossoms that perfumed the lengthening days. But what should have been a season of grace seemed to Lucy only a cruel taunt. The flawless days and mild nights mocked the mood of the household. To a passerby, she thought, they must appear the perfect portrait of a contented family sitting on the veranda on this sunny Saturday morning. Lin was helping Cal build an elaborate castle of blocks, while Bethie sat tatting the edge of a handkerchief. Nick had pressed Selina to play a game of cards, and Lucy was ostensibly reading, though she had not turned a page in over half an hour.

Abel looked up from the letter in his hand. "Mama," he said, grinning, "Herr Schmidt says the first vintage is ready. We did it, Mama!" He waved the letter triumphantly in the air. "The Pastora Vineyard is launched on a river of wine!"

"Did he say how it tastes?"

" 'Dry with a pleasant hint of the fruit,' " he read. "Herr Schmidt wants to know if he should pack some bottles in straw and send them down."

Beth glanced up from her work. "Oh, no! Mama, let's go to Saint Helena. It wouldn't seem right not to sample the first wine up there, in the vineyard."

"Could you get away from the office?" Lucy asked Abel.

"Perhaps, if it was only for a day or two. I'll inquire on Monday."

"I shan't be able to go," Nick said, studying the cards in his hand, "not that it matters."

"Nick," Abel told him, "I wish you'd consider coming. This is an occasion we should all share."

"It's your land. It's your vineyard. Enjoy it." He changed the subject. "Selina, my dear, you're much too clever at this game. You've trapped me in a pretty pass here I'm afraid."

"Aide-toi, et le ciel t'aidera."

"What the devil does that mean?"

"Help yourself," she said sweetly, "and heaven will help you."

"I wasn't asking for one of your high-flown lectures, my dear." He slapped his cards down on the table.

"See here," Selina objected, "there's no need to be insulting."

"I'm sick of sermons. I can't so much as make an idle comment in this house without one or another of you throwing out some kind of veiled challenge."

"You're being overly sensitive, Nick," Lucy said smoothly. "Selina meant no harm."

"But if the shoe fits," Beth put in without looking up, "then perhaps—"

"That's enough," Lucy cautioned her.

"Let her say whatever she wants," Nick replied bitterly. "It's no secret that you all sit in pious judgment of me. There's nothing wrong with my eyes or ears. I see the suspicious, sidelong glances. I hear the reproach in your voices."

"Lin," said Lucy, "take Cal inside to wash his hands for dinner."

659

"No, Grandmama!" he cried. "I'm not finished with my castle!"

"Let him stay, Lin," Nick ordered her sharply. "And you, Calvert, you can stop staring at me like that."

"Leave the boy alone," Beth told him.

"He's my son, too. You can treat me like a pariah if you like, but I'll not have a six-year-old passing judgment on me."

"Why don't we all go inside," Abel suggested. "It's almost time to eat."

Nobody stirred. Selina gathered up the cards from the table and put them in their box. "I've quite lost my appetite."

"My fault, no doubt," Nick said drily. "Forgive me, my dear, for upsetting those refined Yankee sensibilities of yours."

Abel's jaw tensed. "Spare us the sarcasm, Nick."

"Yassuh," he drawled. "Yo' the head o' the house. Yo' the bossman. Whatever yo' say, suh."

Beth gave him a look, a cinder-black gaze, burnt-out and hard.

"Surgit amari aliquid," Selina murmured.

"Ah," Nick said, "the smugness of those obscure pronouncements."

"I only meant—"

"Selina," Nick told her, leaning toward her over the table, "I don't give a tinker's damn what you meant."

Selina rose, her face flushed. "I will not tolerate such language."

Abel went to her side. "I believe you owe my wife an apology."

"The devil take it. I'm fed up with her pretentious claptrap."

Selina stiffened. "Never mind. I no longer expect anyone in this godforsaken city to appreciate true refinement."

"Were the circumstances different," Abel said slowly, "I would be forced to demand satisfaction."

"In God's name!" Selina cried, turning to Abel. "How could you even suggest anything so barbaric? This city has contaminated even you!"

"Selina," Lucy said, "you're overwrought—"

"Yes! I am. As any decent woman would be. I've had all I can stand of this place! How can any virtuous woman be expected to keep her sanity here? Everywhere I look, I see depravity. Common prostitutes plying their trade on the public streets, gambling-hells operating openly, Chinee slaves pressed into immoral servitude! Here you think culture is a minstrel show and you allow lunatics to come to tea! Well, I shan't stay any longer than I have to! May God protect me from being corrupted like the rest of you."

Abel put a hand on her arm. "My dearest—"

Selina pulled away. "I never should have allowed you to bring me to a house stained with the blood of two killings. I should have known such a thing could happen only in a place where madness and evil flourish like weeds. Qnd now! You expect me to live under the same roof with a depraved creature who sinks further and further into the muck of his vice with every passing day— and fouls our lives in the process!" Abruptly, she stalked toward the door.

"Selina," Abel called out, following her, "if it's only a matter of finding another house—"

The door closed behind him. There was silence on the porch. Cal's face was pale, and his small hands were trembling. Beth went to him and put her arms around him.

Finally, Nick spoke. "Selina has quite a way with words, don't you think?"

"You started this," Beth told him. "It wouldn't have happened if you hadn't insulted her."

"Blame everything on me, my dear wife. I am the cause of everything and anything that goes wrong in this house."

"Be still, you two," Lucy snapped. "There's been enough quarreling for one day."

"Mama, do you think I ought to try to talk to Selina?"

"No, Bethie. She and Abel will have to work things out between themselves."

Looking at Abel's face, Lucy was reminded of a time when he was a small boy and had been stung painfully. He had not even seen what it was that caused his cheek to blow up and turn livid and throb so sorely that it kept him from sleeping. He had looked puzzled and hurt, the way he did now. It had taken Selina only a day to put her affairs in order and book passage to Boston. Despite

Abel's entreaties, she was determined to sail on Thursday next. Simon Waite had informed him of her intention to seek a divorce. "A measure," he'd told Abel sternly, "unheard of in the Mountford family."

"Mama," Abel said quietly, staring down at the carpet on the floor, "how did I fail her? What did I do wrong?"

Lucy went to him and put an arm around his shoulders. "You did nothing wrong. Neither of you is at fault. Some roses can't survive transplanting, Abel."

"I thought she'd be as happy here as I was in Cambridge."

"You both made the same error in judgment. You mustn't condemn yourselves or each other. You made a mistake, but you're both young, and you mustn't allow it to mar the rest of your lives. We must see to it that Selina leaves a loving, understanding family without rancor. It's important, son, that when you look back on this you have no regrets on your own account. Do what you must and do it like a gentleman. It's the worst of times that shapes our character. Don't do or say anything to Selina that might cause you remorse or guilt. They are intolerable burdens, Abel. I wouldn't wish them on either of you."

They tried, she and Beth, to raise his spirits in the wake of Selina's departure, but he appeared deaf to their overtures. Adversity, Lucy reflected, had always had a way of bringing out the Indian in him. Withdrawn and laconic, he masked his feelings behind the stoic countenance of his mother's tribe. He had been like that ever since she could remember. "Let him do things his way, Bethie," she finally told the girl. "Sometimes you and I forget that there's a part of him that's different from us."

It was not until they went to the vineyard that Abel showed signs of rallying. He took to the hills, alone, walking for hours on end, returning only for the evening meal, tired yet relaxed, the strain gradually disappearing from his face. He would always be a child of the land, and the land alone possessed the peculiar, subtle means to restore and refresh him. Lucy understood this.

Chang had prepared a banquet fit for his gods. Herr Schmidt and Hong erected a pair of board and sawhorse tables outdoors, below the veranda. Lucy and Beth laid the china and cutlery while Frau Schmidt decorated the white cloths with crocks of wildflowers. The main house, the bunkhouse and the Schmidt's cottage were emptied of chairs. In a wooden tub filled with cold well-water lay half a dozen bottles of wine. Chang, assisted by the bunkhouse cook, emerged from the kitchen with platter after platter of crisp duckling, savory pork, tender, spicy bits of chicken, dumplings, vegetables and steaming mountains of rice. Herr Schmidt motioned to Abel. "It is for you to offer the wine."

"Hong," Abel called, "give me a hand. You serve the men at your table, and I'll serve the five of us at ours."

They uncorked the bottles. Hong moved about the coolies' table with the solemnity of a holy man dispensing balm to his flock. When the wine was poured, he sat down.

Abel raised his glass. "Thanks be to God for His gifts," he said. "And a toast to the blessed memory of my stepfather, Seth Slade. He is with us today in this vision he made possible."

As Lucy brought the wine to her lips, the scent of its bouquet, fresh and fragrant, filled her nostrils. She took a sip. It was dry but not tart. It was light but with sufficient body to please the palate. But to Lucy, it tasted of nothing so much as memories. In it were the bright, green days of spring, the scent of the earth after rain and the faint, fruity aroma that wafted from vines laden with ripe grapes. She looked up from her glass. "Dear God," she said softly, "we've a miracle in a bottle."

Abel's face broke into a broad grin. *"Vivat vinea!"* he shouted. "Long live the vineyard!"

Herr Schmidt and the others laughed and applauded. Even Frau Schmidt, usually so diffident, seemed effervescent with the spirit of the feast. The coolies jabbered ebulliently in Chinese, their chatter rivaled by a group of chirruping birds that gathered on the porch railing and in the branches nearby, hopeful of crumbs. Beth's face was glowing, her cheeks slightly flushed from the warmth of the sun and the effects of the wine. "Abel," she said, giggling, "you and Herr Schmidt look stern as owls. What are you muttering about?"

Abel smiled and squeezed her hand. "The vineyard. What else? We have to decide how much of this vintage to market. Herr Schmidt says the harvest this year should be even better and bigger."

"But why do you have to talk business now, when we're all having such a good time?"

"The winemaker's work is never done," Herr Schmidt told her. "Last year, this year, next year, the past, present, future—they sit always on his shoulders, like invisible birds, pecking at him for attention."

"But surely today you could make an exception. Abel, do take a walk with me. I've eaten more than my fill. If I don't stir from this table soon, I'll petrify on the spot."

"What a fine picture!" He laughed, pushing back his chair. "You'd make a pretty hitching-post for the horses."

"In that case," she retorted airily, "I shall stay right where I am."

"Oh, yes?" Giving Lucy a wink, he reached down and tickled Beth about the waist.

She let out a small yelp and sprang from her chair. "Beast!"

"I thought that might persuade you. You always were a ticklish brat. Come on, Bethie. Let's go."

Frau Schmidt looked after them as they walked down the lane. "How fortunate you are," she said wistfully to Lucy, "to have two children so beautiful. Like this, they are," she clasped her hands. "Close. There is no *preis*—"

"Prize," Herr Schmidt corrected her.

"*Ja*, prize. There is no prize so valuable as a happy family."

It was so, Lucy thought. They were happy together, brother and sister. Though they looked alike, with their black hair and dark eyes, it was their differences that allied them. Their contrasting temperaments complemented each other. Beth was a capricious, fun-loving, gregarious girl. Abel, on the other hand, had always been contemplative, earnest and reserved. He had a steadying influence on Beth, as though his nature provided a kind of ballast which tempered her wayward inclinations. And she, more than anyone else, had the ability to amuse him and to enable him to make light of himself.

"Oh, Mama," Beth said the night before their departure, "what a glorious holiday it's been. Just the three of us, like old times. I almost hate to go back. It's been so good to forget my troubles for a little while."

"It was a welcome diversion, I agree. But troubles don't shrink with distance, Bethie. Unfortunately, they're with us wherever we go. Where is your brother, by the way? It's nearly bedtime."

"You'd best leave a lamp lit for him. He's with Herr

Schmidt, looking over the ledgers. You know how those two are when they're discussing the vineyard. Mama, Abel seems better, doesn't he? Being here has improved his spirits."

Lucy rose from her chair. "I think Selina's leaving so suddenly took him by surprise more than anything. He was as stunned as if he'd been struck by lightning. I expect he's just now beginning to sort out his thoughts." She gave Beth a good-night kiss on the forehead.

"He was so smitten with her that he couldn't even see the obvious. Poor Selina," Beth said, yawning sleepily, "she was never right for him. She could never have understood him the way you and I do."

XXXV

THEY BROUGHT back four large hampers filled with wine. "We must give a grand *soirée*," Beth urged Lucy. "Our friends have been hearing about the vineyard for years. We ought to share the proof of the pudding. Now that our year of mourning is passed, we could make it a gala occasion. Mama?"

"Bethie, dear, I haven't your enthusiasm for the undertaking, but do as you wish. All I ask is to be invited." Lucy might as well have invited an ant to the sugarbowl, she realized, knowing Beth's penchant for parties. But if the girl was willing to attend to all the details herself, and if it gave her something to take her mind from her worries, Lucy had no objection.

On the night of the party, as Lucy passed through the hall and looked into the thronged rooms, she decided that this was in fact the most pleasant way to entertain. Beth had seen to everything. Lucy had only to dress and greet the guests. The drawing room was cleared for dancing, and the entire house was perfumed by the flowers that adorned every table and mantel. The musicians played almost continuously, perspiring slightly despite the open windows that admitted a cooling breeze. The wine was poured and the glasses raised, sparkling with the reflection of the candlelight. Toast followed toast. "At this rate," Abel whispered to Lucy, "we'll have more buyers than we can supply wine."

"Oh, come," Beth chided, overhearing him. "Is that all you can think of? It's meant to be a party, Abel, not a business venture."

"Nevertheless, my dear, the Pastora Vineyard has now

converted these seventy-odd folk into customers. Congratulations, Bethie. You couldn't have done better if you'd planned it this way."

"Well," she replied, grinning mischievously, "the thought did occur to me. You're not the only one, you know, who has a stake in the vineyard. Will you escort me to supper?" she inquired, glancing around the room. "Nick seems to have disappeared."

"I saw him in the library with Deborah Vanderhoef," Lucy told her. "Shall I fetch him?"

"Don't bother," she said, taking Abel's arm.

"Mrs. Slade." Simon Waite touched Lucy's shoulder. "How proud you must be."

"I had precious little to do with it, Mr. Waite. We're fortunate that my late husband hired a fine winemaster."

"No, no," he said, laughing. "The wine is excellent, of course, but I was referring to Abel. I've high hopes for that young man. It's a pity," he added with a fleeting frown, "that Selina was so adamant in her dislike of San Francisco. Believe me, that son of yours is going to make his mark on this city one day. Did you know he's interested in politics?"

"He always was, even as a boy."

"Simon," Amy Winslow called across the room, "won't you and Lucy eat supper with Warren and me?"

"Go ahead," Lucy told him. "All this noisy festivity has quite taken away my appetite. Perhaps I'll join you later."

Doctor Vanderhoef caught her arm as she passed through the doorway. "Where are you off to, Lucy? I was hoping for a word with you."

"I thought I'd rest for a moment in the sitting room. I've a slight headache."

"I'll come with you. Lucy," he asked, joining her on the window seat, "are you feeling well?"

"I don't feel ill, if that's what you mean, but I still tire easily. And . . ." She hesitated. "Martin, this really isn't fair of me. You should be with the others, enjoying yourself."

"And what? What were you going to say?"

"It's nothing. Only this persistent headache."

"Is it very painful?"

"No. Just a dull, annoying ache."

"Lucy, you're much too pallid for my liking. I want

667

you to pay me a visit. Unless I miss my guess, you're anemic. A simple test will tell us."

"What does that mean? It's not serious, is it?"

"Rarely, my dear. Call it thin-bloodedness, if you will. Treated with something called Blaud's pill."

"You're sure it's safe? I'm wary of pills. After seeing what's happened to Nick . . ."

"My dear." He took her hand. "I hardly blame you, but I assure you I wouldn't recommend anything that would have any ill effect on you. It's merely carbonate of iron. Do come to my office on Monday, won't you?"

It was exactly as the doctor had suspected. Lucy accepted his prescription, feeling somewhat relieved that her malaise possessed a name.

"I'll want to see you again, toward the end of summer," the doctor told her as he ushered her to the door. "By that time, there should be a noticeable impovement in the way you look and feel. Take care of yourself, Lucy."

"I will, Martin. Thank you." She kissed his cheek. "You've been a good friend to us."

He shook his head resignedly. "I wish there were more I could do for Nick. Please tell him that if he wants my help, I'm always ready to give it. But it all depends on him, Lucy. He has to want to quit dosing himself with that stuff before anyone can do him any good."

Lucy gingerly approached the subject with Nick. He listened to her, his jaw stubbornly set, and replied, "I don't want his help. I don't need anyone's help. I'd appreciate it if you'd all stop trying to interfere in my life. Leave me alone, please."

He dined with them less frequently now, preferring to take his evening meals elsewhere. If Cal was bothered by Nick's absences, he didn't show it. Instead, he turned instinctively toward Abel, who had always been so paternal in his affection for the boy that a stranger might easily have assumed them to be father and son. Cal awaited Abel's arrival home from his office each afternoon, full of the small news of the day—a skinned knee, a new spelling word, an odd shell gleaned from an excursion to the beach. These three, Beth, Abel and Cal, are healing each other's wounds, Lucy thought. Sometimes she envied them. But no amount of loving closeness could relieve the anguish she concealed. She must be content to know that the children, at least, found comfort in each other.

Lucy sat with Abel, Beth and Cal on the veranda, watching the summer dusk overtake the hills. Abel set his glass of whiskey on the porch railing and stretched.

"Tired?" Beth asked.

"Relaxed." He inhaled deeply. "I'll be hanged if those white roses of Seth's don't smell as sweet as a bottle of scent."

"They do," Lucy agreed, laying aside the newspaper. "Abel, what do you make of this transaction with the Czar of Russia? The papers say it's going to cost the country millions. Why would Secretary Seward want to spend so much money on that expanse of wilderness, when we're only beginning to recover from the War?"

"Bite your tongue, Mama," he said with feigned shock. "Time was, when folks would have felt the same way about putting money into California. That territory could prove useful someday. Meanwhile, there's one less foreign presence on North American soil." He reached for his glass, but it slipped from his hand and landed in the branches of the azalea bush below the railing. "Ah, well," he said, retrieving the empty glass, "let's hope the azalea has a taste for Hotaling's whiskey."

Cal plucked at Lucy's sleeve. "Grandmama, do you remember when Grandpa Seth sat through the earthquake without spilling his wine?"

"I do indeed. What a memory you have, child."

"I miss Grandpa Seth."

"So do I," she said.

She had aged since his death, she thought as she left the children and went upstairs for her shawl. His ardor and his enthusiasm for life had been contagious. There were times now when she inadvertently caught her reflection in the mirror on the landing as she mounted the stairs, and for a moment she would stare at this slight, wan woman, her hair graying, her shoulders stooped and wonder that the image bore so little resemblance to herself. But it was she, there in the glass. The hollows beneath the eyes, the wrinkles on her brow, the gauntness of the face were hers. It seemed to her sometimes that the secrets she harbored were gnawing away at her, consuming her from within. She paused now, as she often did, to straighten her shoulders and smooth her hair. She had always been slightly vain, she supposed, though she dared admit it only in retrospect.

"I'll get it, ma'am," Septimus called up to her, as the sound of the doorknocker interrupted the morning quiet of the house. He laid his dustcloth on the hall chair.

Lucy peered over the bannister from upstairs. A tall woman of indeterminate years stood at the door. She was dressed in black, and despite an unbecoming coal-scuttle bonnet that shadowed her face, Lucy could see that she was darkly handsome. She spoke quietly to Septimus, regarding him aloofly from beneath full, heavy eyelids that gave her an oddly hooded gaze. He stepped out onto the porch with her and closed the door behind him.

Lucy waited for him at the foot of the stairs. "Who was that woman?" she inquired.

"Ain't nobody you know, ma'am, nor nobody knows you, neither."

"Do you know her?"

"Not so's you could say so."

"But who is she then?"

He seized his rag and began to dust the grandfather clock, mumbling something which Lucy did not catch.

"Septimus?"

"Mammy Pleasant. That's who."

"And who is Mammy Pleasant?"

"No friend to me, ma'am, nor to Biddy. Ain't nothin' but trouble, that woman."

"Yet she calls herself Mammy Pleasant?"

"No, ma'am. Miz' Mary E. Pleasant."

The name jogged her memory. "Isn't that the woman who brought charges against the omnibus company last year for putting her off the bus because she was colored?"

"Yes'm."

"But what did she want here?"

"I don't rightly know," he said, avoiding her glance.

Lucy walked over to the clock and stood facing him. "Then perhaps you'll tell me what she said."

He gave her a pained look. "Nothin' to concern yourself with, ma'am."

"Septimus, Mrs. Pleasant paid a call on this house. It is my house. I demand to know why she came, especially since you seemed so anxious that she not set foot inside. I do not like the idea of servants carrying on hushed conversations with visitors on the veranda. Tell me what happened, please."

He glanced about nervously. "Miss Bethie, where's she at?"

"She's upstairs in the nursery, giving Cal his lessons."

Septimus reached into his pocket and withdrew a gold watch and chain. He handed them to Lucy. On the watch-case were engraved the initials N.S.

"It's Mister Nick's watch."

He nodded.

"But how did Mrs. Pleasant come to have it?"

"He lost it. She found it."

"How did she know to bring it here? His name's not on it."

"Mammy Pleasant, she knows a peck of things. She knows too much, that woman."

"Is she acquainted with Mister Nick?"

Septimus shook his head. "No, ma'am. But I 'spect she knows somebody who is."

"A young lady, you mean."

He gave her a dour look. "That ain't for me to say."

"If I recall correctly, Mrs. Pleasant is known for finding positions for domestic servants—young women mostly."

"Yes'm."

"Is that all she does? Look at me, Septimus," she demanded. "Don't shilly-shally."

" 'Pends on what you hear."

"I see." She slipped the watch and chain into the sleeve of her dress. "I'll put these in Mister Nick's drawer. We'd best keep Mrs. Pleasant's visit to ourselves."

"Yes, *ma'am*. That woman ain't good news to nobody."

An afternoon sun cast lengthening shadows on the drawing room carpet. Beth sat at her piano, playing a Mozart sonata. Lucy closed her eyes and listened to the music. Abruptly, Beth struck the keys with a loud, jangling chord that caused Lucy to break from her reverie with a start.

"Damn Selina, anyhow!"

"Bethie! I beg your pardon!"

"I'm sorry, Mama. I'm envious of her sometimes. I can't help it. She's sailed away from her marriage, free as a bird."

"You don't know that. You have no way of knowing how she really felt or what it cost her to do what she did."

"If you ask me, she was as cold and hard and unfeeling as a stone. There are times I wish I were more like her."

"Bethie," Lucy said slowly, "are you saying you want a divorce?"

"I wish it were that easy." She sighed. "There's a part of me that still believes in Nick. I keep thinking that one morning he'll wake up and put the past behind him, and we'll all be happy again. Am I a fool, Mama?"

"It's never foolish to hope for the best."

"Meanwhile, we could spend the rest of our lives in this wretched, strained pretense of a marriage."

"Hush, Bethie. Look out the window. Here he comes."

"But not for long, I'll wager. He'll change his clothes and be off to fight the tiger before we even sit down to supper."

"Bethie, does he lose much money at the gaming tables?"

"I don't know. He only tells me when he wins, and I'm never sure whether or not it's the truth."

"Afternoon, ladies," he called through the open porch window. He let himself in and came into the drawing room. "Where's Calvert?"

"Septimus took him downtown in the carriage to fetch Abel home from the office."

"Nick," Lucy said, "I hope you'll join us for supper."

"Not tonight. I've pressing business to attend to."

Beth's eyes challenged him. "Faro or *vingt-et-un*? Or the sort of pressing business that sends you home reeking of cheap scent?"

"Bethie," Lucy told her, "I'd rather not be a party to this conversation. If you two have something to discuss, please do it privately."

Beth changed the subject. "Martha and Nathan Morse are giving a dance two weeks from Saturday. The invitation arrived today."

"You know very well I'm uncomfortable at dances."

"Nick, please—"

"Hello! We're home!" Cal cried, bounding up the porch steps with Abel close behind. He ran into the room, his cheeks aglow with excitement. "Septimus let me drive the carriage all the way back!"

"And very handily, too," Abel complimented him. "It was such a smooth ride that I nearly dozed off."

"Nick, please," Beth persisted, "say you'll go to the dance."

"I feel like a beached whale at those things. I sit there like some ungainly freak. I make everyone else just as uncomfortable as they make me. Go if you want to, but don't expect to drag me along."

"Abel," she demanded impulsively, "will you take me? Martha and Nathan are giving a party, and I do so love to dance."

He glanced at Nick. "Only with your permission."

Nick shrugged. "Go ahead. I'll find some other way to amuse myself."

"Calvert, be a dear," Lucy said, "and close that window. It's becoming chilly, now that the sun's going down."

"I believe I'll have a whiskey." Abel started toward the library. "Nick," he called over his shoulder, "will you join me?"

"No, thank you."

"Sherry, ladies?"

"Yes—"

The window fell with a crash, and Cal let out a shriek of pain. Abel leapt across the room and gave the sash a quick, upward blow with the edge of his palm, freeing the boy's fingers.

"There, now. Let me see your hand."

Sobbing, Cal gave it to him.

"It's all right. There's nothing broken."

"Make it better, Uncle Abel. Hold it."

Abel sat down and took him into his lap, stroking his blonde curls. "Slip your fingers into my waistcoat pocket. That's right, just like that. In a minute or two, they'll begin to feel better."

"Is it a magic pocket?"

"It is." Abel nodded soberly, hugging the boy close. He took out his handkerchief and dried Cal's tears.

"If you will excuse me." Nick reached for his crutches and rose from the sofa.

"Nick," Lucy said, "don't go so soon."

He turned and glanced from Beth to Cal. "Why not?" Without waiting for an answer, he left the room.

Abel's dessert was untouched. He leaned forward over the dining-table, intent on what he was saying. His fingers drummed a tattoo on the tabletop. "Something has

673

to be done, I tell you. The waterfront's as savage now as it was years ago when the Sydney Ducks ran rampant there. It's the shame and scandal of San Francisco."

"Why do you carry on so about it?" Beth asked him. "I don't see what it has to do with you."

He looked toward Lucy with a faint smile. "Don't you remember, Bethie, what Mama used to say about the Good Shepherd Home? The problems of the city are ours, because we are the city."

"But what on earth could you possibly do to purge the waterfront?"

"I'm not sure, Bethie. But I know what should be done. The undesirable elements must be flushed out, beginning with the prostitutes."

"Isn't that a rather unsparing point of view?" Lucy asked. "We're a seaport, after all, continually thronged with sailors who mayn't have seen a woman in months. If you banish the harlots from the area, you'll have a lot of men—most likely loosened by drink—attempting to foist their baser instincts on innocent women and girls. It seems to me you'd be making the streets less safe, not more so. I believe the harlots serve a purpose."

"Mama," Beth said tartly, "has always been notoriously tolerant of the weaknesses of the flesh."

"Bethie, that was an unnecessary remark."

"But she does have a point," Lucy observed. "I find it difficult to pass judgment upon others. We are none of us without our sins."

"I'm not passing judgment on prostitution, *per se,* Mama. Though it flouts the law, in my opinion it's more a matter of moral conscience than anything else. But you have to understand, I'm not talking now about your fancy parlor houses. Prostitution is the nucleus of all the crime that flourishes on the waterfront. It's no wonder people are calling it the Barbary Coast."

Beth looked puzzled. "Are you saying that the harlots are committing criminal acts?"

"More often than not, they're accessories. And many a time they themselves are victims."

"Let's go into the drawing room," Lucy said, rising. "Septimus will be wanting to clear the table."

"You see," Abel went on, following her across the hall, "the women lure the men into places where they're drugged and robbed—or worse, shanghaied. If the victim is strong and fights, he'll like as not be washed up on the beach in a day or two."

"But how did you become involved in this?" Beth demanded.

"Warren Winslow's assembling a committee to try to clean up the area. He's enlisted Simon Waite, and when he told me the facts, I volunteered my services, too. It's hellish down there, Bethie, totally without the law."

Lucy glanced at him. "This isn't another Vigilance Committee, is it?"

"No, Mama. We simply want to make the citizens aware of the problem so that they'll agitate to have the laws enforced. And if the existing laws aren't firm enough, we'll press to have stricter ordinances passed. We're working within the law, not outside it."

"Simon Waite mentioned that you were interested in politics. Have politics anything to do with this?"

"Everything. If our elected officials won't act, we'll prevail upon people to vote for men who will."

"Land sakes, Abel," Beth said with a grin, "I haven't heard you rattle on like this since the death of James King of William."

He returned her smile sheepishly. "I'm a bit wiser, now, Bethie." Abruptly, he grew serious. "But some action must be taken. The vice, the depravity, the crime on the Barbary Coast are out of control. As it is now, any man with two bits in his pocket runs the risk of having his throat slit in an alley. The cribs are hotbeds of disease. The wretched Chinese slave girls, once they've worn themselves out, are often shut up in hillside caves to die. The average working life of any prostitute is four years. After that, if she's not killed herself or been killed, she's usually lost to drink or disease."

Beth frowned in distaste. "Is that what you meant when you said they were victims, too?"

"It's worse than that, Bethie. It's nothing to discuss in the presence of ladies."

"It's all right, Abel," Lucy said. "You have my permission. Go on."

"I'd rather not, Mama. Suffice to say that the crimes perpetrated against these women are unspeakable. As a mild example, for instance, the proprietors of some places compel their girls to drink while soliciting customers. If a girl gets sufficiently drunk to fall unconscious, she's abused by any number of men, and the proprietor pockets the proceeds."

"Dear Lord." Beth shuddered. "What an inhuman situation."

"And we live cheek-by-jowl with it, my dear. I've not even scratched the surface of what goes on there."

"Tell me," Lucy asked him, "if you use the letter of the law to stop prostitution on the waterfront as a means of preventing crime, won't you have to close down the traffic as a whole?"

"Yes. That's true. The quality houses will have to close their doors, too. It must be done, if we're to redeem the waterfront."

"It won't work. You're battling the world's oldest profession. There will always be prostitution of one sort or another. At least the better houses are clean and orderly, and the girls there are scrupulous about disease. Wouldn't it be wiser to legalize prostitution, so that it wasn't forced to be part and parcel of the criminal element?"

"Mother!" Beth cried.

"I was only inquiring, dear."

"It's out of the question, Mama." Abel answered. "The good people of San Francisco wouldn't stand for it."

"Mama," Beth said, "I do hope you're not thinking of airing your views anywhere but in the privacy of this room."

"I'm not espousing any causes. I leave that to Abel. But one of the few luxuries of age and experience, my dear, is the freedom to speak one's mind. If it's any comfort to you, you may regard my opinions as the eccentricities of a prattling old lady. Nevertheless, I shall continue to say what I think."

"But don't you want to see those dreadful practices stopped?"

"Don't be silly, Bethie. Of course I do. I'm just posing some logical questions that your brother will have to confront if he intends to become deeply involved in this matter."

Abel nodded knowingly. "A devil's advocate, as Father Crowley would say."

"Precisely. Follow your conscience, Son. You may rely on me to see another side of this issue."

"What can I do to help?" Beth wanted to know.

"Very little, I'm afraid. But you might urge the ladies

676

to see that their husbands take a stand. There are times I'd like to see women given the vote. In a matter like this, their civilizing influence would be invaluable."

"Don't hold your fire 'til that day, my dear," Lucy said, "or your guns will be rusted over."

"What if," Beth said thoughtfully, "circulars were mailed by the committee to every lady listed in the San Francisco directory, stating the problems as succinctly and politely as possible? Surely that would prompt them to bring the matter to their husbands' notice."

"No," Lucy countered. "It wouldn't be correct for a committee of men to address women they'd never met. The ladies would be offended."

"Then I'll sign the letter, and I'll find other women to sign it, too. Mrs. Winslow would, I'm sure. And I know I could call upon Martha and Naomi and Klara."

"You'd do that, Bethie?" Abel asked her.

"Certainly."

He reached across the sofa and gave her a hug. "What a capital idea! Unleashing the persuasive powers of every wife in the city. What a clever little wench you are."

Lucy stood up from her chair. "I believe I'll go upstairs and read a while in bed. I'll leave you two to settle the fate of San Francisco. By the way," she said, pausing in the doorway, "I shall be interested to know if Eleanor Gibbs signs your circular letter."

"Well, Mama," Beth crowed, waving a sheet of paper aloft in her hand as she entered the library, "I've ten signatures! Abel says that's sufficient. He came to our Good Shepherd meeting today and spoke to the ladies. When he left, I passed around the letter that he and I had written. A few foolish old biddies wouldn't sign without speaking to their husbands first, but the rest wrote their names bold and clear. Mrs. Gibbs, too. Why did you ask about her?"

"I'd thought her sentiments closer to my own. Good work, Bethie."

"Now we must have the letter printed and mailed. The gentlemen on the committee have asked their office clerks to divide the city directory between them, so's to make it less of a chore to address the envelopes. Honestly, Mama, it makes me feel so proud to be able to do something like this. Mrs. Winslow told me that her husband thinks Abel has a real talent for politics."

"That, my dear, is not necessarily a compliment."

"But wouldn't it be splendid if he became a congressman or senator?"

Lucy laid her pen in its tray and pushed her chair back from the desk. "Don't encourage him in that direction, Bethie. If his background were to be made public . . ."

"But how could it be?"

"Nothing is impossible. Meanwhile, Indians are not allowed to vote. And half-breeds remain suspect. I wouldn't want to see him invest his time and energy, striving for something beyond his grasp."

"Nonsense. Abel knows what he's doing."

Lucy had to admit that the response to their circular was phenomenal. The members of the Ladies' Union Beneficial Society invited Beth to address their group, a prospect which both flattered and terrified her. She left the house, trembling and fighting off an attack of nausea, having verified her sheaf of facts and statistics with Abel for what seemed the hundredth time. She returned flushed with triumph. "They actually applauded! I felt like a cross between Dorothea Dix and Adah Isaacs Menken in *Mazeppa*."

"Lord have mercy," Abel chuckled. "They'll be no clipping the girl's wings now that she's taken flight."

"Damned foolishness," Nick muttered, "making a spectacle of herself. It's not becoming for a lady to speak of such things."

"And why not?" Beth challenged, "If our sensibilities are indeed more delicate than men's, then we are more shocked and revolted by these conditions than they. As a consequence, we're even more vehement that they be rectified."

"Hanged if you don't sound like some fire-and-brimstone preacher. It's not seemly for a woman to sermonize. You'll be a laughingstock if you keep it up, mark my words."

"I shall do as I please. I find it exhilarating to stand up and speak out for something so important."

"To be seduced by the sound of your own voice is more like it."

"Better that than some other things," she retorted.

"The company of a virago ain't much to my liking. Excuse me, if you will. I shan't be home until late," he said as he left.

"Bethie," Abel cautioned her, "please don't make this undertaking a point of contention between you and Nick."

"Anything I do these days arouses his antagonism. He resents the lot of us, just because we know how spineless he is."

Lucy spoke up. "Nick was a gallant and courageous soldier."

"That was then. This is now."

"All the same," Abel said, "he's suffering enough self-recrimination without your contribution. God knows what it must be like to lose control over one's own life."

"That wouldn't be the case if he had any strength of character. He's weak-willed, and there's nothing can be done about it."

"Bethie," Lucy cautioned her, "don't make things worse than they are. Leave this reforming business to Abel. Do it for my sake, if you will, and for the peace of this household."

"If I can't speak out loud, I shall do it silently. I'll help Abel write and rehearse his speeches."

"What speeches?" Lucy asked.

Abel grinned sheepishly. "The committee has elected to throw me to the lions, Mama. I'm to appear before the Hibernian Society and the Frenchmen's Benevolent Association next week."

"And the Jews want him to speak before their Concordia Society," Beth added. "Even the men's athletic clubs have made inquiries. The Olympic Club has written twice."

"But why you, Abel? I'd think one of the older members of the committee might carry more weight."

"Mama," Beth said with a tinge of awe, "you should hear him speak. He's a regular Steven A. Douglas."

"Indeed?"

"She flatters me, Mama. But Harvard did teach me the fine points of debate. And the gentlemen felt that a new face might be effective. I expect they think youth and novelty will attract more listeners than old, familiar faces adopting yet another cause."

"Still," Lucy mused, "you must come off well, or they

wouldn't have made you their spokesman. I'm proud of you, Abel. I'm proud of both of you."

"Mama," Beth said, looking puzzled, "you don't agree with Abel and me, yet you encourage us. Why?"

"If experience teaches us anything, Bethie, it's the ability to harbor disparate points of view. I admire you and Abel for your well-meaning zeal, though I don't necessarily endorse all of your opinions. Reed Pierce cautioned me once that the world was not to be understood in black-and-white but in more subtle shadings. I know now what he meant."

Abel rose and kissed her cheek. "Bless you, Mama. Come on, Bethie. Fetch a pencil and paper, and let's shut ourselves up in the library while I shape a speech for the Hibernians."

"You ought to ask Father Crowley for his suggestions," Lucy called after them.

"Good advice," Beth replied. "I'll call on him in the morning."

Fragments of Abel's speeches began to appear in the *Alta* throughout the autumn of eighteen sixty-seven, though Lucy had no way of knowing whether this was a tribute to him or to the principles of the committee. Still, she reflected, it was gratifying to see her son's name alongside Mark Twain's well-read letters from abroad. Those who eagerly scanned Twain's colorful accounts of travel among the Bedouins and Moors could hardly fail to notice the name of Abel Bates so often repeated on the same page.

Lucy winced as Doctor Vanderhoef pricked her ear. He took a sample of blood and applied a bit of cotton to her skin to stay the bleeding. "I'll be with you again in a moment."

"It's been a while since we talked, Lucy," he said, returning to the examining room, "though I'm certainly aware of what Abel's been doing with himself all summer. That young man is attracting a lot of attention to the iniquities among us."

"He gives his every spare moment to the committee, and Bethie has become his collaborator, stenographer and sounding board. For a woman who never cottoned to politics, I seem to be in the midst of that mix. How things change. Calvert begins school this month, can you believe it?"

"And Nick?"

"The same."

Doctor Vanderhoef sighed. He put his hand under her chin and moved her face toward the light from the window, tilting it one way, then another, examining her complexion. "Are you still troubled by that headache?"

"Yes." She smiled apologetically. "I'm afraid I always was a stubborn patient."

"Have you any other aches or pains?"

Lucy thought for a moment. "It's a peculiar thing, Martin, but I understand now what 'bone-weary' means. I feel sometimes as though my very bones ache with fatigue. But then, I suppose that doesn't make any sense at all."

"Not necessarily. Lucy, would you have any objection to my consulting another physician about your condition?"

"But why, Martin? Is it serious after all?"

"It's puzzling, and I'm quite as stubborn as you are. I don't like puzzles. You took our pills regularly, as I prescribed?"

"Yes."

He frowned. "There are still far too many white cells in the sample I just took."

"What does that mean?"

"It means you're still anemic. The treatment failed to have the results I'd expected. You're an extremely intelligent woman, Lucy, so I am being completely candid with you."

"Don't ever be otherwise, Martin."

"Some doctors would commence treatment with an arsenic compound, but others, like myself, have increasingly less faith in that alternative. Also, the accompanying effects can be unpleasant. I'd like to call upon Doctor James Blake. Do you know him?"

"No."

"He's an Englishman who spends much of his time here and in Sacramento. He's a specialist in blood disorders. There are few men in the world who know as much as he about such matters. I'd welcome his opinion."

"By all means, ask him."

"It's a wise decision, I think. I'll let you know when he can see you. I'll be on hand, of course." He took the bit of cotton she'd been holding to her ear. "Wait a moment," he said as she started to go. "It's still bleeding. Did you pinch it tightly?"

"Yes."

"Let me apply a styptic. It will smart a little, but it will halt the bleeding."

Lucy pursed her lips as it stung her. "Has it stopped?"

"Yes, but be careful not to scratch or rub there inadvertently. Lucy, I want you to continue taking your pills. And be careful not to go about where there's any illness. Whatever your good intentions, don't visit any sick friends. Anemia seems to make one prey for any diseases that present themselves. There's no sense compounding your condition."

"Martin," she asked, fixing him with a steady gaze, "should I be worried?"

"Do you think it would help?"

She laughed. "Well said." She raised her chin defiantly. "I shall go my way resolutely confident that your Doctor Blake will have a simple remedy for this nonsense."

"My dear," he replied gently, "he's only a physician, like myself, not a miracle worker. Don't burden the poor man with a halo. Let's wait and see what he says."

"You will tell Doctor Blake to be straightforward with me, please."

"You have my promise."

Abel laid aside his newspaper as she came into the drawing room. Beth looked up from her music and rested her hands on the piano keys. "What did Doctor Vanderhoef say?"

"He said not to worry," she answered cheerfully. "Abel," she exclaimed, giving him a perplexed frown, "where did you find those clothes? You look like a common vagabond."

"Deliberately, Mama. As soon as it's dark, I'm to meet two other members of the committee for a night-long reconnaissance of the Barbary Coast. Father Crowley has provided a grizzled old salt to guide us around the more shady retreats. I should look quite at home, don't you think?"

"Will you be safe?"

"Safer than most. At least I'm aware of the dangers, and I'll have an experienced guide."

"Must you do this?"

"Statistics are all well and good, but first-hand observation lends them more meaning."

"In God's name, don't let anything pass your lips. There's no way of knowing what might be in the food or drink."

"And don't dally with the ladies," Beth added.

"You needn't be concerned, either of you. I'm after facts, not sport."

"Nevertheless," Lucy went on, "I shan't feel comfortable until you're safely home."

Abel smiled. "I thought Doctor Vanderhoef told you not to worry."

"About my health. All mothers worry about their children. It can't be helped."

"I'm hardly a child, Mama."

"Age has nothing to do with it."

He gave a resigned sigh. "All right. I shall tap on your door when I return, though I shan't enjoy disturbing your sleep."

"Never mind. Do that."

Lucy woke with a start. The house was silent and dark. Only a faint suggestion of moonlight filtered through the fog beyond the curtained windows, casting a pale sheen across the sill. She heard a soft knock at her door and reached for her robe.

"I'm sorry to wake you, Mama," Abel said as he entered the room. "I knocked three or four times, but you didn't hear."

"I was wondering what had awakened me. Let me light a lamp. How was it? You weren't in any trouble, were you?"

"No, nothing like that." He seated himself on her rocking chair and crouched forward, resting his folded arms on his knees. "I saw Nick, Mama."

"There?" Quickly, she lowered her voice. "On the Barbary Coast?"

"In a gambling den."

"But I don't understand. If he must gamble, why can't he do it among gentlemen? There are private clubs for that sort of thing. Why must he consort with ruffians and criminals?"

"I can't answer that. I saw him long before he noticed me. I watched him. I'd never seen him like that before.

His eyes were glazed and feverish, and he was sweating like a racing horse. His shirt was wet through."

"Was he drunk?"

"No. Yes," he corrected himself. "I suppose he was, in a way. He was intoxicated by the game. It was as though he were risking his life on each roll of the dice and the danger excited him to the pitch of frenzy. But I didn't come to bear tales, Mama. Something he said has bothered me all night."

"Go on."

"When he finally saw me, he came away from the table so flushed and furious that I thought he was going to raise his crutch and swing it at me. But he just stood there, facing me, and very quietly he said, 'She sent you to follow me.'"

"But that's not so!"

"I set him straight, of course. He stared at me for a minute without replying, and then he gave me a queer, crooked smile and said, 'You've no need to tell her. The bitch is already in heat.'"

"In the name of heaven! He used those words?"

"I know, Mama. It was foul of him to speak of her that way, but—"

"She's his wife! How dare he refer to Bethie as if she were a slut! It's he who indulges his baser instincts like some witless animal. You are to say nothing to her of this, do you understand?"

"But what the devil did he mean by it?"

"Who knows? And who cares? Nick is beyond all reasoning. You yourself said he looked like a wild man. There's no accounting for what goes on in that mind."

Abel stood up. "Whatever he meant, I wish to God he'd never said it. I feel as though he'd spilt something putrid all over me and now the stain won't wash away."

"You'd do well to forget this episode. Perhaps he didn't even know what he was saying. Try to understand how jealous he is of you, Abel. He's been bitter as gall since he lost his leg. You're young and whole and healthy. You're your own man, and he's a slave to that damnable drug. Don't listen to him when he spouts his venom. Try to see it for what it is."

"How can you not detest him for speaking like that about Bethie?"

"I despise what he said, but I can't despise Nick. He's

to be pitied. Yet I won't deny that I wish he weren't married to my daughter."

"She could divorce him."

"She won't. I suspect it's for Cal's sake."

"Nick's hardly a father to the boy anymore."

"Still, it would have to be her decision and hers alone."

"Or his."

"No gentleman divorces his wife. It's out of the question."

"He's not behaving like a gentleman these days, Mama."

"Leave it alone, Abel. Go get some sleep. Bethie will be up first thing in the morning, badgering you with questions about conditions on the waterfront. She told me she wants to take notes so that you'll have a stock of examples to use in your speeches."

He gave Lucy a weary smile and kissed her cheek. "I doubt that very much of it is appropriate to air in public. I'll have to brush up my euphemisms."

Lucy found the Englishman, Doctor Blake, a punctilious sort, stiffly correct and meticulous in his examination. His manner matched his accent. He was crisp and precise. "If I may, ma'am." He pressed his fingertips along the base of her neck and made a noncommittal sound in his throat. He turned to Doctor Vanderhoef. "Here," he said, tapping lightly at a place between her neck and collarbone.

Doctor Vanderhoef probed the spot gently and nodded.

"What is it, Martin?" Lucy asked.

Doctor Blake took her hand and laid her fingers against the spot. "How long have you had that slight swelling, Mrs. Slade? Can you recall?"

"I never knew it was there 'til now. Is it important?"

"Quite. Now, if I may take a blood sample, perhaps you'd be kind enough to wait outside in the anteroom while Doctor Vanderhoef and I examine it and review your history and symptoms."

Lucy glanced at the clock on the waiting room wall. Nearly an hour had passed since the doctor had dismissed her. She looked down at her hands folded in her lap. The pattern of veins showed clearly under her white skin, like a trellis of blue painted on a porcelain plate.

685

The door opened. "Lucy." Doctor Vanderhoef beckoned her inside. "Take a seat, won't you?"

She looked from one to the other. "What is it?"

"Doctor Vanderhoef insists that I be completely frank with you, Mrs. Slade."

"As do I," she replied. "I've every right to know the condition of my own health. I'll thank you not to sugarcoat the facts." She caught Doctor Vanderhoef's gaze. "It's not good news, is it, Martin," she said quietly.

He shook his head.

"Explain it to me, gentlemen, please."

Doctor Blake cleared his throat. "You've a serious blood disorder, Mrs. Slade. Unfortunately, very little is known about it at this time. In fact, nothing at all was known about it until about twenty years ago, when two doctors named Virchow and Bennett identified the disease."

"And is the swelling in my neck a part of it?"

"Yes. An enlargement of the lymph glands. Mrs. Slade, under microscopic examination, your blood shows a disproportionate number of colorless corpuscles."

"Doctor Vanderhoef said that meant I was anemic."

"That's true, Lucy," Doctor Vanderhoef told her, "but you have a virulent type of anemia."

"What is the cure for it?"

"There is none as yet, ma'am," Doctor Blake said. "Neither the cause nor cure is known."

"But I feel no pain! How can it be so serious? Are you sure?"

"It is unlikely that you will be in any pain, Mrs. Slade," Doctor Blake assured her. "The disease is gradually debilitating, but it is not, of itself, painful."

"My God." She looked up at the two of them. "You are telling me that I am dying, is that it?"

"We are all dying," Doctor Blake reminded her gently. "Does any of us ever really know when the call will come?"

"How long do I have?"

Doctor Vanderhoef took her hand in his. "We don't know, Lucy. There is just not enough information on the disease to make that prognosis."

"What you are saying, Martin, is that some vile mystery is destroying me internally, and there's nothing in the world to stop it."

He looked pained. "Lucy, I—"

"For pity's sake, Martin, stop acting as though you were responsible for my condition. You're not to blame."

"I'm sorry, Lucy."

She gave him a wry smile. "So am I. Is there no medicine to at least delay the inevitable?"

"None that has been found effective," Doctor Blake replied.

"How peculiar that I feel hardly any emotion at all. Not fear, nor sadness, nor even desperation. If anything, I feel vaguely angry. Isn't that odd?" She didn't wait for an answer. "Death has brushed by my side so often in my life that it holds no terror for me. I've always been conscious of its presence, just as day puts me in mind of the coming night. But this time is different, isn't it?" She glanced at the two men. "This time it has stopped to take my hand. Martin, I must consider the children. I must put my affairs in order for their sakes."

"You have plenty of time for that," Doctor Blake said. "I foresee no imminent change in your condition."

"Lucy, perhaps it would make things easier for you if you told them. You'd not have to bear this burden alone. It's a heavy secret to carry, my dear."

"Yes, Martin, it is. But I've had a lot of practice. Let me do things my way, please. The children are not to know."

He gazed at her in silence. "All right," he said finally. "As you wish. Both Doctor Blake and I would like to have you come to the office for periodic visits."

"You would be doing us a service," Doctor Blake went on, "to allow us to follow the course of the disease. The more we learn about it, the greater the possibility of finding a cure one day."

"Certainly." Abruptly, improbably, she laughed. "But I don't even know its name!"

"Leukemia, ma'am."

XXXVI

LUCY STARED into the mirror over her dressing table, studying this inhospitable configuration of flesh that had served notice upon her. She felt curiously disassociated from the image in the glass, as though it were a relic of the past, like a photograph, a reminder of something that had once possessed a certain validity but was now merely an illusion.

At first, she had conscientiously attempted to wrest some special meaning from each day, each hour, that remained to her. But the commonplace mocked her. Life went on as usual, unexceptional and uncompromising. The dispassionate sun rose and set, casting its changing rays through the windows, warming each familiar room of this house in which she was now a transient guest. The bittersweet awareness of one's mortality, she realized, altered nothing. It was only an acknowledgment of an omnipresent truth, nothing more or less than a nod of recognition to one's own shadow, that dark likeness that tenaciously dogged each step from cradle to grave.

"I'm becoming used to it, Martin," she said, as Doctor Vanderhoef took her pulse. "We are almost comfortable bedfellows, the old shadow and I. He doesn't even interrupt my sleep anymore."

"I'm glad to see you in such good spirits, my dear. How do you feel otherwise?"

"Surprisingly well. Tired, as usual. But I'm not known as a stubborn old mule for nothing. It's been over six months since you dealt me the black card, and I'm still here. I warn you, I'm not to be got rid of easily."

"You still haven't told Abel or Beth?"

"Why should I? They have their own concerns. There will be time enough; I feel sure of that now. Hiram Berry has seen to my will, and I've left letters with him for each of them. I've written Abel to hold onto the land in the Sacramento Valley, come what may, until the railroad is completed. I wouldn't want to die thinking that anything could stop Seth's last dream from coming true. Sometimes, Martin," she continued thoughtfully, as he tested the swelling at the base of her neck, "I think that our dreams are the essence of all that is real in any of us. You dream of curing the sick and healing the injured, and whether you can or not is less important than your dedication to the dream. My father dreamt of being a successful farmer. Nature defeated him, but his dream never failed him for a moment. And I never thought of him as defeated, any more than I think you a failure for not being able to cure me. The dream prevails, despite what happens, because it is inviolate. The rest is almost incidental." Lucy looked up at him sheepishly. "You see? With the sand running out of my glass, I'm waxing philosophical. I didn't mean to bore you."

"I'm curious. Did you ever have what you call a dream?"

"I suppose I did, though I wasn't aware of it then."

"And what was it, if I may be so bold?"

"You'll laugh, Martin."

"I shan't. You have my word."

"I wanted to be an adventurer."

"Do you mean an adventuress?" He looked incredulous. "You, Lucy?"

"No, no," she laughed. "I'm hardly the type. I wanted to have adventures, to sail forth like a ship on a voyage of discovery, to find new lands and meet strange people and do things that no one else had done. Rather a peculiar dream for a girl, I suppose, but I expect my Pa sowed the seeds with all his fanciful tales of faraway places. It's a funny thing, Martin . . ." She hesitated a moment, then smiled. "I've done just that, haven't I? I've had more than my share of experiences. Perhaps that's another reason I'm not afraid to die. I've accomplished everything I wanted and more. I've no dreams left, save for the happiness of the children."

"And they, Beth and Abel, what do they want, do you think?"

"Abel fancies politics, God help him."

"You don't seem altogether pleased with his choice."

"I'm not—not that I could deter him."

"Why?"

"A life of public exposure has its hazards. If you're finished with me, Martin, I shan't take up any more of your time."

"What about Beth?"

"I don't know." She shook her head. "She's changing. For a time, all she cared about were parties and balls. Now she seems to have caught Abel's enthusiasms. She's quite as outspoken as he. Believe me, it's rather formidable, living with a pair of reformers."

Despite her differences of opinion with Abel and Beth, Lucy admired their dedication and enterprise more than she revealed. Often now, she found herself being introduced not simply by name but, in addition, as "Abel Bates's mother." He was making a name for himself, and his speeches were much in demand. Bethie would show him the requests that had come in the mail, and with her advice, Abel would accept those engagements which promised the largest or most influential audience. He would suggest a particular thrust or theme for his oration, and Bethie, after poring over her increasing collection of facts and figures, would pen an outline for him. Occasionally, he suggested an alteration or two, but often as not he developed his speech according to her notes. At the last, he rehearsed it for her approval, usually making the few small changes she advised. He valued Beth's opinion, and it was plain to see how much it pleased her to be the object of such respect—especially, Lucy thought, since Nick showed her less and less regard with each passing day.

Sometimes, Lucy listened with Beth while Abel rehearsed his speeches, though being of a less radical stripe than he and Beth, she commented only when one of them solicited her views.

"Well, Mama?" Abel asked.

"My dear, is it necessary to keep repeating that exhortation to 'Clean up *Sin* Francisco'? It seems to me a bit inflated and sensational. Besides I don't find it attractive to think of myself as a citizen of a place called *Sin* Francisco."

"But that's precisely the point," Beth argued, looking

690

up from the snippet of paper she was cutting from the *Alta*. "If enough people object to that reputation, they'll do something about it."

"It's only a slogan, Mama. I've used it before, and it's very effective. It seems to be catching on."

"Still, I wish it weren't so undignified."

"Mama," Beth said as she scanned the pages of the *Bulletin*, "politics aren't always dignified."

"I'm aware of that, my dear."

"And," Abel added, "it's sometimes necessary to shock people out of their complacency."

"Listen to this," Beth said, holding the newspaper up to the lamplight. " 'The severely bludgeoned body of an unidentified man was found yesterday in the vicinity of Jackson and Kearny Streets, shortly after he'd accused the proprietor of the Stag's Head Saloon of giving him a drugged cigar.' "

"A favorite trick of the crimpers. The victim puts the cigar to his mouth, and before he wakes he's shanghaied and at sea."

Lucy glanced at Cal, who was sitting at Beth's feet, pasting her cuttings into Abel's scrapbook. "Must you discuss these matters in front of him?"

"In a year or so, he'll be able to read a newspaper for himself," Beth replied. "These things can't be kept from him forever."

"But he's only a child, dear. And that," Lucy added, nodding toward the open book on the floor, "is an accumulation of dreadfully sordid tales."

"All of them true, Mama," Abel said, "and all of them good ammunition for the committee. Come, now. Cal's only playing with paste and paper. There's no harm in that."

"Hello, there." Nick stood in the doorway. "Am I interrupting this intimate little circle?"

"Not at all," Abel answered, making room for him on the sofa.

Nick remained where he was. "Good evening, Calvert. Are you going to favor me with a greeting?"

"In a minute, Papa," he said, carefully gluing a scrap of paper onto the page. He pressed it smooth with the bottom of his fist. "There!" He looked up at Abel. "I pasted every one. See." He scrambled to his feet and

691

placed the book proudly in Abel's lap. "Didn't I do a neat job?"

"Indeed you did. Excellent work, my boy."

"Your boy, is he now?"

Abel glanced at Nick. "Calvert," he said, giving him a gentle push, "go give your Papa a kiss."

"No." Nick raised a hand. "Don't you tell him what to do. Forget it, Calvert. I'm sorry I disturbed you."

"Come along, Cal," Beth said. "Let's wash the paste off your hands before you get it all over everything. Nick, there's some mail for you on the table. A letter from your sister, Regina, and an invitation for us to attend a benefit performance at the Alhambra Theatre. Do you want to go?"

"Not especially. But I daresay that won't stop you."

"I thought Boyd and Naomi might like to go with us."

"Ask whom you please. My leg bothers me if I sit too long in those cramped theatre seats."

"Never mind, then. Abel can escort me."

"Papa," Cal asked, "will you stay for supper?"

"Another time, perhaps." He watched in silence as Beth and the boy went upstairs.

"Come sit by the fire," Lucy said. "I expect it's growing cool outside."

He took Beth's vacant chair. "Not near as cool as it is in here."

"I'll thank you, Nick," Lucy told him evenly, "not to throw my words back in my face. You make it all but impossible to be civil to you. Everyone in this house has tried to be accommodating and sympathetic toward you. I can't speak for the others, but my patience is wearing thin. You might do well on your part to make more of an effort."

"An effort to what?"

"Oh, for pity's sake," Abel said, "you know very well what Mother means. An effort to repair matters, instead of carping at Cal or Bethie."

Nick fixed him with a steady gaze. "That would be like locking the barn door after the mare's gone, wouldn't it? You're not as subtle as you think, you know. I'm aware of what's happened here. You couldn't keep your own wife, so you've appropriated mine. And the boy, too. Very convenient."

Abel's face was taut with anger. "Don't talk like a

692

fool. If you paid more attention to Cal, you'd have no cause for complaint. As for Bethie, you know how she feels about this vice of yours. In God's name, Nick, it's not herself she's thinking of. It's you and your marriage and your son."

"And you're her champion, I see."

"I want her to be happy."

"On your terms."

"What is that supposed to mean?"

Nick gave him a faint, cynical smile. "As if you didn't know."

"I can't think what you're talking about."

"Nick," Lucy said, "stop acting as though Abel were somehow at fault here. You've abandoned your wife and son in favor of drugs and gaming and harlots. You've treated your family's devotion and affection as if they were worthless. You can't expect them not to be hurt by what you've done. How can you be so stubbornly perverse? What you're doing is unwholesome. It's—"

Abruptly, he seized his crutches and raised himself from his chair. He turned on Lucy, his face white. "Don't lecture me. You're no one to talk, when you can't see what's taking place right in front of you. Unwholesome, you say? It doesn't strike you that this sudden, intimate alliance between brother and sister is as perverse and unwholesome as—"

"How dare you?" Abel sprang to his feet, his fists clenched at his sides. "Damn you! That filth you wallow in has poisoned you completely. I wish to God I could beat it out of you!"

"You don't think I can see what's going on between you and my wife? Brother and sister? Murmuring together like a cozy pair of doves? Playing the parents to my son? Dancing about in society, ever the inseparable partners?"

Lucy was shaking. She rose and stepped between them. "Leave now, Nick, because if Abel won't strike you I will. Take your lies and go. For that's all they are, Nick. Lies. You lie to yourself to invent excuses for what's happened, when you are the one who's to blame. And by all that's holy, don't ever again say such things under my roof." Her heart hammered in her chest, and she thought for a moment she might faint. Abel reached out to steady her.

"You heard what Mama said."

"That would please you, I suppose, to be rid of me. But," Nick said, turning toward the door, "you're not. Not so long as she's my wife and she lives here with my son. And mark me, my wife's brother," he called over his shoulder "don't think you'll get away with this scot-free."

Lucy waited until the door had slammed behind him. "God in heaven!" She sagged into a chair. "He's gone mad. What are we to do?"

Abel strode to the mantel and grasped it tightly, as though he might wrench it from the wall. He stared down into the firelight. "We can't do a thing. It's up to Bethie to reach a decision. But this house is your property, Mama, and you can lawfully restrain him from coming here, if you show good cause."

"That would be meddling in their marriage, not to mention risking a scandal."

"The truth is, we're already risking a scandal. How long do you think Nick's debauchery can go unnoticed? Especially with his brother-in-law the chief spokesman for reform in this city. Those waterfront rats would like nothing more than to make capital of the connection in hopes of disconcerting me."

"Perhaps you should resign from the committee."

"The devil I will!" He pushed himself away from the mantel and turned to face her. "Don't you see what Nick's done? He has us all dancing to his tune. At first, we accommodated him out of pity and to keep peace in the house. Now he brandishes lies and threats to keep us bending to his will. The poor, damned fool," he said bitterly. "All the power he has left to him is fraudulent. But I'll be hanged if I'll allow him to manipulate me."

"Abel, you just finished saying that Nick is in a position to cause you public embarrassment."

"I'm prepared to confront that issue, if it arises. If the corrupt influence of the Barbary Coast can claim its victims from decent families like our own, no one is safe from its influence."

"I will not have you exploiting this family to further your own ambitions!"

"Yet you'd allow Nick to coerce me into silence?"

"I should remind you that Nick is not the only one in our family who has flirted with scandal."

He brushed her words aside with a brusque wave of

his hand. "That's ancient history, Mama. You're a paragon of respectability. You founded the waifs' home. Your good works are famous. You defended yourself and your home against that madman who took Seth's life. You're a heroine, Mama—"

She cut him off. "Don't deceive yourself. The past is never dead and gone. Not mine, yours or anyone's. We carry it with us forever. Make no mistake on that account. Tread lightly, Abel. I warn you."

"If Nick's behavior comes to light, I'll have to acknowledge it. I will not attempt to suppress the facts."

"Have you thought of how this might affect Beth?"

"It would be out of my hands. I can only hope that it might convince her to divorce him."

"What about these ravings of his?"

"What about them?" he retorted. "Would you have me turn away from Bethie? Now? When she most needs kindness and affection? Would you allow Nick's demented fancies to do this family more damage than he's done already?" He shook his head incredulously. "I'm not even sure he believes that rot himself. Perhaps he only said those things to bait me. I don't know Nick anymore. He's a stranger to me."

"To us all, I'm afraid."

"And Bethie has to share her bed with him." He passed a hand over his eyes. "Dear God, Mama, what a situation we're in."

"Did Nick leave?" Beth inquired as she returned.

"Yes."

"He forgot Regina's letter." She picked it up from the table. "I'll put it beside the bed where he'll see it when he comes in."

"If you'll excuse me," Abel said, "I've some work to attend to."

Beth looked after him. "What's got into Abel?"

"He and Nick had an argument."

"About what?"

Lucy sighed. "Does it really matter?"

Beth picked up the newspapers she had left piled by her chair. "No."

The morning sun streamed through Lucy's bedroom window, flashing against the silver-backed hairbrush in her hand. Deftly, she twisted her hair into place and secured it. "Lin," she called toward the open door of the dressing room, "are you there?"

"Yes, missee," she replied from her room beyond.

"Be a dear, please, and fetch me the green bonnet with the egret feathers."

Lin emerged from the dressing room, the bonnet in her hand.

"Is my blue dress clean? I'd planned to take it with me to Saint Helena tomorrow."

"Yes, ma'am. You want to take the lilac and the gray, too?"

"Just the gray. We'll only be gone three days. What about Cal's things?"

"I am packing them now."

"I'm sorry you won't be coming along, Lin, but as it is, Cal will have to sleep with Abel. Now that he's no longer a baby, we really need another room." Lucy pinned her hat and took her gloves from the dressing table. "Lin," she said, studying her, "why don't you see if my lilac dress can be altered to fit you? I expect it won't need much more than a hemming."

She smiled broadly. "Thank you, missee. It's my favorite dress."

"Here." Lucy reached into the drawer. "I kept an extra yard of the lilac ribbon. It's yours."

Lin took the ribbon and twined it through the black braids coiled at the nape of her neck. "How does it look?"

"Beautiful." Lucy stood for a moment, gazing at her. She was a young woman now, yet her shy ways still gave her the air of a child. She was slim and small-breasted, almost boyish in the narrowness of her shape, though her lithe movements and gentle demeanor were becomingly feminine. Left to his own devices, Li Fu would have sold her into the cribs to give herself to anyone who'd pay his fifty cents. Like as not, she would have died long ago, abused and debased, her sweet soul warped and blighted like a bud exposed to the indifferent frost. Impulsively, Lucy kissed her cheek. "I must be off now. I've errands to do before we leave for the vineyard."

Lucy paused for a moment inside the entrance to Wells Fargo, listening to the murmured conversations between the tellers, officers and patrons. Was it this hushed hum hinting of mysterious, weighty confidences that always gave her a slight thrill of excitement? Or was it the music of the silver and gold coins, a sound like the urgent chimes of a clock, exhorting one to hurry about one's business? Let the rest of the country content itself with limp scraps of paper; in San Francisco, the jingle of coins prevailed. Commerce was thriving, and inside these marble walls she sensed the throbbing pulse of it, powerful and exhilarating.

"Mrs. Slade." Mr. Biggs rose as she approached his desk. "Please have a seat. What may I do for you?"

"I came to make a withdrawal. We're traveling to Saint Helena for a few days."

He dispatched a clerk to fetch her money from one of the tellers. "May I be of any further service?"

"Yes, you may, though not immediately. Mr. Biggs, you've been looking after my affairs for nine years now, and I thank you for your continued interest and concern. It's given me a sense of security to have your good advice, since I know so little about finance."

"You flatter me, Mrs. Slade."

"Not at all." She folded her hands on the desk. "I'd very much appreciate it if you'd extend this same personal service to my son and daughter, should they want it. I'm not growing any younger, and I'd rest easier knowing that they could call upon you for counsel. Abel is conservative about such things, but Beth has a tendency to be flighty and knows even less than I about financial dealings. Neither of them is particularly interested in such matters. Abel is likely to overlook opportunities, while Beth is inclined to spend without thinking."

"I'd be glad to help either of them. Is there anything in particular I might do?"

"Not as yet, but I daresay the time will come. It's important to me to know they can rely on your personal attention."

He reached across the desk and shook her hand. "Indeed they may. You have my word that I shall look after them personally. I've watched those two grow up, Mrs. Slade. Why, I remember when Beth was scarcely tall enough to peer over the top of that counter there." He chuckled. "She used to jump up and down in hopes of getting a glimpse of what went on behind it. Are she and Nicholas in their new home yet?"

"I beg your pardon?"

"I'd understood they were buying a house. Nicholas told me as much when he closed his account."

"No, they're still in the Bush Street house at present." She hesitated a moment, then took a chance. "You're referring, I presume, to the account opened with the five thousand dollars I gave them for a wedding gift."

"Yes. Ah, here we are." He received her money from the clerk and gave it to her. "Wish them well for me in their new place, won't you? And enjoy your trip."

Lucy debated with herself as to whether or not she should speak to Beth of Mr. Biggs's disclosure. Perhaps Beth knew and had said nothing about it. Perhaps they actually were considering moving, in hopes of making a fresh start. Still, it seemed unlikely, and even less likely that Bethie wouldn't have mentioned such a plan. Lucy doubted that she would have agreed to Nick's withdrawing the entire amount, especially now, when they seemed on the verge of divorce. She broached the subject as tactfully as she could.

"I had a talk with Mr. Biggs at the bank today," she said as Beth came into the library. "He's offered to assist you and Abel with any financial questions that might arise."

"Oh, Mama, you know how little I care about business affairs. No offense meant, but it's hardly ladylike to concern oneself with those things. Finances are a man's occupation."

"Still, someday you might want to spend some of your money, to invest it in real estate perhaps."

"You and Seth had all the talent for that. I'd most likely come a cropper if I tried, even with Mr. Biggs's help."

"I think," Lucy said cautiously, "that ladylike or not, you ought to give some attention to your funds. Bethie, what became of the money I gave you for a wedding present?"

"Nick put it in the bank. Why?"

"In whose name?"

"I don't remember. Everything was so rushed, what with his going on to war. Is it important?"

"Mr. Biggs let it slip that Nick told him he was going to use it to buy a house."

"For whom? Not for us, certainly."

"Nick withdrew the money from the bank, Bethie. He closed the account."

Beth stared at her, dazed and unbelieving. She looked as pale and fragile as a porcelain doll. Slowly, she sat down. At length, she bent her head and covered her face with her hands.

Lucy went to her and knelt beside her chair. "I'm sorry I had to tell you."

Beth shook her head. "It doesn't matter. I would have found out sometime."

"Perhaps there's an explanation. Don't judge Nick before you hear what he has to say."

"What does it matter if there's an explanation?" she asked hopelessly. "He did it behind my back. Mama, don't you see?" She raised her head and looked at Lucy. "There's nothing left now."

"Dearest, it's only money . . ."

"It's not the money. He's betrayed me. I tried to believe in him, in spite of everything. I kept hoping he'd change. But he's lied to me. He's been unfaithful to me. Cal and I mean nothing to him anymore. And now he's destroyed the last shred of faith I had in him. He's cheated me." Her voice rose. "Damn him!" she cried. "He has debased and ruined every fine and decent thing I had to offer him. I have nothing left to give!"

"Hush, Bethie—"

"I hate him for that. He has bankrupted me, and I'm not talking about the money. I feel used up and hollow, Mama, like an empty husk. No more," she said, her voice suddenly calm. "He's done his harm. There's nothing left for him to destroy."

The front door slammed. Beth stood up. Lucy took her by the shoulders. "Don't act in haste, Bethie. Don't do anything you'll regret."

Beth looked at her as though she had not heard. "Nick, is that you?" she called. "Would you come into the library, please?"

"Afternoon, ladies—"

Beth cut him off. "What happened to the money we were saving? The five thousand dollars Mama gave us for a wedding gift?"

The question took him by surprise. He glanced uncertainly from Beth to Lucy.

"If you'll excuse me." Lucy moved toward the door.

699

"No, Mama. I want you here."

"Bethie," Nick said, attempting a smile, "it'll be replaced. I borrowed it, that's all."

"You closed the account."

"I'll open another. I'll have it all back in a few days, a week at most."

"You lost it at the gaming tables."

"Temporarily, Bethie, only temporarily. A run of bad luck. But these things don't last. One good night, and I'll be well on my way. Don't worry," he said blandly. "Don't make such a fuss about it."

Beth gazed at him, her face without expression. "Get out. Leave this house, once and for all, and don't come back."

"Now, Bethie," he countered, "surely you're not going to send me packing just because of—"

"Now. You may come back for your things after we leave for the vineyard tomorrow. I never want to see you again."

His face grew flushed. "You can't do this. I've a right to be with my son."

"So help me God," she declared, "if you don't stay away, I shall go to your Uncle Dabney and tell him everything. I'll see to it that your family knows the entire story. And if that's not enough, I'll take the truth to court."

He coughed nervously. "You wouldn't do that. I know you wouldn't," he insisted, "because you wouldn't risk your reputation. You're in this reform movement up to your neck. How do you think it would look if—"

Beth stiffened. "Don't push me, Nick. Who would have more reason to speak out than a woman whose husband had debauched himself with drugs and harlots and wagered away their savings? I swear to you, I'll fling it all out in public if you cross me."

He said nothing. His eyes were on her face. Beth returned his gaze, fierce and intransigent.

"It's what you've wanted all along, isn't it?" His voice was almost a whisper. "You've had no use at all for me since your precious brother came back to rule the roost. I should have expected this."

"Leave Abel out of it," Beth retorted. "I can't help it if you despise him for being everything you're not. I thank God that Cal at least has Abel as an example."

Nick flinched perceptibly, then recovered his composure. He gave her a fleeting smile, pained and cold, as if he had glanced for a moment directly into a white winter sun. "You've seen to it that he plays father to my son. Does he play husband to my wife, I wonder?"

The flat of her hand struck him full across the face. The sound, ugly and harsh, seemed to hang in the air between them like the echo of a sharp, deep, irreparable crack. Nick's knuckles were white on his crutches. Very slowly, he turned away and limped from the room.

Lucy reached for the arm of the chair and eased herself into it. "I wish I'd not been a party to this."

"I wasn't sure but that I'd need a witness." Beth listened for the sound of the front door closing. "He's gone."

"I'm sorry."

"Don't be. I'm glad it's over."

"How will you explain it to Cal?"

"I'll tell him the truth. That his father was being unfair to us, hardly ever at home and acting disagreeable and ill-tempered all the time. I'll tell him I asked him to leave so that we could enjoy some peace and contentment. Trust me, Mama, I doubt it will matter much to Cal. Nick's taken care of that."

Indeed, Cal accepted the news unquestioningly. He was excited about the trip, all the more so since Abel told him the railroad now went as far as Saint Helena itself. On the steamer to Suscol, he was full of questions about the size, the smoke, the noise of the train. Would there be lots of people to meet it at the station, he wanted to know. Would it whistle to tell everyone it was coming? Would it frighten the carriage-horses?

Lucy watched his face as the railroad clattered through the countryside. It was a picture of pure rapture. The might and bluster of the engine, the swaying and rattling of the coach, were the stuff of a small boy's dreams. She reached across the wooden seat and patted his head. "When you were younger, Calvert, there was no railroad to the valley. But before you are grown, there will be a railroad all the way across the United States, and you will be able to see the whole country from a seat like this." She took his hand in hers. "Will you promise me something?"

"Yes, Grandmama."

"Promise me you'll go. Travel as far and wide as the railroad will take you. Do it for me."

"Will you come, too?"

"I doubt it, my dear. But you will be there to see all the sights for me, and maybe you'll remember this day when you first rode on a train with your Mama and Uncle Abel and your Grandmother."

Its whistle blowing, the train pulled into Saint Helena and came to a halt with a noisy gnashing of metal, its engine belching and wheezing steam. Cal stood in the doorway, beaming as though the sounds were an ovation heralding his arrival. Beth watched as he leapt from the steps and ran toward the platform. "What was all that about telling Cal to travel across the country? He'll pester me from now 'til doomsday, wanting to go."

"No, he won't," Lucy said. "He understood."

The second vintage, Herr Schmidt announced, had yielded more and finer wine than the first, though the difference in taste was imperceptible to Lucy's palate. On the slopes, clusters of fruit buds hung on the vines, precursors of yet another harvest to come. Lucy stood with Herr Schmidt, looking over the valley as the lengthening shadows of the hills stretched across the fields below. The coolies gathered up their gear and filed back to the bunkhouse, with Cal tagging behind them.

Herr Schmidt looked after him. "It is good that the boy is happy here. Someday this will be his vineyard."

Lucy reached down and fingered a bunch of bright green buds. "Another year, another vintage. Life goes on. Yes, I expect one day this place will be Cal's pride and joy as it was Seth's and mine."

"May I walk you back to the house, my lady?"

"Go ahead, Herr Schmidt. I'll be along shortly."

The twilight was warm and still. Only the occasional sounds of the night birds broke the silence. Here and there on the valley floor, pinpoints of lamplight marked a house amid the obscured expanse of farmland.

Lucy started and turned at the sound of Abel's voice. He walked up the hill to where she stood by Seth's grave and glanced down at the marble marker glowing whitely in the faint light of the crescent moon.

"What are you doing out here alone in the dark, Mama?"

"I wanted to see what it would be like at night."

"We were beginning to worry about you. Chang's readying supper."

"I lost track of time." She took his arm, and he led the way back down the grassy incline to the path.

"Is anything wrong? You seem so pensive. It's not like you to brood."

"Age makes us all less frivolous and more thoughtful."

"I've been pondering something, too, Mama. Last week, Warren Winslow and John Fiske took me aside after the committee meeting. They asked me to consider running for mayor next year."

She halted. "But that's absurd! You'll only be twenty-five years old!"

"President Tyler began his career in the Virginia House of Delegates at twenty-one. It's not too soon for me. The truth is, though, that I wouldn't expect to win. Not this time. But John and Warren have an excellent point. They're aware I'm keen to enter politics, and they said it would be foolish to waste the splash I've made with my speeches. In their opinion, I should mount a campaign for the mayoralty so's to insure that my name and policies become indelibly imprinted on the public's mind."

"But why do it, if you think you can't win?"

"Because once I'd taken a shot at the office, my intentions would be established, and I could command continued public attention. Then, in 'seventy-one, I'd run again with a good chance of winning, Lord willing."

"That seems very far away. Must you initiate this scheme so soon?"

"Yes, if I'm to take advantage of the publicity I have at present. The object is to keep the fires burning. Warren and John are right when they say that this is a God-given opportunity."

"You know I've not much taste for politics. Ambition makes some men vicious. What if it became known that you weren't what people think you are?"

"That I wasn't your son? Mama, there's as much chance of that as there is of a blizzard in San Francisco."

"Secrets are dangerous, Abel."

"My past is long dead. To all intents and purposes, I am exactly what I appear to be."

"Putting the past away is like trying to kill a snake. You may hack it to pieces, yet it can still turn on you and strike."

"I appreciate your concern, but if that's your only argument against the proposal I shan't let it deter me. Can you think of any valid reason I shouldn't pursue the idea?"

"No, I can't," she admitted. "I presume you've discussed this with your sister."

"She's all for it." He took Lucy's hand in his. "You're chilly, Mama. Let's get back to the house."

"Abel," she asked as they made their way along the trail, "won't this cost a good deal of money, even if it's only an experimental campaign?"

"Have you forgotten that you once put over two thousand dollars in an account for me at Wells Fargo?"

"Lord have mercy!" She laughed. "The sweepings from Celia's that you converted into a small fortune at Abner Gibbs's."

"I've no intention of being in any man's debt. It's not prudent for someone in politics."

"You've obviously given this a lot of thought. Is it my permission you're after?"

"I don't need it, Mama," he reminded her gently. "It's your blessing I want."

Lucy put her arm around his waist. "You don't have to ask for that. You have it always, in this or any other endeavor. What surprises one's children deliver," she marveled. "If I could, I'd stay about forever, just to observe your adventures."

He paused in front of the porch steps. "I'll make you proud of me, no matter what happens. I promise you that."

She glanced up at him. He looked so earnest and solemn in the moonlight that for a moment her voice caught in her throat. "Come," she said. "Chang will be insulted if we keep him waiting any longer."

Lucy pushed aside the wooden bar across the press-house door and stepped inside. It was hot and stuffy from having lain closed these many months. Motes of dust stirred in the bright shafts of sunlight that streaked across the dirt floor. The mingled scents of wood and must filled her nostrils. She ran her hand absently over the stack of baskets that rested lopsidedly against the wall. A ladder leaned against the juice tub, and above it, the crushing tub lay empty, save for the pestles left there since harvest-time.

"My lady?" Herr Schmidt's shadow fell across the floor. "Excuse me. I saw the presshouse was open and could not think why."

"I wanted to look around."

"Everything is in order, I assure you."

"I'm sure it is." She shaded her eyes against the sun as she came out.

Herr Schmidt slipped the bolt across the door.

"Is Abel in the caves?" she asked him.

"*Ja*. He and Hong are packing some of the new wine to take back to the city."

"I believe I'll look in on them."

He caught up with her. "Is anything wrong, my lady?"

"Nothing, Herr Schmidt. It gives me pleasure to see what you and Seth have built. And as I don't know when I'll be back again, I want to take it all in while I'm here."

"You will return for the harvest, won't you?"

"I don't know. I may not be able to come this year, but Abel will. I'm sure of that. Herr Schmidt—" She stopped and turned to face him. "Without you, this vineyard would not exist. I want you to know that I am forever grateful."

He bowed. "You are most kind."

"There's no way I can ever fully show my appreciation, but I've taken steps to insure that you and Frau Schmidt are provided for, so long as either of you lives on this land."

"My lady—" He shook his head in consternation. "I do not know what to say."

"I'd be obliged if you'd say nothing." She continued along the path. "I trust you'll keep this conversation confidential."

"As you wish, ma'am." He paused as they drew abreast of his cottage. "On behalf of my Anna and myself, I thank you."

"It's the least I can do, Herr Schmidt." She went on, sensing his eyes upon her as she walked away.

The wine was packed in hampers and loaded onto the

705

carriage. Abel and Chang carried the bags from the house and set them in the boot. Cal, eager for the train ride, had already climbed into his seat, clutching a parcel of candied fruits from Frau Schmidt. Lucy took her seat beside him. As Abel helped Beth up, Lucy reached down for Chang's hand and shook it. He seemed embarrassed by the gesture and looked away.

"Take good care of the place, Chang."

"Yes, missee. You please tell Lin I plant some Chinese vegetables out back. They came up good, maybe I send some down city."

"I'll tell her."

As the carriage circled the drive, Beth turned to take a parting look at the house. "How pretty it is, Mama, with the morning glories in bloom along the porch."

"Yes," she replied. But she did not look back.

XXXVII

WHEN HARVEST-time came, Lucy remained behind on Bush Street, while Beth and Abel journeyed to Saint Helena to oversee the work. With Cal in school, the house was quiet, yet she found it difficult to rest. Silence held no peace for her anymore. It was no longer something comforting, inside which she might take her ease as if wrapped in a warm, familiar quilt. It was her enemy now, encircling her like some formidable, soft-footed animal, tense and hungry, waiting expectantly, imperturbably, to claim its prey. Her strength was failing, though the doctors professed amazement that her condition had deteriorated so little in the past few months.

"I am staying longer at this party than you thought," she told them, "and I'm still having a pretty good time of it."

"I'm happy to hear that," Doctor Vanderhoef said with a smile.

"Speaking of parties, Abel is having a group of gentlemen for dinner when he returns next week, to discuss his plans for entering politics. Would you and Doctor Blake care to come?"

"Unfortunately, I shall be in Sacramento," Doctor Blake replied.

"I'd be interested in hearing what he has to say."

"Good, Martin. Seven o'clock on Friday next."

"I'll be there. Do you hear anything from Nick, Lucy?"

"Not a word. But Boyd told Bethie that he's become so sullen and bitter that he's hardly the same person. He's grown difficult to work with, he said. The men at the Iron Works try to avoid him. You've no idea, Martin, how angry Nick makes me. He is bent on destroying his life, and here am I, hanging onto the ragged shreds of mine with all my might. What I wouldn't give for the thing he takes so lightly."

"And how is Beth?"

"Too busy to mourn the past, I'm glad to say. She's occupied with Abel's plans. You'll see her next week. She serves as his hostess for these affairs."

"You'll be there as well, I trust."

"If I feel up to it, though I shan't stay long. I'm of no use in these situations. I'm ignorant of politics."

Abel paced the floor in front of the fireplace. "Mama, surely you'll offer your endorsement this evening. It would mean a great deal to me."

"Why? We women don't vote. What do our opinions matter?"

"Don't talk poppycock," Beth snapped. "Your support is important. You're respected. You've been a success at business. You're known for your services to the community. Besides, how would it look if you didn't endorse Abel's aims?"

"Your brother is more conservative in his view than I. I shan't lie to further any man's ambitions, even if he is my son."

"But Mama," Beth persisted, "couldn't you find some way to let people know that you advocate his running for mayor?"

"Leave her alone, Bethie. Don't badger her."

"All right," Lucy relented. "I shan't compromise, but I shan't do any harm to your plans."

As she came down from her room that evening, she paused at the foot of the stairs, listening to the voices of the guests in the drawing room. She could distinguish Simon Waite's bass, like the rumble of a pipe organ, under the tones of John Fiske and Hiram Berry. She could hear Warren Winslow's slightly nasal delivery and the unmistakable laughter of Albert Fearing. Lucy took a deep breath and raised herself erect. It would not do for them to guess that she was a sickly woman with blood like weak tea.

Joe Mason stood in the doorway to the drawing room. For a second, as she approached him, a peculiar look crossed his face. So, Lucy thought, it begins to show. She

708

gave him a cheerful smile. "How good to see you, Joe. How long has it been?"

"Almost a year. You're looking well," he lied.

"I'm feeling a little under the weather. I only came downstairs to bestow a brief, motherly blessing."

"You've not lost your healthy sense of humor, I see." He gave her hand a squeeze.

Abel came forward and took her arm in his. "Friends my mother has a few words to say."

Dabney Stevens and Solomon Brock stepped aside, making way for her. Martin Vanderhoef rose and motioned her to his chair.

"Gentleman," she said, laughing, "I'm honored. You part before me as though I were Moses at the sea."

Abel stood beside her chair. Lucy reached up and took his hand in hers.

"I daresay my son has made his intentions known to all of you."

"Hear, hear," Joe Mason called.

Albert pounded the floor with his cane, as the others applauded and nodded their approval.

"I'd be making a certified fool of myself if I pretended to know anything about politics. But I have lived in this city for as long as any of you. I have observed the character of its politicians, good and bad. As I see it, gentlemen, there are three kinds: those who want to win office for the glory of it, those who want to win for what they can steal and those who are bent on serving the public good. I repeat, I know nothing of politics, but I do know my son as only a mother can. He is of the last category. He is sensible and principled. He cares deeply about our city. And he is utterly determined to faithfully serve its citizens as their mayor one day. That is all I have to say, my friends. I leave the rest to you."

"Bravo!" John Fiske exclaimed.

Abel bent to kiss Lucy's cheek.

"Good luck," she whispered. "Give me a hand up the stairs, would you? I'm feeling a bit weak in the knees."

Beth ran to her and embraced her. "You were wonderful."

"Enjoy your dinner, gentlemen." Lucy shook each of their hands as she left the room. "Do you know," she said to Abel as they reached the hall, "I feel the same way I did on the day I saw Bethie married. We parents must fi-

709

nally deliver our children's fate into the hands of others. It's like losing a part of oneself forever."

Abel put an arm around her shoulders. "You've not lost me, Mama, or Beth either. Nothing will ever come between us."

It was not true, she knew. A shadow was falling between her and the children, between the dying and the living, but she hadn't the heart yet to tell Abel and Beth. Sometimes, when she came upon someone she hadn't seen for months, she would see the same expression she'd seen that evening on Joe Mason's face. It was insidious, this disease, so gradual and subtle in its subversion that not even Lucy, studying herself in the mirror, could discern its daily toll upon her. She could measure her decline only in that first shock of concern she saw on the faces of others. She made excuses for her appearance, claiming fatigue or a stomach upset, which seemed to suffice. At least, she thought, I shan't have them flapping and hissing about me like vultures waiting for the end.

Lucy raised her head from her pillows and glanced at the clock. It was almost eight. She closed her eyes again, dredging her thoughts out of the opaque drowsiness that still clung to her. It is Wednesday, she thought. It is October. And by God, I am still here.

She donned her robe and opened the curtains. The morning was warm and still. A thick, opalescent fog lay wrapped about the house, unruffled by so much as a whisper of wind. She went to her dressing table and reached for her hairbrush.

With a thunderous, hollow rumble, the ground beneath the house lurched sharply sideways. Lucy staggered backwards and was hurled across the bed. Above her, a long, thin crack snaked across the ceiling. The water pitcher fell from the bedside table, splattering her face. The objects on her dressing table skated from side to side as the house righted itself. The earth continued to shudder, then suddenly jerked sideways once again. Lucy seized the bedpost and held fast to it. A shower of plaster sifted down on her. She held her breath in terror, as the house groaned like a living thing being torn asunder. It heaved and shivered and finally was still. She raised herself on her elbows. The floor was littered with shards from the broken pitcher. The clock, her comb, brush, hand-mirror and hairpins lay scattered about the room. She reached down and picked up her pearl and diamond brooch from under the rocking chair. As she rose, she started at the sight of the hoary apparition in the mirror, then realized that her hair was full of plaster.

The door to the dressing room flew open, and Lin ran in.

"Be careful!" Lucy warned. "Don't cut your feet."

"Missee—" Lin gasped.

"I know. It's the worst I've ever felt. Fetch your slippers before your hurt yourself."

Lucy went out into the hall. Abel emerged from his room, his shirt open, his trousers half-buttoned.

"Good Lord," he said. "For a moment, I was afraid it would never stop. I thought we were finished."

Cal's door opened, and he stood peering into the hallway, his face white, his eyes wide with fear. He tried to speak, but the words would not come. Abel went to him and held him close.

"Easy now, Calvert. There's no need to be frightened anymore."

"Hallo!" Septimus called from downstairs. "Anybody hurt up there? Miz' Slade? You folks all right?"

"Yes," she replied. "What about you and Biddy?"

"Biddy burnt her hand from the bacon fat, but it ain't bad. The house sure is a sight, though. Your fancy china tea set's a goner, Miz' Slade. Ain't a whole piece left to it."

"Never mind, Septimus. It's not worth fretting about." Suddenly, she turned to Abel. "Bethie! Where is she?"

They ran into her room. She lay sprawled on the floor at the foot of her bed, clad only in her petticoat and camisole. Abel lifted her onto the rumpled sheets.

"Is she hurt?" Cal cried.

"There are no marks on her. Mama, fetch some salts."

Lucy ran back to her bedroom, searching for the phial of salts amid the welter of debris strewn across the floor.

"It's all right," Abel said as she returned. "She fainted, that's all."

Beth smiled weakly. "I felt as though my heart was going to burst with fright."

Abel stroked her temples. "So did I. It was a bad one, for sure."

She started to sit up, but he took her gently by her bare shoulders and pushed her back against the pillows.

"Rest a minute, angel. You're as pale as chalk. Lie there and catch your breath. I'll fetch some brandy from the library."

He returned with the bottle and three mismatched glasses, as Lin led Cal away to finish dressing. "You won't believe the destruction down there, Mama. Septimus says the pantry looks like it was raining china and glass." He seated himself on the bed and poured a drink for each of them. "The library smells like Hotaling's distillery."

Lucy began to laugh.

"What's so funny?" Beth asked.

"It's wonderful!" she answered, her voice bubbling over. "The devil with the damage! We're alive! We're unharmed!" She raised her glass. "To life!"

Abel drained his drink and set it on the table. He took Beth's hand in his. "Feeling better?"

"Much."

"You gave me a dreadful start when I saw you lying there."

"I'm sorry . . ."

"Don't be." He raised her hand and kissed it. "All that matters is that you weren't hurt." He stood up from the bed and stuffed his shirt into his trousers. "I'd best go help Septimus clear the dining room for breakfast."

The house, as Abel had warned her, was an unholy mess. Not a single room had escaped undamaged. But, as if to remind them of their good futrne, more tremors followed intermittently, some strong, some slight.

Lucy raised the windows in the library, as Septimus rolled up the whiskey-stained carpet. The fog had gone, but in its place a low cloud of gray-brown dust hovered over the city like a premature, unnatural dusk.

Abel had hardly left for the office when he returned. "They're not letting anyone into the building until they're sure it's safe. They've had to abandon the hospital on Rincon Point, and there are scores of people in the public squares, afraid to go back to their homes until the shaking stops."

"Was anyone killed?"

"As many as five, I heard. It's worst where they've filled in the bay. That 'made' land isn't as solid as the rest of the city. By the way, I stopped at the Good Shepherd

712

on my way home. There's a lot of breakage, but nobody was injured."

"That's a blessing," she said, sweeping the last fragments of glass into her dustpan.

"Mama, how much money do you have in the house?"

"Almost a hundred dollars, I think. Why?"

"Would you loan it to me? I'll see if I can borrow some from Bethie, too. I've a little over two hundred in my strongbox upstairs."

"What do you intend to do with it?"

"Those people camping out in the public squares need to be fed. I thought I'd try to persuade the local merchants to pitch in, if I defrayed some of the cost."

"My dear, it's hardly your responsibility."

"And the city's homeless children weren't yours, but you saw the need and came to their help."

She laid her broom aside. "I'll go with you."

"Are you sure you feel up to it?"

"After what happened this morning, I feel as though I've been given a second lease on life."

The sun, filtering through the dustcloud overhead had a peculiar bronze cast to it. They made their way in the eerie light to the heart of the city, past toppled chimneys, ruptured, twisted fences and walls of brick fallen like toy blocks across the sidewalks and streets. They skirted chunks of cornices, some as large as boulders. Doors and windows listed precariously, and splintered glass chinkled and crunched under the wheels of the carriage. Here and there, archways had collapsed, leaving jagged, yawning gaps heaped with rubble. At the corner of Dupont Street, Abel hailed a man driving a wagonload of furnishings, atop which perched two little girls.

"Sir! Where are you bound?" Abel called out.

"My sister's house on Geary. Ain't much left of ours."

"You know the grocery on Sacramento and Kearny?"

"Goldberg's? The place that used to be Kroenig's?"

"That's the one. I'd like to hire you and that wagon for the rest of the day, if you'll meet me there at one o'clock."

"How much?"

"Five dollars. Ask for Abel Bates."

"Done. Aaron Trist, at your service." He clucked to his horse and drove on.

Mr. Goldberg listened in silence, his brows furrowed,

as Abel told him what he wanted. Lucy glanced about the store. Every shelf, it appeared, had disgorged its contents upon the floor. Two clerks were busy trying to restore order to the jumble of sacks and boxes and broken bottles.

Mr. Goldberg stroked his chin thoughtfully. "Enough to tide these people over, you say?"

"Nothing fancy, sir. Just so's they aren't hungry."

"Fellows," he called to his clerks, "bring me every tin of biscuits we have. And all the cheeses. I've another store on Pine," he told Abel. "I'll give you the same from there."

"I don't want to clean you out, Mr. Goldberg."

"I've more in the warehouse."

"About the cost—"

"You can have the lot at what it cost me, if," he said, raising a finger, "you'd be so kind as to say where it came from. Advertising never hurts, Mr. Bates. Say, there's a friend of mine down the street got a big shipment of bananas from Panama a few days ago. Let's stroll over and have a word with him."

By early afternoon, Abel and Lucy, followed by Aaron Trist, set about making the rounds of the campsites. A hastily lettered sign affixed to one side of the wagon read: "Biscuits and Cheeses—Jacob Goldberg; Jerked Beef—Mordecai Coe; Bananas—Bernard Hooks."

A cheer went up from the disheveled, anxious people huddled on their coats and blankets on the grass. They quickly lined up behind the tailboard of the wagon, amazed and grateful. Some smiled broadly and others had tears in their eyes as Abel, Lucy and Aaron Trist doled out their goods.

"It won't fatten you up any," Abel called out to the crowd, "but you'll not starve."

Over and over, Lucy noticed, the same dialogue was repeated. "Which one are you?" they'd ask Abel. "Goldberg, Coe or Hooks?"

"Abel Bates is the name. Happy to be your host."

"We'll not forget this."

"I hope not. I'll be running for mayor next year, and I'll be needing friends like you."

"Did you plan that?" Lucy asked him as they turned homeward in the sunset, waving farewell to Aaron Trist and his empty wagon.

"Did I plan what?"

"To use this disaster to your political advantage."

"You know me better than that. But when they asked who I was, I remembered what Mr. Goldberg said about advertising. I reckoned it wouldn't do any harm. I meant what I said. I'll be needing their support."

"You're a politician, by heaven. That's obvious, though only God knows where you came by such a personality."

"It's purely enterprise, Mama. Learned from the most enterprising person I know. Yourself."

"No, sir! Don't blame me for spawning a politician. You children are well beyond my influence. Power passes from one generation to another; that's the way of life. Lately, I feel like a leaf caught up in this whirlwind of yours."

By nightfall, the house was at least comfortable, if not presentable. There were two light tremors, one at seven, another an hour later, and then, blessedly, calm.

"Not a word from Nick," Beth observed bitterly, "not even a line to inquire if Cal was safe and unharmed. We might as well not exist, for all he cares. What is that bird that sticks its head in the sand?"

"An ostrich," Abel replied, looking up from his reading. "Why?"

"That's Nick. It's easier for him not to face facts."

"Bethie," Lucy cautioned her, "don't go setting yourself on a pedestal. The truth is often hard to bear, and it makes no exceptions."

"If he ignores our existence, I shall ignore his."

It hurt Beth, Lucy knew, to see Thanksgiving and Christmas pass without so much as a word from Nick to Cal, much less a gift to mark the boy's birthday. Were it not for Abel, she thought, those two would be desolate. He was far more understanding and attentive to the child than Nick had been at his best. And brother and sister were so close that it sometimes seemed to her that they thought with one mind and spoke with a single voice. Even their gestures were alike. They laughed at the same jokes and they worked and played together as congenially as they had as children, save that now their common goal was Abel's political career and their diversions were lectures, concerts and plays.

"You must let me have a look at you before you leave

for the theatre," Lucy called from her bed as Beth passed by in the hall. "How I wish I felt up to going with you."

For months, she, like the rest of San Francisco, had watched with a mixture of curiosity and fascination as William Ralston's California Theatre rose down the street, just this side of the junction of Bush and Kearny. It was vast, imposing and lavish. Above the entrance, marked by a pair of massive, ornate lamps, was a long, graceful colonnade with towering arched windows, a sight that reminded Lucy of the pictures she'd seen of stately Greek temples. People talked in hushed tones of what it must be costing Billy Ralston to erect this monument to the arts, though no one asked. The millionaire's penchant for magnificence was becoming a legend, and the city was content to be the beneficiary of this latest expression of his extravagance. After the grand opening, there was to be a masked ball. Beth and Abel had conspired, amid whispers and laughter, to go in complementary costumes.

"I'll give you a hint," Beth said, poking her head into Lucy's room. "We're dressing in honor of John McCullough, since he's the star of tonight's play. What does that tell you?"

"McCullough? He's most famous for his Shakespeare. Not Othello and Desdemona, surely?"

"I shan't say another word."

When they were dressed, Cal ran in and perched expectantly on Lucy's bed. "They're ready, Grandmama!"

"Shut your eyes, both of you," Abel called.

Lucy heard the swishing of silks as they tiptoed into the room.

"Now," Beth said, "open your eyes."

With a sweeping flourish, Abel doffed his plumed, velvet hat. Beth, in pale pink, her hair garlanded with flowers, made a low curtsy.

"But who are you?" Cal asked.

"Romeo and Juliet."

"Who are they?"

"You'll read about them someday," Lucy told him. "Whose idea was it to go as Romeo and Juliet?"

"Mine," Beth answered.

"But only after I refused to play Puck," Abel added.

"You look very handsome, both of you. What's the play this evening?"

"Bulwer-Lytton's *Money*."

"How appropriate," Lucy said. "The thing Billy Ralston loves best. Well, run along, you two, and enjoy yourselves. I shall want to hear all about it."

Beth was still aglow with excitement the next morning. "There's never been anything like it, Mama! You should have seen the procession of carriages—barouches and clarences with liveried coachmen, and the passengers wearing all manner of elegant costumes. Just everyone was there. The Stanfords, the Floods, the Fairs, even Emperor Norton! There were white camellias everywhere and beautiful paintings on the walls and huge, dazzling crystal chandeliers and—"

"Don't forget the curtain," Abel prompted her.

"You should see it, Mama. It's a painted panorama of our bay, that makes you feel as though you're standing on a balcony overlooking the entire coast."

"The Ralston touch," she observed. "It sounds as if he didn't miss a trick."

"The Winslows and the Gallaghers sent you their regards," Abel told Lucy. "Mrs. Winslow means to stop by for a visit. She heard you weren't well."

"Oh, dear. Amy is difficult enough to endure under the best of circumstances."

Beth's smile faded. "Mama, you know I don't want to meddle, but I've been intending to ask you if you don't think it might be wise to see another doctor. This seems as good a time as any to bring it up. Perhaps Doctor Vanderhoef doesn't—"

"I have complete faith in him, my dear."

"Bethie and I think you're making a mistake not to consult someone else. We're both concerned that you don't seem to be getting any stronger. If you won't consent, Mama, I'll have to take it upon myself to make some inquiries and invite another doctor to come have a look at you."

"No," she said hastily. "As a matter of fact, Martin has called in another man. Doctor James Blake. His reputation is impeccable."

"Why didn't you mention it?"

"My health is my affair."

"Not when it worries Abel and me to see you so weak."

"What did Doctor Blake say?"

"He's not sure of anything just yet," she lied. "It's evi-

717

dently rather complex, but I expect we'll know what ails me in due time. I assure you, worrying won't do any good."

"Do you think you'll be able to hear Abel address the Presbyterians tomorrow evening?"

"It won't be a long speech, Mama. That's why I'd particularly hoped you'd come. And there will be ladies present this time."

"I'll be there. You see?" Lucy smiled at them. "Not even Billy Ralston's opulence can tempt me like a speech by Abel Bates."

Amy Winslow placed her teacup and saucer on the table and pressed her napkin to her lips. Age, Lucy observed, had softened her face, giving her features a slightly melted look, like those on a marble statue perennially exposed to the elements.

"Lucy," she said, laying her napkin aside, "I've not seen Nicholas lately. Every time I meet up with Beth, she's with her brother. There's nothing wrong, I hope."

"He's no longer living here, Amy. He and Beth came to a parting of the ways."

She seemed taken aback. "I'm sorry to hear it. How sad. First Selina and now Nick, and you feeling unwell, too. But I must say," she added brightening, "Beth seemed in excellent spirits when I saw her Thursday evening. My twin sister, Florinda, who's visiting with us, thought her quite the most beautiful woman there." She laughed. "She asked me when they were going to be married."

"Who?"

"Beth and Abel. 'How well suited to each other they are,' she said. She assumed they were engaged. A perfectly natural mistake. Watching them together, anyone might have made the same error. But under the circumstances," she said with a sudden frown, "I wonder."

"Wonder what? Under what circumstances?"

"Now that you tell me Nick and Beth are living apart, do you think it is altogether discreet of her and Abel to come dressed as Romeo and Juliet?"

"For pity's sake, Amy, they're brother and sister."

"Of course. Perhaps that's where the difficulty lies. They're obviously so close to each other and so affectionate toward each other that it must be hard for a husband or wife to compete with that affinity. Poor Warren told

718

me when he married me that Florinda and I were so close, being twins, that he felt like an interloper coming between us."

"Amy, any speculation about Beth's or Abel's marriage is just that. Speculation. And any talk about them is gossip. In my opinion, gossip is nothing more than the mischief of idle minds."

"I had no intention of prying!"

"Forgive me. Perhaps I'm overly protective of my children."

"I should say so! You pounced on me like a she-bear."

"My apologies. Amy, I don't mean to be rude, but will you understand if I tell you that I must rest now? I promised Abel I'd hear his speech tonight, and I'm afraid I shan't be up to it if I don't rest beforehand."

"You're not angry with me, are you?"

"Should I be?"

"I was only curious as to how two such auspicious marriages could go amiss."

"Then you must address your questions to the children. It's not my place to speak for them." Lucy stood up from her chair. "Please give my regards to Warren."

Amy hesitated a moment. "It was Warren who wanted me to ask."

"Warren? But why? Can't he talk to Abel?"

"Lucy, it's my turn to apologize." She rose and took Lucy's hands in hers. "I don't actually know why he wanted me to draw you out on the subject, but now I'm angry that I consented. I hope with all my heart that you'll not hold it against me. I assure you, whatever Warren's motives, he was acting in Abel's interests. Are we still friends?"

Lucy kissed her cheek. "We've known each other too long to be anything else."

Amy gazed at her at length, her hands still clasping Lucy's. "Do take care of yourself."

Lucy looked around the crowded hall, trying to discern the effects of Abel's speech from the expressions on the faces about her. The listeners were attentive and respectful, occasionally applauding or murmuring agreement with his words. She herself felt a mingling of wonder and pride at seeing this unfamiliar, public side of him. It was,

719

she reflected, no less an essential part of him than the private side she knew so well. In fact, perhaps this speaker, this aspiring public servant who so engrossed his audience, was far closer to the truth of Abel's nature than the dutiful, affectionate son she knew. For here, in public, his dreams found expression. Here, he rose to stand before these people in an act of faith in himself, faith in their response and faith in the future of this city they shared. In the earnest passion of his pledge to them, he laid open his most cherished hopes. Watching him, Lucy realized that he was not so much her son but his own man. And in this public side of him, the inmost properties of his character were illuminated.

"This city and I," he was saying, "grew up together. We came of age together. Though we are still young, it is time for us to assume a position of responsible leadership. I put it to you, however, that such a position must be earned. That," he said, smiling, "in part explains my appearance before you tonight."

Lucy glanced at Beth. The girl's face was raised toward the rostrum in such admiration that it reminded Lucy of a rose turned toward the sun. For some reason, Beth's expression disturbed her. She returned her gaze to Abel.

"Before we can point with rightful pride to our city, we must eliminate the rot that would infect and corrupt it, blighting its potential just as surely as a tree-rot warps and blasts and finally brings down one of nature's noblest examples of all that is lofty, strong and fruitful. But before we can do this, we must be willing to identify and confront that corruption which threatens to pervert our greatness. This is why, ladies and gentlemen, I have brought these facts and figures to your attention this evening. Not to shock you, not to dismay you, not to dishearten you. Rather, to point out the urgency of taking action. We, you and I, *are* this city, for without us, its people, it would be a vacant pile of wood and brick, left to the ravages of time. We citizens of San Francisco are the heart and soul that inspire it with human life. And we are, each of us, responsible for the quality of that life. Every day, every moment wasted, in effect condones and abets the forces that would bring us down. There is no time to be lost. The future takes shape at this very hour. Soon the transcontinental railroad will bring thousands more to settle on these shores. I ask you: what will they find here? Will they find law? Or will they find chaos? It falls to us to provide the answer." He paused. "Thank you."

There was an explosion of applause. Beth's cheeks were flushed with excitement. "Wasn't he superb, Mama? Hear how they clap and cheer!"

Lucy raised her voice over the tumult. "What an ovation! I can scarcely believe that remarkable man is my son."

"Isn't he an inspiring speaker? No wonder he's becoming so influential. Just think!" Beth explained. "Someday when Abel is mayor, we shall be the first family of San Francisco."

Lucy regarded her thoughtfully. "That would please you, Bethie, wouldn't it."

"Of course! I'd think it grand to play hostess for all those important meetings and receptions."

Lucy reached over and took her hand. "Tell me," she asked, suddenly solemn, "is that one of the reasons you encourage him so enthusiastically? Be truthful with me, Bethie. I know your character too well not to realize how much that sort of pomp means to you."

"Great heavens, Mama." She looked dismayed. "Do you think I'm some kind of parasite, feeding off Abel's ambitions? How could you say such a thing? I want the office for his sake. He deserves it. And this city deserves to have a splendid leader like Abel. I only meant that we'd enjoy it, too."

"You, perhaps. I am past enjoying power. But make no mistake, young lady. If I thought you were manipulating Abel for your own purposes, I would speak out very sharply."

"I couldn't do that, Mama. I love him too much."

"And who's to say he won't take himself another wife in the meantime?"

Beth raised her eyes to the speaker's platform where Abel stood, his arms outstretched to the audience. She watched him for a moment as he nodded and smiled in acknowledgment of the lingering applause. "He wouldn't do that," she said.

Oddly, Lucy knew she was right.

"Bang!"

Lucy started, as Cal ran into the sitting room, blowing

721

an imaginary puff of smoke from the barrel of his wooden rifle. "Guess who I am, Grandmama!"

"Johnny Reb, perhaps?"

"I'm Buffalo Bill Cody!"

"Are you, now? How many buffalo have you killed?"

"Twenty hundred."

"Did you eat them?"

He grimaced. "They're too ugly to eat."

She smiled. "Ah, but you're wrong, Calvert. Buffalo steaks are very tasty."

He sat on the floor in front of her chair. "Did you ever have them?"

"Yes, indeed. And drank the milk, too. And slept under a buffalo robe."

"Was that when you walked to California?"

She nodded. "Sometimes we ate mule, too. It wasn't very good, but it was all the food we had. And we drank melted snow because we had no water."

"And the Diggers attacked you."

"That's right."

"Were you scared?"

"Very."

"Here, son," Septimus said from the hallway, "don't be plaguing your Grandmama. You know she needs her rest. You come keep Biddy and me company in the kitchen 'til Lin comes home." He glanced worriedly at Lucy. "You all right, ma'am?"

"Yes, thank you. Where did Lin go?"

"She jes' took a little walk, ma'am, with a friend."

"The boy may stay with me, Septimus. He's no bother."

"Yes'm. Calvert," he warned him, "don't you go jumpin' about and makin' your Grandmama tired, you hear?"

"I won't," he promised soberly. "She's telling me about the olden days."

Sometimes he would sit quietly for hours, listening to Lucy's reminiscences. He liked to hear about the trackless prairie and how the wagons were hauled up the Sierras. He was full of curiosity about the Miwok children she'd taught and how gold came to be in the rivers. His was such a different life, she reflected, a city life of street railways, gas lamps and man-made wonders like Woodward's Gardens. "How fast the world changes," she murmured, more to herself than the boy.

"Will my world change, too?"

"I'm sure it will. Let's see, when you are my age, it will be nineteen-ought-one. You'll be living in another century, Calvert. Think of that." She stopped abruptly, catching sight of Lin in the hall. "Mercy, Lin, what on earth are you wearing? Come, let me look at you."

Lin hung back in the shadows of the hallway. She was dressed in black cotton trousers, a pale blue jacket and cotton slippers. "You don't like Chinese clothes?"

"It's not that, dear. It's only that I'm not used to seeing you in them."

"They were a gift. From the wife of Wah Ming."

"The fruit vendor? Why would his wife send you clothes when you don't need them?"

Lin shrugged and looked acutely self-conscious.

"They're most becoming, dear," Lucy reassured her. "Run along with Lin now, Calvert. Your Grandmother is all talked out." Lucy closed her eyes and leaned back in her chair. Even the mere effort of entertaining the boy wearied her.

She had meant to rest there for only a few minutes, but when she opened her eyes the room was in darkness. She could hear Beth and Abel talking quietly across the hall. After a moment, they came into view, standing together in the drawing room doorway, silhouetted by the lamplight behind them. Beth laughed softly. Lucy sat upright, her hand on the arm of her chair, suddenly alert. Something in Beth's low, whispered laughter unsettled her, a sound as ominous to her ears as the rustling of leaves on a windless day. Lucy watched as Abel turned back into the room and Beth walked away toward the stairs. She frowned, wondering what it was in that innocent exchange that had troubled her.

Lucy emerged from the darkened room. The drawing room was empty, and the door to the library beyond was closed. Abel had closeted himself with his papers and law books, working, as usual, until suppertime.

In the dining room, Septimus was setting the table. He glanced up as she passed by. "You have a good nap, ma'am? I didn't light the lamps in there for fear of wakin' you."

"Thank you, Septimus. I believe I'll take my supper in bed this evening. Would you or Biddy be kind enough to lay a tray for me?"

He put down his handful of knives and forks and came

723

to her side. "Take my arm, Miz' Slade. I'll help you up the stairs."

"Tell me," she asked him as they reached the top, "does Miss Bethie seem happy to you?"

"Yes, indeed. I ain't seen her so cheerful since Mister Nick used to come courtin' her."

"That was my impression, too. Perhaps I am not so daft after all."

He chuckled as he turned and went back down. "You ain't got no worry on that account. You're jes' about the sanest woman I ever did see."

"That's what I was afraid of," she said softly.

XXXVIII

On FAIR days, the sun shining through the window panes cast a lattice work of light and shadow across her coverlet. From her bed, Lucy watched the clouds floating inland, buffeted by winds from the sea, drifting across the valleys, mountains and deserts to the east. Sometimes, her thoughts drifted with them, and she saw once again in her mind's eye vast vistas of plains, peaks and barren wastelands lying under the same blue sky that now hung like a painting on her wall, encased by the window between the fireplace and her dressing table.

Beth knocked at her door and brought in the newspaper. She laid it on Lucy's bed. "Mama, Mr. Winslow is downstairs."

"To see me?"

"No. He wanted to speak with Abel. Mama, I think something's wrong. He looked upset. What would bring him calling without notice on a Sunday afternoon?"

"Was Abel's speech well received last night?"

"As far as I know."

"Then I shouldn't fret. Maybe you're mistaken. Maybe he was only preoccupied."

"I'm scared, Mama."

Lucy glanced at her. "What is there to be scared of?"

Beth shook her head. "I don't know. I can't seem to grasp it. I feel as though something were going to happen."

"Silly girl, something always happens. Is it me you're worried about?"

"Yes," she confessed, "but it's something else, too. I feel as if it's like an earthquake, something I can't prevent."

I pray it's not an earthquake. That's hardly a rosy—"

Beth. Mama. May I come in?" Abel looked from one
e other. "I'm not interrupting anything, am I?"
ethie told me Warren was here."
            nodded. "I don't quite know what to make of his
            He sat down in the rocker, a perplexed expression
on his face. "He wanted to know if I was keeping anything from him that might hurt my prospects."

"What did you tell him?"

"I asked him to be more precise. I wasn't sure what he
meant."

"And?" Lucy held her breath.

"Of all things, he wanted to know if there was any
scandal connected with Selina's leaving San Francisco."

"Selina?" Beth looked incredulous. "She'd be the last
person in the world to be involved in anything scandalous."

"I'm not sure that's what he meant." Abel frowned.
"I'm not at all sure what he did mean. He wouldn't say.
He told me that a friend of his at the *Bulletin* came to
him with an anonymous letter that had been mailed to the
paper."

"Did you see it?" Lucy wanted to know.

"He didn't bring it. He said if what was in it was untrue, there was no reason to trouble any of us."

"But what did it say?" Beth demanded.

"It contained what Warren called 'scurrilous innuendos'
about the reasons for Selina's departure. That was all I
could get out of him."

"Who would want to slander Selina? And why?" Lucy
asked. "She's been gone for over a year."

"I don't think it was aimed at Selina, Mama. It was me
they were after."

"I trust the *Bulletin* doesn't give much credence to
anonymous letters."

"Of course not. But evidently, when Warren discussed
the letter with John Fiske, John confided that he'd heard
the same rumors. He'd dismissed them as nonsense."

"Don't you think you ought to see John?"

Abel put his hands on his knees and pushed himself up
from the chair. "The sooner the better, I guess."

"Son . . ." Lucy reached up and took his hand as he
passed. "Politics is a dirty business. There will always be
someone to throw mud. You'd best learn quickly how to

respond to this sort of thing. It's a pity, I know, but you mustn't avoid the issue."

"That's the hell of it, Mama. If I knew what it was, I could put the matter to rest. Talking with Warren, I felt as though I were wrestling with a phantom. Well," he said, squaring his shoulders, "let's see what I can pry out of John."

Toward evening, Lucy felt well enough to dress and go downstairs for supper. Though these rare excursions tired her, it seemed somehow essential to reaffirm that, weak as she was, she was not yet, by God, incapacitated.

At the sight of her, Septimus rushed to the bottom of the stairs and ushered her into the drawing room. "What you mean, comin' down them stairs by yourself when all of us is here to help? You put a fright into me. What if you'd chanced to fall?"

Lucy cut him off with a wave of her hand. "Yes, yes, yes, I know. Quit braying at me, Septimus. My patience isn't what it used to be, either."

Muttering an inaudible protest, he knelt to light a fire in the grate. The stoop of his shoulders seemed more pronounced than ever, and the white frost at his temples forecast the winter of his years. He rose slowly from the hearth, grasping the mantel to steady himself.

"Ah, Septimus," Lucy said quietly, "our dancing days are over, I'm afraid."

He nodded ruefully. Slowly, his face creased with amusement, and he shook his head from side to side, softly. "You sure danced fine, ma'am, and you learnt me to dance fine into the bargain. I taught Biddy every step. Hanged if that old woman of mine can't still tread light n' quick as a butterfly."

"Oh." Beth appeared in the doorway, looking disappointed. "I heard voices. I thought Abel was back."

"You keep your Mama company, Miss Bethie. I got to get back to work."

Beth seated herself at the piano. "Mama, what would you like to hear? Some Beethoven, perhaps?"

"Something loud and lusty."

"Lusty?"

"And gay."

"If you say so." With a flourish of her fingers, she struck up "Oh, Susannah," and by the time she launched into "Billy Boy" they were both singing.

727

Can she bake a cherry pie, Billy Boy, Billy Boy?
Can she bake a cherry pie, charming Billy?

"What the devil?" Abel strode into the room, visibly confounded by the racket. Seeing Lucy, he smiled. "I declare, Mama, I should have known. This house is a sight quieter when you're confined to your bed. Why, it sounded just now like I was walking into the Bella Union melodeon."

Beth jumped up from the piano. "Never mind that. What did John Fiske have to say?"

His gaze faltered slightly. "Nothing worth discussing."

"But surely you can tell us."

"Rot, that's all. What's for supper?"

Beth frowned. "Abel, what's the matter? Don't try to evade the issue."

"Someone is spreading false rumors. Damnable, dirty, outrageous lies."

"Then it's nothing to do with Castalia," Lucy said.

"No."

"Was it about Selina?" Beth asked.

"Not really."

"But if it's untrue," Lucy told him, "you need only expose the rumors and refute them categorically."

"No. I wouldn't foul the air with such filth, not even in the privacy of this room."

"But something must be done," Beth argued. "Who on earth would spread obscenities about you?"

"Almost anyone who'd stand to lose by seeing the Barbary Coast purged. That means every crimp, crooked gambler and whore-monger in the city, not to mention their patrons. A few thousand people, more or less."

"Is there no way you can get to the bottom of this?" Lucy asked him.

"I need to find Nick."

"Nick?" Beth looked astonished. "But why Nick?"

He hesitated a moment, then sank resignedly into a chair. "Because," he said, his voice strained, "every damned one of these insinuations bears the echo of his voice. He frequents those places, Bethie. You know how he can rave on. If he's been spewing venom at the gaming tables, there are plenty of ears to pick it up and too many tongues to repeat it."

"You're the last person in the world he wants to see," Beth said. "Don't expect him to be cooperative."

"I daresay he'll cooperate if I threaten to sue him for slander."

"I beg you, Son, don't indict Nick for this on the basis of coincidence. You're only guessing."

"That's why I have to talk to him. If he's not at fault, maybe he knows who is."

Beth leaned over the back of his chair and laid her hands on his shoulders. "Do what you must."

Abel reached up and clasped her hands in his. "Dearest Bethie, how I wish to God it had never come to this. Understand me; I loathe being suspicious of Nick."

Lucy sat in the rocking chair in her bedroom. Cal tapped at her door and came in to give her a peck on the cheek. "Lin and I are going for a walk, Grandmama." He drew back and looked at her, his young face troubled. "Will you be able to take me for a walk someday soon? Just the two of us?"

"We'll see. Bundle up warmly, dear. There's a heavy fog coming in."

"Missee," Lin inquired from the hall, "you need us to bring you back anything?"

"Nothing, dear. Thank you."

Lin, Lucy noticed, was dressed in her cotton jacket and trousers. She seemed lately to prefer Chinese clothing, plain though it was, to the skirts and shirtwaists which Lucy thought more flattering to her figure. But, she reflected, Lin was no longer a child and could dress as she pleased. Perhaps, being shy by nature, she felt less conspicuous wearing the dull, somber plumage of her people than affecting the fine feathers and fripperies of her white sisters.

Lucy gazed out the window as the fog slipped slowly inland, flowing in a silvery tide through the channels between the hills and inching its way upward to swirl about the heights. She never tired of the spectacle in all its myriad variations. It softened and blurred the sharp edges of existence and transformed commonplace views into nebulous ambiguities. Was that the shadow of a carriage passing below or of a great, gray whale swimming through the turbid depths? Were those the faint glimmerings of gas lamps or the phosphorescence of rare, submarine creatures? The mist teemed with enticing intimations. It scudded by, close and confidential as a whisper, breathing of things unseen, of veiled possibilities and fugitive fancies. It was, she realized, the weather of dreamers, hazy and subtle and infinitely more to her liking than the glare of a clear and cloudless day which laid bare merely that which was, void of all suggestion as to what might be.

The moon rose over the billowing ocean of fog, making it luminous now. It seemed without beginning or end. Lucy remained at the window, looking out at the clouds.

"Mama?" Beth came into the room. "Don't you want the lamps lit?"

Lucy turned to her. "I vastly prefer dreams to facts. Never underestimate the power of dreams, Bethie."

"Are you all right, Mama?"

"Yes, my dear." She watched as the room took shape in the lamplight, each object distinct and finite, casting precise shadows on the walls. She caught her image in the mirror. It is no use, she thought suddenly. My mind tries to fly from this room and beats against these walls like a moth, the dust falling from its wings.

"Bethie? Mama?" Abel shouted up the stairs.

"We're here, in Mother's room."

"I've Nick's Uncle Dabney with me."

Beth glanced at Lucy. "That's curious." She called to Abel, "I'll be there in a moment."

"I'm coming, too," Lucy said, taking her arm.

Dabney sat on the sofa with Abel, facing the two women. He seemed uneasy, hunched forward slightly as though ready to leap up at any moment. He rubbed his palms to and fro on his knees. "I don't know where Nick is," he blurted out.

Beth stared at him. "I beg your pardon?"

"He cleaned out his desk and left without notice. I assumed he'd told you."

"Nick and I have been apart for some time. I thought you knew."

With obvious reluctance, he nodded. "Boyd had mentioned that you were having some difficulties. But I never thought," he went on earnestly, "that you two weren't in communication with each other. I mean, what with the boy, Cal . . ."

730

"I think," Abel said to him, "that you ought to le Bethie know the whole story."

Dabney averted his eyes from her gaze. "It was the money. God knows, I gave him every opportunity to pay it back. He was borrowing, Beth. First only from Boyd and only small sums at that. But it became a habit, and finally Boyd had to refuse him. He took it in good spirits, didn't seem offended and promised Boyd he'd be repaid every cent he'd given him. I knew nothing of this, of course. Not until later."

"What happened then?" Beth asked.

He took a deep breath. "It came to my attention that he was borrowing from his subordinates at the Iron Works. My clerks, my laborers. And none of them willing or in any position to press him to return the money. He'd put them in an awkward situation, and he knew it. I told him to his face that I felt he'd exploited my workers. It was a dishonorable thing to do and harmful to the morale and loyalty of the men. I said it had to stop, that I'd asked the employees to provide me with a list of his debts and given them my words that they'd be reimbursed. I showed him the paper."

"What was the amount?" Beth wanted to know.

"Over two thousand dollars."

Her eyes met Abel's. She said nothing.

"Beth, please believe me," Dabney went on. "I gave him every opportunity to settle matters. For a few weeks, he made some small sporadic payments, but after that he became lax. I warned him I'd have to deduct the money from his salary. We had angry words. He accused me of not trusting him. And in fact, I hadn't much reason to. It was a nasty argument. He seemed to feel that Boyd and I had turned the workers against him. He quit, Beth. I haven't seen him or heard of him in nearly two months. I paid the men back out of my own pocket."

Beth shook her head. "Naomi never said a word to me."

"Boyd probably didn't tell her," Dabney replied. "It wouldn't have served any good purpose. All this time, I assumed Nick had told you he wasn't at the Iron Works anymore."

"I've not seen Nick for almost a year." Beth reached out and took his hand. "Uncle Dabney, I know you did your best for him. We've all tried to help him. He has so many problems. More than you know."

731

"I feel very sorry about this, Beth. Nick is Stevens flesh and blood. I could never have conceived of anything like this happening in our family."

"All of us feel the same way, Dabney," Lucy reassured him.

"When Abel told me that you didn't know, I felt it my duty to inform you myself."

"Abel," Lucy said, "perhaps Dabney would like to have a glass of whiskey."

"I mustn't," Dabney said, rising from his chair. "Rose will be wondering what's become of me." He clasped Abel's hand, then bowed to Lucy.

"Let me see you to the door." Beth took his arm and led him into the hall.

Lucy looked at Abel. "Nick's disappeared. What do you make of it?"

"People don't disappear. He's around here somewhere."

"Abel, you're not thinking of notifying the authorities, are you?"

"No, no," he assured her. "But I'll find him, sooner or later."

Despite the warmth of the sunny, spring day, Lucy rose from her dressing table, went to the window and closed it. She felt faintly feverish, as though she might have caught a mild chill. She fetched a light shawl and wrapped it about her shoulders.

"Mama!" With an excited whisper, Beth rushed into the room, then quickly pressed a finger to her lips. She shut the door behind her and leaned back against it, her eyes wide. "You won't believe it! Lin has a beau! The son of Wah Ming, the fruit vendor. And of all things, he's asked to see you!"

"Wah Ming?"

"The son. He's downstairs now."

"What does he want?"

"I don't know. Lin asked me to come into the kitchen, and there he was. He bowed most respectfully and said he had a matter of great importance to discuss with the lady of the house. I said he might tell me whatever he wished, but he answered, 'Thank you, ma'am, but it is only correct that I talk with Mrs. Slade.' "

"He speaks English?"

"Perfectly." Beth laughed uneasily. "What on earth shall we do?"

"Call down to Lin and tell her to bring the young man up."

"Mama, you can't invite a strange Chinaman into your bedroom!"

"I'm feeling a bit poorly, Bethie, and I'm not keen on having to take the stairs. It's not as though I weren't dressed, my dear. Besides, if the young man is a friend of Lin, I shan't be ungracious to him."

"What if he wants to sell you something?"

"Bethie, do be a dear and let's get this over with."

Lin paused in the doorway, as though unsure of her welcome. Beth beckoned her inside and seated herself on the bench in front of the dressing table. Tentatively, Lin advanced a step into the room. Behind her stood a young Chinaman, as rigidly erect as a wooden soldier, his skull-cap clasped so firmly in both hands that he looked to be wringing it dry.

"Lin?" Lucy inquired from her rocker.

She started at the sound of Lucy's greeting. "Missee," she said in a small voice, "may I present Wah Jung, the son of Wah Ming?"

"How do you do?" Lucy said.

The young man bowed swiftly and with such precision that it seemed for a second that he might snap in two. "I am honored, ma'am," he replied, clenching his fists still tighter about his cap.

"And what is your business here, Wah Jung?"

He fixed his gaze somewhere on the wall above Lucy's head. "I have come," he said, aiming his words into the space between them, "on a matter of much consequence." He spoke with the strained circumspection of a student addressing his teacher.

"Your English is excellent, Wah Jung. My compliments to you."

He seemed momentarily disconcerted. He gave Lin a sidelong glance, but she was staring down at the floor.

"Go on," Lucy told him.

"I wish to marry Li Lin." Wah Jung looked startled by his own words.

"No!" Beth cried.

Lin's head flew up. An expression of panic crossed her face. "Missybet!"

"No, I mean—" Beth shook her head, flustered. "Mercy, I only meant—"

"This comes as a surprise," Lucy said. "How long have you known each other?"

"Three years, ma'am."

"Why, Lin!" Beth exclaimed. "You sly-boots! You never let on!"

"Marriage is a very serious step," Lucy said thoughtfully.

Lin nodded. "Yes, Missee."

"Wah Jung, Lin is not used to Oriental ways. She lives in a Western household and is accustomed to being treated as one of us. I do not think she fully understands the difficulties that the Chinese experience in America. Your affection for Lin is commendable, but you are asking her to risk much heartache."

"Ma'am," he answered, "begging your pardon, but she is one of us. She may live among your people, but she can never be one of them."

"Lin," Beth asked, "are you unhappy here?"

"No, Missybet, never! But someday," she said wistfully, "I, too, would like to have a family."

"No matter what happens," Beth declared, "you may always think of this family as your own."

"Where did you learn to speak so well, Wah Jung?"

"When I was seven, ma'am, I went to work for Bigelow, the bookbinder. It was he who taught me English. Now I wish to know more."

"More?"

"My father," he said, casting an awkward glance at Lin, "says Li Lin has no dowry. I say this is not so. She can teach me the American ways. She is a refined lady. I wish to raise a fine, American family. I have much to learn from her."

"And can you do this on the wages of a bookbinder's apprentice?"

"Oh, no, ma'am." He suppressed a smile of pride. "For over a year now, I am a fisherman. My uncle has two shrimp boats. Soon I will have my own boat."

"Wah Jung, Lin does not even know how to prepare Chinese food."

"No, missee! I help Chang. I watch him. I know many Chinese dishes."

"What she does not know, my mother and sisters w:
teach her."

"Lin," Lucy addressed her gravely, "I am only concerned that you have been among us too long to live comfortably as a Chinese. And, my dear, I do not want you
to suffer unnecessarily from the insults of ignorant, insensitive whites. I don't want you disappointed or hurt."

"Mrs. Slade," Wah Jung said, reaching for Lin's hand,
"I will care for her. There will be no unkindness under
our roof. I shall see that it is turned away at the door. I
promise you that."

"Lin has a mind of her own, Wah Jung," Lucy warned
him. "She thinks like a Western woman."

"Yes." He grinned. "She will be an American wife."

"And your parents? What do they think of this?"

"They are old, and new ways do not come easily to
them, but I was born on Sacramento Street. I have lived
here for all my nineteen years. They know I must do
things differently. I respect the wisdom of the old ways,
but I must also learn the new if I am to succeed in America."

"You are an ambitious young man."

"I am."

"Lin," Beth asked her, "are you sure this is what you
want? Such a big change . . ."

"Yes, Missybet. I love you all, and I am glad and grateful to have lived here so long, but it is time for me to be a
wife."

With effort, Lucy rose from her chair and went to them.
She took their hands in hers. "You are both determined
to marry, I see. I cannot stand in your way. I give you my
blessing."

"When do you plan to do this?" Beth wanted to know.

"We must first consult a fortune-teller," replied Wah
Jung. "He will choose the best day for us."

"Bethie, we'll send for Chang to prepare a wedding
feast. Wah Jung, do you think you can find the proper
place for it to be held?"

"I will find such a place."

"Oh, Lin!" Beth cried and ran to kiss her cheek. "I
miss you already!"

"I will come to see you. I won't be far away."

"Good-bye, Mrs. Slade, Mrs. Stevens. Thank you."

Lucy looked after them. "Bethie, it must be made clear

to Lin that she can return here at any time, if things go badly for her."

"Of course, Mama."

"Help me to bed, dear. My head feels stuffed with cotton wool, and I think I'm feverish."

Beth laid a hand on her forehead. "It feels warm. I'll make you some camomile tea to help you rest. I daresay this excitement has been too much for you. Shall I send for Doctor Vanderhoef?"

"No. Just let me lie down for a bit."

Abel came into the room, bearing Lucy's supper tray. "What news! When Bethie told me, I couldn't believe my ears. Lin is fluttering about like an agitated sparrow, with her feet scarcely touching the ground."

"Abel, I want your word of honor that you'll make it your business to see that Wah Jung and his family treat her well."

"I swear to it, Mama."

"It was bound to happen. I always knew the time would come when Lin would look to a life among her own kind. I often wondered if it was right to treat her as one of us. When I'd see the expression on the face of Wong, the laundryman, or the looks that some of Hong Hing-wing's coolies gave her, I'd wonder if I hadn't inadvertently been cruel, turning her into something unnatural, something that people gawked at, like a dancing bear. At least," she allowed, "Wah Jung seems a decent sort. I suppose I should have suspected the die was cast when Lin began to wear Chinese clothes again."

"You always had Lin's interests at heart, Mama. She knows that. And from what Bethie told me, she's exactly what Wah Jung has been looking for in a bride."

"Uncle Abel!" Cal burst into the bedroom and dashed to his side. "Look what I won in school!"

"As I live and breathe, a shiny, new nickel!"

"Look, Grandmama! I was the only one who did all his sums right."

"Don't come too near, dear. I feel as though I'm coming down with the sniffles."

Abel drew the boy onto his lap, but he wriggled away. "I'm too old to sit on anyone's lap."

Abel made a pained face. "Calvert, what will I do with this lap if you won't sit on it anymore?"

"You could get another baby." He looked puzzled at their laughter. "He could, couldn't he, Mama?" he asked as Beth entered.

"Could what, dear?"

"We could get Uncle Abel another baby to hold, now that I'm too big."

Beth looked at Abel, a scarlet flush coloring her cheeks.

"Perhaps," Lucy suggested, "Uncle Abel might borrow one of your dolls, Calvert."

He giggled at the thought.

"Let's put the nickel in your bank, dear," Beth said, "before you lose it."

"What would I do without those two?" Abel murmured when they had gone.

"You'd be sharing this house with a tired, failing, old woman."

"Bite your tongue, Mama. I will tell you this, though," he said thoughtfully, "They are like my own family."

"They are your family, Abel, your sister and your nephew."

"Yes. Of course." Abruptly, he stood up. "I must wash up before we eat."

Lucy stared down at the food on her tray, regretting that she hadn't the appetite to do justice to Biddy's efforts.

In the morning, she felt no better for a night's sleep, yet she insisted on leaving her bed.

"You're in no condition, Mama," Abel told her. "You're not well enough."

"Don't contradict me," she retorted hoarsely. "This is my home, and I shall do as I please in it."

"I still say—"

"The devil with you!"

"Don't be angry with me. I'm only trying—"

"I *am* angry! I resent being ill. I despise being frail. I am reduced to fuming helplessly while age and illness steal away my options. And now you'd deny me the simple pleasure of escaping from this room for a few hours."

Under protest, Beth laid a bed for her in the window seat of the sitting room. With Abel at her side, Lucy made her way downstairs. Bethie tucked a quilt about her, glaring at her in disapproval all the while, as though Lucy were a spoiled, fractious child. "Are you satisfied now?"

"Yes, dear. Thank you," she replied sweetly. "Run 'ong. I'll sit here quietly and read the paper."

But the fine print of the *Alta* swam and swirled before her, and after a few moments she gave up trying to make it out and closed her eyes. When she awoke, Beth was sitting close beside her, busy with her mending.

"You slept for almost two hours," she said accusingly. "You shouldn't be out of bed, and you know it."

"I was only resting my eyes," she lied. "Is that the doorknocker?"

"I'll answer it," Abel called from the other room.

Through the window curtains, Lucy discerned the shadowy shape of a carriage at the gate. "Are we expecting callers?"

"It must be someone for Abel."

The striking of the grandfather clock drowned out the murmuring voices in the hall. Abel came to the door of the sitting room. "Bethie——" His voice sounded hollow and unnatural. "Bethie," he said again, "there's a gentleman to see you. From the police."

Beth clasped her mending to her, as if to shield herself. "Something has happened to Nick."

Abel beckoned toward the hall. A tall, red-haired man whose florid mustache looked like a grotesquely downturned smile came to his side and stopped there, seemingly reluctant to disturb the two women.

"This is Officer Leavitt, Bethie."

She swallowed hard and nodded.

"Come in, officer," Lucy said. "Sit down, please."

Abel went to Beth and stood by her chair. She reached for his hand and held it tightly.

Leavitt stared at the curtained window. "It's my sad duty, Mrs. Stevens, to inform you——"

"Nick is dead," Abel interrupted. "By his own hand, Bethie."

"No!" The clothes she was mending fell from her grasp. Instinctively, she reached for them, retrieving them from the floor and carefully smoothing them in her lap, as though trying to piece together the fragments of some shattered object.

"How did it happen?" Lucy asked quietly.

Leavitt shifted uncomfortably in his seat. "He was found hanged, ma'am, by the young woman whose lodg-

738

ings he was sharing on Washington Street. She discovered him when she returned to their room late last evening."

"Who is this woman?" Abel wanted to know. "Have you questioned her thoroughly?"

"Yes, sir. Her name is Ella Park." He glanced up, looking for a sign of recognition. "She is an unemployed domestic." He hesitated. "A woman of color."

"Are you satisfied that she is telling the truth?" Abel asked.

"Yes, sir. Evidently Mr. Stevens had been ill, suffering hallucinations and the like. She'd taken him in a few days earlier."

Beth wept silently. The tears trickled down her face and neck, but she made no move to dry them.

"Go on," Lucy said.

"Miss Park returned, saw what had happened, and in some shock and confusion she sent for her mentor, Mrs. Mary Pleasant. It was Mrs Pleasant who summoned the police."

Lucy raised herself on her pillows. "Am I to understand that Miss Park is a protegée of Mrs. Pleasant?"

Leavitt's face was without expression. "I believe so, ma'am."

"I see."

"Mrs. Pleasant advised us to notify the family. She provided this address. Miss Park had no knowledge of any family."

"Who is this Pleasant woman?" Abel asked him. "How did she come by her information?"

"Never mind," Lucy said. "I know who she is. She called here at one time."

"Did Miss Park offer any plausible reason why he should have taken his life?"

"Yes, sir. She said he was deeply in debt at the gaming tables. He had fits of severe melancholy, she said, and his senses sometimes deceived him."

Abel slipped his arm around Beth's shoulders.

"I—" Leavitt stared at his hands as though he did not know what to do with them. "I have a letter."

"He left a letter? Where is it?" Abel demanded. "Give it up, man."

He cast Abel a warning look. At length, he withdrew a folded piece of paper from his pocket and held it before him with both hands, making no move to relinquish it.

"Sir, I think you ought to know," he said, turning it over and over, "that it contains some very strong statements. Mr. Stevens made some harsh allegations. Perhaps the ladies might not—"

"No," Beth protested. "Let me read it. He was my husband."

Leavitt handed the paper to Abel.

"This is all? There was no envelope addressed to anyone?"

He shook his head. "It was lying unfolded on a table nearby. Can you verify that it's Mr. Stevens's handwriting?"

"It is."

"Give it to me, Abel."

Abel waved her words aside, his eyes on the paper. After a moment, he looked up at Leavitt. "Who saw this?"

Leavitt cleared his throat. "Myself and two of my men, Miss Park, Mrs. Pleasant and the landlord, too, I expect. He was there by the time we reached the room."

"Good God," Abel muttered.

Beth reached up and took it from his hands.

"Bethie!"

She pulled away, quickly scanning the paper. With a cry, she sprang up, hurling it aside. "In the name of heaven!" she shrieked. "How could he write such lies? What a vile, unspeakable act!"

Abel put a hand on her arm. "Try to stay calm. He wasn't himself, remember."

"But to leave something like this! Full of the most horrible insinuations and falsehoods! To do something so evil with his dying breath!"

Lucy picked the paper from the floor by her seat. With shaking hands, she read it, forcing herself to focus her eyes on what was written there. When she had finished, she folded the letter and allowed it to fall again to the floor. "I don't suppose," she said, her voice little more than a whisper, "that it would make any difference, Officer Leavitt, if I were to swear to you that there has never been any impropriety between my son and daughter—"

"Don't, Mama! There's no need to defend Abel and me!"

"The reasons given in that letter for Selina's departure," she went on unsteadily, "are untrue. The things Mr. Stevens supposedly witnessed were largely figments

740

of his imagination. His mind was unsettled. He saw plot against him where there were none. Neither his wife nor son was ever disloyal to him, much less—" She motioned toward the paper. "Much less anything of that sort."

"Yes'm." The officer's face was pained. "I regret it was my duty to pass the letter on."

"You're arguing with a dead man, Mama," Abel told her bitterly. "Don't bother. It's no use."

"What can we do?" Beth asked. Despite the presence of the others, she looked suddenly as desolate and bewildered as a lost child.

Abel took her into his arms. "Dearest Bethie," he murmured, stroking her hair. He reached for his handkerchief and gently dried her tears.

Leavitt glanced away uneasily.

"Abel," Lucy spoke up. "Show Officer Leavitt to the door, if you please."

Leavitt raised a hand. "There is one more thing," he said apologetically. "As a matter of routine, we ask that a member of the family confirm the identity of the deceased."

"Do you want me to come with you now?" Abel asked.

"That's not necessary, sir. We're sure it's Mr. Stevens. We have his personal effects and the word of Mrs. Pleasant and Miss Park. But as soon as you feel up to it—"

"Yes, yes. Just allow me an hour or two here with my sister and mother."

"Certainly." He paused, halfway to the door. "I very much regret having to bring you such distressing news."

Abel took his arm and ushered him from the room.

"Mama, the treachery of it!"

"Hush." Lucy laid a finger against her lips. "Don't say another word, Bethie." She waited until she heard the door close. "It's all right now. He's gone."

"Nothing is all right! Nick is dead, Mama. How will Cal feel to learn his father was a suicide?"

"He must be told. It wouldn't do for him to hear it as gossip."

"I don't trust myself to do it without betraying my feelings."

Abel came into the room, his face grave and tense. "Good Lord, I would gladly have given Nick the money, any amount, if it would have helped."

"No, Abel." Beth shook her head. "Don't blame yourself. He wouldn't have accepted help from any of us. He hated us too much. You read the letter."

"Regrets are useless, children. What's happened is bad enough, but the fact that half a dozen people saw that letter makes the situation far worse. It's too much to expect that none of them would say a word. Abel, were those the rumors that concerned Warren Winslow and John Fiske?"

He nodded.

"He meant to destroy us." Beth's voice was flat with despair. "Think what the scandal could do to Cal. And Abel's career depends upon his reputation."

"Used to," he said. "It's past saving."

"Abel, fetch Septimus," Lucy told him.

"Why?"

"Don't ask questions."

"Miss Bethie." Septimus bowed his head to her. "I'm so sorry."

"Thank you, Septimus."

"Septimus," Lucy demanded, "how well do you really know Mammy Pleasant?"

He was taken aback. "Well's I care to, which ain't much."

"But you know a good deal about her."

"I s'pose so."

"Would you trust her with a secret?"

He glanced hesitantly at each of them.

"It's important, Septimus," Abel said.

"No. I wouldn't."

"Why?" Lucy persisted.

"Because that woman trades in secrets, that's why."

"How dangerous is she?"

He let out a deep breath. "Mammy Pleasant's 'bout the most dangerous woman in San Francisco, believe you me."

"I believe you," Lucy said. "You may go now, and thank you." She waited until he was out of earshot. "That's what I was afraid of."

"Who is this Mrs. Pleasant?" Beth asked. "How do you know her, Mama?"

"She came to the house once. Afterwards, I made some inquiries. It seems she places her protegées as servants in the homes of men of high standing."

"For what purpose? Blackmail?" Abel asked.

742

"Perhaps," Lucy told them. "In any event, she and five others read Nick's letter. The fuse is lit. Something must be done before this thing explodes and causes irreparable injury to you and Cal. Nick's fantasies of—of immorality—"

"Say it, Mama. Incest."

"Abel!" Beth cried.

"That's what he wants the world to think, Bethie. That you and I have—"

"No! No!" She clasped her hands to her ears. "It's a lie!"

"Is it?" Lucy said quietly.

Aghast, Abel turned on Lucy. "For God's sake, Mama!"

"Perhaps it was a lie when he first concocted it to salve his own guilts, but it has become the truth—and you know it as well as I do."

Beth's face went white. "What are you saying?"

"Mama, it's not the time to speak of such things."

"I swear to you, nothing shameful has ever happened between Abel and me!"

Lucy looked at Abel. Unflinchingly, he returned her gaze. Like two hostile animals, they stared at each other in silent defiance, each refusing to give ground. "That's not the point, Bethie," Abel said finally, his eyes still on Lucy, "is it?"

Instinctively, Beth flung her hands up in front of her face as if to ward off a blow. "Please, Abel, please! No!" she gasped. Then, like a fluttering banner suddenly bereft of wind, she slowly collapsed, limp and powerless against the truth.

He seized her in his arms. "Don't," he begged her. "It's nothing to be afraid or ashamed of, my dearest." He brushed the damp hair from her cheek and kissed her. "It couldn't be helped."

Beth shuddered involuntarily. "Hold me. Don't let me go."

"I won't let you go, Bethie."

"My children—" Lucy summoned all her strength to speak. "My children, don't you see? Now that the truth is out, Nick's lies can't hurt you." Her voice was scarcely audible. "The only lie left to harm you is the one we ourselves have fostered." She closed her eyes, unable to continue.

"Mama," Abel sounded alarmed, "let me get you to bed."

"Yes," she whispered, "I think you'd better."

"Don't try to walk. I'll carry you."

"You must go to the police. You must get that over with."

"I will, Mama. Bethie, make her bed ready."

Beth sat beside her, holding Lucy's hand in hers, as she drifted in and out of a shallow slumber disturbed by fugitive anxieties that refused, like shifting shadows, to fall into focus. Once, when she awoke, she found Beth with her face in her hands, weeping noiselessly. "Hush, child. All things pass. Somehow we'll find way to deal with this."

"But how, Mama?" she implored her softly. "How?"

XXXIX

LUCY AWAKENED to find them both in the room, sitting together in silence, their hands joined, keeping watch over her.

"Bethie has sent for Doctor Vanderhoef, Mama."

"Was it Nick?" she asked.

Abel nodded. "I've arranged to have the service on Wednesday. He'll be buried at Laurel Hill Cemetery. I told Cal."

"How is he taking it?"

"He seems puzzled more than anything else. I expect at his age it's difficult to conceive of someone wanting to die."

"Bring your chairs closer. I've not the strength to speak loudly." She waited until they were at her bedside. "The truth must be told."

"No." Tears welled up in Beth's eyes. "It would be the ruin of everything Abel has worked and planned for."

"Is a political career that important?"

"It's the life I've chosen, Mama," Abel said gently. "You know very well that no city in this country would knowingly elect a half-breed to office. People like myself are part savage in their eyes. We're barely domesticated, not to be trusted any more than a tamed coyote."

"You underestimate yourself, Son. The citizens of this city believe in you."

"And you underestimate the depths of their prejudice," he argued. "Besides, they would feel I had gulled them and made fools of them."

"That's a chance you'll have to take."

"Mama, you can't ask him to deliberately risk destroyng his career! He might not even be allowed to practice law if the truth gets out."

"Tell me, my children, do you love each other?"

The looks on their faces were response enough.

"Never mind." She held up her hand. "It's not necessary to answer that. But even if this scandal subsides, what kind of life do you imagine for yourselves, under the circumstances?"

"I shall take care of the house, as I do now, and be hostess for Abel's meetings. I'll help him and—"

"And live a life of deception, filled with fear. What if there were children?"

"Mama!"

"Don't look so shocked, Bethie. You're lying to yourselves if you think it won't come to that."

Abel passed a hand over his eyes. "God knows, I don't want to bring disgrace upon this house, much less upon Bethie. But as things are, I cannot make her my wife."

"And if you could?"

"I would."

She glanced at Beth. The anguish on her face was so palpable that Lucy ached for her. "Bethie?"

"I can't let him sacrifice his future on my account."

"It is the only way, if either of you hopes for a single scrap of happiness together. You must dare to take the gamble. If Abel's background remains a secret, Nick's letter will likely ruin your lives, and if by some miracle it doesn't, you have only a life of stealth, duplicity and fear ahead of you. You have no choice. The truth is your only hope."

"We need to think this out, Mama. Give us time."

"We mustn't allow panic to force us to act hastily," he said.

"Abel's right. Perhaps there will be some opportune time—"

"Time," Lucy interrupted her, "time, you say, time. You are young yet, and you can still talk about time as though the future were forever." See paused to catch her breath. "Listen to me. I have no future of my own. You two and Cal are all the future left to me, and I refuse to die with this shadow over you."

"Don't talk like that!" Beth cried.

Abel bowed his head. "Why, Mama? Why did you insist on keeping it from us, when we worried so over the way you were failing?"

"It's quite enough to be dying without being surrounded by people wearing pallbearers' faces. I've known for months."

"We begged you to see another doctor!"

"It wouldn't have helped. It's a blood disease for which there is no cure. Martin Vanderhoef called in the finest specialist in these parts." She gave them a faint smile. "And I fooled them both. They're amazed I lasted this long. Please," she said, reaching out for Abel's hand, "do as I ask."

"So much has happened—" His voice broke. "I promise you, I'll consider what you say. I must sort out my thoughts first. Bethie and I have so many things to discuss before—"

"Missee?" Lin knocked at her door. "Doctor Vanderhoef is here."

"Come in, doctor," Beth called.

Abel rose to leave.

"Martin, I have just told the children."

He looked from Beth to Abel. "I wish there were something I could do."

"We understand that you have done everything possible." Abel shook his hand. "Thank you. Bethie, I'll be in the library."

The doctor laid his palm on Lucy's forehead and frowned. "How long have you had this high temperature?"

"Two or three days."

When he had finished his examination, Doctor Vanderhoef rose from the bed and closed his bag. "It looks like pneumonia." He turned to Beth. "See that she takes plenty of fluids. She must also have complete rest."

"Don't rush me, Martin. I shall have that soon enough. Bethie, dear, give me a moment alone with the doctor, if you please." She waited for Beth to shut the door behind her before she told him about Nick. "Martin, there is something you must do for me," she concluded. "It is imperative. Take down these names, please." She paused a moment, gathering her wits about her. "Warren Winslow, John Fiske and Simon Waite. Albert Fearing, Joe Mason and Boyd and Dabney Stevens. Most important of all, leanor Gibbs and Father Crowley. I must see them all together."

He looked up from his notebook in alarm. "Lucy, you can't. I forbid you to ignore my orders. I won't allow you to squander your strength. In your condition, the slightest exertion—"

"Martin, I haven't much time left to me, and we both know it. Let me spend it my way. On my oath, Beth's and Abel's lives hang upon this. Believe me, it must be done, or I shall die knowing that my children are destined for a life of misery. I beg you to help me. It is the last thing I shall ever ask of you. And by God, Martin, if you won't do it, I'll get those people here somehow. I swear it."

"You are asking me to go against my principles. How could you expect me to do such a thing, knowing it could only harm you?"

"I am beyond harm. The children are not. Trust me."

"Lucy—"

"Please. Don't make me get down on my knees, Martin. I doubt I'd be able to get up again."

He gazed at her at length. "When?"

"Nick's funeral is Wednesday. It had better be Thursday."

"Lucy you may not be able—"

"I'll be able. I must."

"Are you absolutely certain this is so important that you'd risk your life to do it?"

"My life is already over. All that matters now is that I remove the one remaining obstacle to my children's happiness. You can't deny me that."

"I see it's useless, as usual, to argue with you."

"But Martin," she said, patting his hand, "think how you'll miss it when I'm gone."

It was essential, Lucy knew, to husband her waning strength. She slept, or tried to, and lay as quietly as possible in her waking hours, marshaling her thoughts, going over and over what she knew she must say, until the words came readily to her.

Lin held a spoonful of broth to Lucy's lips. "Only a little more, missee. Biddy will put the blame on me if you don't finish it. Good. It's all gone." She laid the bowl on Lucy's tray. "Wah Jung wishes me to tell you that he is unhappy at your distress."

"Tell him—" She broke off, coughing, and fought to catch her breath. "Tell Wah Jung that my distress is less, now that he has promised to take good care of you."

Lin lowered her eyes. "Missee, I could not say that."

"Does he read English?"

"Yes."

"Then fetch me a paper and pencil."

Lin hesitated.

"Do as I say, you foolish girl."

on the page. It scarcely seemed her own hand, this disjointed, meandering scrawl. She felt suddenly as though all the essential properties which defined her character were falling away, one by one, like leaves from a blighted tree. "There," she said as she pressed the paper into Lin's hand. "Wah Jung must know how much your happiness means to us. Old ways die hard, Lin. You must strive to make him respect you, or you'll not be able to respect yourself."

She nodded. "Missee, you are shivering. What is it?"

"I don't know," she gasped.

"I'll fetch Missybet."

"Don't." Lucy caught her arm. "They're only just home from the cemetery. Let Missybet be for a while."

"Calvert!" Lin cried, seeing him at the door. "You may not come in now. Your Grandmama is too ill. Go away, child."

He stared at the figure in the bed, his gaze dark with anxiety. "You're shaking, Grandmama."

"She's burning up with fever. I'm going to get the doctor," Lin said, darting out of the room before Lucy could object.

Cal lingered in the doorway, as though he did not dare to take his eyes from her. "They put Papa to sleep in the ground," he said abruptly.

"He was in pain, Calvert." Lucy heard a wheezing in her breath as she spoke. "He's found relief now. He's at rest."

"Is he with Grandpa Seth?"

"Yes, he is."

"Then he won't be lonely."

"No, dear." She tried to keep her voice steady, despite

ner trembling. "They'll be happy together, and you must try to be happy, too. Go along now," she whispered hoarsely. "I have to rest."

Doctor Vanderhoef undid the top of her nightdress and slipped it from her shoulders. Methodically, he tapped his fingers against her chest and back in several places, then helped her back into her gown. Lucy lay down, and Beth pulled the covers about her shoulders.

"I don't like the sound of that cough," he said. "Have you any pain?"

"In my side. Here," she said, showing him. "It's quite sharp, but it comes and goes. The coughing seems to bring it on."

He took both her hands in his. "Lucy, I think that you must reconsider—"

"No!" she rasped.

"For the sake of my own conscience, let me warn you—"

She shook her head fiercely. "I won't listen, Martin."

Beth frowned. "What is it, Doctor?"

"Nothing," Lucy told her.

Doctor Vanderhoef gave Lucy a long, penetrating look. She matched his gaze defiantly.

"You're a mule," he muttered as he stood up. "You want a veterinarian, not a physician."

She clasped his hand. "You tried, Martin."

"I'll see you tomorrow, God help us."

"Bethie, you and Abel must be here."

"Here?"

"Tomorrow morning."

Beth looked puzzled. "Of course, Mama. We'd not leave the house with you so ill."

Lucy woke from a fitful sleep. A thin shard of sunlight slashed through the narrow gap between the curtains. She took a deep breath and winced, her lips parted in a silent cry of agony. She waited until the pain subsided and with effort reached for the crystal bell on the table by her bed.

Lin answered her summons, bringing her morning coffee.

"Close the door, Lin. I don't want Beth or Abel coming in."

"Yes, Missee."

"Bring me my comb and brush and some hairpins, please." Lucy took the brush from her and began to stroke it through her hair, but the exertion of raising her arms brought back the pain. The brush fell from her hand and clattered onto her breakfast tray.

"Let me, Missee." Lin perched on the bed. Carefully, she brushed and combed Lucy's hair into a thick coil and pinned it into place. "There, that's better." She slid off the bed and surveyed her work.

"Now, Lin, fetch my dark purple silk and the garnet mourning jewelry."

Lin stared at her.

"You heard me. I must get dressed."

She took her head vehemently. "Doctor Vanderhoef would not allow it."

"Doctor Vanderhoef knows all about it. In an hour, he and some others will be expecting to see me. I shan't face them dressed like an invalid."

Lin gave no sign of moving.

"Help me, please. I can't do it by myself."

"Missybet would be very angry with me."

"It's for Missybet and Abel that I must do this. If you have any love for any of us, you must help me now."

Stubbornly, Lin stood her ground. "It is no good for you."

"I am doing the right thing. You must believe me."

At last, reluctantly, the girl went to the wardrobe and brought out the dress. Without comment, she fetched Lucy's undergarments and shoes and laid them on the foot of the bed.

The ordeal of dressing left Lucy faint with fatigue. Several times, she'd had to stop and rest, gasping from spasms of pain that made her eyes water. Her clothing was suddenly too large for her. It hung loose and ill-fitting on her body, as if it were not hers at all but belonged to be someone else.

Lucy made her way to the rocker and sat down. "I shall need Septimus to carry me downstairs."

"Missee, please—"

"Mama?" Beth flung open the door and gaped at the sight of her. "For pity's sake, what's going on here? Are you mad? Lin, how could you let her do this? You've no business being up and dressed, Mama. And what is Mrs. Gibbs doing here? She says you sent for her."

"I did. Run along, Lin, and tell Abel I want to see him right away."

"Let me get you back into bed, Mama."

"Stay where you are."

"You're not thinking clearly. It's the fever, I'm sure."

"I have never thought more clearly in my life."

Abel halted in the doorway and glanced from Lucy to Beth. Beth spread her hands helplessly. "She won't listen to me."

"Dabney and Boyd are here. And I saw Father Crowley coming up the walk. What's this all about?"

"I intend to tell them the truth. No!" She raised a hand to stay their arguments. "Listen to me, both of you. Living with a lie is intolerable. I cannot permit you to bring such anguish upon yourselves. Secrets destroy. They have cost me more suffering than you will ever know. And now, one of them, lying in ambush all this time, has trapped us." She closed her eyes and pressed her lips tight against the pain that overtook her. "Bethie, Abel," she whispered, "I don't want to die knowing you're not free to try to find some happiness together. Let me die in peace, I beseech you."

Beth blinked back her tears. "But Mama, Abel's future—"

"I'll survive, Bethie," he said quietly. "Mama's right. We can't live a lie without its eventually corrupting every decent thing that we have to share with each other."

"Abel, please, don't be rash. You must think about—"

"I've done my thinking, Bethie. I've done little else for the past few days. We owe our friends the benefit of the doubt. Perhaps they can accept the truth of me. Perhaps not. Mama has more faith in them than you or I do. Maybe she knows them better than we." He looked momentarily exhausted. "I'm not sure of anything, anymore, except that I want nothing to come between us ever again."

"It's not only our friends you have to consider, Abel. There's a whole city out there. What if people were to turn their backs on you now, just when you've a chance to realize your ambitions?"

"Then we'd go someplace else where we could make a fresh start without the burden of scandal."

752

Beth's voice fell to a whisper. "Abel, I'm so afraid."

He put his arms around her. "So am I, dearest. But i we take the risk, maybe we'll never have to be afraid again."

"Ma'am." Septimus rapped at the open door. "What's this about goin' downstairs?"

"It's all right, Septimus," Abel told him. "I'll carry her. Easy, now, Mama," he said as he bent over her chair, "relax." He lifted her effortlessly and strode toward the hall, carrying her as lightly as if she were a child.

They rose as one, shocked into silence at the sight of her. "Lucy—" Albert Fearing began, but his words caught in his throat. He coughed and turned away, reaching for his handkerchief.

Tenderly, Abel set her on the sofa. Doctor Vanderhoef arranged a pile of cushions at her back.

"Sit down, my friends, please."

Joe Mason took the footstool by Albert's chair. Only Warren Winslow, John Fiske and Abel remained standing.

"It will come as no surprise to you to learn that I am dying."

"My dear . . ." Father Crowley reached out to touch her arm.

"Bless you for coming, Father. Bless you all. I shan't keep you long." She stopped, waiting for the pain to pass. "We've had too much sorrow in this house of late. I want no more, not on my account or anyone else's. Warren, I'm aware of the rumors."

Warren Winslow looked startled.

"I gather you and John both heard them."

John Fiske glanced anxiously at Warren.

"The rest of you might as well know. Someone has been spreading scandalous tales of an unwholesome relationship between Bethie and Abel."

Joe Mason's head snapped up. A flush spread over his face. Beth turned to him and attempted a reassuring smile. He seemed embarrassed and looked away. Abel's eyes rested unwaveringly on Lucy's face.

"That person was Nick."

Dabney Stevens gasped.

"Dabney, Boyd, you know yourselves that Nick's mind was unsettled. He fancied people were plotting against him. He saw his family and friends as enemies. He imag-

…ned evil where none existed. His last act was to write a letter so damning as to ruin Beth's, Cal's and Abel's lives." A fit of coughing overcame her. She fought for breath. Doctor Vanderhoef knelt beside her. "It's all right," she said finally. "Fetch me some brandy, Martin."

He frowned, then rose and went into the library.

"Something happened to Nick," Boyd said in a strained voice. "I don't know what. He changed. He was a different person."

Abel spoke up. "I don't think he meant to lie, Boyd. He lost his reasoning. He thought that all of us, you, your father, Bethie, myself, even Cal and my mother, had conspired against him. It's all in the letter the police found by his body."

"He must have been insane," Dabney muttered.

"I fear that's true," Lucy said. "But the lies he left behind can still do a great deal of harm."

Simon Waite cleared his throat. "Some of us are not without influence in this city. Our words are sufficient to refute this kind of thing."

Albert Fearing nodded agreement. "It wouldn't be the first time unsavory rumors have circulated around a public figure. There's no need for anyone to know where the stories originated. It would be enough to dismiss them as an outrageous and transparent attempt to undermine Abel's political strength."

Lucy took the glass Doctor Vanderhoef handed her, holding it fast with both hands so as not to betray her unsteadiness. She drank the brandy down, glad of the burning sensation inside her, as though its warmth might rekindle her dwindling strength. She set the empty glass aside. "These insinuations are as false as they are venomous, but I felt the need to confront them openly. It is useless to fight slander with subtlety. The truth is the only antidote for such poison."

"Lucy," Doctor Vanderhoef said, "you must rest now. You've done what you had to—"

"I'm not through, Martin."

The color drained from Beth's face. She faltered as if she were going to fall from her chair. Abel reached out and caught her elbow to steady her. He looked at Lucy, his dark eyes wary.

"There are sins of omission, are there not, Father, as well as sins of commission?"

"Yes."

"And there are lies of omission as well as lies of commission. Each is equally dangerous. I've dealt with the latter. I must now—" She halted as a wave of vertigo seized her. "No, Martin." She motioned the doctor away. "I must now speak of a lie that was never uttered, though I myself am guilty of having countenanced and fostered it." Lucy's hands were trembling. She clasped them together tightly. "It concerns a woman. She is dead now. I never knew her given name. I never sought to learn it, or much else about her, despite the fact that her care once saved Bethie's life. I have often regretted that I was so callous and stupid as not to show her more kindness. She needed kindness. She lived among strangers. She was lonely, I believe. She was a good and humble woman, religious after the fashion. By the way," Lucy said, glancing up, "did I mention that she was an Indian?"

There was a faint, almost imperceptible movement among them, as though a slight earth tremor had jarred the house.

"No," Simon Waite answered, "you didn't."

Eleanor Gibbs stirred uneasily.

"Yes," Lucy said, "it makes a difference, doesn't it? This good, humble woman who saved my daughter's life was won by a white man in a game of cards. She was what we called a China article. An article, friends, a piece of goods. But not prime goods, mind you, like our fancy French harlots wearing their money on their backs." She saw Joe Mason avert his eyes from her. She drew a deep breath, indifferent to the pain. "This woman would not have fetched a dollar in a place like the Bull Run, or even fifty cents in the cribs, like the Chinese and the Negroes. You see," she said, "I have kept abreast of your committee's research. The Mexicans, I believe, are considered to be worth twenty-five cents, two bits. The woman I speak of was worth only the pips on a card. It is a disgraceful story, I grant you, but you gentlemen of the reform movement are familiar with such tales."

With an expression of acute discomfort, John Fiske pointedly inclined his head toward Beth and then in the direction of Eleanor Gibbs. Lucy fixed him with an uncompromising gaze.

"Your committee has made no effort to stop the degradation of human beings, whether they be sailors vic-

755

timized by crimps or Chinese slaves or, I presume, squaw wives—though, of course, there are those who consider the Chinese and Indians less than human."

Warren Winslow stared out the window. Albert Fearing examined the silver head of his cane minutely, tracing its embossed design with his fingers.

"But I ask you," she went on, "what of a man who beats his dog because he thinks it only a dumb beast? Is he not the more bestial of the two? And those who debase others; do they not at the same time debase themselves? I leave the answers to your individual consciences. Eleanor—"

Nelly glanced nervously at Father Crowley.

"Eleanor, I've asked you here as a friend, to bear witness to what I have to say, in the presence of your confessor."

Nelly froze. Father Crowley rose and went to stand by her chair. "Lucy—"

"Bear with me, Father. Joe," she said, "Eleanor and I did not meet for the first time when you introduced us. She was kind enough to indulge my small deception."

Joe Mason looked perplexed.

"You see, we'd met many years ago in Castalia. For certain reasons, I did not wish to acknowledge that earlier acquaintance. Eleanor obliged me, and I am grateful to her. She kept my confidence. But now I must ask her another favor."

Her face was white. "Pastora—"

"Tell them the rest of it, please."

Nelly stared at her. She spoke, almost inaudibly. "Why now?"

"There are good reasons."

"Go ahead," Abel told her.

Beth's face was streaked with tears.

"The boy—" Nelly began. "A few of us knew, like myself, but only the ones who'd come early to Castalia."

"I don't understand," Father Crowley said.

Her voice quavered. "The boy was not Pastora's own. He was adopted. His parents were dead. The father was a trapper who'd turned to farming sheep."

"His name was Luther Moore," Lucy said quietly.

"The mother—" Nelly broke off. Her eyes sought Lucy's. "Pastora?"

"Abel's mother was the wife of Luther Moore. She was an Indian of the Modoc tribe."

Nelly nodded. "It was common knowledge."

No one moved or made a sound.

"I am indebted to that woman not only for saving Bethie's life but for giving me the son I never had. Were she alive today, I could still never fully repay her for her gifts to me."

John Fiske put his hand on Abel's shoulder. Warren Winslow fumbled for a cigar and lit it.

Lucy was suddenly short of breath. "You see," she went on, her voice scarcely audible, "his roots here run even deeper than yours or mine. He is California's child more than he is my own. It's little wonder he feels so strongly for this place and its people." She gasped for air. Her chest felt as if it were under a great weight. Despite the pain, she struggled to fill her lungs.

"Quickly, Beth—" Doctor Vanderhoef lifted Lucy from the sofa. "Help me put her to bed. This has been too much for her."

Beth took Abel's hand in hers and kissed it. She ran from the room to prepare Lucy's bed.

"Thank you, Mrs. Gibbs," Lucy heard Abel say.

There were other voices, too, voices that purled and eddied about her and some that rose and fell like breaking waves, all of them echoing hollowly in her head as though they were reverberating from the dank, green-coated walls of some seaside cavern.

"There is an accumulation of fluid in the left lung," Doctor Vanderhoef said. "Has she been coughing up much phlegm?"

"Yes," Beth answered. "It's rust-colored . . ."

Lucy opened her eyes. Doctor Vanderhoef was nowhere to be seen. Her room was dark, save for a single lamp burning on the mantel. Beth and Abel sat talking together in hushed tones.

"What time is it?"

Beth rose and rushed to the bed. "It's past midnight, Mama." She reached down and took a damp compress from Lucy's forehead. She rinsed it in a basin of water on the table and wrung it out. "There," she said, laying it back on her brow, "does that feel better?"

She nodded.

"You've had no food all day. Biddy left a pot of soup warming on the back of the stove. I'll go and fetch some."

"Abel." Lucy motioned him to her side. "What happened?"

"You collapsed, Mama. You've been feverish and delirious since this morning."

"No. I meant, what happened downstairs? Afterwards. How did they take it?"

"I'm not altogether sure," he confessed. "John Fiske, Joe and Father Crowley all shook my hand as they left. I had the impression that Mrs. Gibbs was glad to slip away. The others—" He frowned. "Well, perhaps they need time to digest the news. I don't think they knew how they felt or what to say. I sensed that Warren Winslow was a bit distant, but that might have been my imagination."

"And Simon Waite?"

"He was courteous, as always, but he looked at me as if his eyes were trying to bore their way into my soul. I don't know what to expect from him."

"And you. How do you feel?"

He took her hand in his. "I don't give a damn what happens, so long as Bethie and I are free now. We're both strong and resilient. We'll make a life for ourselves somehow." He bent to kiss her cheek. "Don't talk anymore. It tires you so."

Lucy hazily remembered taking the soup that Beth had brought, and then some camomile tea—or perhaps that had been later. She heard the sound of Cal's voice in the hall outside her room. She looked at the clock. It was nearly noon.

"Bethie," she asked as she entered, "why isn't Cal at school? He's not ill, is he?"

"No, Mama. It's Saturday. You've been slipping in and out of awareness. I expect your mind wants to rest now and then."

"Open the window."

"It's too foggy, Mama."

"Open it a little, then. I need air."

A light breeze played at the hem of the curtains. Lucy tried to lift herself on her elbows, but the feat was beyond her. "Raise me up, Bethie, so I can see out the window."

"It's nothing but gray. You can hardly make out the hills, much less the bay."

"Please."

A flock of birds wheeled about the sky, tracing dark wreaths against the pearly mist. The shrouded sun, pale and diffused, tinted the churning clouds here and there with traces of color, like the faint glimmering of embers in a bed of white ash.

"The sky is on fire."

Beth glanced at her with a frown of concern. Abel came into the room. He drew a chair to her bedside. "How are you feeling?"

"I'm so very thirsty, Seth. May I have some water?"

Abel lifted the glass to her lips and held it while she drank. "I've had a letter from Herr Schmidt," he said. "The new vintage is ready for tasting."

"Is that you, Abel?"

"Yes." He leaned close to hear her.

"Take me there. To the vineyard."

"You're not well enough to travel."

"After. Think of Seth and me as you drink the wine."

"You know I will."

Lucy closed her eyes and slept.

Her hands were cold. She remembered Doctor Vander-hoef holding them and rubbing them. "Where are my gloves?" she asked.

"You don't need your gloves, Mama," Beth told her gently.

"I seem to have mislaid them. Ask Seth if he's seen them."

"Yes, Mama." She walked to the open window where Abel stood gazing absently at the sun on the bay. He put his arm about her shoulders.

" "What was your name in the States? Was it Jackson or Johnson or Bates?' "

Beth looked back toward Lucy. "That's the rhyme we used to recite as children, isn't it, Mama?"

"It was never Bates, was it, Mr. Collier?"

"She's rambling, Bethie."

"Is it May?" Lucy whispered.

Together, they came to the bed. Beth glanced down at icy and nodded.

"It's twenty-five years."

"Twenty-five years, Mama?"

"Since I left Saint Joseph. It was May then, too. Listen," she murmured. "Bells."

"No, Mama," Beth said. "Your mind is playing tricks on you."

Abel hushed her. "She's right, Bethie. Listen."

Through the window came the steady clangor of fire-bells and the muted thunder of cannonfire. Above them, the distant bleating of steam whistles carried plaintively across the hills.

"It's the railroad," Abel said. "I'd all but forgotten that today was the day. The news must have just come over the wire from Promontory."

"The last stray lamb." Lucy smiled weakly. "My flock is delivered."

"Your flock, Mama?"

"She's wandering again, Bethie."

"No," Lucy raised a hand in protest. "The dreams." Her hand hovered, trembling in the air for a moment, like a spent bird working its wings vainly before it fell.